The Womb of Uncreated Night

The Womb of Uncreated Night

BY

CHRIS ANTONIDES

iUniverse, Inc.
New York   Bloomington

The Womb of Uncreated Night
A Novel

Copyright © 2009 Chris Antonides

All rights reserved. No part of this book may be used or reproduced by any means, graphic, electronic, or mechanical, including photocopying, recording, taping or by any information storage retrieval system without the written permission of the publisher except in the case of brief quotations embodied in critical articles and reviews.

This is a work of fiction. All of the characters, names, incidents, organizations, and dialogue in this novel are either the products of the author's imagination or are used fictitiously.

iUniverse books may be ordered through booksellers or by contacting:

iUniverse
1663 Liberty Drive
Bloomington, IN 47403
www.iuniverse.com
1-800-Authors (1-800-288-4677)

Because of the dynamic nature of the Internet, any Web addresses or links contained in this book may have changed since publication and may no longer be valid. The views expressed in this work are solely those of the author and do not necessarily reflect the views of the publisher, and the publisher hereby disclaims any responsibility for them.

ISBN: 978-1-4401-5741-7 (sc)
ISBN: 978-1-4401-5743-1 (dj)
ISBN: 978-1-4401-5742-4 (ebk)

Library of Congress Control Number: 2009937237

Printed in the United States of America

iUniverse rev. date: 10/20/2009

. . . For who would lose,
Though full of pain, this intellectual being,
Those thoughts that wander through eternity,
To perish rather, swallowed up and lost
In the wide womb of uncreated night
Devoid of sense and motion?

—John Milton
Paradise Lost

Part One

1.

AFTER MONTHS OF EAGER ANTICIPATION, the Batmobile was outfitted and ready. It was time for Batman to take it for a test drive before he could cruise the city streets, ready to right wrongs. Brewster donned his costume with the help of Hippias, followed a side road from the Lodge down to the eastern edge of Inwood Hill Park on Payson Avenue.

Though there were few pedestrians, the distinctive appearance of the "Batmobile" immediately excited the attention of occasional passersby. Decked out in that absurd costume and driving a futuristic car resembling an earthbound spacecraft, Brewster could hardly have thought that he would be able to drive around Manhattan in the thing without creating a stir. Who would not be startled at seeing it? Inevitably, the "Batmobile" engaged the interest of a patrol car. The police fell in behind him and turned on their flashers. Having installed "booster rockets," Brewster tried to elude them with a sudden burst of speed. Unfortunately, the boosters propelled him through a red light and into a vehicle at the intersection of Dyckman Street and Broadway. Neither driver was injured. Ordinarily, such an accident would merely have led to traffic citations and insurance claims. But Brewster in his outlandish disguise had not taken into account the necessity of carrying a driver's license. It was an understandable oversight. After all, "Batman" did not carry identification in the expectation that he might be stopped by the police, like ordinary citizens. There was nothing felonious or deceptive about this good-natured booby. But driving without a license, an accident compounded by the flamboyant "Batmobile" knock-off? The officers in the patrol car thought that merited a laugh-in at the precinct.

Brewster docilely submitted to "spread 'em" against the car while one of the cops frisked him and his partner called in to the precinct. Both men were laughing. Spread-Em confiscated the utility belt, then told Brewster to remove his hood. Brewster refused and the cop moved to assist him. Brewster instantly assumed a defensive karate stance, and the astonished cop burst out laughing again. Call-In came out to assist his partner. Unable to remove the hood because they were laughing so hard, the cops managed to handcuff Brewster's hands behind his back and ran him in to the precinct station. The "Batman" costume and Brewster's insistence that he was Bruce Wayne drew mock-serious reactions at the station.

"What have we got here?" the sergeant at the desk exclaimed as soon as the arresting officer brought Brewster into the precinct station.

"This guy says he's Batman," Spread-Em intoned solemnly, while Call-In stood by, enjoying what was to come. Two detectives in the room sat at their desks. They both looked up at the same time. One snorted derisively, and got up from his desk for a cup of coffee, tonelessly chanting the Twilight Zone theme, "Doo-doo-*doo*-doo,/Doo-doo-*doo*-doo." The other pushed his chair away from his desk, stretched, and folded his hands across his paunch, nothing astonished. He had seen it all, but he was impressed with the remarkable authenticity of Brewster's appearance. This went beyond even the most meticulous costume ball reproduction. Then a thought came to him.

"Hey, they must be shooting a Batman movie in town!" This observation stirred the derisive curiosity of the station. "Who could this actor be? Keaton?" "Nah," chorused the detectives in unison with the desk sergeant. "This guy's breastplate don't have nipples," quipped Twilight Zone. "Must be Christian Bale. And who are *they*? Gotta be a big production able to afford a get-up like that." Whoever he was, thought Twilight Zone, he was a powerful-looking sucker. Arnold Schwarzenegger? Nah! Still wearing his hood, there was no clue to his identity or his age. Here was this hunk with bland vacant eyes, docile, yet formidable. From boots to pointy-eared hood, he looked to be as tall—no, *taller!*—than the tallest men in the station. A frame out of a comic book panel come startlingly to life and ready to star in some as yet unannounced Big Studio Movie. This of course was perplexing. Why would a Hollywood Studio surreptitiously begin a production that cried out for media hype? Yet how else explain a comic book character come to life?

"Yeah," retorted Twilight Zone, "and we're all gonna be called as extras!"

"You wish!" joshed Spread-em.

But Brewster gave no encouragement to their cinematic aspirations. He stood there, stoic, aloof, too dignified, really, for a Hollywood actor. A Broadway show? "Batman, the Musical?" Was this character real or had the station house really gone off into the Twilight Zone?

The sergeant marveled at his silence.

"Don't ya hear what they're saying about ya?" the sergeant asked, meaning the subtext, not the surface of their words. But Brewster said nothing, so that the sergeant marveled all the more. If this guy thought he was Batman, he certainly went to a lot of trouble to look like it. And the men at the precinct reacted the way most people react to the apparently impossible, however improbable. Brewster was a huge joke.

"Batman, eh?" said the sergeant, ruffling his fingers over the keyboard on his desk as if preparing to enter the name into his computer. "Is that with one 't'? You got a last name?" Then confidentially, "Tell me, are you really *The* Batman?" With exaggerated seriousness, he entered "AKA Bruce Wayne" using his index finger.

"Whatever you say," said Brewster quietly.

"Doo-doo-*doo*-doo,/Doo-doo-*doo*-doo!" chimed Twilight Zone under his breath, but loud enough for others to hear and guffaw at.

Now the sergeant liked a put-on as well as any other man, but only when he could play King of Subtlety. He began to get the uncomfortable feeling that he had lost track of who was sending up who in this intricate, if ungrammatical, battle of wits. Tiring of indecision, he ordered Spread-Em and Call-In to "Get that stupid mask off him!" While they took odds on whether the hood and the cape were of one piece, or whether the hood was attached to the breastplate, and argued about the best way to get it off, Brewster simply flipped the hood away from his face to the back of his head to expose his face, glistening with perspiration. After all, a knight upheld the spirit of the law even when he seemed to be operating outside of its letter. The men gasped. Could this kid, even a superkid, be a Hollywood movie star? Had he even begun to shave? They had supposed he was a man, not an overgrown boy. Then they collectively shrugged. Hollywood's pickin' their leading men younger all the time.

But since Brewster declined to identify himself beyond claiming to be *The* Bruce Wayne, the police had no option but to lock him up till they could figure out who he really was. Then notify his parents or Bellevue. Maybe both. And although Brewster at seventeen was a big strapping fellow, he was obviously a minor.

"So?" the arresting officer asked the man at the desk. "In the tank?"

The sergeant frowned at the officer's lack of humanity. "He's just a kid."

"Yeah, but he looks like he could take care of himself."

"In that getup? You wanna start a riot? C'mon! Put him in an isolation cell."

"Oh, yeah!" smirked the officer, rolling his eyes. "The one we use for *murderers*."

The modifications made on the Batmobile by Brewster and Hippias had obscured the vehicle registration number, so that added another charge to the blotter. Brewster spent the weekend in jail. He might have been there longer. Some wag at the station, thinking there might be enough to the Batman-movie angle to shake up precinct doldrums with sensational publicity, leaked the story to the media. The connivance of the entire personnel of the station house went so far as to allow Brewster to remain dressed in his Batman costume rather than require him to change into less sensational garb. Imagine the surprise of the Wainwrights when they saw their son behind bars, resolutely turned away, but unmistakably Brewster wearing that ridiculous costume, on the six o'clock news and heard the anchor chortling, "Batman in the brig—An unknown Hollywood movie star in a *restrained* publicity stunt?"

Fuming, Augustus Wainwright had his legal team pull strings to get the media out of range. Then his attorney descended on the station full of wealthy wrath to claim his employer's dotty offspring. The attorney berated the police for having allowed the son of a prominent citizen to become the center of a media freak show. He insisted that the boy had merely been dressed for a masquerade ball. He threatened to sue the media and the police department for having allowed an innocent caper to balloon into a major scandal. He conceded that Brewster had shown poor judgment and recklessness in causing an accident and driving without a license. The police, for their part, were startled and a bit cowed at the revelation that such a prominent and influential man was the boy's father. But the story had made news and there was little they could do in retrospect to hush that up. The prosecutor agreed not to press charges provided Mr. Wainwright made restitution for the property damage and agreed to have his son evaluated by a court appointed psychiatrist. He agreed to hush up the arrest as much as possible, withholding the boy's identity, and letting the media story die of information-starvation. Mr. Wainwright's attorney agreed that the "Batmobile" was an attractive nuisance and that Brewster should not be allowed to use it in the future.

Augustus avoided civil litigation with the driver of the car wrecked by Brewster—a teenager, himself, who thought being wrecked by "Batman" was "cool," and who had luckily escaped serious injury—with a handsome financial reimbursement for which he readily agreed to sign a confidentiality agreement. The fiasco put an end to the "Batmobile."

Both Amalia and Augustus concluded that Brewster's behavior had finally got beyond the limits of youthful imagination and parental indulgence. Their son not only had told the police that he was Bruce Wayne, but that during the following psychiatric evaluation, repeated the story during preliminary examination. He added that the Wainwrights were really surrogate parents, his real parents having been murdered several years earlier during a street mugging, and that he was in the FBI's Witness Protection Program. He did not feel that he was jeopardizing his anonymity with the psychiatrist because no one ever suspected that Batman was in reality Bruce Wayne, no matter how obvious it was to the reader of a comic book. Besides, whatever he revealed would be privileged information. The psychiatrist reported back to the prosecutor at a meeting with Wainwright's attorney that Brewster was seriously deluded, probably schizophrenic, and recommended immediate hospitalization. But through his attorney, Augustus Wainwright coldly refused to have Brewster committed to an institution. It was a family matter and it would be handled privately. Brewster would undergo psychotherapy. His attorney made it quite clear to the officers of the court that he expected the matter to be dropped and threatened dire consequences to their jobs, not to say the city, if anything Brewster had told them leaked out to the media.

From all indications to the court's psychiatrist, Brewster appeared to really believe what he had said about his alter ego. And though Augustus blustered and threatened, the Wainwrights were clearly alarmed about Brewster's mental state. Through his influential connections, Augustus was put in touch with Dr. Ferencz Sandor, Chief Psychiatrist at the prestigious Psychiatric Institute. Sandor had begun as a classical Freudian, but gradually had come, like Carl Jung and Alfred Adler, to reject Freud's emphasis on infantile sexuality as the basis for mental disorders. Jung he found too preoccupied with the collective unconscious and myth. He preferred Adler's interpretation of the unity of the individual conscious to Freud's compartmentalization of the psyche into ego and id.

The Womb of Uncreated Night

Sandor interviewed Brewster, then ordered a battery of standard psychological tests. The results were mixed because Brewster removed his contact lenses prior to the evaluation sessions and, using the techniques that he and Hippias had developed, tried to conceal his myopia from the testers. When the tests involved motor skills and tactile puzzles, he seemed to have an uncanny knack for solving them quickly and efficiently. "Almost without looking," marveled the tester.

But the tester was baffled by Brewster's performance on multiple choice tests. While Brewster had appeared to toss them off so effortlessly, the pages on which they were printed looked as if they had been peppered with random pencil marks and squiggles. The tester put it down to dissociative unresponsiveness. And Brewster's unconcealed mirth at the interviewer's evaluation only seemed to confirm it. The tester added irrelevant humor to the list of Brewster's personality deficits. He lost no time in reporting this aberrant behavior to Dr. Sandor.

Sandor doubted that Brewster's condition was serious enough to engage the head of a prestigious psychiatric facility. As Richard Korngold's former training analyst, he always believed that Dr. Korngold would make a fine therapist if only he would give up metaphysical leanings and pop culture that smacked of Jungian myth-making. Their differences often led to heated exchanges. But they managed to displace latent hostility in playful ironic jabs that fooled neither of them. If Sandor regarded Korngold as something of a mountebank, a metaphysicist with a medieval turn of mind, and Korngold, in turn, challenged Sandor on his pompous authoritarianism, they both sheathed their knives in friendly banter. Nevertheless, Sandor thought Korngold would be a suitable choice as Brewster's therapist. And of course, he expected that he would be kept informed.

Sandor telephoned Korngold. After an exchange of the usual personal and professional banalities, which were nothing more than a thinly disguised jockeying for advantage between colleagues, each testing the other's professional reflexes, Sandor smoothly interjected, "I wonder if you would consider taking this so interesting case I've just come across . . . as a personal favor to me?" he added, as if he conceded something of greater benefit to himself than to Korngold. "It should be right up your alley."

"Along with the other trash," muttered Korngold. Sandor then ran through Brewster's symptoms as if lecturing from notes to a graduate class. "The results of the psychological tests, together with his behavior at testing sessions, suggest that the young man might possibly be said to show mildly schizoid tendencies. But he shows a surprising grasp of reality for someone with so highly organized a delusion . . . he says he's Batman." He paused for Korngold's reaction.

"He thinks he's *Batman*?" exclaimed Korngold. And Sandor thinks he presents mildly schizoid tendencies? What's he up to? wondered Korngold.

"Whether a delusion centered on a comic-book hero," continued Sandor after what he regarded as Korngold's respectful silence, "is sufficiently bizarre as to be distinguished from a simpler delusional disorder . . . He does have some grandiose perception of himself as a kind of juvenile savior . . ."

Korngold chuckled. "Grandiosity being something you understand so well," laughed Korngold. The sudden intake of breath in his earpiece suggested that perhaps Sandor had not found it as up to their usual banter as Korngold intended. "Well," he added hastily, "that certainly qualifies, doesn't it?" The kid must be fruit-loops and Sandor sounds as if I'll have him back on planet earth in a few weeks.

"It may only be a shadow," said Sandor, ignoring the interruption, smiling to himself, and savoring the metaphor enough to repeat it, "only a shadow of schizophrenic affect. The cryptic smile, as if he were contemplating some private joke. A certain flatness in mood. The case is certainly intriguing, and not without interest . . . from a metaphysical point of view," he added slyly.

"What about hallucinations? Social functioning?" Korngold cautiously sidestepped the provocation, thinking that the old windbag wasn't about to get *his* goat today.

The Womb of Uncreated Night

Yes, yes, thought Sandor, miffed that his invitation for Korngold to come out and play on his turf had been declined. Korngold's mother-ego was wide awake and alert to the interests of its little boy. Very well, Richard. Cool and professional it is. "No, no hallucinations, as far as I can tell. The boy's behavior has been bizarre, but not dysfunctional. He seems to be completely self-possessed. But, a comic-book hero. Batman! The boy is very intelligent and extremely well read. You'd think his heroes would be—" Sandor left it hanging in a vocal shrug.

"Less 'pop'?" Korngold obligingly filled in. Are you sure that you really weren't thinking right up *yours*, Sandor, old boy? "Obviously, such a fixation is an unhealthy sign, especially in a bright kid from a wealthy family whose heroes ought to be drawn from the classic myths of high culture," Korngold laughed. "It's a sign of the times."

It was Sandor's turn to step around a dig. Richard knew that he disapproved of Jung's archetypes, but if Richard wouldn't come out, Ferencz certainly wouldn't play his game. When Sandor described the circumstances of the "Batmobile" episode and the obvious flight from reality, Korngold wondered if Brewster were psychotic enough perhaps to need hospitalization.

"Well," resumed Sandor in his grand old man demeanor, "outside of his Batman fantasy, he sounds quite rational and lucid, as intelligent schizophrenics often do. Perhaps it could be a rational interlude between psychotic episodes." He paused, considering a disagreeable possibility. Much as he would enjoy Korngold's discomfiture if his colleague couldn't handle the kid and Brewster did have to be hospitalized, some of the egg on Korngold's face might stick to him and the Institute, too. Wainwright wouldn't take kindly to that, and out the window would go any hope of a lucrative grant. "No, I wouldn't say he's likely to be a custodial problem. At least, not yet. You know how these things go."

"How long" said Korngold, warily, "has this been going on?"

Worried about your reputation as usual, eh, Korngold? Sandor thought, unsympathetically. "The onset of his delusion has been gradual—not a good sign—and progressive . . . since about puberty? If he hasn't gone completely around the bend after several years, as near as I can tell, the prognosis seems good. But with delusional disorders of whatever type, who can say?"

Sandor was being entirely too nonchalant. Korngold hesitated. "What about his parents? Are they likely to be a problem during therapy?"

Sandor hesitated, letting suspense build, and tried to sound as ominous as he could. "They are firmly opposed to hospitalization."

Great! thought Korngold. But it was an almost irresistible challenge, as if Sandor had flung out a dare that Korngold could not refuse without suggesting that he wasn't up to it. "That's understandable enough." Then, off-handedly, "Why aren't you taking the case?"

Sandor paused to enjoy the moment. Was Korngold running out of justifications for avoiding a commitment to this spoiled, obstinately neurotic, even psychotic, scion of one of the wealthiest families in the city? And was he now trying to maneuver Sandor into the position of foot-dragging? "Well, I'm sure you can understand that I'm increasingly preoccupied with the administration of the Institute and could not possibly take on another patient just now . . ." Better your reputation than mine, he thought, already considering how he would disengage himself and the Institute from a fiasco.

Could it be, Korngold wondered, that Sandor was something of a snob and was turned off by popular icons? The thought stirred up his democratic sympathies. Despite his noncommittal responses, the case intrigued him. If he could get a handle on the kid and bring him around, who knew where it could lead? He, too, might get to be Chief Psychiatrist of a prestigious psychiatric facility. An inner voice breathed caution. It would be just like Sandor to dump a really dangerous psychopath into his lap. But if he accepted the challenge, he would be one-up and gain the moral high ground. He agreed to evaluate Brewster's condition, but promised nothing.

He promises nothing, gloated Sandor as he hung up the phone, but he is hooked. And he will likely find the boy a virtual tar baby! Once engaged, it would not be easy to deny Augustus Wainwright. Caught in a tar pit with a saber-toothed millionaire prowling the perimeter! Sandor was finding that he really enjoyed administrative work.

When Brewster showed up for his first session, Korngold was not prepared for what he saw. After many years of practice, he knew that many psychotics do not fit the popular stereotype of the raving lunatic. That quite seriously ill people can look perfectly "normal," not even remotely unbalanced. But he was somewhat awed by Brewster's physical presence. Brewster was over six feet tall and powerfully built. He came into the office warily, as if it were too small for him, as if afraid of bumping into things and knocking them over. There was nothing furtive or clumsy about him, but there was a faint aura of caution in the way he smiled and offered Korngold his hand.

"Good morning," he said, and waited deferentially for the therapist to sit before seating himself in the chair Korngold indicated. He was polite but reserved, almost shy—surprising in a young man whose physical appearance alone generated a certain awe that might have led to adolescent self-assurance, even cockiness. His face had the vacant symmetry of a comic book hero or a model advertising underwear, and Korngold wondered for a moment whether the blankness of expression was put on for his benefit or if it was the genuine reflection of an athletic booby. It was only a fleeting doubt. There was nothing slack-jawed about this jock. And the large, sharp blue eyes—contacts? wondered Korngold—pierced the mask in spite of the vacant expression and nailed Korngold to his chair. A mane of neatly trimmed, intensely black hair contained the face and kept it from floating away out of sheer, studied vacuousness. He had the imposing but not yet fully developed physique of an Olympic athlete, and he wore a casual sport shirt, Levis, and sneakers that affected a casual grace that was oddly out of touch with his demeanor.

Good manners often conceal hostility, and although Korngold himself was a six-footer and in his younger days had some prowess in self-defense, he felt that if antagonized, this young man would be a formidable adversary. But however resentful of the present procedure he may have been, Brewster was reassuringly in control of himself, rational, and clearly eager to make a good impression. Not that Korngold felt in any way threatened by his manner. In fact, he was a masterpiece of self-control and what used to be called "good breeding." You sensed it the way you sensed the contained power and sleek design of a faintly humming dynamo. The desire to make a good impression was part of his artful concealment.

He was affable enough, as the interview began, but reticent. Ordinary conversational gambits did not draw him out. He responded to questions directly and succinctly, then lapsed into silence. He was obviously blocking, and Korngold hesitated to broach the matter of his recent escapades and the fantasy behind it too directly, feeling that, like prodding an inflated balloon with a finger, he would simply bounce away. He had just had a potentially serious scrape with the law. Unless he was completely out of touch—something Korngold doubted on the basis of preliminary observations—he should be able to recognize the impropriety of driving without a license. A normal adolescent could be expected to be somewhat abashed at having been involved in an accident. But he gave no evidence of any such affects. No sign that masquerading as "Batman" might be considered peculiar. Since Korngold did not want to begin by alienating him, he tactfully avoided any reference to his adventure. Instead, they made small talk about conditions at home, his schooling, his social life—what might be considered non-threatening matters.

"Tell me about your interests," Korngold began, thinking he might tell about his obvious interest in physical training, in sports, girls, and other teenage concerns. Korngold discovered instead that he had a surprising amount of knowledge about the mammalian order, Chiroptera—bats—and was prepared to go on at considerable length

The Womb of Uncreated Night

about their genera, species, habits, and physical characteristics. This was clearly a ploy at avoidance. He became almost voluble on the subject, until he detected something in the way Korngold was letting him run on that brought him to an abrupt stop.

"Why have you stopped?" He had at least begun to open up and go beyond mere laconic responses. And however earnest his attempts at blocking, he was revealing important matter in spite of himself. The talk about bats was clearly relevant to his "Batman" alter ego.

"Oh, I get carried away, sometimes. I realize that not everyone shares my enthusiasm for these creatures. In fact, most people find them pretty repulsive."

"And you don't."

"No, I don't. Most of them, like the Megachiroptera—the fruit bats—are quite harmless. And the Microchiroptera—the insect eaters—are useful. Even cute and furry. Only the Desmodontidae—the true vampire bats, which are quite small—feed on blood and are true parasites. And then there's the Megadermatidae—the false vampires—which are carnivorous but not blood-drinkers. Funny how humans think they're the only ones who should eat meat."

Korngold understood the revulsion. He himself had no special horror of the creatures, and some of the pictures he had seen were indeed reminiscent of the "cute" qualities one sees in furry kittens and puppies. But vampire bats have ugly snout faces, like demons. And they are dangerous vectors for rabies and other diseases. He chose to maintain a healthy distance from them—if he thought of them at all. And then Brewster surprised him.

"Even their mating ritual is cute."

"Oh?" said Korngold, noncommittally, surprised at the possibility of a significant affect so soon in their relationship.

"Well, yes. It's initiated by the male while the female is asleep. He rouses her with little bites on her neck, and when she is fully awake—But we aren't here to talk about hobbies, are we?"

"What are we here to talk about?" Korngold asked, wondering if

- 15 -

this would drive Brewster back behind his mask. And Brewster did for a moment lapse again into silence. He looked past Korngold and out through the window beyond the desk.

"What do you see?" Korngold nudged, hopefully. Brewster continued to stare out the window.

"I see—I see—" Then he turned his gaze back to the therapist and smiled. "I see that you are trying to draw me out."

"About what?" Korngold returned his smile. The game was afoot and it was on to the hunter. Brewster was giving no indication that he sensed anything amiss in himself. But he was aware of the hidden agenda.

"I suppose you want to know about the Batmobile accident?"

"Only if you would like to tell me about it."

"It wouldn't do any good. You wouldn't believe me any more than Dr. Sandor believed me. Or the police."

"Or your parents—?" Korngold ventured. Had he told the *police* that incredible story about the Witness Protection Program? If he really believed it, then he did not regard the Wainwrights as his real parents. How did he relate to them? Korngold wondered. And how had they reacted to the news that he did not consider them his real parents? It must have been quite a revelation.

"My *parents* . . . ," said Brewster with a cryptic smile, "can't be bothered."

"Tell me about your parents."

"They're dead." He said it so matter-of-factly and with such utter finality that Korngold gasped and hesitated before continuing. After all, Freud had said that when the patient and the therapist disagree about factual matters, the therapist would be correct. And he knew that the Wainwrights were very alive.

"I see," said the therapist, not seeing at all. "When did they die?" Did he think he was adopted?

"The DC account has my parents getting murdered on a side street. But you know how inaccurate news reports can be."

The Womb of Uncreated Night

Korngold was not sure if he caught his impulse to laugh in time. Surely a smile slipped out? He managed to ask, matter-of-factly, "DC?"

"*Detective Comics.* You know, Batman."

Years of practice keeping a straight face when patients made outrageous statements kept him from blurting out something that would have damaged any further relationship with Brewster. "I see," he said noncommittally.

"Yes. Well, actually, Bob Kane's account got it somewhat garbled."

"Yes?" Korngold's mind leaned forward alert and intent, but he let his body sag impassively.

"Yes. They were shot and robbed in the tunnel that leads from Pennsylvania Station to Sixth Avenue."

"I see."

Interlude

"Flying high above the city—"

Whee! "We're in an airplane or a helicopter, right?"

"Of course not," said Brewster. We're in your office. It's like Marley's ghost and Scrooge."

"I see," said Dr. Korngold. "But which of us is Marley's ghost, and which," with a sly smile, "is Scrooge? And where are the chains and cash-boxes?" He lit a pipe and puffed up smoke around him that smelled of burnt cookies.

"The chains and cash-boxes of the mind, though invisible, are quite real, as you shall presently realize."

"Yes. But Marley's ghost didn't fly Scrooge. It was the ghost of Christmas present that flew him. Are you a ghost?"

"In a manner of speaking, I am. Flying high above the city—"

"Are you Past, Present, or Future?"

Brewster sighed. "Despite Mr. Dickens, ghostliness is inherently 'past.' There really is no future. And the past," he shrugged, "just another word for memory in whatever form that appears. As for the present, which paradoxically keeps slipping into the past the instant that it *becomes, that is* apparent only in memory."

"Which is the past."

"Which is the past. The past is memory. Memory is the past. So there's not much point to the present, is there?"

"But surely there is a now?"

"Now? What is *now*? When is *now*, anyway? Now lapsed into past the moment you uttered it. The moment decays in the moment. *Now is* merely the transition between a future event that doesn't yet exist until it becomes apparent once it has occurred in the lapse of the moment. It's an anticipation of the past that slips away as you try to identify it. *Now is a convenient abstraction, like an imaginary number such as the square root of minus one. Something unlocatable that can locate something that is locatable. Like a zero.*"

"*An interesting paradox. Let's see if I have this straight. If I throw a tomato at a freight train as it rattles past, doesn't that mark a* now?"

"*But the tomato splattered and smudged as it passed.*"

"*Well. Aren't the splatter and the smudge a* now *event? The train is traveling faster than my pitch. Suppose my throw could match the train's velocity. Wouldn't that mark a precise point—oh, and let's say it's something that doesn't splatter, like an arrow shot from a bow. And since we're being very precise, the arrow strikes a wooden boxcar, not a metal tanker that would deflect an arrow.*"

"*Even as you shoot that arrow, the point at which you were aiming has passed. And at the precise instant that arrow digs into the siding—*"

"*Aha! That 'instant' when the arrow digs into the siding. Isn't that a* now?"

"*But that* now *on the side of the train is not* your now, *because its* now *is in your past. It's a* now *only in the past, as I've already said, a theoretical abstraction. By the time your mind perceives it as* now, *that instant will have moved away into the past. If you were able to aim, shoot, and perceive infinitely fast, that would be the theoretical* now. *Even if, in terms of human experience—which is, after all, what we're talking about, no?—the difference between the event and its perception, however slight, however imperceptible, that difference is nevertheless real. Its location in time and space might perhaps be statistically, but not absolutely, determinable. So* whose now *is it?*

"*If our perception of events were a series of discrete frames, say, like in a movie, which we could stop at will so that our brains could simultaneously perceive one of them as an event as it occurs, we could perceive a real* now *event. But for practical purposes,* now *is no more real than an imaginary privy. It accommodates the basic urge of a moment which is corrupted in the moment. There is always a lapse, be it as infinitesimal as a nanosecond, between the event and our perception of it that places it in the past. The persistence of perception may blur such lapses, but* now *is only an illusion. That's what drives us nuts.*"

As he spoke, Brewster's eyes drifted into some remote point beside

Korngold. Korngold subtly shifted his body so that it occupied the space Brewster had been staring at in order to refocus his attention. "But surely you agree that there will always be another instant, another hour, another tomorrow. A future. The future is simply what's to come."

Brewster sighed impatiently. "Well, but don't you see? It's not real until it's past. We only know that time flows forward because it's what we remember. But we know that only because it's in the past. Yesterday, you were sure that there would be a today and planned for it. And here you are. But you didn't know that yesterday. And what you know today has already slipped into a yesterday that will come tomorrow."

While Korngold debated whether to laugh or toss him back to Sandor, Brewster pressed on. "What if, as some physicists theorize, time could be reversed? You see that the future would be the past. So the future is nothing more than a conundrum."

"Science fiction," scoffed Korngold. "Even those theoreticians can't agree among themselves whether time is reversible. And whether it can or cannot be, until the matter is settled one way or the other, it's of no practical use."

"Use is a matter of perception," said Brewster. "Who was it," he mused, "said God wouldn't deceive us through our senses?"

"I think Descartes said something like that."

"Yeah. Well, illusion is deception. So either God allows us to deceive ourselves through our senses or maybe our senses allow us to deceive ourselves about God."

"You do get things tangled up."

Brewster smiled. "Actually, it's God. Being everywhere at once he's bound to get things tangled up. God is like the square root of minus one. In the past."

"Then even the past, which you say is real, is deceptive? Illusory? Another paradox?"

"That's why it's always being revised. But reality and truth aren't necessarily the same thing. It's all in the spin you give them."

"I see," said Korngold, grimly. "Reality is in a constant state of flux. You can't step into the same one twice! Truth is in the wrist. So your past,

The Womb of Uncreated Night

which is what we're here to discuss—" Korngold threw up his hands. "Well, then, if you are not The Ghost of Christmas Present, or the Ghost of the True Illusion of the Present, since these things cannot be, you must be the Ghost of Christmas Past?"

"Only if you really believe you are Scrooge and I am Marley's ghost," guffawed Brewster. "Now there's a spin for you! Scrooge psychoanalyzing Marley's ghost!" He paused for a *now* in which Korngold uttered something between a groan and a sigh. "But this has nothing to do with Christmas. Besides, it's not Marley who is transformed, but Scrooge. Come to think of it, . . ." he added with a sly look at Korngold.

"But," he resumed briskly, "*flying high above the city*—"

"'Ghosts are!'" interrupted Korngold, seizing on Brewster's use of present tense. "If there's a present tense," he said, "maybe ghosts can fly. Maybe *you* can fly. But I can't. Why should I risk my neck for you? Who are you—*really*—anyway?"

"Maybe that's what we're here to find out," replied Brewster. "Someone in the evanescent moment that keeps eluding you in the past. Well, consider me, um, the storyteller who exists as long as someone listens, and who, in turn, exists only so long as I continue to tell the story."

"A very interesting solipsism," said Korngold. "What happens to you and me if I stop listening?"

"We merge into the cosmic slurry, become very dense, and form a black hole from which nothing—not even imagination—can escape. Then, when we have absorbed all conceivable moonshine, we reach critical mass and explode, spewing absurdity over the universe, regenerating it in a new past. Fifteen billion years ago. Illusory, of course. Okay? Have a little faith. Flying high above the city—"

"Faith! Fat lot of good faith would do anyone if he splattered all over the pavement," said Korngold, laughing. "We're thirty stories up. The pavement may not be moving away from the tomato, but the effect will be remarkably similar. One can't fly on faith alone, but with wings and engines!"

"I'll be your wings and your engine."

"Hm . . . faith," said Korngold, "is the 'quest for an ideal that transcends the passing flux of immediate things.' But I'm not sure that faith in your words has enough lift to keep us aloft for long."

"You left out 'hopeless,'" said Brewster. "Alfred Whitehead said that religion was a hopeless quest. An attempt to anchor the past in an imaginary now *in order to resurrect and revise the future;* yeah, that's pretty hopeless."

"Not all ideals are hopeless," said Korngold. Then added chuckling, "We're certainly flying high this afternoon. I think I'm even getting a touch air-sick!"

So Brewster began again. "Flying high above the city . . ."

2.

IT ALL BEGAN WHEN GOD said, "Let there be light!" He never said, "Let there be darkness!" did he? From this it follows that like primordial chaos he was uncreated, eternal, and one with the darkness. If God-in-the-darkness always was, without beginning or end, then everything that followed must already have existed in him and with him. Or did the unformed matter and energy he was made up of coalesce, cohere, and explode into light? Either way, isn't it curious that a God of light should have had the same origin as darkness?

But if everything already existed in that darkness, why did God need light? Was darkness unsatisfying? If so, perhaps his creation of light was an act of rebellion, a protest against chaos. For the creation of light unbalanced the forces, made them visible so that they could be sorted out and evaluated. In dividing the primordial realm into light, which he called *Day*, and darkness, which he called *Night*, he *saw* that the light was "good." Evil was created by default.

But *Day* is merely a temporal convenience on earth. He did not create only the sun for the geocentric mind of man but liberally sprinkled the universe with *lights*. Perhaps God set those lamps in the sky for us to follow. Or perhaps the lamps were meant to light his own way through streetless space. One thing seems fairly certain. When humans brought the lamps to earth and subjected the wilderness to logic and order, the creatures God created and placed on the earth divided day and night among them. Everywhere the human race went, they lit fires against the night, and night and its creatures retreated before them. But if God in all his radiance did not banish night from the cosmos, what did humans hope for on earth?

New York City's Central Park was once a part of that night, a barren wilderness of swamps, bluffs, and rocky outcrops dotted with an occasional Indian camp. By the mid-nineteenth century, the site had been overrun with random shacks and shantytowns whose residents cut down the sparse mature trees and scattered pig-pens and bone-boiling factories among the saplings, poison ivy, rock-bound bogs, briars and thorny undergrowth. Now it is a triumph of landscaping, 843 acres set among outcroppings of ancient schists and gneisses, with paths tunneling in and out among underpasses and overarching trees until they open into gardens, playgrounds, and zoo.

Almost in the center of the park, Belvedere Castle perches atop Vista Rock, a natural focal point of the park, thrusting its turret high above the steep rocky embankment that falls into Turtle Pond from which mists rise late at night—as if some occult emanation—shrouding the castle in the chill night air. Stories once circulated that it was haunted by a mysterious figure, some obscure European aristocrat who had fled the Continent in the 1870s and disappeared shortly after he had taken up residence in the castle.

Perhaps this fanciful little fable was no more than the vengeful invention of a shanty-town bone-boiler dispossessed by the park's planning commission, intent on scaring parents out of letting their children visit the future park, an obbligato to the night music of recurring cycles of decay and disintegration that lurked beneath Olmsted and Vaux's grand greensward plan, as if the land resisted being dragged into the light and some inner event horizon pulled it back into primordial darkness. From 1856 at the beginning of construction to 1859 at its peak, the park was often bogged down in practical, political, and ideological controversies, and sometimes quite literally

The Womb of Uncreated Night

in bogs and quicksand. While pitched battles over political patronage and inefficient management were fought outside the park site, the "grubbers" who cleared the area of undergrowth and brush were subject to fevers contracted from the deep, mud-filled, filthy yellow bogs like the one that stank and stagnated southwest of Vista Rock. Clay pipes laid down in the first phase of construction had, by the 1880s, disintegrated, plugged the drainage system, and turned the lakes and meadows into stagnant malarial swamps. Parents were warned to keep their children away.

Perhaps. As the surrounding City tightened its grip on the perimeter of the park over the years, its growing population horse tram trundled up and down the island from row after monotonous row of dreary row-houses to the stifling towers of commerce, the park gradually buried the urban clamor under its sylvan serenity. It offered residents a refreshing respite from urban dissipations and vices and an elitist dream of a haven for spiritual and aesthetic awakening. Despite the havoc created by the bearers of light as their economic and ideological squabbles led to repeated disruptions and reconstructions, clashes over jobs and wage scales, complaints over political corruption, shoddy materials and the costs of replacements, inefficiencies in management and performance that led to frequent cost overruns—the cost of the park on its "completion" was more than three times the budget for the entire City at the time work on it was begun—despite all of this, Olmsted and Vaux's pastoral vision of light gradually overcame the sinister inclination of the land to sink into night. Nocturnal myth scrubbed away by matter-of-fact innocence of public day.

Of course with a six-day work week and an average working day of ten to twelve hours, most residents could enjoy the park only on Sundays, when they flocked to it. The rest of the week, on late afternoons and early evenings, it was enjoyed largely by the wealthy, as they "took the air" in their carriages—and the unemployed. With the illumination of the paths at night and the shortening of the working week, light renewed its encroachment on darkness.

The Belvedere was for a time converted into a weather station, but the readings of meteorological conditions were so erratic—as if some local condition of soil or bedrock disturbed magnetic and electrical phenomena and skewed the readings—that use was eventually given up, and in fact, the building virtually abandoned until the city decided to turn it into a tourist attraction.

All of this—the social, economic, political, and aesthetic turmoil surrounding the creation of the park—a rumored mysterious inhabitant who disappeared, the disturbances of meteorological readings, the building's dramatic setting—lent the place an eerie aura fit for haunting, the kind of icon that draws ghouls and demons—or children—on Halloween and casts a romantic spell over even otherwise staid citizens. The civilizing influence of gardens, playgrounds, and even a maintenance facility in the transverse sunk below an overpass next to the Belvedere, did little to dispel the haunted atmosphere. These were carefully contrived so as not to intrude on the mythic appeal that wells up out of some unreasoning, primitive vital principle animating the darker imagination. Something that revels in forbidden rituals, deifies the unexplainable, and lurks in forgotten pockets of the landscape. It resists the prosaic transformation that grew up around it. The Great Lawn, an oval of grass once the site of the old reservoir, sweeps away to the north where it ends in a line of trees, flanked by a pinetum, and a playground. At the southern edge of the Lawn, a path skirts Turtle Pond sunk below the brooding presence of the castle, circles around it to the east past the equestrian statue of Sigismund Jagiello, two swords crossed above his head against the spell of the Belvedere, winds back west and clambers nervously up a flight of dimly-lit steps hewn out of the bedrock on which the Belvedere sits. The path opens onto the Terrace and Pavilion breathing deeply in the open spaces of the Overlook before plunging back into the claustrophobic thickets of the Ramble on the south. Here, the labyrinthine paths, writhing, twisting and turning, escape the relentless, pounding, grid-locked walls slammed down on Midtown Manhattan.

The Womb of Uncreated Night

The enticingly contrived, intricate coil of the Ramble, still appearing as one of the wildest and most "natural" parts of the park, leads away from the Belvedere, straggling down another broad flight of hewn steps, straying through arched overpasses and unexpected passages quarried through massive granitic domes, then sinks gradually past a running brook that cascades into the Lake. The Lake lies in what appears to be a depression gouged out of the bedrock by glaciers during the last Ice Age, filling it with their melt as they retreated, and striating the surrounding bedrock. But it actually lies in a shallow basin constructed by gangs of Irish and German laborers, fed by the Cascade and the Spring-Rock Waterfall. The Ramble broadly and unevenly arcs around the top and east sides of the Lake, and is reached from the west across two bridges: the Bank Rock Bridge spans the top of the Lake where a toe of Vista Rock swells up over the 79th Street Transverse to the promontory of The Belvedere to the north; and the Bow Bridge, a graceful cast-iron collar spanning the neck of the lower lake where it washes up to the Bethesda Terrace on the south and the boathouse on the east. Paths through the Ramble are lit by lamps shielded in wire mesh cages against target practice. But sometimes, the cage hangs open, its light flown out. The surrounding wild areas are dark, the pools of lamplight absorbed into the dense, shuddering shrubbery that by day politely edges the paths but at night roughly shoulders them. The gloom is not so much pierced by these bursts of light as the light is somehow crystallized out of hunkering darkness—gelid haloes, swept by gusts of wind into static, phosphorescent maelstroms. Here and there, a lamppost lurches drunkenly, drawing away from some unknown assault, its eye cast askew.

The surrounding city is sometimes obscured by the convoluted paths or the overhanging trees, though the glow of the cityscape, always smudging the night sky just above the treetops at the edge of the park, ventures out overhead only when the sky is overcast and the eerie pale fires of the city char the lowering clouds. The trees and shrubbery muffle but never stifle the breathing of the great organism that coils around the perimeter. As one approaches the transverses, or nears a ventilation shaft piercing down to the subterranean transits that honeycomb the bedrock under the Park, the rush of an automobile or the rumble of a subway train startles the darkness, scattering it in disarray. Only momentarily fluttered, the night quickly nestles in again among the foliage, and the leaves of darkness once more enclose, constrict the arteries of view. Or, around a suddenness of some brooding bronze, skyscrapers loom up in the distance against the sky, glowing windows mirrored in the eddies of the Lake, so many stars fallen to earth.

3.

The final triumphant fanfares of Bruckner's monumental Eighth Symphony had hardly come reverberating to an end in Avery Fisher Hall when the stout, starchy, balding little man with shiny threadbare coat and beaked nose sitting next to Guinevere leaped to his feet applauding and cheering. Claudio Abbado could hardly have given the Philharmonic a more decisive downbeat. Guinevere and Brewster smiled at each other as the audience came in on cue from the little man. The more enthusiastic among them joined him on their feet, cheering. Guinevere and Brewster had enjoyed the performance as much as them. But as the acclaim continued for several minutes, during which the conductor signaled various instrumentalists in turn to stand and share the applause with him, Guinevere grew restless and wondered how soon they could decently leave. Following the lead of others who were as enthusiastic about leaving as the standing audience was about shouting approval, Guinevere nudged Brewster toward the aisle, apologizing and trying not to step on feet.

After the closeness in the hall, even the warm city air was refreshing. The fountain in the piazza surrounded on three sides by the temples dedicated to theater, opera, and concert filled their eyes as they left Fisher Hall, dazzling water and light whose twinklings intensified as they radiated in all directions and splashed back from the wall of shops and cafes embedded in the high rise buildings across Broadway. Through the side streets, hollow and mysterious, oozed the dark, dense mass of Central Park. Brewster wondered how he was going to tell her. These things had to be handled delicately or they wouldn't come off. There was the reasonable, logical approach. There was the nonchalant, cavalier approach—"Oh, by the way . . ." Whichever he used, there was some risk. But secrets had a way of festering.

"You're unusually quiet this evening," said Guinevere responding to his pensive mood.

For all the sense of liberation as they stepped into the plaza, humidity and traffic soon added to the weight of Brewster's thoughts.

"Let's take a stroll in the park," he suggested. "All right?" He took her hand and gave it a little squeeze.

They crossed Central Park West and stepped out of the artificial day of the avenues into the genuine night of the Park. A cool breeze lifted the oppression of the city. They were absorbed into one of those rare New York nights when the air was relatively free of pollution, the sky clear enough to see the stars. Street noises blurred into city, and city hovered behind its nightly mask to peer out over the park through a thousand yellow slits. The soft darkness of the scene set off the fiery eyes as velvet sets off precious stones. The pervasive, pungent smells of horse dung on the riding path and the straggling parade of horse-drawn carriages along the West Drive mingled with the faint aura of cherries, crabapples, and wisterias. Darkness stirred the treetops, reached down into bodies to rouse desire, and drew out strollers as cold draws heat. Though it was now well after 10, Brewster and Guinevere shared the unconscious security of others, strollers, bench-sitters, an occasional couple lying in the grass exchanging intimacies.

"You don't often hear a Bruckner symphony that's almost exciting," said Guinevere, breaking into Brewster's thoughts. "Especially the Scherzo."

"A variation on 'penny for your thoughts'?" laughed Brewster. "I liked the performance, too, but I'm not sure I have anything original to say

The Womb of Uncreated Night

about it." Should they talk about the various editions commented on in the program notes? Abbado had chosen the generally preferable Nowak edition, but wouldn't it be interesting to hear the Haas, which combined the original and revised editions? Or that Bruckner had introduced three subjects in the first movement, instead of the traditional two? No. Phony sophistication didn't seem the right way to lead into secrets.

"Some people think Bruckner's symphonies are all right to knit by."

"They are long," agreed Brewster.

"*Think* of all the baby caps and blankets for needy children that women could produce instead of riffling their programs through their 'heavenly length'!"

"'Heavenly' being a euphemism for interminable," chuckled Brewster. "But I suppose with enough zip, even the interminable might seem heavenly." As he spoke, the breeze brushed the treetops. "Like that breeze up there."

But Bruckner was beside the point. Guinevere was eager to hear what he wanted to say. And Brewster wanted to say it, wittily, debonairly, even casually. After several weeks, he was sure that she wanted to share more with him than casual sex. Before their relationship went further, it was only fair that she know about his other self. He had to do the right thing. But how? His tongue stuck between his heart, which assured him that she loved him enough to understand, and his head, which told him that she would find it absurd. How to broach it subtly, not blurt it out and expose himself to disbelief, or worse, ridicule? He squeezed her hand as he weighed his options. If he bared all in a suitable spot, mightn't he be able to kiss away whatever went wrong? But to lead up to it from *Bruckner*? His mind echoed aimlessly in the great symphony that seemed to have no outlet.

Guinevere caught his hesitation and waited patiently. After a few minutes, suspense got the better of her. Brewster was on the verge of saying or doing something that she knew would be important, something she really wanted to hear. "Sometimes," she said, "it's best to just say—or *do* whatever it is . . . like the fragrance of the wisterias on that pergola we passed through back there . . . effortlessly, without worrying about the how."

Each lost in hope, they had walked quite deep into the park, over the Bank Rock Bridge and through the Ramble Arch. The city disappeared behind Gothic scenery. A scooter cop had stopped three young men, cautioning them that ". . . the Ramble at night is notorious for drug pushers, muggers, and homosexuals . . ."

It didn't occur to Brewster that this might have been an inauspicious moment to declare himself. "Well—it's about who I really am. About this other life I lead."

For a moment, Guinevere almost laughed. Oh, no! she thought gaily. Is he going to tell me he's a mugger? A drug pusher? Gay? Ridiculously out of character. She had never met a man more upright than Brewster. What secret could he possibly have been harboring during their deepening intimacies over the last few weeks?

But Brewster did not notice her amused puzzlement. As they turned up the path along Burns Lawn, he could see the outline of Belvedere Castle, like a ghostly presence brooding over a stage setting fit for a nineteenth century opera. He led Guinevere there. From that promontory, everything would look different. A strange contrast with how the castle would appear in a few weeks when, just on the other side of Turtle Pond, the Delacorte would be wrapping up an evening's performance around this time of night. Then the area would be brilliantly lit, the Pavilion overlooking the rocky outcropping on which the Belvedere sat decked out in striped awning, and people would be milling about, their feet and murmuring voices a placid backdrop to the actors and sound effects bursting like cannon-shot across the Pond, renamed Delacorte Pond for the occasion. How would his impromptu production measure up to that? The little scene he was about to stage-manage should be far less dramatic.

But now the ambience was dark and hollow and *miserere*, a single lamppost preventing the scene from caving in on itself. Suspense mounted with each step up the path. Despite his best intentions, when

The Womb of Uncreated Night

the curtain of doubts and hesitations lifted, Guinevere would react in a way that he could only guess at. Only the "higher purpose" motivating his improvisation gave him the courage to play out his part. Brewster's feet followed the path leading up to the castle over the gradual rise of steps carved into the metamorphic stone. It was a fitting destination, a suitable setting for climactic revelations . . .

"I was just remembering," said Guinevere, trying to lighten the mood as they walked, "what Toscanini said about Bruckner's music."

"What's that?"

"That you could tell from listening to it that Bruckner had never been with a woman—no doubt because it took him forever to reach a climax!"

They both laughed, but the unintended irony stung Brewster. Was she inviting the thrust needed to close the gap between them, to reach the side he had never shared with someone he'd been intimate with? He chuckled and gave Guinevere's hand a squeeze.

"Poor Bruckner," he said. "His students so badgered him into allowing them to 'improve' his symphonies that he spent a major part of his declining years undoing their misguided revisions. Sensing the approaching end of his life, he prayed that God would allow him to live long enough to finish his Ninth Symphony. He never did."

"Maybe God thought his symphony was long enough," quipped Guinevere.

They laughed again. But Guinevere sensed Brewster's uneasiness. She grew as anxious about what he was stumbling over to tell her as he was. A smile, no more than a shadow in the uncertain light, passed over her mouth.

"Frantic old woman," she began, "goes to the doctor.

"'*Dokter! Dokter!*' she cries, '*Ich kan nisht pishen!*'

"The doctor looks at her thoughtfully. '*Vi alt bist du?*' he asks.

"'*Achtsik yor.*'

"'*Pishen genug!*'"

Brewster's laughter fell with a hollow thud among his steps. He, too, had pissed enough and ought to say what he had to say before *he* reached eighty.

"Guinevere," he said at last. "There's something I've been trying to tell you. I'm just not quite sure how to put it." He was dribbling again. They were quite close, but doubt still yawned between them. He shook his head, perplexed, and looked at the pavement as they walked ever more slowly. But the answer was not there.

Guinevere closed her eyes and gently rested her head against his shoulder. She raised her face to him, hoping that the mute invitation would ease what had become seriously awkward.

Brewster tried to speak again, his emotions a muddle of poetry and kitsch. "Guinevere—." His blood bloomed. Every organ in his body swelled. The touch of her body, her scent as she leaned against him . . . his heart cleaved to the roof of his mouth. He was dizzy with conflict. If only they would float off, she and he, words dropping away like so much ballast tethering them to the ground. He ached for her, desperate enough to take her right there against the nearest stone outcrop like a common thug, dissolving doubt in ecstasy and release. But inner coarseness trickled away in outer refinement. Long-winded as Bruckner was, even he announced his themes earlier than this. But then Bruckner's themes weren't secrets teetering on the edge of absurdity.

How much simpler everything seemed when they'd first met . . .

4.

BREWSTER'S CHILDHOOD SHOULD HAVE BEEN typical of the healthy children of wealthy New Yorkers. As a child, he had the usual illnesses, the passing turmoils expected in adjusting to the well-intentioned, if occasionally misguided, intrusions on his persona inflicted by parents, peers, and the rest of the world. His parents were a bit remote, but they wanted to instill in him a sense of tradition and social responsibility. They did this by leaving him in the care of nannies at home and sending him to public school, for a time, in the fashionably aristocratic belief that associating with social inferiors would give him the common touch.

But from infancy, Brewster had been visually impaired. He was so near-sighted that Amalia and Augustus feared that he might be blind. By the time he was one year old, he responded to movement, but only a few inches in front of his face. Dr. Cacamati, an ophthalmologist specializing in children with impaired vision, held out the hope that as the boy grew, the focal plane of his eyes would increase so far that corrective lenses would enable him to see well enough to develop in a reasonably normal way. That proved to be overoptimistic. At two years, Brewster's focus had extended to slightly more than twelve inches. Dr. Cacamati was still cautiously optimistic, but warned the Wainwrights that Brewster would probably need corrective lenses for most of his childhood. Perhaps even through his adult life.

"What about laser surgery?" asked Amalia, yielding to Augustus' impatience with imperfection.

"We'll see. When he gets older. Brewster's eyes will still be developing well into his teens. Even then, a procedure may be impermanent. All in good time."

At three, Brewster had to wear glasses with heavy lenses in order to see clearly beyond a few feet. Dr. Cacamati assured the Wainwrights that the clumsy devices would be necessary only until he was old enough to wear contacts. But Brewster delighted in flinging the clumsy things away and gleefully running about, crashing into objects for the pure physical joy of it. His mother called it mischief, his father called it perversity. In either case, no child of affluent parents would be raised without the services of a nanny.

Amalia wanted to engage a woman capable enough to provide a gentle touch for Brewster's infantile physical needs, and hardy enough to be able to take the strain of his boisterousness. She had in mind someone like a no-nonsense German hausfrau. When Miss Worthit showed up, Amalia thought she looked too delicate for the job. She certainly looked gentle enough, and she had letters from previous employers attesting to her capability and experience. But she was far from the stolid woman Amalia had in mind. Moreover, the letters recommending her were so similar in style and content that they should have aroused the suspicions of any scrupulous reader. Augustus, coming into the room where Amalia was interviewing her, noticed that Miss Worthit was young and pretty. He seldom interfered in the hiring of domestic staff, so that when he took an interest in the interview Amalia was surprised. She hesitated to say anything more until after the woman's recommendations were verified. But after Miss Worthit left, Augustus overruled Amalia. He thought that she was just the person Brewster needed. He also thought that he might occasionally have need of her services . . . elsewhere in the household.

Amalia saw that her husband's mind was made up. She gave in without fuss, a little investment in compromise that she would cash in another time.

The Womb of Uncreated Night

Worthit soon learned to consider Brewster's romps demonic. At three, Brewster was tall for his age, physically robust and active. He greeted every physical presence rather like a St. Bernard puppy, which he somewhat resembled in size and motor skills, with an affectionate bound. Coupled with his defective vision, such enthusiasm could only lead to calamity. His eyes could tell him about the presence of physical objects only vaguely, but instead of making him cautious or uncertain, he rushed to embrace them. He used his hands and arms the way a happy puppy uses its tail, to sweep everything off surfaces at the same level. If the surface happened to be a coffee table with the usual illustrated books and magazines, there was little harm. But when he exuberantly burst into the drawing room, one Sunday afternoon, and embraced his mother's tea service like a puppy greeting its long-absent master, the results were catastrophic. Amalia and a few ladies of her social set were quietly chatting over tea and cakes when Brewster, who had become adept at eluding his nanny, literally crashed in. The tea and cakes ended up on rather than in the guests. Amalia was inclined to laugh at the stupefied expressions on her guests' faces, but the disapproving glares of one or two made her swallow her mirth.

"I'm so sorry!" She got up and rang for the servants. "Where in the world could Worthit be?"

"It's nothing, really!" smiled an elderly lady with snow-white hair sitting on the sofa and dreamily stroking the boy's shaggy dark hair. But her daughter, a woman with a sterner disposition sitting next to her, bridled.

"Really," she muttered through clenched teeth, "you would think that a grown woman with excellent sight could be relied on to keep track of one nearly-blind child!" A moment later an exasperated Miss Worthit, her clothing in disarray, came hastily into the room, a tousled Augustus glaring from the shadows in the hallway, grabbed the delighted boy by the hand, and led him out.

Because Brewster was not by temperament inclined to be sensitive or reclusive, the nanny tried to put a damper on his social life. Miss

Worthit took him to public parks and playgrounds where other nannies often walked with their charges. At first Worthit sheltered Brewster from casual contact with other children for fear they would make fun of his owlish glasses. She also feared that his habit of flinging off the cumbersome things and rapturously bounding into every obstacle could lead to serious injury. She did not have to worry much about Brewster's impact on other children. Because he was inclined to greet other children as enthusiastically as his mother's tea service, the other nannies saw him not so much as an object of ridicule but as a menace to the lives and limbs of their children, which is to say, a liability to their job security. But Brewster's open and friendly nature was irresistible. It led to acquaintances with a few of the hardier children, even to a certain degree of encouragement by the nanny of a bully who welcomed collisions with Brewster as a salubrious corrective to her boy's aggressiveness. And from Miss Worthit's perspective, as long as Brewster was colliding with other children he would not be embracing horses on the nearby bridle path, automobiles on the street, or other sprightly conveyances.

Eventually, Miss Worthit and the other nannies relaxed their vigilance enough so that the children were able to carry on a lively black market in comic books, bubble gum, and sweets, things they imagined nannies would surely forbid and valued according to the estimated degree of prohibition.

For all the inconvenience of the lumpish glasses, Brewster became an avid reader. He devoured the books in his father's library, even plodding through those that were beyond his understanding. He would laboriously page through volumes of arcane words which he looked up in the several unabridged dictionaries or plague Worthit's limited vocabulary and patience to define, absorbing bits of information even when he lacked their syntactical sense. He delighted equally in those with illustrations, especially those that were strongly centered in human anatomy or wildlife. When Brewster's questions taxed Worthit's patience—or proved embarrassing—she suggested that he find some less challenging matter to relieve his mind of excessive study. This gave

The Womb of Uncreated Night

Brewster the chance to pore over the comic books he had bartered for. He was particularly taken with Detective Comics.

He was fascinated by the natural environment. Outdoors, he would throw himself on the lawn and through his owlish glasses study a blade of grass until he was satisfied that he had the essence of grassiness. Or he would come armed with a magnifying glass and fall to examining the minute world of ants or other insects. He once caught a grasshopper and examined it under the glass so intensively, that he unintentionally scorched the insect. Amazed at seeing wisps of steam and brownish ichor oozing out of the creature, he watched as it burned to death. Brewster wondered at a device that let him see so well that it would destroy what he saw.

Like all small boys, Brewster developed favorites among nature's creatures. Steeped in Detective Comics, he soon developed a particular affinity for the bat.

For three seasons of the year, the Wainwrights resided in a Georgian mansion on Midtown Fifth Avenue which they quaintly thought of as a town house. This location was convenient for the social life of Amalia and Augustus Wainwright, providing all the amenities of their cultural and commercial interests, and being across the street from Central Park, provided Brewster with a wholesome place of recreation. During the summers, the family took up residence in what was supposed to be a modest "country house," The Lodge, but was as much a mansion as the one on Fifth Avenue. Built in the 19th-century on the northern tip of Manhattan, it perched atop the escarpment overlooking Inwood Hill Park to escape the swelter of lower elevations with cooling breezes coming down along the Hudson River.

Brewster's prankishness at the expense of the domestic staff at The Lodge encouraged them to avoid him whenever possible, thereby increasing his solitariness. From a very early age, wild things drew him. He spent as much of the time as his abstracted parents and distracted nanny would allow exploring the woods and closely observing the creatures there. Once, late in the season when the school year had begun before the family moved back down to Fifth Avenue, he found a solitary bat hibernating in one of the "Indian Caves." He gently took it into his hands intending to bring it to school for show-and-tell. He placed the creature in a pocket of his coat and took it home, where he transferred it to a brown paper bag in which he thoughtfully punched holes. He prepared for his classroom presentation by reading about bats in an encyclopedia of the Mansion's substantial library. By the time he got to the classroom, however, the warmth of his handling, his room, and the school had revived it. When he opened the bag to show his prize, the bat flew out over the heads of his classmates. In the screaming chaos that followed, it was hard to tell whether the children or the bat were more hysterical.

Even the teacher took refuge under her desk, demanding, between shrieks, that Brewster "Get that creature out of here!" For his part, Brewster watched in admiration this unexpected turn of events. After initially screaming and cowering in their seats with hands flung over their heads, some of the children—led by some of the more mischievous girls and nearly all the boys, who saw chaos as a way of escaping the classroom—scrambled over each other and fled, still screaming, into the corridor. Before long, children in the adjoining classrooms, alarmed at the commotion—or perhaps mischievously sensing a way of disrupting the school's boring orderliness—and unrestrained by their teachers, joined the throng, and very soon the entire school was in an uproar.

Indignant at the commotion, the principal came out of her office to discover what all the fuss was about. She grabbed one of the girls running past her and demanded that she calm down and tell what was happening.

"Here!" she shouted, "Why are you carrying on so?"

"It! It!" cried the girl, struggling to get free of the principal's grip. "*IT!*" she shrieked, pointing toward the door of the classroom.

Just then, the bat managed to find the door and swooped through the corridor. "What's that? A bat? But how did it get into the building? Oh, come now! You aren't afraid of a harmless little creature like a bat, are you?" The bat brushed by the principal's head so close that she imagined that it actually got tangled in her hair. She, too, flung up her hands and ran screaming out of the building. It was not long after that the entire building had been evacuated and everyone, principal, staff, and children, huddled shivering in the autumn air, glaring balefully—the mischievous kids hiding their glee behind this façade—at Brewster as he walked sedately out of the building pursing his trembling lips. Was he shaking with fear of repercussions or repressed laughter? It was hard to tell.

When the janitor, laughing heartily, finally had captured the frightened bat in a net, the principal found some composure, collected her tattered dignity and marched back into the building. The children were sent home with instructions that their parents inspect them for scratches or bites that might become infected. She carefully avoided mentioning the possibility of rabies, realizing what a panic that could start and the ugly legal complications that would follow. Brewster was summoned to her office. He was inclined to think that the bat's performance in the classroom was far more instructive than anything he could have said about it. But neither the principal nor the teacher, when he faced them that afternoon, found the incident enlightening. The bat, unfortunately, met a worse fate at the hands of a pathologist looking for signs of rabies.

Brewster's cordiality toward nature's more sinister creatures endeared him neither to his classmates at school nor the domestic staff at Wainwright Mansion. Bat jokes and fights followed Brewster around the schoolyard. Since he saw so poorly without his glasses, aggressive children thought that all they had to do was knock them off in order to leave him at their mercy. That strategy worked only as long as they stayed beyond arm's reach. If Brewster got his hands on them, he gave as good as he got. He became so skillful at sensing malicious presences, that he gained a reputation as "bat-boy, the kid with echolocation."

But he sometimes came home bruised and torn anyway. A teacher once found him in the school yard groping on the ground for his glasses. The school recommended that Brewster be sent to a school with facilities for special education. This was less out of concern that Brewster's defective eyesight might disadvantage him than as a wedge to drive a problem child out of the school.

On another excursion in the woods, Brewster found a garter snake and delightedly grasped it by the tail for closer scrutiny. Studying his specimen intently, he carried it home and entered as he often did at the kitchen door. Cook was preparing an afternoon snack for him. Hearing the boy come in, she turned around as Brewster, waiting behind her, held the snake up in front of her face for her to admire. With a piercing shriek that surpassed anything when Brewster had brought the bat into the classroom, Cook dropped the glass of milk and plate of cookies in her hands. Neither his parents nor the servants were ever quite sure whether Brewster's interest in these bizarre creatures was exuberant innocence or sly deviltry.

The incident of the bat at school and the anxiety Brewster was causing among the domestic staff left Augustus brooding over the child he had never fully accepted as his son. This clumsy, oafish, near-blind child—could it really be his? He had put up with it for eight years out of regard for public appearances and accepted the responsibilities of parenthood for the boy. And *this* was his reward! He had never lost a sense of hostility to the boy's presence, a mindset he did little to conceal from Amalia and the child. Brewster accidently learned about this resentment when he inadvertently overheard his parents heatedly discussing the matter. He had come into the room unnoticed. Augustus had raised his voice to Amalia.

"Who is that boy, anyway?" demanded Augustus. "No one in *my*

The Womb of Uncreated Night

family ever had such defective vision. Who could he have inherited it from? Damned if I don't think that he was switched with our baby at the hospital!" Then he added, muttering, "If you were ever pregnant with my child!"

Amalia stared at her husband shocked and disbelieving, unwilling to respond to her husband's accusatory tone. She did not want to believe that Brewster had been switched with someone else's baby at the hospital. She was indignant that Augustus continued to resent having been forced to marry because of the baby. Augustus could easily determine his paternity with a simple blood test, if he really doubted that he was the father. Still could! But she did think that her heavy drinking during pregnancy was to blame for Brewster's defective eyesight. Her sense of guilt made her bite her lip and bear her husband's reproaches in silence.

Whether Augustus really was the father, or Brewster was not even the son born at the hospital but a baby switched at birth, her instincts displaced as much reticence about motherhood as any upper class lady was capable of. The baby had been inconvenient for her, as well. Once her lying-in passed, however, she did not let whatever maternal feelings or the vestiges of girlish rebellion interfere with her new sense of social responsibility. She kept Brewster as close as someone in her position could. She was learning to cope with her husband's rejection of her son and finding subtle ways to get back at him.

Brewster was devastated at what he had heard. He left the room as unnoticed as he had come in, and clambered down to the base of the cliff above the Indian Caves. Who am I, he wondered, if they are not my parents? He began to climb back up the cliff. Who would I be, if not Brewster Wainwright? When he had almost reached the top, dirty and clothes torn, he turned to look down through the trees the way he had come. It would be so easy to let go and slide away down to the Caves . . .

Augustus was indignant at the suggestion that anyone living under the Wainwright roof, even if of dubious lineage, should be sent to a school for rejects. He fumed until Amalia, with a cooler head, came up with the simple, obvious alternative always available to the affluent, and one that would gratify Augustus' elitism. They would engage a tutor. A mollified Augustus agreed, but demanded that Amalia hire a man with strong masculine presence to instill manly qualities in the boy. One that could free Worthit for other duties.

So Amalia redeemed her husband's questionable choice of a woman with unverified credentials by engaging the scholarly Mr. Trifle, whose slight build, receding chin and hairline were as far from the manly man Augustus had in mind as Miss Worthit's shapeliness from Amalia's hausfrau. Mr. Trifle's qualifications could hardly be faulted. He had some experience in teaching gifted children and would be able to begin Brewster's education with primary instruction in languages, mathematics, and the sciences. That appealed to Amalia. She had a moment's hesitation about him. His academic credentials were so substantial that she wondered why he would settle for a job as tutor. She accepted his explanation that he did not care for academic infighting, and hoped for greater freedom to pursue his own interests.

Mr. Trifle would supervise Brewster's education in basic curriculum. He would supplement those studies to fit the boy's intellectual growth, at least until Brewster was nine or ten and old enough to wear contact lenses. Then they would see. The vain little man thought this arrangement gave him some authority in the household. He mistook his importance so far that it did not sit well with Miss Worthit, especially when he thought it entitled him to hit on her.

If Brewster's poor eyesight did little to impede his interaction with the environment, the interventions of Miss Worthit and Mr. Trifle did less. Without his glasses, Brewster delighted in losing the two to whom his parents had entrusted him. The vague, furry environment he perceived without the lenses seem to conspire to absorb him as willingly as he embraced it. The chase for this rascally fugitive usually began when Worthit or Trifle heard a crash and found the glasses lying where Brewster had flung them—on the floor, in a pot on the kitchen range, in one of the mansion's several fireplaces, with or without fire. He was not choosy about places to ditch them. If one or the other of them picked up the spoor soon enough, they could quickly locate his whereabouts by following the path of overturned furniture, broken knickknacks, or books strewn around the rooms. But the mansion had many rooms and connecting corridors. If there was any delay, Brewster might double back over a cold trail, complicating the search. Then Worthit and Trifle would team their efforts, one of them holding out Brewster's glasses like some forlorn lure, and in the manner of game beaters, starting from opposite ends of the mansion hope to drive their quarry into the other's clutches.

Miss Worthit discovered, after one of these exhausting searches, that if her eyes were out of focus she could more readily spot him. It was a secret she never shared with Mr. Trifle. Once she spotted Brewster, she would sort of sit with her chin on her hands and watch the proceedings, as amused at Trifle's futile searches as Brewster in eluding both of them. It got to be a kind of unspoken contest between Worthit and Trifle to see who would find him first. Of course, even with unfocused eyes, Miss Worthit's vision was much sharper than Brewster's. But walking around unfocused in pursuit of a child does pose hazards. Miss Worthit did sometimes run into things she would otherwise have avoided—toys or books Brewster left lying on the floor or purposely left where an incautious adult could be expected to trip over them. More than once her search technique yielded a twisted ankle. She almost came to serious grief on a darkened stairway. Such misadventures provided Mr. Trifle with a few moments of reciprocal amusement.

Interlude

Brewster had fallen silent. With annoying deliberateness, Dr. Korngold took the pipe out of his mouth, emptied its bowl in the ashtray on his desk, and laid it atop the ashes. Complacently, he folded his hands across his slight paunch and finally looked intently at his patient, a sly smile at the corners of his mouth.

"You might follow Thoreau's advice not to fritter away your life in detail."

"Yeah, yeah, 'Simplify, simplify,' and all that, sounding like he wanted to reduce life to mere survival, but clinging to books and all the detail of their content. Isn't searching for simplicity in life a kind of sifting through its detail? When Thoreau said frittering, wasn't he making a distinction between living in the detail and thinking about it? *Walden* is full of detail."

"And you seem to be bent on matching it," *chuckled Korngold*. "But, then, we all have our own little ways of answering nature's call, don't we?"

5.

THE WAINWRIGHTS OFTEN WENT TO soirées and benefits attended by the stars of the opera, and took a special interest in Mme Villiards during her prime. As long as she was the reigning diva of the Met, they cultivated her friendship, nurtured it during the years of her declining vocal equipment, and preserved its memory after her retirement. MmeV, as she was familiarly known to them, was in her heyday a strikingly handsome woman. In her youth she was full-figured, admired by opera-lovers as "statuesque"—and disparaged by opera-haters as "fat."

But the "statue" was as ingratiating off the stage as she was stately on. After her retirement, Mme V remained socially active in a number of charities and community projects, but the Young Artists Group was closest to her heart. She gathered around her a network of neurotic protégés, partly in an effort to justify what she felt was her undeserved wealth—a kind of noblesse oblige— but partly because she genuinely liked people, especially artistic young people down on their luck. She quietly contributed modest sums to their projects, enough to keep them from giving up but not so much as to make them dependent on her. In those aspiring young faces, she saw a reflection of her own early ambitions, and she led a rich, if vicarious, life in the twilight.

Mme V also arranged with the owners of radio stations, art galleries, and coffee houses for one-day performances or displays in more formal settings. Of course, some of the members of her group were not quite ready for actual performance—those who hadn't yet really produced anything substantial for private or public scrutiny, those who merely wished that they would someday produce something but probably wouldn't, and those who pretended to creativity but really were hangers-on—interested in the arts, but not really participants except as spectators. She opened her luxury apartment on Central Park West to social occasions for them in which to interact, find stimulation, and demonstrate their budding talents. Aspiring writers read portions of work in progress. Would-be artists displayed drawings and paintings. Musicians gave recitals of chamber and solo piano music—Mme Villiards had a magnificent Bösendorfer—of established composers, or the new compositions of their colleagues.

Having no children of her own, she mothered her protégés as aggressively as any stage mother, gave them advice on their careers, and corrected their speech and their manners. She interceded with influential people on their behalf, allowing others to gauge their relative merits, and indirectly encouraging those others to lend their support in a way commensurate with her protégés' abilities and the inclinations of potential benefactors. She enlisted the support of Augustus and Amalia Wainwright, who were staunch supporters of opera—perhaps more concerned with its social prestige than love of the medium. But she could also be a stern mama if her charges violated her standards of taste and decorum. She had disapproved of smoking as a young woman because it irritated her voice, and though her voice as she approached seventy was no longer a matter of concern, she did not tolerate the merest whiff in her apartment. Vulgar language offended her ears and was severely rebuked. Persistent offenders were ousted. Sexual displays offended her eyes, though her heart was warm and she encouraged romances—even going so far as to play matchmaker—as long as they were carried on discreetly.

After her return from Europe, Susannah and the Wainwrights renewed their closeness. Augustus and Amalia made it a point never to

The Womb of Uncreated Night

miss a performance by Susannah. The Wainwrights, like most other New York families of wealth and prestige, had a long association with the arts. And the glitz and glamour of horseshoe-shaped opera houses had always proved a powerful magnet. The family tradition of "owning" a box at the opera dated back to Augustus' great-grandfather Hosmer, who vied with other wealthy New Yorkers for the limited number of boxes at the old Academy of Music on Union Square, and who was among the coterie of new magnates behind the movement that eventually led to the creation of the original Metropolitan Opera House on Broadway, specifically so that they could all have boxes at the opera.

At eight, Brewster was considered old enough to go to the opera. Time enough for him to learn how to behave at the theater. He would have to sit still and listen instead of drawing attention to himself and causing an uproar. It would be a valuable asset to his social development. He would have the privilege of hearing Mme V's admittedly fading vocal equipment. The whole heroic spectacle of opera would appeal to him and become an important shaping influence on his mind. Augustus, however, was less enthusiastic. The flap following the bat incident at school was still fresh in his mind. He imagined paper gliders made out of pages torn from program notes sailing out across the auditorium. Nor did he wish to be encumbered with the child at after-theater soirées. He suggested that Amalia take him alone to a matinee. Besides, he argued, an evening performance would keep him up past his bedtime. But Amalia did not want to go alone with Brewster. Neither did she wish to miss out on the late parties. She finally won over Augustus when she suggested that Brewster would be less trouble if he were a bit sleepy. Worthit would be able to cope with him when they returned home.

On the morning before the performance, Mr. Trifle prepped Brewster for the occasion.

"So that you will not disgrace your family or me," he said, with a bit more emphasis on the latter, "you will sit in your seat quietly and enjoy the music." The way he said it implied that no one in his right mind could either honestly sit still through an opera, much less enjoy it, but that it was socially correct to have the good manners of at least appearing to do so. Hypocrisy at short order being the crowning social grace. "I will identify the dramatis personae for you, and explain the plot." Seeing that Brewster was slouched forward in his chair, his elbow resting on the table in front of him and his chin in his hand, Mr. Trifle eyed him disapprovingly. "One sits up straight and well back in his chair so as not to obstruct others' view of the stage." Brewster took the hint and sat up straight with hands in lap. Gratified, Mr. Trifle relented a bit. "Since you will be sitting in a box, you are allowed to sit at the edge of your seat, if you wish. You may even lean forward in anticipation when something especially exciting is about to happen. You will know that is to occur when the singers, the soprano especially, begins to sound as if she were practicing scales at the piano, and the orchestra will become so loud as to try to drown her out. When she is thoroughly exhausted by this unequal competition, she will collapse, and the audience will applaud. The more enthusiastic members, nearly as hysterical as she, will probably cheer ungrammatically. They will shout 'Bravo!' whether to a woman or a man or a group.

"I will now give you the rudiments of Italian grammar so that you will know better. The feminine ending is -a. The masculine, is -o. The plural, -i. So, how should one address approval to a woman?"

"Brava," Brewster responded dutifully.

"And to a man?"

"Bravo."

"And to a group?"

"Bravi."

"Bravo," he said with tasteful restraint. "Excellent! You have now mastered Italian." He broke off, wondering if Brewster were yet capable of understanding irony. They had not yet covered it in the rhetoric. He shuddered involuntarily. The whole idea of exposing him to three or four hours of boredom bordered on child abuse. But the mind of a child is like a garbage dump. He shrugged and decided to dump Italian

The Womb of Uncreated Night

into a curriculum that already included French and German. "If you grow restless," he cautioned, "study your program. That will impress your parents."

"Shall I cheer, if others do?"

"No. Only the claque cheer. Another time I shall tell you about the claque. But as you can hear from the sound of the word itself—you remember our discussion of onomatopoeia?—they are a thoroughly disreputable lot."

He then carefully explained the characters and plot of the opera, and lectured him on the composer and his relation to historical period. "This evening, you are to see and hear Richard Wagner's *Die Walküre*, or in English, *The Valkyrie*." My God! he thought. His parents are mad to expose the child to opera for the first time by inflicting Wagner on him! "Observe that the preferred pronunciation places the accent on the second syllable, not the first. The action concerns the misdeeds of the Teutonic Gods and their effect on mortals."

All this, of course, was entertainingly scaled down in colloquial vernacular. But for all his eight-year-old innocence, Brewster was quite sophisticated. At times, Mr. Trifle droned on so that he almost put himself to sleep. When he managed to rouse himself, he found that Brewster was studying him closely, and strove to appear more alert.

"If this is a German opera," wondered Brewster, "why would the audience cheer in Italian?"

"Ah. Such contradictions are to be expected at the opera since the audience are as illogical as they are ungrammatical. *'Tutto nel mondo è burla,'* 'All the world's a joke!' But that's another opera."

Mr. Trifle need not have worried. For Brewster, the opera was Batman Comics come to life. Opera, like the comic book, is mythic and archetypal, its action neatly panelized, and much is communicated through grandiloquent flourishes. It seemed to him as if the Flatlanders had suddenly torn a wormhole through their constricted space-time continuum—even two-dimensional creatures can conceive of time—and run amok in our three-by-four-dimensional existence. Brewster tolerated the unexpected language barrier. His grasp of German fell far short of the conventions of operatic diction—often unintelligible even to those who were far more fluent than he. Perhaps some of the drawn-out dialogues eroded his attention, but there were some stirring sounds in the orchestra. And as the tension mounted in the second half of the first act, Brewster found it rather exciting, in spite of the few low points. Mr. Trifle would have been surprised.

Brewster eagerly looked forward to the second act at the intermission. His parents were so far pleased with the tutor's preparation. Unfortunately, the second act was another matter. The air in the house had become as stale and flat as an uncovered soda. Tempest and passion were replaced with domestic squabbling between Wotan and his wife Fricka, interminable dialogues with Brünnhilde, his favorite warrior-maiden daughter. Mme Villiards was imposing as Brünnhilde, the Valkyrie. She was tall, with an erect carriage and a presence that drew all eyes when she was on stage. She was most memorable in this role, standing on a rocky crest, a spear confidently poised in her right arm, a shield in her left, her radiant face swept back from the tip of her Roman nose into delicately arched eyebrows. The line of her high cheekbones seemed to extend into the wings of her helmet from which fell her long auburn hair—a living, breathing, singing statue worthy of Phidias or Praxiteles. It was this image that first attracted the Wainwrights—and many others—to her and held their rigidly compartmentalized imagination.

Even so, the extended dialogue between Brünnhilde and Siegmund over the coming battle with Sieglinde's husband was beginning to make Brewster nod. He fidgeted or whispered impatient queries which tried the patience of his parents. But after a few disapproving looks that plainly enjoined questions until the intermission, he managed to contain himself. Brewster had almost dozed off with Sieglinde when he recalled Mr. Trifle's critique of Mme Villiards.

"Imagine the absurdity of seeing Brünnhilde, whose willful defiance of the supreme god, Wotan, brought about the end of the Teutonic gods,

The Womb of Uncreated Night

". . . just imagine her playing the Japanese teeny-bopper Cio-Cio-San in *Madama Butterfly*, and putting up with a horny American sailor!"

"But didn't you mention Teutonic gods?"

"Oh, Wotan is the god-father, a randy fellow who gives his word and breaks it. You will see the extent of his duplicity in his dealings with the giants, Fafnir and Fasolt. Wotan had disguised himself as a wolf and fathered a human child, Siegmund—"

"Half-*human*? Half *wolf*?" exclaimed Brewster.

"I'll give you, 'Victory-Mouth' is a weird name even for a wolf-child, but it's appropriate. He is a mouthy sort. He turns up on the lam from an enemy clan that's out for his blood and ends up at the house of Hunding, who, it turns out, is also a member of the clan that's chasing him. And to top it off, Hunding's married to Victory-Mouth's sister, Sieglinde—"

Brewster had gasped appropriately, then asked, "Which means—?"

"Victory Mild. But Victory-Mouth doesn't recognize his sister and she doesn't recognize him, even though they're twins, because they were separated as kids. Right away, they turn each other on, sort of like falling in love with your own reflection in a mirror, and Hunding is understandably miffed. When Hunding wants to know his name, Victory-Mouth tells him it's Woeful-Wolf. Sly, eh? Of course, everyone in the audience roots for the kids, who've obviously got some kind of hormonal condition. Hunding, of course, is supposed to be a big fat slob. Even his music sounds big and fat and slobbery. Anyway, at dinner, Hunding sees Victory-Mouth giving Victory-Mild the eye while spouting off for like twenty minutes about what a hero he is. And Hunding, villain that he is, notices the resemblance between the two."

"Funny how heroes are so stupid and villains, so smart. So where does Brünnhilde—? Hey, she's their sister too!"

"So she is. But we'll come back to her. Hunding has it all figured out before Victory-Mouth and Victory-Mild know it, and he tells Victory-Mouth that the laws of hospitality require him to protect a guest under his roof, but next day—look out."

As Brewster struggled to stay awake, his recollection—almost a dream—was more compelling than anything happening on stage. "Victory-Mouth is going to need more than his mouth. Does he have a weapon?"

"No. He lost it in the fight with the clan. But his father, Wotan, as Wälse-Woeful-Wolf, told him that some day when he needed a weapon, it would be there for him. Guess what? It's the sword stuck in the tree growing through Hunding's living room. Dunderhead that he is, Victory-Mouth doesn't realize it. But Victory-Mild knows, and she's slipped Hunding a Mickey during dinner, tells Victory-Mouth about the sword, they finally recognize each other as brother and sister, sing about the moon in spring for another fifteen minutes, and go off considering themselves man and wife.

"Meantime, Wotan is getting his Valkyries—"

"There's an awful lot of incest going on here!" said Brewster, uncertain about the moral improprieties of opera.

"Wotan was big on incest."

"And the Valkyries?"

"They are Wotan's daughters, nine Amazons who pick up heroic corpses and schlep them up to Valhalla—don't ask why. He's getting them ready to protect Victory-mouth in the clash with Hunding's clan."

"Why does Wotan need nine Amazons to pick up one hero?"

"Oh, you know. Gives them a chance to leap from pinnacle to pinnacle shouting battle cries amid flashes of lightning while Wagner whips up orchestral fireworks in the pit. I never said that myth and opera were logical, did I? Anyway, Brünnhilde is his favorite—a chip off the old block, and more Wotan than Wotan. He tells her at first to protect Victory-mouth. But his wife, Fricka, who is against philandering, divorce, and incest—sort of a pagan fundamentalist— knows that he has been fooling around with a human woman, and that Sigmund and Sieglinde are his children. She tells him to forget about Victory-Mouth. So poor hen-pecked Wotan tells his favorite Amazon not to protect Victory-Mouth in the upcoming fight.

"Well, she's a big, goodhearted girl who's soft on heroes and knows

The Womb of Uncreated Night

that Wotan's heart is really with Victory-Mouth Woeful-Wolf. When she goes to tell him that he's about to become Geschlagenmund and has to go up to Valhalla with her but can't take Victory-Mild with him, he threatens to kill Victory-Mild and himself."

"What's Victory-Mild doing while all this is going on?"

"Oh, she's asleep. She's preggers and tires easily—"

"Already?"

"Well, they've actually only been on stage for like two hours. But it seems longer. Anyway, the Amazon is filled with admiration at Victory-Mouth's devotion to his sister-bride, and decides to go with Wotan's Plan A. Needless to say, all hell breaks loose when Wotan learns what's going on. But the Amazon spirits Victory-Mild away while Wotan is attending to Hunding's brawl with Victory-Mouth."

"And—?"

"And Victory Mouth is Geschlagenmund, poor guy. Brünnhilde is grounded. Wotan puts her to sleep—along with a sizeable portion of the audience—on a rock and surrounds her with fire through which only a fearless hero can pass and awaken her."

"That's it? Does the hero ever come? Is she awakened?"

"Yes, by her nephew Siegfried—Victory-Peace, Victory-Mild's son—who is too stupid to be afraid because he's never met a woman. He kisses her—how he ever figured out to kiss a woman when he's never before met one is beyond me—wakes her up, and off they go, husband and wife. Fortunately, the audience wakes up and goes home before that happens."

"Yes," said Brewster, "but how can anyone capable of playing such an Amazon also play a diminutive Japanese butterfly?"

"I suppose if you squint a little."

The opening of the third act perked up considerably. A few fortissimo zips in the strings, a mad whirling in the woodwinds, and prancing horns, and Scene One was off and galloping. The Ride of the Valkyries was taken at such a reckless tempo that Brewster thought the singers might fall off their horses as they swooped to their battle cry,

"Ho-jo-to-ho-o!" But whatever it lacked in horsemanship and musical restraint was more than made up in sheer visceral excitement. Mme Villiards was in good voice as she pleaded with Wotan for compassion, when things quieted down in Scene two, and at the end, the Magic Fire Music quite lifted everybody by the ears.

Brewster was perplexed when his mother and father stood up and cheered Brünnhilde. "Bravo!" they shouted. "Bravo!" But since they knew Brünnhilde, he figured that grammar and logic must not apply to them. He was unable to resolve the thought that they belonged to that claque which Mr. Trifle had spoken of so disparagingly. He shrugged, remembering Mr. Trifle's words, *Tutto nel mondo è burla!* His parents took him backstage to meet Mme Villiards.

"Where are we going?"

"We've been invited to Mme Villiards' dressing room," his mother replied.

"Oh? why?"

"Wouldn't you like to meet the lady who sang so beautifully?" His mother was really very patient. Brewster didn't know what to make of it. For him, Brünnhilde was the lady Wotan put to sleep at the end of the opera. As far as Brewster was concerned, the lady was still up on a rock, surrounded by a ring of fire through which no one but a fearless hero could penetrate. True, he had been puzzled when that same lady came from the wings to take bows and cheers. Wouldn't she afterwards go back to her rock and the fire? Why, then, were they going to this lady's dressing room?

Though exhausted after her all-out performance, Susannah Villiards was glowing. She sat facing the mirror on her dressing table, but Brewster found the room and her presence overpowering. She wore a loose-fitting gauzy pink gown, oddly delicate on someone who still looked raw and heroic. Instead of flames, a ring of flowers surrounded her, and she was removing her makeup. A pungent mixture of sights and sounds and smells came rushing at him. What looked perfectly natural in stage lights can look bizarre enough off. Seeing

The Womb of Uncreated Night

her reflection in the mirror, the makeup half-removed from her face, Brewster's first impression was that it was dissolving. He was horrified but transfixed. The flowers flooded his nose with their perfume, but beneath it he detected something sour. Could it be coming from this regally imposing lady? She was much larger than his mother in every way, in body, in gesture, and in odor. The scents nauseated and at the same time intoxicated him. Sometimes Worthit smelled a little like that. But there never was such an odor about his mother.

While Mme Villiards finished removing makeup and arranging her hair at the dressing table, she exchanged greetings with the Wainwrights and modestly accepted their compliments. Then she turned to face them.

"Brewster," said Mrs. Wainwright by way of introduction, "this is Mme Villiards, the lady who sang Brünnhilde." Brewster was not entirely willing to accept the second half of his mother's introduction, but he decided to keep mum. He had not yet accepted the idea that the life on stage was supposed to be independent of the life outside the theater, as if somehow what happened in the opera was not as real as the other improbabilities he experienced in or out of it. If a character died on stage, why, then, he or she ought really to be dead. He wondered if singers might forget that they were supposed to be dead, and that if they remembered, they would drop dead on the spot? He tactfully resolved not to remind them. And as he and his parents were all invited to a little party at Mme Villiards' apartment the next afternoon, he had another reason for deciding it would be inconvenient to remind them that the Valkyrie was supposed to be asleep on a rock surrounded by fire. Mme Villiards was staying up past her bedtime.

Mme Villiards' dresser poured her guests some champagne. The little party toasted Mme Villiards, and Brewster was allowed a little sip from her flute, carefully turned so that the trace of lipstick on the rim of the glass would be on the other side. More champagne went up his nose than into his mouth and they all laughed as he sputtered.

6.

Nearly all of the lampposts in Inwood Hill Park were regularly scalped by vandals. Metal baskets installed to protect the lights from target practice by mischievous boys never kept them from climbing the poles, breaking through the protection and smashing the lights.

At the age of eleven, Brewster often sat in the woods of Inwood Hill, which were separated from the formal gardens of the Lodge perched atop the cliff at the northern edge of the park. They appealed to him partly because of the illusion of wilderness, and partly because he could read the adventures of Batman in Detective Comics without fear of discovery by his nanny or his tutor. The park was once the site of spacious country houses. These were later replaced by privately endowed institutions, and now were reverting to a natural state, which nowadays meant demolition by predatory youngsters. The park covered 196 acres and was full of steeply winding, sometimes forgotten and unused, paths. The Lodge, an anachronism from that earlier gilded age, hugged the eastern slope of the cliff overlooking the Harlem River, sheltered from the oppressive drone of traffic approaching the Henry Hudson Bridge on the western slope by the towering spine of rock, and from the playing fields edging the river by the city's only stand of native forest climbing up the debris at the base of the cliff.

At some time in their rambles, local youngsters inevitably discovered the Indian Caves while clambering over the base of the rugged 230-foot escarpment of schist and Inwood limestone that made up the northwestern tip of Manhattan. The caves are overhanging slabs of rock that have tumbled down the ravine on the exposed eastern edge of cliff. Kids and souvenir hunters soon ransacked the site for its bits of arrowheads, potsherds, ornaments and other debris of lives before the invasion by Europeans. By the time Brewster discovered the caves, such treasures were pretty well depleted, and the caves mostly ignored except for an occasional visit by school children on a field trip. The caves themselves, used by the Wiechquaesgeck tribe of the Delaware nation, were perhaps 20 feet above the path that follows the ravine leading down to the legendary spot where Peter Minuit was said to have purchased the island of Manhattan for 60 guilders' worth of beads and trinkets.

The caves were easily seen from the path through the shrubbery. Brewster enjoyed crawling into them, exploring as far as he could without getting stuck in their tapering interiors. In his early explorations, Brewster noticed a narrow triangular fissure in the cliff rising behind and to the side of a large overhanging ledge. It was filled with crushed fragments of weathered marble and granite, the gravelly debris of decayed rock and soil wedged into the space. Powdery granules and dirt had begun to sift down among the larger pieces. The base of the crevice was effectively screened from view by trees and shrubs that had grown out from the gravelly soil at its base.

Curiosity and impulse led Brewster to dig into the soil. He had no clear purpose. It was just that he enjoyed digging. He liked the feel of the dirt and gravel in his hands. The more he dug, the more he felt. At first, he dug with the frantic enthusiasm of a terrier after a buried prize. But as he continued, a deeper, subliminal rhythm took hold. His hands explored the cleft in the rocks, firm where he sensed that the soil was resistant but not impenetrable, gentle, where it yielded readily. Sometimes, his whole hand and arm up to the elbow sank into rich, friable, sour-smelling loam which he could remove and stroke with one luxurious sweeping movement. At others, the face of the rock sweated and stank of fetid, decomposing organic matter and dissolving minerals that almost made him retch. At yet other times, he panted with exhilaration. But always, he penetrated deeper into the rocks.

Unknown to Brewster, Miss Worthit had followed him to the site of his excavation after he returned home one day covered with dirt. As she watched, concealing herself from view behind nearby shrubbery, his hands, so strong for such a young lad, gently prodding the clefts in the rock, stirred something inside her. Unable at last to restrain herself, she pushed through the shrubbery, grabbed him and hauled him away, struggling. By the time they got to the Mansion, both were covered with dirt, and she insisted on an immediate bath. She undressed him in the bedroom, big for his age as he was, and scolded. Her voice caught when he stood before her, completely naked. Protesting that he was perfectly capable of undressing without her help, he nevertheless allowed her to drag him by the arm into the bathroom and order him into the tub. She began to scrub him with grim determination. In the process, she was splashed with water. She remembered that she, too, had gotten grimy. When she reached his groin, her hands lingered over his genitals. She undressed herself in front him and climbed into the tub. Brewster stood in the tub, stunned by her behavior and by her woman's body, which he had never before seen. And very different she was from boys and girls who showed each other "theirs." She sponged herself as he gaped, devouring him with her eyes. As Miss Worthit ran a sponge first over his genitals, then her own, he was aroused. She reached behind him to scrub his back, pressing herself against him and burying his face in her breasts.

Not long after that, both Brewster and Worthit began having restless nights.

When Miss Worthit had first discovered Brewster at his work near the cave site, her impulse was to forbid it. But after that day when they had both got back to the mansion hot and dirty, she welcomed his excursions as an excuse for frequent baths. There were few parts of the boy's body Miss Worthit's sponge did not linger over. Brewster was both alarmed and excited at her attentions. The warm, moist, sensuous caresses of the woman began to stir between his legs uncontrollably. This grew. Having thoroughly probed him with her sponge, she would then hand it to him and guide his hand into all her private places. Brewster's restlessness at night increased. Miss Worthit took him into her bed to calm him.

Satisfied that she had her charge under adequate scrutiny, the governess allowed Brewster greater freedom of activity during the day. He used to have to sneak away from his studies to the excavations whenever Miss Worthit was otherwise occupied, which was not very often. But now he found that Miss Worthit was often otherwise engaged and he could get away whenever he wished.

Enticing as the diggings and the bathings were, they were also accompanied by an underlying sense of shame, as if somehow Brewster and Miss Worthit had crossed into some forbidden zone. He became increasingly guilt-ridden and withdrawn. He had enjoyed Miss Worthit's fondling, but the feeling that it was wrong grew. Though both the elder Wainwrights remained cool and aloof from Brewster during this period, Amalia, being a mother, noticed things that escaped the father. She began to have doubts about Worthit, who, unlike her credentials, had seemed at first to be as trustworthy as she appeared to be competent. Amalia could see, in her fleeting glimpses of Brewster, that something was troubling him. When a normally boisterous kid becomes reticent, even reserved, the vacuum can hardly escape notice.

Vaguely disturbed by Brewster's moodiness Amalia sent for Worthit. She had noticed Worthit's absences. Sometimes they understandably coincided with Brewster's, sometimes with Augustus's. But especially at night, she absented herself from the premises entirely. Amalia chided herself for being perhaps too demanding and tried to rationalize Worthit's neglect of her duties. She remembered all too vividly how her own family circumscribed the freedoms she felt entitled to. Worthit was entitled to some time for herself in the evenings. But a mother's concern did occasionally override more liberal feelings.

When Worthit came into the library she seemed curiously out of sorts and fussed at the collar of her dress. Since Worthit had always been a meticulously groomed young woman, Amalia was annoyed. There was some subtle change in the woman's whole demeanor that she could not quite put her finger on. It made her uneasy. She looked narrowly at the nanny, wondering if she ought to draw attention to the slight smudge at the edge of her collar.

"Worthit" . . . she hesitated . . . "are you quite well?"

A pause. Then, "Of course, ma'am. Why do you ask?"

"Oh—it's nothing I'm sure. Just my imagination, perhaps." Amalia was puzzled by Worthit's manner. The nanny avoided her eyes. "But tell me. Is Brewster quite well?"

"Brewster, ma'am?"

What *is* wrong with the girl! "Haven't you noticed a change in Brewster's behavior?" As how could she not?

"A change, ma'am?" replied Worthit, her eyes briefly met Amalia's, then quickly looked away. She absently adjusted the collar of her blouse. "What sort of change would that be?"

"Come now, Worthit," said Amalia, growing impatient. "Surely you've noticed that Brewster has become suddenly very quiet? It's not like him."

"Oh." Another pause. "Well, children do go through phases. Like the moon." She managed a wan smile—"Perhaps this is just his dark side?"—and forced a little chuckle.

Baffled and irritated by Worthit's unresponsiveness, Amalia sent her away and asked her to send Mr. Trifle. Trifle was a busy little man who seemed active even in repose. He came bustling into the room as energetically as Worthit had entered negligently.

"You sent for me, madam?" He was almost agog with attention.

"Yes, Trifle." Amalia decided to use a more oblique approach. "How are Brewster's studies going?"

The little man's expression momentarily hooded, but quickly brightened. "Well, now that you mention it, he does seem to have become a bit listless and inattentive of late. But I didn't think it was serious enough to trouble you with. Boys will go through these moods, won't they?"

"Do you think so? I wonder if he's quite well?"

"Oh, assuredly. Moody, perhaps. But ill?" Trifle thought about it for a moment. "No, madam. I think not ill. Perhaps all he needs is a change of air." He wondered if that sounded too obviously as if he were angling for a cruise in the Caribbean. Or better yet, the Mediterranean. *He* certainly could bear a change. And a nice cruise in the tropics, even with Worthit and the boy—

"Miss Worthit," Amalia broke in on his daydream, "have you noticed anything—out of sorts—with her?"

The rivalry between Worthit and Trifle had always been amicable enough on the surface. But underneath it lay the submerged hostility of the disappointed suitor. The truth is that Trifle had always hungered for Worthit's voluptuous body but she had spurned his advances, always under the guise of competition for Brewster's approval, of course. This had wounded him deeply. And here was the Grand Lady of the Manor offering a golden opportunity to give Worthit a thrust she could not refuse. The little man fairly seethed with a passion which he himself could not consciously admit.

"Uh—n-no, madam. Nothing out of the ordinary." *Could* there be a connection between Brewster's demeanor and Worthit's? "Perhaps Miss Worthit could use a change of air, too?" And of course, not to forget Trifle. He left the suggestion hanging hopefully.

But Mrs. Wainwright was not open to hints at island cruises.

"But then she and I see little of each other," with a tinge of genuine regret in his voice, "except when our duties with Brewster overlap," wistfully wishing for a different kind of overlap.

Amalia wondered whether to bring the matter to Augustus. He would be very cross and probably put it down to her imagination. Trifle was beginning to look ill at ease.

"Thank you, Trifle. That will be all for now." Could he be right? Did they all need a change of air? It was a bit early in the season for a cruise, but if Brewster continued to mope about, it might be a good idea.

During the next several days, Amalia kept the matter from her husband to await developments. Not only did Brewster not snap out of his moodiness, but Worthit's too grew worse. The nanny was increasingly absent from the mansion in the evenings when she ought to have been on hand to look after Brewster. She would leave and return, unexpectedly, without a word of explanation. Amalia assigned some of her duties to the housekeeper, who rightly felt herself put upon. To make matters worse, Worthit was becoming downright untidy. The girl often fussed with her dress, as if she could not get her collars quite right. Was she actually scratching herself in front of others? Amalia was on the verge of bringing the whole thing to Augustus when he came to her.

"What has become of Worthit," he complained. "She wasn't available a few evenings ago, and last night I was looking for her again. To help me with some paperwork," he added hastily. And there it was. The situation was taken out of Amalia's hands. Worthit made another one of her unexplained departures one evening and never returned. At least, not that she knew of. Brewster told Trifle that he thought he saw someone or something prowling around under his bedroom window. Trifle was skeptical but dutifully reported the alleged incident to Amalia, along with his belief that the boy was imagining.

Amalia hired a temporary nurse to keep an eye on Brewster until new arrangements could be made. Brewster was getting a little old for a nanny, but the nurse might alleviate any separation anxiety he may be feeling at the departure of Worthit. At night, she was stationed at a window in an adjoining room to reassure everyone that Brewster's imaginary intruder was just that. On her first night, the new nurse thought that she, too, detected something moving in the shadows. An investigation turned up nothing tangible. There were no further incidents on the following nights, and the whole thing was put down to imagination.

The Womb of Uncreated Night

Mr. Trifle really had not fully appreciated the extent of his fixation on Miss Worthit. After her disappearance, he began to pine. And since the Wainwrights were not disposed to send him on a cruise to the Caribbean, much less the Mediterranean, he decided that he would take his savings and blow them on a cruise himself. He could not, however, bring himself to depart as unceremoniously as Miss Worthit. It was not in his very proper character to do that. So he gave his notice, offering at first to stay until a new tutor could be found.

But the Wainwrights dragged their feet in finding a replacement. Trifle at last had had enough of what he regarded as their stalling, packed up and left. Perhaps Amalia was reluctant to replace another important member of Brewster's caretakers so soon after the sudden departure of Miss Worthit. Brewster seemed to be taking it well, though he had lost his former exuberance. That actually pleased Augustus. Perhaps that boy was his son after all, the quiet, aloof offspring he had wanted all along, outwardly reserved, even repressed. When the time came for the boy to sow his wild oats, Augustus would be ready with his checkbook. There was hope for him yet.

Amalia resigned herself to Brewster's new self-sufficiency and tried to share her husband's approval at the passage of infancy. She had found Brewster's high spirits rather appealing and was frankly puzzled by the ease with which Brewster accepted the sudden departures of the nanny and his tutor. She could understand a sturdy preadolescent outgrowing the nanny, and the nebbishy Trifle did not have an endearing personality. But whatever had been troubling him leading up to the departures had apparently eased up. Had they something to do with his malaise? She temporarily apportioned among the household staff the routine matters of seeing that Brewster's immediate needs were met, and if she fretted about how Brewster was occupying himself, it merged into a search for replacements.

Freed of the sometimes overbearing supervision of Worthit, Brewster returned to his excavations. Digging with just his hands had become increasingly difficult for him as he met resistant surfaces. Pretending to take an interest in landscape gardening, he approached the gardener, Antonio. He got him to show him something about techniques of natural landscaping and the use of various tools. Tools began to disappear, and when Antonio made a fuss to the Wainwrights, to reappear. They thought that poor Antonio was getting senile.

Using the "stolen" tools, Brewster eventually penetrated quite deep into a cleft between the rocks. As the work progressed, he noticed that the piles of dirt he had excavated were threatening to give away his excavations. He took care to be more discreet by randomly distributing the dug out material across the face of the cliff. After each dig, he inspected the site for obvious signs of digging and checked to see if it was visible from below. For days at a time, he paused in his penetration into the side of the ravine to contrive a deceptively natural-looking blind of shrubbery and debris. If someone strolled or jogged nearby, he stopped digging and pretended to be examining the caves. To a casual eye, his dig appeared to be only one more jumble of nature struggling to assert itself through the tangled undergrowth.

7.

The underground passageway connecting Herald Square with Pennsylvania Station was always dirty, littered with newspapers and other scraps of paper, cans of soft drinks — some seeping their unfinished contents, plastic coffee cups, cigarette butts. The tunnel smelled of urine. Halfway down its length, in a blanket of cast-off newspapers and corrugated paper, a homeless man huddled, disheveled, infested with lice, addicted to alcohol, muttering incoherently. He lived inside concentric mazes—city streets, underpasses, subway; the innermost, his head—a worm burrowing through a blur of graffiti from which he peered at passing shadows, mining an occasional coin. When he lurched to his feet, flitting shadows sucked him into their vortex. He staggered through crowded subway trains, mutely begging with a dirty plastic cup thrust at passengers.

His age was indeterminate, though he appeared to be in his forties. He wore a dingy dark, frayed overcoat, with the collar turned up and held the lapels close to his throat with his other hand. He shivered. He seemed not to be wearing a shirt or undergarment. He had no shoes, and his naked feet were bruised and covered with sores. His dark skin was dull and gray from having lived so long underground, unwashed. His eyes were vacant, glassy, deep in their hollow sockets, looking almost as if they had no pupils. His thick uncombed mat of wiry dark hair molded by the pavement or walls against which his head had rested at some time past was flecked with dandruff and bits of unidentifiable detritus. Sometimes, as he lurched through a subway train, a passenger would drop a coin in his cup, anxious to divert the aggressive thrust and send him on his way. Or the frowning white man, out of nastiness or loss of balance as the moving train swayed from side to side, stepped on a bare foot, causing Hippias to howl in such anguish that almost everyone in the car hastily fished out a coin to drop into the cup. Or the seated black lady, on her way to work, took out a dollar bill and stuffed it into the cup. Sometimes a reluctant donor hardened his heart because he thought that charity would only encourage the beggar's dissipation.

Back at his usual place in the dimly-lit passageway, sitting amid the scattered newspapers, Hippias suddenly stopped his vacant muttering, as if a particular passing shadow had startled him into attention. Everything washed into a flood of focus. Glaze became purpose and his eyes filled with what they saw.

Still shaky on his feet, he steadied himself momentarily with a hand against the grimy, sweating wall he had only a moment before lain stupefied against. A slight smile stretched his unaccustomed lips, as if recognizing someone or something he had not seen for a long time. His lips began to move. But instead of incoherent mumbling, he began to speak quietly but distinctly. The words at first did not form complete sentences. Gradually, his voice grew from long untapped reservoirs of resonance. The words took firmer hold. And he spoke at last in full periods as he walked slowly and steadily to the tunnel's exit and mounted the stairs to the street.

"Only in the harmony of the senses and the spirit can we find true perfection," he began, addressing the crowds gathering at the intersection of 33rd Street waiting for the light to cross over Seventh Avenue to Pennsylvania Station or hurrying elsewhere Up- and Downtown. He walked slowly down the middle of the sidewalk, haranguing pedestrians brushing impatiently past him, his voice bouncing over the surface of traffic. "Reason, residing in the spirit, for the spirit *is* reason, must not yield to the senses. Nor must the senses be dulled or diluted, for it is through them that the spirit is able to orient itself in the material world . . ." Surprised by such rational-sounding speech from such an unlikely source, the passersby who heard him nevertheless shrugged it off as the random lucidity of lunacy. But this was no passing fluke. Hippias proved himself capable of sustained rhetoric, and soon became a center of curiosity. He stopped walking. Without raising his voice to rant, as some street-preachers do, without threatening hell-fire or damnation, nor calling on sinners to repent, his voice accompanied by the rumblings arriving and departing below ground, the echoing steps of busyness, the babble of voices in conversation or peddlers hawking rip-offs or cursing mishaps, the blare of traffic in the streets, his voice somehow cut through the hubbub. Though he sometimes lost the ear hurrying past in its maze of concerns, and sometimes found an uncharitable jeer that made him the target of a misdirected ego, he also sometimes arrested the thoughtful in their harried flight, arousing sympathy and concern.

When asked his name by some would-be benefactor, he gave only Hippias, which soon turned into "Hippie." It was at once oddly anachronistic and ironically funny. So "Hippie" became his street name.

Eventually, "Hippie" became a bit of a celebrity. The news media took him up and discovered that before he dropped out onto the streets of New York, he had been well-educated, a member of an affluent and cultured African American family, among whom he had begun to show signs of instability. Embarrassed, his family had been uncertain what to do with him. Reluctant to have him institutionalized, alarmed at his increasingly bizarre and irrational behavior, they were finally mystified and perhaps a little relieved when he dropped out of the family circle and was absorbed into the great heap of anonymity accumulating in the streets of Manhattan. Wary of his notoriety in the media, they welcomed him back into the family and tried to hush up the whole business.

The Wainwrights had not yet found a tutor for Brewster. Augustus reluctantly agreed with Amalia that Brewster probably no longer needed a nanny. But he would still need a tutor for a few more years. He wistfully yearned for a woman who would have the endowments of Worthit and the credentials of Trifle. But he realized how improbable that was. Besides, hiring the household staff was Amalia's domain and he did not want to risk a row.

When Hippias's story was circulated and recirculated in the media ad nauseam, Augustus was unsettled by the gleam in Amalia's eye. According to the human interest stories which persisted in the news media despite the family's efforts to suppress them, Hippias's background had been investigated—as if they had any notion of a proper investigation! he scoffed—and were impressed by his educational background, his dual accomplishments in areas as classical as the man's name, and advanced studies in theoretical physics. Hippias Goldspiegel! Something about a character in an obscure philosophical eighteenth century novel by some obscure German, he muttered. Really! That was sure to rouse Amelia from Wainwright complacency! Augustus never could understand the perverse streak that made her sympathize with the disreputable and the downtrodden.

Amalia, on the other hand, saw in Hippias an opportunity to slip "deserving underprivileged" and "ethnic diversity" past Augustus' stark conservatism. She knew that the instability leading to the squalor of Hippias's life on the streets would make Augustus hesitate—Ha! she corrected herself—outright refuse! But she had given in to him on matters she felt strongly about, and he knew that too. That would be enough to keep him on edge. She would bide her time, and then when he thought that she had moved on to other concerns . . .

Amalia found him in the library, celebrating a recently acquired controlling interest in a revolutionary new technology without having risked any of his own capital. She, of course, knew nothing about such matters. So she found him in an expansive mood when she came in looking preoccupied.

The Womb of Uncreated Night

Augustus looked up at her and smiled graciously. "Well, now, is something wrong?"

"It's Brewster," she said, sitting down on the edge of the chair beside him.

"I suppose he's been up to some mischief, eh?" he chuckled, sipping his whiskey. "Boys will be boys."

Amalia spoke hesitantly. "We can't always have our way, can we?" she responded guilelessly. "It's really too bad, you know." She paused to gaze out the library's tall windows. "About Worthit, I mean. She had such a way about her," she turned and looked at him directly, "didn't she? With Brewster, I mean. To have left without even saying goodbye . . . But there's no help for it, is there? And besides," she smiled comfortingly and patted his hand, "Brewster *was* getting rather old for a nanny. We couldn't have kept her on much longer. Could we?"

"She was useful in other ways."

"Yes, of course. But Brewster really does need a tutor. It's time we did what's best for him and replaced her. What if, at the same time, we could do something for the community, even if only indirectly . . . ?"

Augustus stirred restlessly in the haze of his drink and the flush of his success for some rebuttal. This conversation was taking an ugly turn. But he had not quite lost his buzz, and the prospect of favorable social comment made him reflect. However avaricious he might be in business, he was not above making public gestures to get it—he swirled the ice in his drink and took another sip—both public favor and an improved business climate.

"Well, then," she said brightly, "wouldn't it be quite a coup if we could pick up that brilliant man who has just recovered from his ordeal on the street and give him gainful employment which might keep him from sliding back. It would be so good," she hurried on, "for Brewster to see at first hand the value of reaching out and aiding such a deserving recovery, to say nothing of how it would enhance your philanthropic image . . . which could use a bit of polish."

Augustus, grudgingly swayed but unwilling to surrender control entirely, insisted that he personally would see to it that the man's background and academic credentials were minutely scrutinized. "Any blemish, the minutest speck on the man . . ."

When Amalia interviewed Hippias for the position, Augustus sat in discreetly in the background. The Wainwrights found Hippias cleaned up and dressed in a worn but serviceable three-piece suit. He wore no jewelry, but he sported a watch-chain, the one adornment his family had preserved for him, across his vest. His oxfords looked worn and down at the heels, but the shoes were polished. He looked like a business man, Augustus thought, a banker or stock broker down on his luck. When he spoke, he was quite as lucid as he was learned. As they talked, he drew the watch out of his pocket, dangled it by the chain from the index finger of his right hand, and began to swing it like a pendulum in time with his speech. Amalia ignored this quirk. Augustus rumbling in the background wondered if Hippias was trying to hypnotize them.

Actually, Hippias had no need of such gimmicks. He had a fine deep resonant voice which he used with an assurance that only occasionally showed traces of recent neglect. His manner was spellbinding and the interview went smoothly. He outlined a program of study for Brewster that would seamlessly pick up where Trifle had left off. He was perfectly at ease in discussing basic academic curricula, and despite his . . . hiatus . . . showed a grasp of current academia. He had even had some classroom experience as an undergraduate teaching apprentice at local schools. He made a strong impression on Amalia, and even the cynical Augustus thawed a bit. Hippias was not over-concerned about the usual practical matters, prospective duties, living accommodations, salary. He was sure these would be satisfactory. Amalia broached the matter of Brewster's visual handicap, and Augustus hinted that the boy was, as a result, a bit odd. Hippias assured them it was something he could handle.

The interview took an off-the-wall turn when Brewster was brought in to meet his prospective tutor. At a passing mention of Brewster's interest in Batman, Hippias lit up and at once expressed his admiration for the character's mythic qualities without any trace of condescension or sucking up. Augustus assumed it was appropriately both, though he disapproved of the subject. It gratified him that Hippias knew his place. Amalia quietly wondered in passing if Hippias might encourage Brewster's unwholesome fantasizing. Both parents were favorably impressed. But this time, Augustus and Amalia agreed, they would thoroughly verify the man's credentials.

Hippias and his family had come through the scrutiny of his past before his life on the street without a blemish. Augustus was satisfied that the family were respectable, upstanding business people. Black *and* Jewish. Amalia had hit a home run! There was no criminal record. Hippias had indeed received undergraduate and graduate degrees in the classics at prestigious universities and gone on to earn graduate degrees in the natural sciences and technology. He had distinguished himself in all areas. Why the devil hadn't he been snapped up by some Think Tank or Industry? He might have spared us all. But he had suddenly become unstable. He slumped, all his youthful brilliance and drive sucked out of him. His family did not know what had become of him until the media picked him up.

Hippias was offered the job. He accepted and prepared a curriculum based on Trifle's careful records. By late summer, Hippias had settled into The Lodge with the Wainwrights and begun gathering materials for lessons. He and Brewster often walked about the grounds atop the cliff, talking together and getting to know each other. Though their shared interest in Batman, Hippias developed a free and easy manner with Brewster, and easily overcame any doubts he may have had. Their relationship gradually eased so far that Brewster casually asked about babies switched at birth. Intrigued, Hippias questioned his pupil about his reason for asking. Gradually, Brewster recounted what he had overheard between Augustus and Amalia. This information, too, Hippias took matter-of-factly.

The speech with which Hippias Goldspiegel had emerged from his homeless frame of mind was never very far from his thoughts. In the doubts about whether Augustus was Brewster's natural father, Hippias found the ideal syringe through which to inject the harmony of sense and reason into the Batman mythos and nudge Brewster in a way wholly unexpected by the Wainwrights. Only after tutor and pupil had settled in together did Hippias set his plan in motion.

"Have you noticed," he mused one day, as offhandedly as he might have mentioned the fragrance of the roses in the gardens, "the similarity of your name to Bruce Wayne's?"

Brewster nodded thoughtfully. "I suppose I did. I once brought a bat to class. It escaped and caused a humongous commotion. After that, the kids at school started calling me 'Batman.' Maybe *they* made some connection."

Hippias waved away speculation about what other children may or may not have thought. "But isn't it interesting," he said, "that if you had been switched with another baby at the hospital the Wainwrights would not really be your parents?"

Brewster shrugged. "Isn't that what you'd call circular reasoning?" he said.

"Yes," replied Hippias. "But don't you see that, like Bruce Wayne, that makes you an orphan and points you in the same direction?"

Although an idea like that might readily stir the fantasies of any preadolescent boy, Brewster found an obvious flaw in it. "My parents haven't been mugged or shot," he said drily.

"True," said Hippias with a smile, for he saw that Brewster had at once realized what followed.

"Ah, I see! If the Wainwrights aren't my parents . . ."

The Womb of Uncreated Night

"Exactly!" Hippias was pleased that Brewster fell into the spirit of the game so readily.

"Then my birth parents *may* have been mugged and shot without my knowing about it." He turned over the implications in his mind. "Or if they have not, they may yet be. Huh!"

But another problem occurred to Brewster. "But the Batman story has already been written. How could I actually be Bruce Wayne?"

"Yours would not be the first case of a prophecy foretold in a myth. The Dalai Lama of Tibet is held by many to be a reincarnation of a Bhodisattva of the fifteenth century. The legend of the doppelgänger offers another way of seeing how one human being's life could be duplicated by another."

"Oh, I remember reading about reincarnation and karma, how your actions in one life determine your spiritual status in the next. But the doppel—"? Brewster hesitated.

"—*gänger*," finished Hippias emphasizing the umlaut. That's sort of an evil twin. The doppelgänger is virtually identical to a good person something bad is going to happen to."

In bringing up the curious correspondence in the names, continued Hippias, "I'd like you to look beyond the limited significance of the bat-image intended by Bob Kane. Instead of just being a symbolic disguise designed to play on the superstitious dread and cowardice of the criminal mind as he saw it, perhaps Kane had an unconscious wish for a positive figure to offset the archetypal vampire figure, a heroic bat as antidote to the sinister side of mankind. Sort of like a reverse doppelgänger. In a way," he added, "I think that's why you're so fascinated by bats and the Batman character. It's a little like the monks of Tibet searching for the next Dalai lama. If a small child is found who shows familiarity with the possessions from the life of a previous Dalai lama, that is considered a sign of the reincarnation."

"But I already knew all about Batman when I was a small child," said a disappointed Brewster. "So familiarity with Batman's life and possessions wouldn't count. And if I'm Bruce Wayne's doppelgänger, wouldn't that mean that make me an evil twin?"

Hippias laughed at Brewster's willingness to enter a game he might lose. "No, no, not at all! We don't need to be so literal. I only wanted you to consider the parallels for now. We are all born with the capacity for good or evil. We may even be predisposed to one or the other. But we also have intellects that make it possible for us to choose which path to follow. I think that your inner choice was already revealed in your taste for Batman. I think it showed your true nature asserting itself."

"But there must be lots of kids who feel the same way," objected Brewster.

"That's true. But none of them have your unique abilities or the opportunity to validate that nature."

"What unique abilities?"

"Ah, we're getting ahead of ourselves. They will reveal themselves if you give them a chance. That's what education is really all about. Not just learning how to do something or other, but learning how to find our true selves in what we do. You know, Brewster, if we let ourselves be defined by some occupation, which is a only step above letting ourselves be taken over by our senses, we are alienated from our true nature. We can only reach that through the harmony, the balance, of reason and spirit.

"We need our physical senses to orient our selves in the material world." Seeing that Brewster had begun to look uncomfortable, Hippias hastily added, "The marvelous thing about our senses is that we can compensate for deficiencies in one by enhancing the others. Some individuals hear better than others. Others have greater dexterity. Yet others have sharper senses of taste or smell. Sometimes these abilities show themselves in early childhood. Sometimes they have to be developed. You've already learned how to supplement the limits of seeing with feeling, haven't you?"

Brewster was not sure how to respond. He had casually mentioned the pleasure of digging at the base of the cliff. But he still felt shame mingled with pleasure at recollecting Miss Worthit. Taking Brewster's silence as attentiveness, Hippias continued.

"Reason lives in the spirit which is informed through our physical senses. Spirit is that indefinable inner awareness of who we are as individuals, that self, that *me* living inside our heads."

"Is that what some people call *soul*?"

"More or less the same things. Let's just call it the *self* for now. If that *self* is overwhelmed by gratifying the senses, its reason is weakened and the spirit which guides our behavior crumbles. They must always be kept in balance, for if one or the other gets the upper hand, we lose our true selves. Do you understand?"

"Sort of," said Brewster.

"Good enough for now. So, education consists of learning how to keep reason and the senses in harmony."

"Not just learning how to do things?"

"To do what things? That's for the spirit and reason decide. If the *self* develops in discontinuity with the external, material world, its perception of the world is distorted, and the individual's place in it is disoriented. You wouldn't be the first, feeling himself so different from those who claim to be his parents, to wonder if he were a changeling. The Wainwrights keep themselves so aloof and distant, doesn't it seem at times as if they were play-acting?"

"Oh, like a conspiracy?" This tutor was something else. He offered Brewster an alternate reality straight out of science fiction. The most convoluted video game in a living arcade. If he often appeared to be on a different dimensional plane, even when they were talking about the same thing, that only enhanced the impression. And he had that odd habit of swinging his pocket watch like a pendulum whenever they had these earnest chats.

"Sort of," echoed Hippias with a smile. "The word 'conspiracy' covers so many levels of pretending. For instance, have you ever heard of the Witness Protection Program? The Government often relocates witnesses who can testify against criminals to protect them from retaliation. It sets them up in new homes and gives them new identities. When your parents were mugged and shot in the 33rd Street tunnel I used to live in—" Seeing that Brewster was about to interrupt, Hippias answered before he could ask, "No, I never witnessed such an event. But suppose that *you* had. The shock of such a traumatic event could easily lead you to suppress the memory."

"But Bruce Wayne *did* see the shooting," said Brewster. "And it wasn't in the 33rd Street tunnel." Hippias said nothing. He merely waited for Brewster to follow the line of thought that had opened up. Walking beside Hippias on the path, Brewster could not see into his face, to gauge how far he ought to go. "So, Bruce Wayne, or someone like him outside the comic book that the Government didn't want anyone to know about, might've put him in Witness Protection and conspired with Bob Kane to create a whole new scenario to cover it up?"

Hippias left the question hanging in Brewster's mind, contemplated his pupil for a moment. Then, "Have you ever heard about people who, under hypnosis, are able to recall their lives in former existences? Perhaps . . . under hypnosis you could recall the event."

"What an intriguing idea! That sounds like fun! And you're saying that *I* may really have been Bruce Wayne in some former life, only I've forgotten?"

"Like all energy, the vital energy of life is not lost. It is merely recycled."

"That's awesome!" cried Brewster in admiration. "Do you know how to hypnotize people?" Hippias smiled cryptically.

"Some people are more susceptible than others," he said, and put his watch away. "But I suspect that you have a strength of mind that would be highly resistant to suggestion. We might try it some time. If your mental strength is as formidable as I suspect, it may take some doing. On the other hand, you may be able to recapture your former self without hypnotic suggestion. Perhaps by playing the role of Bruce Wayne as detailed in your comic books."

It was not unheard for kids to refer to comic books as "joke books."

The Womb of Uncreated Night

But that they might be something more, truly *real* . . . or could the *real* merely be a joke in an alternate frame of reference . . . ? Could Hippias mean that Batman was something more than a "joke" because Bruce Wayne was somehow encoded in Brewster's past? That he might even grow into Batman?

"Could a person," thought Brewster aloud, "give reality to a comic book hero, or could a comic book hero give reality to a person?" Further wrinkling the boundary between Fun and Games was Hippias's reinvention of the death of Bruce Wayne's parents—his?—in another life. He pondered the significance of such a death. While Death was simulated in the panels of the comic strip, Life went on between them. When he got wrapped up in *DC Comics*, he did feel, in a way, that he had lived Bruce Wayne's experiences. His present life might be the Life Between, a kind of continuum outside the panels from which he could observe his former life within them. That could explain how the Waynes could be his parents, murdered on the streets of New York, while the Wainwrights were his surrogates. Then a thought troubled him.

"But Dr. Thomas Wayne and his wife were shot to death on the streets by a mugger, not in a tunnel," objected Brewster reluctantly, afraid that he was stumbling over an out-of-place detail that would bring on the collapse of this newly discovered alternate Life he eagerly wanted to try on.

"Even the most careful reporter may nevertheless make the clumsiest factual error," Hippias responded airily, "due either to reporting under stress or to faulty sources of information. Mr. Kane may not have been the most acute observer. His story may have been an imagined reconstruction. You know, it's the sort of thing Woodward and Bernstein 'reported' in the Watergate scandal."

"Or like Truman Capote's *In Cold Blood*?"

"Exactly! And think of all the non-fiction fiction written in the years since, people reporting what others are supposed to have said. People love to reinvent history, not to say themselves. It gives them the illusion of control over an irrational universe and their otherwise insignificant lives."

"Oh," said Brewster, brushing against some viburnums they were passing. He cocked his head as another thought occurred to him. "But if you witnessed a murder in the tunnel, wouldn't you be put into the Relocation Program too?"

"Hah! Nobody would pay any attention to me. I would not," Hippie said with an enigmatic smile, "be considered a credible witness. Nobody would take me seriously. But as I said, I never witnessed such a thing."

Brewster looked curiously at the man walking beside him but said nothing. After a few more steps of reflection, he returned to the real-life comic book unfolding itself before him. "And the Wainwrights back at The Lodge, my . . . parents?"

"Caretakers. Surrogates . . . As you are underage, the authorities could not allow you to fend for yourself. Aside from the murderers of your parents, there would be the disagreeable possibility that the juvenile authorities would have placed you in an orphanage. You would not have liked that."

Brewster was frankly puzzled. He sounded out his doubts. "If I've been reincarnated, and the Waynes were my actual parents in a former life, why couldn't the Wainwrights be my actual parents in this one? Do events in *this* life have to repeat events in that past life? They needn't be dead. Yet." He paused to kick a stone.

Hippias smiled enigmatically. "At the moment," he said, "we are only entertaining possibilities."

They had reached the end of the path in a little clearing looking out over the cliff. Two-hundred and thirty feet below lay the Indian Caves. The paths of Inwood Hill Park curved and branched off through the trees and shrubbery. "Do you see those paths below, Brewster, how they twist and turn off into side-paths? They all interconnect. If you walked casually along them, you would see ever changing vistas through the trees and upthrust rocks concealing where they branched off. Choosing one path over the other would transform the experience, and in so doing, you. Even if you retraced your steps over the same path, your perception would not be the same as if you had not chosen it. But the exact nature of that transformation depends on how your choice affects you, how your spirit and reason respond to the surroundings your senses have shown you as you walk. Yet you would not perceive the unity of the paths' design." Hippias turned to look searchingly into Brewster's face. "If you returned to the Lodge right now, would you be exactly the same person you were when we started out. Or have you perhaps acquired some new outlook?"

Brewster was about to reply.

"No," said Hippias. "Don't try to answer now. We will discover the answer in time."

8.

BREWSTER FACED A CONUNDRUM. WHAT had seemed so certain to him yesterday, appeared less so today. Standing close to a rhododendron at the rim of the cliff, he peered thoughtfully at a bud in its rosette of leaves. If it survived weather, disease, and pests, it would emerge as a leaf or a flower. But the choices of a boy almost twelve years old were infinitely more complex and bewildering. They swirled in his mind like a dust witch. If the answers must come from within, as Hippias implied, did that mean consciously trying to figure them out would unbalance his true, inner self? Would reasoning it out disrupt "the harmony of the spirit and the senses"? Did he really have choices? Hippias couldn't have meant that he should go about blindly bumping into life the way he did when he was a little kid, knocking things over because he couldn't see without his glasses. But *how*? How did that bud "decide" whether it would be a leaf or a flower? His season come one day, would he look in the mirror and reveal to himself, to the world, Bruce Wayne, a foundling, his reincarnation? Or his doppelgänger . . . ?

How do you stop reasoning things out anyway? Another moment's reflection and Brewster decided that the Wainwrights and their mansions were probably not typical foster homes anyway. He didn't know much about such things, but he wondered why a wealthy couple would bother to give a home to a half-blind foundling. Brewster was still lost in puzzling them out when Hippias came looking for him.

"Ah, there you are," said Hippias.

"I was thinking about what you said yesterday," said Brewster. "About choosing and not choosing and the foundlings and reincarnation and the doppelgänger—" Hippias held up a hand to stop the outpouring.

"Perhaps we need to slow down a bit," he said, "and consider these matters more carefully. When I outlined choices for you but then told you not to choose just yet, I meant only that you should not rush to a choice. It's not that you don't ever choose. You can't help choosing. It's just that until your senses have filled you with sufficient knowledge, your choices are blind; reason and the senses are not yet in harmony, and one or the other may lead you to an unfortunate choice. And while you're waiting to see what choice is best for you, we have Fun and Games, where you can try some of the choices on, so to speak. Do you see?"

"I think so," said Brewster doubtfully. He hesitated. Yesterday, too, he thought he "saw."

"Well, then, shall we play?" Hippias placed his hand on Brewster's shoulder and turned around. They walked on a path skirting the cliff. Trees and shrubbery hid its precipitous drop.

"There are larger pictures than those in our daily comic panels," resumed Hippias. "And they provide the background for the next phase of our games. What was magical to the early humans when they first contemplated the forces of nature was magnified thousands of times when they placed these in the context of the universe. Imagine! A cosmos inhabited by gods and spirits and demons. Skepticism has eroded that magic and replaced it with reason and empirical observation. Humans once did not doubt that the whole universe was permeated by an Oversoul. They called it by any number of names, but people all over the world, having no knowledge of each other, agreed that *something* was out there," Hippias's arm swept across the sky, "an eternal essence, a prime cause from which everything was created."

Hippias paused on the path, thinking to give Brewster a chance to catch up. He only nodded.

"And this *something*," Brewster said with a shrug, "this Oversoul. God, of course."

Hippias returned the nod. "Yes, God is one of the many names they gave it. What made it even more meaningful to them, this essence, was that they possessed a fragment of it. It was a part of them and they were a part of it. That was the original belief. Ancient peoples did not think of the 'self' as separate from that Oversoul because that would have destroyed the harmony of the universe, and isolated them from the spirit living in all things. Such a thing would have been incomprehensible."

"And science," said Brewster, "has done just that?"

"All but!" replied Hippias. "If that essence is present everywhere and in everything, and yet eluded all the scientific data-gathering gadgets available, can it be anything more than a figment of the imagination, at best, or mass psychosis at worst?"

This time, Brewster stopped dead in his tracks. Hippias walked on a few paces. Then he too stopped and turned to face Brewster. "Science has eroded the certainty of Oversoul, but traces persist. Aside from the stubborn refusal to accept only what all our senses and instruments are showing us, the question remains whether our senses and the instruments designed to sharpen their perception are too limited to penetrate into cosmic nature. Furthermore, the more scientific instruments tell us about the universe, the less certain we are that what they show us is really all there is to see. At the subatomic level our instruments become uncertain. They show us that *something* is happening, that electrons circle a nucleus, but they don't allow us to say exactly where they are. And finally, there is that sense of self, completely unscientific, that refuses to believe that it will really die."

"Did the ancients think of themselves as . . . *selfs*?" asked Brewster, vaguely uncertain whether the solecism or the tautology were more troubling.

"*Selves*," corrected Hippias. "The Ancients had words like that, but they did not use them as we do today. Their 'self' did not separate them from the rest of humanity, for in that separation lay absolute death—

The Womb of Uncreated Night

not just the body's, but the *self*'s as well. Their only hope of surviving physical death lay in partaking of the Oversoul, of that fragment of the immortal being which lies beyond their fragile body's shell."

"God."

"Close enough," smiled Hippias. "Well, with the increasingly skeptical outlook encouraged by industrialization and technology, in a word, science, the concept of soul has been demystified. It has degenerated into the self, the ego, the 'I.' Everything," said Hippias, his eyes going out of focus for an instant, as if Brewster were *out there* somewhere, "everything has been reduced to 'I.'"

"Um, then if people thought that the universe had a soul because they had a soul, that must be why they also thought that it had a body like theirs, with a head and arms and legs? And a brain that reasons and calculates?" Hippias did not respond. Brewster had to work out imponderables for himself. "Then where is this body?"

"Might as well ask the atoms that make us up where *our* bodies are," Hippias replied.

"But paleontologists can reconstruct a prehistoric man from just a few fossils. I've even read that forensic specialists can reconstruct a murder victim's physical appearance from an arm or leg bone, even reconstruct a face from small skull fragments. Why can't they reconstruct God from the structure of the cosmos?"

Hippias smiled indulgently. "Inferring anatomical structures from known species, or from species resembling those that are known, is vastly different from inferring the structure of the universe from the Milky Way. Scientists don't yet know as much about the universe as they know about our bodies. The more they learn, the less they know with any certainty. Consider, then, how infinitely more difficult it would be to infer the structure of the Overself."

"Then how do you know that there is an Overself, a God, or any other universal self?"

"There is intuition. There is faith. We feel that we know without really knowing. Whatever Overself exists may have evolved out of the same 'dust' as ourselves . . . or may simply be a figment of our minds."

"But if this universal being evolved first," said Brewster, still puzzling out origins, "couldn't it have become intelligent enough to create us?"

"Several possible answers," Hippias began slowly, "follow from your question. First, the one that many people today believe, that a Super-being, the one called God, somehow pre-existed the physical universe. Truly supernatural. Second, a proto-being may have emerged from the physical stuff of the cosmos, either already having super-intelligence or evolving it and somehow mastering the principles of life. Then in turn that 'God' created other life forms less evolved. If so, then perhaps one day—no doubt eons from now—these lesser forms may evolve into Super-beings like the one who created all the forms of life we know and may yet discover. Finally, that 'God' may be no more than the sum of our imaginings. These three don't necessarily exhaust all the possibilities."

"Then how do we decide which is the real possibility?" asked Brewster. "Or don't we need to?"

"No one knows beyond an affirmation of faith which answer is the definitive one. My intuition leads me to suppose," said Hippias, as if looking into the cosmic void like a fortuneteller consulting a crystal ball, "that if anything like the 'God' of the Judeo-Christian creed exists, he is a product of the cosmos, not its cause."

Hippias paused again for Brewster to catch up.

"Well," said Brewster, frowning in possibilities, "if we can't say for sure whether the universe creates the Overself or the Overself creates the universe, how can we ever be sure what to believe and how to live our lives according to that belief?"

"Intuition can't answer 'which came first' questions any more certainly than faith."

"Intuition sounds a lot like faith," said Brewster. "But isn't intuition based on what you see without knowing that you see it? I mean, you have hunches about things that you've never seen before because you don't realize that they remind you of things you have seen. But faith . . . ?"

Hippias nodded approvingly at his young charge. "Faith affirms. Intuition gropes. Both are blind. Doubt is the stuff of a scientific

The Womb of Uncreated Night

outlook, that we can know only what we can *see*. Finite minds bounded by what they see between birth and death can't really grasp infinity. Everything we can see has a beginning and an end. It's hard to comprehend that there ever could have been a vast *unseen*, without substance, form, or sentience, out of which *the seen*, in substance, form, and sentience came. *Something* must have been there, all along, eh? If there ever was an *unseen*, where did *the seen* come from?"

"So whatever goes beyond the finiteness of our sense of self," said Brewster, struggling with abstractions that were making him giddy, "we fill in with 'intuition?'"

Hippias squinted. "Or faith." He thought for a moment. "Of course, what we see are extensions of mind, of self. And there is a connection between them that may be invisible. We can sense the impulses connecting them with mechanical instruments, but we can't *see* them directly.

"And then there's the question of self. What is the self, anyway? Everyone agrees that he or she is aware of an inner self. But no scientific method, no instrument yet devised can show it to us. *Intuitively* we *know* who we are. But sometimes we are uneasy because we can't scientifically *see* it. Sometimes," he said almost inaudibly, "we get so tangled up in self-doubt that we can even become self-destructive."

The path curved back from the escarpment that overlooked the confluence of the Harlem and Hudson rivers. Through a break in the trees, they could see the Bronx on the north and the Palisades on the Jersey shore to the west. They paused to take in the view.

"Yes. Yes," said Hippias as if in answer to a question from some unknown source. "The mysterious *self*. Does physical matter groping for form discover intelligence, self? Or does intelligence underlying physical matter discover form? Everything on earth supports and nurtures us as we, and all our kindred fragments, here and across the galaxies, nurture the Overself. *There* is the harmony!" Hippias looked back at Brewster expectantly.

But Brewster was not quite ready for the leap into space. "What happens to our 'self' when we die?" he asked. "Does it go on being us? If we come back as someone or something else, do we still know . . . " Brewster was momentarily stumped," . . . do we still know who we are . . . who we were?"

"Do you think the atoms that make up our bodies know who they are? Or that the food we eat retains its former identity? I don't mean to suggest that they have a consciousness such as ours. For all we know, the gap between the universal Oversomething and our sight or grasp may be as great."

"Okay. So there's this universal harmony we ought to tune in to," pursued Brewster, skeptically. "Do we tune in by going to church?"

"Church? Worship is the outcome of primitive belief in the supernatural. To bow before a mysterious power that is capable of punishing or rewarding, something you fear and hope to propitiate— ha! you clean and care for your body, but you hardly expect your atoms to sing you hosannas!" He paused to let off some of his exuberance. "But yes, I suppose you could say there is a kind of worship in it. A kind of communion. Yes." His eyes turned dreamy. He tuned in again to some distant, secret communication. Then his eyes refocused on Brewster, all tutor again.

"Let's take a look at the two kinds of awe that applies here, shall we?" Hippias settled himself on a rock outcrop at the edge of the precipice and invited Brewster to join him.

"We can easily see two broad categories of power, that which is exercised through physical force, and that which is exercised through psychic force. The one compels the body. The other compels the mind. The great unseen power of the universe that we sense—what is it, but an idealized, emotional extension of the power of a parent? a ruler? or a priest? presiding over some ritual confirming its authority? At each stage in this transference, its focus becomes less powerful as it becomes less tangible, less visible—"

"But if you defy your parents, a king, or a priest," interrupted Brewster, "you're punished. And the punishment is pretty tangible."

The Womb of Uncreated Night

"Punishment, my boy, is the physical exercise of power, inflicted on flesh and blood. In its most concrete form, it's raw, primitive brute force. But power also has a psychic component. Authority is its abstraction. Like consciousness, we *know* it's there. It awes us. We shudder at its unseen threat. We are born in pain. However far we may evolve out of our bodies and into our minds, we never lose the primitive dread of that primal pain. That is the origin of awe. That is the psychic engine that drives all power. But if it is seen *only* in terms of physical punishment, power loses its cosmic awe. The persons over whom brute power is exercised either collapse into abject slaves, or rebel with their own physical power, or find some other way to escape its influence."

Brewster mulled over his tutor's words. "But didn't you say that physical power compels the body while psychic power compels the mind? Haven't you just got psychic power compelling the body?"

"Ah!" said Hippias smiling indulgently at his pupil. "But it's an evolutionary process, don't you see? Primitive dread is reasoned away by the mind as the child matures. And when it is fully developed, the mind is able to put aside childish fears. Suppress them, but not eliminate them."

"Then awe gets its power by suspending physical punishment without ever giving it up?" said Brewster doubtfully. "But if we learn awe from physical punishment, no matter how evolved it gets, isn't all authority tainted with brutishness?"

"Hah!" said Hippias, triumphantly. "The trick is to learn how to wield it with such finesse that brute force is never resorted to. Raise authority to an exquisite abstraction, to an invisible retaliation that may or may not come, tap into unconscious wonder and dread, and you have the power to paralyze even the most sophisticated reasoning. Then you may believe in something beyond your self, and sway others. That's *awe*, that's true power. It transcends punishment. It's the ability of the inscrutable to puzzle, baffle, bewilder that ruffles our engrams and makes our scalp crawl. Inscrutability drives religions. A completely predictable god becomes impotent because it can be manipulated. But an unknowable god shrouded in mystery, ah, that raises monuments and sacrifices blood . . ."

Hippias trailed off into abstraction. How to let off more fizz, keep it light without threatening the universal harmony? Too much fizz and he would float off into space, where Brewster was not yet ready to follow. Too much gravity, and the weight would crush the boy's fragile belief. He returned with a shift and a chuckle.

"Awe!" he said as if he tasted the concept. "Awe is an undercurrent flowing through our desire to break the cycle of birth-death-rebirth. The desire to escape this cycle is the desire to escape . . . call it 'fate?' 'destiny?' 'God?' Your question of what happens to our 'I' when we die smacks of rebellion. Curiosity is the beginning of rebellion."

"But, if the mind evolved from the body, how could its curiosity be considered rebellion against the natural order?" wondered Brewster.

"It's not a rebellion *against* the natural order. Rebellion is an integral *part* of the natural order. It's the nature of intelligence, which begins with curiosity. First, it asks 'why?' An innocent desire to know. Then, 'why not?' From there, it's a small step to demanding, simply because it conceives of possibility. Base matter generates intellect which, in turn, generates the Overself, the God, that self-beyond-self, then challenges it!" The fizz erupted into a maniacal laughter before Hippias could tame it into a merry smile.

Brewster was startled and bewildered by the unexpected force of that laughter and the bizarre implications of Hippias' last words. He jumped off the rock they were sitting on and faced his tutor. "But—" he stammered, trying to get the words out, "but—if God either created us, or even if he? it? was created by us, why would we challenge him—it?"

"It would be as if the food we ate declared its independence, wouldn't it?" laughed Hippias gently. "Refusing to be assimilated, resisting even our ingestion of it. The revolt of the foods! No, no, that would be altogether too disharmonious, wouldn't it? Mere self-ish-ness!"

The path now led back to the mansion.

"So we're food for the Overself who's really a projection of ourselves?" Brewster laughed, too, though he didn't know whether from the absurdity of the whole discussion or simply because he couldn't resist joining in what sounded like a joke.

"The Hindus, Buddhists, even Jews, Christians and Muslims," said Hippias, "each in their own way, try to break the cycle of death and rebirth. They all imagine that they will be reborn after their death in some form or other. Hindus and Buddhists, in *this* world, Christians and Muslims, in the *next*. They all imagine that this cycle will continue until some grand *event*, whether self-willed or divinely ordained, brings a final end to life on earth. Sadly, some of them have trouble distinguishing the divine purpose from their own. So they spend their lives trying to 'tune in' to the divine harmony through discipline and worship, with sometimes disastrous consequences for the rest of humanity. On the surface, Christians, Jews, and Muslims appear to be more in a muddle about the afterlife. They believe that all life in this world will end in some divinely decreed extinction. Yet at the same time they believe that they will live in the next world 'in the flesh,' as they lived in this one! Except in that life, the virtuous will experience only the joys of this world, while the unworthy suffer all the ills. They are full of desire and contradiction.

"That puts them at odds with Hindus and Buddhists, who seek ways to end desire. But a common thread runs through all of them: once the Great Harmony is achieved, they will be transformed, one by one or en masse." Up to this point, Hippias had been speaking in his best tutorial voice. He spoke now in ordinary tones. "And while the poor fools flounder around, waiting for the grand transfiguration, the All Powerful turns parasitic, feeding on those over whom it holds power."

"No wonder people want to break the cycle," said Brewster, uneasy about the feeding metaphor.

Hippias focused on Brewster again. How much had his pupil really understood? Like a fisherman trying to land an elusive fish, he felt the urge to reel Brewster in. Had the boy reached the threshold of acceptance that would allow him to take the next step? Was Brewster ready for the net?

"It's the difference between merely listening to music and creating it," he said.

"Listening is nice."

"Yes, but when the music ends? What then?"

"Oh. Well, I suppose it's the internal and external that makes universal harmony? But religion turns everything inside out?"

"Something like that. But all is in harmony if inside and outside are continuous."

"Like a Möbius strip!"

"A Möbius strip! Yes. We need only find a way to focus our existence and direct it along such a continuum, and eternity is ours."

Brewster fell silent and thoughtful as Hippias climbed down off the rock. He knew some little about death, picked up from whispered comments at home or blaring headlines in the media. It was a sort of operatic abstraction, a diva retiring from the stage to her dressing room after a climactic grand gesture, to remove her makeup and afterwards throw a celebratory party. There had been little concrete instruction. The body of a cat or dog rotting in a gutter where it had been negligently tossed by some unseen accident—not that he had been allowed to see many gutters. Or a pestering insect swatted in a reflex of annoyance. Or the unintended victim of forces brought to bear in ignorance, observing a grasshopper with a magnifying glass . . .

But these seemed so distant. In polite society, such unpleasantness was kept at a distance. The subject of death was taboo. Like farting, or what you did in the toilet, or exploring your body. There was a kind of shame about it. It was a fact of life one didn't talk about. Or if one did, it was in hushed tones. Proper people, if they died at all, did it discreetly. Not grossly, in the streets . . .

And what about Dr. Wayne and his wife, gunned down in front of Bruce? That was a poser. They were certainly proper and should have had the good taste to act with discretion. Was a public sacrifice needed for some higher purpose, suspending etiquette? The inverse of great crimes allowed to outstanding individuals? In order to create awe?

Death inflicted on others violated good manners and had to be made up for somehow. In that former life, Bruce Wayne had tracked down the thug who murdered his parents and brought him to justice. Wasn't the thug serving a higher purpose? Why, then, had vengeance fallen on him? Because it was pure brutishness? Apparently, it wasn't just *serving* a higher purpose, but *how* you served it that made the difference. More etiquette. Christians, Jews, and Muslims were not the only ones in a muddle.

The death of the Waynes had become a conundrum of Fun and Games for Brewster. Perhaps it defined the boundary between the two. Would the Wainwrights, too, be murdered in the streets? After all, his twelfth birthday was not far off. The Wainwrights were a pain, sometimes. But he wouldn't wish them any harm, however discreet. If they were killed by some thug, would he have to avenge them by taking on the identity and burden of Batman with Hippias to help and guide him? There was a lot more Games than Fun in this prospect.

But none of this prepared him for experiencing death in himself. It never occurred to him to expect to live forever. He simply did not expect to die, like so many things people do but don't believe in. This Overself that Hippias was talking about raised as profound a mystery as had ever occurred to him. Until Hippias said that it was possible that we might not *have* to die, Brewster had never contemplated the *necessity* of dying.

"Why do we *have* to die?" he asked, still trying to locate the boundaries of Fun and Games and bad taste.

"Why, indeed?" said Hippias. "In this world of uncertainties, death is the only ultimate certainty. But there is still some, well, let's say, 'magic' hidden away in life that may get some of us around that final necessity. Perhaps Christians have come closest to realizing what that is . . ." He paused speculatively, then half-aloud, "Unless, of course, the Maya . . ."

"The Christians? Oh, how?"

"Through the blood of the Master. Imagine, if you can, that by drinking the life's blood of the Overself, one drinks the very stuff that gives life beyond life."

"Do Christians drink blood?" said Brewster, astonished. "Does the

Overself have blood? And . . . they drink it? How is that possible if we can't see arms and legs?" Not that the idea would be particularly appealing even if the limbs were visible.

"Yes," said Hippias, "the possibility is in us. We and the Overself are of one spirit and one blood. Some Christians drink it symbolically. Others, actually. Or so they believe. The *awe* lies in the drinking of the blood—and the belief that it nourishes and immortalizes the soul. Little do they realize how close they come to physical immortality . . ." Hippias trailed off, knowing that this child could not yet understand.

"And if drinking the blood of the Overself gives us immortality, what does the Overself drink?"

"In a sense," said Hippias, "us."

All this disturbed Brewster and threw Fun and Games into such disarray that he wondered if he was supposed to laugh or shudder. Everybody feeding off everyone else? He was inclined to shudder a little at the thought that some Overself—God?—dined on human bodies and drank their blood the way Augustus ate and drank at table. How would the blood be served up? When wine was served at dinner in the Wainwright household, it was with a great deal of ceremony. Augustus carefully scrutinized the label, noted the year and whether it was a grand cru. After the butler opened the bottle to let the wine "breathe," Augustus sniffed the cork, savoring the bouquet with narrowed eyes. Before allowing it to be served to the table, he sampled a small portion the butler poured into his glass, swirling it about in his mouth. Only when this ritual had been performed to Augustus's satisfaction was the wine shared. Was this the way God wined?

And while God and Augustus wined, Hippias would have him playing Bruce Wayne-Batman. Would Brewster emerge full-blown as the character from a comic book? Would it really matter, then, which came first? Whether he consciously decided to be a foundling or a reincarnation? Some games are won and lost. Some games always end in a draw.

9.

OVER THE NEXT FIVE YEARS, Brewster was almost wholly absorbed by the extensive and intensive program of academic studies Hippias heaped on him during the Wainwrights' winter residence on Fifth Avenue. But in summers spent at the Lodge, lingering doubts about possible identities, reincarnation, and doppelgängers were kept in abeyance while pupil and tutor enthusiastically threw themselves into developing the "Bat Cave" Brewster had begun at his first tentative dig.

They worked on the triangular fissure previously dug into by Brewster, using hand tools and carefully distributing the excavated material among the trees and shrubs along the base of the escarpment. Penetrating deep into the fissure they broke through a stratum of Inwood limestone underlying the cliff's granitic mantle. Gradually, they cleared away the debris of rock weakened by joints and cracks and opened up a sizable gallery. They ran a concealed electrical cable down the cliff from the Lodge and strung up lights to work by, digging as quietly and stealthily as they could, mostly under cover of darkness, or in inclement weather when the park was deserted. Hippias set up a surveillance camera and an alarm that would be audible only to the two in the cave to alert them to anyone on the paths close enough to discover their operations.

When they had finished excavating the "Bat Cave," Hippias determined that they had dug into a fault line along a downfold that dipped to the east and under the park. From the geologic studies of the area that were available, he speculated that erosion continued down the limb of the fold which would rise up in the vicinity of Broadway below street level but above the terminus of the Independent Subway at 207th Street. If so, the vein of crumbled rock might make it possible to dig a tunnel that would eventually connect with the subway.

Although Hippias discouraged eavesdropping on personal conversations of strollers, or the intimacies of lovers who made out in the park picked up by the surveillance system, these scraps of affairs gave them useful information about the habits of the park's visitors and added zest, really bringing the great cosmic game of Fun and Games down to earth.

As Brewster grew into his teens, he and Hippias spent more time in their observation post during the summer months keeping careful records of events in the park. They witnessed a few muggings and destructive gangs roaming within the range of their surveillance equipment, which they promptly and anonymously reported to the police. There was an occasional arrest based on their tips, but little effective prosecution because, unless the police responded promptly enough to catch perpetrators in the act—which, they noticed, was not often—the malefactors got away. And because they could not come forward without revealing their presence in the cave, Brewster and Hippias were confronted with a serious moral dilemma, only partly relieved by the knowledge that they sometimes prevented more serious crimes.

For the first few years, Hippias, in addition to attending to Brewster's education, had overseen his physical development, setting a moderate agenda of exercise which he thought suitable for early adolescence and especially Brewster's size and build. But Brewster grew and matured as robustly as his rambunctious infancy had suggested. Hippias soon realized that Brewster needed more expert instruction in weight-lifting, gymnastics, and martial arts than he was capable of giving. Hippias searched for and found a superb but glum trainer in an over-the-hill athletic director of a New York State college out on Long Island. "Rooster" Bantam was of average height and had plainly been roosting too much.

The Womb of Uncreated Night

But he had keen gray eyes and he could size up potential in others even when he neglected his own. When Rooster first met Brewster in casual street clothes, he saw a thirteen-year-old bookish nerd who was big for his age but otherwise unimpressive. He did not want to be bothered with a spoiled rich kid. And one that was almost blind to boot. His idea of physical training for over-privileged twerps like Brewster was "a kick in the ass." He became less reluctant when he learned about the generous stipend offered by Hippias—funds supplied by the Wainwrights and vaguely defined as "expenses for field trips."

The first session was grudgingly routine and far below Brewster's capabilities. Rooster learned from Hippias about the boy's poor eyesight, so he expected little and asked for less. When Brewster first appeared in the gym wearing trunks and tennis shoes, he was surprised by the boy's imposing but undeveloped physique yet unrelenting in his disdain. He told Brewster to warm up, lift some weights, do some waist bends and stretching exercises, then sit on a stationary bike until his return. Rooster went off and left him there, figuring that the kid would not do half the prescribed activities, quit in less than half-an-hour, and he himself ahead a few bucks for goofing off. When he came back over an hour later, he found Brewster on the stationary bike, perspiring but unflagging.

Rooster eyed him suspiciously for a moment, wondering who was playing who for a patsy. But he found no flicker of amusement in what the kid was doing. He softened a little and decided that the kid at least had gumption. He stopped Brewster and spent a few minutes explaining workouts on the parallel bars. Still a bit cynical, he outlined much more than any novice could be expected to master. He made as if to leave again, but stood where he could observe Brewster without being seen. Brewster's first attempts at the workouts were uncertain and clumsy. But he very quickly improved. In less than a quarter hour he had the routines down pat. In another quarter hour, he was performing them so smoothly that Rooster was amazed and, though he had trouble admitting it to himself, delighted. It was a pleasure to watch him. At the end of the second hour, Brewster was executing even advanced routines flawlessly, with no sign of slowing down. Growing concerned that this kid would work himself into physical exhaustion, Rooster stopped him. He hid his budding admiration under a gruff, "Okay. That's enough for today. Hit the showers."

If Rooster thought that Brewster was going to stand around and wait for praise, he was surprised. Brewster matter-of-factly did as he was told, got dressed, and left without a word. From then on, Rooster had new respect for his protégé. When Hippias suggested that Brewster might also benefit from some martial arts training, Rooster arranged for a skilled instructor. He saw no need to inform the sensei about Brewster's eyesight. The boy needed no coddling. Brewster enrolled in a class with others of his age and soon became a star pupil. Under the guidance of this team, Brewster became an accomplished athlete by the time he was sixteen. All of this without the knowledge of the Wainwrights.

For his sixteenth birthday, Brewster's "parents" presented him with the roadster. Brewster engaged a local teenager who, despite a precocious "druggie" rap sheet with the local police, was a brilliant mechanic. And with Hippias's help, Brewster and the mechanic designed a removable outer "skin" for the roadster, incorporating as much of the comics' Batmobile design as feasible. The "skin" was to be molded of newly developed impact-resistant plastics approaching the strength of sheet metal. Although secrecy was paramount, Brewster did not consider the drugged-out mechanic much of a security risk. When the guy was stoned, which was most of the time, he spouted such futuristic and paranoid-sounding rubbish that nobody much heeded him. It took more than a year to complete the modifications to the car.

While the roadster was being outfitted for its alter ego in the shop, Brewster and Hippias were eagerly developing Batman's skin. The form-fitting tights worn by Batman allowing the same freedom of movement enjoyed by dancers and acrobats presented no problems of design and fitting. But providing the protection of some kind of body armor without hindering the wearer's mobility presented challenges. For that, Hippias hit on a theoretical method of spinning carbon nanotubes

The Womb of Uncreated Night

into threads that could be woven into a fabric lighter, stronger, and suppler than Kevlar. With his theory in hand, he approached Augustus. Hippias had kept the leveraged buyout of the corporation developing practical applications for nanotechnology five years earlier simmering gently at the back of his mind. And here was a perfect application.

Hippias laid out his proposal for the "nanokevlar," stressing the commercial benefit of a fabric that could protect law enforcement and military personnel, yet weigh no more than underwear. Augustus was so impressed by its potential, that he immediately gave Hippias permission to pursue the idea with Woodrow Eastman, a specialist in nanotechnology at a leading research institute. Backed by Wainwright's wealth, Hippias promised him the moon. Eastman had already developed such threads, but they had an inherent brittleness which weakened the fabric. With Hippias's ideas and the Wainwright fortune dangling in front of him, he was soon able to overcome the problem. Hippias left the matter of commercial application to the elder Wainwright's business interests. They did not need to know about his and Brewster's furtive plans. But Brewster would be bullet-proof.

The trunks modeled on the costume worn by the comic-book Batman presented a different kind of encumbrance.

"What do heroes do when nature calls?" wondered Brewster. "There's nothing in the Batman or Superman lore about toilet breaks. Don't heroes need to relieve themselves?"

Hippias thought about it. It was, of course, an important matter. At first, Hippias was inclined to simply dispose of the problem by suggesting that they work a "motorist's friend" into the regalia. But that lacked aesthetic appeal.

"How heroic can you get?" muttered Brewster, shaking his head.

Then Hippias had a thought. "You know," he began casually, "at the nanoscale the essential properties of common materials undergo radical changes. Solids disintegrate. Liquids vaporize. I'll bet that with a little more prodding Eastman could come up with a way to incorporate into the nanofabric a component capable of breaking down urine and feces into volatile fluids that could quickly be wicked into the fabric of the costume and vented into the atmosphere . . ."

The expression on Brewster's face stopped him. "Being covered with piss and shit, in whatever nanoparticulate form, for whatever nanoparticulate duration is asking a bit much, don't you think? Even for a hero. And the *smell*?"

Hippias stopped short of expanding "further development" into a nanodeodorant, though he was sure that that, too, was perfectly feasible. He shrugged.

"Then you'll have to purge yourself before putting on the outfit, and limit your intake of food and liquid."

Brewster shrugged in turn. "Heroes don't usually stop at Starbucks for coffee and doughnuts while on duty."

The most skillful and discreet tailors in town were employed in making various parts of the costume so that only Hippias and Brewster knew how the full ensemble would be assembled. Augustus did not bother about the details. He approved of any venture that would keep his batty son and the zealous tutor occupied. The tailors were told only that the material was for a top secret military uniform under development, and only someone with top-level security clearance could know about it.

The hood presented further challenges. The tailors fitted a lightweight, rigid mask of reinforced nanofabric over Brewster's head and down the back of his neck. Like a helmet. Nanofabric was worked up to join the mask just below his chin. The hood was still flexible enough to allow Brewster to move his head freely. But it tended to restrict peripheral vision and somewhat muffled his hearing. It also had the disconcerting tendency of not always following precisely the movements of his head. A sudden turn of the head, and he sometimes found his nose stuck into a bat-ear. Bruce Wayne never had that problem. Technologists working with Eastman found a way of stacking the nanoparticles in layers so that they slid smoothly over each other. The fabric followed the minutest head movements like a second skin.

The Womb of Uncreated Night

The eye openings were enlarged to improve peripheral vision, and the skin around his eyes and forehead darkened with a perspiration-inhibiting salve so that Brewster's light skin would not reflect light at night and perspiration would not leak into his eyes. Electronic hearing devices were installed in the bat-ears and one end fit into Brewster's ears. They found that there was no need to compensate for any muffling effect of the hood. The hearing devices were state-of-the-art, and were adjustable for distance and direction by sensors that responded to the muscles of Brewster's skull. These worked like a kind of radar that would enable Brewster to move about in total darkness by echolocation. The process was more complicated than ordinary radar because the frequency of the "radar" was beyond the range of human hearing and had to be stepped down, increasing the possibility of distortion and error. It depended on Brewster's subjective ability to differentiate pitch, intensity, timbre, and harmonics. Through trial and error, the devices would enable him to judge the size, shape, and distance of objects. Far trickier for Brewster was learning to distinguish and interpret the sound signatures of familiar objects solely on the basis of complex sounds returning to his receivers. After weeks of practice, he was able to do a kind of rough sort, to differentiate hard objects—stone, metal, or wood—from soft—flesh, fur, cloth. With quick, slight movements of his head, he could form some idea of the shape, size, location, and state of rest or motion of an object and guess at its identity.

Brewster could usually distinguish small animals, say, a dog—even if it were not moving—from a bench. He could tell the difference between a tree, a man, and a lamppost. The massive forms of buildings made them easy to identify, and he could even tell by the subtle shifts in the audio spectrum whether they were made of stone or glass or metal. Hard objects produced a series of distinct, sharp pings. Soft objects varied from fuzzy pings through dull thuds and murmurings. The first time he panned his head from one side to another, the resulting blur of sounds made him lose his balance and stagger. For all the crudity of his orientation, he was able to negotiate his way through a maze of obstacles Hippias set out for him. After a few trials, with the obstacles rearranged by Hippias each time, Brewster was able to run the course rapidly. But Hippias added a new wrinkle. Brewster ran blindly into a badminton net stretched across his path and tore it from the posts. He and Hippias stretched it out again, and Brewster "stared" at it with his echolocator for some time. Finally, Brewster thought that he could make out a faint, fuzzy signature. On the next run through the maze, he quickly ducked under the net without touching it.

Eventually, he and the tutor thought that he would be able to refine his locational skills and be able to recognize finer objects and make subtler distinctions. They practiced both outdoors and in, using only a blindfolded hood and the utility belt, and dispensing with the rest of the costume. Hippias kept trying to challenge Brewster's perceptions, tripping him up with a rope stretched a few inches above a rug covered floor between two pieces of furniture. A brick placed over a concrete path made Brewster stumble and fall, tearing a hole in his trousers and bruising his knee. The housekeeper began to wonder whether she ought to inform Amalia that Brewster seemed to be returning to his childish clumsy ways. They practiced on spider's webs until Brewster thought that he could detect the sound of stickiness.

Hippias designed gauntlets and boots whose gripping surfaces were impregnated with nanofibers mimicking the hundreds of microhairs on a gecko's toes that enable the lizard to cling upside down to panes of glass. These, he theorized, would make it possible for Brewster to cling to walls and even ceilings. The material was pressure sensitive, so that by tensing or relaxing the muscles in his hands and feet, Brewster would be able to cause the fibers to adhere to a surface or release it. Hippias devised exercises that help him develop the necessary muscular control. Brewster learned to independently relax one set of muscles while tensing another. To make the exercises more challenging, Hippias devised various distractions to break his concentration.

Coordinating muscular controls so that they would become subliminal responses to complex situations proved tricky. It was like playing a musical instrument. Brewster had to master the technique using each individual piece of the costume, like fingering the strings on a violin. At first, focusing on controlling his hands in the gauntlets, he sometimes tensed up and got stuck to the surface he was trying to negotiate. Or he relaxed too much and lost his grip. Through trial and error, he learned just how much muscular tension allowed him to grip any surface, and how much relaxation to release it. He mastered this technique so thoroughly that he could climb hand over hand up any wall. He got so adept at it, that he soon was able to clamber up to the ceiling as fast as he could stride across a comparable distance on the floor.

He next applied himself to mastering the muscles in his legs and feet so that he could duplicate that control with his boots. But neither Brewster's agility nor the ingenuity of Hippias and their technical advisors, could get the cape right. The material had to be pliant enough so as not to restrict the freedom of movement afforded by the tights, but stiff enough not to flap unnecessarily—during a high speed chase or in a crosswind, for example. Their combined efforts were unable to create a cape capable of gliding with the weight of a man attached. Nanotechnology was no help here. They considered various forms of retracting and telescoping ribs and ways of attaching them to Brewster's limbs, but that was complicated and cumbersome. And there was no way of attaching them reliably so that they would not restrict movement. Everything that gave them the required freedom of movement ended like the open umbrella kids use when they jump off the garage roof.

Brewster reluctantly resigned himself to not being able to glide from tall buildings. He contented himself with exploiting the capabilities of his nanogauntlets and boots. He delighted in climbing the walls, then in crawling across ceilings using only the fingers of the gauntlets and the tips of the boots. He grew so adept in pushing the costume's limits, that he felt encouraged to plant the soles of the boots on the ceiling and slowly stand upright, that is, he dangled from the ceiling upside down like a bat in a cave. But his first effort ended ignominiously. After a nanosecond of success, gravity won out over balance between tension and relaxation. Brewster's feet just slipped out of the boots. He fell with a resounding thud that echoed through the mansion.

Brewster's parents, who at that moment were taking tea in the drawing room, exchanged startled glances.

Mr. Wainwright frowned. "You don't suppose that boy is running about without his contacts now?"

"I'll speak to Hippias about it," said Amalia pouring out the tea.

But Hippias, finding that Brewster had escaped serious injury by tumbling and rolling, simply shrugged his shoulders and admonished Brewster to "Try again!" And try Brewster did. Eventually, he made the necessary muscular corrections over the walls and ceilings of the Wainwright residences and no longer reminded the household of its boisterous occupant. Control became second nature, impervious to distractions devised by Hippias. In the final stages of training, Brewster worked out coping mechanisms that allowed him to distinguish between trivial distractions, and genuine emergencies.

Despite its spacious dimensions, the library had a curiously claustrophobic feeling. Entering it, Brewster felt as if sight and sound were being absorbed. The walls and ceiling were paneled in deep-hued teak. Bookshelves clung to every niche between beams with raised paneling rising from the floor like square pillars and continuing across the fourteen-foot high ceiling. Brass sconces with translucent shades of green glass stood out from the pillars. Broad double doors with raised panels were of the same rich teak. Every shelf was lined with books bound in fine-grained, hand-tooled Moroccan leather. The upper shelves, accessible by a ladder attached to a rail near the ceiling, glided effortlessly over the polished floor on brass-clad rubber wheels. A large Persian rug with subdued floral design cushioned the center of the marble floor. Flanked by leather club chairs with tufted backs and antiqued nailhead trims, brass urn-shaped lamps on armchair tables atop Palladian columns, a fireplace with marble facing and hearth set into deep red-brown mahogany paneling hardly disturbed the gloom. Cut crystal goblets and decanter glinted on the tables. At the far end of the room stood a massive desk of solid mahogany, its grain aswirl like cream in unstirred coffee. Behind it, mullioned windows rose from floor to ceiling, flooding that end of the room with gold-tinged light. Drapes of rich green brocaded silk hung at their sides.

Because the room was out-of-the-way and largely deserted, Hippias had Brewster orally solving increasingly complex problems in mathematics, physics, and chemistry while clinging to the massive doors by his left hand and foot and simulating a rescue of a damsel in distress with his free hand and foot on the right. Unsupervised by Hippias, Brewster climbed to the top of the sturdy shelves and read books selected at random while dangling upside down to see what effect blood rushing to his head would have on his mental acuity. Brewster even took to "walking" on the ceiling of the library while reading. By chance discovering Brewster in this activity, Hippias decided to make the situation more *interesting*. He set fire to paper in a wastebasket placed directly under him, then he stood back to observe how Brewster would extricate himself amid the ensuing uproar in the household caused by sprinkler system and smoke alarm. After such diversions, he nonchalantly asked Brewster for a detailed account of what he had been reading.

Brewster became so absorbed in the novelty of climbing walls and pacing across ceilings that he was oblivious to what was happening on the floor below him. So it happened that while he was hanging out on the ceiling of the library with a volume of *Principia Mathematica*, Augustus came into the room to retrieve a document from a lower drawer of the desk. Not being the sort who could easily be diverted, Augustus failed to notice the ceiling's novel appendage. And Brewster, intent on Newton's argument that the laws of motion presupposed the existence of an absolute space and time in which motion is not merely relative, failed to notice his father. Augustus might well have left the room as unobservantly as he had entered. But the pages of the volume Brewster were reading were uncut. When Brewster slit them with a letter opener he had taken from the desk, he sliced through more than paper. Though faint, the sound neatly cut through the silence. Like many people whose brains deny what their eyes see, Augustus froze, speechless . . .

Brewster found that it was necessary to have Hippias help him into his costume. Like Batman's Alfred. Of course, at sixteen, Brewster had not achieved his full growth, so this costume was a work in progress. Brewster wondered if later developments in technology could overcome the practical limitations of the cape. But costume and physical development were harmonious enough so that, on occasion, he could intervene in a mugging, or drive off an assailant in Inwood Park or the heights of its hulking companion across Dyckman Street, Fort Tryon Park, all under the watchful eye of Hippias. Confident in his impervious costume and the knowledge of how the Batman game played out, Brewster never worried about the dangers of confronting local villains. Muggers, after all, were cowards who preyed on the weak and defenseless. Even so they might rely on the security of cohorts or the menace of a weapon.

But Brewster was not foolhardy enough to enter a situation where he might be overmatched. He always had the element of surprise on his side. The spectacle of a comic-book character leaping to rescue some victim caught even the most hardened thug off guard. That alone gave Brewster an edge. Even if a mugger thought the sight of him was ridiculous enough to scoff at or laugh off, Brewster wasted no time on macho-flexing. His attacks were swift and decisive. If the mugger did not flee, Brewster simply overpowered him, trussed him up, and left him for police notified anonymously by Hippias. A mugger who might be so totally zoned out or uncool as to tell the cops that he had been trussed up by a comic book character was either jeered into recanting or sent off to Bellevue for observation. But any competent thug would be protective enough of his reputation to claim that he was the victim of some local hood. If it happened that several attackers had been bested by Brewster, they would rather have it believed they were victims of a rival gang than try to convince the police they had been attacked by a six-foot flying mammal.

Once the costume was on, the awkwardness of donning it discouraged Brewster from taking it off oftener than necessary. Eventually, he became quite accustomed to wearing it around the cave. So natural did wearing it seem to him, and so deeply absorbed in the technical problems of his Batman persona did he become, that on one occasion he forgot to remove it.

An unseasonably warm spell in October had encouraged the Wainwrights to open up the summer mansion for a weekend in the country. They had invited a number of houseguests to share the weekend, and on this night, a harvest moon cast a rustic glow over the ridge above the Spuyten Duyvil. The house blazed with light casting ghastly shadows that plunged into the darkness beyond the lawn that ended abruptly at the edge of the cliff. The house had the three-dimensional darkness-against-moonlit sky of a Magritte painting. The Wainwrights were having a formal dinner-party.

They had invited prominent business people and patrons of the arts. Brewster walked into the dining room just as the guests had begun the first course. Augustus, sitting at the head of the table, from which he had a full view of the entrance hall through the open doors of the dining room, caught sight of him first. He froze with a spoonful of steaming soup half-raised to his half-open lips. The soup dribbled down the front of his dress shirt. His stifled gasp of outrage at spilling his soup and Brewster's appearance in that outlandish getup caused a stir at the table. As if at a prearranged signal, all the guests politely turned to look at the strange presence. Ignoring the distraction, Amalia calmly ate her soup. She had long since passed through the various stages of maternal amusement, tolerance, and finally indifference to her son's idiosyncrasies. She knew at once that only some off-the-wall action of Brewster's could have caused her husband's reaction.

Recognizing at once the source of his father's consternation . . . oops! . . . Brewster nonchalantly continued into the room pretending that nothing was amiss.

"Good evening," he said, "I hope I'm not too late to join you?"

"Good evening?" sputtered Augustus. Following the incident in the library, he had sent Amalia to warn Hippias not to encourage his son's erratic behavior. No self-assured figure of authority could stoop to upbraid a servant directly. Since Brewster had curtailed his ceiling strolls, he assumed that what Amalia had told Hippias had been handed down to Brewster, and that had ended the matter. But here he was again in that outlandish getup!

"Good evening, Brewstuh?" he said, regaining his composure. "Halloween is still two weeks off. Are we trick-or-treating early, this year?"

The guests tittered uncomfortably. Brewster beamed at everyone and sat down at a place left vacant for him. His mother continued eating her soup without looking up.

"I thought we might have a costume ball," said Brewster. "For charity, eh? A Batman theme would provide plenty of characters for everyone to dress up as." Augustus bit his lip. Looking around the table, Brewster recognized patrons of the arts, "How about a benefit for the arts. MoMA? The Met?" He drew murmurs of approval from the guests who knew Augustus well enough to suspect that the weekend would cost them something. And the lad's suggestion sounded like fun. Their positive reaction smoothed Augustus' face into a semblance of benevolent approval.

10.

AFTER THE DISASTROUS FIRST OUTING of the Batmobile, Brewster and Hippias realized that it was impractical anyway to zoom around New York City in an automobile at any hour of the day or night. Moreover, the episode had so incensed Augustus that he was ready to fire the tutor on the spot. Amalia managed to defuse his anger by pointing out how well Brewster was adjusting to his visual handicap under Hippias's guidance and how self-assured and independent he had become.

"*Independent!*" sputtered Augustus and went dumb with rage.

"*Too* independent, of course!" soothed Amalia. "Hippias will have to be put on notice that another such incident would not be tolerated. After all," she reminded him, "Hippias had developed the nanokevlar concept which was proving to be lucrative and had claimed no interest in the profits." Surely, Augustus should weigh these benefits against encouraging boyish eccentricities? "And with the court-appointed psychiatrist to supervise, we should have an end to such embarrassing episodes. Boys will be boys!" she said brightly. Augustus bristled at being outmaneuvered once again by his whimsical wife. He relented. But silently he fumed.

So Brewster and Hippias did what most people do when their actions above board become too conspicuous. They went underground. Hippias returned to his hunch that following the fault line that struck toward Broadway would bring them within reach of the IND. A careful inspection of the station at 207th Street revealed an access shaft at its south end. Using portable power tools, they might be able to dig through to it by the end of the following summer. There, Batman would have access to the subway and be able to drop down unobserved onto the roof of a train once it had left the brightly lit station. The vast network of underground shafts and tunnels that honeycomb Manhattan, supplying steam, electricity, and water, and especially the subway system, should enable Batman to move efficiently to any area of the city.

Few of the teeming New Yorkers bustling about on the surface, hurtling up and down the high-rise buildings, laboriously climbing the steps of five- or six-story walk-ups, browsing at shop windows, or exploring the brightly-lit underground promenades of such grandiloquent public structures as Rockefeller Center or Grand Central Station or R.H. Macy's that tease the eyes with brilliant displays of clothing, jewelry, household furnishing, notions, and books, or tease the nose with gourmet delicacies or more plebeian fast-foods, give much thought, if any, to the vast, hive-like networks that lie beneath these solid-appearing façades. What they see is the magician's surface, a veneer behind which, little-observed, the nether world of pipes, conduits, ducts, tunnels, catch-basins, drains, sewers, pipes, cables, airlocks, and ventilation shafts carry the essentials of life and provide access for repairing, modifying, or enlarging them.

If they think about them at all, the underground is often embroidered with urban legends of alligators and other exotic creatures living in the sewers that raise goose bumps on the gullible. More frightening is the Norway rat: millions of voracious foot-and-a-half-long monsters capable of gnawing through cinder blocks and lead insulation, able to swim any water and climb any wall. But as long as they are not seen, or at worst only fleetingly glimpsed, imagination sustains the illusion that the city and its human inhabitants are secure.

The Womb of Uncreated Night

In such a milieu, Hippias reasoned, Batman might blend in as just another urban legend.

New Yorkers are notorious droppers and tossers, completely indifferent to the surfaces they move over or stand on. It's a tradition. In the 1830s and 1840s, they used to toss the contents of chamber pots out into the streets, along with household garbage for pigs to roam through and eat. All through the 1950s, dogs were allowed to shit all over the sidewalks. Then the city passed an ordinance requiring dog owners to pick up after them. Not that all dog owners scrupulously observed the ordinance. Cats, of course, have always enjoyed the privilege of doing as they pleased. Besides, how often does one see a cat squatting in public? But some people are indifferent to unsanitary conditions. Men demurely piss behind the nearest tree in public parks—not to say vestibules of buildings, viaducts, and underpasses; or in more flagrant cases, directly into street gutters or against the walls of buildings in plain sight.

So drop and toss they do without a qualm. Cellophane and foil wrappings from packages of candy, gum, cigarettes; tissues; sales receipts; ticket stubs; the effluvia of pocket and purse—all are deposited wherever they happen to be standing or walking or transporting. The innate need to drop and toss is never more apparent than during a ticker-tape parade. In an orgy of symbolic purging, they empty their inhibitions—and sometimes their washrooms of toilet paper—in one grand ritual gesture. This ritual reversion to emptying chamber pots into the streets—this perpetual ticker-tape parade—is only partially suppressed the rest of the time. Without the least self-consciousness, concern, or even awareness they trash the spaces they live in. Out the windows of cars and trains. Onto the floors of elevators. Up and down the subway steps. Even in churches. Drop and toss, the deft flick of cigar ash or cigarette or butt. Quite professional-looking people, carefully groomed and neatly dressed, are as prone to this absent-minded behavior as the scruffy types one might expect it of.

Above, on the city's streets, the debris accumulates into a wind-driven tide that ebbs and flows, rushes in torrents, swirls in eddies, or stagnates in gutter-pools. Below, in the subways, this trash, whether dropped or tossed on the station platforms or directly onto the track beds, is swept along by air currents generated by rushing bodies and trains. And since the city cleaning crews cannot compete with the rate at which this stuff is dropped and tossed, it sits and offends eye and nose. Sometimes a stray spark from the third rail or the unlawful lighted cigarette tossed by some defiant smoker sets the junk to smoldering or even actively burning. The resulting confusion snarls up train traffic until a crew can be summoned to cope with it. And if a train approaches as the crew gets the trouble under control, they stand aside from the tracks in recesses in the subway walls provided at intervals for just such emergencies.

Having at last broken through to the access tunnel under Broadway, Brewster and Hippias found it deserted. They made their way to a ventilation shaft that opened into the top of the subway tunnel. They let themselves down metal rungs embedded in the recess of a wall a few hundred feet from the platform and peered diagonally across to the well-lit platform. Seeing the trash that had accumulated between the tracks and under the third rail, Brewster turned to Hippias.

"Surely," said Brewster, "littering is not unique to New Yorkers?"

"Of course not," replied Hippias. "Any place as congested as New York City is bound to promote, even intensify, slovenliness. The lack of order is rooted in imperfect socialization."

"Well, then," mused Brewster, "I guess it's bound to be imperfect, isn't it? Maybe we're biologically incapable of conforming to social norms imposed on us as children?"

Hippias did not answer. Nor did Brewster expect one. Some kids, of course, readily manipulate the rules, obeying them in public but freely ignoring them in private. The more defiant ones refuse to pretend to knuckle under to such "bullshit" and flout the civilized veneer encoded in "standards." They create an atmosphere of nonchalant daredevilry, a kind of absolute self-reliance in which only what you think matters,

The Womb of Uncreated Night

matters. It affects even otherwise well-mannered juveniles unconsciously who act in ways they *know* they shouldn't. That *knowing*, after all, is just more of the bullshit imposed by uptight standard regulators.

For all that they despise traditions, they freely adopt those that reflect the underside of civilization, as when they delight in the ancient tradition of graffiti to protest against the tyranny of walls. Every restriction becomes a canvas for a declaration of self-expression.

The less artistically inclined find other ways of declaring their independence. In broad daylight, kids can be seen hopping onto the backs of buses for a free ride. They grab onto the minute ledges and clefts in the buses' metal outer skin, onto the framed advertisements, on the most precarious of hinges and projections, leap onto the bumpers, and cling. Sometimes they hang on only until the bus stops further down the street, just showing off. At others, they hang on until the bus is well out of sight, more serious travelers. But the most ambitious and reckless kids go underground.

Batman hovered in the shadows of the subway tunnel, waiting for the A Train to pull out of the station. Inside his confidence, Brewster eagerly anticipated his first outing. He thought about the subway surfers, who ranged from the deranged to the defiant. Some are just stupid kids who think they can stand atop a speeding train with their arms outstretched, avoid all the low spots at the tops of tunnels, and keep their balance as the train hurtles around a sharp curve. Brewster smiled a mixed smile. His way of getting around town was sure to be seen as the same kind of reckless and irresponsible behavior as his less well-equipped counterparts. Only he and Hippias would know about the relative security of nano-enhanced gloves and boots. He would also have more sense than to pretend he was flying or surfing a wave on the ocean. Adding to the mix was how outraged Augustus would be, more from the scandal than parental concern, if he ever found out. Although teenaged daredevils courted visibility, Batman had ample reasons for staying out of sight. But he would have to run the risk of being seen. All in a good cause, of course. Brewster could not admit anticipating the pleasure and excitement of ratcheting up Fun and Games to a new level.

Brewster's surfing, initially, was to familiarize him with the trains, the tunnels, timing journeys of varying lengths, and the means of entering and exiting the subway system. He did not at first make use of these apertures, but explored emergency escape routes only far enough to determine where they gave onto the streets. This information he logged and studied after he had returned to the cave. When he and Hippias were convinced that he had mastered this mode of transportation, Brewster cautiously began to leave the safety of the emergency exits and to explore the neighboring areas. He made sure that no passersby should spot him, though an occasional street person might be lying nearby, asleep or unconscious, huddled against the warmth coming out of a nearby grate in winter. Since Brewster restricted his explorations to late night, and exposed himself only in areas that were dark and relatively deserted, his dark costume gave him a sense of semi-invisibility.

Lying flat and immobile along the top of the car or hanging on to the rear, his figure was noticed by few as the train clicked off the stops, hitting 60 miles per hour between 145th Street and Cathedral Parkway. As the train approached the Cathedral Parkway station, it slowed down and the figure arced over the edge of the car on which it rode, hit the track bed at a run, and disappeared though the steel beams separating the express and local tracks. Moving over to the local tracks, the figure again became immobile and invisible among the shadows.

For all of Brewster's acrobatic stunts in mounting or dismounting moving trains, discovery was inevitable. A passenger who just happened to turn as the light from a train passing on an adjacent track silhouetted his form; a passenger who just happened to be standing near either end of the platform when Brewster was leaping off of or onto the moving train; a station master, preoccupied with making change or popping his fingers to the latest rap blaring out of his glass cage, just happening to look up as a train with a fantastically caped appendage whisked by. An imaginative person catching sight of this phantasm probably stared dumbfounded.

"What the hell was *that*?" Or, "I'm hallucinating!" The more prosaic or jaded merely shrugged off the phenomenon as another example of juvenile dementia, "Another wild kid risking life and limb in a crazy stunt!" Yet others just laughed. But there were also those self-possessed, basically responsible but officious whistle-blowing types who seem to be forever itching to raise a hue and cry at any departure from convention. The woman who ran to a station's toll booth to report the phantom atop the train looked Into a face behind the glass that was as blank as the whistle-blower's was frantic. The Manhattan Transit Authority had long since resigned itself to the futility of preventing surfers from endangering their lives, and seldom pursued them unless coincidence brought them to the same place at the same time. There was only so much that could be done. Only after the passenger's cries became hysterical, alarming the other passengers in the station, did the woman in the toll booth alert the transit police. The cop who appeared moments later assured her that the next station would be alerted.

On the last car with his head pressed against its roof, Batman's electronically enhanced hearing began to pick up some unusual stray static clicking on and off, the kind you hear when someone is using a walkie-talkie. He did not actually hear what was being said between motorman, conductor, and transit cop, but he sensed that something was wrong. There was a considerable stir at the station. The transit cops, unable to close the station or clear out the passengers in advance, had ordered those on the platform waiting for the train to stand back until they gave the all clear. The passengers were understandably curious, some even alarmed but as avidly eager, at the presence of several tense cops, hands on side arms, looking as if they were about to apprehend a mass murderer on the train. Despite warnings from the cops, passengers were milling about, and their combined mutterings amounted to a muffled rumbling that Brewster could distinguish from the noise of the train. The lighted space of the station was just visible around a bend in the track, and there was just enough clearing between the top of the train and the tunnel's ceiling for Brewster to raise his head to see. At the moment he saw the dark blue uniforms and picked up their warnings to be prepared, he rolled off the slowing but still rapidly moving train and, with his nanogloves and boots gripping grappled the wall of the tunnel, gracefully swinging against it, and slid into the shadows.

When the transit cops inspected the top, rear, and far side of the train, leaning out of the control cab's windows, two of them even leaping gingerly down onto the tracks to peer at the undercarriage, they found nothing. They searched the tunnel for some distance behind the train, looking for evidence of a body that might have fallen from it. The following trains were rerouted, and a service car was sent along the tracks to search for any sign of an injured body. No one could have conceived the notion that someone might have leaped from a rapidly moving train and vanished without a trace. After seriously tying up the subway system for the better part of half an hour, while passengers grumbled at the delays, the investigating team was baffled. It was impossible for anyone to have gotten off a moving train without injury. And a thorough search showed that there was plainly no injured body in the tunnel. The whole thing must have been the product of an over-zealous imagination, or a hoax, someone's sick idea of a practical joke. Much to the disgust of the Transit authorities, the media got hold of the story and gleefully spread it across the city with TV interviews of passengers and Transit cops on the six o'clock news, in garish headlines, in radio news stories crackling with excitement.

The Phantom Subway Rider became a legend. And with subway passengers, however skeptical, alerted to its presence, further sightings were inevitable. Those who caught sight of the Phantom quickly recognized the costume of the comic book Batman. And Brewster, when he saw that concealment was becoming increasingly problematical, began to enjoy his status as a kind of folk hero, waving to the passengers as the train he was riding pulled out of a station, the passengers cheering and applauding. He also enjoyed eluding the police. For a time, they were never able to catch sight of him, let alone catch *him*. The idea that somehow the passengers had entered into a conspiracy to flout them in some kind of bizarre protest against the dangers of subway surfing seemed incredible. The police increased their vigilance. Brewster increased his wiliness. His exploits spread by rumor, and many a TV station rushed its mobile unit to the site of a reported sighting only to find the passengers hugely enjoying the joke of their discomfiture when they found their bird had flown.

Inevitably Brewster was spotted by the transit cops. He began to show off a little, hopping on and off trains where passengers could get an occasionally clear view. Even in their perpetual rush to be somewhere else, some would cluster at the ends of platforms in the hope of glimpsing the spectacle. Some passengers would even miss a train if the flurry of activity at a station hinted at Brewster's presence. It was the greatest show in New York City for a couple bucks. Brewster's performance had the effortless grace of a circus aerialist, and when he had made his death defying leap onto the back of the train, he turned and flashed a friendly smile and a grand wave of his free arm as he moved down the tunnel.

Only then did Brewster notice the anxious rookie transit cop who happened to be mingling in one such crowd. The cop whipped out his sidearm and aimed at the caped figure as it faded in the darkened tunnel beyond the end of the platform. The cop, of course, had meant merely to intimidate a misguided kid showing off on the train. He could not have risked discharging the weapon in a crowded place. The last thing the cop and the passengers saw as the Phantom form vanished in the shadows down the tunnel was a gloved hand wagging a finger at the cop, who was hooted and booed, red-faced out of the station.

A local train arrived while the express waited to make connections. Passengers moved from one train to the other, some moving up the steps at either end of the platform. A trio of rowdies whooped and ran laughing up the steps at the north end of the station. The express pulled out, and the local followed. The dark figure again gracefully sprang onto a passing car and climbed to the roof as before—103rd Street. 96th Street. 86th Street. 81st Street— then fleetingly revealed in the light of one of the train windows as he dismounted. Having previously explored the emergency exits, access tunnels, and utility passageways, Batman was able to enter Central Park unobserved. He moved to the area around the Belvedere Castle, and waited for what might not come that night, perhaps, but for what he knew in his heart would surely come.

Interlude

Subway surfing made the news in the tabloids from time to time, usually after some kid managed to get himself mangled or killed. Inevitably, Brewster's adventures would surface and catch the attention of Korngold and the Wainwrights. At first, Korngold reasoned with Brewster about the of dangers of his activities. But when rumors continued to circulate about the "phantom of the subway," Korngold recommended that the Wainwrights dismiss Hippias as a pernicious influence on Brewster's Batman fixation. This time, Amalia was neither able nor willing to intercede for Hippias. The matter had gotten out of hand.

Augustus had planned to buy him off, but Hippias simply disappeared.

Brewster suspected Dr. Korngold's involvement. When he confronted the therapist, Dr. Korngold sidestepped the issue.

"What do you think could have happened?"

"I thought you might know. I think Mr. Wainwright was getting ready to fire him," said Brewster.

"Why so?"

"I suppose he must've heard about the subway surfing."

"Maybe Hippias got wind of his impending dismissal and left of his own accord? Are you concerned about him?"

"Of course, I'm concerned!" said Brewster impatiently. "Hippias was my friend and mentor for five years. I've heard about his life before he became my tutor. If he's relapsed into dementia—" Brewster broke off the unpleasant thought. "And since his departure, I've heard rumors of a homeless man resembling Hippias not only around his old haunts in Penn Station, but also in the vicinity of the Belvedere in Central Park."

"Did you try to find him?"

"Yes, of course. The Penn Station area—it's easy to spot panhandlers in spite of the crowds."

"You went in mufti?" said Korngold straight-faced.

"Yeah, not as Batman."

"So, you think he might have reverted to his former dementia?" Brewster did not answer. After an awkward silence, Korngold continued. "We're using the term, dementia, loosely. With only anecdotal history to go on, it's impossible to say whether his former symptoms were brought on by organic disease, substance abuse, trauma," he shrugged, "any number of possible factors. Or even if he suffered from dementia at all. He may be bipolar. There are other possibilities. Not all such disorders are static or progressive."

"You think maybe he could go into remission again?"

"Have you considered the possibility that he may not have regressed at all? That he might have just left the area?" Brewster did not answer. "What about the Belvedere?"

"Yeah, I've looked there too."

"As Batman?"

Brewster hesitated. He did not want to lie. But he knew that Korngold and the Wainwrights—they were plainly in cahoots—would give him a hard time. "Only at night," he said at last.

"Using the subway to get there?" Korngold kept his tone noncommittal.

Brewster sighed heavily. "Yes, surfing the subway."

Korngold looked down at his desk thoughtfully and toyed with his pipes. Then he looked up again and directly at Brewster. "That's most unwise," he said. "Your parents—"

"The Wainwrights," Brewster corrected.

"The Wainwrights," conceded Korngold to avoid haggling, "and I have cautioned you about that. We thought that with Hippias gone—"

"So you did have something to do with getting Mr. Wainwright to dismiss him! I knew it!"

"Not so fast! I agreed with him that without Hippias' encouragement you might stop putting your life at risk. The rest was up to your parents."

This time Brewster did not correct him. "That's a cop-out! You and they have put his life at risk!"

"My responsibility is to my patient. That's you."

11.

DOCTOR RICHARD KORNGOLD STUDIED HIS image as he stood naked in front of the full-length mirror in the bedroom he shared with his wife, Sydney. His tall, sturdy build had begun to sag a little. He had put on a bit of weight. He sucked in his slightly bulging gut. It wasn't really a paunch. But at thirty-five, he was already bald. When he saw a patient, horn-rimmed glasses and smoke from his pipe diverted attention away from the wide swath which inconsiderate genes had plowed across the top of his head. Patients found his voice mellifluous. He smiled frequently and indulgently. As he stood there, smiling dourly at his reflection, a smile of a different kind crossed Syd's face.

"Everything satisfactory, Major Winchester?" Syd made it her mission in life to deflate her husband whenever she thought he was feeling too good about himself. She teased him by comparing him to Major Winchester in the TV series, M*A*S*H, whom he somewhat resembled. He would let her have her little joke, pluck the barb from his conscious mind, and toss it away along with the rest of the good-natured venom they mildly injected into their married life.

Almost as tall and two years older, Sydney was what most people considered a "handsome woman." She wore four inch heels that made her appear taller than him and added "statuesque" to her appearance. She wore her dark lustrous hair in a skullcap cut, emphasizing a well-shaped head and the sharpness of her nose and chin. It also fit the self-image of a professional woman whose proper name was Sydney. Richard knew perfectly well that she hated nicknames like "Syd." But it was one of those little needles they pricked each other with. She was as lively and vigorous as any professional could be. Like Korngold, her background, too, was in psychiatry. But without a medical degree, she was qualified to practice only as a lay analyst, at which she was every bit as successful as her husband. They practiced their professions, separately, in a residential suite large enough to accommodate their two offices with separate entrances into the hallway. Apart from their professions they shared lives without ever making them a life. Their shared interests, amusements, food, were as compartmentalized as any two people sharing living spaces could make them. Even in bed, their intimacies were routine and distant. And yet for all their analytical skills neither of them ever bothered about how two people living so closely could live so separately.

Dressing in front of the mirror, Dr. Korngold thought about his afternoon appointment with Mrs. Wainwright. Brewster had been his patient for four years. Following the disappearance of Hippias, Brewster had become hostile, blaming Korngold for having deprived him of his friend and mentor. Once that hostility had run its course, their sessions had been, if not placid, at least civil, and finally dull and unproductive. Korngold knew that the resentment had submerged and tried without success to get Brewster to vent his feelings. Brewster would only admit to making half-hearted efforts to locate Hippias, but even those had become infrequent and less urgent. If the Phantom Surfer only made sporadic news in the tabloids, Korngold assumed that Brewster was limiting his Batman episodes to Inwood Hill Park during the summer.

Brewster's fantasies confirmed the "shadow of schizophrenic affect" that Dr. Sandor, had originally suggested. Korngold, too, had observed "the cryptic smile, as if he were contemplating some private joke." Then an idea, as improbable as intriguing, came to him. What if it really was a private joke? Could Brewster, could anyone, sustain such a pretense for four years and not be seriously unbalanced? Whichever

The Womb of Uncreated Night

it was, as long as Brewster was able to function, Korngold kept to a conservative course. If this little game got worse and endangered Brewster or others, he could always fall back on psychotropic drugs. If at all possible, Korngold would not subject him to the too-easy routine of pill-popping all too common in current medical practice. He did not think that Brewster would require hospitalization.

But clearly, something more was needed. Korngold was not yet ready to concede that he had exhausted treatment options. He was fascinated by the spectacle of a young man masquerading as a comic book hero, developing high tech gadgetry to aid him in his fight against crime. On the one hand, it was ludicrous, even pathetic. On the other, absurdly heroic, but heroic nevertheless. And in a world without real heroes, naïve and even sweet. Or was it, perhaps, a more mundane hunger for sensationalism, the arrested development of a kid who had been alienated from his parents and society? If Brewster was a nut, he was a harmless nut.

From all that he had learned about Brewster's past and the sources of his Batman fixation, Korngold doubted that the Wainwrights had any insight into Brewster's nature. Aside from generalized progress reports, Korngold had told them only that their son still fantasized about Batman and further treatment was advisable. Yet so much more remained unsaid. The Wainwrights knew that with the help of Hippias Brewster had equipped himself with sophisticated Batman gadgetry. But like Korngold himself, they probably knew no more about the content of Brewster's comic books than what might have haphazardly drifted through their elitist screens. Only after he had felt compelled to run through back issues of Detective Comics for insight was he able to understand how deeply Brewster's character had integrated with Bruce Wayne's. It was always about saving the world, one crime at a time. When he started to speculate about where in Manhattan Brewster could possibly have found a "Bat Cave" as a base of operations . . . He had to break off. He realized he was being sucked in to the fantasy.

In time, he assured Augustus, he and Brewster would be able to work through the problem. He wanted to discuss with them a recommendation he thought would hasten that end. By that time Augustus was livid. He thought Dr. Korngold was stalling, lying, or just plain incompetent. He would have fired him on the spot if Amalia had not stepped in. She persuaded Augustus to leave the matter to her and packed him off to the Lodge, fuming, while she remained behind on Fifth Avenue with Brewster. After a week, Augustus had had enough time to cool off. Then she sent Brewster up as well and summoned Korngold for a conference.

Except in Hollywood, psychiatrists do not ordinarily make house calls. But a summons from Mrs. Wainwright was no ordinary occasion. It was therefore unremarkable to Sydney that Korngold left his office early in the afternoon to visit the Wainwright mansion.

Dr. Korngold entered the Wainwright mansion on 71st Street off Fifth Avenue. A maid led Korngold through the cavernous Entrance Hall and down a cool and dimly lit corridor to the library where Amalia would be awaiting him. Their footsteps echoed off the marble tiles in the hollow silence of the almost empty house. When the maid ushered in Korngold, Amalia was standing, silhouetted in thought at the tall window overlooking the garden. She turned and walked toward him, her outstretched hand materializing first out of the brilliant sunshine at the window, then her smile. They sat and exchanged pleasantries as the maid returned with a tea cart.

When he turned the conversation to Brewster, Korngold aiming at lightness struck a nerve, "Even bats," he said, need to get out of their caves once in a while."

Amalia poured out the tea and offered him a tray of sandwiches. "I do wish you wouldn't joke about it," she said. "After all, Brewster is not exactly a recluse. Mr. Wainwright and I have regularly taken him to the opera and concerts. He's often at the museums and art shows where he meets the very finest professionals, business people, artists, critics, writers. His father and I encourage him to participate in all the social events . . ." she trailed off hesitantly. It did sound stuffy.

"His eyes were never very good, you see," she resumed. "He was such a clumsy child. Perhaps I've tended to shelter him overmuch from physical activities." She sounded apologetic. "Even after Dr. Cacamati had corrected his vision with contact lenses . . . one would never know, to look at him, just how handicapped he would be without them . . . we thought that the strenuous activities of—well, you know—*normal* boys, sports, for instance . . . A sudden blow to the head or face might knock the lenses out and leave him almost blind. Or what if someone—not out of malice, you see, but simply in enthusiastic play—what if someone struck his eyes and caused the lenses to injure them?"

How ironic, thought Korngold. How much of what she said was genuine concern for her son, and how much was the lament of a society matron who had so little time for raising her offspring that she had left him almost entirely in the hands of nannies and tutors? Korngold recognized that Amalia was more interested in her son than Augustus. But if Augustus was more to blame for having created the cold and indifferent family dynamic, that hadn't eased its effect on Brewster. They had offered so little personal contact with their son that he had grown up ready to believe that his real parents had been murdered and that she and her husband were surrogates . . . or perhaps unconsciously wishing that they might yet be murdered.

Korngold wondered what she would say if she knew that Brewster had been regularly working out at a fitness center under the supervision of a competent physical trainer as early as his thirteenth year. Or that Hippias had enrolled him in a martial arts class and her son had earned a black belt at sixteen. Brewster at twenty was, in fact, far more physically accomplished than most "normal" boys.

"But does Brewster really have much of a social life," observed the doctor, "I mean with people his own age? You've filled his social life with an enriched fare that would benefit the development of any young person. But while doing that, his tutors heaped studies in the liberal arts and sciences on him—all necessary and useful," he added hastily as he saw Mrs. Wainwright was about to protest. "When their vigilance lapsed, he escaped into comic book fantasies. Hippias continued to saturate him with sciences and technology. But he also shared Brewster's fixation on Batman. That, along with the isolation from his peer group caused by his visual handicap, only furthered his substitution of comic book vigilantism for social interaction."

"Augustus and I *do* emphasize the arts!" protested Amalia. "Hippias *did* school him in literature. And we *did* try to curb Hippias' encouragement in fantasies . . ."

Korngold acknowledged that everyone had given Brewster valuable insights into human motivation. "Brewster has a sharp mind in a big strapping body. If his Batman role playing shows nothing else, he's learned to handle himself very well physically. He's become a robust young man and needs to get out and interact with young people his age. He's long past the need for your protection."

"I have to tell you that all these media rumors about a 'Batman' vigilante have upset Mr. Wainwright so badly that he feels you have been dragging your feet through Brewster's therapy."

"These things," said Korngold with head cocked to the right and raised eyebrows that reluctantly acknowledged Mr. Wainwright's understandable, if unconstructive, criticism, "take time. There are few quick fixes in medicine. But if you and he lack confidence in my handling, I can refer him back to Dr. Sandor."

Amalia held up a restraining hand. "That would only prolong a resolution. Mr. Wainwright has left the decision to me. I am still interested in hearing what else you had in mind. You were about to suggest some new approach for Brewster? Short of throwing him into Hell's Kitchen and letting him play vigilante there?" she laughed.

"That's not a bad suggestion," Korngold laughed along with her. "But I think we can ease him into something less drastic, a broader milieu that isn't too radically different from what he's already familiar with. Then nudge him further, if he needs it. It wouldn't hurt to draw him into a circle where I could observe him outside of the office from time to time, yet remain in the background."

"Mr. Wainwright will be very hard to manage if there are any more episodes in the media. There were those adolescent escapades, years ago. But he's no longer an adolescent. We can disapprove, but we can no longer restrain him. As long as he's living in our household, Mr. Wainwright expects him to abide by his decisions." She sighed. "But young men always find artful ways of dodging restrictions."

"You know Susannah Villiards quite well, I believe?"

"Certainly. She's an old friend. Brewster met her when he was a little boy. I believe she made quite an impression. I'm afraid we haven't seen much of her since she retired from the opera."

"Do you know her work with the Young Artists Group of New York?"

"Oh, yes. She sponsors talented young people in all the arts. Arranges musical soirées, poetry readings, even small art shows. It's her pet project. She's always in need of support from members of the community who are in a position to help encourage her more gifted protégés. Augustus and I regularly contribute."

"Well," said Korngold, "perhaps you could take a more active role in supporting the group?"

Amalia looked doubtful. "Our time is pretty well committed," she began hesitantly.

"Indirectly, at least. You could encourage Brewster to take an interest in the group, have him attend some of the meetings. He could meet young people who are just as committed as those professionals he's already met. They just haven't met with much success yet. They come from all social classes. They're a good mix. I'll bet they will give him an outlet that he will take to the next level without our help." Korngold could see that such an environment meshed well with Amalia's own program of enlightened interest in the arts, a direction she approved for Brewster. It was nothing radical or "strenuous." Just a gradual airing out of a young man's musty mind.

"And if he took a shine to some of the members and wanted to help them out," continued Korngold, "encourage them, perhaps offer them some small financial assistance? You would be able to manage that, wouldn't you? That would draw him out of himself, develop new friendships, and give him a chance to exercise social reform without resorting to vigilantism. Not quite as exciting as swinging through a comic book adventure. But a tangible benefit to his peers, and through them, the larger community. And that's what Batman is all about anyway." Amalia silently mulled over the wholesome sound of this proposal, more to avoid any appearance of haste than out of any real doubts about it.

"And you attend these—soirées, are they? You could keep an eye on him and give me occasional progress reports?" Korngold was, in fact, more or less doing that with several members of the group who were in fact his patients. Sort of group therapy. But she did not need to know that.

Mme Villiards' condominium tower on Central Park West overlooked the park. With her condo's spacious living room opening onto a terrace through a wall of French doors Mme V could accommodate gatherings of thirty to forty people. In the center of this wall a raised platform ample enough to accommodate a Bösendorfer concert grand piano in ebony splendor and room to spare gave easy access to the terrace. The polished parquet floors of the dais as well as the main portion of the room was sparsely furnished with pieces that could easily be moved to the sides so that folding chairs might provide seating, as in a small auditorium. Across the opposite end of room, a large alcove complementing the piano's stage had been recessed into the wall. It had a large fireplace flanked with a long sofa and several club chairs. This arrangement worked well for solo recitals and readings, but was too cramped for chamber ensembles or other group performances. Mme V had dropped hints with the Wainwrights, hoping that they would offer the use of their ballroom for occasions calling for larger forces. When she learned that Brewster would be coming to the next Wednesday night meeting of the Young Artists Group, she was determined to pursue the matter with him.

Brewster arrived at that meeting and found Dr. Korngold and Mme V quietly conversing in a corner of the living room while the young artists were taking refreshments from a well-furnished sideboard on one side of the alcove at the back of the room. Korngold beamed when he caught sight of him and whispered to Mme V. She had not seen Brewster since his childhood and would not have recognized him but for Korngold's cue. She smiled in genuine delight and held out her hands to him.

"Can this be the same little boy who drinks champagne through his nose?" she said, taking Brewster's hands in hers. Because he was a full head taller, she blew him a kiss instead of the usual peck on the cheek reserved for favorites. "What a handsome young man you've grown into!" Brewster endured the usual pleasantries, shook Dr. Korngold's hand, smiled and laughed politely. He was glad enough when the diva cut through the dreary amenities.

"Now, Brewster, you're to mingle with people your own age and not stand around with us old folks," said Mme V, not quite winking at Korngold. "Get to know some of the young people." She pointed out some of her talented charges and briefly filled him in with enough background on each to get him started.

"See if you can find Nick Artsynick," added Dr. Korngold. "I've taken a special interest in him. He has serious ambitions as a composer. I believe we're to hear one of his pieces this evening?" he said, turning to Mme Villiards, who had turned away to greet another guest and did not hear him. "He's written several things that show considerable promise, but he's a bit of an oddball. I can't figure out whether he's the genuine article or has such a great musical intelligence that he gives the impression that he is!"

"I hope you'll take an interest in them, Brewster, dear," said Mme Villiards, rejoining them. "They're all very deserving. Perhaps a bit full of themselves." Brewster dutifully began the rounds of the room, numbed at being thrust into a role he had not been prepared to play. So he had been maneuvered into coming here as some kind of Lady Bountiful in drag? He introduced himself to several people as "George Farquhar," and wondered if anyone would care.

Dabney Addler was known as "the Dabbler" to his acquaintances because he was a polymath with the inclinations of a dilettante. And it sounded like his name. Nobody ever used his real name, not even Pilar, his common-law wife. Dabbler and Pilar were not native New Yorkers, but being both quite liberated sexually, they readily adjusted to the Big City and quickly settled in the Village. They "bought" a small basement apartment in a rundown tenement where West 4th Street and West 10th Street illogically cross. The former tenant, when they called to inquire in response to an ad in *The Times*, told them that they would have to buy $1,000 worth of furniture. "It's not worth $1,000, but that's the way it is."

When they showed up at the address, they found the typical areaway and basement floor about three feet below street level, behind an iron fence and gate. The tenant showed them into the apartment. It was indeed a basement, the front rooms closed off from the furnace and utility rooms at the back of the building by a gypsum drywall partition through which they could hear the sounds of the super sloshing water in the laundry. The ceiling was low, and ducts and pipes were exposed along its length. The rooms, really two large rooms partitioned so as to divide the apartment into a kitchen-living room and bedroom, were freshly painted a kind of off-pink, and looked clean. As in many older tenements, the bathtub was in the kitchen, covered over with a metal lid when not in use. The john originally down the hall and padlocked, was accessible through an opening knocked out of one of the bedroom walls when indoor bathrooms and central heating were required by ordinance in the late '50s.

The $1,000 furniture consisted of a linoleum covered deal table in the kitchen, a pair of nondescript, mismatched chairs, and a sofa that looked as if a cat had been sharpening its claws on it. In the bedroom, there was a metal bedstead that sagged slightly in the middle and looked as if it would squeal rhythmically during love-making, a single nightstand, and a bureau whose top drawer was missing. Dabbler looked at Pilar with questioning eyebrows, but neither spoke until the tenant moved into the other room. They briefly wondered if they could bargain the tenant down, but knowing that living quarters were at a premium, they hurriedly agreed to take the place, and Pilar, who kept the finances, wrote out a check. They were ready for Village life.

Robert-Peter Fairfield was one of Dabbler's collectibles. Dabbler called him R-P, and that eventually became Arpie. Arpie had a round face, straight, prematurely gray hair combed and parted, with a few resistant tufts standing upright. He had bad teeth, revealed by a tendency to let his lips hang open most of the time. He was slightly near-sighted. One eye, the right, had a pronounced cast. He had to close this eye, or turn his head so that both eyes were aligned, in order to focus the left eye more clearly. He wore thick, horn-rimmed glasses that gave him an owlish look. He held his head slightly tilted back because his glasses otherwise kept slipping off his straight short nose. This made him look as if he were looking down at people with a smug, superior air.

When Nick first met Arpie, Eric Satie's *Three Pieces in the Form of a Pear* leaped into his head. Arpie's torso could only be described as pear-shaped. He spoke with a New England accent though he was raised in New York. He sometimes scratched himself, absently, complaining to acquaintances of hives, never associating his rashes with the tiny, tell tale spots of blood on his bed sheets that would have suggested an entirely different cause.

A collector of "geniuses," Dabbler introduced Arpie to Nick and his other friends and had encouraged him to come along with Pilar and Nick to the Young Artists Group. Nick had wandered off somewhere at the moment, but Dabbler introduced himself and Pilar to Brewster and a knot of acquaintances gathered around Dr. Korngold.

"We're sort of en famille, don't y'know," said Arpie with a chuckle. "I've got an I.Q. of 157."

"Oh? Really?" said Guilemot. "I've never seen one that big. Could you take it out and show us?" Guy Guilemot, a francophone from Montreal, insisted that his name be pronounced *ghee gheelmó*, "à la française." That inevitably led to teasing him as "Ghee-Ghee," Clarified Butter, or to pronouncing his last name like the bird, "Done any diving lately? Ha! ha!" He arched an eyebrow above the good-natured hostility of such gibes, too suave and sophisticated to respond. He was in his mid-twenties, always elegantly attired in suit and tie. Dr. Korngold dubbed him "le suit." Tall, cadaverous, with the nose and haughty expression of an over bred collie, he combed his long straight hair back to conceal a bald spot. He looked down at Arpie with the air of the caterpillar interrogating Alice. He would have blown smoke rings at him if Mme Villiards had not forbidden smoking in her condo. Even when not smoking, his voice could convey the arched eyebrow and fingers absently flicking ashes from a nonexistent cigarette. Those fingers were long, tapered, and might reach a twelfth at the keyboard. Everyone knew that he was an accountant whose only talent consisted of having acquired an artist-wife. That was proof enough that he was a connoisseur, with an authoritative opinion about art.

Gaby, "a very promising young artist whose work showed high technical accomplishment," standing nearby, preened in her husband's repartee. Barely out of her teens, attractive, a bit impractical, but outgoing and vivacious, she knew that she was a more finished artist than any of the other members of the YAG, "amateurs." Ghee-Ghee returned his wife's admiration. He was sure that her gifts, which, whatever they lacked in quantitative measurement, exceeded any number Arpie could come up with. "In a college production of *A Doll's House*, Gaby understudied for Nora, and in rehearsal, when it came to the scene where Nora dances the tarantella, you know? Gaby danced out right behind her in perfect sync, without," he almost sang, "missing a step." They beamed at each other.

Gaby had joined the Group in the hope of finding a benefactor, a patron, or a commission. And Mme V, who had happened by, provided

The Womb of Uncreated Night

just the opportunity she had been hoping for by casually suggesting in passing, "Perhaps we could exhibit some of your paintings here, some time, dear?" Before she could turn away to greet other guests, Gaby pounced.

"Oh, thank you, Madame! That would be wonderful! I would be delighted to put together a show for one of the regular meetings of the group." The alacrity of Gaby's acceptance took Mme Villiards by surprise. She had only meant her offer as encouragement, the way people who do not see each other regularly suggest that they really must get together some time. But as long as it remained in the limbo of possibility, she was not really concerned that Gaby might hang her pictures and dance tarantella in front of them. Besides, she mused as she moved away, a few paintings tastefully arranged along the walls of the apartment wouldn't be amiss. Guests could admire the art and sample hors d'oeuvres while some of the young musicians performed their music. Some nice, genteel background music—she set her jaw firmly—*undanceable* music. Why, yes, it could make for a pleasant change of pace.

She was still musing about arrangements for the possibility of an "art show" when she overheard several young women admiring the handsome "George Farquhar." Wondering who could be introducing himself as an eighteenth-century comic dramatist, she turned and saw that they were eyeing Brewster. She pounced on him with mock indignation. "Now Mr. Farquhar, you wicked boy!" she said, pulling him aside. "You are not to put people on so." She brushed away his protestations of innocence. "There's young Artsynick. Go and introduce yourself properly."

"Unjustly accused," said Brewster as he went off smirking in search of Nick Artsynick at a window behind the Bösendorfer, overlooking a terrace, and beyond it, Central Park. "I understand you're a composer?" began Brewster. "Will you be playing something of your own for us this evening?"

"No, I'm too busy composing my masterpiece," said Nick, turning, wondering who was this phony pretending to take an interest in him? "An opera. I've already begun writing the prelude as I stand here, containing motifs to be developed in the opera—not the usual compositional procedure, of course. But then I tend to do things ass-backwards."

Brewster laughed. "Tell me about it."

"Yeah, sure," said Nick with a shrug.

"No, I mean really," said Brewster. "I'd like to hear more about it."

"Oh? Right. Let's see, do you know the story of Abelard and Heloïse? Wonderful subject for an opera. Fulbert, canon of Notre Dame around the middle of the twelfth century, hires Abelard as his niece Heloïse's tutor. Grand opening scene in the cathedral where Abelard first sees his prospective student. Grand orchestral peals in the opening bars of the prelude," said Nick, getting caught up in his head. "Solemn, but ominous, too, you know? Hinting at the, well, *coup* to come." He strode over to the piano, smirking, and played double octaves, pianissimo, on f-sharp, alternating with thunderous chords, d-major in the deep bass against g-minor in the upper treble. Several of the Young Artists in conversation around the dais jumped and glared at him. Delighted at their reaction, Nick laughed and broke off, playing the restrained chorale tune that followed. "Abelard of course immediately falls in love. That's followed by the early lesson scene, really a love scene with double-entendres. Then the seduction scene."

"Doubling of another sort, eh?" said Brewster.

"Yeah. I'll pencil that in. After Heloïse gets pregnant and bears a son, they marry to pacify uncle Fulbert. But uncle Fulbert treats her badly and Abelard spirits her away to the convent at Argenteuil. Thinking that Abelard is about to abandon his niece, uncle Fulbert hires thugs to cut off his balls."

"A bit too late, wouldn't you say?"

"Maybe, but an interesting trope on the concept of climax. At the beginning of the opera, Abelard is sung by a baritone. After the castration scene, he rises from the spot where he has fallen, a countertenor. Singing florid roulades."

"A real coup de théatre!" laughed Brewster. "Did you really make that up just this minute?"

Nick shrugged, got up from the piano and Brewster, puzzled, followed him back to the group that had gathered around Dr. Korngold near the fireplace in the alcove. The musical part of the evening was about to begin. Mme Villiards introduced a young woman who had studied with a fashionably avant-garde composer as a child. She played a dissonant and polytonal two-part Invention of her own composition, apparently written for her teacher, an impoverished disciple of Boulez. It sounded suspiciously like an exercise in which she had been told to take a Two-Part Invention by Bach and "do everything he does." Atonally.

Nick sat on the sofa with Dabbler and Arpie, awaiting his summons. Brewster was prepared to display all the socially correct hypocrisy. But when he caught sight of Guinevere Glimmerglass, he quickly inserted himself at the end of the sofa, crowding Nick who did not like being pressed against Arpie Fairfield and got up grumbling, stepping around to stand behind the sofa.

Guinevere was sitting on the floor with her head leaning back against the armrest of the sofa where Brewster sat. He could almost feel her through a scant inch of separation. Her face was slightly turned away, as if she were listening raptly to the music. Her soft throat rose smoothly to a fine, firm chin, then to full lips tucked into a sly corner. He followed the line of her gracefully curved nose up to her closed eye and slightly arched eyebrow. He traced her forehead with the tip of his thought up to her long, chestnut hair, which went without a hairdresser's art and hung loosely down to her shoulder. An almost iridescent sheen, as from platinum blond highlights underneath, made her face, without makeup, seem to glow in the lamplight. He wanted to scoop up handfuls of her hair and inhale. What color would her eyes be? As if she had caught his thought, she turned her head and looked up at him. Her eyes were the russet shout of autumn leaves. His lips moved, wanting to say something brittle and witty. Something with a casual breath to stir but not rattle those leaves. But her eyes laughed in his. She took his hand, and introduced herself. Her touch was soft and cool. Her subtle scent cut through Korngold's unlit pipe, Mme Villiards' musky sweetness, Arpie's armpits, and Guilemot's suit, permeated with stale cigarette smoke, like an oboe piercing through a thick orchestral texture.

Korngold stood prominently in front of the fireplace tapping the pipe against his teeth, as if to test Mme Villiards' ban on smoking. She sat in a chaise facing him, frowning. Guilemot stood at the other end of the sofa whispering to his wife who was sitting on the armrest between Arpie and him. As the atonal Invention came to an end, they applauded politely.

Discussion followed. Some of the audience got up to take more refreshment. One who had remained seated and noticed Bach buried under dissonance got up and went to stand beside the pianist. He asked her to play the opening bars of her invention, then inserted his hand behind hers and played the beginning of the Bach. "I was wondering when someone was going to notice that," she said with an uncomfortable smile. As the discussion continued, Ghee-Ghee turned to Nick.

"Your piece isn't going to give us warmed over Bach in modern clothing, is it?" he chuckled.

"More like cool Schönberg under a wig," said Nick. "Some people carp at anyone who presumes to compose these days. If you write something traditional, they'll say, 'I've heard that before.' If you write something that breaks with tradition, they'll complain, 'It isn't music.' Or if they haven't even heard your music, they'll question your presumption in writing it, like 'Who do you think you are, anyway?'"

"So what are we going to hear from you tonight?" asked Ghee-Ghee.

"Unless a composer wants to break completely with the past for the sake of originality," shrugged Nick, "he's bound to imitate something. But no. My piece follows traditional models and uses a dissonant style—"

"Something old, something new, something borrowed—anything blue?" smirked Ghee-Ghee. "A wedding march, perhaps?

"It follows sonata-allegro form," Nick growled.

At this, Korngold intervened. "You know, Goethe made the most significant link between virtue and the arts, equating humanism, the inborn qualities of mind and body which raise men above the animals, as the source of goodness. But his was only among the first of the Romantic voices to say so. Maybe the Romantic philosophers wanted to model society on the arts because they were mesmerized by aesthetics."

Brewster snickered at this. Korngold turned to him with a questioning look, but Brewster said nothing. "You don't agree?" prodded Korngold.

Brewster skeptically cocked his head left and slowly shrugged, almost as if he were stretching or yawning. "Of course," he said. "It had nothing to do with the fact that the rulers those Romantic philosophers served encouraged the arts in order to glorify their own sleazy empires, even distract the masses of people with dazzling displays."

"But they also serve to provide us with perspectives that are absent from the scientific method," protested Korngold.

"Ah, perspective!" smiled Brewster, wagging his head. "Those grand boulevards that Baron Haussmann plowed through Paris under Napoleon III, they really beautified the city, didn't they. Nothing whatever to do with facilitating the movement of troops and cannons to put down protests. Power *is* pretty, isn't it?"

"You sound like a Communist," sneered Ghee-Ghee.

While this exchange had been heating up, Arpie, whose grasp of music never went far beyond analytical elements—key and time signatures, strict observance of metronome markings and the mathematics of scales and harmonies, as much science as art—had been turning over in his mind the advisability of lodging a protest of his own. He broke into the discussion for the first time. "But isn't perspective a *science*?"

"Only when viewed from a mechanistic point of view," Korngold quickly replied, relieved that Arpie had sidetracked the escalating confrontation between Brewster and Ghee-Ghee.

"They say that Bach had great mathematical abilities," said Arpie.

Korngold nodded. "It's true enough that without a mathematical basis, architecture, all art, including music, would be impossible. Goethe understood that. But he also understood that there is an aesthetic of human emotion which goes beyond measurement. Power in perspective," he said, turning pointedly to Brewster, "can indeed be 'pretty.' The perspective applied by the Greeks in the construction of the Parthenon actually took that into account when they oh-so-subtly calculated the amount of distortion needed to make the columns look perfectly straight when viewed from any angle."

"Well, that's inherent in optics—" began Arpie.

"But clever mathematical calculation," Korngold continued, "could never work for a Shakespeare, or a Dickens—"

"Or a poet," put in Guinevere.

"Or a poet," agreed Korngold. "Or any other art that's not primarily visual. The eye is not by itself an entirely reliable guide to the world. Yet it's the sense we most rely on."

"That's why we need five," said Brewster. "If one of them is defective, the other four can compensate." Even before Dr. Cacamati's contacts had corrected the worst of his near-sightedness, Brewster had never been overly sensitive about his eyes. "And then there's that mysterious sixth sense." Brewster was not thinking in mysterious psychological or metaphysical terms. Hippias and he had found the means of enhancing his other senses beyond what any of them could have imagined. No one needed to know that *his* sixth was a nano-sense.

"Proportion and perspective in the arts really comes down to selective distortion, doesn't it?" said Nick, who had been struggling with his own inner perceptions as the time neared for Mary Beckonwith to play his sonata. It shamed him to think that his pianism wasn't up to playing his own composition.

"You can fool some of the senses some of the time," said Ghee-Ghee seizing the moment, "but can an artist fool all of the senses all of the time?"

"That usually isn't necessary," said Korngold.

"No," guffawed Ghee-Ghee. "For that we have psychiatrists!"

Touché, thought Nick, as everyone laughed. "Or accountants," he muttered. From the eye-down-the-nose he got from Ghee-Ghee he knew that he had been overheard.

"And just which part of the body do your proportion and perspective stir?" sniffed Ghee-Ghee.

The Womb of Uncreated Night

"Maybe we should just wait and hear how Nick's music stirs us," placated Korngold.

Ghee-Ghee turned to Dr. Korngold and said, "What possible humanitarian purpose could the sonata-allegro form serve anyway?"

Before Nick could retort or Korngold, intervene, the post-mortem on the atonal invention at the other end of the room wound down. Mme Villiards made her way to the dais to announce that Mary Beckonwith would play Nick's sonata. To make sure that Nick did not linger and get into another altercation, Mary, who had sat quietly, rolling her eyes as the group around Dr. Korngold had held their own cultural caucus, got up, took Nick firmly by the hand and led him to the piano. She placed the music on the stand in front of her. She pushed Nick onto the chair behind her, ready to turn the pages.

Just as Mary started to play, a disturbance in the foyer diverted everyone's attention. A grim young man in the grip of a determined-looking older woman bustled noisily into the room. Mme Villiards immediately recognizing the young man as Leon Barvim exclaimed in delight. All smiles, she ran to greet him and his mother. Mary stopped playing. She and Nick looked at each other uncertainly then back at the new arrivals.

Mrs. Barvim let go of her son as soon as she had realized that all eyes were on them. She basked in Mme Villiards' gracious welcome while her son stood there looking out of sorts. An accomplished but unwilling pianist, he had come at his mother's instigation. She and her husband, who had begged off that evening because of pressing business affairs, were Russian émigrés. Though his father was the only parent who played a musical instrument, the violin, both parents were music lovers. Mrs. Barvim, whose black hair in late middle age was either dyed or had not yet begun to turn, played the piano vicariously; that is, she played upon her son with the same commitment to perfectionism that drove such virtuosos of pre-Revolutionary Russia as Heifetz and Horowitz, pushing him toward a concert career he had never wanted since reaching the age of puberty. He played, grimly, vengefully, to drown out his mother's threats to cut him out of the family's substantial commercial interests if he did not become a concert pianist. Any resistance was countered by Mrs. Barvim's withering, sarcastic, "You're such a smart aleck!" The elder Mr. Barvim was inclined to shrug at his son's recalcitrance and play a little Tartini in his spare time. After years of this internecine skirmishing, Leon's polished pianism demonstrated an idea that would have outraged W.S. Gilbert, that anger-driven technical mastery could convincingly carry "merely corroborative detail" so far as to give it the verisimilitude of artistry.

After a whispered discussion with Mrs. Barvim and her son, Mme V went back to Nick and Mary still seated at the piano, with Leon in her wake. The whispering now included a protest by the pianist, during which Nick sat dumbly by and Leon's face lost some of its grimness. Disregarding Nick and Mary's consternation, Mme Villiards turned a pleased face on her guests and announced that, "We have a special treat, this evening. Leon B—"

"Lon," he corrected her. "I go by 'Lon.'"

"—Lon Barvim," she smiled apologetically. "Lon is going to give a recital next week at Town Hall. Tonight, he's going to play a part of that program for us." She paused for the excited murmurs and applause. "He is not yet a member of the Young Artists Group," Mme Villiards went on, "but perhaps if we give him a hearty welcome, he'll consent to join us regularly." She led the renewed applause and returned to her place near Korngold as Lon edged Mary away from the Bösendorfer. Arpie, in an aside to Brewster, whispered that Barvim had shortened his name to "Lon" because he thought "Leon" was too Jewish. It also sounded macho.

Nick returned to the group around the sofa, stung at having been deprived of his moment. He watched as Barvim, looking glum, sat fussing with the adjustable bench, flexing his fingers, squirming into position. A privileged guy preening under his shining moment, thought Nick bitterly, a moment that should have been his. He remembered that a reviewer had written of Leon that he was a young pianist who was making a name for himself in music circles. Not so, Nick scoffed. His parents' money was buying him a name. What would Leon's prospects be if they hadn't been able to buy his way into Town Hall? For the briefest moment, Nick tried to think sympathetically of what it must have been like for the parents, Jews living in Russia. Persecuted, the grinding poverty they might have endured. And even if they had been relatively well off, the hatred that hung over them and threatened at any time to crash down on them. But the Barvims had escaped. He had not. They had instead come down on him.

Arpie whispered to Brewster, confidentially. "We went to high school together, you know. We used to chum around together and hang out in Central Park. I never thought much of it until he started talking about how the bible condemned homosexuality. 'Let's go to the park,' he'd say, 'and if we meet any homosexuals, we have the right to beat them up and take their money.'"

"And did you and he ever beat up homosexuals and take their money?" asked Brewster, absently, annoyed at the distraction from his contemplation of Guinevere.

"He also had his hair straightened because it was too curly," added Arpie. "Too Jewish," he chirped.

"Beethoven," announced Barvim tersely, and immediately attacked the piano. He fumbled the opening fanfare leaping from the bottom to the top of the keyboard. He stopped, frowned and shook his head, while his mother glared, the YAG murmured and stirred. He compressed his lips, inhaled audibly, and began again. This time he managed the opening salvo with only a minor slip, and thereafter had the notes firmly in his fingers. But throughout the entire performance, the frown never left his face except to deepen into a scowl.

At the first note of the music, Nick recognized what Barvim was playing. He was stunned. Beethoven, indeed! Bad enough to have to follow Beethoven—*any* Beethoven—with a sonata that was stylistically somewhere between Hindemith and Schoenberg. But the *"Hammerklavier"*? A monument that dwarfed anything written before or since! And unless Barvim played like Toscanini, it would last a good forty-five minutes! Would there even be time for Mary to play his sonata afterward?

12.

... THE DEVELOPMENT section of the "Hammerklavier" drew to a close, and Nick back into the music. Fugue. Flight. What was Beethoven flying from? Away from his deafness or into it? Penetrating deeper and deeper into his inner sound, away from the distractions outside? Becoming more human as he withdrew further into his inner awareness? An earway for others to follow . . . ? Flight . . .

Dabbler and Pilar were well settled in when several months later they encouraged Nick to come to the City. When he arrived at their digs, he was offered the sofa, but preferred the floor. It would be adequate until he could make other arrangements. Fresh from the hinterlands, he was utterly bewildered. The hard buildings confining the streets slammed into his face and imprisoned his vision. Even the sky seemed constricted. They gave him a headache.

Nick was shocked by Dabbler and Pilar's casual habit of removing all their clothes as soon as they came home. Dabbler defended this quirk simply by insisting that clothes are uncomfortable. At first Nick declined to strip off his own clothing out of some vague sense of impropriety as much as his reaction on first seeing the lubricious Pilar in the altogether. But gradually, he accepted Dabbler's rationale, beginning with removal of his shoes, and in a month-long strip-tease, his shirt, undershirt, and pants. For a time, he was content to accommodate the Addlers' nudity by

The Womb of Uncreated Night

moving around the flat in shorts and socks. But eventually he managed to shrug off the last of his inhibitions to imitate their odd—for him—quirk. Perhaps, he thought, nudity was "cool," New York being such a sophisticated place. Although the three of them generally got along well, an occasional misgiving rattled Nick's composure. Something about being in the altogether went beyond literal exposure. There was a psychic exposure as well, a sense of vulnerability. But to what? Nick couldn't have said. Why stir up bourgeois prudery and guilt?

Dabbler carried himself with a certain boldness and confidence. Yet his face and mannerisms were those of a child. His straight, pale blond hair gave his head a certain softness, almost a delicateness, that reached into his face, hairless except for even paler eyebrows that faintly traced the ridges of his brow. Beneath these, an almost exact bilateral symmetry studded by faded blue eyes gave his expression the vacuous innocence of a six-year-old. He looked naïve, even sweet.

People tend to believe someone with a face like that when they aren't trying to take advantage of them. Shortly after moving into the Village, Dabbler walked into a Brooklyn machine shop and told the foreman that he was an experienced machinist. As it happened, the shop was short-handed and needed a skilled worker. The foreman without further ado took him over to a metal-working lathe, told him to set up a job and go to work, turned his back and left him. Dabbler simply stared at the lathe.

"My goodness," he had said when he told Pilar about it later that day, "I was afraid to touch anything. The machine was so complicated that the least little mistake could have ruined it!"

"What did you do?" asked Pilar between mirth and awe.

"I just stood there, staring at it, until an experienced old-timer on a nearby machine came over and showed me what to do." And before the week was out, Dabbler was a skilled machinist and the fair-haired boy of the shop.

He was tall, lean, and athletic, surprising when you considered that he ate constantly—anything and everything within reach—and never seemed to exercise. Tiring of the routine at the machine shop after a few weeks, he simply quit and went to work washing dishes at a Chinese restaurant because the owner kept urging him to eat: "Are you sure you've had enough?" he kept asking anxiously. Dabbler assured him that he had, then went home and began rummaging in the cupboards for food. Pilar did not know about this change of profession until she came home after work and a trip to the supermarket in the evening, surprised to find him sitting in his usual dishabille at the deal table, listening to WQXR, reading a bible, and pouring Karo corn syrup over slice after slice of bread. By the time she arrived, he had eaten almost an entire loaf. It was the only food left in the place.

"The sink is full of dishes," she exploded when he told her what he had done, "and the grocery is full of food. Did it ever occur to you that you might wash the dishes and replace what you eat instead of just eating everything till it's gone and expecting me to replenish it and clean up after you?" Dabbler was uncertain about whether she was annoyed more over his giving up the machinist's trade or his eating habits. He slammed his bible on the table, got dressed, stalked out to the corner grocery, and returned fifteen minutes later with a bag of apples. He had cooled off and stood in the kitchen like an overgrown kid caught sneaking a between-meals snack.

"I suppose," mumbled Dabbler by way of apology, "I unconsciously expect every woman to react like my mother."

"We do things together, I hope, that you never did with your mother!" retorted Pilar.

Dabbler shrugged in acquiescence. Then noticing that Pilar had been washing the dishes in his absence, decided he had better say something complimentary. "You're a good housekeeper," he said.

⁂

. . . The fanfares of the "Hammerklavier's" coda subsided into awed silence, and Barvim began the brief, playful scherzo. For a moment, Nick again became aware of Arpie's armpits before drifting off again . . .

Arpie paid his first visit to the flat shortly after the spat between Pilar and Dabbler. Neither of them bothered to dress for the occasion, and Nick affected an embarrassed nonchalance about it and followed suit. Or unsuit. That three naked people casually sharing a flat in a sophisticated city should imply anything more than the mild infraction of a prudish taboo had been relegated to a remote place in his thoughts. Nick rationalized the nakedness of the ménage as natural, the way people in a nudist colony must do. How they must feel when outsiders come to peer at them was outside his experience. But when Arpie raised his eyebrows and smiled knowingly but fully clad, Nick was vaguely irritated. What's he thinking? His cool pose inwardly thawed and he felt compromised.

Arpie had impressive mathematical and verbal skills, and a certain cockiness that did not fully compensate for his sense of being an outsider. He wanted to be admitted to Nick and the Addlers' shared interests in the arts, music, and chess. Although not a chess-player, Arpie picked it up as an entree into the group. The ease with which he picked up the fundamentals would demonstrate his genius.

There was something in the way he first came to the board that said, "Although I've never played chess before, because I am a genius I'll be able to outplay you cold." As a result, his first contests with Nick were disastrous. Supremely confident that his high I.Q. allowed him to make preposterous moves, his first games were less than brilliant. He committed the novice's blunder of moving his queen in front of his king in the opening moves of play. Even though Nick gleefully demonstrated the folly of this approach by quickly castling and trapping Arpie's queen with his rook, Arpie persisted in it. Was he being pigheaded enough to keep falling for the same trap? Or did he think he would find a way to outwit Nick if he kept at it? Or, a slyer motive—was he trying to ingratiate himself with Nick by letting him enjoy a cheap victory? Nick was never sure that the latter motive wasn't the real one. But eventually Arpie began to play more thoughtfully and became a good match. He became so good that he began to beat Nick often enough that Nick thought that he might eventually be able to forgive Arpie's smugness.

. . . The slow movement, one of the longest Beethoven ever wrote, can sing with tragic intensity. And although Barvim had shown himself to be accomplished in the difficult, even brilliant passage work of the first and second movements, Nick thought he played this most soulful of all music a little coolly, even mechanically. Or was he carping because his own music would so pale beside even a mediocre performance? But the music began to sing in his head in spite of himself. For a time, it teased him out of his grievance. To be brushed aside by Beethoven, well, who would not be? If he dwelt on Beethoven, could he ever again put pen to paper? But to be elbowed out of the way by *Barvim*? Even that sting began to be absorbed into the music. Then the Adagio faded away. The last movement slowly built an introduction out of an inner silence, like the searching recitative spun out by a heroine in the charged atmosphere of an opera, now reflective, now agitated. Only instead of leading up to an aria, it launched into a gigantic fugue. Full of every pianistic device, rapid scales, wild leaps, rumbling arpeggios, and whirling trills, it makes superhuman demands on a pianist's technique. There was something oddly appropriate about the grim, Romantic look on Barvim's face as he came to grips with them and perspiration broke out on his forehead . . .

Dabbler was a little like that, if in a less focused way. He was as brilliant and personally appealing as he was indolent. He read abstruse treatises on non-Euclidean geometry and the functions of a complex variable with as much apparent facility as most people read novels. Since few of his friends indulged in such pastimes, their attention tended to wander when he held forth on arcane puzzles with that sweet, serene unruffled face. Except that whatever struggle he had with those recondite ideas, he never broke a sweat. Friends were willing to take his word for his ability to penetrate those subjects. Their ears not being attuned to the music of mathematics, they could not hear any wrong notes or ragged tempos in it. But the mild exterior was deceptive. When he was angered, those pale eyebrows condensed unexpectedly out of his unblemished skin as a storm out of a cloudless sky, his mouth turned down and his chin jutted out in a moue that looked more petulant than fierce, the kind of face an actor learning to project *deep disapproval* might practice in front of a mirror before trying it out on an audience. And out of that spoiled serenity would pour a continuous torrent of the foulest epithets that ever blistered an ear, until his passion or his spectacular vocabulary had been spent.

When he wasn't dissipating his talents between jobs by writing poetry and sometimes music, wasn't reading the bible, pontificating about morality, or conning his way into a new profession, Dabbler sometimes turned to painting. This, like everything else he did at home, in the nude, using Pilar as a model. Shortly after Nick joined them, Dabbler between jobs began painting a mural on the blank unbroken surface of the back wall in the bedroom. He installed fluorescent light fixtures with tubes that supposedly duplicated the spectrum of natural sunlight. He kept the wall covered with a drop-cloth when he was not working on it, and used the cloth to screen off the room when he was. It was curiously inconsistent—the artist, nude, while the work was modestly covered.

At last, Dabbler, his torso splotched as any palette, removed the drop-cloth to display the finished work. The effect was startling: the composition was straightforward enough, Pilar—it was a recognizable likeness—rising from the sea like Aphrodite. Not the serene Botticelli goddess seductively cloaking her genitalia with long blond hair, but a virago, almost predatory female in an Afro who looked more ready to devour than to entice. She was either stripping the water from her limbs or splashing it over them. Behind her, a halting, groping, overcast sky in which lurked sinister, half revealed forms. And the color and texture of the sea looked odd, tinged with a pale, reddish hue reminiscent of capillary blood when viewed against a strong light, a kind of nubbled, grainy texture—almost a pointillistic effect that, viewed a few feet away, coalesced in the eye to create the impression of a wash of color as if each droplet of water was at the same time separately discernable from the next. Only, when you looked more closely, you saw that the water droplets were really tiny human body parts. Pilar-Aphrodite was bathing in a sea of bleeding humanity.

Pilar stared at it wide-eyed for several minutes, then turned on Dabbler and scolded him for portraying her in a scene of such wanton cruelty.

"What do you mean by portraying me like some—some monster!"

Dabbler was startled. "But sweetheart—not a monster—a goddess!" Then he tried to rationalize his intent. "It's—it's—" He hesitated, groping for a satisfactory response. He had not seen Pilar's monumental figure as monstrous. He almost laughed at the absurdity of such an image, as if King Kong had been summoned out of the depths of an uncharted jungle by Pilar's gong. But he quickly checked his merriment this side of Pilar's scowl. "It's The Great Mother," he said at last. Put in that light, he was at a loss why Pilar did not see it as an homage. He had begun painting without a conscious agenda, scarcely aware of what he had been doing. He had stared at the wall until he felt a vague sense that something was there, a hazy design he needed to paint the blankness away from to reveal. Like Topsy, it just grew. And this simply was what it had grown into. What did it mean? Did a painting have to *mean* anything at all? Could a creation have a meaning its creator did not have? Could his work take on a meaning that the creator never intended? He struggled to give it a meaning that would defuse wifely outrage. As he mulled over these thoughts, Pilar's body language suggested that he had better come up with something fast.

"Well," he blurted out, trying to sound confident in the certainty of a formula, "If nothing else, see it as . . . well, a harmonious composition of form and color. After all, that's what Whistler did with the portrait of his mother. What's good enough for someone's mother ought to be good enough for someone's wife, right?" Or some such relationship. He was getting muddled and further away from an answer that would erase that look on Pilar's face. "Had Whistler's mother felt slighted about being reduced to an *Arrangement in Gray and Black*?" Then he caught himself on the term, "reduced," and hastily added, "Isn't that pleasing in and of itself?" Pilar continued to glare at him.

Dabbler was getting nettled, the pompous professor lecturing the recalcitrant student. "It is not a creator's responsibility to explain his creation. That is the responsibility of the audience. It is the creator's function to create. If you don't understand it—" he shrugged "—walk away. If you meet someone who thinks he understands it, ask *him* what it means."

"And ignore him if you don't like the answer!" said Pilar.

"Well, uh—if it has to have a meaning beyond the compositional," said Dabbler desperately, something clicking into place at last, "you could say it's a sort of The Great Mother rising out of the sea—"

"A *bloody* sea!" stormed Pilar.

"Well, all births come out of blood, sweetheart. Or maybe a symbolic protest against man's inhumanity to man." That had an appropriate ring of social redemption that ought to appeal to the populist in Pilar.

"That's not a man taking a bath in bloody human bodies!"

"Well, you could think of it in terms of a protest against men dominating women. A Great Mother rising out of a sea of men's bodies and stripping them of power."

"A Great Mother! A parody. A twisted goddess of love. Me!"

"But sweetheart—"

"It's ugly. Is that what you unconsciously really think of me!"

More heated words followed, and finally, Dabbler, exasperated, burst out, "There's no such thing as an unconscious. The whole idea is a load of crap! I don't believe it exists."

"Then explain what you meant the other day when you said that you unconsciously expected every woman to act like your mother!"

Dabbler, taken aback by this, drew himself up. "I perceive that you are thinking more clearly than I, at the moment," he said with a pomposity that undercut the concession. "But I have found that it is a waste of time to try to explain things to people who do not understand what I mean!"

"Oh!" exploded Pilar, "and I'm a donkey!" She marched stiffly into the bedroom and put on her clothes. She remained sullenly clothed for the rest of the day to deprive Dabbler of the sight of her body. He hovered around her, naked, making conciliatory little noises, but Pilar steadfastly ignored him as she attended to minor domestic chores in keeping with being "a good housekeeper." And Nick, unwilling to take sides, but uncertain whether getting dressed himself would be interpreted as showing support for Pilar or remaining naked expressed support for Dabbler, sat on the sofa in a funk. Never before had he felt so exposed. His eyes met Dabbler's once or twice, and he wondered if he saw an appeal for help or an unspoken suggestion that he get out. Since they all condescended to get dressed before they left the flat, he finally decided on the latter as the most neutral course. As quietly and unobtrusively as he could, Nick dressed himself and left without explanation.

Evening crept out of the corners. Pilar had just finished washing the dishes and placing them on the drainboard. Dabbler, who ordinarily made no effort to help with domestic chores, turned on a light, reluctantly picked up a dish towel, and slowly reached for one of the dishes on the drainboard. Pilar snatched the towel out of his hands and glared at him. Wearying of being rebuffed and hoping that she would hear his stomach rumbling and think of preparing supper, Dabbler made a grim mouth, sat at the kitchen table and silently began reading the bible. Exasperated at what she saw as the ultimate in pious hypocrisy, Pilar threw the dish towel at him and went off in a huff into the bedroom. Throwing her injured pride and a few personal belongings into a laundry bag, she left for parts unknown. Dabbler, after he had stopped fuming, dressed and set out to find her.

When Nick returned an hour later, optimistically believing that the tension would have eased, that Dabbler and Pilar would have made it up, that Pilar would have supper ready, and the three of them could resume their innocent ménage, he found darkness and abandonment. Something cold and alien had sifted into the place. He turned on all the lights in the flat, but the sense of dislocation only scuttled into the shadows like so many cockroaches. He did not at first understand what had happened in his absence. There were the dishes Pilar had washed. The kitchen-living room actually looked unusually neat. But when he went into the bedroom, the dresser looked like a mouth with its teeth knocked out, its drawers gaping open or scattered at random

The Womb of Uncreated Night

on the bed or the floor. Odds and ends of undies and stockings dangled forlornly from them. Facial tissues, a sanitary napkin, and a shoe were scattered across the floor where Pilar in her haste had dropped them. Presiding over this disorder, The Great Mother calmly continued to bathe ironically in a sea of human indifference. Nick shivered.

So they were gone. Left to himself, Nick no longer went about the flat in the nude, keeping himself and The Great Mother carefully covered. Still not completely acclimated to New York City and with his only close friends gone, he became increasingly uneasy and haunted by a sense of anomie. That was when he had become a patient of Dr. Korngold's. On one of those damp mornings in a New York December, when the wind driven mist clawed at the world with talons of ice, scrabbled at windows and doors to be let in, he opened the outer door onto the areaway and found a cat soaked, shivering, and huddling against the warmth of the crack under the door. He took it in and, as he toweled her dry, felt his inner fractures start to mend. A few days later, he took in a stray mongrel. The cur and the cat responding to Nick's hospitality didn't seem to mind that he wandered aimlessly about the flat fully clothed. But they were not at all quite sure at first that they wanted to share it with each other. Eventually, of course, they settled into an uneasy truce, and by degrees developed an open affection for each other. Nick named them Dabbler and Pilar, and if his spirits did not soar, he found that they could stand and walk.

Nick's vague irritation with Arpie was sharpened when he dropped by after his roommates had been away for some time. Nick was having difficulty managing the rent on his own and feeling edgy. They were having coffee, sitting at the deal table, and Nick had fallen silent, staring off into the unfocused vacancy somewhere above his cup. As if there were a design somewhere under the layers of the ambient noise in the apartment, and if only he could clear away the racket beautiful music would emerge. He hadn't asked Arpie over, and really wanted to get back to composition. Without a piano, he had no difficulty following Shostakovich's injunction against composing at the piano.

Nick wondered idly what would emerge if Arpie were cleared away. Would he "drop by" unannounced to pry? Perhaps to check on Nick's dishabille now that his friends were gone? At the moment, R-P was lost somewhere in the haze beyond the space above the cup. Arpie's presence was a strain, and to ease the tension, Nick got up and turned on the radio. WQXR was playing a recording of Stravinsky's *Pulcinella*, based on music attributed to the eighteenth-century composer, Pergolesi, and he and Arpie listened as the last scene played to its exuberant close. When it ended, the announcer read some comments about how Stravinsky had "become enamored of the songful young Italian . . ."

"Whoops!" said Arpie, leering.

"Oh, yes!" snapped Nick, "and you'll no doubt want to make something of *Le Baiser de la fée*!" He had to admit to himself that a fairy kissing an allegorical Tchaikovsky had a certain piquancy these days. How was Arpie's French? The sharpness, if not the meaning of the question, created a semantic lapse of several minutes.

When Arpie brought the conversation around to Nick's friendship with Dabbler, Nick was not paying him much attention.

"What happened between Dabbler and Pilar? Why did they leave?" asked Arpie.

"Oh, they had a fight," Nick said absently. Pilar left, and Dabbler took off after her. That's the last I heard of either of them."

"You were closer to Dabbler than to Pilar, weren't you?"

"Well Dabbler and I go back to high school. Yes. He and I are long-time friends. He shacked up with Pilar after he met her out here. Then I met her when Dabbler suggested I move to New York and share their digs till I got myself together."

"But you had more of a relationship with him?"

The space over the cup coalesced into a point in R-P's cast eye. The rest of Arpie came into focus around it. He eyed Arpie coldly.

"A relationship? We were friends."

"It's a relationship I always envied," said Arpie with a shy smile.

That set Nick's teeth on edge. "Are you suggesting that his friendship

The Womb of Uncreated Night

with me drove a wedge between Dabbler and Pilar?" he bristled. Nick told himself to remain calm. He remained so calm, in fact, that when he slammed his cup down onto the saucer on the table, breaking it into several pieces, he was serenely unaware of the damage. Arpie, on the other hand, visibly started at the shattered china, and seeing the grim look on Nick's face, logically deduced that he had touched on a sensitive matter. Dabbler and Pilar cowered behind the couch. After several minutes of awkward silence, he left without finishing his coffee.

By late winter, a certain uneasiness had crept back out of the corners of Nick's mind and pushed away the tentative tranquility that had come in with cat and dog. Was it the prolonged absence of his former roommates? No, it was something more disquieting. Something seemed to be pushing away the surface of his existence, as if it were a curtain of water that could be parted by unseen hands. He began to feel as if he were being watched. Nick stood absently staring out over the areaway through the barred windows of the flat. It was raining.

The sooty particles that filled New York City's air and silted through the window frames and under the sashes and collected on the inner sills would, at least for a day or two, be washed from the sky. The street shone in a hiss of streetlamps as night rumbled in on thunder more felt than heard. Dabbler and Pilar came and sat beside him, ears erect and tails curled protectively around their paws. As if electricity had leaked out of a frayed wire and played along the surfaces of the room, Nick felt the hair at the nape of his neck prickle. They all looked at each other, eyes opened wide, and the animals' hackles rose. The spell lasted until an ear-splitting crack of thunder sent Pilar diving under the sofa, Dabbler scurrying into the kitchen, and Nick trying to allay his own agitation by coaxing them back to his side. He tried to speak soothingly, but his voice quavered.

"There! there! It's all right. You're not afraid of a little thunder are you? I'm still here with you. We're all safe. Nothing has happened. We're in this together." But neither cat nor dog nor Nick himself was reassured at the imminent prospect that the three of them might all perish together.

Over the next several days, the uneasiness grew. The super, who didn't like animals, discovered that Nick was keeping pets. At first he watched, unseen and silent. But when he found a stool in the areaway, he scooped it up with a shovel, knocked loudly on Nick's door, thrust the evidence at him and gave him an ultimatum—get rid of the animals or get out.

13.

. . . Lagging behind Beethoven's fugue, rumbling all a-trill in the bass and cascading in the treble, Nick's recollections coiled around some mysterious spool yet never reached its core. Whatever is in the pattern of life that reminiscence cannot recall, nor thoughts can think, nor yet words can say, can music encompass it . . . ?

Arpie was, like Nick, one of Dr. Korngold's "pro bono" patients—a tactful way of saying "charity case." As a soul-searching would-be writer, his therapy was a series of paraphrases. Early in his sessions he thought he was full of sparks that were never fanned to flame. Later, he decided that his problem was divine sparks in his heart and a mouth full of ashes. Finally, he was sure that the flames were in his mouth but the ashes were in his heart. Korngold tried to be patient with him.

Arpie's genius, like Dabbler's, lay in his grasp of mathematics, language, and science. He played the piano passably, if mechanically, so he edged into the Young Artists Group. But he wanted to be a writer. He wrote science fiction in a spare, hard style that strived for Hemingway in outer space. Yet his characters, when they were human at all, were not "he-men." Instead, they were often pathetic androids or humanoid aliens trying desperately to be human. They struck Nick as more like the prim Truman Capote with a tinge of lisp-and-mince facing down Pain Is and Life Goes On in The Great Beyond. But of course they always lost out to the Inevitable.

When he was not soliciting others to accept him because of his I.Q., Arpie was an amiable raconteur. He was full of anecdotes that skillfully nailed the defining quirks of just about everybody he knew, however well or casually, all of them amusingly embellished. If they sounded like ideal character sketches for his stories, they lost something in his outer space.

But Arpie was as generous and well-meaning as Nick found him socially inept. It was through him, in fact, that Nick got his first job in New York. Nick had come to the city with a little money in savings and had not immediately felt a pressing need for a job. While he, Dabbler, and Pilar shared the flat, dividing the rent and household expenses between them, he spent the first few months "getting oriented" in town. That turned out to be a mistake. By the time Dabbler and Pilar had split, he was running low on funds and desperate for income. Arpie suggested that he try the Orpheus Music Company on Lower Broadway, where he worked.

The Orpheus Music Company occupied a loft above one of those fashionably funky stores that catered to disaffected young people with the means and the cool to thumb their noses at the mainstream by playing at Goth and vampire. The boots, bags, beads, and bangles, faded jeans with torn-out knees, and leather jackets trimmed with silver ornaments clung to the walls below posters of young men and women scantily clad in the goods on display. The store throbbed Satanic purpose in relentlessly pounding disco-heavy metal sound for which social barriers like walls served only as transducers; the windows, trimmed with metal and framed with wood, buzzed and broadcast their contribution to the racket of Broadway traffic. Inside, clerks with liberally pierced noses, mouths, and ears, purpled lips, and spiked hair greeted customers with cold, hard, glittering eyes and underpaid faces. When the business had first opened and begun sending its amped-up vibes through the store's stamped metal ceiling and the floor of the Orpheus, Mr. Kahlenholtz had complained often and almost as loud to the managers of the store and the building. The new tenants finally agreed to soundproof the ceiling.

The Womb of Uncreated Night

The Orpheus was widely regarded as the go-to place for sheet music of all classical genres and orchestral study scores. Open bins ranking the center of the floor invited customers to browse through music neatly displayed in vertical files arranged alphabetically by composer and genre, and the high-ceilinged walls stuffed with file-boxes expanded the offerings. Customers flipped, riffled, and sorted under the watchful eyes of Mr. Kahlenholtz. Indifferent to the niceties of handling fragile sheets, they were often inclined to misplace or jam them back into their bins or boxes without regard for the creases and frayed edges that turned "new" into "used." Mr. Kahlenholtz expected Arpie and the new hires, "Miami" Bernwall and Nick Artsynick, to keep their wits about them in expanding his surveillance. If Mr. Kahlenholtz ringing up a sale, Arpie atop a ladder assisting another customer, and Nick and Miami hesitating over which of them ought to intervene and how, provided an opportunity for careless cramming, Mr. Kahlenholtz's sixth sense about impending profit loss kicked in. He immediately dropped whatever he was doing, strode ominously glaring and snorting, grabbed the sheets out of a culprit's hands, put them to rights and efficiently stowed them safely inside the folder, returning it to its proper place in the bin. Then he went back to what he had been doing, flinging a stern In-case-you-were-wondering-that's-how-it's-done look at Nick and Miami on the way.

Arpie would open the store at 9 a.m. and handle the till. Mr. Kahlenholtz usually arrived an hour or two later from his apartment in the Bronx. Thereafter, Arpie busied himself at the bins and box-files, checking for selections that needed to be restocked, items misfiled or damaged. Nick and Miami's first duty as soon as they arrived was to sweep the floor with push brooms. The floor boards, exposed for years to air bone-dry from steam heat in winter, air conditioning in summer, and the daily schlep of street-schmutzed feet, creaked and squeaked. The muffled thump and bump from the shop below made the floor vibrate in barely visible puffs of perennial dust and dirt only partly swept away by the new-hires' brooms. That chore done, Miami and Nick used intervals between customers to familiarize themselves with the contents of the bins.

Technically their supervisor, Arpie was not bossy. In fact, when neither Kahlenholtz nor cash customers were around he left them to their own devices, becoming so inconspicuous that Nick and Miami felt virtually alone in the store. At times, he was nowhere in sight. Without bothering to explore, they idly wondered where he had wandered off to. Was he in the back office writing a novel? Had he slipped out to the coffee shop next door? But if a customer stood near the cash register or the store filled with customers, he reappeared at once.

As they stroked the aisles with their brooms first thing in the morning, they whiled away the monotony with coworker chitchat.

"Do you go for opera?" Miami paused to ask soon after they had been working together for a few days.

"Do I go for opera," repeated Nick, blankly, looking up from his broom and staring at the file-boxes on the opposite wall as if they might suggest how to answer. "Are you a singer?" he asked, turning to look at his chunky coworker.

"No, I'm not a singer," said Miami with exaggerated patience. "I play the clarinet."

"Oh," said Nick, turning back to his broom.

Miami stood for a minute with half-open mouth, watching Nick. "Well?"

Nick stopped sweeping again. "Well," he echoed.

"You didn't answer my question," said Miami. "About opera."

"Oh," said Nick, turning back to the broom. "I was turning it over in my head. I must've gotten sidetracked by the sweeping nature of the question."

"So?" persisted Miami, exasperated now.

Nick sighed and continued to sweep. "Do"—sweep—"I"—sweep—"'go'"—sweep—"'for opera?"—sweep, sweep. He went silent for a moment longer. Then without further pauses, "Do you mean like 'going' to the john? I like some operas, but they don't make me want 'to go.' Although," he added with a little laugh before Miami could react, "I might have 'to go' if they dragged on too long. But ordinarily? No, I don't 'go' for opera."

The Womb of Uncreated Night

Seeing that Nick was being a smartass, Miami tried not to let it get to him. "You know what I meant. 'Go for,' as in *like*, ok? I go for Italian opera, myself." Nick grunted and continued to sweep. "How about Verdi?"

"The King of Oompah?" responded Nick. "I detest him."

"But *Otello*! *Falstaff*!" protested Miami.

"Worst things he ever wrote!" snapped Nick.

Miami looked thunderstruck. Then, with a suspicious squint, "Are you a Wagnerite?" he asked.

"The trouble with Verdi," said Nick, posing as musical progressive in sweeping condemnation of Italian operatic tradition, "is that he feeds audiences what they want without advancing musical form and expression. He's a dead end."

"What's wrong with giving audiences what they want?"

"It caters to the lowest common denominator of taste. And what's wrong with asking audiences to stretch their ears?"

"You can't blame Verdi for the tastes of the audience. They go to the opera to be entertained, not to be tortured on the rack! They want to leave the theater whistling an aria, a good tune. How many people leave the theater after a Wagner opera—oh, *excuse* me, *music drama*—whistling a leitmotif?"

"At least Wagner's operas have a coherent dramatic flow that isn't interrupted every five minutes by applause."

"Yes, and don't you wish they did so you could get up to 'go!'" retorted Miami as he swept away into the back room.

The eviction notice served on a shovel coincided with the depressing burden of rent that had been straining Nick's meager salary from Orpheus.

An eerie, arm's-length companionship shared by Nick, Arpie, and Miami was based on a common love of music and cemented by an unspoken distaste for each other. As the days of spring grew longer and winter tensions eased, they occasionally met at a greasy spoon on Broadway for coffee, diffidently, the way regular commuters in a train station are unavoidably thrown together and acknowledge each other with a grudging camaraderie. They occupied rather than shared a common space at a table, their thoughts joining the march of the city past the grimy plate-glass windows to their desperate, disparate destinations. Each wondered why he was not elsewhere, but made no move to go.

Arpie's ovoid butt, like his thoughts on the verge of toppling off their wall of isolation, hung over the flimsy, metal backed chair. Miami's slack-jawed silence caressed a reminiscence of some diva singing Verdi. And Nick's uptight veneer shielding his privacy threatened to come unglued over his urgent need for economical living quarters. Of the two, he would have preferred quarters with Miami. There would have been endless arguments over music in general and opera in particular. Nick would have been preferred that to Arpie's constant prying. But Miami lived comfortably with his parents in Brooklyn, so that was out of the question. Arpie, on the other hand, lived alone in a four-room shotgun and had plenty of space for a roommy to share expenses. It galled Nick to have to suck up to him.

Arpie had jumped at the idea of sharing expenses, but he hesitated when Nick insisted on bringing his dog and cat with him. Nick made it clear, however, that he would not consider moving in without them. Arpie relented. Once they all had settled in, the animals weren't much trouble.

Nick soon found that Arpie had an unfortunate problem with flatulence. He made matters worse by drawing attention to it, announcing the event by exclaiming, "Oops!" whenever he was about to fart, loudly relieving himself, and grinning apologetically. On one such occasion, he and Nick were sitting in the kitchen drinking coffee at the table. He suddenly exclaimed, "Oops! Oops!" leaped to his feet, ran into a closet and slammed the door after him. The door was snap-locked on the outside, and when Arpie had closed the door after him, the latch snapped to, followed immediately by a spectacularly loud fart.

The Womb of Uncreated Night

After a moment of silence, Arpie tried to open the door and realized that he was locked in. A few moments later, rattling the door knob, and finally knocking sheepishly on the door, he begged to be let out.

Calmly sipping his coffee, Nick ignored Arpie's pleas. Let him enjoy his afflatus. In his own mind his first symphony was forming. A Fart Symphony. It would begin with loud blasts in the brass, followed by a mincing main theme in the strings. Perhaps he could even borrow a page from Scriabin's book and have a smell kit representing different sections of the music passed out to the audience as their tickets were taken. Each scent would be impregnated on a card coded with a number, and a TV monitor installed at the back of the orchestra would cue the audience to a corresponding scratch and sniff... Why not? Something like that had been done on an experimental production of Prokofieff's *Love for Three Oranges*. Bliss had written "A Color Symphony." "A Fart Symphony?" Might sound as if he were slapping himself down. How about "A Sniff Symphony?" Well, he'd have to be careful that everyone understood sniff in its core sense of inhaling through the nose. It wouldn't do to have the audience sniffing at his symphony. There was always plenty of sniffling and hacking during any concert performance anyway. "Snuff Symphony?" What if the conductor interpreted snuff as an invitation to whip out a pistol and, say, shoot the concert-master or the first horn? Or worse, what if he whirled about on the podium and shot the composer! Wouldn't do. Safer to add a wind machine and call it, "A Wind Symphony."

Nick loved the double entendre. It'd have critical success built in. When the critics said, "This symphony really stinks!" they'd be praising it! The air conditioning system could be goosed up to blow gales of fresh air through the auditorium between the first and second subjects, even varied in intensity as the music modulated from key to key, so that the smells could be kept distinct or allowed to blend as in the development section, or the coda. Of course, the wind intensity could also be varied with the wind machine. The suspense of exactly when it would blow the music off the stands would be as exhilarating to the musicians as the audience. And many a conductor during a performance of impassioned music has imagined himself atop a mountain with a howling wind blowing through his hair. The score would be marked, "air cond. and wind mach. ad lib." The percussion section would love it! And that would provide a wonderful aleatory, with musicians scrambling across the stage to retrieve their parts, creating a whole new spectrum of sound when the violins ended up playing from trombone parts transposed up an octave or two, or the bassoons sight-reading the clarinet parts, without transposing from B-flat, A, or E-flat to concert pitch.

The development section would be quite . . . complex. Imagine the counterpoint in a farting fugue! And through it all there would be that fateful knocking motif, from an embarrassed request in the timpani intensifying as each sequence of farts—from bowel-rumbling double basses to long drawn-out plaintive wheezes in the woodwinds, anguished urgent squeals in the strings—steadily mounting, crescendo, to climactic demands, basso profundo ma con espressivo, from trombones, contrabassoon, and tuba, to be let out of the closet. Everyone would be so . . . well . . . relieved when the whole thing was over. There wouldn't be too much of a clean-up problem in the auditorium following the performance if the audience held on to their programs.

The performance in his mind over, Nick drained his cup of coffee, got up, and trailed out with the rest of the audience. Odd how that rapping motif persisted in one's head. When he returned, two hours later, he found Arpie sitting sullenly at the kitchen table, virtually in the same position he was in before his earlier outburst, glowering into the vacant space above his coffee cup. Nick casually walked over to the closet and inspected the door, running his thumb over the splintered frame where the latch had been. He made a show of looking for it on the floor, and looked surprised when he saw it sitting on the table next to the coffee cup he had left there.

"Say, Arpie. You've damaged the door. Will you be able to fix it, or should I call the super?"

The Womb of Uncreated Night

. . . Barvim brought the finale to a thundering close. Applause drowned out the reverberating strings of the final chord. Barvim stiffly acknowledged the applause and circulated through the room. From the dais, he had caught sight of Guinevere in the conversation group around Korngold. He brushed past well-wishers to make his way to them.

Mme Villiards intercepted him. "That was wonderful," she beamed. "Your program at the recital should be one to hear . . ." Barvim nodded his thanks and tried to push past her. She put out a hand to restrain him. "But tell me, why do you look so angry when you play?"

"I don't like to play," Barvim said curtly. He looked at his mother, graciously accepting the compliments of the people standing beside her.

"You certainly don't play as if you don't like to play," said Ghee-Ghee.

"All this artsy-craftsy crap is for sissies," Lon said flatly, and loud enough for his mother to overhear. Mme Villiards' jaw dropped, Brünnhilde about to let out a war-whoop. Mrs. Barvim continued to smile at the flattering comments of those near her, but her body stiffened and the lines of her face curdled into a warning that could cost a smart-aleck his allowance. He ignored the warning and added defiantly, "It's all a lot of swishing. Charles Ives nailed it when he called American composers 'pussy-boys.' But he didn't go far enough—"

"Now hold on!" interrupted Korngold All the great thinkers around the world would agree with Thomas Mann that 'Music by its very nature leads men out of absurd artificiality into fresh air, into the world of nature and humanity.' Maybe you could ease up a little and let that universal thought sink in."

"Yeah," scoffed Barvim, "I heard about *him*."

Arpie turned to Brewster for his reaction. But Brewster was too absorbed in Guinevere to pay attention to the consternation Barvim was causing. Rather than asking Barvim to leave, Mme Villiards turned away indignantly. Barvim continued his campaign to twit his mother. "My parents made me take piano lessons and practice six hours a day when I was a kid," he griped.

"There are other things than musical instruments that could stand some practice," chided Korngold. "Once a person is wise enough to put his feelings into definite order, the spell of immaturity is broken. That skill requires more than an oppressive taskmaster. Then he might realize that there's nothing so gratifying as mastering experience through art, a piece of music, painting, or poetry. And when he gets that, he'll be able to do his bit with a better grace."

"Oh, I'll do my bit, all right," said Barvim, turning toward Guinevere. She was more interesting than annoying his mother or Dr. Korngold and his groupies. While the others around Dr. Korngold had been debating the course of civilization, she and Brewster had withdrawn into each other. They had hardly spoken beyond a simple exchange of names, but their eyes carried on a lively conversation. Barvim interrupted. He leaned over her, his face almost touching her hair, inserting himself between them and cutting Brewster off. He introduced himself and took her hand, conversationally launching into suggestive innuendo. Guinevere snatched her hand out of his grasp. Brewster got up stiffly, about to slug Barvim, thought better of it, and went to stand next to Korngold.

Ghee-Ghee, who apparently had been pondering about the significance of the passage from Mann that Korngold had quoted, chose this moment to ask, "What's the difference between 'artificiality' and 'absurd artificiality' anyway? Isn't all artificiality absurd?"

Mme V caught the mischievous look that passed between Brewster and Korngold and glared at them before it burst into laughter.

"Of course!" said Brewster, trying to sound earnest as he looked the elegant Ghee-Ghee up and down. "How could Mann have neglected the distinction between genuine artificiality and absurd artificiality?"

Ghee-Ghee flushed. Guinevere shook Barvim out of her face and also stood up. "And do you think music, or for that matter any of the arts, could take us out of all that and restore us to nature?" she said in a voice that took in those nearby. "When they're so full of artificial boors, I mean?"

"My mother wanted me to flit through nature like a fairy," said Barvim on cue. "When I got wise to all the phoniness, I made up my mind to quit as soon as I was old enough."

"Then perhaps there's hope for the arts after all," smiled Guinevere.

"Hope," said Korngold, "doesn't come in a deluge. It trickles. But a steady trickle fills without destroying. If the arts can change a few hearts at a time . . . And once you have changed men's hearts—"

"And women's?" put in Gaby. "Though come to think of it, men's hearts do seem to be more impervious to change."

"Yes, of course," laughed Korngold. "A few *human* hearts at a time. Change is a contagion that can infect both genders."

Mme Villiards had gone back to the piano to announce that Nick's sonata would conclude the evening's music. Mary Beckonwith had gotten up and started to move toward her. Seeing Nick hang back, she went to him and urged him along with her. As they stepped forward, Nick noticed that the audience had grown restless on returning to their seats.

"They won't sit still for the work of a nobody after Beethoven!" Nick hissed. Mary glared back at him. She dragged him determinedly to the piano. She had prepared a substantial and difficult piece, she said, and she was not about to sacrifice all her effort for Nick's pathetic ego.

"Okay, okay!" Nick groaned. "But just play the scherzo. This place needs a joke." That led to a whispered argument during which there was considerable buzzing and scraping of chairs in the audience. Mary grasped the restlessness of the group. She conceded Nick's point and began to play "the joke." After thunder and lightning, a little laughter—no matter at whose expense—might lighten the mood.

As she played, the group around Korngold fell silent, apparently listening. Barvim persisted in following Guinevere as she moved away to avoid him.

"Yes. I think I see," said Brewster. "Music has the power to integrate ourselves with each other and our environment rather than to exploit each other ruthlessly." But his eyes were focused on Barvim as he pursued Guinevere. *If I cocked my head,* he thought, *squinted a little, and clipped him right there on the chops . . .* Face turned to Dr. Korngold, Brewster moved casually toward Barvim. "But can we really do the one without the other? Oh, sorry!" he said as he cut off the pianist's pursuit. "It sounds easy enough for a person of means," continued Brewster like an overzealous buttonholer as Barvim tried to sidestep him, and to avoid him—"oops!"—Brewster stepped back into his path . . . "whether he has inherited them as wealth or genes, to learn to exercise power responsibly as an artist, a musician." *A good swift knee in the groin.* Seeing that Brewster was determined to keep him at bay and that he was outmatched, Barvim gave it up.

"Or a poet," added Guinevere,

"Oh, yes," said Brewster, turning toward her. "A poet has great power." Brewster thought that he could listen eagerly to anything Guinevere would care to pour into his ears. That might drown out the urge to batter Barvim.

Mary had finished playing Nick's scherzo. The group applauded politely, not quite sure what to make of the piece. Nick got up from his position behind Mary and tried to smile appreciatively. He felt hurt that Barvim had been creating a disturbance that distracted Korngold and Brewster during the performance. Had they even heard it?

The soirée was breaking up. The group milled about chatting, and preparing to take their leave of Mme Villiards. Guinevere lost sight of Barvim. She thought she had at last escaped his attentions and slipped out onto the terrace to look out over Central Park and wait for him to leave. She caught Brewster's eye as she stepped through the French doors and hoped that he would follow. As she stood looking out over the park, she sensed the presence of someone contemplating her from the door. She turned expectantly and saw to her dismay that Barvim stood in the open door. With an ugly smile, he closed and locked one side of the patio doors and stationed himself in the open half in such a way that she would have been unable to pass through it and back into the living room without brushing up against him. Annoyed, Guinevere was considering how much skin she would have to scrape off his leg before she could get past him. Brewster saw what was happening as he threaded his way through the departing guests.

"Excuse me," he said, towering over Barvim and without waiting for him to move, roughly shouldered him aside. Guinevere smiled at Brewster and took his arm as if it had been prearranged. Barvim, looking almost as glum as he did when playing Beethoven, had to step aside to let Brewster escort her past him.

Brewster and Guinevere together took their leave of Mme Villiards.

"This is a really grand thing you're doing here, Mme V," said Brewster with a twinkle in his eye. "Perhaps we could have one of these soirées at the Wainwrights'? Hire a chamber orchestra? Serve a buffet? Make it a real occasion. What do you think?"

"Now, Brewster," said Madame Villiards, doubt reining in eagerness, "don't tease. I hope you're not joking."

"Why Madame V," exclaimed Brewster looking hurt, "you cut me to the quick! That you'd think I could be insincere!"

But the possibility of the soirée meant too much for Madame Villiards to take at face value what was offered so breezily by a young man who was capable of a gesture meant to impress a young lady on his arm. "That's a generous offer," she said with a cautious smile. "That old ballroom of yours wants a bit of use." She paused to reconnoiter, then pushed on. "You know, we have a very talented clarinetist, William Bernwall—the young people call him 'Miami' because he came back from Florida babbling about the place after a trip there with his parents. He's become quite a virtuoso on his instrument. He's been wanting a chance to play Mozart's Clarinet Concerto with a chamber orchestra. But there's no room here. Our next meeting is scheduled for Wednesday, June 5th. If you really think . . ."

"Done!"

Outmatched by Brewster in his conquest of Guinevere, Lon Barvim ditched his mother and left Mme Villiards' apartment without a word. Bristling and stiff with anger, he smashed his fist against the elevator's call button. When the car arrived, he pushed into it before the doors had fully opened. Through the lobby, grunting curtly at the doorman who greeted him politely and held the door open for him, Barvim turned and stalked up Central Park West to 77th Street. He paused at the entrance to the tunnel leading to the 86th Street subway station in front of the Natural History Museum. The gate to the tunnel would be closed at this hour. He started to walk past the statue of Theodore Roosevelt, then stopped.

He was still fuming as he crossed the avenue to the low stone wall that marked the western boundary of Central Park, walked back down to 77th Street and entered the park at the Naturalist's Gate. As he crossed the bridge over the bridle path and the filled-in Ladies' Pond, he had no purpose other than walking to vent his frustration and humiliation. Two young men leaning against the stone balustrade of the bridge stopped in their conversation to check him out as he approached, but seeing the hostility in his face, they shrugged and continued their talk.

By the time Barvim had crossed the West Drive and stepped onto the path along the Lake, his fury had congealed into thick intent. He turned down along the path to the Bank Rock Bridge that led into the Ramble. He picked up a large rock as the path wound past the Ravine. He followed a tall skinny kid down the sloping path leading to the little stream called the Gill. The kid turned his head to the side nervously as he became aware that he was being followed. Just before he reached the parting paths at the bottom of the slope, Barvim spoke.

"C'mere, honey," he said with sinister sweetness.

The kid smiled, thinking to turn away his pursuer with some pleasantry. As he turned, Barvim raised his arm and brought the rock down on the kid's face full force. He raised his arm again and struck the kid again above his eye. Barvim turned and walked away as the kid sat down on the path clutching his head in his hands.

14.

FOR THE NEXT WEEK, BREWSTER and Guinevere met daily. Most of their time together, it was enough to stroll down the street, hand in hand, Brewster sometimes inclining his head to bring their faces close so they could murmur in each other's ears. During these murmurings, Guinevere told Brewster that her parents were dead, that she had a small inheritance from her grandfather, and that she had come to New York and lived in Greenwich Village . . .

Although it was true that she was living on a small inheritance, her parents were actually very much alive and living in New England. When she turned eighteen, they insisted that she make a "suitable match" to consolidate their social position. But she wanted to live in New York and become a poet. When they refused to consider such a bohemian scheme, she went to live with Rodrigo, the son of a local Portuguese fisherman who had fallen in love with her. A common fisherman's son, and Portuguese ancestry to boot! Totally unacceptable! Just as fiercely proud, the fisherman was convinced that the girl was a frivolous airhead from a family who looked down on him and his son.

"Rodrigo would never be accepted by her family," the father stormed. "She would fill his head with silly ideas that he was better than he was and turn him against his father. And they were *Protestants*." No matter that the father was not a devout Roman Catholic and her family was only vaguely Episcopalian. The fisherman would not hear of his son living with the daughter of Protestant snobs. True to their respective dogmas, family and fisherman promptly disowned their offspring. The lovers decided to pursue her dream in New York.

Guinevere, who had an idyllic, romantic vision of life in an artists' colony, was startled to find "The Village" divided into East and West, with little resemblance to her quaint image. The charm of the crisscrossing streets laid down over old Indian trails, rural paths, and boundaries in the West Village had succumbed to bustling commercialism and ethnic and cultural chaos. The scruffier East Village offered something closer to the bohemian scene she imagined. They found a large, one-room apartment on St. Mark's Place behind the office of a retired dentist who lived on the floor above with his wife and a very strange son who never went out during the day. Guinevere quickly adjusted to the new place, despite the Upstairs Son's unsettling habits of rattling the doorknob each time he passed on his nocturnal excursions and playing Chopin's *Funeral March* on a horribly out of tune piano at 2 a.m. This gave Rodrigo fits, and more than once Guinevere had to restrain him from going up to punch out the lights of the Upstairs Son.

She knew that Rodrigo's irritation was not entirely caused by the Upstairs Son's peculiar habits. He loved to take Guinevere into his arms, evenings, and listen to her read the poetry she had composed during the day. Guinevere's small allotment was enough to meet minimal living expenses. But the young man had little work experience or training beyond hauling in the catch on his father's boat, and few prospects in the Village. He was having a hard time finding a job, and a harder time living off his woman. After several months of actively looking for a job that would satisfy his need to control their economic circumstances, he began to wander aimlessly. Eventually, he became as erratic as the Upstairs Son, leaving the apartment shortly after the doorknob rattling and not returning until after Chopin, evasive and uncommunicative. She did not know that he had fallen into the dismal duet of the drug culture, using and dealing. And then, one night, he went out and never came back. She had read a newspaper account of a young man answering to his description who had been killed in a drug deal gone bad. But Guinevere could not accept the image of his body lying anonymously in a gutter, his life oozing out of a torn throat.

No.

He had caught the disease of the doorknob, and had left to rattle all the knobs in the Village. He would come back to her when he had rattled them all. How long would it take? A year? Two? She began to welcome the rattlings of the Upstairs Son as a sign of the return. Even running to open the door in anticipation. And then it became a nuisance. And then it was lost in the background of city noises . . .

But there were so many other things to murmur about. She and Brewster went to the Palisades and sat dangling their feet over the edge of a five-hundred-foot cliff, gazing out across the Hudson River, silently admiring the Cloisters perched on the opposite shore and the towering steel skeleton of the George Washington Bridge. Wouldn't it have been a pity if they'd fleshed it out with stone, as originally planned?

Mornings, often, they rented horses from the riding academy on 89th Street and entered the bridle trail in Central Park. On the first day, they rode south over the badly eroded stretch to where the exhausted trail finally puddles away into stinking mud near the Heckscher Ballfields. They turned back and thereafter confined their riding to the northern loop past the Reservoir and into the rugged scenery of the northern end of the park. Afterward, they lunched on a mediocre meal and good drinks on the terrace at the Tavern on the Green, or ambled down to the fast-food café at the zoo to munch on hot dogs, gulp orange crush, and watch the two o'clock feeding of the seals, or stroll across to the Boathouse café for Pasta Primavera and wine. They rented a rowboat, and Brewster would ply the Lake while Guinevere read some of her poetry to him, or parts of romance novels with covers featuring the Italian hunk with a name that sounded like a brand of detergent. The heavy breathing protagonists had them doubled up with laughter. Once Brewster laughed so hard and pulled back so vigorously on the oars before they were full in the water that he fell over backwards into the bilge. Guinevere buried her face in the book and hooted. Before long, they were reenacting some of the novels' steamier scenes in Guinevere's East Village apartment. After collapsing in unromantic hilarity on their first tries, they eventually found that they could generate their own kind of steam.

On the third day after they had begun these outings, they strolled through the Ramble by way of the Bank Rock Bridge, passed under the stone arch, and approached the steps cut into the base of Vista Rock leading up to the Belvedere. From Vista Rock, they could circle back down along the northern edge of the Ramble, weave through the sinuous paths at its heart, and gradually reach the Boathouse for their afternoon on The Lake. It was weird and exhilarating, as if in following this route they were enacting a secret ritual whose purpose and significance neither of them could have expressed in words, making a commitment to each other, the nature of which neither consciously understood. There was something as inevitable about it as Olmsted's plan that Vista Rock should be the focal point of the lower part of Central Park. Neither voice nor thought gave the feeling external form. But it drew them on. It was enough.

The sky was overcast. Ambient light softened the twisted, churning, intricately folded rotting schists and blurred glacial grooves. A solitary birder had strayed from the depths of the Ramble, indifferent to the fact that early morning offered best sighting, avidly pursuing a Blackburnian warbler through the first southwest wind of May. Lured on by its high-pitched call scaling the limits of ordinary human ears, he stumbled through the shrubbery along the path, lost sight of his elusive quarry's blazing orange head and throat high in the trees and almost crashed into Brewster and Guinevere. He cursed under his breath as he stumbled onto the path in front of them. The birder looked crossly at the couple, as if it was somehow their fault that he had lost sight of his

The Womb of Uncreated Night

prize. At almost the same moment, something dark flitted through the sky and plunged toward the Belvedere, then pirouetted back up into the air, catching Brewster's eye. Brewster flashed a conciliatory smile at the birder and pointed out the gyrating creature. The birder eagerly raised his glass, but his face puckered.

"Why, that's not a bird at all. It's only a brown bat!" said the man, annoyed, "although it's an odd time of day for a bat sighting. Probably disoriented by the overcast sky," he muttered, moving quickly away so as not to be encumbered further by anyone who couldn't tell a bird from a bat.

As the grouchy birder stamped off, Brewster cocked his ear at a thin voice piping so high on a gust of the southwest wind as to be almost pitchless, quickly followed by a brief chirping flourish, faint and almost lost. The warbler perched invisibly atop a nearby oak. The bat darted up from the Belvedere turret again. Guinevere shivered.

Brewster lay beside Guinevere. Lost in reverie, passion spent. Dreamily, he stroked the "shocking fur," as e e cummings had put it, now quivering at the mouth of a warm, moist cave. He chuckled.

"What?" asked Guinevere.

"I've found your bat."

"What!" said Guinevere, in mock alarm.

"Well, maybe it has a cute furry face. I can't see."

"Ew!"

"I thought the image would appeal to a poet."

"Yes. But comparing a lady's pudenda to a revolting creature, however 'cute,' isn't as romantic as you seem to think. Not to say politically incorrect."

"Mm. If it's politics we're into here, let's have another run for office." She giggled as he rolled over onto her. They struggled, laughing, for several minutes. Then Guinevere pushed him away and sat up. "But how embarrassing! It's like a woman's worst fear!" She shuddered.

"How's that?" asked Brewster. Still laughing, he drew her back down beside him so that her shoulders rested on his arm.

"A bat tangled in the hair on your head is bad enough. But between your legs!" She shuddered again.

Brewster stopped laughing and looked searchingly at her.

"What?" she said, giving him a blank look.

"Oh, nothing." For a moment his thoughts flapped wildly about the ceiling. "Are you really so afraid of bats? They couldn't really get tangled in your hair, you know."

"Oh, yes they could!" insisted Guinevere.

"But their echolocation, like radar. It enables them to avoid obstacles. They can fly through a room strung with fine wires and not hit a one."

"If they get into the house and are frightened, they frantically fly around trying to find a way out, their wings can brush your hair in spite of . . . radar. If the hooks on their wings got snagged in your hair, they could easily get tangled up in it. And then how would you get them out in a place that's so hard to reach or see?"

"Extremely unlikely," sighed Brewster. He stroked her face with the back of his right hand. "An irrational fear." His left arm had begun to grow stiff under the weight of her body.

"Unlikely, maybe. But not impossible. And anything that is not impossible, however irrational, must be possible!" retorted Guinevere, pushing his hand away from her cheek and propping herself up on her elbows to look down at him. "And even if it *is* irrational, what's that got to do with anything? Irrational fears are very real nevertheless! So why bring it up?" She lay back again, feeling vindicated.

He gently pulled his arm out from under her and sat up. What would Dr. Korngold say? That bringing it up was a way of getting an irrational fear out into the open where it could be dissected, like a specimen on a laboratory table, and left in a non-threatening pile to be assimilated by the intellect? But how could merely *talking* about a fear, especially a shadowy, half-formed imaginary one, be beneficial? Any more than mere exposure to civilization, to culture—not just art, literature, and music, but the ethical systems and sciences, too—could make a human being decent? And if such exposure alone doesn't do it, is it necessary at all? It's all . . . so much talk—

"It's all so much *talk*!" Guinevere broke in on his thoughts, startling Brewster at this sign that their minds, like their bodies, could move in complementary rhythms. Yes, so much talk. But if talk sometimes was empty, it was still the most human form of communication. Behind talk lurked an infinitely regressing sequence of intricate perceptions that unfold into possible realities that silence would otherwise conceal. Is reality only a reductionist order at some level of conversation? Or is it the other way round? Does talk open up the chaos concealed by the reality of silence? Does Occam's razor apply here?

"Well, talk can be nice, too," he said, lying down again and nuzzling her ear.

"Fine. Let's talk, then," said Guinevere, staring up at the ceiling.

"What'll we talk about?" Brewster again brushed Guinevere's cheek with the back of his hand. She did not push it away this time, but she did not return the tenderness.

"We were talking about bats in the hair."

And castles in the air, thought Brewster. He grunted and rolled over on his back, seeking her eyes on the ceiling. "They're such repulsive creatures," she said. "Imagine one of them getting caught on top of your head where it would thrash wildly about and you couldn't get at it. Or it might have fleas! or lice! Ooh!" She shuddered. "Or rabies! And even if you tried to get it out of your hair without hurting it, how *could* you go at it blind, with its wings flapping, its body wiggling, and the horrid creature squeaking with fright?"

Chaos.

He couldn't find her eyes on the ceiling. Brewster didn't want to say anything further to agitate the bizarre turn of fantasy thrashing frantically about the room. The only window he could think to open and hope it would flutter out of was silence.

15.

. . . At the very moment that Brewster and Guinevere reached the top of Vista Rock and stood in the terrace of the Belvedere, a casual stroller near The Point at the southern end of the Ramble—a finger of rock thrust into The Lake as if to poke at the Bethesda Fountain on the opposite shore—was startled when a tall, pale, wraithlike form flitted across the shadowy paths and disappeared into the shrubbery near the Bow Bridge. One moment, the path was clear and the trees and shrubs among the rock outcrops were motionless, silent, as if the weight of their brooding presence impeded the passage of time. Then something violently agitated the shrubbery, as if a sudden gust of wind blew through it. A form materialized out of it and moved so swiftly and noiselessly that it was little more than a pale blur. The few people who saw it were unable to form a clear impression of it. Was it an animal? a man? Its skin was ghastly pale. Naked? But in the dim lamplight filtered by shrubs and trees, no one could have said for sure. No one had caught sight of its head or face, but they thought the figure had a dark, flowing mane.

Brewster led Guinevere to the Pavilion overlooking Turtle Pond and the Delacorte Theater. Afterward, they could descend the steps behind the castle that would take them along the south side of the pond, past the dark equestrian statue, through the underpass below

Cleopatra's Needle jabbing at the dark sky, past the Met's after-hours glow, and out onto prosaic Fifth Avenue.

"But you were saying?" prompted Guinevere, as they approached the mystery, wondered again if, after all the fumbling over what he wanted to say, it hadn't better be left unsaid. Yet she was impelled by a foreboding fatalism to play out the scene like some perverse interactive video to an uncertain but pre-programmed end.

When they reached the Pavilion and the terrace of the Belvedere overlooking the barren Delacorte and the flat, dark waters of Turtle Pond, for all the expansiveness of the Great Lawn spread out beyond them, the night drew inexplicably tighter around Brewster. The secret finally gnawed its way out of the closeness. He tried to finesse brightness, optimism, and sophistication out of the fluttering darkness inside him.

"Listen, Guinevere. I—my real name, that is—I'm really Bruce Wayne!"

"Wh-what?" The Scherzo from Bruckner's Eighth whispered in gusts over the barren rocks. Soft horn calls and tremulous violins shivering in and out of the clefts below the Belvedere, *allegro moderato*, sent Guinevere's mind reeling. Cellos chanting a child's rustic rhyme. Background music? There is no music to accompany real life, though much is scherzo. Guinevere was as startled as if he had struck her. Of all the possible denouements she imagined, this was one she was totally unprepared for. What had she expected? That he would sweep her into his arms like in some romance novel, kiss her, tell her he loved her, that he wanted to share his dark, mysterious life with her, but she could never ask his true identity? He certainly had the deep, dark secret of a gothic hero. Dreading, instead, that he would confess something sordid, that he enjoyed kinky sex, had some disgusting fatal disease, or that he really preferred men? And really, much as those would have disappointed her, she was prepared to be oh-so-understanding. Even tragic. But this—this! Beyond comprehension!

"What?" she said again, inanely trying to brush the insistent, whispering, whirling music out of her head.

"I'm Bruce Wayne," he asserted simply, beginning to suspect that he had thoroughly bungled bright sophistication and was now deep into salvage. "My real parents were shot and killed by gangsters when I was just a kid," he added, helpfully.

"*What?*" The music was getting too loud. She had to raise her voice to be heard above it. "But—but the Wainwrights?" she protested.

"Oh, they're not really my parents. My real parents have been replaced with imposters. My real parents were Dr. Thomas Wayne and his wife, Martha. The Wainwrights are just caretakers assigned to me by the Witness Protection Program after my parents' murder. Apparently, I witnessed their murder when I was a kid, and the trauma has caused me to lose all memory of them. You know, the government provided a sort of safe house for me."

Guinevere stared at him in disbelief at this incredible revelation, *what?* reverberating among the cellos in her head. Remembering what he had been told, Brewster rushed on, desperately hoping that an overload of information might somehow erase her look of alarm and close those delectable lips opened incredulously. But her consternation only increased as he unfolded his story. How his childhood had been cut short when his parents had been shot to death by hoods in the underground passage that ran from Pennsylvania Station to the old Gimbel's Department store on Seventh Avenue. That wasn't the Detective Comics version, of course, but it was his mordent to the unembellished melody of history. How he had grown up intent on avenging his parents' death by fighting the criminals who preyed on the powerless and the unwary. How he had assumed the role of Batman to play on the superstitions of the criminal mind . . .

Brewster could not account for the effect bats had on Guinevere. Criminals were not alone in their superstitious dread.

"You are a beneficial, misunderstood, and terrifying insectivore with a cute, furry face?" said Guinevere through a shattered smile, trying to regain her composure and hoping to josh Brewster back to reality.

But once released, a secret for so long repressed had an irresistible momentum . . . How he had embarked on his crime-fighting mission, patrolling the night streets like a medieval knight-errant, helping those being threatened or attacked. How he hoped that by chance he might one day confront those who had deprived him of his parents and bring them to justice. He described the lengths to which he had already gone to master the complex network of underground passages and tunnels that would enable him to move quickly and efficiently to almost any spot in the city.

"Oh?" interrupted Guinevere, still trying for a smile. "Not the Batmobile or a Batcopter?"

"A Batmobile in grid-locked Manhattan? Actually I tried that. Turned out to be as practical as a hundred-yard dash in a maze." He passed over a twinge of conscience at omitting how he had acquired that wisdom. "As for a 'Batcopter'—" he shrugged, "we decided that would probably prove as impractical as the Batmobile." Guinevere did not pursue whom he meant by "we." That was a logical question worth a rational discussion. But this was not a rational moment, and besides, she was too nettled to point out that a "real" comic book hero would have solved all the impractical stuff. She made an impatient gesture as if to bat away the absurdity of the paradox. And Brewster had become so caught up in his story that he lost all sense of inhibition in telling it. He was completely oblivious to the effect it was having on her.

He was so earnest, and he told this bizarre and wildly improbable story with such a straight face that she gradually grew to hope that he was having her on. But she wasn't sure and didn't want to commit the *faux* of revealing her uncertainty. Should she defuse the constricting gloom gripping her and toss off the whole thing with a laugh? *But this is crazy!* Ridiculous as the story sounded, she could not laugh at it. It wanted only a background display of fireworks to turn this whole production into the farce it ought to be. She tried to search his shadowy face for any sign that would cue in her laughter. But his eyes were as sincere as his voice. He, at least, did not find what he was saying incredible. If he was gulling her, it was a masterful performance.

Finally noticing that Guinevere seemed to be imploding, Brewster began to feel that perhaps he had gone too far. He smiled, whether to reassure her or out of nervousness at the way she was taking his story might not have been immediately apparent at the edge of the circle of light.

Grasping at straws, Guinevere took the smile as her cue and laughed in desperation. "Oh, *Brewster*! What a hoot! You almost *had* me there!"

As he looked at her uncomprehendingly, it came bursting through to Guinevere, triple forte—Triple woodwinds—8 horns—3 trumpets—alto, tenor and bass trombones—contra-bass tuba—timpani . . . and those dizzy, ditzy, whirling children screaming their demented ring-around-the-rosy . . .

"You're serious! This—this—comic book fantasy?" she gasped through the hysterical round whirling in her head. "*This* is what you wanted to say to me!"

"That I'm really Bruce Wayne in private life and secretly the Batman." He laughed nervously. "Uh—yes," he added simply, struggling to maintain his bright, optimistic tone. Blurting out a story that he knew was absurd on its face, he had bet love against incredulity . . . and lost. Shadows banked his inner fire.

And Guinevere—what could she think? He's made this up to test my limits? Could he be holding back something worse behind this whopper?

"Well . . . that's—interesting," she said as calmly as inner denial allowed. She moved out of the lamplight.

"You understand, then?" said Brewster, surprised and thinking he might have succeeded in spite of his doubts. "You—uh, don't mind?"

Guinevere was beginning to get annoyed by what was obviously some sort of grotesque joke. "*Mind?*" said Guinevere, feeling as if she had lost her mind. "How could I possibly mind?" And she wondered whether she had lost hers or he had lost his. "I suppose you want me to be your Batgirl," she added, bitterly, "so that when we married we could have a flock? a pack?—oh, whatever it is!—of little bats and the whole family can go flying off through the night to the strains of Bruckner's Eighth Symphony . . . uh-h-h!"

The Womb of Uncreated Night

Brewster, for his part, was at a loss. "Well, I knew it was a lot for you to take in . . . You know, if you'd take me seriously." Between laughter and chagrin, Brewster realized that things had gone horribly wrong. Perhaps he should have thought this through more carefully. After all, he was no longer an adolescent and Guinevere was certainly not his tutor. If a mind can wring its paws and pace nervously about, Brewster's did. Scurrying about, making little chucking noises that nervous otters make.

Guinevere thrust her face at him and stamped her foot. "You *are* being serious? You expect me to believe this rot! I thought at first you were *joking*. I *hoped* that you were joking! My God, you *should* be joking!" Then, in a less indignant, almost plaintive, even pleading tone in which she shed her sophistication as a virgin sheds her clothing, "*Are* you joking?"

Brewster's mind abruptly stopped its frantic pacing. Of *course* he should not have expected his quirky confession to go over the way he intended before he had prepared a declaration of love to plant it in! Of *course* Guinevere would be upset at such a fantastic revelation. What fool would think otherwise? How many women learn that they are in love with a comic-book hero? He was afraid to say anything for fear that he would burst out laughing inanely at his own absurdity. But before he could frame an adequate reply, Guinevere's indignation mounted again.

"Why are you saying this to me?"

"Well, Guin—if we are to have any kind of long-term commitment—I mean—we *were* about to make a commitment, weren't we? I felt—well—honor bound, you know, to fully reveal myself to you—so that you would know what you were getting into—"

"What *I* was getting into! What *I*— And you—this *joke!*—"

"Guinevere," Brewster burst out in spite of himself, "this is no joke!"

"No, it certainly isn't! It *should* be, but then we would be laughing, wouldn't we! But it's that rarest of jokes, so clever no one gets it!"

Brewster turned away in vexation and stared out over the parapet at the ruin of the scene he had created. Guinevere began to walk stiffly back down the path they had come up, but then she broke into a run that took her into the depths of the Ramble. Brewster started to go after her, but paused in the terrace of the Belvedere. He watched her departing form going back down the steps they had climbed, standing there dismayed for several minutes— Should he go after her at once or should he wait awhile until she had a chance to cool off? She was, after all, a sensible woman. Surely she didn't doubt the sincerity of his love for her. That she'd soon rationalize his blunder into fey nonsense that neither of them had to take seriously. That she'd laugh it off and forgive him. As he stood pondering his options, he thought he heard a terrified cry some distance off and realized the danger he had allowed Guinevere to expose herself to. He ran down the steps she had taken, casting about for some trace of her.

He searched frantically, calling her name down the maze of intersecting paths, hoarsely muttering, "No! No!," alarming strollers and a young couple making out on the grass. At the ominous sound of this hurtling menace, the young man on the grass leaped up, eyes blazing and fists clenched, ready to defend his girl. But Brewster ran past him, calling out for Guinevere.

When he gave up trying to find her on his own, he ran back to the call box at the Belvedere. It was not working. Desperate, he ran down the west staircase, past the Shakespeare Garden to the Swedish Cottage nearby. The place was deserted, but a call box on the building worked. He had barely begun to speak to the officer at the other end of the line when he spotted a patrol car moving along the West Drive, dropped the phone, and flagged down the car. The two officers in the car told him to get in, drove over the broader sidewalks, edged past the Great Lawn and the Turtle Pond, and entered the parking lot east of the Ramble. From there, one of the officers, a young rookie named O'Brian, accompanied Brewster to the area on the north side of The Lake where Guinevere was last seen, while the other waited for back-up.

The two men began a search, and the officer spotted signs of struggle in the grass. They found tracks as if something heavy had been dragged some distance across the damp lawn between the outcrops of

The Womb of Uncreated Night

the Ramble. A shoe, Brewster was sure it was Guinevere's, though he hadn't really paid much attention to her footwear, evidently had come off as she was dragged along. They lost the traces among the paths that wound among the rocks and strayed almost to the stream that ran down to the waterfall and into The Lake. Two young men sat smoking in the rustic gazebo along a nearby path. O'Brian asked them how long they had been there, if they had seen or heard anything unusual. One of them pointed back in the general direction of the boat house, and said he had heard someone crashing around in the bushes. He started to snicker but was cut off at a poke in the ribs from his comrade's elbow. O'Brian pressed them for more specifics, but Brewster had already run off in the direction indicated. By the time the officer joined him, he was carefully examining the shrubbery.

"Looks as if someone has been in here recently," he said.

"Nothing unusual about that around here," said O'Brian, shining his flashlight into the dark recesses. "But let's have a look."

Guinevere's body lay in a thicket off one of the darker side paths that Brewster could not have clearly seen into without more light. The beam of the officer's flashlight picked out a bloody triangular clot on a vein in her throat just above and to the left of her collar bone. Her hair was disheveled and her blouse torn, exposing her neck and shoulder. She showed no signs of life. The night had turned chill and misty tendrils had begun to rise from Guinevere's inert body. Brewster shivered, his feelings as inert as the body on the ground. The officer, who thought he should be hardened to such cases, checked for pulse and breath automatically. He turned to Brewster with a hopeless look, as if he would shake his head.

"What could make a wound like that?" he wondered aloud.

Looking down at the ruin of his love, Brewster spoke unguardedly. "Vampire bat."

O'Brian stared at him. "You okay?" *This guy seen too many Bela Lugosi movies.* "Don't look like no animal bite to me. I mean, fangs don't leave no mark like that."

Brewster shook his head. "No, not fangs. Not the kind of wounds you get in stories about human vampires. Those are more like the kind of bite marks snakes leave. Two neat punctures wouldn't bleed enough to drain the blood out of even a small animal, let alone a large animal like a human. If a human attacked anyone with their canine teeth, they would end up tearing flesh the way dogs do." Sarcasm, he thought. Tearing flesh. "And the human jaw just isn't hinged to bite only with the incisors, leaving only fang marks. No. This is the mark of a vampire bat."

The cop took a step back away from Brewster, his hand instinctively resting on his side arm. This was *nuts*! What's wrong with this guy? How could he talk like that—like he was giving a lecture, so cool, while his girl friend lays there dead? People in shock might do crazy things, but he never heard of no one under stress so detached—like maybe a coroner's report. Not from the victim or the victim's lover at the crime scene. That was nuts.

"Take it easy. Back-up'll be here soon."

But Brewster was lost in bewildering speculation. Vampire bats, after all, were tropical. Such creatures couldn't survive in the climate of New York City. Could a specimen have escaped from a zoo or private collection? "The bat makes an incision that bleeds profusely," he continued, oblivious of the officer's increasing wariness. "But this mark, it's larger than any bat's. Sort of in the form of an inverted triangle, like you'd expect from bites inflicted by canines and close-set, sharp lower mandibles . . ."

"Sure. Sure, Mr.—" Brewster had identified himself in the patrol car when he had first gotten in. But under these disturbing circumstances, the rookie had momentarily forgotten his name. "Sir," he ended, lamely.

"The bat even secretes an anticoagulant so that the victim's blood won't clot. Its saliva has a remarkable enzyme that prevents clotting better than any other substance known to medical science. But the vampire bat doesn't suck up the victim's blood. It laps it up."

O'Brian was completely unnerved by Brewster's composure. It must be the shock. Yeah. "Easy. Easy." He tried to sound soothing, but his voice had gone hoarse.

The Womb of Uncreated Night

"Vampire bats usually attack while their victims are asleep," mused Brewster. "Could Guinevere have been rendered unconscious first, and then her body drained of blood? But no mere bat could have dragged her here. First a mugger, then an attack by a bat? Let's see if there are any other marks—" and he bent over the body, intending to exam it for signs that Guinevere may have been knocked unconscious and left for—

"Hey!" barked O'Brian. "Don't touch that body!"

The curt order cut through Brewster's intellectual detachment and sent him reeling. This was no puzzle to tease the mind. This was not a picture in the tabloids of some stranger's body that stirs the compassion of aroused citizens. He gave a muted, constricted cry, "Guinevere!" His throat clamped shut and he could say no more.

O'Brian was still baffled by Brewster's former behavior, but this sign of genuine grief relieved his anxiety and made him more sympathetic. In a calmer tone he added, "You might disturb evidence."

Lingering doubts about Brewster's stability were scattered by the squealing brakes and flashing lights of squad cars on the other side of the rock outcrops near the boathouse. Back-up had arrived. Brewster was no longer O'Brian's responsibility. Slamming doors, running feet, and voices set off a disturbance in the surrounding undergrowth at the face of the rock outcrops. Something moved there, quick and furtive. Instinctively thinking that the disturbance had been caused by an assailant who might have concealed himself there, both Brewster and the officer sprang to investigate. They were joined almost at once by the men who had arrived in the squad cars, and while O'Brian was explaining how he and Brewster had discovered Guinevere's body, the commotion in the shrubbery, and Brewster's strange talk about vampire bats, Brewster returned to the site of Guinevere's body.

She was gone! His exclamation of alarm brought the policemen to his side. With several flashlights trained on the spot, they could see the impression left by Guinevere's body. But there was no sign of the woman.

"Didn't I tell you not to touch the body?" growled O'Brian, grabbing Brewster by the arm. "What'd you do?" Brewster only stared

- 185 -

at him uncomprehendingly. He and Officer O'Brian were instructed to stay where they were.

"Watch him!" one of the cops said, before he and the others went off to search the surrounding area. They followed the sporadic signs of recent disturbance in the adjacent undergrowth as well as they could, their flashlights jabbing inquisitively everywhere, their bodies casting sinister, flickering silhouettes against the mists thickening in the cooling air. Brewster was in any case too stunned to have said or done anything more. An uneasy silence fell over the scene.

As the police searched for Guinevere, a small knot of curious passersby gathered on a patch of lawn at a discreet distance and silently observed. Standing well back in the shadows beyond the fringe of the group, a pudgy man wearing an opera cape and a silk top hat created a momentary stir. He muttered stifled curses, brushing himself furiously and slapping at his exposed skin as hordes of mosquitoes swarmed around him. The onlookers paid scant attention as he turned and fled down a path. His eyes, as he passed a lamp still vigorously swatting at the insects, were agitated. What little of his face showed under his hat was swollen and flushed. Looking raven black in the garish light, his shaggy hair and beard covered most of his face. He vanished around a bend in the path.

After a thorough search of the immediate area, which seemed to take longer than it actually did, the searchers returned empty. They had done as much as they could for the night, they said. They would have to come back next day to continue their search. It was not unusual to see signs of nocturnal activity in the area, so they could not be sure of much. Inspecting more closely the site where Guinevere's body was found, they were surprised to find a few drops of blood. Considering the wound in the woman's throat which had presumably led to her death, one would have expected to see more blood on the ground where her body had lain.

The police focused on Brewster, but saw nothing to suggest that he had killed and spirited away the woman's body. What could he be

The Womb of Uncreated Night

up to? Could Brewster and O'Brian have been mistaken about the severity of the wound? Could she have recovered enough to wander off, semi-conscious, while Brewster and the officer were distracted by the commotion in the bushes?

Brewster drank from that straw of hope.

The police insisted on taking him to the precinct to make a statement. He clung to the belief that Guinevere had only been wounded and was perhaps wandering about the park. The police assured him that the regular night patrols in the park had been alerted and they would keep a sharp eye out for her.

What if she had left the park and was wandering about the city dazed and helpless? The streets, too, were being patrolled and the police on the lookout for her. Since Brewster's family had been contacted and a chauffeur dispatched by the Wainwrights to pick up Brewster, the police had ample assurance that he would be available for further questioning. But O'Brian's report on Brewster's behavior at the scene of the crime left them suspicious. Brewster had not been alone with Guinevere's body long enough to have stashed her away in the bushes. The area had been searched. Could he have had an accomplice? Possibly. What about motive? Nothing tangible. One of the detectives remembered something about an accident, a few years back, involving a kid dressed up like Batman driving a souped up "Batmobile." Was there any record of such an incident, or was it one of those whoppers that power rumor mills?

When Guinevere failed to return to her apartment next day, any hope that she could still be alive was muted. And Brewster's little disquisition on vampires had meanwhile leaked to the media and caused a storm that submerged his concern for Guinevere's well-being under sensational and misleading headlines.

VAMPIRE BAT ATTACKS SOCIALITE. WHERE IS GUINEVERE?

MILLIONAIRE GOES BATS!

Even the sedate *Times* ran a story on the front page sporting a more accurate headline:

MYSTERY SURROUNDS DISAPPEARANCE IN CENTRAL PARK

Neither Brewster nor Guinevere, of course, was a socialite. And, of course, the TV news anchors and their teams exchanged the usual exclamations of wonder and disbelief over the incredible story. Officer O'Brian related his strange encounter with Brewster Wainwright. And female reporters enjoyed a good shudder at the notion of vampire bats flying around the city intent on getting caught in their hair.

Interlude

Brewster arrived for his four o'clock appointment almost a quarter of an hour late. He came in without a word of apology for his tardiness and sat down. He waited.

Dr. Korngold silently studied his patient who seemed almost indifferent to—he could hardly be unaware of—the sensational turn of events around him.

"Well," said Korngold, picking up the pieces of Brewster's recent escapades, "was it a joke, Brewster?" He wanted to provoke an adequate response without heaping inappropriate or counterproductive guilt on the guy. But he had to get Brewster to focus on the flaws in his back-story.

"Surely you were aware of the dangers of the Ramble so late at night, especially with few people about?"

"Well, you know, as Batman I've learned to handle dangerous situations pretty well. I guess I felt confident in my ability to deal with any ordinary kind of attack, even without my Batman gear." Korngold groaned inwardly as he saw years of therapy going down the tubes. He had begun to think that the "Batman" obsession was fading. But he could see that it was strong as ever. "I'm pretty good with my dukes, you know," Brewster said with some of that self-confidence of young men who have developed skill in martial arts, but have not yet suffered real defeat.

"I can well believe it," said Korngold. In the four years since he had first taken Brewster on as a patient, he never stopped being awed by the guy's ability to overcome a severe visual handicap and reach such superb physical development. "And did you acquit yourself well that night?" he added ironically.

Brewster smiled ruefully at the barb. "Obviously, a different sort of skill was required that night. One that I wasn't up to."

"So you ignored the danger."

"Well—it was somehow—exciting—you know? I mean, being with Guinevere . . . the danger of a woman's rejection. The risk of exposing my secret identity—"

"*Your real identity as Bruce Wayne.*"

"Exactly—that cop's warning we overheard—in short, the whole atmosphere of a precarious tryst . . ." He shrugged and tossed his head dismissively.

"Like Tristan and Isolde," prodded Korngold sarcastically.

Brewster made a wry mouth at the mockery. "Yeah, I could've handled King Mark, Melot, and his courtiers, I think. But I was too deeply involved with Guinevere to expect what happened. I mean, I think part of me wanted Guinevere to need me, so that I could challenge her disbelief in what I was telling her. Pretty selfish of me, huh?"

Korngold nodded, puffing on his pipe. "Of course. Danger can be exhilarating, and like all exhilarations when they reach a certain pitch, interchangeable. And it's that very interchangeability that confuses you and exposes you to the dangers that excite you."

"I guess I let Guinevere down pretty badly."

Korngold puffed on his pipe.

16.

VERY WARM FOR MAY, GOES the title of a forgotten musical. And "the promised song of springtime" in New York in May can turn downright tropical. Temperatures in the second week of May that year soared into the 90's and even touched 100. When two detectives showed up at the Wainwright Mansion to follow up their investigation into the disappearance of Guinevere that week, they wore the customary suits and ties in spite of the heat. Perspiring freely, they looked as wilted as the spring flowering plants in the garden beds outside the mansion. The butler showed them into the library and left to fetch Brewster.

Brewster came into the room, cool and comfortably dressed in slacks and a polo shirt open at the throat. One of the detectives, a paunchy, balding, middle-aged man of medium height, with a thrust-back face and a moustache that only partly concealed the meanness of his mouth when he was not talking, was mopping his face with a handkerchief. His polyester suit jacket with unfashionably broad lapels which had come back into style, hung unbuttoned and somewhat soggily, sweat stains showing through at the armpits. An indifferently tied four-in-hand with school colors not likely his had been yanked desperately away from the shirt collar revealing a missing button. The shirt looked as if it had been laundered by an unwilling spouse who was having a bad hair day. The other, taller and silent, positioned himself discreetly behind his partner, whether out of deference or an embarrassed awareness that he smelled strongly of armpits, Brewster could not say. He had a dreamy, boyish face, hardly one to intimidate anyone into a confession, and was trying not to look too wilted, notebook in hand, attentive but clearly subordinate.

Looking from one to the other, Brewster's heart sank. They *looked* like detectives. What should detectives look like? You'd think that they would be so disarmingly ordinary as to pass unnoticed on the street. Sort of protective coloration. But these two, though physically unalike, were instantly recognizable as fuzz. And in this weather! A certain indefinable something implied that they knew more than they were letting on. But those detective faces said that whatever these men knew more about did not include anything about Guinevere's whereabouts. He fell into abstraction and did not at first return the detectives' greeting. He stood, staring down at the man's exposed throat. Reading Brewster's bearing as a criticism of sartorial disarray, the detective grunted, tightened the corners of his mouth, and loosely straightened the tie over the lost button.

"Mr. Wainwright? Would you mind answering a few questions—?"

And they asked detective questions. *Mind*? How could he possibly mind at a time like this? Why should he mind interminable questions that get nowhere? *Of course I mind, you blockhead!*

"We need to review the details of what happened the other night."

Although he was wary but devastated, and demoralized by his own sense of guilt in having allowed Guinevere to come to harm, Brewster felt his resistance to these legal thugs draining away and shook his head fatalistically. "It's all my fault," he murmured, indifferent to the sudden splinter of steel in the detective's eyes. The man with the lapels had that flat Jersey accent that always sounded so blasé, as if everything he said ended with "Is that right?" whether he actually said it or not.

"Oh, how's that?" said Lapels. Is that right?

"Well, I suppose I shouldn't have allowed Guinevere to run off after a silly quarrel, should I? I mean, especially late at night. And in a dark and ill-lit place."

The Womb of Uncreated Night

"And what was the quarrel about, if I might ask, sir?" "Sir" sounded almost an afterthought. Isn't it amazing how some men can be as hot on a trail as any baying hound but manage to affect a veneer of such polite and utter disinterest? Is that right?

Brewster couldn't very well tell these men about Batman. If Guinevere's comical disbelief bordered on hysteria, and from someone he felt close to, what could he expect of these guys? His off-the-cuff dissertation about bats in Manhattan . . . Officer O'Brian had duly reported that. The Wainwrights hushed up the affair of the Batmobile, but the police may not have respected the court order sealing the file as much as the Wainwrights supposed. After five or six years, you would think that the whole matter had gotten properly buried. But here were these mock-humble public servants circling around him looking too—what?—too stupid to be so stupid. Or was he being over-sensitive because he felt so guilty?

"Whatever engaged couples quarrel about. You know."

"What," said Lapels, "sex?" There was no "sir" this time. How could anyone say "sir" right after "sex"? Sex, sir? Sex-er? Sex-err? As awkward to think as to say.

"There's more to a relationship than sex," said Brewster impassively.

Lapels, tacking to catch a breeze, sailed on over Brewster's unwrinkled surface. "You say you were engaged? You set the date? She maybe pressure you about a commitment?" Is that right?

"It was just a lover's spat. Guinevere went off in a huff, and I stood around like a jerk before I realized the danger of letting her go."

"And just when did you realize there was danger?"

"Well—a woman alone in the Ramble—late at night in those twisty-turny paths in the dark— Even if there wasn't anyone around to molest her, she could stumble and hurt herself—I mean, isn't it obvious?"

"So, you say there was a spat . . . 'whatever lovers quarrel about?' Sometimes those can get pretty heated," said Lapels mopping his brow. "You manage to stay crisp and cool in all this heat."

"It's the air-conditioning," said Brewster drily.

Armpits chuckled. "As I recall, sir, it was pretty warm and

- 193 -

muggy that night. You have a portable air-conditioner you carry around with you?"

"Underarm deodorant is usually good enough," snapped Brewster. He looked away to conceal his annoyance with himself at coming down to his level.

"Of course, a man of your means," continued Lapels, "would never need to worry about a woman running away from him. Maybe that's why you hesitated. You figured she'd come back, eh? Like you said, there's more to a relationship than sex."

"Whatever," said Brewster with a shrug. "I was momentarily startled by her running off. I thought she was just being melodramatic. Temperamental. You know. Then, as I told the officers on the night we searched for her, I heard a scream."

"Still," said Lapels, turning to his partner confidentially, "a well brought-up young fellow like Mr. Wainwright here would know how to keep his cool even when things run hot. So why would he hesitate when his true love runs off into the night? Considering his options, perhaps?" he said turning back to Brewster. "And maybe he figured, if she didn't come back to a prize catch she wasn't worth the trouble?"

The barbs found their mark. Brewster flared inwardly at the suggestion that he had behaved unchivalrously. But Batman would never have done that. Nor would he give such a clod the satisfaction of punching out his lights. He clothed his thoughts in black hood and cape.

"You say you heard a scream?" Lapels turned again to his partner, who consulted his notebook and murmured, "... heard a muffled cry."

"Not exactly a scream," Lapels said. "How far away would you say the 'muffled cry' was?"

"Far enough so that a scream might have sounded like a muffled cry," replied Brewster with elementary logic.

"And how far would that be, sir? You understand, we're just trying to get the facts so we can help find your fiancée. You want to help us do that, don't you?"

And maybe pin a bum rap on me, thought Brewster. Are these

The Womb of Uncreated Night

guys for real? wondered Brewster. Do real detectives talk like this? It's a little like hearing a recording of your own voice. We think, "Do I really sound like *that*?" We get used to the face in the mirror, reversed as it is, and begin to think that's what we really look like—in reverse. Do we *hear* in reverse too? Is that why we don't recognize our own voice? Words can be perfectly reasonable. But the tone of voice can reverse them in an insinuating spin. Is that right? Sarcastic putz.

"Of course. But what's the point of rehashing what I've already gone over several times?"

Armpits intervened. "It's our duty to get all the details right, sir. Your first report was made under stress, at a time that must have been very traumatic for you. There's just this matter of a—" he hesitated, unsure whether he had been the butt of some locker room joke at the station house, or Officer O'Brian had been the butt of a lunatic's sense of humor, or merely embarrassed at mentioning an utter absurdity, "—a vampire bat? That's what you told the officer on the scene, isn't it, sir?"

Whee! *Here* we go! Brewster snugged into mask and cape. "That was just speculation. I've made a little study of bats"—Lapels smirked—"and the wound on Guinevere's throat . . ."

"Yes, sir. But I was just wondering. Officer O'Brian said you seemed to be, well, let's not say *un*concerned, just pretty cool and collected for a guy whose sweetheart is laying dead at his feet . . . Just take your time, sir," said Armpits. So Brewster clenched his jaw and repeated what he had told O'Brian.

"As I said at the time, it resembled the bite mark of the vampire bat, that vampire bats are tropical, and that they couldn't survive the winters this far north."

"Almost word for word," said Armpits, consulting his notebook.

"And this business about the shape of this wound?" said Lapels. "You think maybe someone's filing his incisors?"

"Either that or wearing falsies."

"So if we discount someone wearing an appliance, you think maybe someone's exotic pet got loose?" persisted Lapels with a wink at

Armpits he made no effort to hide from Brewster. The two detectives looked as if they might burst into laughter at any moment. They smiled without showing their teeth, and Brewster had the eerie feeling that if they did they would reveal filed incisors.

Brewster played out the charade. "It's not impossible, however improbable . . ." He shrugged.

"'However improbable, must be the truth,' eh? Say, maybe someone in one of the high-rises has a—whaddaya call 'em," said Lapels turning to Armpits.

"Aviary," offered Armpits.

"Yeah, aviary. Those rich dudes have some pretty weird tastes, eh? Say, somehow the door to the cage got left open—"

"Yeah," chimed in Armpits, "like when the guy goes to feed the pet bat, his wife screams that one of the kids has cut himself with this Exacto knife the kid uses in some exotic hobby—"

"Enough to rattle anyone's cage—"

"So he forgets about the open door and out comes the bat—"

"Looking for the kid's blood—"

"Only the window's open, too—"

"So out flies the bat—"

"Yeah. Freedom. More blood in Central Park. And the rest—"

"And the rest, as they say, is history," finished Lapels, who, like a Trock having executed an improbable series of entrechats and fouettés, which is to say, a lot of fancy jumping and whirling about, finishes en pointe, poised for a pratfall.

When, twenty minutes later, Brewster had not "slipped up," Lapels decided that he could not be shaken that day. He and his partner might have to come back again in a few days and see if Brewster's story still held together, "word for word," like a well-rehearsed story, or if the weight of guilt would cause his defenses to collapse into a pile of confession. Brewster was sure that Lapels sensed that he was concealing something. Or was it simply the air of self-reproach that hung about him, hinting he knew more than he was letting on?

The Womb of Uncreated Night

The detectives left, muttering about "wasting their time on a friggin' loonybird!"

Several days of diligent search by the police failed to turn up any trace of Guinevere. She was missing and presumed dead.

Hot. Muggy. Monday. One of those summery late spring days when a dome of polluted air pressed down on the city and made you feel as if you were covered with grime as soon as you stepped out of an air conditioned space. Dr. Richard Korngold sat in the study of his apartment that served as his office waiting for Brewster, his last appointment of the day. He was moody and irritable.

The media had been turning the disappearance of Guinevere into the usual sound and light show. Bad enough that the news was saturated with reports of casual violence and that a young woman he knew and liked had been its latest victim. Now it was that garbage about a "vampire"! It was sure to have a negative impact on Brewster's emotional state and seriously set back the progress he had been making with him over the last four years of therapy. And it would stir up the "Batman" fantasy all over again. Matters were made worse by Brewster himself over that absurd story about a vampire. None of this boded well for his emotional stability, which was already fragile, what with his "Batman" fixation and the loss of Guinevere. There were rumors already that the "Batman" vigilante prowling around Central Park might in some way be responsible for the attack on Guinevere. That coupled with a number of reported disappearances which the police were unable to trace placed Brewster in a highly vulnerable position.

The previous Friday, Korngold had been hoping to ease into a lazy weekend with a quiet dinner. As the telephone rang he could not help reflecting, impatiently, that every form of communication, every conversation, gesture, contact, every experience, was a fractal—a fraction of existence like a Chinese water flower, a sliver of infinity compressed into the finite folds of a piece of crepe paper. A ring of the phone, a knock at the door drops it into the mind. The intricately folded design expands and crowds out the comfortable drift of thought. The borders of the mind fray at the edges into trackless spirals, complex at every level of scrutiny until it blurs--

The phone rang again.

He sighed and picked up the receiver. It was Mrs. Wainwright. Had he heard the news about Guinevere? "Brewster is under suspicion in the girl's disappearance—something about a vampire attack? I'm so worried."

"Is Brewster at home now? Good. How is he taking it? If necessary I can arrange to see him right away."

Brewster was in a funk. "He's locked himself up in his room and refuses to see anyone."

"That's understandable," said Korngold reassuringly. "In itself, there's no cause for alarm. Just keep an eye on him. If he continues to shut himself up, I'll drop by and try to talk to him." He fumed inwardly as he stood staring out the window at the skyline, the earpiece barely touching his ear. What good did it do to struggle against the chaos of this city? He knew he was allowing himself to get over involved. Mustn't take this so personally. Brewster had another appointment for Monday. If he got through the weekend without further to-do, they could talk it out then.

"But this talk about a vampire—" agonized Mrs. Wainwright, "and that vigilante masquerading as Batman—?" If she had consciously or unconsciously made the connection between the "vampire" rumors and the comic book fantasy, she was probably too horrified even to mention it.

"Sheer coincidence, I'm sure," said Korngold to reassure her. But he wasn't at all convinced. Layer after layer had been unfolding over the past four years. And still he had not found the nub of Brewster's illness. Each time he thought he had it, he discovered that it was only a ripple

The Womb of Uncreated Night

in a very deep and turbulent pond. He could not even tell whether what roiled up was the silt of the patient's own traumatic experiences or a reaction to his probing. He chuckled to himself ruefully. Ah, Bea Lillie! There are pebbles at the bottom of my patient!

Korngold had urged Mrs. Wainwright into calm enough so that she could mercifully ring off. If Brewster was masquerading as a comic book hero, whether he was actually playing the vigilante or merely promenading in costume, there was enough real danger in it. Either way he exposed himself to street violence. Neither could be dismissed as the harmless hobby of a wealthy crank. That Brewster was indeed batty in more than one sense of the word, Korngold was quite certain. Brewster appeared to be convinced that he was Bruce Wayne, that his parents had been killed when he was quite young, and that, like his comic book idol, he was obsessed with avenging the victims of street violence, possibly even encountering his parents' imaginary murderer—

He had kept that last detail of the fantasy from her.

Then Guinevere! Until this latest episode, Brewster's obsession with Batman had seemed innocent enough. Could her rejection of it have awakened a more active, darker phase of the fantasy, resulting in her disappearance and probable death? Could the attack on her represent a lethal spin on his parents' "murder"? The "death" of the Wainwrights, which Korngold suspected was part of an elaborate practical joke, began to show the fangs of an alienation deeper than he wanted to believe. Sucked into the psychotic fantasies of Hippias, could Brewster have "murdered" them for having "rejected" him, and could that rejection compounded with Guinevere's have ratcheted up the whole fantasy into full-blown violence?

17.

When you wake up, you know, however blearily, you're *you*. That is, you gradually become aware that you inhabit your own skin. You feel with your own touch, see with your own eyes, hear with your own ears, smell with your own nose, even taste the crud of your own mouth. The signals are all being processed by the brain where you know you're awake. You don't announce yourself to yourself. Name, address, phone number, occupation, marital status, and all the utter clutter of the rest of the day are suspended for that transition from sleep to full awake.

What if when you go to move you find that your body doesn't respond in a wakened way? What if your eyes and ears and nose and mouth were stuffed with white gauze? What if you try to brush away the gauze and find that you can't move your hands? If you try to swing your legs over the side of your bed and find that you can't? Or try to sit up and find that you can't do that either? You *know* that you're helpless. But are you awake or still asleep dreaming that you're awake? *Who* you are is less significant than *whether* you are. But terror doesn't require a fully conscious state to be real.

When the young woman with the snow-white hair opened her eyes, they were glazed. White gauze was everywhere. Her head was full of it. Her face was smothered under it. Her eyes were scratched by it. A brilliant glare bulged in at the window and the whole room reverberated

The Womb of Uncreated Night

with whiteness. She tried to brush away the gauze with her hand, but discovered that her hands and feet were bound. She struggled to free herself, but couldn't. Terrified, she began to scream.

"LET—ME—GO!"

A smudge appeared in the gauze. It hovered over the bed on which she lay and a voice spoke gently to her. But she didn't understand. "Please," she begged. "Please let me go."

"Where do you want to go?" said the voice. The woman was baffled by this question. Where *did* she want to go? "You're all right, here. We had to tie you down with the sheets so you wouldn't fall out of bed and hurt yourself. You're still pretty groggy." The Voice patted her shoulder reassuringly.

"Do you know where you are?" it asked.

The white-haired woman only stared up blankly at the blur expanding and shrinking in the haze.

"What's your name?" Another blank stare. The voice repeated the questions several times. No response. The woman strained to see more clearly. The dark spot stretched and spread into a figure that towered over the bed. It grew appendages that reached out to a gleam of red suspended beside the bed, its color seeping through the gauze like a draining wound. The figure shrank again into a blur and disappeared. Left alone, the white-haired woman's awareness slowly condensed into thought. *Where am I? Who am I?* Then, like the redness in the gauze, her consciousness trickled away into nothingness.

A dreaming minute later, two white figures, a man and a woman, brought awareness with them some time later. The man repeated the same questions asked by the earlier voice. "Do you know where you are? What's your name?"

This time, the white-haired woman spoke. "Where am I? What's my name? Who is Jennifer?"

"Jennifer?" asked the doctor. "Is that your name? You're in New York Hospital, Jennifer." Then he gently shook her shoulder because she was beginning to drift away again. "Jennifer. Do you know your last name? Do you have a family, Jennifer? Or a friend you want us to notify? Jennifer?"

But "Jennifer" had drifted away. The gauzy glare scratched against her eyes, and since she was unable to rub them with her hands because they were still tied, she closed her eyes to blink it away and wait. Wait for what? She didn't know. For a moment, the glare pressed in through her shuttered eyelids. Then from somewhere deep inside, cool inky night came pooling up and drowned out the whiteness. When she opened her eyes again, she saw the darkness. She wondered in a daze if somehow an interior well had spilled ink out of her eyes and obliterated the world. Gradually, she began to make out forms in the dark. Lightless things hulked, immobile, square, rectangular, and oblong. Other lightless things fluttered at the large, vacant space that penetrated the plane of deeper darkness a few feet away. The forms fluttered and swayed as if they would pounce. She cried out in fright and a nurse came running into the room. The nurse snapped on the overhead light. The glare blinded Jennifer. Jennifer wrenched a hand free of the sheet, threw it in front of her eyes and cried out again.

"What's the matter?" asked the nurse in a quiet, reassuring voice. She turned out the overhead light and turned on the bed lamp so that it would not shine in the patient's eyes. "That better? Did you have a bad dream? Are you in pain?"

"Those things—!" stammered Jennifer—"at the window—those curtains—oh, window! curtains!" And she giggled in embarrassment. "I thought—I thought—"

"Everything all right, then?" said the nurse. "It's very late. Would you like something to help you sleep?" Jennifer shook her head. "Well, you can talk to the doctor about it tomorrow. Try to get some sleep. Would you like to leave the lamp on? Yes? I think we can leave your hands free, now. If you need anything, just push the call button."

After she left, Jennifer reached up and switched off the lamp. She lay back, staring out the window, no longer seeing phantasms in the window curtains. Her eyes adjusted to the comfortable darkness and she could see a few stars. As she watched, she seemed to drift out among them. Dark nebulae loomed above her then broke over her like waves and dissolved away.

Hearing about this interesting amnesia case, Dr. Korngold, the hospital's consulting psychiatrist, visited the patient known only as "Jennifer" on his rounds. He walked into the room frankly, smiling, intent on projecting an upbeat image. He almost stumbled when he caught sight of Jennifer's eyes. The irises almost faded into the whites. She looked so frail and vulnerable that he was deeply moved. And something else about her appearance, something half-familiar, teased his mind. The massive loss of blood had been replaced and gave her skin an ethereal quality. Her skin was almost startlingly pale, but a rosy glow had begun to suffuse it. Her face was drawn, but the fineness of her features gave it an innocence and sweetness at odds with the tension.

Korngold was transfixed. Strange, half-formed images born of superstitious dread stirred in his imagination. But a scientist could suppress the occasional oddities of existence suggesting that the world, like Thoreau's loon, eluded science. How had Jennifer's blood been drained? No ordinary parasite could have removed such a massive amount as to leave her unconscious and in shock. No, she was the victim of some violent attack. Some anemic psychopath suffering from a morbid sensitivity to sunlight prowling about the Ramble at night? He dismissed as idle fancies anything more sinister. Veiling the trouble in his own eyes, he read her chart. What was this about the presence of an unknown virus in her blood work?

He smiled encouragingly and asked Jennifer the usual questions about who she was and what she could remember of what had happened to her, but found her shocky and lethargic. Still, there was something vibrant in her that drew him to her. She would have to be probed more deeply when she was more alert. As he prepared to leave, he took her hand reassuringly and was startled by the warmth with which she returned his grasp. She raised her head and shoulders slightly, looked at him searchingly for a moment, then relaxed her grip and turned her head and her gaze away.

Strangely disturbed by the encounter, Korngold went in search of the hospital's Infectious Disease specialist, Dr. Buckyballs. He found him in the research lab. A slender, wolfish man in a soiled lab coat hunched over a microscope looked up when Korngold came in. His bushy hair, of a mousy color that gave little clue to his age, grew over his head and into a beard that gave his face—what could be seen of it—a gaunt, almost haggard look. Dreamy gray eyes barely penetrated the glasses he wore and made him appear half asleep. The butt of a cigarette, smoked so relentlessly down to the end it almost disappeared into the beard it was about to ignite. Ashes clung to his hair like bits of dandruff and spilled down the front of his lab coat. He absently brushed these off as he got up to shake hands when Korngold introduced himself. Even the backs of his hands were unusually hairy. How old was he? wondered Korngold. He was no kid. And yet there was something youthful about him. Probably some former whiz kid who never grew up.

A routine check of Jennifer's blood type prior to the transfusion had turned up an anomaly. The blood cells behaved in a manner that suggested something very unusual was going on. A lab technician suspected an unknown virus, and brought it to the attention of the I.D. specialist who examined a blood sample under the scanning electron microscope. What he discovered was indeed something like a retrovirus. He found that its genetic material was typically RNA, with an enzyme that could copy RNA information into DNA molecules. These were integrated into the host cells in Jennifer's blood—the red corpuscles at the molecular level—and were apparently using the genetic apparatus of the host cells to replicate the parasitic cells, as in other retroviruses. But this was not cancer, or HIV.

Could these in some way be responsible for Jennifer's condition? Were they in some way contributing to Jennifer's severe blood deficit? She was responding well to whole blood replacement, and follow-up tests showed that the anomaly was in remission. Since the parasitic cells were capable of self-replication, this spontaneous remission was strange. Korngold asked Buckyballs to speculate on its etiology and possible treatment.

"Well, we know that this thing behaves like the typical retroviruses, except that transfusions send it into remission. I have seen no sign of interferon, which might've inhibited its growth. As such, if that's what it really is, it won't respond to drugs. If it flares up again, we might try to block its penetration into host cells with experimental drugs."

"But you don't have any idea of what it is. How did it get started in the first place?"

"Possibly a mutation of some sort—in the genes of an enzyme? It's extremely small, even for a virus—somewhere around 100 Angstrom units, its capsid has an unusually asymmetrical, lopsided polyhedral shape."

"You mean like the complex mixture of arrangements of the pox or bacteriophage viruses?"

"I mean lopsided. The thing is weird. It *looks* like DNA, and it *behaves* like RNA. And it contains enzymes, as many human viruses do. And—" he hesitated, uncertain whether to go on.

"And?" prompted Korngold as the hesitation lingered.

"Well, as I've said, they replicate themselves very efficiently by parasitizing host cells. But just as they're about to set up shop in earnest, they—they—you aren't going to believe this . . . I'm not sure I believe it myself." Korngold grew visibly impatient, and Buckyballs continued, "Well, they start parasitizing each other!"

"Wait a minute. Don't mutating viruses sometimes destroy other, similar viruses? Why is that so unusual?"

"Destroy others, yes. But set each other on one another? This is different. Viruses go on multiplying until they run out of cells to parasitize or encounter some antibody. These just reach a certain critical point and then . . ." Buckyballs shrugged. "It's like macrophages turned cannibal. The cells are attracted to each other, then one breaks into the capsid of another and absorbs it!"

"The one with the bigger mouth wins, eh?" said Korngold, wondering what had they gotten hold of.

"I told you, you wouldn't believe it. But the cannibalism might explain why this particular strain of virus has gone into spontaneous remission." He laughed. "They lose their taste for alien cells, get tired of each other, and go dormant!"

"Cannibalism!" Korngold squirmed. "One of those topics we evade but can't avoid. But in viruses? I've never heard of such a thing."

"Well," hesitated Buckyballs, "actually I have. Or something similar. About nine years ago. There was this homeless man, big black fella who'd been living in the subway in a kind of stupor. Suddenly he became a media headliner and was brought here for examination. The Infectious Disease consultant I was working under at the time wrote off the anomaly as a blip in the data. He asked for my opinion, and innocent young fool that I was, I gave it. He really expected me to confirm his own perception. I pushed for further investigation. He nodded tolerantly. But I kept analyzing the data and pushing for a careful review of what I'd found. He kept ducking it. Finally, I pushed once too often. He grabbed my elbow and said, 'Look!' with a finality that clearly meant 'drop it!' I've been hatching out an explanation—I won't call it a theory. Too wild . . ."

"I don't suppose there could there be some doubt about your present analysis?" interrupted Korngold anxiously. "I mean, you're no longer young and innocent."

A strange look passed over Buckyballs' face, a kind of cryptic amusement. But he only raised his eyebrows and let Korngold's remark pass. "Believe me, I'd rather there was some doubt. But we've observed this phenomenon directly and checked the imaging. You can see the damned things eating each other. Then they sort of metamorphose into more typical asymmetries and . . . they just quit."

"Damnedest thing I ever heard of."

"Maybe not. As for how it got started—the puncture on her neck is the likeliest source of infection by a carrier playing vampire." With the merest hint of a twinkle in his eye, Buckyballs nonchalantly tossed another pebble into Korngold's complacency. "There's something else. Those dummy sections at the ends of our DNA, the telemores that eventually get used up as we age? In the samples I examined, they showed signs of, well, *growth*."

"*What?*" exclaimed Korngold with a laugh. "You've discovered the Fountain of Youth! Why man, you may have stumbled onto immortality!"

Buckyballs merely removed the butt that had become a fixture of his face and lit up another cigarette. The suspense built up to a flippant climax: "Jennifer may live longer than her normal life span. And if her telemoric DNA continues growing, getting longer . . . ?"

"*IF* vampires really exist, and *IF* they were immortal," scoffed Korngold.

Buckyballs shrugged. "I'm not prepared to claim those are facts. Whatever the long term effects of the virus may be, the anomaly in the specimens I've seen so far is only temporary. But the facts in this case have set me to wondering. You did ask me to speculate. What if the virus, once it is introduced, settles into a steady state, flowing smoothly along in the blood stream, growing and accumulating until it reaches a certain critical concentration, and then begins to . . . *wobble?*"

"A kind of turbulence, eh?" Korngold's skeptical tone was tinged with sarcasm. "And I suppose the 'vampire' effect continues as long as this virus *wobbles?*" Korngold himself was beginning to wobble, and sputtered in exasperation. "Are you trying to tell me that . . . *turbulence* . . . in the circulatory system is creating some kind of . . . of . . . pathological craving for human blood? And the longer the wobble the longer the life!"

Buckyballs serenely pursed his lips around the cigarette and raised his eyebrows again, as if to say, would this face lie? It was impossible to tell if he was suppressing a smile under all that hair. "Who can say what effects would be produced by a virus that could eddy viscously throughout the body, especially in the brain? Maybe it isn't viscosity at all. There may be another explanation."

Korngold made a wry face that showed he had had enough of Buckyballs' explanations for one day, but mustered enough professional courtesy to thank him and left. Buckyballs was, after all, widely respected for sound research and judgment. If he chose to cover up the fact that in this case he hadn't a clue about this "vampire virus" by floating out some sci-fi fantasy, it was probably meant as a good-natured joke between colleagues. It was an understandable response to his own impatience and skepticism. Had he sounded derisive? No doubt his attitude made Buckyballs defensive and he chose this way of reasserting his authority. And, Korngold admitted with a chuckle, the guy was right. He *had* invited speculation. Buckyballs had nevertheless given him some disturbing data to sort out. A pathological condition caused like drag in the Alaskan pipe line! Vampirism the result of wobbling viruses! Indeed! It was, he had to admit, a very good joke.

Next day, Korngold visited Jennifer again. The snow white hair against her pale, almost translucent skin held him. There was something compelling about her. She still had no memory of recent events. Except for the amnesia, and the loss of some blood, Korngold determined that she would soon be able to function outside the hospital. But she had been severely traumatized, and though she was unable to recall the attack, the trauma was apparent. She would need extensive therapy to help her regain her memory and cope with the emotional shock that was sure to follow. He enlisted the help of well-endowed charitable agencies in setting her up in a residence near his office and providing her with a small stipend for daily necessities. He arranged to treat her without fee after she was released from the hospital.

The Womb of Uncreated Night

Troubled by strange dreams and her inability to remember recent events, Jennifer was grateful for Korngold's offer. When she came into Korngold's office for the first time, she looked anxiously around the room, as if lost and uncertain about what she was expected to do. Korngold was seated at his desk, so Jennifer sat in the chair next to it. Her eyes were shaded pale blue, delicately accentuating their sockets and giving her expression a hollowness that Korngold found somehow enticing.

"Do I lie on the couch?" she smiled wanly.

Korngold was still more disconcerted by what Buckyballs had told him than he cared to admit. The effect that she was having on him only compounded his discomfort. "It's a bit early in our relationship, don't you think?" he said, and instantly regretted it.

A smile slowly spread across Jennifer's face.

"If that would make you more comfortable," he added.

"I thought it was standard procedure," said Jennifer. "The patient lying on the couch, I mean. With the therapist sitting out of sight taking notes."

"Only in classical psychoanalysis. We can sit here and chat, if you like, or you can lie on the couch and tell me whatever comes into your mind. But there are preliminaries I'd like to discuss with you. And I'll take notes in or out of sight." Korngold pieced together a brief history of who she was before the blackout. There were significant gaps even before the traumatic event. Whether she was simply unable to recall parts of the past or was consciously repressing them, he could not say for sure. But part of what she did recall, or at least, what he was able to make out of her sometimes fragmentary recollection, had an aura of plausibility.

Jennifer leaned back in the chair at the side of Korngold's desk, adjusting the collar of the turtleneck around her throat, as if it chafed despite the air conditioning. Her voice, as Korngold heard the bits and pieces of her story, sounded oddly out of character with her body language, as if she had been describing someone else.

"Now, Jennifer," said Korngold, reassuringly drawing at his pipe. "We'll do everything we can to help. Your family—"

"My family probably wouldn't care," interrupted Jennifer, frowning.

"How can you be so sure?" Jennifer's frown only deepened, and Korngold wondered why she resisted the idea of locating them. Just how deeply did her long-term memory reach that it could not, or would not, get past her bitterness? "Well, then, your friends here in New York are undoubtedly concerned about your absence and looking for you. Surely, they'll have notified the police that you're missing. Word will be circulated to hospitals. Eventually, we'll get wind of inquiries and we'll take it from there."

But Jennifer would not be reassured. She gave him such a penetrating look that he found it hard to breathe. What was happening to him? He looked away to the windows. "We'll find them," he said. Then, when the momentary queasiness had passed, Korngold turned back to her in a business-like manner. "In the meantime, you need to keep meaningfully, even if only temporarily, active while we sort out who you are—who you were, and whether you really want to be that person again."

"Who I want to be," she echoed vacantly. And Korngold once more experienced a kind of unprofessional yearning. "Wouldn't I want to be who I was?" She shook her head in vexation. "Who I *am*. I mean, am I who I am now, or am I the memories of who I was?" She shook her head again, trying to dislodge the distracting particle *I/me/was/am* rattling around in her head like a BB in a pinball game. Or was her head the BB rattling around in the *I/me/was/am* game? "What if there's something in my past, my memories . . . something shameful, something so morally repugnant to me that I've blotted it out . . .?"

Korngold struggled to be reassuring but truthful. And in this case, the two simply did not square with each other. At the back of his mind, that absurd "vampire" virus had thrown everything out of kilter. Obviously there *was* something in her past she could not face. But was it the past that predated the trauma or the trauma itself? Or were they both somehow fused in those memories that she had locked down out of reach? Could her condition possibly be complicated by emotional factors that had led to a Dissociative Identity Disorder that existed prior to the trauma? Multiple personality, indeed! Before Jennifer, he had never taken the condition seriously. Like many in his profession, he doubted the authenticity of the reported cases, suspecting that the therapists themselves had, unintentionally, to be sure, suggested alternate "personalities" to their patients under hypnosis...

Well, there was Brewster and that irresponsible governess. But surely Brewster was borderline schizophrenic? *Two* cases of D.I.D? Korngold sighed in frustration. If one was unlikely, two were utterly preposterous! In spite of official recognition by the American Psychiatric Association, the few authentically documented cases of multiple personality sounded like humbug... identities paraded on a walkway like so many mannequins at a medical fashion show... coutures by mountebanks trading on the pathetic delusions of schizophrenics... a modish personality for every occasion! But in Jennifer's case... could it be some new episode attributable to the pernicious effects of that new virus? And Brewster? Could he somehow have been infected with the virus, too? Korngold would have to find a way to get Brewster to submit to a blood analysis. For the present, he could only fall back on the pat and the platitude, the last resort of the morally stymied.

"Most cases of amnesia eventually clear up by themselves. Recall returns, bit by bit." He squirmed uncomfortably. "We all have something in us we're not exactly proud of because we live in a world where we are conditioned, directly or indirectly, to believe that perfectly natural behavior must be adapted to moral principle, which is about as *un*natural as you can get. Impossible to live up to without bending your psyche out of shape. And in such a contorted environment, you're unusually vulnerable to almost any shock. You've had a terrible ordeal of some kind." How could he tell her that a "vampire" had been at her throat, when he believed that the only "real vampire" he could conceive of was a jejune morality that symbolically preyed on humanity and sucked the life out of its character? And sent its victims to psychotherapists, he added, sardonically. What, Dracula incarnate—if flesh it was—flying around the Ramble and pouncing on hapless passersby! Just thinking about it was giving him heartburn.

"Apparently, you couldn't bear to face . . . whatever it was." Later. Later. Time enough to face "it" later. She knew she had been attacked. She needn't be told by what just yet. Had she been abused as a child? Would she "remember" under hypnosis that her parents had sexually . . . He broke off that line of thought. "Still are unable to face it. But shameful? Wrong? Such judgmental terms are counterproductive. The victim is hardly to blame for having been exposed to violence. The shock of the attack itself alone might have been unbearable enough to drive you from yourself. If it was further complicated by some buried, unresolved moral debris you've accumulated over the years . . . ? Those are possibilities we need to explore. The important thing to understand now is what you feel *now* and why you feel that way."

"What do I feel now?" Jennifer asked, as if Korngold knew what she felt and could tell her, if only he would. Her tone was flat, sounding as if she were uncertain about when "now" was. For a fraction of a second, an echo of Brewster's nonexistent *now* flashed through Korngold's mind. But Korngold's mind hurried off before the thought had fully formed.

Jennifer stared at the curtains above the air conditioner in the window. The afternoon saturated them. They hung limp, dripping with sunlight. The glare burned her eyes and made them teary and red. She closed them around the muffled murmuring of the traffic in the streets outside the room, now and then interrupted by a wailing siren, the screech of hard-braking tires and the indignant blare of horns. Like clouds of vapor given off by streams rushing through a flume, these distant sounds billowed up from the streets and seeped into the room as shapeless as *I/me/was/am*. Her ears strained to hear the captive sunlight gurgling through the guts of the air conditioner.

"Now," she said. "Now. I only want to feel . . . what I felt before, whatever that was. I want to feel at home in my head, not a stranger wandering around inside it. I want to have my own familiar thoughts about me. That can only happen when I recover who I was . . . Without knowing who I was, how can I know who I am?" She opened her eyes suddenly and looked at Korngold the way a mouse being chased by a

The Womb of Uncreated Night

cat looks at a hole. "I mean, you don't just take off and put on who you are . . . like changing clothes?"

"Why don't you just tell me what readily occurs to you? Not all memory begins in a clear point in time and place. Instead, it's like—"

"A vapor. A shapeless mist of *I/me/was/am*, with the identity-things I'm seeking diffused in it, scattered like sunlight in the atmosphere. A sky of *me*."

The cool, fragrant smoke of Korngold's pipe had turned acrid in the air conditioned closeness of the room. ""That's very poetic," he said, "but not quite what I had in mind. Metaphors of identity are prized by Freudians, and are probably profoundly insightful in dream analysis. I don't do dreams. I think we need a more prosaic, factual foundation for the restoration of who you are. That will only happen if you give your thoughts time to assemble."

Jennifer, looking at the windows, mused aloud. "Odd how you can be in a cool room yet feel the heat throbbing in the windows. As if it's knocking to get in. As if it seeks permission."

"I'm not quite sure what use we can make of that metaphor," said Korngold. "I suppose we could say that memory can be like that. What do you think?" How to break through? Jennifer's fixation on poetic images was unsettling. Korngold did not want to deal with them. Still, it might be the only way to reach her. He tried to visualize the problem, his skin prickling. "It's as if your conscious mind had lowered a curtain between your former self—the world you knew—and your perception of the present," he said, feeling clumsy. There was more affect in his feeble attempt at metaphor than he was willing to admit. There was something about her. Almost hypnotic. "As if, standing in front of the curtain, you could sense what's on the other side," his voice grew husky and shook with repressed desire, "you can almost feel it—some of it, filters through—but something has rendered your conscious mind powerless to reach through to whatever activated that screen . . ." He began to falter. He wanted to reach out and tear through that curtain, to enter Jennifer.

Jennifer listened, leaning her side uneasily against the backrest of the chair, nervously rubbing her throat just below the scar. Korngold got up and stood over her. His knees almost touching hers. His mouth dry.

"Is the wound bothering you?" There was something almost sensual in the way her hands caressed her throat. Jennifer did not answer. Korngold bent over her, his face close to her throat. "Let's have a look." He stroked the area of the wound with his hand. Jennifer shuddered. "No, no," he said, "it's all right. I just mean to examine the site of the wound. It isn't infected, is it?" He thought that she would draw away in anxiety. But instead she raised her face to his, keeping her eyes a moment longer on the curtain in the window. As he gently palpated the area around the scar with his finger tips, her eyes turned full into his. He was surprised at the unsteadiness of his hand. There was no serum discharge, and the wound seemed to be healing well.

"We'll have to keep an eye on this," said Korngold, leaning close to her at the edge of the chair. "There's still a slight chance of infection."

"At the hospital . . . I overheard the nurses whispering . . . About a vampire . . ."

Korngold drew back, visibly annoyed. "That was very unprofessional of them. You were in no condition to have heard about that."

18.

After the widespread notoriety of Guinevere's disappearance in Central Park, a woman began haunting the Ramble late at night. Her long, straight snow-white hair flowing over her shoulders and down her back made her head seem to glow in the dark, an effect enhanced by the simple dark dress that obscured her body and gave her head the eerie effect of floating ghostly above the paths. Her features were patrician but blank, her face, youthful and unlined but somehow suffused with mature suffering. She appeared at irregular intervals, tracing the same path each night, beginning just to the east of the gazebo near the lake, carefully avoiding other strollers, and winding her way up to the Belvedere, where she vanished. If approached, she faded back into the unlit areas among the shrubbery and trees. So faithfully did she follow this pattern each time she appeared that she became the subject of local rumor, an object of awe and superstition among the more susceptible visitors to the Ramble.

Once the Delacorte Theater's Shakespeare-in-the-Park season began, the mysterious woman avoided the area until the theater crowd had dispersed. The curiosity-seekers among them sometimes lingered in the area hoping to catch sight of the apparition, or more likely, to join in the possible fun of exposing it as a fake. The park police were dubious and inclined to dismiss the rumors as either a practical joke or mass hysteria, but as a precaution the park patrol were instructed to keep a sharp lookout.

If the apparition was disinclined to giving command performances, there were a number of over eager ghost-spotters who imagined that a lamp or some light-colored object glimpsed through wind-tossed trees answered their purpose. There were even a few hoaxers who heated up the rumored sightings when interest seemed to be cooling off.

Such pranks were not limited to teenagers, who might be expected to engage in such mischief. On one occasion, an elderly woman with snow-white hair and wearing a dark dress created a minor furor after she left the Delacorte just after the play—it was *Hamlet*—had begun. She had escaped notice in the theater because her hair had been done up in a bun and was partly covered by a dark scarf of sheer silk. She had reached the steps at the western approach to the Belvedere just as Bernardo and Marcellus were trying to persuade Horatio that they had seen an "apparition."

> Mar. Horatio says 'tis but our fantasy,
> And will not let belief take hold of him
> Touching this dreaded sight, twice seen of us.
> Therefore I have entreated him along,
> With us to watch the minutes of this night,
> That, if again this apparition come,
> He may approve our eyes and speak to it.

She removed the scarf, as she climbed, undid her hair, which was quite long, and let it fall down her back.

> Hor. Tush, tush, 'twill not appear.
> Ber. Sit down awhile,
> And let us once again assail your ears,
> That are so fortified against our story,
> What we two nights have seen.
> Hor. Well, sit we down,
> And let us hear Bernardo speak of this.

> Ber. Last night of all,
> When yond same star that's westward from the pole
> Had made his course t' illume that part of heaven
> Where now it burns, Marcellus and myself,
> The bell then beating one —

In the minute or so it took to play these lines, the woman had reached the promontory near the Pavilion where she was sure to be seen in the brightly lit aura of the theater lights at the very moment when Marcellus cries,

> Peace! break thee off! Look where it comes again!

The Ghost, in this production, was not actually supposed to appear, merely a hollow sounding voice via the theater's sound system to suggest something awesomely supernatural. Supposedly visible to the players but invisible to the audience, the ghost was scheduled to "enter" at stage left which, as it happened, was in a direct line with the Belvedere. So that when "Marcellus" pointed in that direction, he was astonished to see an apparition on the promontory far more compelling than the hollow voice emanating from the concealed loudspeakers. The audience, reflexively following where he pointed, gasped, and murmured in surprise and consternation as they caught sight of her. Her dark clothing set off the whiteness of her face and hair so that her head, glowing in reflected light, seemed to float in space. Some of the audience, too, began to point. The other actors, perplexed at the commotion, were caught off guard, momentarily dropped their lines and involuntarily looked before trying to resume. Straining to be heard above the surging commotion, they almost shouted their lines. But the situation had gotten out of hand. Some members of the audience stood up to get a clearer sight—a few stood on their seats—which provoked those who were not interested in the impromptu performance on the promontory, kept their seats, and clamored for more art and less matter.

In vaudeville days, theater managers used a variation of the shepherd's crook to yank mediocre performers off stage. A patrolling cop happening to come up the Belvedere's eastern steps leading from the path along the southern edge of Turtle Pond served that function here. Alarmed that the woman so close to the edge of the precipice might do something desperate, or perhaps a student of the theater by day who disapproved of amateur improvisation, he ran up behind her and pulled her away from the edge and back out of sight of the Delacorte's audience. The audience had followed this unexpected drama in various stages of distraction while the actors tried to ignore it, and when the cop yanked the woman back from the precipice and out of sight, they laughed, cheered, and broke into applause. The play continued, but when Marcellus said, "Thou art a scholar; speak to it, Horatio," the audience burst into laughter again. And when Horatio said, "What art thou that usurp'st this time of night . . . ," the audience broke up into such uproarious hilarity that the theater manager finally had to come on stage and scold them for their unruliness before they were once again able to suspend their disbelief so far as to let the play proceed without further outbursts—not without an occasional incorrigible titter.

News accounts, next day, reported that the elderly lady had been arrested for disorderly conduct. The police let out that this mischievous old lady—whose identity was not revealed because she was the dotty dowager of a respected prominent family who had been disappointed in a career on stage—accounted for the UNIDENTIFIED FLOATING HEAD OF CENTRAL PARK, as the headlines blared it. She had even hastily smeared her face with phosphorescent makeup that enhanced the glowing effect. The police considered the matter closed. The lady was fined and released into anonymity. An elderly lady claiming to be the ghost of the Belvedere parapet sold her story to the tabloids. It was spiced up with the assertion that she was really an ectoplasmic manifestation of the ghost of Hamlet's father who had been trapped in inter-dimensional space where sex changes occurred spontaneously without surgery.

The Womb of Uncreated Night

🦇

Two nights later, the mysterious floating head reappeared on its customary rounds. As it went along its usual path near The Lake, the shadows stirred and came to life. A darker form suddenly enveloped it. There was a muffled cry, a groan. The shining head fell to the ground, the darker form at her throat. Then silence broken only by faintly rustling leaves and brute lapping. An instant later, a second form, a large bat, leaped out of the darkness and grabbed the attacker by the scruff of his neck. The dark form reared up and flung the bat against a tree. Attracted by the commotion, a few late-night strollers warily approached the scene. Others fled. Within moments, a squad car on the East Drive had slammed to a stop, one of the cops had climbed up and over the steep slope, a scooter cop arrived on a Segway. The attacker had seized the bat by his throat, but sensing the gathering reinforcements, let go and disappeared back into the darkness out of which he had leaped. The bat ran to the fallen head, lifted it, and gazed searchingly at the face. But the new arrivals converging on him caused him to gently lay the head back where it had fallen, and take off, whether in pursuit of the attacker or to escape the gathering onlookers they were unable to say.

The two cops stayed with the unconscious victim to assist and await backup.

"Looks like that old lady was at it again," said the cop from the squad car, noticing the white hair.

"Yeah," said scooter. "Bad move." He shined a flashlight on the woman's head. "Hey, wait a minute. That's no old lady!" Though her hair was snow-white and she wore a dark dress, the face and body clearly belonged to a young woman in her twenties. Her skin was ghastly white, and there was a bloody triangular clot on a vein in her throat just above and to the left of her collar bone. Her hair was disheveled and her blouse torn, exposing her neck and shoulder. "Jeez! Another one!"

They turned to question the onlookers about what they had

witnessed, which was disappointingly little. When they turned back to check on the victim, she was nowhere to be seen.

Brewster in full Batman regalia moved through the shadows of the Ramble until he stood under a tall oak atop the hill on the north shore of the Lake overlooking the Bow Bridge. On the opposite shore, the angel with outspread wings hovered benevolently over the basin of her fountain in the center of the Bethesda Terrace. She stood out stark and dark against a background of lights which still festooned the Terrace. Above and behind her, the 72nd Street transverse obscured the now abandoned Naumburg Bandshell where a jazz festival had been held earlier in the evening. Strings of lights still hung in the haze over the terrace, cascaded down the Victorian staircases, and tunneled through the arches of the underpass. A few stragglers lingered around the fountain as a park crew dismantled the display and swept up debris.

Behind Brewster lay the dim-lit paths of the Ramble. Out of the corner of his eye just over his left shoulder two young men came from different directions on a path skirting the hill met, kissed, and went into the bushes. The muggy air clung in pale haloes around the lampposts along the paths. As Batman watched, a light winked through the shrubbery. A bulb in a lamp blinking before the bulb burned out? A moment later, it flickered in a different spot along the path. It had to be the Floating Head catching the light from the lampposts!

He was about to run to intercept it, but Brewster hesitated. His intent was not to confront, intimidate, or terrify the UFH, but to learn who she was and why she was wandering around the Ramble. And maybe discover what had become of Guinevere. So how could he expect her to react when Batman hove into view? Any Head in its right mind would flee. And suppose he did not scare her out of her wits, how would he speak to her? What, casually lean against the nearest lamppost and try a pickup line you might use in a bar? "Oh, hi, there! . . . Come here often? . . . Like your hair . . . "

Shaking his head over the absurdity of the situation, he trailed her on a parallel path, his feet rather than his mind guiding his steps through shadows as much as possible. The path curved around a dark rock outcrop that obscured his view. He silently clambered up it. Several paths wound around other outcrops and intersected beyond trees and shrubbery. He would have to risk approaching her as directly and gently as possible or risk losing the chance to meet her. Remembering the old saw about the unseen being more frightening than the seen, he would plant himself casually under one of the lampposts ahead of her on a path she was sure to follow. What he would say, when and if he got the chance to say anything at all, would have to come on the spur of the moment. Yeah, he thought with a disgusted shake of his head, even if he stammered something brilliant, like, "Come here often?" or, "What's a nice girl like you . . . ?" or even, "Um . . . " or "Er . . . " Of course, she just might double over with laughter and be unable to run. But he decided against snappy pickup lines.

So Batman selected a lamppost where the light could stream over him and he would be plainly visible. He chose a spot far enough away from a bend in the path so that when she rounded it he would not suddenly loom up in front of her. Once there, he paused indecisively. He experimented with folded arms, then let them hang loose by his sides . . . He leaned against the lamppost, one leg propped against it as any lurker might do. He decided on folded arms. A moment later, she floated around the bend and caught sight of him. She hesitated, then stopped. She stood contemplating him. She neither came nearer nor ran off. He tried not to look tense. Then it hit him that although she had been ambling casually enough, she had avoided other pedestrians. Even though she did not seem to be frightened by his appearance, he had to admit that an oversized bat casually hanging on a lamppost along an ill-lit path in a lonely place might not be reassuring. He looked away, feigning indifference. She stayed where she was. She smiled. He lowered his leg, stood on both feet facing her, smiled, and lifted a hand in greeting. It was lame. She turned away without a sign and disappeared up the path she had come down. She *had* smiled. Had it been derision? Brewster wanted to go after her. But if he had not appeared threatening before . . . ?

19.

SMILING SMUGLY AS HE WATCHED the nightly parade on the path facing the Gill, Lon Barvim stationed himself on a bench to watch and wait. He had chosen the more secluded spot near the rustic bridge that spanned the Gill where it paused to collect into a pool before plunging over the waterfall, really no more than a trickle, down the Ravine and into the Lake. Its indecisive flow paced the steps of furtive men and boys as they, too, straggled among the less-worn channels of the Ramble. As he sat, sure of Moses' authorization, a light detached itself from the lamps along one of the paths and floated down beside him . . .

A few days later, a glum-looking young man whose curly hair looked as if it had been straightened was found unconscious near the wooden bridge spanning the Gill. He was at first taken to the emergency room of New York Hospital. He had lost several pints of blood and was comatose, but still alive. When the laboratory technician discovered the same anomaly in his blood that had been previously been reported by Buckyballs, he immediately notified the I.D. specialist. Buckyballs and Korngold conferred with the attending resident. The man's blood cells also showed the mysterious virus, only his infection seemed to be more severe. When Buckyballs and Korngold went up to his room to examine him, they found that the young man had vanished without a trace.

From the description of the man given by the hospital staff, Korngold guessed his identity. The realization that it might be Leon Barvim, filled him with new anxiety. First Guinevere Glimmerglass, then Barvim, both associated with the Young Artists Group! Brewster was flying around the Ramble looking for some clue to the vanished Guinevere, whose disappearance he blamed on a "vampire," Jennifer was running serious risks by returning to the Ramble hoping to trigger some association with her identity, and now probably Leon Barvim. All of these people were in some way associated with the YAG, however incidentally—and with him! Korngold was now genuinely alarmed.

The following week, there was a new twist in the attacks in Central Park. A man who had been sitting on a bench in the Ramble late at night had been approached by a stocky young man.

"How much money you got?" the young man said, looming over the seated man.

"Oh, coupla bucks."

"Hand it over."

"But—" the seated man raised a finger to protest. The other man hit him in the face and broke his nose. Seeing the blood on the man's face triggered uncontrollable violence in the attacker, who now beat him so severely that he lost consciousness. When the battered man regained his senses, he staggered to his feet and stumbled his way onto the West Drive and into the path of an oncoming patrol car. The driver slammed on the brakes, barely missing him. He and his partner warily scanned the sides of the road for signs of an attacker. Who could this man be running from? The driver called in for an ambulance while his partner searched his pockets for identification. Finding none, he concluded that the man had been beaten and robbed. They had been alerted to report just such suspicious circumstances.

When the ambulance arrived, the man was taken to a local hospital for emergency treatment. As soon as he saw the victim, the emergency-room intern whistled. "Son of a bitch! This guy's jugular has almost been bitten through!" The victim had obviously lost a lot of blood. The intern called for blood typing and with the help of a nurse began to close the wound. The man's vital signs were weak.

"Jesus!" whispered the doctor. He turned to the EMT who had not yet left. "This poor schmuck was not only beaten, but it looks as if he's been bitten as well. Were you able to find any identification on him? He might not make it, and we need to notify his family in any case."

"Naw. Except for the bite, looks like a routine mugging," said the EMT driver. "You think maybe some dog bit 'im while he was out? Like maybe watch out for rabies?"

"That's no dog bite on his throat. Savage teeth marks—" The intern shook his head.

"Maybe a rat?" said the driver.

The intern shook his head again. "Looks like one of the 'vampire' attacks that've been in the news. I'm going to notify the folks at New York Hospital. They've had experience with this sort of attack. We're not really equipped to deal with it here."

"What you saying, doc? You think this vampire's now beating up and robbing his victims?"

The intern shrugged, cocked his head, and phoned New York Hospital to report his suspicions. He was advised to begin blood transfusions as soon as possible and to send blood samples for study by Dr. Buckyballs. If the blood tested positive for the new virus, they would make arrangements to have the victim transferred to New York Hospital—assuming the patient could survive long enough for transportation. Under no circumstances should the victim be released before the I.D. specialist's report on the blood samples. He was further advised to keep the matter quiet to avoid alarming the public about vampires.

Lots of luck with that, thought the intern as the EMT crew left.

Brewster was early for his appointment with Dr. Korngold. He sat in the lobby, idly watching the elevator doors open and close, waiting until it would be time to go up. He was surprised when the doors opened and Arpie got off. He smiled his recognition, adding a slight nod. Arpie, always eager to meet someone to talk to, took the smile as an invitation to sit and chat.

"Are you here to see Dr. Korngold?" began Arpie.

"Yes," said Brewster. "You?"

Brewster was not in a mood for idle conversation with someone likely to probe every word for hidden meanings. One psychoanalyst was enough. But he suppressed a sigh and resigned himself to the inevitable.

"He's seeing someone right now. I was hoping that his next appointment wouldn't show up or come late so that he could squeeze in a few minutes with me."

Sorry to disappoint you, thought Brewster.

Before the conversation could take the ugly tone Brewster feared, the elevator doors opened again. A woman got off. She was dressed somberly in a basic black, simple shift that hung loosely from her shoulders. Her long white hair was slightly disheveled and muted by a gauzy scarf that caressed her face like a mantle. Stray strands partly obscured her face. She held her head up so that her throat rose softly to a chin made firmer by her bearing. Her lips, startling red without apparent makeup, were set in a thin line quivering with hidden excitement. A gracefully curved nose swept up to delicate brows arched over eyes colorless but gleaming through the veil of hair. The palest of blue shadow, like sunlight on new-fallen snow, washed over her china cheeks and flowed into the hollows around her eyes. Her prominent forehead floated ethereally over her eyebrows.

Her appearance was oddly familiar. Brewster drew in his breath sharply and almost spoke to her. But as she passed by and moved across the lobby, the woman seemed hardly aware of her surroundings, much less of him and Arpie. Ignoring Arpie as he was saying something about why he wanted to see Dr. Korngold, Brewster stood and watched her. He could see the subtle, sensual curves of her back and waist and hips as the shapeless dress yielded to the rhythms of her shifting gait. Despite the implications of the white hair, her supple, effortless movements were not those of an old woman.

As she walked away from him toward the entrance, she was briefly framed and silhouetted against the brilliant sunshine in the street. The striking white hair haloed her head. Brewster continued to watch, spellbound, as the woman's form passed through the plate glass swinging doors and turned west toward Third Avenue. On an impulse, he decided to follow her. He abruptly turned and left Arpie with his mouth open in the middle of a sentence Brewster had not heard a word of.

The glare of sunlight reflecting off glass, steel, and stone in the street dazzled him. In the few moments it took his eyes to adjust, the sidewalks, filled with pedestrians and the woman was absorbed into the light. Brewster hurried toward Third Avenue, jostling the occasional pedestrian bent on getting in the way. He turned downtown on Third, hoping he could catch sight of her again. But when he reached 76th Street he realized that he had lost her. He stood indecisively for a minute or two at the cross street, indifferent to the jostling pedestrians he now seemed perversely bent on getting in the way of. He circled the long blocks between the avenues, but finally gave up the futile search. He hurried back to keep his appointment with Dr. Korngold.

By the time he got back to the building, paced impatiently for the elevator to arrive, rode up the scraping shaft to the thirtieth floor and stepped out into the corridor leading to Korngold's office, his hour was half over.

Arpie had managed to get in to see Korngold in the interim. But whether Brewster would show up or not, the doctor was not in a mood for one of Arpie's petulant screeds. He insisted that he had other matters to attend to, and asked Arpie to excuse him. Reluctantly, Arpie got up and made as if to go, but Korngold knew he would not leave. He could never simply go directly to the door, open and walk through it when his time was up at the end of a session. Korngold sighed. Arpie would invariably linger at the door with his hand on the doorknob, sometimes even hold the door tantalizingly ajar to heighten the implication of imminent departure. Or he would go to the door, make as if to go, even actually cross the threshold into the hallway but not risk locking himself out by fully closing the door and letting the latch bolt snap to, then turn back to deliver the ultimate, the penultimate, or the antepenultimate parting word. Walking away and turning back were not, for him, two separate sentences, but twin halves of a line enclosing an anticlimactic caesura of interminable length performed by a performer with absolutely no sense of the syntax of an exit.

Arpie had once miscalculated and inadvertently closed the door all the way. The bolt snapped to. Korngold could see the doorknob being rattled and hear Arpie's plaintive knocking. Damned if he'd get up and start the farewell dance all over again! The rattling and knocking had stopped after a while, and Korngold turned back to some notes on his desk. Arpie had then begun to call his name in a singsong plaint. Korngold had thrown down his notes and looked at the clock on his desk. He wondered how long it would take an I.Q. of 157 to grasp the situation. After an annoying minute that seemed far longer than the sixty seconds ticked off by the clock, silence. A pause. And the relief of the sound of elevator doors opening and closing down the hall.

But Arpie had mastered the technique of dieresis since then. He never again allowed the door to swing too far. How did he do it? thought

Korngold in an admiration of despair. Did he practice on the doors at home? Jascha Heifetz could not have gauged an interval more precisely!

On this occasion, Arpie had just paused as usual in the doorway of Korngold's office to consider how he might stretch his purloined visit by another five or ten minutes. He was cut off in mid-lacuna as Brewster suddenly burst through the door with a thud and a hasty, "Oh, sorry!" Arpie was flung back several steps and stood slack-jawed as Brewster energetically strode over to Korngold's desk and dropped into the chair beside it. Korngold, as startled by Brewster's brusque entrance as relieved by an interruption that hastened Arpie's departure, fixed Arpie with a significant look. Arpie reluctantly left the room and closed the door all the way. Korngold could not help holding his breath for the satisfying finality of the bolt snapping to. He then turned back to Brewster.

"Sorry I'm late. Something odd just happened." Brewster saw that Korngold was tense as soon as he had sat in the Ergonomic Chair. Arpie could have that effect on people. But Brewster sensed something beyond that. And what was with the rumpled clothes. He looked as if he had been rolling around on the floor.

Korngold, whose thoughts were still churning after his session with Jennifer, had become even more agitated by Arpie's intrusion. He was startled by Brewster's words and shifted uneasily in his chair. Something odd, indeed! Would there be no end of oddities that "just happened" in the last few days? Brewster lapsed into puzzled silence at the therapist's demeanor. Korngold stirred himself out of his funk. "Something odd," he nudged," just happened . . .?"

Brewster was returning a decidedly odd look. "Something happened?" Korngold repeated. "Just *now*?" he prompted. He waited for Brewster to go on, wondering if he would say anything about last night. But Brewster continued to study him with a puzzled expression. Korngold shrugged and decided to wait him out. After a few minutes the silence began to weigh down on him. He tried again.

"Something—"

"You remember the young woman with the white hair who was attacked in Central Park?" Brewster interrupted.

"The woman who was mugged two nights ago," responded Korngold. "The Unidentified Floating Head."

"Yeah. Well, I think I just saw her." He waited for some reaction, but Korngold merely looked back at him and waited for him to go on. "Leaving this building. I followed her."

Korngold's heart was in his mouth. He waited for more. Brewster seemed to be gauging his reaction. Korngold struck a match and lit his pipe, concentrating on the flaming match as he sucked at the stem until the bowl glowed and fragrant smoke covered his face. He slowly shook the match out and dropped it in the ashtray on the desk, settled the pipe in his teeth and folded his hands over his slight paunch. Then he looked back at Brewster. The afternoon sunlight beginning to reflect off the buildings on the north side of 78th Street struck the lenses of his glasses so that they shone like mirrors. "Did you—," speaking between puffs as he looked closely at Brewster's face through two-way mirrors and smoke, "did you speak to her?"

"No. I didn't get the chance. She disappeared.

"Disappeared," said Korngold smiling and looking down at his desk in relief. "What, into thin air, in broad daylight? Yes, I'd certainly say that qualifies as 'something odd'!"

"As a matter of fact," said Brewster testily, "she disappeared in a glory of sunshine." Then, "Speaking of sunshine. Do you mind?" he got up and adjusted the blinds to subdue the blinding light. Korngold's eyes slowly materialized behind the mirrors. "She passed by me in the lobby, and when I followed her out the door the sunshine dazzled me. In the few moments it took my eyes to adjust to the glare, she was gone. I ran after her a couple blocks down Third Avenue but didn't catch sight of her again." He paused again, waiting for Korngold to react.

"I see."

"I was wondering. What would she be doing in this building?"

"What do you think she would be doing here?" said Korngold.

"She might've been visiting . . . somebody," said Brewster with a dismissive toss of his eyebrows. But he kept his eyes on what he could see of Korngold's through the smoke. "Who knows? Maybe seeking help."

"Help?"

"Sure, help. This is both a professional and residential building, after all. The Directory in the lobby is full of doctors' names. Including yours."

Korngold looked impassively at the blinded window. "It's a big building with a public entrance," Korngold said diffidently. "There are any number of possibilities. Visiting a friend . . . ?"

"Or a therapist?"

Korngold shrugged. "Perhaps. Let's go back to something you said earlier," said Korngold. "You saw a woman in the lobby and you thought you recognized her? Can you remember where you might have seen her before?"

"Well, there was all that foofaraw about the white-haired old lady masquerading as the 'Floating Head.' That was Mrs. Eldritch, by the way. The Wainwrights know her family, and I met her when I was a little kid knocking over tea tables. I don't think she was quite right in the head then, but she seems to have gotten dottier since. Anyway, right after the cops picked her up, the real woman with the floating head reappeared and was attacked. The news media reported that she was a young woman with prematurely white hair, someone possibly in her late twenties."

"Yes?"

"That description certainly fits the woman I saw in the lobby. I mean, granted, the description was pretty general. But there aren't that many women in their twenties with prematurely white hair, are there?" Brewster was silent a moment, and Korngold could see that something was puzzling him.

"And?" prompted Korngold.

Brewster continued in a reflective tone, "And . . . except for the color of her hair and maybe a slightly—I don't know how to put it, exactly—," he looked closely at Korngold, "a slightly maturer? air about her, I'd almost think it was . . ."

Korngold glanced at the clock on his desk. "Let's pick it up next time."

After Brewster had left, Korngold went to the kitchen for a snack. Sydney seldom joined him for meals during the day, so he had the kitchen to himself. He turned on the small-screen TV sitting on a counter. He watched the news and made a sandwich. As he picked it up to eat, there was an announcement that the unidentified man who had been attacked last night had died at New York Hospital earlier that morning. What would Buckyballs make of this latest "vampire" attack? Korngold still resisted the idea of the myth. But he was no longer scoffing. Somewhere in the I.D. specialist's cockamamie speculations there had to be an underlying order. He left the uneaten sandwich on the counter near the sink and went to pay him a visit.

"Consider this," said Buckyballs, assuming his best professorial pose. "Let's assume some vector, like a vampire bat, for instance."

"A vampire bat in Manhattan?"

"Hypothetically. A convenient metaphor. A creature like a vampire bat. The vampire bat secretes an anticoagulant enzyme to keep its victim's blood from clotting. All of these attacks have been in the area of the victim's throat, where blood flows plentifully and accessibly. But it's also the part of the body a victim would be most defensive about. It's puzzling, I'll admit. In most of the cases, there was no sign that the victim had been physically overpowered—no sign of bruising or other indication of restraint—"

"There is at least one case of a victim having been beaten up," interrupted Korngold.

"Yes, I'm familiar with the case," said Buckyballs, looking as if he disapproved of the unruly vampire. "But that seems to have been an isolated case. Some kind of aberration from the pattern of attack—"

The Womb of Uncreated Night

"Meaning?"

"Meaning that in most cases, the victim seems to have submitted willingly to being bitten!"

Korngold looked at him with growing uneasiness. "And how would you account for that?"

Buckyballs raised his eyebrows and spread his hands in an expression that said that Korngold would like what he was going to say. But what else was there? "How much do you know about the vampire in literature and folklore?"

Korngold hesitated. "A little. I've read about John George Haig, 'the smiling vampire of London,' Fritz Haarman of Hanover, and the Countess Elizabeth Bathory of Hungary—even Sergeant Bertrand, the Phantom of Montparnasse,' who were all clearly psychotic. There isn't much to choose between myth and mass hysteria where psychosis is concerned." For Korngold, these were deranged human beings, not reified creatures of superstitious dread. Could they have been the victims of a virus-induced psychosis? Rot!

"Traditionally, the vampire has always had a strongly erotic nature, sometimes subtle or even unconscious, sometimes overt and gross. In Bram Stoker's *Dracula*,—"

"Ha!" broke in Korngold.

"—Jonathon Harker meets the three female vampires in Dracula's castle, and felt 'a wicked, burning desire' to be kissed by them. Eastern Europeans believed that intense sexual drive gave the vampire immortality. And the vampire seems to have hypnotic powers. Imagine being able transfix any girl you want to make out with just by giving her the eye! Don't laugh! Fantasies have their counterparts in reality, as any good shrink will tell you." Buckyballs could not help snickering at the consternation that flashed over Korngold's face.

"Well," continued Buckyballs, "getting back to the enzyme. The anticoagulant associated with this new virus is similar to *Draculin* secreted by vampire bats. But it has a unique feature. What if, in transduction, the process by which an enzyme transfers genetic material from one organism to another, the vampire virus invades the bloodstream of its host, creating an intense erotic blood lust?"

"*What if?*" scoffed Korngold. "*What if* you had some evidence to support such a preposterous idea?" Then curiosity got the better of his skepticism. "*Do* you have evidence?"

"I would've expected you to take an interest in the etiology of vampire mania," said Buckyballs, playing foxy grandpa. "But you seem to be more familiar with the fictional vampire than you were willing to let on a few minutes ago. Or was that merely understated irony?"

"You were pulling my leg," Korngold said.

"Maybe a little," admitted the specialist, amused. "But in the recent cases no one's been caught drinking somebody's blood. And you'd pretty well have to catch them at it red-handed before you could—"

Korngold groaned. "Look here, I'm not sure I'm ready to buy your enzyme theory, but it has a lot more going for it than this vampire bullshit. An enzyme that causes some mental derangement? Yes. One that creates an infectious blood lust? Farfetched but not implausible. But an enzyme that carries hypnotic powers! And even . . ." he was puzzled that Bernwall had regained his memory soon after a blood transfusion. But Jennifer had not. "Do you suppose that memory loss could be triggered by the virus in its active phase, then return when the virus is quiescent?"

Buckyballs cocked his head speculatively. "An interesting suggestion," he said, getting up to pace back and forth across his office, as if considering how such a mechanism might work. Then he stopped pacing and broke into laughter. "By George, I think you've got it! No, really," he added, brushing over Korngold's sour look. "The unpredictability of the virus's phases working differentially in different individuals works like those old werewolf stories. You know, the hero turns into a werewolf during a full moon and wakes up next day naked and with no recollection of what he'd been doing the night before. Say, maybe we could call it the *werevirus!*"

Korngold uttered a sound of disgust, abruptly turned his back on Buckyballs and walked out of the office, muttering, "Or better yet, the *buckyvirus!*"

Buckyballs sat down laughing, still in a mood to have some fun with his so-serious colleague. "Oh, come on!" he called out to the departing form, "I promise to behave!" And Korngold, more interested in a dramatic gesture than in cutting off further conversation, turned back to confront this mischievous imp.

"What I was trying to say," he spoke with the exaggerated patience of someone who had lost all patience, "before I let my mind veer off track only to bushwhacked by your flippancy, was that your whole catalogue of symptoms is farfetched enough without adding the ability to project hypnotic powers into the mix! And you still haven't given me a shred of evidence!"

Relishing Korngold's chagrin, Buckyballs was unable to resist pushing the envelope. "But consider," he laughed. "Say it's possible. Say the carrier has a magnetic personality, sex appeal. He is somehow allowed to get close enough to kiss or nuzzle, bites the victim's neck instead, and is strong enough to overcome any resistance. Crazy as it sounds, how else to explain the facts . . . such as they are. Hypnotic suggestion, from whatever source, makes sense."

"Set up nonsensical criteria and nonsense 'makes sense.' Where's your evidence?"

"Yeah, the evidence is still pretty sketchy. But the study of enzymes since the nineteenth century is full of farfetched ideas that eventually panned out. We now know that enzymes are capable of complex metabolic changes. They can induce variable interactions with other enzymes."

The fusion of banter and science that Buckyballs spun grated on Korngold. He did not appreciate being twitted by a colleague. "You promised to behave," he chided, not wanting to be considered a grouch.

"So I did." Unperturbed, Buckyballs resumed. "But look at it another way. Suppose that the infected organism, a human being after all, that's really what we're considering here. Suppose a human being's metabolism were thrown off by a viral infection. Suppose further that he or she had been bitten by a bat. Couldn't a suggestible person traumatized in that fashion develop a mania about vampire bats and perhaps even start acting like a vampire? After all, there are those documented cases of people who parasitized humans for their blood. Nobody has been able to convincingly explain away their motives."

Korngold thought bitterly how Sandor considered *him* prone to "metaphysical" theories, and here was Buckyballs out-spooking him! He thought of the bizarre cases of men and women infected with AIDS deliberately infecting others out of some sick desire for revenge. He thought of people, men and women, who know they are infected with venereal diseases and yet continue a promiscuous life style out of malice or simple indifference. Or like some uncontrollable addiction.

"I suppose," Korngold said after meditating on these abnormal behaviors and shifting ground away from the absurdity of hypno-eroticism, "that there could be a link between this new virus and delusions in which someone imagines himself a vampire. But some of these bodies have been completely drained of blood. It's a bit much to think that a man or woman could drain off five or more pints of blood at a single sipping!"

"Who said anything about a single attack? Why not repeated episodes over a period of days? Before the victim's body would have a chance to replace the lost blood. Let's suppose the presence of the virus could create some kind of—well—derangement of a psychic nature, since that's in your field. The victim probably simply couldn't resist repeated bleedings—might even welcome them!"

Completely absorbed in his theory, Buckyballs got up again and paced back and forth with his eyes on the floor. Was he trying to avoid eye contact? wondered Korngold. Like a caged animal."Imagine. A fully developed human 'vampire'—yes, yes, I know," Buckyballs held up a hand to restrain Korngold's objections, "*hypothetically* speaking. Let's just apply the term to anyone who develops a morbid craving for blood, not Bela Lugosi turning into a bat! This 'vampire' secretes an enzyme which is the vector for transmitting the vampire 'virus.' If the victim of such an infection is not completely drained of blood, he or she survives and, in turn, develops a craving for blood. But the virus has not yet reached that critical mass that is self-sustaining. So after a while, the virus stops reproducing and the craving for blood wears off."

"And you're suggesting," said Korngold, "that the victim of this 'vampire's' bite is driven by a kind of hallucinogenic ecstasy, and develops a craving for blood to replace blood lost to the original 'vampire'? That victim attacks another person, spreads the virus, and . . . we've got an epidemic!"

Buckyballs nodded. "The hallucinogenic analogy makes a lot of sense. The fully developed vampire as a kind of drug pusher and his parasitized victims are his users!" Buckyballs seemed to be enjoying an epiphany. "If the victim is completely drained of blood, of course, he or she dies and never becomes a vampire. If the craving goes along with sexual excitation, tremendous changes in the body are produced, and *that* triggers the enzyme secretion. Like fleas that go into a feeding frenzy and breed when a rabbit's ears are engorged with blood when the rabbit is sexually excited during mating . . ."

"This is too weird!" cried Korngold, for the moment astonished out of the Apollonian poise he had adopted as a kind of apology for having been so tactless in his first interview with Buckyballs.

But Buckyballs, tightly wound up in his cocoon, was still pupating. "The infusion of this enzyme into the victim's bloodstream induces a psychotomimetic ecstasy similar to the effects of psychedelic drugs. It must therefore be addictive and create a craving for the enzyme. Eroticism is a powerful addiction! Blood alone does not satisfy the victim. Otherwise, he or she could simply find ways of obtaining whole blood by less . . . colorful . . . means than pouncing on somebody's throat.

"If the victim infected by the original vampire's bite is not capable of regenerating the enzyme—some of it must be lost each time it's transmitted to another victim?—that could make the victim dependent on the original—what?—*master* vampire, who alone is capable of regenerating the enzyme. The victim must return to him for a 'fix.' A critical level of enzyme must be reached before the immature vampire can mature, that is, regenerate the enzyme by himself, and that level is controlled by the master vampire through his ability to grant or withhold it. Only when the *master*, the 'dealer,' allows it to reach the critical level in the 'user' does the victim become a fully independent vampire. From time to time, therefore, the 'user' vampire must return to the 'dealer' vampire with a supply of blood obtained from others, and is rewarded with a re-infusion of the vampire enzyme."

Korngold looked at Buckyballs like an adult looks at a kid who tells an incredible lie so audaciously, that the more incredulous the adult looks, the more inventively the kid embroiders his whopper. Only Buckyballs embroidered *his* whopper seemingly indifferent to or unaware of Korngold's skepticism. And Korngold was having the queasy feeling that if this whopper kept coiling around reality it might squeeze across some inexplicable threshold of truth.

"And how many *master* vampires do you suppose we have on our hands?" he asked skeptically.

Buckyballs shrugged. "Since the present outbreak is recent, and the number of victims few, my guess is that there is only one. So far."

"But how would the . . . *vampire*," Korngold spoke the word with the kind of mingled indignation and puzzled acquiescence of a sane man who finds himself in a rational conversation with the inmate of a mental institution, "how would he overcome his victims before he transmitted this psychotomimetic enzyme in the first place?"

Buckyballs never faltered in his insouciant chimera. "Why, the vampire would have to be powerful enough physically or psychically to overcome the victim."

"One would think," said Korngold, "that you had a vested interest in this thing."

Buckyballs paused in mid-stride and looked up at Korngold impishly. "You mean," he said, with a leer and a mischievous look, and speaking in an exaggerated Hungarian accent, "am I . . . one of *them*?"

"I'm relieved to hear that you're treating this as a joke. I was beginning to think you really believed your vampire myth."

The I.D. specialist looked at him thoughtfully. "Many a truth, you know . . . I'll admit that there isn't enough hard evidence to verify my

The Womb of Uncreated Night

mythologizing, as you would have it. But it fits what little we have so far. And I'm working on a theory that's even more elegant!"

"Hah! Well, let's go along with the hallucinogenic angle. That you've found a new 'virus' in the blood of these victims, even that it acts like a psychotomimetic drug—that makes a kind of crazy sense. I suppose that since the wounds on the victims we've seen resembled infected hickeys, it's conceivable that people are transmitting the disease in this way." Korngold shook his head in sardonic disbelief. "A virus-induced psychosis that creates a mania for blood with an orgasmic payoff!"

Buckyballs shrugged again. "The 'vampire' was only a convenient analogy. As I've already said, I'm not committed to people morphing into bats that fly around at night."

"Let's just drop the vampire image. The pusher-user analogy seems adequate. Occam's razor cuts through your byzantine embroidery, I think."

"Yeah, but looking for a pusher among pushers—this thing shouldn't be confused with simple drug abuse. That might just confuse the cops and the public."

"Better to risk confusion over an exotic drug pusher than a panic over a supernatural terror. You'll pardon me, Bucky, but you sometimes sound like you're playing soccer with the atoms of reality."

Buckyballs smiled. "No more implausible, I think, than that the chemical and mathematical feasibility of exotic carbon molecules with sixty or seventy atoms should be conjectured and experimentally synthesized—after extensive research—only later to be discovered occurring naturally in the cracks of rocks."

Korngold returned Buckyballs' smile, enigma for enigma, and clapped him on the shoulder. "Dr. Soccer Balls!"

Off to a rocky start since morning, Korngold found himself even more unsettled after his visit with Buckyballs. Uneasiness lingered through his other appointments that afternoon. He listened, listless and less interactive than usual, retreating into the pose of the classic analyst. He listened, almost without comment while his patients unraveled, interjecting an occasional perfunctory grunt, or a "How did that make you feel?" or a nod of the head to give the illusion that he really was listening. Mostly, he stared out the window, his thoughts still on the implications of Brewster's encounter with the Unidentified Floating Head—no! Useless to pretend that it could be anyone but Jennifer. Yet he refused to follow that awareness beyond the immediate hazards to Jennifer of wandering around the Ramble late at night, in spite of his attempts to caution her against doing so. What if the vampire attacked her again? That was what vampires did—he shook his head in irritation.

Listen to yourself! he thought. You've let yourself be taken in by a lot of romantic claptrap, thinking like a character out of a hokey novel. There are more possibilities for harm than from a persistent vampire! When the last patient left his office a few minutes before four o'clock, he tried to review his notes, but abruptly flung his notebook on the desk, got up, and hastily left his office. He was not sure where he was going, but once on the street, he turned east to the river. He stared for a few interminable moments at the barges sluggishly bucking the current, then turned resolutely downtown to Sixty-Eighth Street. He again found Buckyballs in his office, the perennial cigarette stub dangling from his lips, doing some paper work. When Korngold came in, Buckyballs seemed relieved to have an excuse to chuck the papers and hear what his colleague had to say.

Seeing plainly that Korngold was down, Buckyballs broke in grinning broadly. "Buck up, old boy!" he said, vastly amused. "Tell Uncle Bucky what's on your mind!"

Korngold found it impossible to remain seriously annoyed with this rascal. "You remember Jennifer?" he said, uncertain just how much of her nocturnal rambling he ought to reveal. Buckyballs of course remembered. The grin faded and he listened seriously. Korngold told him of his concerns for her safety.

Buckyballs shook his head slowly, reflecting. His look grew distant. "Some of these victims of the vampire disease, they seem to grow reckless. As if they considered themselves immune to danger." Then his eyes focused on Korngold again. "Well, this Jennifer. You've been treating her, haven't you? Why do you suppose she'd take such risks?"

"She still suffers from amnesia—"

"*Sustained?*" said Buckyballs, surprised. "No intermittent remissions?"

It was Korngold's turn to express surprise. "You think it has something to do with the virus?" When Buckyballs only answered with a shrug, Korngold continued. "She thinks haunting the place will jog her memory. It's possible of course. I've cautioned her. But she's a very determined young woman." Then, sheepishly, he asked Buckyballs whether he thought the vampire—he had given up trying to use any other term of identification—might, like the fictional prototype, obsessively pursue someone who had been bitten.

Buckyballs chuckled at Korngold's unscientific question. What he knew about the virus, he said, came through a microscope's lenses. The rest he surmised from what he had observed and read about human behavior. And about that, he shrugged again, he would defer to Korngold.

Back again in his office, Korngold could not shake off the uneasiness stirred up by the day's encounters. He went to the window and raised the blinds. The reflections off the buildings across 78th nearly blinded him. But the heat slamming into him failed to sweep away troubling thoughts. As his eyes adjusted to the glare, he could just see the Triboro Bridge shimmering through the waves of heat. Like a mirage. What was wrong with him? Some premonition . . .

20.

"Talk about bad pennies always turning up!" Korngold said to Buckyballs as the two looked down at the unconscious form of Leon Barvim. There was no doubt about his identity. He was found in The Ramble and brought into the ER of New York Hospital fully clothed. The police had found identification in his clothing. He had lost several pints of blood and was barely alive. The lab technician found the same anomaly in his blood that had been discovered in the earlier attacks. The intern on duty ordered an emergency blood transfusion in a desperate hope that his life could be saved. Korngold was dismayed at this second attack on the same man. He struggled against admitting to the one common factor he could be sure of: The Young Artists Group. And Brewster. Ever since Barvim had sparred with him over the affections of Guinevere, had he become a marked man? Korngold could not believe that Brewster's masquerade as Batman was anything but benevolent. He had never viciously attacked the rascals he apprehended. His vigilante excursions which gradually trailed off after the disappearance of Hippias had reemerged without significant incident. His comic book crusade to save the world had been rechanneled into a search for Guinevere. And Korngold could think of nothing in their sessions that could have triggered an outbreak of violence. But then there was this new virus. What if Brewster had been infected . . .?

The Womb of Uncreated Night

Korngold's visits to Buckyballs were becoming routine. Since the whole vampire business had begun, they had developed a sort of chumminess that went beyond formal collegiality. So he was completely at ease in approaching the hematologist yet again. Buckyballs was so intent on a document he was studying that he was unaware of Korngold standing in the doorway of his office. When Korngold rapped on the jamb of the open door, Buckyballs hastily covered his reading matter with a manila folder, then turned with a smile to greet whoever had come in.

Korngold was a little surprised by his appearance. Buckyballs' shaggy hair, beard, and perpetual cigarette appended to his mouth and trailing ashes all over the place had never struck him as especially tidy. But today, there was an indefinable something that made him look more disheveled than usual. Maybe just tired, he thought. Yes, he does look tired. He shrugged to himself and returned Buckyballs' smile.

"I heard about the latest victim," he began.

"Ah. You have some interest in him?" asked Buckyballs. "How did you know him? Was he a patient?"

"Just a passing interest. Maybe you've heard about the Young Artists Group meeting at the apartment of Susannah Villiards, the former diva at the Met. No? Well, I heard Mr. Barvim perform there a few weeks ago. That was the extent of our acquaintance. But because I've been active in sponsoring the group meetings, I felt the responsible thing to do would be to check in on him. Thought you might be willing to accompany me when I went up to interview him about his attack?"

Buckyballs slowly shook his head. "With the amount of blood he's lost, I doubt he's survived," he said. But nevertheless he accompanied Korngold. When they entered Barvim's room to examine him further, his bed was empty.

"As I expected," said Buckyballs with a shrug. "He must've passed away this morning."

When they approached the charge nurse to learn the time of death, the nurse was alarmed. Barvim had not died. He should still be in his bed! She almost ran to his room and stood stunned at the empty bed.

"He shouldn't have been able to get out of bed, let alone wander away!" she exclaimed as she rang for the call nurse. The consternation of nurses and orderlies scurrying about in search of the missing patient soon included the intern on call for the ward.

"How the *hell* did he do that?" he scolded the charge nurse, wonder, and even admiration overlying the possibilities of an article for the medical journals. "Did he turn into a mist and drift out the window?" Hospital Security was notified and the hospital put on alert. But it would take days to verify where he could be on the premises.

Korngold and Buckyballs returned in silence to Buckyballs' office.

"He survived!" exclaimed Buckyballs in astonishment as they got there. "I mean, I learned about the massive loss of blood when the examining physician sent me a sample to examine for the—forgive me—*werevirus* does stick in the head. I was sure he was a goner."

"I assume the blood tested positive for the—" Korngold rolled his eyes. "I'm sorry, I just can't use your term. For the virus."

"Well," said Buckyballs, perched on his stool and again offering Korngold the creaking chair, "I think we ruled out a vampire bat in Manhattan. But consider what we've agreed on we've agreed on . . . *hypothetically*, of course. A convenient metaphor, remember? . . . A creature *like* a vampire that secretes an anticoagulant enzyme to keep its victim's blood from clotting. All of the attacks have been on the victim's throat, where blood flows plentifully and accessibly. In the cases of victims who've died, we assume that it's from repeated attacks. We don't have any other explanation for massive blood loss. We must also assume that once the vampire stops feeding normal coagulation resumes, or else the victim would bleed out."

"Yes, of course," said Korngold, indifferently. His old skepticism was returning in spite of his wish to be less judgmental."

"And you accept the master-vampire suggestion?"

"Your pusher-user theory offers a more plausible suggestion for why a victim exposes his throat to an attacker. After all, no one in his right mind is going to stand around while someone takes a chunk out of his throat!"

"No one on drugs could possibly be in his right mind," smirked Buckyballs. "And so far, at least, there have been no signs that the victims have been physically overpowered, no sign of defensive bruising or other indication of violent resistance . . ."

"With one exception," said Korngold, holding up a finger.

"With that one anomaly, which hasn't been accounted for," agreed Buckyballs.

"And just like that," said Korngold musing aloud, "this man of science has brought the twin columns of science and order crashing down into mysticism as calmly as an accountant justifying two columns of figures!"

"Buck up, ol' boy!" said Buckyballs raising his eyebrows and spreading his hands in an expression that meant Korngold would not want to believe what he was going to add, but what else was there? "In our last talk, you told me that you knew about real-life vampires as well as the usual literary and folkloric ones."

Korngold sighed. "Yes. Well, my reaction then was that it was all a lot of rubbish."

"But you're having second thoughts?"

Korngold nodded. "I'm no longer convinced it's all explainable as hysteria or psychosis. Although I still think some of it is," he added doggedly. "A virus-induced psychosis is more plausible than I formerly thought." He shrugged in resignation. "And we've already gone over the influence of the nineteenth-century novels, so let's not do *Dracula* again."

"Of course not," laughed Buckyballs. "But recall our discussion from last time about the Eastern European's association of vampires' and sexual virility. Did you know that it stemmed from their having exhumed male corpses with erections?"

"If hypnotic powers gave men erections, they wouldn't need Viagra!" snorted Korngold.

"Well, not everyone is equally susceptible to hypnotic suggestion. To say nothing of how many men would be skillful enough to use it. And remember, the seductive vampire may also be a woman." Korngold knew that Buckyballs was pushing his buttons in collegial fellowship. But it rankled nevertheless. "Anyway," continued Buckyballs, "getting back to the enzyme and the virus, we're in unknown territory there. Somewhere in the transmission, in the enzyme or the virus itself, who knows what effects may yet be discovered? The process by which the virus creates a blood lust invades the host cells and reprograms them to reproduce itself—? So far, that's as mysterious as the vampire's hypnotic powers. *Hypothetical* hypnotic powers," added Buckyballs hastily as Korngold started to object.

"But there's a difference between vampires' erotic nature in folklore and their hypnotic powers in Stoker's novel," protested Korngold. "Until *Dracula*, no vampire had the power to put his victims into a trance."

"Yes," laughed Buckyballs, "let's *not* do *Dracula* again! But maybe the folklore simply considered erotic magnetism transfixing enough?" "At any rate, I understood your interest in the occult was a favorite hobbyhorse. This is the first I've heard you taking it seriously." Korngold frowned. "Well, hypothetically, at least? Korngold still wore disapproval. For the sake of argument?" he added.

"A hobbyhorse does not transport you into the real world, but out of it," said Korngold sternly. "Out of habit, I entertain, but do not encourage patients wound up in their own nonsense." Buckyballs' eyebrows shot up. "Not that I consider you a patient," he added drily.

"Of course not. But what other explanation for the victim's passivity under attack can there be? Maybe pheromones? Like the high level molecular aldehydes emitted by flowers to lure insects? Pleasant odors so intense that they intoxicate the victim? Which orifice of the vampire's anatomy do you suppose would emit them?" He laughed uproariously while Korngold struggled to be patient. "Well, whatever tranquilizing agent is at work, it clearly would have to take effect *before* the enzyme or the virus enters the bloodstream."

"We're back to that?" groaned Korngold

"I wonder if anyone considered examining victims for puncture wounds?" Buckyballs laughed. "Maybe the vampire stalks them, tranquilizer gun in hand." The sour look from Korngold ended that line of discussion. "But consider," he lit up another cigarette, "suppose . . ," he puffed, "well, we've gone over this before. However he or she manages that neck-nuzzle, it's without a struggle. Some people like kinky sex . . . After all, a lot of strange things go on in The Ramble at night. But then, do the victims share similar personalities? Or does the vampire have a knack for recognizing victims who are into that sort of thing? What do you suppose they have in common?"

Korngold started. The consternation that flashed across his face might have been reluctance to concede any point that led to a fantastic conclusion.

"Okay," continued Buckyballs, "If it's not organic chemistry or fatal attraction, what then? Purple brain-power? Electromagnetism?"

Oh, *Lord!* protested Korngold's thought. He's beginning to sound like Brewster! He thought of the bizarre cases of men and women infected with AIDS deliberately infecting others out of some sick desire for revenge. He thought of men and women, knowingly infected with venereal disease continuing a promiscuous life style out of malice or indifference. Or some uncontrollable impulse.

"I suppose," he conceded at last, anxious to move on, "that there could be a link between this new virus and delusions in which someone imagines himself a vampire. But some of these bodies have been completely drained of blood. No apprentice vampires in dead bodies."

"Well, addiction does make a lot of sense. An ambulatory victim would crave repeated bleedings, and try to replace the blood with yet other victims."

"A victim who loses blood, develops a craving for it, yet enjoys losing more of it. Then victimizes others, creating a chain-reaction of epidemic proportions. And if a victim loses too much blood before it can be replaced by other victims, he or she dies. What a disheartening prospect!"

"Well," said Buckyballs, "something you said yesterday about the virus having active and inactive phases was insightful. If the virus has not reached that critical stage of infection that is self-sustaining, it goes dormant, and the craving for blood weakens. That would indicate that we have primary and secondary victims, an active and an inactive phase!"

"So," Korngold cut in, the chair creaking as he got caught up in following the hematologist's thought, "in the active phase, the victim, in a kind of ecstatic frenzy of blood lust attacks others unaware of what she is doing." When Buckyballs suddenly stopped pacing and looked at him intently, Korngold took it as a kind of affirmation. "In the inactive phase she still carries the disease, ready to break out at some unpredictable moment."

"Yes," said Buckyballs pacing again, "that sounds right. Secondary victims, then, would be only mildly affected by the original infection because the amount of blood taken and enzyme communicated to the victim falls below the level of sustainability. The secondary victim would likely recall the episode. But the primary victim would experience a hallucinatory oblivion that swallowed up all recollection of the attack . . ."

"Yes, of course," reflected Korngold. Amnesia."

"Why not? We have plenty of evidence that hallucinogens can create memory deficits. We just don't know exactly how this particular hallucinogen works. We don't even know if it's the enzyme or the virus that determines the victims' mental response. If they craved intimate contact with the vampire without knowing why, we have some inkling about the erotic side effects of the blood lust. And greater contact leads to greater memory loss."

"Until, at last, the victim is . . . a slave of the vampire master," said Korngold, awed.

"What little we know for sure, so far, fits," said Buckyballs. And like a student promising his professor that he would study harder, "I'll work on making it more elegant. We scientists like 'elegant solutions,' don't we? They satisfy the unrequited coldness of disinterest."

"Hah! What's elegant about vampires running loose in Central Park? That you've discovered a new virus in the blood of the victims, that you've also found an enzyme that helps to spread it, that victims suffer some loss of memory," Korngold shrugged, "to call that elegant . . . The hallucinogenic angle sounds promising. The wounds on the victims' necks resemble hickeys. That's consistent with 'love bites' and eroticism." Then

Korngold shook his head in dismay. "Blood lust disguised as love bites! A virus-induced psychosis that creates a mania for blood with an orgasmic payoff! If that's your 'unrequited coldness of disinterest' . . . My God!"

"Well," said Buckyballs, "at least it's not people morphing into bats that fly around at night." Then, unable to resist he added slyly, "Not yet, anyway."

"Let's drop the vampire analogy, shall we? The pusher-user is adequate."

"Even persuasive."

"So," said Korngold, the chair squealing as he rose, "soccer balls with reality it is! Good ol' Dr. Buckminsterfullerene!" he laughed.

He started to leave, then hesitated at the door and turned back. "Still," said Korngold shaking his head, "there ought to be some hard evidence to prop up your speculations, even if only something that crawls out of the cracks of rocks!"

Buckyballs opened his mouth as if to speak, hesitated, then reached under the manila folder and pulled out a battered-looking journal bound in cracked and flaking leather. "You might find this of interest," he said, handing it to his colleague. Seeing that the book was very old and fragile, Korngold, who was fond of handling rare old books, took it carefully and examined it. It was a journal, neatly handwritten in German. Some of the pages were blotched with brownish stains, a few were torn, others were stuck together. He looked up at Buckyballs in surprise and delight. "Your German is probably better than mine," Buckyballs said. "But I've been able to read through it a couple times. It's at least a hundred years old."

"These brownish blotches?" said Korngold indicating a discoloration, some of which had come off on his fingers as a powdery residue.

"Dried blood that hadn't been absorbed into the paper. Some of the pages were stuck together. I'm afraid I damaged some of them when I tried to separate them."

"Where did you find it?" asked Korngold, still turning its pages, trembling with delight.

Buckyballs smiled into his beard, lit a cigarette, and contentedly took a few puffs before answering. "I was combing the files in the old morgue in the basement of Bellevue, looking for old autopsy reports from the nineteenth century when I came across a file box with this journal and a vial of brownish substance. The medical examiner who performed the autopsy didn't know what to make of it. The journal was found next to a body discovered near the Belvedere in Central Park a hundred and thirty-odd years ago, evidently the victim of foul play. In spite of remarkably good facilities for the period, including a refrigeration room, the report has very little beyond a preliminary examination.

"All bodies were usually photographed for identification and held up to seventy-two hours, depending on the weather. The body described was that of a tall man of spare build whose throat had been cut or torn. He was apparently mugged, stripped naked, and died of exsanguination. Only the journal was found lying in the vicinity of the body. From that the M.E. naturally concluded that the victim was a foreigner. The M.E. apparently had no German and didn't know what to make of the journal. There were no other means of identifying the body. Evidently the M.E. saw something unusual about the remains, for he went to the trouble of obtaining a small sample of the man's blood which he preserved in this vial," said Buckyballs holding up a small, sealed glass tube, "and placed it in an evidence box along with the journal."

"Then there must have been a photograph," said Korngold, intrigued.

"Yes. The body was photographed as usual. But before the M.E. could perform a full autopsy, the body vanished."

"What, into thin air?" exclaimed Korngold.

Buckyballs laughed. "For all anyone knows."

"And the photograph?" asked Korngold, eagerly.

"The photograph," Buckyballs shrugged. "The evidence box also contained an exposed plate with a fogged image. It showed a vague form that may have been a human body."

"I suppose," Korngold speculated, a little disappointed, "I

suppose the body was found in the summer, and the colloids used then were unstable . . .?"

Buckyballs tilted his head thoughtfully. "You may be right. The body *was* discovered in the middle of hot summer, and that might have had something to do with the fogging, directly or indirectly. "Haste, careless handling, faulty technique," he shrugged again. Who can say?" He paused. "But an image on a photographic plate would have been printed on paper. The paper photograph, not the plate would've been stored. No, I think that for some reason, the plate image didn't pan out."

"Then why would the M.E. preserve a useless image in the evidence box?"

"Why, indeed! There must've been something highly unusual about the corpse for the M.E. to have done that." Both men reflected silently about the implications of what might have happened. Then Buckyballs spoke again. "Aside from the items I've mentioned and a notation on a formal report that the body went missing prior to a full autopsy, there was no other information available. So the box was shelved and apparently forgotten."

"Have you analyzed the contents of the vial?"

"The vial?" Buckyballs studied the vial, rolling it between fingers. He puffed thoughtfully on his cigarette until a long column of ash dangled from it. "Hm. It's blood, probably drawn at the time."

"The side effects of the virus," wondered Korngold. "You don't suppose . . . how long do you suppose the virus would be viable? And anyway, it couldn't really transform a person's physical appearance?"

Buckyballs' beard twitched and the cigarette's ash dropped onto his lab coat. "You mean," smiling absently and brushing off the ash, "like Dracula turning into a mist and drifting away? Or maybe getting younger as he fed on blood and aging when he didn't? The 'fountain of youth,' you called it. Ho-*ho*! Either would be a useful exit strategy!"

"Yes, of course. May I borrow this?" Korngold held up the journal.

"Yes, of course," said Buckyballs. Korngold left with a smile and the journal.

21.

A WEEK BEFORE THE SOIRÉE at which Miami Bernwall was scheduled to play Mozart at the Wainwright mansion, Ghee-Ghee showed up unexpectedly at Mme Villiards' apartment just as the diva was about to go out for the evening. She had, in fact, opened the door as Ghee-Ghee was about to ring the bell.

"Oh, how thoughtless of me! I didn't realize that I might be interrupting—" he apologized, but made no move to leave.

"Not at all, my dear," Mme Villiards said, glancing at her watch. "What can I do for you?" She signaled her intent not to be delayed by closing the door to the apartment and taking Ghee-Ghee's arm. "Walk with me to the elevator."

"Gaby thought we should take you up on your promise to let her show some of her work at a regular meeting of the Young Artists Group." Mme Villiards stopped dead in her tracks. Ghee-Ghee should have been fully aware that the next meeting at the Wainwrights' had already been planned well in advance. "Oh, I know it's an imposition, Madame! But it would mean so much to dear Gaby. A gallery expressed great interest in seeing her work when I said it would be shown at your apartment."

Mme Villiards planted herself firmly in the middle of the corridor, her mouth agape at the presumption of the man. She tried desperately to recall exactly what she had said to Gaby. *Had* she promised and forgotten? That moment of indecision cost her the initiative. Ghee-Ghee rushed in before she could get over her hesitation.

"I know it will mean postponing the soirée at the Wainwrights', but I've already called Mrs. Wainwright and asked her if she would agree to sponsor Gaby by doing that."

Mme Villiards continued to stare at Ghee-Ghee, dumbfounded. If her "promise" *had* come home to roost, and if, considering the amount of time and trouble Amalia had put into preparations, she was willing to postpone the event . . . How could Susannah stand in the way of a young woman just starting out in life? Mme Villiards resumed walking toward the elevator. Indignation tempered by kindness and generosity comes perilously close to gullibility, and when manipulated by the fraudulent can wear away even the most resolute defenses.

"Well," she said at last, "if Amalia is willing to go to the extra trouble, I guess it would be ungracious of me to withdraw my . . . 'promise.'" She would telephone Amalia in the morning to coordinate their events.

Ghee-Ghee escorted her onto the street, where the doorman hailed a taxi for her. Then he turned back into the lobby and used the courtesy phone to call Mrs. Wainwright. When she heard that a man from the Young Artists Group was on the line, she took the call. She learned from him that a previous commitment made by Mme Villiards to an artist required a change in schedule for the soirée at the mansion. Since Mrs. Wainwright had not yet completed arrangements for the Mozart concert, some technical difficulty with a clarinet Mr. Bernwall was supposed to play, she was actually relieved at having another week for preparations.

On the evening of the exhibition Mme V had been trapped into promising, Gaby and Ghee-Ghee arrived later than expected to set up the paintings. Instead of "a few" paintings anticipated by Mme V, Gaby had chosen over two dozen, plus pen-and-ink sketches and silk screen prints. They had rented a van to transport the work. The cost of the rental put a crimp in their budget, but Ghee-Ghee would spare no expense for his wife. He picked up the van the night before so that he could take advantage of alternate side of the street parking, managing to squeeze into a space near their brownstone on West 83rd. He had wanted to load the van immediately, but Gaby fretted about leaving her valuable work in the van overnight where thieves might break in and steal it. Waiting until the next day meant that they had about two hours for Ghee-Ghee to get home from the office, load the van, and make the short drive down and across town to Mme V's condo. That was cutting things close, but if a few people arrived early, well, they could enjoy watching the exhibit being set up.

Next day, Ghee-Ghee managed to leave his office at a quarter of 5. The subway platforms were already mobbed by people with similar intentions. Preoccupied with ordering the evening's preparations in his head, he allowed himself to be crowded into the wrong train and soon found himself going uptown on Lexington Avenue instead of Broadway. Well, he'd just have to take the 42nd shuttle to Times Square. The express would still get him up to 86th Street by 5:30 or 5:45, tops, despite the usual delays. He should be home by 6. He and Gaby would have the van loaded by 6:30 or so. They might even have time for a snack, though Mme V could be counted on to provide a good spread. Even if they ran a little late, they wouldn't go hungry for long.

Ghee-Ghee reckoned without all the things that could go wrong during rush hour. He planted himself firmly near the center doors of the car, tightly gripping one of the steel posts. But he was so pressed by waves of passengers determined to get on *this* car and no other that his grip was soon torn away and he found himself squeezed between riders pouring through the doors on either side. At 42nd Street, the surging passengers were as impenetrable as they were deaf to his shouts of "Coming out, please!" preventing him from getting off before the doors closed. The onslaught had inadvertently pushed him nearer the doors at the end of the car. He swore under his breath, set his jaw, and

The Womb of Uncreated Night

grimly determined to get off at 59th. He *would* get off, run downstairs and catch the express back to 42nd.

As the train pulled into 59th Street, a black woman behind him began digging her elbows into his back. "I'm getting off here, too," he said to her, like, Get your damn elbows out of my back, lady! "WHADDOICAREWHATYOUGONNADO!" she snapped back. But Ghee-Ghee clawed his way out with the woman's elbows spurring him on when the doors opened, rushed downstairs to find the Downtown train had just pulled out, and waited, full of wrath, for the next one.

Gaby could see that he was in a foul temper and sweating when he arrived at the apartment a few minutes after 6. They hastily loaded the van in silence. They had intended to wait, anyway, until after the worst of the rush-hour traffic would be over, so it was not a serious set-back when they finished about 7 o'clock. They had just enough time to drive over to Columbus Avenue, skirt the Museum of Natural History down to 79th, over to Central Park West, and voilà! Mme V's condo. Even with possible traffic delays, they should have half-an-hour to unload and set up.

It was nearly 7:30 by the time they had executed their plan. Ghee-Ghee double-parked the van near the service entrance, causing a minor traffic backup, much indignant horn honking, and raised middle fingers. With the help of one of the condo's custodians, they unloaded the van onto the sidewalk. Ghee-Ghee left Gaby and the custodian to load the paintings and their display racks into the service elevator while he took off in search of a parking place on Amsterdam. By the time the paintings and equipment had been unloaded into Mme V's apartment, Ghee-Ghee got there, breathless, with the first arrivals.

Energized by the altercations of the evening, he fell to work with Gaby's assistance, unceremoniously moving furniture, rolling up Mme V's priceless Persian rug to one side, scraping the parquet floor, and creating near-calamities. Mme V stood aside, aghast, with a hand over her mouth to muffle strangled little cries when vases teetered, the buffet service rattled, or potted plants careened. The easels and display racks, jury-rigged by Ghee-Ghee from scrap wood and salvaged curtain stretchers, were set up so hastily that paintings and sketches sprawled randomly across the raised alcove and along the walls on either side. Not the aesthetic progression envisioned by Gaby, but it had an impromptu vitality.

When Gaby and Ghee-Ghee were done, a few gouges left in the floor could be covered up by carpet until the floor could be refinished. But Mme V was galled at the chaos. Her beautiful Bösendorfer was completely obscured, its open case even serving as a prop. And there was no place for the musicians to play their tasteful background music. Most of the guests, who had been steadily arriving as the Guilemots worked, remained huddled uncertainly near the foyer. Ghee-Ghee, having worked off the evening's grievances, smiled at his wife, pleased that they had not held things up too long—it was only 8:10, fashionably late! They strolled to the opposite side of the room to admire the effect of their handiwork.

But the hastily assembled racks were not completely stable. As the guests came into the room, a subtle shift and shudder crept through the array. The racks sighed as if tired and slowly began to creak and lean to the floor in a sustained groan. The paintings and props fell in on each other in a cubist clutter of shatters and jangles. Ghee-Ghee was panic-stricken. But Gaby's eyes sparkled, and with a sweeping gesture, "Ladies and gentlemen," she cried, the triumph of revelation in her voice, "my installation, 'A New York Minute'!"

It sounded like a catchy title for an unintended disaster. The guests gasped. There was an awed silence of about thirty seconds. Then ugly rumbling as they contemplated tattered sketches—paintings of city streets pierced by the points of broken canvas stretchers, the eye of an unrecognizable face, the limbs of some unidentifiable victim, smudged pastels, even an oil which had not yet had time to dry running across a street scene in defiance of gravity—lay in a twisted rubble heaped across the polished floor of the Bösendorfer's alcove. Discrete words were flashing out of the clouds of muttering, "Shocking!" "Poor taste!" "Too soon!" "Capitalizing on tragedy!" "As if 62nd Street wasn't a painful enough reminder!" Ghee-Ghee collected his tattered ego and scrambled out of the debris to cover his wife's dicey crapshoot. "Ladies and gentlemen, it's in the steps of Picasso!" This announcement was at first met skeptically, then some grudging head-waggling, and suddenly broke into acclamation as the guests rallied around the alcove acclaiming Gaby's brave and brilliant insight. "Audacious! Terrorism as Art!"

A Soho gallery owner just happened to be among the guests. He immediately offered to show "A New York Minute" as soon as Gaby could reassemble it. "As soon as she and Ghee-Ghee could collect the dice and roll them again," grumbled Nick, who had joined the throng of oohs and aahs around Gaby.

"This has given me a fantastic idea!" he said. "Why not enhance the effect of the collapse—er, the exhalation?—with chance music for a capella chorus: low murmuring basses, wavering sopranos, altos and tenors antiphonally declaiming Gertrude Stein, *sprechstimme*, all combining into one final, sustained, lingering, synchronized groan as the paintings, sketches, and music settle to the floor! In perfect sync! An Aleatorio!"

Gaby only looked at him sidelong, with suspicious, narrowed eyes. Ghee-Ghee muttered, "Surely, you jest!" Nick later heard a rumor that the Whitney was considering an exhibit. Gaby was on her way without him.

22.

Not long after arriving in New York Nick had discovered that the subway system was a marvel of efficiency. The trains went everywhere. He was never more than a few blocks' walk of where he needed to get to. So he dawdled until almost half an hour before he planned to leave, half-heartedly picking over the compositions he would use to test the sincerity of Brewster Wainwright's interest. In the end, he cut the culling short and stuffed as many as he could into an oversized mailing envelope. The soirée postponed by the Guilemot encroachment had been rescheduled for that evening. It really belonged to Miami Bernwall's performance of Mozart. But Brewster had expressed interest in Nick's compositions, and Nick saw no reason why he should not at least try to make something of an opportunity.

As he came up the steps to the street from the flat he shared with Arpie, the air was warm and muggy, the sky overcast. He would stroll across Eighth Street to Fourth Avenue and take the Lexington train up to 68th. The walk over to the Astor Place stop and back across to Fifth Avenue at the other would probably take longer than the ride uptown from Astor Place, but Nick had gotten used to walking. And he would arrive fashionably late.

Climbing up the steps of the 68th Street station, he heard the deep rumbling. Was it a train roaring past the station? As he came up to the street sheets of rain drove into his face. The streets wavered in steamy mist, as if a matrix of pixels in his head needed horizontal alignment. Or like trying to see in the bathroom mirror after a shower had steamed it up while turbulent vapor drifted across his vision. He ducked into the doorway of one of the stores on Lexington, pulling his shirt out of his pants and shoving the envelope up against his chest. Few passersby cringing in the rain bothered to notice his sartorial disarray. He hurried up Lex to 70th Street, then across the three interminably long blocks—well, two-and-a half blocks, to Fifth Avenue. The entrance to the mansion was some distance off Fifth. By the time he reached the steps of the entrance, the rain had stopped.

The soirée featuring Miami Bernwall's performance of Mozart's Clarinet Concerto, which was supposed to have taken place at the next meeting of the Young Artist's Group, had already been preempted once by Gaby Guilemot's "Installation." The normally unflappable Mme Villiards had good-naturedly shrugged her shoulders and, with the friendly accommodation of Amalia, rescheduled the performance for the following week. All the arrangements had been made. The Wainwrights had gone to the trouble of opening the Fifth Avenue mansion in summer so that the YAG would have a convenient venue in the center of town, even sharing the cost of engaging the musicians. And the extra week had given Mrs. Wainwright time to send out invitations to a few prominent citizens. The caterers, who had already been contracted, too, did not object at the extra time to prepare an elegant buffet for a larger group. It was to be a genuine social event.

But with the disappearance of Guinevere, Mme Villiards anxiously worried that the Wainwrights might cancel out of consideration for Brewster's feelings. While the Wainwrights had been glad enough that their son had developed "an interest," and were concerned about his feelings, not to say appearances, they were determined to encourage Brewster to keep a stiff upper lip and not allow him to retreat back into Batmania.

Despite Augustus Wainwright's distaste for his wife's cultural enthusiasms, there was to be no turning back. The soirée would take place as scheduled. Mr. Bernwall would tootle his clarinet, or whatever he did with it. The musicians and the caterers were engaged. The mansion's ballroom was set up with a long row of tables arranged for various courses, appetizers, entrées, salads, and such. The guests' munching would hopefully drown out the sounds of the orchestra hired for the evening. Augustus had instructed the butler, Frederick, to stand near Brewster and keep a watchful eye on him as well as the catering staff, who were circulating among the guests with trays of hors d'oeuvres and drinks. Augustus' impatience with the Young Artists Group was aggravated by the suspicion that Brewster was up to something and had put Amalia up to supporting him in some prank.

Several dozen guests circulated around the tables and clustered in small conversational groups. A gallery ran around the second story of the ballroom, and a vaulted ceiling with skylights and sylvan scenes painted around them. Below the gallery on the far side opposite the main entrance to the hall, French doors opened onto an elegant and expensively maintained garden. Thunder rumbled ominously in the distance. If a storm broke, it would keep the guests from circulating into the garden and spoil the one thing in this affair that mattered to Augustus, a chance to show off *his* taste, not Amalia's. The Lincoln Center with its operas and the Philharmonic, they were the right venue for culture. There was nothing grand or heroic about the scale of an overwrought amateur night! That a storm might frustrate this opportunity added to the possibility of Brewster's pranks and put Augustus in a foul mood.

In addition to the Mozart Concerto, the orchestra would afterward break up into smaller chamber groups of various configurations to entertain the guests. Those who were not playing, at any given time, could exercise the democratic freedoms bestowed by the egalitarian

The Womb of Uncreated Night

Mrs. Wainwright. The well-known "original instrument" scholar and conductor, Christian Hogwash, had been engaged to conduct from the harpsichord. The orchestra would perform on "original" instruments. Actually, these were carefully reconstructed instruments following documented and surviving models. But Miami, following common practice, would play a modern clarinet.

On one side of the gallery, places had been set for 17 musicians: 4 violins, 2 violas, 2 violoncellos, double bass, pairs of flutes, oboes, bassoons, and horns, stands and music arranged around the harpsichord. The soloist, of course, was expected to play from memory. Some of the instruments lay on the chairs or, as in the case of the 'cellos and bass, leaned against the pillars at either end of the balcony. Seeing the vacant balcony, Augustus turned to his wife, frowning.

"Where are the musicians? Why aren't they fiddling or tootling?" The musicians, in fact, had mingled with the Young Artists, eating, and chatting about youthful aspirations. When Augustus had first heard that the evening's concert was to be performed in period style, he was pleased, thinking that, as in the historical period when aristocrats treated musicians as menials, they would be dressed in livery and perhaps sporting powdered wigs. Amalia, mindful of his repressive mindset, had stipulated they should mingle with the other *guests*.

"Why, Augustus, they get hungry just like everyone else. Don't you think it creates an amiable atmosphere? Come and meet them." Taking his arm, she tried to urge him into the ballroom.

Nick was backed into a corner by Miami near the staircase leading up to the gallery with his clarinet, stoutly resisting conversion to "original instrument performance."

"Isn't it incongruous," said Nick, "to perform the concerto on a modern instrument accompanied by so-called original instruments? Why not compromise on an orchestra of modern instruments?"

"Christian doesn't compromise," retorted Miami.

Nick smirked and pointed at the clarinet. "Isn't 'original instrument performance' where purists play old music out of tune? Sort of like creationists opposing evolution, isn't it?" Miami's mouth dropped open, but before he could retort Nick went on. "I remember a recording of an 'original instrument' performance of Handel's *Royal Fireworks Music* where the intonation was so bad I wondered if it was some kind of joke. You're only going along with a fashionable trend. As for Hogwash not compromising, why aren't you going to play the Mozart on a basset clarinet, which is more like the one he originally composed it for? After all, the range of the modern clarinet in A—you're not playing a Bb instrument, are you?—can't play the lowest four notes of the 'original.' The version you'll play on that thing you're waving around is bound to have had whole passages transposed and rewritten by some hack."

"No one knows for sure," retorted Miami with the exaggerated patience an adult uses to explain a difficult concept to a child, "exactly what kind of clarinet the concerto was written for. We don't have Mozart's autograph score. Basset clarinets are rare and hard to come by, while the modern instrument is readily available. Should his music for clarinet not be played because your ears are still stuck in the period when 'original' instruments meant limited technique and bad intonation? Besides, no one in the know uses 'original instrument performance' any more. The preferred term is 'authentic performance.'"

"Or just plain 'period instruments.' Didn't I hear something about Hogwash having a clarinet constructed along the line of instruments Mozart's clarinetist, Stadler, was familiar with?" Nick shot back, brushing aside the revised name-tag.

"Yes, a type of basset clarinet. But it wasn't available. There was some problem with it, something to do with the size of the tone holes and the way the keys worked. It couldn't be corrected in time for tonight's performance. It's not exactly the kind of instrument everyone is familiar with. Besides, substitutions are consistent with performance practices in the eighteenth and early nineteenth centuries. They don't make the performance any the less authentic—*valid*!" he corrected hastily before Nick could jump on the outmoded term. The other musicians had begun climbing the stairs to the gallery and Miami seized the opportunity to cut off further debate. "You know," he said, as he started up after them, "you're the worst kind of purist after all."

The thunder rumbled nearer. The first scattered drops of rain fell with a splatter like Amalia's scattered efforts to get Augustus to mingle.

"This is all Brewster's doing," Augustus grumbled. "And yours. The two of you may play host and hostess. But as for me . . ." He pulled away abruptly and retired to his study, shaking his head when Amalia chided him for his bad manners. She smiled and went into the hall to join Brewster's guests.

Several of the Young Artists Group regulars clustered around Dr. Korngold and Mme Villiards. Hogwash, himself, had joined them briefly to exchange pleasantries before going up to join his musicians.

Mme Villiards made a special point of drawing Mrs. Wainwright's attention to Gaby, looking radiant as she stood next to her husband. She tried to submerge the irony she felt as she introduced, "The inspired artist who had created 'A New York Minute,'" in admiration for Gaby, and in pride that it had been unveiled at a meeting of the Young Artists Group.

"Is this the young lady who has stirred up so much talk in the gallery circuit?" said Amalia. "How charming, my dear!"

Gaby beamed and tugged Ghee-Ghee into her glory, "And this is my husband and able assistant. Without his clever constructions, the 'Minute' and all its successes would never have happened." At this, Ghee-Ghee, who towered elegantly above his dainty wife, preened in her aura, suavely fingering the cuff-links of the French cuffs on the shirt he habitually wore with his suit.

"Well, you're both to be congratulated," said Mrs. Wainwright warmly.

"Yes," added Brewster. "You've added art to the list of things that are collapsible and portable. A boon to traveling exhibitions! It puts me in mind of the first computers, room-filling vacuum tubes and circuitry which in one short generation were miniaturized onto microchips. And now, everyone has a personal computer. Just think of the possibilities of miniaturizing an art installation that everyone could have!"

Ghee-Ghee continued to smile, but his eyes hardened.

Det. Lapels, had come at Brewster's invitation. He suspected that he was being set up. But he was off duty and could not resist a big bash and free booze. And there was the possibility that Brewster might somehow give himself away and then—*got'im!* When Brewster jovially introduced him to Korngold as "Police Commissioner Gordon," Lapels knew that he was the butt of some joke. Like everybody else at the Precinct, he knew something about Batman movies and heard rumors of someone masquerading as the "caped crusader." But not being a Batman fan, he had no clear idea about the role he was supposed to play. Seeing his puzzlement, Korngold chuckled, shook his hand, and breathed a congratulatory, "Of course you are!"

With "the Commissioner" reluctantly drawn into the circle, conversation soon turned to the "vampire" attacks and the activities of the "Batman." Hogwash excused himself and climbed the stairs to the gallery. The musicians, who had been warming up with a cacophony of snatches from the concerto, fell silent as Hogwash at the harpsichord and oboist traded *A*'s for them to tune to. The drone of the musicians as they began to tune their instruments was occasionally absorbed by the thunder echoing through the ballroom. As the rain fell steadily with a long drawn out hiss in the garden, the rumbling eased and the musicians began the first movement of the Mozart.

"Tell me, er—Mr. Gordon?" snickered Ghee-Ghee, wondering if he might have had more fun addressing him as *Commissioner*, "what's your take on 'Batman'?"

Lapels found himself in an exquisite muddle. Was this guy playing along with Brewster's joke, or was he just a twit? Should he make a snappy comeback or piss all over him? Feeling foolish, he did not want to give himself away. Should he play it straight, pretending to go along with a gag he did not get, or act like a clown pretending not to know how foolish he was being made to feel? While he was debating the niceties of his situation, the clarinet took up the First Subject of the concerto.

"Whoever the guy is," Lapels said sourly, "he's breaking the law."

"But aren't citizens supposed to aid the police in apprehending lawbreakers?" asked Brewster wide-eyed.

"No one asked him," said the detective.

"He hasn't harmed anyone, has he?"

"Maybe he has, maybe he hasn't," snapped Lapels. "So far, there's no evidence that he has. Doesn't mean he hasn't. Like lovers who quarrel and one of them disappears," he added pointedly. "The law moves on evidence."

"Or suspicion," said Korngold. He was listening to "Commissioner Gordon," but closely observing Brewster. He was still uneasy about the possibility that he might have been infected by the virus. "There are so many day-to-day situations that might arouse suspicion, it's difficult to know at what point intervention is warranted."

"So you think it's okay if a citizen decides to take the law into his own hands 'just in case'?" shot back Lapels.

"That's not what I said. I was merely observing that our society has become so complex that violations of citizens' rights are endemic. It creates an atmosphere of doubt and suspicion, in which people—police *are* people, aren't they?—act inappropriately."

"Yeah, but police are trained professionals and know how to spot troublemakers." Korngold turned away with a smile. Ghee-Ghee guffawed. "Okay, okay!" added the detective. "So they make mistakes. Like you said, doc, we're people, too. You ever make a mistake with your patients?"

As the players of the concerto, who Nick thought he alone had been listening seriously to, reached the haunting second movement, an uneasy silence fell over the group. Nick, in spite of the contempt he had expressed to Miami, felt that the balance of modern clarinet and "original instruments" was coming off rather well. He was so carried away by the music that, as he felt his scalp crawl and his hair rise, he thought that the others too had fallen under the spell of the music. They looked around uneasily at each other. A flash of lightning crackled in the garden, setting off a clap of thunder. The lights flickered and went out. The musicians, who had up to then seemed oblivious to the storm, stopped playing. Muffled alarm gave way to excited murmuring.

"It's the Unidentified Floating Head!" said Arpie in awe.

Sparks danced through the room. A mysterious glow floated along just above the balustrade of the gallery opposite the orchestra and vanished in another flash of lightning followed by another thunderclap.

When the lights came back on, the musicians, after some whispered instructions from Hogwash, resumed playing the second movement.

Arpie insisted that he had seen the Unidentified Floating Head of the Ramble. Several others agreed.

"Commissioner Gordon" ventured drily that the lady who had perpetrated the hoax in Central Park had been released after the incident, but had been referred to Bellevue after trying the stunt again. She was being detained for observation and consequently was, regrettably, unable to put in an appearance.

"But there's another one," persisted Arpie, lowering his voice conspiratorially, "the original. That mysterious woman who's been haunting the Ramble recently."

"No reliable witness has come forward," said Lapels. "You've got nothing but hearsay, rumor, and maybe hysteria tossed in."

Unexpectedly, Korngold agreed. "Where is she, then? There's nobody up there," he said, indicating the gallery where "she" had been seen.

"She could've ducked out while we were blinded by the lightning," objected Arpie.

Ghee-Ghee chuckled. "Or perhaps it was a hoax perpetrated by someone," he said with a sidelong stage leer at Brewster, "who has the means and resources to play a holographic prank."

Several members of the group came to Brewster's defense. Nick expressed surprise that anyone would take Ghee-Ghee's farfetched conspiracy seriously when they could be listening to Mozart. Others were indignant at the thought that anyone in their circle could be capable of such a stunt. The disbelieving look Brewster had fixed on Ghee-Ghee only inspired him to heap on further innuendos. Mme Villiards thought that overnight success had made Ghee-Ghee ungracious. She inwardly dismissed the preposterous insinuation, yet, like many reasonable people who get caught up in absurdity, she could not help trying to make sense out of something that was really senseless.

"But what possible motive could anyone have for such a vulgar prank?" she protested rhetorically.

Still basking in afterglow, Ghee-Ghee was unable to resist one more shot at Brewster. In the rapt attention of the group, Ghee-Ghee could not hold back. "Guilty conscience over complicity in the loss of a loved one? They say grief like that can drive even rational people to extremes."

Mme V now stared at him in disbelief. "Not only grief," she said.

Brewster stiffened and looked about to lunge at him. Mrs. Wainwright hastily interposed herself in front of him. She fixed him with a stern look. Then she turned to Ghee-Ghee, smiled sweetly and took him by the arm. "Wouldn't you like something to drink? To celebrate," she said as she led him to the bar.

Korngold, too, had tensed. The other members of the group looked on, startled into immobility. For a few minutes, the spell of Mozart seemed to have oiled the troubled surface. Finally, thought Nick, they're actually *listening*! But unreason teases insidiously at the most tranquil mind.

"And how could he have timed the event with the storm?" wondered Mme V aloud, as if no time had passed since Ghee-Ghee had spoken. Escaping from Mrs. Wainwright and returning drink in hand, Ghee-Ghee shrugged.

"A combination of weather forecast—"

"Weather forecasts being so reliable," broke in Dr. Korngold, who had been uncharacteristically silent as he studied Brewster's reaction.

"—instruments that are capable of measuring electrostatic buildup, and serendipity," Ghee-Ghee went on. "In very poor taste."

"Unless," said Korngold, "unless of course, the whole thing was merely some atmospheric effect—ball lightning, for instance. That combined with the natural anxiety induced by the storm may have led the more imaginative among us," he avoided Arpie's petulant face, "to imagine the Unidentified Floating Head."

The performance ended, unnoticed at first because almost everyone below the gallery had clustered around to hear Korngold's explanation. After an awkward silence, they applauded the musicians all the more enthusiastically.

When Miami came downstairs, Nick congratulated him on his performance, then added that despite his initial fear that the horns might overbalance the other players in such a small ensemble, he was impressed at how well they had been kept in check and added just the right weight to the tuttis. That was more important than phony concerns about "authenticity."

"To be fair," Nick said to Miami, "you played the concerto beautifully. There was a special eloquence to the Adagio. The piece hardly called for the big sonorities modern instruments are capable of. But the mellow quietude you were able to give it—Stadler couldn't've done it better. Maybe," added Nick, unable to resist, "the contrast between the brilliance of the modern clarinet and the astringent sound of the older instruments set you off too prominently and occasionally offset the balance in the outer movements?"

And they were off again. They argued about everything, each trying to outdo the other on "authentic performances," the virtues of modern instruments, the pointlessness of recreating what could only be guessed at, while the others were still preoccupied with the UFH.

After the rowdy interruption of the storm and the conclusion of the Mozart concerto, the guests drifted into small clutches of shared interests. The musicians were mingling with the others as they sampled the buffet. A young composer hungry for a performance of his music accosting a violinist, a cellist enduring another who wanted to form a small ensemble to play his work, the musicians nodding tolerantly. As

The Womb of Uncreated Night

long as there was something to eat and drink before they were expected to play again. Something light. Maybe some jazz.

While this one-sided bargaining played out, Lapels battened on Dr. Korngold who was looking around the ballroom like someone who wants to be elsewhere.

"You weren't going to leave us already, were you?" said Lapels. "Join me in another drink."

"I think I've had my limit," said Korngold. Then looked closely at the detective, thinking, *And maybe you have, too.*

"So what you think of the vampire attacking people in the park?" Lapels' eyes had begun to glaze, and his words slightly slurred. "Think he's some *psycho*? Like maybe it's this 'Batman' creep."

Korngold shrugged. Might as well try to reason with a "psycho" as someone who's had too much to drink. But even someone who is tipsy might benefit from therapy. "As a scientist," he smiled, "I'd object to the derogatory use of 'psycho' almost as much as the term 'vampire' in any sense but the literary."

"Implying that you'd rather believe in this Batman fella than the vampire?" put in Ghee-Ghee, who had been hanging back.

"Perhaps that's because I have no idea who the 'vampire' really is."

Ghee-Ghee arched his eyebrow skeptically. "Are you saying that you actually know who the 'Batman' is?" he said astonished.

"Why, yes," said Korngold, turning on Ghee-Ghee the same smile he had bestowed on Lapels. "As a matter of fact, I know all about him." Brewster's dismay competed with Ghee-Ghee's surprise.

"Well?" said Ghee-Ghee and Lapels simultaneously.

"He's—" Korngold cast a mischievous wink at Brewster—"he's Bruce Wayne!" Ghee-Ghee and Lapels groaned simultaneously. Korngold only laughed.

"Who the hell is Bruce Wayne?" demanded Lapels, at which Korngold laughed all the harder and was joined by Brewster and Ghee-Ghee.

"As for the 'vampire,'" Korngold added, "he, she, or even they—yes, there may be more than one—are probably suffering from a disease like porphyria. Of course, there are also these vampire cults in which disaffected young people with the means and the cool to play at Goth thumb their noses at the mainstream. Who knows when their 'play' may not have turned dangerous? Like subway surfing," he said, looking again at Brewster.

"Well," said Ghee-Ghee, "there are rumors that Batman is the Phantom Subway Surfer." He turned to Lapels. "Why aren't the police doing anything about *him*?"

"The police can't be everywhere at once, y'know!" groused Lapels.

"Yes," said Brewster, relishing the moment, "that's why you need an occasional vigilante!"

"Don't you think you've had enough?" said Korngold as Lapels was about to have another drink.

"Besides, this Batman," said Lapels, oblivious to Korngold's concern, "he's turned into some folk-hero. Citizens boo the police when they try to nab him."

A bass player, a violinist, and one of the cellists at the harpsichord had begun jazz improvisations on popular ballads. An all-night party got under way.

Korngold sought out Mrs. Wainwright who had been catching up with Mme Villiards. "It's getting very late," he said, "and I really must go. This has been a great evening. You've really put the Young Artists Group on the map," he said. He took his leave from the little circle gathered around him. "Brewster, I'll see you tomorrow afternoon. Good night."

As soon as he stepped out into the street, Korngold did not feel as triumphantly secure as he had let on. The storm had passed, the sky had cleared, a scent of moisture in the cool air should have been refreshing after the stuffiness of the ballroom. Yet an unaccountable uneasiness clotted the badinage of the soirée as he crossed Fifth Avenue and entered the park at the Inventor's Gate at 72nd Street. He strolled aimlessly down

Pilgrim Hill, skirted the Conservatory Water, and paused a moment at the Lewis Carroll statue to recollect the *New Yorker* cartoon of a father and his little girl standing in front of Alice and her Wonderland companions. The little girl wore an evil smirk, while her father glared down at her, "No, she isn't some kind of a nut! *You're* some kind of a nut!"

As he walked back along the path that would lead through the Trifoil Arch to the Old Boathouse, he could not help smiling at his own unwillingness to believe anything Brewster told him. In a role reversal, the child would tell the father that *he* was the nut who could not believe in fantasy. Following the path along the Lake with the Loeb Boathouse on his left and the eerie emptiness of the parking lot on his right, an odd sense of dislocation swept over him. What was it? a piece of loneliness torn loose from the cult of companionship? He soon found himself walking through the badly lit paths of the Ramble. He began to have the unsettling feeling that he was being watched. The sounds of the city sifted through the trees and settled in an eerie hush over the ground. When he came to the Point across from the Bethesda Terrace, its angel brought him back to himself. He retraced his steps back to Fifth Avenue and up to 78th Street and across those long blocks to Madison, Park, Lexington, and finally, Third.

By the time he reached his apartment, it was long past midnight. He felt so out of sorts that he went directly to his office. His terrier, Pascal, was in his usual non-pensive mode and set up a racket that threatened to wake up Sydney until he admitted him to the office and sternly shushed him. He was riffling through Wagehalsen's journal, with Pascal contentedly curled up at his feet under the kneehole, when the dog suddenly sprang out, barking furiously, and rushed at a window . . .

Interlude

Korngold sat at the desk in his office, sailing through the siren song of myth and mysticism in the arcane literature that lined the bookcases behind him, securely lashed to reason by scholarship and science without risk from the reefs of the supernatural, as contentedly as Pascal at his feet, the smoke of fragrant tobacco from his favorite briar curling up to the ceiling . . . A passing interest in sheng fui led him to set the desk at a right angle to the two large windows looking out at and past the tall apartment and office buildings across 78th Street, and down over the roofs of nearby rowhouses. In the distance, through the gaps between the buildings, the lights atop the cables of the Triboro Bridge spanning the East River hovered above the headlights of motor vehicles intermittently blinking as they swept across to the FDR Drive or disappeared into the maze of Queens. An occasional scow, all shadow and running lights, blared a warning as it inched upstream toward Ward's Island. The city's lights scattered through the dark background—like glowing eyes in the night.

Poking restlessly through the papers on his desk after the unsettling walk through the Ramble, he had come upon the journal Buckyballs had lent him. Its fragile, blotched pages had gripped and disturbed him. As he picked it up and began to read, he felt again that he was being watched. He looked up and was startled by two red eyes that appeared suddenly among the city lights. He jumped violently back from the desk, upsetting his chair. A hand reached into the light shining through the window, tapped politely at the pane, then saluted him, touching the rim of a top hat on a head lost in the reflected light of the room. Pascal leaped at the window barking furiously. A face—ghastly pale, but oddly wavering, brooding—a bitter, rueful mouth from which a wan smile slipped forlornly into its corners— and the outline of a body moved into the light and settled on the sill.

Korngold was startled as much by this man's—was it human?— singular appearance as the improbability that anyone should be sitting on a narrow ledge 300 feet above the street with no visible means of support, not

The Womb of Uncreated Night

to say how he might have got there in the first place. The recollection of the discussion about a holographic projection struck him as absurd then as it had in the mansion. But absurd ideas sometimes have a way of sticking in the mind. Who could possibly engineer such things? Some deranged window washer playing some sort of prank, perhaps? Maybe, thought Korngold, I had too much to drink at the soirée.

The man's skin—if man it was—was so wrinkled that at first glance Korngold thought he must be impossibly old. Then, peering through his shock at this absurd apparition draped in cape and opera hat reclining nonchalantly on the window sill, Korngold saw that the network of arteries, veins, and capillaries normally obscured by the epidermis stood out clearly, webbed the surface of its face and hands and gave it the puckered look of someone who has sat in the bath too long. It had the unsettling appearance of an old man's skin fitted grotesquely on a handsome young man's face, as if some demented tailor had fitted it with a suit of skin several sizes too big for his customer's skeleton, then shrunk it to his frame. His head, a halo of darkness washed over the face in mirage-like waves as available light was drawn into it. The features of the face enigmatically blurred and refocused, as if a photographer constantly adjusted a lens. The room spun around Korngold, and the city streets, ablaze with lights a moment before, faded and grew bright again.

Korngold came to himself, picked up the terrier, still barking and snarling furiously, put him out of the room, then turned at the closed door to look again at this unlikely fluttering phantasm just outside his window. An illusion that he saw but spooked the dog? Nonsense! His agitation at an illusion conjured up out of fatigue and reflections in the window, that's what upset Pascal. Yet the image persisted. After a few moments more of perplexity, he strode quickly across the room and threw open the sash to dispel this illusion caused by some trick of light or sooty air on the window pane. He was disconcerted to find that the image was even more palpable, that it smiled more broadly, and addressed him by name.

"Good evening, Dr. Korngold," said the Apparition.

"Who . . . who are you?" marveled Korngold, disconcerted that something so unlikely could speak to him so clearly. "What are you?" It was one thing to hear one's own thoughts as if they were voices in his head. It was quite another to see the speaker. While he was puzzling about it, the eyes of the Apparition darting around the den came to rest on the shelf holding Bram Stoker's novel.

"Perhaps it would be simplest to think of me as the spirit of Count Dracula, eh? I knew him, you know."

"Count Dracula! Is this a joke?" If one's mind can play tricks, why not a joke?

"Well, perhaps only a protégé of that great man. Permit me to introduce myself. Actually, my name is Heinrich Wolfgang von Wagehalsen."

"Wagehalsen, eh?" Aha! thought Korngold, I have you now. Mind games! At this hour of the night, I seem to be as open to wacky ideas as sound ones. "Why are you risking your neck up here? And why should I think of you as Count Dracula?" The obvious answer, that both were figments of imagination, was too simple and straightforward for such a bizarre situation.

"A whimsical subterfuge. I was sure that you knew the name of Dracula. Whereas my own name—"

"Your own name is as phony as you are. I don't doubt your identity. Only my sanity."

"Do you doubt the reality of your own senses?"

"My senses are real enough. But their perceptions may not be. I've just returned from a late-night party and may be suffering from dyspepsia. I expect you'll next untie a handkerchief from around your head and drop your jaw in some ghastly way."

"Alas, Herr Doktor, as you can see," he said doffing his hat, "my head is without handkerchief! But how droll to think of me as Marley's ghost! And you, then, are like Scrooge—or perhaps you have the guilty conscience of a Scrooge? Well, then! Take my hand and we will fly high above the city beyond the reach of conscience . . ."

Korngold drew back.

"Tell me," continued Wagehalsen. Since you don't believe in me, why did you bother to open the sash?"

"*I was trying to determine whether you were some odd reflection in the window or if you—or something—was really there.*"

"*And—was I there?*" chuckled Wagehalsen.

"*You're only a projection of my own imagination.*"

"*But imagination is everything! Surely an alienist knows that even hallucinations are real in the sense that they exist in the time and the space of the mind? So . . . May I come in . . . for a drink, perhaps?*"

"*Ah, the threshold! Dracula can't cross it unless he's invited in?*"

"*Come now, Herr Doktor. You know that is not true. Dracula could turn himself into a mist and drift through keyholes and cracks under doors! One does not require permission when one has the ability to do as one pleases. But to observe the niceties of hospitality, that is no more than common courtesy.*"

"*Courtesy!*" laughed Korngold. "*How courteous to ask your victims if you may bite them on the neck and drink their blood!*"

"*Oh,*" sighed Wagehalsen, "*only a little sip now and then. Like friends who share a bottle of wine. But as to the invitation, what is a little invitation, after all,*" he wheedled, "*but a means of overcoming social distance? Mere formalities! We harbor many things in our minds that our mouths deny.*"

Korngold was set back by this insight but smiled cynically. "*Forgive me for being inhospitable, but no. Bad enough to imagine you out there. You seem to be in no danger of falling, which, believe me, if I were in full possession of my faculties you would be doing. Besides, if you have the power to hover out there on your own, a little thing like my refusal shouldn't be much of a barrier.*"

Wagehalsen shrugged. "*Some denials are more formidable than others. But acceptance,*" he said, "*is a form of invitation, is it not? Denial, even retreat is a kind of acquiescence, whether it originates in fear or overt welcome. One does not bother to deny or refuse what does not exist.*"

Korngold leaned forward, thrusting his face closer to the apparition's, bemused by the circularity of denying what he denied was real. All the while, Wagehalsen perched nonchalantly on the window sill, oblivious to the height and the consternation of his unwilling host. Like many older

New York apartments, the windows of the apartment were deep enough so that Korngold's mind, at least the imaginative part, had enough space on the ledge to share with the Apparition.

And Wagehalsen, apparently, was going to stay there for as long as it took to sort him out. After the silent confrontation had gone on for some time, Korngold hoping that the Apparition would vanish, the Apparition awaiting its summons, Wagehalsen spoke.

"You know, as well as I, Herr Doktor, "that as long as you keep me out here, I am really already in there."

Korngold recognized the inescapable logic of the situation. "Yes. That's a conundrum, isn't it? It's the old ontological argument that the ability to conceive of a thing must imply its existence outside of the human mind. Philosophers since the seventeenth century have squabbled almost as much over that idea as pro-lifers over exactly when life begins. Pro-lifers, at least, haven't gone so far as to claim that life begins with the gleam in a man's eye. Not yet, anyway.

"At what point in imagination does the real begin?" he continued, musing aloud to himself. He could not have felt woozier if he had actually been sitting out there on the ledge. Imagining this thing out there placed it in here as well! It was a precarious place to be. And a long way down.

His professional position, which he considered essential to all psychiatrists, had been that of all the scientists who have to face a world of indeterminacy and chaos, only the psychiatrist clings to the certainty that he knows the difference between what is real and what is not. Under the circumstances, that idea rebounded ironically. He had considered himself "open" to the inexplicable, willing to entertain the exotic and even the supernatural for what it may have to teach him. Science and reason made him immune to the effects of wild imaginings—he could learn from others' delusions, even enjoy them to a certain extent, as long as he did not succumb to them. Yet here he was with this! Whatever he might yet learn from it, he certainly wasn't enjoying it.

The fantasies and delusions of his patients were for him a laboratory in which to study. He accepted them as "real" to the extent that his patients

The Womb of Uncreated Night

accepted them as real. He did not judge them. He was more concerned with the effect of imaginary symptoms on his patients than with the reality of their imaginings. No one could deny that the effects were real, no matter what bizarre form their imaginings might take. A patient presenting with hallucinations would of course be taken seriously by any competent therapist. He would probe the source of the disturbance until he found a way to integrate it with their existential selves, even if that meant entering into their delusional world in a search for internal flaws. He would then find a way to draw them to the attention of the patient and let the person's own internal rationalizations undo the fantasies. Sometimes, irrationality was self-correcting, persisting in its hold on the imagination in spite of contradiction or apparent impossibility. In such resistant cases, he conceded that nothing could be done and reluctantly dismissed them as "incurable."

It came, therefore, as an immense surprise to him when he confronted Wagehalsen outside his office window. He at last faced two unacceptable possibilities: either a vampire really existed outside of the fantastic inventions of the ignorant, the superstitious, the mentally unbalanced, or that his own mind had, in some way he was unwilling to admit, harbored its own phantoms. He desperately sought some flaw in the manifestation of the apparition before him in order to believe or disbelieve.

He shook his head vigorously to dispel the problem. When he looked again, the image slowly faded . . .

Part Two

23.

As Brewster stepped out of the elevator on the thirtieth floor into what should have been the familiar hallway leading to Dr. Korngold's office, he felt a peculiar sense of dislocation. At first he thought he must have gotten off at the wrong floor. The hallway was bare of furniture or ornament, but always had been. Wall sconces lit it well and sunlight streamed in through the window at the far end. The carpet was the expected dingy red. Faint cracks in the nondescript beige walls were beginning to betray typical shoddy high-rise construction. The ceiling was the usual white plaster. What could be wrong? Holding the elevator door with his hand, he ducked his head back inside the car and glanced up at the floor indicator above the opening. All the numbers were dark. The light must have gone out. The absence of the indicator light must have worked its way into his subconscious, he reasoned, and skewed his perception. Then, when he got off the elevator, it triggered this sense of alienation. Funny how such a trivial thing could send shivers down your back. He would report it to Korngold, who would notify the super, the light would be fixed, and the shivers would be gone. In the meantime, the number on the door to his left was reassuringly 30B.

Brewster entered the foyer which served as waiting room. The inner door to Korngold's office was ajar, and he could hear a tenor singing in German. He recognized the music as Schubert's, but the words were indistinct and he was unable to identify it. He knocked, but hearing no response, stuck his head through the doorway, rapping again. Korngold was seated at his desk with his back to the door, a shadow against a window.

"Dr. Korngold?" No response. Brewster spoke again. This time, a subtle tremor passed through the outline of the shadow. Without moving away from the window, the shadow responded.

"Yes, Brewster. Come in," said the therapist's voice to the window. The sense of dislocation came over Brewster again. Could the malfunctioning elevator floor indicator have created an aura of malaise so subtle yet so pervasive as to be projected into someone's tone of voice? Brewster pushed the door open all the way and stood in the opening. Korngold finally turned to him. "Come in." There was something hesitant in the way he said it. His face haloed with shadow, a little incidental light dimly smudging it. Like a blackboard hastily erased, thought Brewster as he settled himself ergonomically, expectantly. Korngold still hesitated at the window, as if uncertain how to begin some new therapeutic approach. Instead, "Excuse me a moment," he said, turned abruptly and left the room by a door leading to the living quarters.

Drawn by the music to the stereo behind Korngold's desk, Brewster got up and picked out the album notes from the CD's jewel case. It was a recording of the Goethe-Lieder by Peter Schreier. The tenor had just begun "*Der Fischer.*"

> Das Wasser rauscht', das Wasser schwoll . . .
> The water rushed, the water swelled . . .

A fisherman sits on the seashore, calmly contemplating his fishing rod, unmindful of the rising tide around him. A mermaid rises out of the waters and reproaches him for using human wiles to lure unsuspecting creatures from their cozy element.

"Do not the sun and moon delight in bathing in the sea?" she asks. If only he knew how blissful life was down there, he would dive in and join it.

The Womb of Uncreated Night

Brewster knew the poem and did not need to read further, how the mermaid beguiled the fisherman in peril of the sea. He smiled at the mermaid's plaint. Who was luring whom? Literature is full of treachery overlain with beauty, sirens and mermaids who lure men to their destruction. But in Goethe, there is a curious balance between this other-worldly menace and the human unconscious. As if the mermaid were a projection of the man's own perception of the sea, she speaks to him, she sings to him. Half she pulls him, half he sinks; never wholly the one or the other. If earlier poets shared with mariners the superstition that Nature wove spells to tease unwary humans out of reason, tempting them to unforeseen dangers, Goethe's ballad does not seem sinister. Even the half-aggressive ending makes the fisherman a willing victim. And Schubert's music blithely daps along.

Leaving the fisherman to his fate, Brewster wandered around the room scanning the books on the shelves which honeycombed it. Near the door through which Korngold had left the room, he found the usual technical manuals on abnormal behaviors, the *DSM-IV*, classic studies of Freud, Jung, Adler, Brill, Lindner's *The Fifty-Minute Hour* . . .

In his haste, Korngold had left the door to the adjoining room open a crack. Brewster heard low agitated voices. He recognized the voice of Dr. Korngold. The other was a woman's. Mrs. Korngold—? He paused for a moment to contemplate the window brilliantly ballooning in afternoon glow. Schubert's song ended, as if it would swallow up the blazing heat in its cool depths.

. . . The voices from the next room faded in and out of Brewster's awareness between the bindings of the books. The voices were heated, but the words were indistinct, the woman's tone accusatory . . . half a shelf devoted to chaos theory . . . angry, Dr. Korngold's apologetic . . . another shelf-and-a-half to the social history and legends of the nineteenth century . . . placating. Commentaries on the Arthurian legends, the works of Chrétien de Troyes, Robert de Baron, Wolfram von Eschenback, and Thomas Malory. Curiously abutting these, vampires and vampirism, at the end of which stood Bram Stoker's *Dracula*.

As the voices dropped to a barely audible murmur, Brewster turned his head to contemplate Korngold's desk. Except for a blank legal pad and pen, the pipe rack and pipes he was always fiddling with, the ash tray into which a bowlful of burnt tobacco had been emptied, and a box of tissues for the lachrymose, it was free of clutter, the kind of workspace one keeps not so much for the sake of neatness, but to prevent compromising matter to straying eyes. One other item caught his eye. A tattered journal. Its yellowed pages lay open. Some were stained in places with faint brown blotches. Reflexively, Brewster skimmed the pages where they lay. Despite faded ink and occasional illegible bits, he made out the neatly handwritten German text, turning the pages with growing interest. The voices in the other room faded away entirely . . .

The Wagehalsens of Weimar claimed descent from a bastard son of Bernhard of Saxe-Weimar and the Ernestine branch of the Wettin dynasty in the Thuringian territories of central Germany. Bernhard was duke of Weimar, Protestant hero of the Thirty Years War. The Wagehalsens' bastard, one Friedrich Bernhard, was supposedly sired in the duchy of Franconia in southern Germany, one of the newly created bishoprics of Würzburg and Bamberg in 1633 during the Swedish phase of the war. Franconia had in fact preexisted as one of the five stem duchies of medieval Germany, but this rearrangement gave the Swedes a way of rewarding Bernhard for his services against the Holy Roman Empire. He did not enjoy his trophy for long. The new Franconia was reabsorbed into the old Franconia when his army came to grief with the imperial forces at Nördlingen shortly after. Easy come, easy go. Thus the son who was not a son was born in a duchy that was not a duchy, and lost in the endless divisions, subdivisions, and re-divisions of Thuringia among the legitimate Wettin heirs, the sons of Friedrich II, Albert and Ernst.

The Womb of Uncreated Night

The duchies of Saxe-Altenburg, Saxe-Coburg, Saxe-Eisenach, Saxe-Gotha, Saxe-Meiningen, and Saxe-Weimar which eventually became Saxe-Weimar-Eisenach shifted from one line to the other as one or the other failed to produce a male heir. As a result, the line of Friedrich Bernhard became so obscure that the Wagehalsens could not even agree on whether he had been born in Würzburg or Bamberg, eventually leading to a collateral split between the Würzburger and the Bamberger branches. Neither branch actually lived in either of those Bishoprics, their supposed patriarch presumably having made his way to Weimar during the final, French phase of the war. Family rumor had it that he had fled southern Germany in order to escape the fighting between the French and Swedes on one side and the imperial armies on the other. But as he would have been only fourteen when the Peace of Westphalia was signed in 1648, no one really cared.

How the bastard Wagehalsens managed to root their family tree in such shifty ground is a marvel of tenacity. Although they were roundly snubbed by the legitimate Wettins, both branches of Wagehalsens tried to exploit the gaps left by the failure of male heirs in the Wettin line through the Salic law of succession in order to validate their illegitimate place in it. They were fiercely proud of it. So proud were they of the legitimacy of their illegitimacy that they constantly clarified their claims by thinning the overgrown branches of the family tree with judicious pruning of "deadwood." When they were not at each others' throats or eliminating superfluous heirs by sending them into the military or the clergy, the survivors enhanced their pretensions by naming themselves after established descendants of the Wettin line. The redundancy of Ernsts, Alberts, Friedrichs, Bernhards, Wilhelms, running to as many as eleven or twelve in some cases, and paraded among the Wagehalsens in such combinations as Ernst Bernhard, Friedrich Albert, Johann Friedrich, Friedrich Wilhelm, etc., privately irked members of the legitimate lines, whose refusal to recognize the dubious claims even by denying them, only encouraged their persistence.

Eventually, the Bamberger Wagehalsen line failed to produce

an heir in 1741, so the game was resolved by default in favor of the Würzburgers. Whether the legitimate Wettin heirs subsequently bought them off with land just to shut them up, or they simply overwhelmed opposition with their progeny—they certainly were a fecund lot—the Würzburgers contented themselves with their newly acquired land holdings and settled into complacent, but wealthy, insignificance. Along with their comfortable social niche, they also picked up Pietist beliefs, which favored direct, personal revelation through devout bible study over established church doctrine as the source of righteous living. What could be more revelatory than wealth? They did not care if they had become old-fashioned at the turn of the nineteenth century. Their righteousness was confirmed by their prosperity and energetically maintained through shrewd management. They also avoided the fragmentation that sapped the Wettin dynasty by sending off younger males into the army or the clergy instead of dividing up their lands among them.

The twelfth Friedrich von Wagehalsen, born in 1798, was an intense, romantic youth. As a child, his love of music was tolerated, even encouraged. But when he reached adolescence, his parents urged him to put away this childish interest. He soon got caught up in the intellectual ferment of the time, which in 1813 was hardly distinguishable from the political. Scarcely fifteen, he steeped himself in the patriotic poems and articles appearing in periodicals, mostly denunciations of that arch fiend, Napoleon. His father, Ernst Wilhelm, who had continued Wagehalsen prosperity under the Confederation of the Rhine, and was deeply concerned over its unraveling after Napoleon's disastrous invasion of Russia, disapproved of his son's patriotic fervor. He shared with Goethe and Hegel a suspicion that animosity toward Napoleon was an expression of mass mediocrity trying to bring down a great genius. Under Dowager Duchess Amalia and her son, Karl August, Weimar had become a famous cultural center, and the common people—landowners, local officials, merchants, even the peasantry—were more concerned that bringing down the French would disrupt local prosperity and the art, literature, and music that flourished.

The Wagehalsens especially felt that patriotism was all very well, but what of Christian living, the ethical pillar of economic and social stability? In this atmosphere, unchristian frivolity and mediocrity were frowned on. When Friedrich wanted to attend Heinrich Luden's suddenly popular course on the history of the German *Volk* at the University of Jena, his mother vehemently objected. She was not ready to let her son leave the sumptuous nest that had been built under righteousness for that sty of riotousness. She knew, indirectly of course, what kinds of goings-on he would be exposed to. Besides, she hoped that he could find favor at the court of the duke Karl August, perhaps even be taken under the wing of the great Goethe. If there were frivolity or riotousness at court, at least it was discreet, a far cry from the notoriety at Jena. The father hesitated, half in sympathy with his wife's misgivings. But the lord of the manor was inclined to indulge his son as much as to assert himself over his wife.

"Oh, let him try his wings." Ernst Wilhelm argued that the trip—only some thirty kilometers to the east, after all—was a way of giving the lad some experience of the world. A trusted servant would accompany him, and supervision by his cousin's family, the Ehrenhofs of Jena, would keep him out of serious mischief. Besides, though the idea verged on frivolity, real experience might reveal Luden's feet of clay to his son and eventually purge his youthful idealism.

And so Friedrich was packed off to Jena, accompanied by the son of one of the family's most trusted servants. Hans, hardly a year older than Friedrich, gave off an air of folk wisdom that could be mistaken for a maturity that reflected his father's trustworthiness. Never having been away from the Wagehalsen manor, much less charged with an important responsibility, wisdom and maturity had gone untested. Ernst Wilhelm and his wife could not have known that he was at heart a scheming adolescent only too eager to shuck off the stifling Pietism of the Wagehalsen manor. As Friedrich lay asleep in the room they shared at an inn midway through the journey, he abandoned his young master. He shrewdly left Friedrich enough money to complete his journey. Not out of any spirit of generosity or fellow feeling. He was counting on the boy's pride to go on alone, giving Hans plenty of time to evade pursuit. And he was sure Friedrich's cousins would eagerly assist the boy in order to put the Wagehalsens in their debt.

At the University, the lecture hall was so packed with students that Friedrich, who had arrived late, had to stand with others crowding the corridors. By arriving earlier on subsequent days, he was able to insinuate himself into the back of the hall and stood entranced by what he heard, ideas well nourished afterwards in beer halls with fellow students. Friedrich delayed the news of Hans's defection from reaching Weimar. He had the willing collusion of the Ehrenhofs, who hoped to oblige Ernst Wilhelm by sharing their home with Friedrich. Inevitably, news of Hans's defection reached Ernst Wilhelm from traveling acquaintances. Far from the gratitude which the Ehrenhofs had hoped to earn, he felt that they had betrayed his trust. At last he yielded to his wife's reproaches and summoned his Icarus home before the intoxicating licentiousness of Jena could melt his wings.

When he returned home before the end of the academic year, Friedrich was still so fired up over the mangled history, mysticism, and nationalism of *Volk* that he pleaded with his parents to allow him to join Adolf Freiherr von Lützow's volunteers gathering against Napoleon for the coming "War of Liberation." Had he not shown admirable initiative in coping with Hans's treachery and coming through the temptations of university life unscathed? Surely that more than made up for his trivial deception in not having informed them in a timely way. His parents were not entirely in agreement with their son's lofty defense of dishonesty. But they were genuinely alarmed at the turn of his eagerness to go off to war, to soar from one blazing sun to another. They flatly refused to let him go.

"Let him try his wings!" Frau Wagehalsen scolded. "Just see where he wants to fly!" With both parents firmly in opposition for once, the boy's hopes were quashed. Ernst Wilhelm sighed and silently bore his wife's rebukes, spoken and unspoken, for having opened the door to this idea, feeling that they were justified. Friedrich bore his disappointment at missing the Battle of the Nations at Leipzig, "only two days' journey"—80 kilometers away—on October 16-19, with less grace. Nor was it eased by the news of the terrible casualties which his mother kept throwing up to him.

The Altendorfs, who owned lands abutting the Wagehalsen estate, had an ancestry just as good as the Wagehalsens', though they were a bit miffed at being unable to claim a bastard as illustrious as a Wettin's. For their part, the Wagehalsens were always eager to extend their hold on the countryside. They readily agreed to a marriage of the Altendorf heiress, Sophie, to Friedrich. The contract had been arranged when she and Friedrich were children. The claim implied in the "von" of both the Wagehalsens and the Altendorfs would not hold up under close scrutiny, but each family thought that the other might validate their tenuous claim to nobility through the union. Uniting spurious claims gave them greater strength than either alone. And consolidating adjoining properties enhanced their value. So the bargain, concluded according to custom, was more property management than any regard for the feelings of the boy or his future bride. By the time Friedrich was old enough to have an inkling of what marriage would mean, he had been willing enough to accept the match as a dutiful son. But having been deprived of the "Battle of the Nations," he rebelled. Not because he had seen and found his bride-to-be physically repulsive—which he later found was quite the contrary—but rather out of sheer spite at having been cheated out of the glorious defeat of Napoleon.

Sophie, for her part, harbored antagonistic feelings of a different sort, though she was normally a docile, sweet-natured girl who accepted what her elders thought best. In an age when most girls were generally not well educated beyond instruction in domestic skills, she was uniquely privileged to have been tutored in languages and mathematics. As a little girl of five, it meant nothing to her that she had become engaged to the eight-year-old boy-next-door. The fact that "next door" was actually over the hills and several kilometers away and that she had never seen the boy fit neither the syllabus nor the syntax of her studies. So long as *engaged* was merely an abstract hypothesis, Sophie remained complacent.

Even in an upper class girl's life, unromantic reality eventually overtakes symbolic allusion, and casual chit-chat metamorphoses into duty. At first, only warm, fuzzy hints of what *marriage* meant filtered through the golden haze of girlhood. Visions of reenacting the public daily rituals of her mother and father did not alarm Sophie. Her idyllic childhood would just expand and grow socially, just as her body did, physically. Bit by indirect bit, her nanny pricked this juvenile smugness with increasingly graphic hints and suggestions. By the time Sophie was twelve, the hints had grown to grim awareness. She felt betrayed and indignant. No boy was ever going to do *that* to her.

Hormones have a way of changing a girl's outlook. A year later, the two families arranged for their children to meet. Though her mind was still shocked by her nurse's stories, her body was becoming curious. She had privately begun to be aware of feelings that she never would have admitted aloud. But what would this boy be like? Prepared for the worst, Sophie was brought into the great chamber where Friedrich, well turned out but sulky and scornful, and his parents sat in state, waiting to receive her and her parents, contracts in hand. When he saw Sophie, standing in dust-laden sunlight streaming through the tall windows, the parched air suddenly bloomed. He unfolded and throbbed, his inner harp plucked and strummed. He bit his lip and modestly folded his hands in front of his breeches. The effect on both was transformative, as if uncaged longings had leaped across the space between and reshaped them.

Had Napoleon not escaped from Elba and once again threatened Europe in 1815, they might have been married at once. But Friedrich, just turned seventeen and not sure that marriage to a pretty girl was worth giving up glory for, more confidently asserted himself. Any lust for Sophie at their first meeting was obscured by the memory of Luden's lectures and the legendary Black Troops of General Lützow that he had not been allowed to join in 1813. Smoldering patriotic embers stirred by the writings of Friedrich Ernst Schleiermacher, Ernst Moritz Arndt, and Friedrich Ludwig Jahn, now burst into flaming desire to show off for his lovely fiancée. What did it matter if visions of throwing off French oppression and setting up a new German nation were little more than a ballet of paramilitary drills, fake Teutonic symbols, and classical poses? There was a real fight brewing, and he would be in it. How glorious if he could fight for the Fatherland and return to his bride-to-be, victorious, to sire a new race of perfect beings who would forge a new state, a higher service worthy of the nobility and Protestant virtue!

His parents disapproved of this new rash of patriotism as vigorously as they had the old, but recognized that Friedrich at seventeen was not as easily denied as he had been two years earlier. He threatened to run away and join the army without their approval. By this time, too, anti-Napoleonic sentiment had slightly thawed the surface of glacial parental anxiety. Reluctantly, Friedrich's parents gave their consent, thinking it better that he leave with their blessing. They were more afraid that if he left without it and some great harm befell him, they could never forgive themselves. But they could not accept their son's romantic desire to serve as a common foot soldier. Ernst Wilhelm scoffed at the idea.

"You have no idea what you are about. Do you imagine that it will be some camping trip where everybody roughs it in good fellowship as a test of endurance against the elements? Aside from the discomforts and indignities of life in the field which are the lot of an ordinary soldier, you will also be exposed to increased dangers in battle, so much fodder for the front lines. You would be among the first to be wounded or killed. No! My son will not endure that. We will buy him a commission." Ernst Wilhelm assured his wife that a commission would minimize the risks to their son. He would hear no further protests. It was settled. Friedrich bent to his father's will. Besides, he rather fancied charging into the thick of the fray on a snorting stallion.

The Altenburgs thought the Wagehalsens were foolish to let their daughter's future ride into uncertainty. However much they admired youthful courage, they privately feared he would not come back and they would be unable to find another son-in-law as suitable. If Friedrich managed to survive, so much the better for both families. For Sophie, visions of matrimonial life were so much girlish anticipation. She liked Friedrich and looked forward to his company. But she also admired his fire, unaware of the kinds of burning that a soldier might endure on or off the battlefield.

No sooner had the French engaged the Prussian forces under Blücher at Ligny on June 16, than Friedrich's horse was shot out from under him. The shell fragment that downed the horse narrowly missed him, but the horse rolled over on him as it fell, crushing his leg. By day's end, the Prussians had been badly mauled. Napoleon then turned toward Waterloo to meet the forces commanded by Wellington. Friedrich lay in shock with the dying horse on top of him throughout the battle. He was not discovered until well after dark. His commanding officer knew his family, admired the lad's spirit, and fearing for his life under the inadequate medical treatment available in the field, paid a local peasant to transport him immediately to Brussels, some 50 kilometers northwest. He was loaded onto a rude wagon and set off over poor roads and rough terrain.

In the confused aftermath of battle and darkness, the peasant, trying to avoid the road taken by the French who were marching in the same general direction, strayed, approaching Brussels from the south rather than the west. Late in the morning of the 18th, he realized his mistake. He could hear men and horses trampling the woods and fields on the outskirts of Waterloo. The road to Brussels was blocked. As he hesitated, shortly before noon, the bloody fighting began. Frightened by the sound of muskets and artillery moving in his direction, the peasant leaped from the cart and fled for his life, abandoning Friedrich to his fate.

That battle was over in one long, horrifying day. Napoleon engaged Wellington's forces, over one hundred thousand men, horses, and guns crammed into a quarter-mile front just south of Waterloo between the village of La Belle Alliance and the ridge of Mont Saint Jean. They fought through mud and mist of a nasty, wet day from late morning until nightfall. The steadfastness of the British regulars under Wellington withstood the advantages of men and guns under Napoleon until Blücher, who had rallied his men, arrived. The French retreated and Napoleon fled.

Friedrich lay in the wagon that night in a feverish, barely conscious delirium. He was discovered next morning by a reconnoitering British cavalry officer, who sent word to the Prussians. Friedrich was finally delivered to hospital, where the doctors, overburdened with sick and wounded, almost lost him. But young bodies can be remarkably resilient, and by the end of summer, he was strong enough to return home. His crushed leg had been amputated, but the medical staff congratulated themselves on having saved his life. The extent of his injury and the ignominious way it had been inflicted embittered him. He was ashamed at having lost his leg, at having to return home an unheroic cripple.

The homecoming was subdued. Sunk in depression as he was, his parents feared for Friedrich's sanity. The boy was fitted with a wooden leg, which he at first vehemently rejected. But practical necessity overcame his revulsion, and it even made him heroic in Sophie's eyes.

His younger brother Albert Wilhelm, who had languished in his brother's shadow, had secretly hoped that Friedrich would not return from the war. When he returned, missing in body and spirit, Albert Wilhelm secretly rejoiced. He had neither the desire to join the army nor the humility to enter the clergy. He would have been quite happy managing the family estates. He had even fancied himself in love with Sophie and hoped to win her for himself if Friedrich failed to survive.

Like most fantasies, this one got a rude setback on Friedrich's return. It briefly revived when he saw that his brother was maimed and despondent, especially when the Altendorfs brought Sophie to visit Friedrich and he turned away in shame. Sophie and her parents accepted the damage with a good grace, and agreed to give him time to heal mentally as well as physically. But the Altendorfs frowned on a marriage with Sophie before Friedrich was again healed in body and mind.

Albert's hopes were finally dashed when his brother's spirits, however haltingly, revived. Friedrich was to have Sophie after all, and would in time inherit the combined estates of the two families. But their mother was especially fond of "her baby," and disapproved of the Wagenhalsen practice of disinheriting the younger son and turning him into a vassal of some mean benefice. She quietly provided that some land and her very large personal fortune would go to Albert Wilhelm. Since she outlived his father, Albert eventually became a very rich man without opposition.

The Wagehalsens and Altendorfs saw Friedrich and Sophie settled into a suitable estate nearby on the outskirts of Weimar, bestowed by Sophie's family. And in the following year, they had the first of two sons, Heinrich Wolfgang. A second son, Johann Ernst, was born at the end of the next year, in 1822. Albert Wilhelm never overcame his bitterness over his brother's recovery, and set about getting back at him by undermining his authority over his first-born son. He never married, and made Heinrich his principal heir, a fact that he lost no time in communicating to his nephew when the boy was barely old enough to understand. For his part, Friedrich had for a time regained something of his youthful outlook.

Heinrich Wolfgang was exceptional among the Wagehalsens. Not only was he named after a patriotic lecturer on the history of the German *Volk* at Jena rather than a Wettin, but also after Mozart, whose music his father loved. The latter proved to be a fateful influence.

Interlude

The voices in the adjoining room rose in pitch and volume, joined by Pascal's frantic barking. All were cut off by a slammed door. After a few minutes of silence, Korngold came back into the room. He found Brewster now seated at his desk and deeply engrossed in Wagehalsen's journal. In fact, he had completely forgotten about Brewster during his altercation with Sydney. He stood in the doorway, silently observing him, mildly astonished to find him still there. The controversy in the adjoining room had drained him as well as the afternoon.

For his part, Brewster had become so taken with Wagehalsen's history, that he had not even been aware of the passage of time. When Korngold spoke, Brewster was startled. He hastily got up from the desk and began to apologize for his intrusion. Korngold only took a deep breath and waved him off, pleading the lateness of the hour and an unforeseen event. They could take up the journal next time.

Then, "Wait," he said, as Brewster got up to go. "What would you say to increasing our sessions to five a week for the next two weeks?"

Brewster nodded.

24.

When Albert Wilhelm made Heinrich Wolfgang his principal heir, he meant to alienate the boy's affection for his father. But that was not enough. No. There had to be more. He kept his feelings patiently concealed as he searched for a better way to get at his brother. Eventually, a promising opportunity would present itself.

For his part, Friedrich bore Albert no ill-will. In fact, he could afford to be generous enough to pity his brother's loneliness. So that when Heinrich, as a toddler, showed remarkable musical precociousness, compassion and the remnants of his own youthful romanticism and love of Mozart overcame his otherwise sternly practical nature. His conviction that "art" could never be anything more than a frivolous pastime was offset by a genuine desire to make Albert feel useful. He had no inkling of his brother's submerged hostility, or suspicion of ulterior motives. When Friedrich offhandedly suggested that Albert might oversee his son's musical education, he was only too pleased when his brother eagerly accepted. Friedrich's offer was not entirely disingenuous. He believed that developing Heinrich's musical abilities would keep both his son and Albert out of mischief until the boy was old enough to undertake more serious matters. After that, Sophie and he might find a suitable match for Albert so that he could raise a son of his own.

The child had a keen ear for music and unusual dexterity, learned to play the piano and the violin soon after he began to walk, and even began to compose little pieces for the amusement of his family. He was soon improvising at the piano on themes that were sung or played for him. Albert at once engaged the services of a pianist and a violinist from the court theater of Karl August. They would be answerable only to him. The trio began nurturing Heinrich's considerable talents just after his third birthday. By isolating Heinrich from Friedrich and Sophie for most of the day, Albert subtly interposed himself between them and their son. Gradually, he displaced his brother as father figure so completely that Heinrich began calling his uncle, "Vati."

Although the pianist Herr Hochenpochen spoke no French and the violinist M. Hautecul spoke no German, rivalry served as their common language. They soon managed to learn derogatory nicknames for each other. Hochenpochen lampooned the violinist as "Herr Crincrin." Stung, M. Hautecul's indignation went unrequited because he could not bring himself to mouth such un-Gallic mouthfuls as "Monsieur Pimmelklimper," even though what *prick strummer* lacked in Gallic finesse had a certain je ne sais quoi. He had to content himself with a cloud of French epithets for which there were no German equivalents. Besides, how could that vile language possibly have a verbal vessel strong enough to hold the vitriol he would pour over the head of that *boche*!

They understood each other very well. From the first, the two fenced for dominance over their precocious pupil. When they were not using the boy's mastery of the technical demands of their respective instruments as rapiers with which to skewer each other, they were sneakily undermining each other's reputation, each determined to exploit Heinrich as a child prodigy on *his* instrument. Herr Hochenpochen puffed himself as a pupil of Weimar's own Johann Nepomuk Hummel. He never tired of reminding everyone that Hummel had lived and studied with *Mozart* when he was 8 years old and toured Europe as a Wunderkind. Like many refugees from the ugly events in France during the 1790s, M. Hautecul had been attracted to Weimar by its peace and the highly cultivated society of Duke Karl August. But he was still *French*. He sniffed that *he* had studied with Pierre Baillot, the great *French* violinist and composer, at the Paris Conservatoire.

Needless to say, all this petty squabbling in two different languages wore on Uncle Albert. He was at first amused at the way they traded insults with each other, even taking an occasional liberty to spice up the translations by adding his own barbs. But eventually, he listened with increasing impatience. Besides, it cut into the time for tutoring his nephew, which really did not matter much. Hochenpochen was often speechless in admiration and uneasiness at the ease with which Heinrich mastered his exercises. At times he worried that there would soon be nothing more he could teach him. But there was no holding Heinrich back, and the teacher had to earn his keep in his pupil's reflected glory. Each time he showed off the boy's accomplishments, he tried to catch the eye of "Herr Crincrin," claiming the boy's achievements as proof of his teaching skills. He would introduce the *Kind* to some new technique only to find that he either already understood or mastered it almost at once. All Hochenpochen could do was stand aside and cast about for some pianistic stunt which the boy might not toss off so easily.

At the same time, he brushed off the boy's proficiency on the violin, while Hautecul experienced the same anxieties, marveling yet worrying that he might all too soon find the boy had reached the limits of anything he could teach him. And the violin teacher was no less dismissive of the piano. That led to a new debate about the relative merits of their instruments.

In spite of the constant bickering, by the time Heinrich was five, he had made such progress on both instruments that word of mouth brought him to the attention of Goethe, and through him to the Grand Duke Karl August. Goethe had met the twelve-year-old Mendelssohn when that prodigy had come to play for Weimar's celebrated native son, Hummel, in 1821, the very year Heinrich was born. He had shaken Mendelssohn's hand and said, "You are my David, and I am your Saul." He was curious to hear this Wagehalsen phenomenon for himself and used his influence with the Grand Duke himself to arrange a performance at court. The stigma of bastardy which hung over the Wagehalsens had kept them from any standing there. But with a favorable reception from a close friend of the Duke's such as Goethe, Friedrich thought his son's talents might redeem the family name. He began to reconsider the value of music. With such favor and patronage, what might not even a *musician* accomplish? His son would be another Mendelssohn whose amazing gifts would amuse the Duke. And gain preferment for the family at court.

When the expected summons to court came, however, Friedrich was away in another province on business. Uncle Albert was delegated to accompany Heinrich Wolfgang and Sophie to Court. Both Hochenpochen and Hautecul tried to worm their way into the occasion, but the Duke's invitation had stipulated family only. There, Heinrich stunned the court with his skills on both keyboard and violin. Karl August and the Grand Duchess Luise of Hesse-Darmstadt, condescended to congratulate the child. Goethe patted him on the head and solemnly shook his hand.

"And here," said Albert smiling with undisguised satisfaction at his own cleverness, knowing that the great Goethe would appreciate the allusion to his meeting with Mendelssohn, "here is your Magic Carpet!"

"Ha-ha!" chuckled Goethe. "Yes, yes! A Magic Carpet to sweep over everyone!" He patted Heinrich's cheek. "You shall be my Solomon!"

The Duke assured Albert that he would take a keen interest in the boy's future. Friedrich was so gratified when he learned of his son's success and the Duke's interest that, when Albert proposed taking the five-year-old boy to Vienna to meet the great Beethoven, he agreed at once. But Sophie and Heinrich's teachers were aghast. Sophie fretted about the hardships such a journey would impose on her son, while Hochenpochen and Hautecul worried about the impact on their jobs. Hautecul, especially, opposed the journey out of fear that Uncle Wagehalsen might take his nephew on the tour with Hochenpochen alone, and he would lose out to that vile *salopard*. He agreed with Frau Wagehalsen that the boy's health would suffer on such a journey. He pointed to the sad plight of Heinrich Wolfgang's namesake, Mozart, during his father's exploitation of the young prodigy. Furthermore, though he was still actively composing, Beethoven was by then profoundly deaf. A meeting with him, he protested, would be difficult to arrange. And it was well-known that he hated child prodigies. They would be lucky to see him at all. Even if it could be managed, what could they possibly hope to accomplish with a deaf musician? Hochenpochen shared his rival's misgivings, but he shrewdly let him bear the brunt of opposing the uncle's will. Still, Albert believed that the interest expressed by both the Duke and Goethe, one of Beethoven's friends, would overcome such qualms. And the aura of such a meeting, argued Albert, could only further the boy's success.

He lost no time in bringing the proposed expedition to the attention of Goethe, and through him, the Duke. He got favorable responses from both, though Goethe, too, had reservations about a meeting with Beethoven. Letters of introduction from Duke Karl August himself and Goethe, the most important addressed to the Archduke Rudolph, brother of Emperor Francis II, patron and benefactor of Beethoven, offered a very good chance that the young prodigy would get an audience. That alone would enhance young Heinrich's career. After that . . . Well, a meeting with the curmudgeonly composer would be an iffy matter best left in the hands of the Archduke and Beethoven's conniving secretary, Anton Schindler. Rudolph had been installed as archbishop of Olmütz in Moravia the year before Heinrich was born, but spent as much of his time in Vienna as his administrative duties allowed. As a member of the imperial family, pupil, friend, and benefactor of Beethoven, Rudolph would be in an ideal position to persuade the composer to tolerate the boy.

Dangling the prizes of a possible preferment at Court and the virtual certainty of a reception by the illustrious brother of the Austrian emperor, Albert easily swept aside all doubts. He also knew that his brother's leg could never stand up to such an arduous journey, so he innocently volunteered to sacrifice his own comfort for the sake of his nephew. Rumors of a possible visit to Beethoven flew about the Wagehalsen manor and were soon transformed into an impending certainty.

Hochenpochen and Hautecul suddenly saw how useful such exposure would be—for Heinrich's career, of course. They vied with each other to praise the farsightedness of Albert's plan. A trip to the music capital of Europe, more important even than Paris! What an opportunity to display Heinrich's gifts! The boy would of course need a coach to keep him up to the mark, and each would willingly accept such a burden.

For a time, Hochenpochen took leave of his senses, rashly proposing that Heinrich prepare Beethoven's Piano Sonata, op. 106, "Hammerklavier," or the Op. 111, both dedicated to and both well beyond the pianism of the Archduke. At fifteen years old in 1803, he had been Beethoven's pupil and was developing into an excellent pianist. But at thirty-nine in 1826, he suffered from gout, rheumatism, and bouts of epilepsy. He continued to compose, but he was no longer able to play the piano. All the more, then, His Imperial Highness would marvel at and fully appreciate the child's virtuosity. It would make an awesome impression.

Hautecul knew that Heinrich would never be able to bring off the "Hammerklavier." No amount of talent could overcome the child's physical limitations. Not to be outdone, he proposed preparing Heinrich in a more modest, more realistic Beethoven violin sonata. Hochenpochen's insane ambition would bring him to grief, and he would be there to fill in. But Hochenpochen quickly came to his senses. He realized how much he was asking of a child. Maybe Heinrich could prepare another of the piano sonatas Beethoven dedicated to the archduke? The "Hammerklavier," and the last in C minor, Op. 111, might, regrettably, be out of the question. Heinrich's hands, even though large for a five-year-old, could barely span an octave. That would present formidable technical difficulties in the extended passages of the late sonatas where both hands were simultaneously executing trills with thumbs and forefingers while playing melodic figures with the outer fingers of the same hands. Hochenpochen admitted it would be unwise to tax the boy's physical limitations with the challenges posed by them. The "Hammerklavier" especially required wide leaps from one end of the keyboard to the other as well as those devilish trills . . . And at three-quarters of an hour . . . too long. No. He must choose something more modest . . . yet spectacular.

Torn between the urge to wow Archduke Rudolph and not risk overwhelming his brilliant pupil, Hochenpochen at last reluctantly but sensibly set his sights a little, if not much, lower. He decided to take a chance on Beethoven's Sonata Op. 81a, "*Das Lebewohl.*" It was certainly challenging enough even for accomplished pianists years older. Beethoven had composed the sonata during Napoleon's bombardment and invasion of Vienna, when the archduke had fled the city with the imperial family. It was the first of the three sonatas Beethoven dedicated to the archduke and would have sentimental appeal. Yes, a most effective introduction! The depth of the composer's feeling for his friend and onetime pupil could be gauged from the original subtitles which Beethoven gave to the sonata's three movements, "*Lebewohl,*" "*Abwesenheit*" and "*Wiedersehen,*" Farewell, Absence, and Reunion. One of Beethoven's publishers, Breitkopf, hoping to capitalize on the more fashionable French, took it upon himself to bring out two editions, one with Beethoven's original subtitles, and another with French subtitles, "*Les Adieux,*" "*L'Absence,*" and "*Le Retour.*" Those enjoyed widespread acceptance. But Beethoven had written *Le-be-wohl* over the first three chords of the score. He, himself, had denounced the changes both in language and spirit. "*Les Adieux*" was the kind of farewell one addressed to a group, not an intimate friend. And "*Le Retour,*" Return, had nothing of the amiable nuance of "*Wiedersehen,*" Reunion. Hochenpochen would prune away the cold pretentions of the French and restore the more *gemütlich* German. That should please both Beethoven and the archduke. And rub it in M. Crincrin's face.

This sonata, too, had many passages of octave work, and in the third movement, the simultaneous sextuple semiquavers, almost trills, of thumb and forefinger against the melody played by the third, fourth, and fifth fingers of the same hand. Though such exuberant devices were not as extensively used as the similar devices Beethoven used in the later sonatas, they still posed a challenge to the boy's reach. But Heinrich had

The Womb of Uncreated Night

already shown that he could break octaves so efficiently that the effect was almost simultaneous. And his fingers were remarkably independent. Hochenpochen had little doubt that the boy would be able to play all the notes. The biggest problem would be in giving the outer notes their necessary melodic emphasis and expression. Beethoven himself tolerated an occasional missed note in his own as well as his students' performances as long as they played with due regard for dynamics and expression. To emphasize the importance of playing expressively, Beethoven even wrote instructions into his piano music, urging that it be played "with feeling and expression throughout," or "with innermost feeling," and similar elaborations.

Well, what could a five-year-old boy, no matter how technically precocious, know of such things? They set to work on *Das Lebewohl*. In a matter of weeks, Heinrich had so thoroughly grasped its technical demands that Hochenpochen began to doubt. Could anyone who so effortlessly grasped technique, whose fingers flew through notes as so many feathers through the air, feel more than the mere exhilaration of flight? Heinrich could, indeed, play all the notes, if at first somewhat mechanically. But then something began to happen. Hochenpochen was at a loss for an explanation. Over the next few months, Hochenpochen coached Heinrich in interpretation, expecting to refine what even in an exceptional child might otherwise be coldly routine, unfeeling. Hochenpochen urged him to play the music from the inside out, rather than the outside in, to play *through* rather than *over* the notes, to draw out the music's *empfindung*, its feeling. Even as he did so, he doubted that this boy, or any child of his age for that matter, could grasp such concepts.

The more Hochenpochen explained, the more the child grasped. And the less Hochenpochen understood. The boy had an uncanny knack for seeing beyond the mere notes on the page. But a five-year-old who could realize what the rest of us earn only through years of toil, a soul? Impossible! And yet . . . Was there perhaps some sorcery by which this boy transformed leaden childhood into gold? Could he really mold it into a semblance—if only a semblance!—of that innerness that

Beethoven demanded? Or was it the knack of a trained monkey to imitate what it saw and heard, and because it was only the performance of a monkey, willingly suspended disbelief in the listener, who then supposed he heard more than he did? Could an automaton be trained to convincingly project contrived feelings so that it seemed to possess a soul? Unthinkable! Trembling with apprehension, Hochenpochen resisted giving up that last scrap of doubt, that last bit of sanity that knew the answer to such questions. But in the end, he threw up his hands and put them into those that barely spanned an octave. Others would have to judge whether his vanity had deceived him into thinking that he had taught the child to play better than he possibly could.

Hochenpochen's work with his prodigy gave him reason enough to insist that he should be allowed to travel with his pupil. But the opportunity to meet Der Beethoven could not be left to chance . . . or to Crincrin. And for all Heinrich's precocious grasp of the sonata, Hochenpochen would still be needed to ensure that the boy would not lapse into mere routine.

Poor M. Hautecul could only lament that Beethoven's only important piece for solo violin dedicated to the Archduke was the comparatively unglamorous Sonata in G, Op.96. Although it had been written for the brilliant French violinist, Pierre Rode, and premiered for the archduke at the soirée of another Beethoven patron, Prince Lobkowitz, it was lovely, but tame. In fact, Beethoven had groused to the Archduke about making concessions to Rode's taste because the violinist did not like bravura style. So he made it more quietly introspective. Not exactly subdued, to be sure, and beautifully lyrical. But it would pale next to what that *chleuh* was offering. If only the Archduke had insisted on giving Beethoven free reign to create a towering *chef d'oeuvre* unhampered by a fussy violinist.

Hautecul also lamented that the accompanying piano part required such self-effacing, delicate inflections that his pianism, assuming he were allowed to go, would not be particularly impressive. Even then, he almost despaired of finding a way to get himself included in the journey. And then, in a flash, it came to him. He approached Albert, busily working out the details for the journey. Cautiously. Any hint that he might be fomenting another squabble with Hochenpochen would be disastrous.

"Monsieur," he began in a mollifying tone, "would it not add to the young master's aura to demonstrate versatility as well as virtuosity? M. Hochenpochen's idea to impress the archduke by having the boy play a work dedicated to him by Beethoven has great"— *not too much! not too much!*—"merit. And the piece he has chosen will certainly display Heinrich's amazing gifts to excellent advantage. But if the boy could also display his skill in an ensemble, would it not show a remarkable range? I suggest, therefore, that we . . . ," he gulped and rushed on, "that we prepare the Trio in B-flat Op. 97, which Beethoven also dedicated to the Archduke. With Heinrich on violin, Hochenpochen," he almost choked on the hated name, "on piano, and myself on the cello. It's sure to please His Imperial Highness." Albert was impressed by Hautecul's willingness to work with Hochenpochen, and the idea appealed to him. He promised to give the suggestion serious thought, and—here Hautecul's heart sank—he would discuss it with Hochenpochen.

Albert summoned both tutors and introduced Hautecul's idea to Hochenpochen, not yet having made up his mind. The more he thought about it, however, the better he liked it. He agreed that it ought to please the Archduke. He called the meeting to discuss the practical aspects of the proposal, and not incidentally, give the rivals a chance to reconcile. But when Hochenpochen dismissed the idea out of hand, Albert was indignant at his obstinacy. He upbraided him for refusing Hautecul's effort to defuse the tension between them without even thinking about it, and decided on the spot. They *would* prepare the archduke's Trio, and with a good grace, too, or he would leave them both behind. And if they created any kind of disturbance on the journey, or in any way threatened his nephew's success with their petty bickering, he would send them both packing at once. Hautecul and Hochenpochen hastily—if grudgingly— made their peace with each other.

The preparations of sonata and trio were so promising that the two rivals persuaded Albert, and even half-convinced each other, that they truly had made amends. Albert was satisfied that their amicable presence as coaches and accompanists for his *Wunderkind* would ensure the success of his nephew's tour. With Albert's positive outlook, Friedrich made up his mind. His son was destined for greatness, and the family, for the court of the Grand Duke. He brushed aside all doubts and reservations, and charged Uncle Albert with arranging to shepherd his son on the journey. A few weeks later, Albert, the newly chastened tutors, a medical attendant, and servants, set off by diligence. If Hochenpochen and Hautecul still abhorred each other, they were at least politic enough not to let on to either Albert or Heinrich.

They arrived in Vienna two weeks later, toured the city and attended concerts, where, among others, they heard the music of Beethoven, and for the first time, Schubert. Heinrich quickly learned to play some of it from memory at the keyboard. Soon, people influential in aristocratic musical circles were inviting him to perform at their musicales. All were loud in their acclaim. News of his accomplishments circulated through the city, and along with the letter of introduction from Karl August, eased his entry into Rudolph's residence.

After his secretary had related the contents of the letter, Rudolph resigned himself to enduring a wretched child whose parents regularly inflicted its overrated abilities—however remarkable at such tender years—on the ears of their betters. He shared Beethoven's antipathy for child prodigies. He would no doubt be expected to kiss the *Bube*, praise its performance inordinately, and give it some valuable trinket. He also fully expected the urchin to have been coached to flatter and impress him with these ends in mind. At length, the boy was ushered into his presence and was asked to play something. Heinrich Wolfgang played the sonata dedicated to His Imperial Highness flawlessly. As the music Beethoven had dedicated to him emerged so assuredly and expressively under the fingers of this urchin, Rudolph leaned back with narrowed eyes. The look of amused boredom melted away into keen interest. Astonished and deeply impressed by the performance—yes, it *was* a performance rather than some parlor trick—he would be willing to arrange a brief concert for his circle of friends among musicians and musically knowledgeable members of the nobility.

He resisted, however, the suggestion of a meeting with Beethoven, even for such an obviously gifted performer. After all, the composer was now stone deaf. Aside from Beethoven's well-known antipathy for child prodigies, what could such an audition possibly hope to accomplish? Audition! What an odd word in the context! The composer had not been able to perform in public since 1815. And even then, he who had been renowned as a brilliant pianist, was so deaf that the last performances had been disasters. Ludwig Spohr, who had played the violin in performances of the Trio dedicated to the archduke in 1814, reported that the composer's deafness had already advanced so far that he alternately pounded on the keys in *forte* passages and played so softly in *piano* passages as to render the piano part incomprehensible.

"But, your Highness," protested Albert, "did not Beethoven bestow on Franz Liszt the *Weihekuss*, the kiss of consecration, at the end of a concert in the Redoutensaal only three years ago?"

"Oh, yes!" laughed Rudolph dismissively. "Would you heed every rumor concocted by interested parties to further someone's career? Beethoven was hounded by his secretary, Schindler, to grant an interview to Liszt a few days before the concert. The meeting did not go well because Beethoven was set against it. Liszt invited Beethoven to attend the concert. Schindler hounded him to go, if only to make amends for his employer's hostile reception. But why would Beethoven have sat through a concert he could not hear? And why would you now want to trouble the man again with a *Wunderkind* whom he also could not hear and would not want to hear if he could?" But when he saw that Albert's purse would open generously for Beethoven, who was always worried about money, he thought he might relax his objections. He saw that this man, too, wanted to trade on Beethoven's approval to further the renown of a child with a new rumor of benediction. He sighed at the repulsive thought of urging his friend and teacher selling his name for *Gelt*. In the end, he decided that he would wash his hands of the matter by writing to Schindler and letting the secretary do the dirty work.

As it happened, Beethoven had recently recovered from a bout of illness, was in excellent spirits and receiving visitors. The conflicts with his nephew, Karl, were close to resolution. And Beethoven was now regularly circulating among his friends. He had even taken to teasing the women of his acquaintance.

So when Schindler conveyed the Archduke's letter, Beethoven was less hostile than he might have been. In an effort to soften the imposition, the Archduke even suggested that Beethoven treat it as a joke. Beethoven nevertheless bridled at the suggestion that he receive a visit from another presumptuous uncle and his little bastard, this one even younger than the last. His hostility to Liszt had until then been dismissed from his mind. Three years had passed since Schindler connived to inflict *that* wretch on him. He dismissed the idea at once. But when he read that Uncle Albert was prepared to make him a gift of 1,000 florins, he reconsidered. A joke, the Archduke had said. A joke, indeed! What kind of imbecile must that child's piano teacher be to encourage a five-year-old to play *Das Lebewohl*! He knew all about doting uncles, and though he did not approve of relatives who tried to promote prodigies, he could not find it in his heart to judge Albert too harshly.

Reading between the lines, he wondered that the musically sophisticated Rudolph had heard and apparently approved of the child's performance. Very well, then! He would "listen" so attentively with his eyes, grateful that he would be unable to hear his music butchered. Remembering that Liszt had been Czerny's pupil, Beethoven thought that it would be a fitting part of the "joke" to inflict the young upstart on him as well! Czerny would at least have to hear the little wretch, while he would busy himself with a composition, and be well paid for the imposition. But he specified that only Heinrich and his uncle would be allowed to visit. Under no circumstances was that blockhead teacher to set foot in the *Schwarzspanierhaus*!

A few days later, Albert and Heinrich arrived on the Glacis, and he and Heinrich climbed the creaking stairs to Beethoven's lodgings in the second floor. Sali, Beethoven's housekeeper, admitted them to his principal living room, where Schindler greeted them and led them to the Broadwood where a smiling Czerny and a frowning Beethoven, awaited them. The instrument was supposed to have a somewhat muffled tone, but since Beethoven would be unable to hear it, it was deemed good enough for the young upstart. Beethoven gestured dismissively at the piano and bade Heinrich without further ceremony sit and play. When Czerny, with raised eyebrows, wrote in his conversation book what piece the child was going to play, Beethoven's frown deepened into a scowl. The impudent little rascal intended to go through with it! Since his feet could not reach the pedals if he sat, Heinrich had to play while standing. He was able to sustain a legato that caused Czerny's jaw to drop. For such a small child to manage such phrasing and tone, it was truly remarkable. At first, Beethoven sat crouched in a corner, ignoring the whole thing, making notes on a manuscript. As Heinrich reached the middle of the first movement, he chanced to look up. He caught a look of such astonishment on Czerny's face that he stopped what he was doing and watched the boy's performance intently, straining to follow every movement of his fingers, ready to judge and immediately correct the smallest fluctuation in rhythm, tempo, or dynamics that he was able to hear only in his head. From the suppleness of Heinrich's hands at the keyboard, Beethoven could not doubt that the boy must be coaxing a singing tone from the Broadwood. By degrees, Beethoven grudgingly admitted to himself that the boy's fingers moved flawlessly over his music. When, after a quarter-hour the boy finished playing, Czerny and Schindler applauded. Czerny turned to Uncle Albert as if he would ask whether there was some deception. It was a well-known fact that child prodigies often misrepresented their age in order to appear even more precocious. Surely, this could be no mere five-year-old? Beethoven patted his head gruffly and went back to his chair in the corner. No *Weihekuss*, thought Albert. But high praise, nonetheless.

Heinrich Wolfgang's successes in Weimar and Vienna went straight to his head. They led him to believe that he was vastly superior to other human beings. His vanity grew along with his skill in music. As Hochenpochen and Hautecul had feared before the journey to Vienna, Heinrich outgrew them. First, having decided to devote himself exclusively to mastering the piano, he dismissed Hautecul. Hautecul protested indignantly to Uncle Albert. Surely, a five-year-old boy did not have the authority to dismiss him? Albert agreed that his nephew should not have presumed to take on the responsibility of dismissing a member of the household's staff. He then fired Hautecul himself. Far from relishing the departure of his rival, Hochenpochen realized that Heinrich's high-handedness would soon fall on him. He knew there was nothing more that he could teach the boy. Heinrich already had the technique of someone three times his age. At this stage of his development, he probably needed to be left to his own devices until he matured a little more. Then his needs might realistically be reevaluated. Rather than wait for the inevitable, Hochenpochen decided to spare himself the humiliation of being fired by a five-year-old and asked Uncle Albert to let him go.

As Heinrich approached adolescence, Franz Liszt's star, which had begun to dim in the 1820s and was almost eclipsed when his father died in the same year as Beethoven, once more ascended. Awed by the virtuosity of Paganini, Liszt began to practice fourteen hours a day, determined that he would be as great a virtuoso as the violinist. As Heinrich grew in age and physical maturity, he was vexed that the court at Weimar, indeed, the courts and concert halls all over Europe, continued to bestow on Liszt the acclaim and adulation that he thought he himself was entitled to, but enjoyed only at home. Although Liszt was ten years older, Heinrich would overtake him. Was Liszt practicing fourteen hours a day? *He* would practice sixteen!

The intense regimen Heinrich followed took a heavy toll on the pianos at his disposal. He often hummed or sang aloud while playing. Uncle Albert Wilhelm sometimes sat in as he played, encouraging his excesses. "But louder, louder, *Jungsi*! I can still hear you singing!

Your playing must drown out everything else from the listener's ears. Shake the rafters! Break the piano!" The strings of a Reicha built with Beethoven in mind obligingly snapped under the impact of Heinrich's thunderous rendition of the opening chords of the *Hammerklavier* sonata. His parents continued to furnish him with instruments by Walter, Seidner, even a Streicher like the one in Goethe's house. Some of these instruments lasted longer, but they were no match for Heinrich. He mangled the keys, jammed the action, or broke the pedals. His parents had to keep him supplied with two or three pianos at a time so that he would always have a playable instrument. In desperation, they obtained a Broadwood from London because English instruments were reputed to be sturdier. Even so, the instruments needed constant tuning. Behind his back, when the servants got over being awed or terrified by Heinrich's musical demolition, they made jokes about his playing and made wagers on how long an instrument would last.

But the feverish pace also began to affect Heinrich physically and mentally. An eleven-year-old boy who spends sixteen furious hours at the keyboard breaks not only the strings of his instrument, but also his health. Uncle Albert said that the hours of practice were paying off, that he was making tremendous progress. Heinrich had already mastered Beethoven's late sonatas. But he showed increasing signs of nervous exhaustion when he played. The servants sometimes found faint traces of blood on the keyboard. His alarmed parents reproached Uncle Albert for encouraging Heinrich to endanger his health. They forbade their son to go on playing. They relented only when he and Albert agreed to cut in half the number of hours of practice. Heinrich resorted to a mechanical finger strengthener, which was becoming a popular fad, to make up the deficit. He succeeded only in crippling one of the fingers in his left hand. He was forced to give up playing entirely while it healed.

Heinrich was crippled in more ways than one. His father's disposition toward him in the intervening years had soured even before the crippling incident. The expected preferment at court effectively ended with the death of the Grand Duke Karl August in 1828. He was succeeded by his son, Karl Friedrich, who allowed Weimar's cultural life to lapse into mediocrity within a few short years. With only a passing acknowledgement of Heinrich's talents, this duke showed little interest in the Wagehalsens. Then Goethe's death in 1832 finally ended all hope that the great man's influence might somehow legitimize the family name among the nobility. The career of his gifted son no longer mattered to Friedrich von Wagehalsen. He grew impatient and snapped at Heinrich, demanding that he turn what remained of his abilities to practical matters. The change in his father coinciding with the injury to his hand bewildered the boy. At first he tried to accept his mother's explanation that pain from his father's leg injury had flared up. But the fading of his grandiose ambition to become a world-famous virtuoso, a serious blow to the boy's self-esteem, was compounded by his father's sudden decision to disinherit him in favor of his younger brother. Heinrich was crushed, baffled by his father's action. Whenever he asked why he was being cut off, Friedrich read aloud whole chapters of the endlessly tedious book of Leviticus to the hapless boy. No longer perfect in body, he could not live up to higher service. He was no longer the unblemished male. Thereafter, he could no longer sanctify whomever or whatever he touched, however much he burned or bled.

In the bitter confusion that followed this rejection, Heinrich grew cynical, the more so as he thought his father might have been more sympathetic in light of his own injury. If Heinrich's injury had made him an outcast, then what of his father's? He felt as if invisible hands had unloaded sinister burdens on him. He began to take it out on his younger brother in sly underhanded ways, fouling his food and blaming the cat, letting the dog have its way with his clothes—and sometimes his bed, and slighting him in front of acquaintances. Johann Ernst was either too naïve to catch on, or so in awe of his talented but now outcast older brother that he could not believe that Heinrich was behind the mishaps.

Heinrich became increasingly difficult. To the extreme embarrassment and annoyance of his parents whenever they had guests, Heinrich took to wandering about the estate, wearing a robe of dirty, unbleached cloth

The Womb of Uncreated Night

which he rent while ringing a little silver bell he carried with him, crying, "Unclean, unclean!" He let his hair grow unkempt down to his shoulders. When his father chided him for being unkempt, he shaved his head. On another occasion, he ordered servants to bring a tub of water into a roomful of guests, and as parents, uncle, brother, guests, and servants gaped in astonishment, he stripped off his robe and washed it. He then scrutinized it as if to see if it was truly clean, but soon tore it, crying, "Unclean, unclean! Body and soul, unclean!"

Uncle Albert was delighted. He took Heinrich's side against his father and secretly encouraged his rebelliousness. As he grew into the wilderness of adolescence, Heinrich took his pranks into the surrounding city and even the countryside, where they soon escalated from practical jokes into libertinism and hedonism. He was linked to scandals of reported child molestation, torture, and rape. None of these charges were ever proved, as Uncle Albert used money and influence to suppress them. But as rumors mounted, fresh disgrace was added to the family name. His parents were stung with the taunt that their son was acting like a bastard. They concluded that Heinrich was not quite right in the head and would have to be sent away to avoid further scandal. But their flesh and blood consigned to a sanitarium would only reflect more shame. No. They would send him to Paris, where his ignominy would be absorbed in the general infamy of that city.

So, at sixteen, Heinrich was sent abroad to Paris with an annual allowance of 800 talers (about F7,000), an income comparable to what actors and shopkeepers in Weimar might earn. But Uncle Albert, who had encouraged Heinrich's deviltry, would not let his brother send his nephew out into the world so miserly provided for. Unknown to Friedrich, he set up letters of credit in Paris and Vienna, so that his nephew would never be far from a substantial allowance.

25.

From its earliest rise in the Middle Ages, Paris stank. Unusually high sulfur content in the soil coupled with streets that were both thoroughfares and sewers combined to raise an abominable stench. So in the twelfth century, Philippe II, "God's gift to France"—but especially to Paris—bestowed pavement on the city, great sandstone blocks laid down on the main streets running east to west, Saint-Antoine and Saint-Honoré, and north to south, Saint-Martin and Saint-Jacques. But that had done little to sweeten the pustulate side-streets and alleyways, the *rues merderais*, not too far beyond the reach of the royal nostrils. There, ladies might lift their skirts above the mire in wet weather, but their noses trailed in shit.

New means of production in the 19th century gave off great light. The July Monarchy of 1830 had rolled out asphalt boulevards for the city's feet and adorned her hair with gas-lit tiaras even as it sucked out its human marrow. Glowing nights smudged the ugly façades of narrow-windowed five-story apartment buildings that filled the spaces of felled trees and gardens.

But even with such improvements, the city was overpopulated and unhygienic. Miasmas from blocked sewers, knackers' yards, and the fecal depots of Montfaucon, gutters and sewers—when they were not blocked—spilled into the Seine from which the residents drew their drinking water. All culminated in a disaster lurking in the narrow, twisting, dirty streets. The cholera epidemic in the spring of 1832 took more than eighteen thousand Parisian lives before the disease had run its course. The government disposed of the bodies at night. They first used artillery carriages to haul them away. But the noise of their metal wheels in the dark disturbed Parisians as they slept. Worse, the unsprung carriages jounced the coffins about, opening them up and dumping corpses into the street, mutilating them and spilling out their guts. A switch to better sprung furniture vans handled more caskets without shaking up their contents. But even in the midst of epidemic, no sooner were the corpses hauled away than the survivors surged back into the streets, put on a carnival, and clamored with mouths and hands and feet to drive the darkness back to the edges.

Like a fashionably world-weary woman of the time, Paris was ever eager for titillation. In every form—food, fashions, books, theater, personal grooming . . . If it was *nouveau* or *nouvelle*, it was socially "in." If it verged on the shocking or the risqué, so much the better. Indeed, scandal easily passed for the "new" and the "news." The only socially unacceptable thing was the failure to amuse. So the success of Sigismond Thalberg amid a city flooded with pianists in the autumn of 1835 filled the press with his praises and set him at the top of the heap. Which was, of course, an open invitation for someone to come along and try to push him off. Unflattering comparisons with Franz Liszt, who at the time was living with Countess Marie d'Agoult in Geneva and playing concerts there, facilitated such a contest.

Arriving in Paris after the end of the concert season in 1836, Liszt gave a semi-private performance of Beethoven's *Hammerklavier* Sonata at the Salle Erard. In the audience was Hector Berlioz, who wrote a review for the *Gazette Musicale* proclaiming Liszt "the pianist of the future."

François Joseph Fétis, the champion of Thalberg's "classical" style of playing, took exception to Berlioz's pushing his favorite into the past. And the game was on. The tension between partisans of the two pianists was further charged when, in January of the following year, Marie d'Agoult wrote a dismissive article under Liszt's name for the *Revue Musicale*. To defuse the mounting rancor, friends suggested that Liszt and Thalberg give a joint concert. Thalberg demurred, Liszt retorted, and all Paris avidly waited for a "duel" between the two. They did not wait long.

Thalberg played a Sunday matinee on March 12 at the Conservatoire for an audience of about three hundred; Liszt riposted by renting the Paris Opéra on the following Sunday, an auditorium that held nearly three thousand. The whole thing came to a head on March 31, 1837, when Princess Cristina Belgiojoso-Trivulzio, a revolutionist and advocate of Italian independence, invited them both to play against each other at a benefit for Italian refugees.

It was against this social set-to between the partisans of the two titans of the keyboard that Wagehalsen arrived in Paris. He found a secluded apartment behind the rue Rossini, ideally located in the city's cultural center. It offered proximity to famous salons, short walks to half-a-dozen theaters, three opera houses, concerts at the Paris Conservatory, or the *Salles* of piano manufacturers Erard and Pleyel. The Théâtre Français was further away, on rue de Richelieu near the Louvre. Between these destinations, his walks would offer opportunities for observing at first hand the salons of the *élites*, the bohemian lifestyles of artists and intellectuals, the studios they worked in, the cafes they frequented, to say nothing of the gambling houses, boutiques, brothels, and all the other infamies in passing. A narrow passageway between shops on the street opened onto a small courtyard. The two-storied building enclosing it on three sides was divided into three two-floored apartments, each comprising a salon, drawing room, and dining room on the ground floors, and two bedrooms on the upper. Wagehalsen occupied the one on the right, angled to the northwest in such a way that direct sunlight hardly ever managed to penetrate the tall French doors and promised some relief

The Womb of Uncreated Night

from hot Parisian summers. The other apartments were occupied but the tenants were seldom at home during his comings and goings.

Having set up his pied-à-terre Wagehalsen furnished it simply. Then, he behaved like any sixteen-year-old in a city full of vices and depravities. Whoring and drinking in the seedier sections of the Left Bank often brought scrapes and bruises. For a few days, he even found a job as accompanist in a music hall, playing the piano in the orchestra pit while gazing up at the legs of the dancing girls instead of keeping his eye on the *chef d'orchestre* or the score in front of him. But it quickly palled. It lacked.

The "duel" between Thalberg and Liszt stirred memories of long hours of practice, and the childhood challenge that Wagehalsen himself had imagined he would make. He visited the showrooms of Erard and Pleyel for a suitable piano. At the Salle Erard, he sat at one of the instruments and began to play the last movement of *Das Lebewohl*, the sonata he had played for Beethoven. As it happened, Liszt was in an adjoining room to book the hall for a recital. When he heard the beautifully executed right hand playing over the almost unnoticeably smudged scale work in the left, his curiosity was aroused. He approached the young pianist who was totally absorbed in his performance, and stood discreetly to the side, listening and observing the fingers of his left hand.

Almost at once, he exclaimed, "Ah, I see the difficulty!"

Wagehalsen stopped playing, annoyed, ready to retort to this intruder. He flushed in embarrassment when he recognized the paragon he had hoped as a boy to challenge.

Liszt smiled sympathetically. "Your ring finger, it gives you some trouble?" he said, taking the boy's hand and examining it.

Wagehalsen admitted that as a child he had overexerted his hand and that finger had been injured. He had been thinking about trying to correct the weakness with a finger strengthening device. "I thought if I could suspend the finger while I practiced with the others, I might be able to—"

"No, no, no!" Liszt interrupted in alarm. "Those contraptions would only cripple your hand further! Consider the plight of poor

Schumann, who just a few years ago thought the same thing and ruined his hand completely. You must come study with me. I will find a way to help you play around this slight imperfection and make it virtually imperceptible. You can learn to compensate with alternate fingerings. Perhaps in time the problem can be eased. I am staying at the Hôtel de France on the rue Lafitte. Do you know it? Excellent! Call on me!" Without waiting for a response, Liszt turned abruptly and left.

Wagehalsen stared at the keyboard for several minutes, thinking about the man he had once thought of as a mere showman. When he returned to his purpose of finding a suitable instrument for his apartment, he left Erard's and visited the Pleyel showroom. He was able to try several pianos without further interruption but was undecided. If the Erard was capable of greater sonority, the Pleyel produced a pearly sound that had its own distinctive appeal. Remembering that as a child he had had more than one instrument, he saw no reason not to have one of each to match his changing moods. He arranged for the instruments to be delivered to the rue Rossini. When they arrived, he had them placed together in the center of the spacious living room, bentside to bentside, so that the two formed an imposing square with keyboards at opposite ends.

Marie d'Agoult was still a married woman when she and Liszt had begun living together two years earlier. They had eloped to Switzerland in order to avoid a scandal in Paris. But when they returned late in 1836 and took rooms at the Hôtel de France, they found their literary and musical acquaintances unperturbed by the affair. When Marie gave several soirées, many prominent figures showed up to welcome them back into society. These parties were so successful that no one took note of the young man with disheveled blond hair who came and mingled until he pushed through the knot of guests surrounding Liszt. When

Liszt greeted Wagehalsen warmly and took him aside for a private chat, Marie was indignant. She had only recently divested her household of one of Liszt's protégés, Hermann "Puzzi" Cohen, one of Liszt's more intrusive pests, and here he was about to take on another hanger-on! No doubt this one would be invited to join in their travels as well!

After the soirée, Marie berated Liszt for burdening their ménage with yet another urchin. But Liszt was too preoccupied with preparations for the "duel" with Thalberg to deal with one of Marie's tantrums. They exchanged heated words. The next day Marie stormed off to George Sand's home in Nohant.

Liszt was also too distracted to begin serious work on Wagehalsen's hand. After his last concert in April, he would leave to patch things up with Marie as George Sand's house-guest. But he did invite Wagehalsen to travel south with him. Mme Sand's house and lifestyle were large enough to accommodate all of them, and was always full of unexpected comings and goings. They would spend the summer at Nohant and then travel together for a tour of Italy. He would be able to see Wagehalsen every day and develop a new technique for him.

Wagehalsen considered Liszt's offer. He did not know that the one of the world's greatest pianists was giving fewer concerts each year in order to satisfy Marie's neurotic need to monopolize him in semi-seclusion. But in the brief time he had known them something he sensed in their relationship made him feel that his presence would not be welcomed by Marie. As he had just settled into his new apartment, he told Liszt, perhaps it would be best to give him time to broach the arrangement to Marie. He could then join them in Italy, at Baveno on Lake Maggiore in August.

The winter of 1837-38 in central Europe was so severe that the Danube River froze. When the river thawed in the following spring, it overflowed its banks and sent a twenty-nine foot wall of water downstream into Hungary. The city of Pest lying directly in its path took the brunt of the flood. Thousands of homes destroyed, those remaining severely damaged, hundreds of people drowned, thousands left homeless, threatened with disease and starvation . . . News of the disaster reached Liszt at a café in St Mark's Square in Venice. He left immediately for Vienna where he gave a series of concerts to aid the victims of the flood. Although he had not been in Hungary since childhood, the plight of those victims stirred a latent sense of patriotism. And many people who heard Liszt's playing at those charity events claimed that his playing was transformed.

Wagehalsen wondered if Marie realized that her stormy relationship with Liszt was hopeless. How could she hope to keep the world's greatest living pianist to herself, keep him from expressing himself? Even as a teenaged onlooker preoccupied with making his own way in the world, he could see that Liszt was meant for the concert stage, and that the harder Marie clung to him, the further she unwittingly drove him away. The call of the concert world, the demands made on Liszt by society, by his pupils, and yes, by Wagehalsen himself, called for loosening a grip she apparently could not release.

On hearing that the Beethoven Committee in Bonn, Beethoven's birthplace, had failed to collect enough money to erect a memorial statue to the great composer, Liszt generously offered to defray the costs himself. He proposed a series of concerts from which he would donate substantial sums to the project. Predictably, Marie opposed it. When in October 1839 Liszt, despite her protests, left her in Florence with one of their children and her maids, and embarked on the tour, she bitterly reproached him for deserting her. He gave a concert in Trieste, and then traveled to Vienna, the city of Beethoven's greatest fame. While there in December, a delegation from Pest invited him to visit Hungary in appreciation for his having raised the largest single contribution for the relief of the victims of 1838.

26.

WAGEHALSEN TRAVELED WITH LISZT'S RETINUE to Vienna, and from there to Pressburg and Pest, Hungary, in December 1839. They traveled overnight from Vienna to Pressburg, arriving in that seat of the Hungarian Diet at 5 a.m., December 18. Liszt was the guest of Count Batthyány, and gave his first concert on the 19th, playing the *Rákóczy March* as an encore accompanied by cries of "Éljen! Éljen!" Only the most hardened cynic could not have been stirred by such a spontaneous, passionate outpouring of patriotic fervor. Austria had oppressed and exploited the country since 1711, when the heroic Francis II Rákóczy was finally defeated by the Austrian forces. Refusing to accept the humiliating treaty negotiated at Szatmar, Rákóczy fled the country and died in exile. Meanwhile, the Hapsburgs had brought in German and Slavic settlers, repressing the native Magyar language and culture.

Liszt's regret, often voiced abroad, that he spoke no Hungarian, was made even more acute here. Wagehalsen was touched by the irony of animated discussions about Hungarian independence in the language of their oppressors, sprinkled with French and occasional Hungarian enthusiasms. He smiled at the naïve optimism. Having experienced alienation from his own family in a country that had been dominated first by Napoleon's Confederation, and then by the Congress of Vienna, he suspected a deeper note of desperation under the bubbling surface.

The Hungarians' enthusiasm for independence would not likely be shared by their Austrian masters.

Wagehalsen had been only nine years old in 1830 when a similar desire for independence in Poland escalated into an uprising that was ruthlessly put down by Tsar Nicholas I. But sympathy for the Warsaw Uprising against Russian domination was widespread and trickled down even into the ears of a precocious preadolescent. And what was it that Robert Schumann had written in an 1836 article, that if the Tsar knew what danger to him lurked in Chopin's mazurkas they would be banned? The music was "cannon concealed among flowers." Fah! What had Chopin's cannonading from Paris done for the Polish cause? Expatriate Poles, no doubt, were deeply stirred amid the flowers while their countrymen at home languished in the Russian desert.

Increasingly uneasy over his own role in Liszt's entourage, and troubled by doubts, charged through though they were with Liszt's electrifying presence, Wagehalsen took to wandering alone in the streets late at night. They were snow-covered and cold, gleaming eerily in moonlight filtering through clouds and an occasional street lamp. The strains of Schubert's setting of Goethe's *Wanderers Nachtlied*, "Wanderer's Night-Song," drifted through his mind:

Über allen Gipfel	Over all the mountains
Ist Ruh	Peace falls
*In allen Wipfel*n	In all the treetops
Spürest du	You sense
Kaum einen Hauch;	Hardly a breath;
Die Vögelein schweigen im Walde.	The birds hush in the woods.
Warte nur, balde	Only wait, soon
Ruhest du auch.	You also will rest.

His feet had brought him to the edge of the icy Danube. The best we can do for mountains hereabouts, mused Wagehalsen, are those hills across the river in Buda. He sensed the shadowy, snow clad Carpathians

The Womb of Uncreated Night

dimly crouching in the darkness 160 kilometers to the north, not near enough to serve as stand-ins for Goethe's Hartz Mountains. The birds, hardly vocal at this time of year, had long since fallen silent. Without a breeze, the dead leaves clinging to the beeches hung stiff and silent, as if fossilized in frozen air. But he could neither wait nor rest. Something about the mountains drew him.

No respectable person would be afoot at that hour in the cold. Homeward bound after Liszt's performance, those who had not stayed for the lavish dinner which lasted the night—unheard of in a city where even the most convivial were in bed by 10:00 p.m.—passed by him in carriages. Perhaps they looked on such a figure with suspicion. Too well-dressed to be a robber. A member of the Austrian secret police? A wayward drunk? Or perhaps something more . . . what? . . . sinister? Who knew about these Hungarians? Late at night and in their cups, even the more educated among them might well smoke up peasant superstitions. Sober as he was, Wagehalsen could not shake off a swirl of dread drifting after the festive carriages. He could not well see into their shadowy interior, but imagined, caught in an occasional stray gleam—someone lighting a cigar or pipe, perhaps—a glimpse of a human gesture. An amiable enough greeting, perhaps, a benediction, while humming, no doubt, something the great Liszt had played. Friends gesticulating, perhaps, in animated discussion about the future of Hungary with such champions as Liszt to bring them honor and prestige among the enlightened Europeans.

More likely, they were half asleep. If there were any gestures, instead of salutation, some of them might instead be crossing themselves or giving him the fig to ward off the evil eye. What more light could the fading aura of brilliant company give off? Independence glistening over snow that would melt in the first thaw of cannon!

Where would István Széchenyi's bridge span the river and unite Pest with its twin, Buda, on the right bank? The project was currently being debated in the Diet, along with the possibility of a title for Liszt. Genius, after all, has a certain nobility. But genius has also a self-aware, arrogant superiority that makes it intolerant of mediocrity. Could the "genius," the spirit of the revolution against classicism in the arts, penetrate the darkness of the Concert of Europe, build a bridge and light the way to a new social order? Independence! Revolution!

Humbug for romantic martyrs!

Genius . . . Goethe's ideal of developing individual potentialities in harmony with oneself and society focused on genius. He considered it the essence of literature, and the creative artist, the individual capable of the greatest integration. But an unrestrained genius, flouting convention, like Beethoven, also posed the greatest threat to worn out social and cultural order. With his greater intellectual resources, he threatens to disturb the layers of mediocrity that cushion society from the shock of genius and unleash forces of destruction and negation. Only innate nobility sets him apart from the common criminal with whom he shares an antisocial image.

Liszt, have a care!

The "noble criminal" could not be dismissed as readily as his base cousin—no, that would strike at the very cultural order which the genius creates. He is nevertheless closely watched. Goethe was acutely aware of that. Intolerant of mediocrity in the arts, he tolerated mediocrity in the rulers of the German principalities who fostered them. Sidestepping social or political solutions to the chaotic forces set loose by the French Revolution, he turned, in his novels, his poetry, his dramas—even in his personal life—toward breathing new life into the Renaissance ideal of man. That allowed him free intellectual range and helped him realize his ideal. If that was not merely a personal solution, it was still a socially reactionary one. To be truly free, an intellect had to throw off passive consent to repressive social norms.

The Renaissance ideal exists in a privileged state conferred by "enlightened" rulers . . . on those who conform. Goethe was able to disengage himself from the revolutionary ferment spreading across Europe under the patronage of the dowager duchess of Weimar, Anna Amalia. Later, Karl August continued his mother's enlightened support of art and intellect under Goethe's guidance. Goethe could afford to remain aloof, a classicist amid the emerging romantic and democratic movements taken up by his restless contemporaries. Under a benevolent benefactor, a man of recognized genius could indulge his poetic tastes, be humble, and live out his destiny observing social conventions.

In short, he set limits for the "free" evolution of intellect, stopping short of threatening the social order which allowed intellect to evolve within those limits. A child submits to suspicious, overbearing parents who monitor his activities as they nurture him. Yet the individual entity, whether a single person or a collective with shared language and customs, like a child, ultimately must grow, develop, and challenge paternal authority or stagnate. A nation's desire to free itself from foreign domination springs from the same impulse as that of a child to escape parental restrictions.

But Goethe's genius flowered in a milieu of political and economic stability presided over by a truly enlightened ruler. What if genius goes unrecognized? What if it is suppressed or misdirected and the evolutionary spark is snuffed out?

When Goethe in the company of Beethoven encountered Napoleon and his imperial entourage, he was prepared to stand aside hat in hand, with bowed head. Beethoven refused to do as Goethe did, and instead, hat firmly on head, plowed into their midst. *They* had to stand aside for *him*. *There* is revolution for you! Genius submitting to authoritarian forces wanders off in lonely, unfulfilled yearning for an unattainable ideal. Ah, but what a lovely longing!

And Schiller? He, too, set the genius at the heart of literature, tilting at the sails of society. Schiller's genius was stifled for a time under the Duke of Württemberg, Karl Eugen. Very different from Goethe's Karl August, this "nobleman" sold his subjects to the British Crown as mercenaries in the American War of Independence so that he could give costly gifts to his British whore. If Schiller had not escaped from the military medical school at Stuttgart, to which the Duke's "benevolent" conscription and prohibition against writing had consigned him, he might have died of the consumption that eventually killed him before he had written *Don Carlos*, and the *Ode to Joy* which inspired Beethoven. He would never have reached Weimar, never become Goethe's friend and collaborator, never written his history of the Thirty Years' War, nor the dramatic trilogy celebrating Albrecht von Wallenstein, the Catholic general who tried to restore peace between warring religious factions, was branded a traitor to the Hapsburg emperor, and murdered. Wallenstein went to his doom trusting blindly in the stars of his destiny which lay in his own breast. How prophetic! The noblest individuals in Schiller's dramas, *Maria Stuart*, *The Maid of Orleans*, *William Tell*, and Schiller himself, were all branded criminals.

Civilization reigns as the greatest of vested interests. To these interests, the heroes of Schiller's plays were noble hostages. But nobility could not ransom them. Notwithstanding the democratic tone of his "Ode," embracing the millions with a kiss of joy for the whole world, peasant, burgher, and nobleman alike, the tokens of universal love plainly come from "above"—from a loving father who "dwells above the starry canopy." All the blessings of mankind flow down through ordained hierarchies, a benevolent God in the world above, the nobility in the world below. Only, by the time benevolence reaches down to the bottom, it is a muddy trickle.

A strange return! The privileges of the upper classes come from the wealth generated by the raw energy of the lower classes. The Patricians feed off them. Yet without the guidance of those bloodsuckers, there could be no civilization which enables some of us to evolve, to rise above the muck. *Us*, thought Wagehalsen. *We*, the Patricians who grudgingly love and work for the betterment of those who sustain us lest they run out of blood. But not too much love, eh? Not too much betterment, lest we run out of reasons for sucking their blood. And then who would we feed on?

The hierarchy is skewed. Genius rightly deserves the place at the top now occupied by vulgarians like Karl Eugen. Both Schiller and Goethe recognized the threat to the established order posed by unbridled individualism chafing against this injustice. The individual of genius had to be reined in, like a horse about to bolt. Civilization is a carriage drawn by genius, whose discarded skeletons jutting up out of the shifting sands of the mass of men jostle the ruling classes as they ride over them.

And Goethe in old age with only social convention to console him? Like the tired, insatiable old Faust of his last work, he realized that sensual gratification was for the moment only, that pursuing the moment of sheer bliss debased human existence. Redemption lay in a mystical yearning for union with "the eternal feminine"—the essence of the Virgin Mary, Gretchen, and Helen of Troy—that draws us onward out of depravity. As in medieval courtly love, honor and virtue—*perfection in imperfection*—lay in ardent desire that was never consummated, but sublimated in noble deeds. Perhaps that puts too sensual a slant on it. It was all summed up in the motto of the angels who bear Faust's soul to heaven: "Whoever strives in ceaseless toil can be redeemed."

But the mass of men are torn between redemption *now* and redemption bye and bye. Could reason lead us to either? Reason requires continuity, an arduous climb step by step up a steep staircase. Of course, there are German romantics—individual, fragmentary entities, like the German states today, remnants of the irrational Holy Roman Empire—who would lead us from the visible world to the world of the spirit through dreams of poetry. Dreams, ah, they soar above the loftiest structures. But do dreams, then, which are of the senses, and senses, which are flesh and blood truly imprison us, as Kant says? Could we escape them into that "real" world which he says lies beyond them and can be reached only through reason? What kind of "reality" exists beyond the senses? Without flesh and blood, reason is incomprehensible. The senses being of flesh and blood, how could the mind dream a dream of reason that would enchant the world of light and the world of night, and cause the shell of the visible world that seems so solid to fall away and leave only a core of spirit?

Wagehalsen walked along the river, scrutinizing the banks. Were the answers he sought encoded there under the snow, or in the Danube running south then east to the sea, or up in the sky, a frayed barrier of clouds through which a few starry lights twinkle in the darkness . . . ?

Fah! Starry lights twinkling in the darkness! How could the poetry of Pushkin and Lermontov even begin to pierce the Tsarist night of Russia? And France! If she had no need of emancipation from the threat of foreign domination, who could liberate France from the French? The Revolution of 1789 had not shaken off the stupid bungling of the upper classes. As for the well-meaning among the rising middle class— well, could the dramas, novels, or poetry wrought from the well-washed hands of Hugo, Lamartine, and Vigny have stopped the cannons and troops ordered out by Louis-Philippe to quell the workers' rebellions of Lyons and Paris? Not all the flowers in Chopin could have done that.

Yet here was the cosmopolitan Liszt, protesting his Hungarianness, futilely hoping to rattle the dotty Emperor Ferdinand and his ruthless Metternich with chords and arpeggios! Born in Hungary of peasant stock, Liszt had lived most of his formative years in France. He might be Hungarian in dream, but in speech and manner he had evolved into the cosmopolitan orphan yearning for a homeland that never was, and tacitly encouraging German-speaking Hungarian aristocrats to trump up Hungarian nobility for a French- and German-speaking musician of Austrian peasant forebears! Indeed!

Wagehalsen's shoulders sagged under the weight of the cold, and the dark. He shuddered and turned back to his rooms, brooding about Liszt's nobility. Well, why not? Nobility, after all, derives from those in power, no matter how despicably attained. If Napoleon had crowned himself emperor a thousand years ago, he, his family, and his heirs would be regarded today as authentic nobles instead of upstarts and usurpers. Time and acquiescence ennoble tyrants. Voilà, the origin of class distinctions! If it took a would-be Hungarian nobleman to press Hungary's claim to independence on the rulers of Europe, so be it! It was an image as worth cultivating for the prestige of a nation as that of a blazing virtuoso for his own. Not that Liszt ever made the bogus claim of nobility for himself. But he did not oppose it. He had got away with playing the

The Womb of Uncreated Night

banned Rákóczy March and that inflammatory patriotic speech—in French!—on being presented with the "Sword of Honor" at the concert in Pest, exhorting his "compatriots" to "shed their blood to the last drop for freedom, king, and country," if necessary. That the Austrian secret police had not arrested him on the spot did not necessarily mean that esteem for the Hungarian nobility had prevented it. Maybe the police simply did not understand French. The incident would be a huge joke in London and Paris. Metternich would probably join in the laughter.

What kind of fulfillment could such flummery offer? A nation asserting itself through its failed individuals? Fanning smoldering rebellion with musical winds would not blow fundamental change through the ruling status quo. With the exception of Count Rákóczy, the same nobility who had hastily proclaimed the short-lived aristocratic Hungarian republic in the eighteenth century had to come to terms with the Hapsburgs. There was something ominous in the euphoria over a march dedicated to a failed nationalistic hero who had died in exile rather than give in to the Hapsburgs. The nobility who had stayed behind, understandably, were ready to protect their vested interests. Grand ideals seldom take precedence over vested interests. The nobility who support independence in the nineteenth century would be no different.

Yet it was all so seductive. Surely, extraordinary gifts, not arbitrary power and kin, were the mark of true nobility? On that basis, Liszt certainly deserved the accolades, not merely the Hungarians', but the whole world's.

After a restless night, Wagehalsen took his leave of Liszt, who through the fog of acclaim swirling around him, hardly acknowledged his going. With no particular destination in mind on Christmas Eve, he traveled by diligence to the east, arriving at Bistritz in Transylvania on New Year's Eve.

A cheery elderly couple welcomed him at The Golden Crown Inn. Herr and Frau Menge were eager to share their New Year's Eve celebration with guests who, for whatever reason, were traveling at such a festive time. Even though the Inn was quite full, the landlord was able to accommodate Wagehalsen with one of his better, more expensive rooms, most of the travelers being of necessity more interested in economy than a well-to-do young gentleman with a "von" in front of his name.

In conversation with the landlord, he learned that he had happened on an inauspicious time to continue his travel to the east. The landlord was troubled about the young man's haste to move on. The innkeeper's wife especially hovered maternally over the restless young man, so far from home. Wagehalsen politely tolerated the solicitude of his hosts, but maintained his determination to press on with his journey. He wondered if the other guests were not as eager as he to resume their travel.

"Do you mean that travel through the Pass is hazardous?" he asked.

"Hazardous. Hazardous." The landlord chewed the word carefully, turning it over and over in his mouth like a wine taster before spitting it out.

"I suppose that the Borgo Pass is under heavy snowfall?"

The innkeeper hesitated. "That would usually be true at this time of year. Especially as almost everywhere else there has been a good snowing."

"But the Pass?" asked Wagehalsen, laughing. "What, must it be negotiated with a sled, as the Russians go?"

"With a sled?" said the landlord, joining in the laughter. "Oh, no! You misunderstand me. The diligence still runs more or less on schedule." Then he sobered. "But here we are, in the midst of winter, surrounded by snow on every side, eh? Enough to slow but not to prevent travel, you see. But in the Borgo Pass? *None*! *That* is what is so strange."

Wagehalsen was puzzled. "But then, where is the hazard in this strange absence of snow? Surely, good road conditions make it easier to travel rather than harder?"

"Ah, my young Sir, do you not see? It is against nature. We in these parts take such omens seriously. We have reason to fear what is unnatural. Especially in *that* place. It is natural for the Pass to be under snow when there is snow everywhere else. It is natural for us to expect some difficulty negotiating it. This lack of snow, now, *that* is *un*natural . . . *too* easy." Wagehalsen waited for the man to say more, wondering what kind of folk these were who objected to an easing of hardship?

"Well," he said, cheerfully, seeing the man was determined to say nothing more, "perhaps we can find someone who does not mind travel that is 'too easy' to take my fellow travelers and me through the Pass? After all, nature does at times play tricks with the weather. I must say your description has piqued my curiosity."

The innkeeper was alarmed. "Oh, Sir, do not joke about such a thing! There are some 'tricks' that go beyond nature. Even if you have no pressing business in Bukovina, I beg you not to think of lingering in that place. And if you do have such affairs there, you must make all possible haste to get through the Pass." He hesitated again. Then, in a cajoling tone, "Wait a bit, at least until it snows there again, eh? A blessing, a matter of a day or two!"

"Whoever heard of such a thing," wondered Wagehalsen aloud, "not to travel when the weather is clear, but to wait until it snows?" Perhaps the landlord was only trying to induce him to spend a few more nights in his hotel with this claptrap. Hold up travel plans and inconvenience his guests for the sake of a little extra rent—?

"Do you mean that none of your other guests are willing to travel through the Pass? Or that a diligence is not available?"

"Oh, yes. Others have been awaiting transportation to Bukovina and beyond. If you are determined to go at once?" he shrugged.

"You would not delay us for a little snow, eh?" Wagehalsen allowed his amusement to show. Had the landlord been pretending to his other guests that the diligence was not available, and at the first snowfall, it suddenly would be?

The innkeeper only sighed.

"I will arrange for the diligence tomorrow at noon," he said, glumly. "If I can find a driver lunatic enough to take you," he muttered. Then, more business-like, "If you make good time, you will reach the Pass at dusk. Even if the coach is delayed . . . well, you may reach it before . . . before it gets too dark. And a few hours later, you will be safely in Bukovina. You will not be able to see much. That will be just as well," he muttered. Then raising his voice again, "You will not reconsider?"

"No. I really wish to press on. Tomorrow noon, then." That would leave little time for lunch. But a hearty late breakfast before leaving should carry him through the journey. No doubt the innkeeper's wife would prepare a snack to be shared among the travelers. This rustic, Wagehalsen thought, is full of old wives' tales. The Pass is probably full of snow and this is some ploy to excuse his liability in case any difficulties arise. Wagehalsen dismissed the possibility that the man was only trying to increase his income. The Menges, after all, had treated him kindly. Nor did he want to reveal just how much the man's story had piqued his curiosity. In fact, he felt as if he were drawn to the place.

The innkeeper did not wish to pry into the affairs of his guest, and as the young fellow clearly was determined, offered no further resistance. "I will make an announcement to the other guests in the dining room at dinner," the innkeeper said.

Wagehalsen nodded, turned, and went up to his room. At table, later that evening, he overheard some of the guests talking among themselves. Some spoke a German dialect that he followed with some difficulty. Others, in a language he could not understand at all. Hungarian? Wallachian? Slovakian? Languages which would be common to these parts. But the drift of what they said was full of superstitious references that made him impatient with them.

The diligence next day was delayed. Something to do with unruly horses. When they finally got under way it was almost three o'clock. The road from Bistritz was, as the innkeeper had said, snow covered, but not impassable. If progress was a little slowed they nevertheless made good headway. The clouds which had hovered over Bistritz had cleared. The sun had set early behind the mountains. Several hours later, the moon had not yet risen and it was quite dark. Only the stars and the feeble light of the carriage lamps lit the way. It must have been nearly midnight as they approached the Borgo Pass. The snow cover had steadily diminished until, at the entrance to the Pass, there was hardly any at all, only mist hovering near the ground. A hush fell over the passengers who, until then, had been chatting amiably among themselves. The moon rose and cast an eerie pall over the mist. Wagehalsen demanded, over the protests of his fellow passengers, that the diligence come to a halt, claiming a call of nature. The others told him to relieve himself out the window, but Wagehalsen demanded some privacy.

Passengers, driver, and horses waited nervously as Wagehalsen ducked behind a boulder. The mists hovering at the crossroad leading through the Pass had become agitated. A form, like night taking human shape, suddenly appeared out of them. The horses reared, neighing in fright, the driver fought to control them as the passengers shouted to Wagehalsen to return to the carriage quickly. He dashed out into the road. The driver cursed as the horses bolted. The carriage careened away recklessly. Wagehalsen saw some of the passengers hanging out the windows, crying out to him in a language he did not understand, and crossing themselves.

He turned to face the source of the panic. The form had solidified into a tall man dressed in black. Solid enough, that is, though wavering disconcertingly, as if not quite sure whether his atoms were correctly distributed. Wagehalsen wondered inanely if he needed a mirror to help him steady his image. In that moment, the shade stopped flickering. It was still so dark as to be almost indistinguishable from the night, almost some trick of moonlight shining through the mist onto the dark rocks. He wore a great black hat that almost hid his face. Below that umbra, bleary eyes, as of someone who has not slept well, gleamed red. They clashed with his skin, ghastly in the moonlight. The man advanced on him. He must have been smiling, for his lips were parted, showing sharp, white teeth.

The young man was startled. From the first, the man exuded some hypnotic power over him. Wagehalsen stood rooted to the spot. But like all adolescents, he considered himself able to hold out against the influence of others. He stood his ground, caught too off guard to take a defensive stance, too reckless to be intimidated. The stranger smiled at the all-too-familiar bravado of a mere boy. He prepared to make quick work of him. Mouth agape, he gripped the youth by the shoulders, the fingers of his hands like the talons of some predatory bird, and turned on him a hypnotic glare that would have burned the eyes of an ordinary man out of their sockets.

But gazing deep into Wagehalsen's eyes he was surprised to find something more than the expected wariness of an innocent. Probe as he might, the man could not find the fear that would turn the boy's will to jelly. He scowled, annoyed. Then, raising his eyebrows, his expression softened and he drew back a little. There was more to this young fellow than empty display. His grip on Wagehalsen's shoulders relaxed and his arm curled around them into a clasp of camaraderie.

"Come, my young friend," he said. "It is too late to be wandering out here alone. You must be tired and hungry. I am Count Dracula, and my castle is but a short distance away. May I offer you its hospitality?"

Wagehalsen turned with him into the mist. It seemed they had scarcely taken two steps when he spied the castle rising out of the mists, towering above them on the edge of a great precipice. In the distance he heard the howling of dogs and wolves.

After he had shown Wagehalsen to a bedroom to freshen up before supper, the Count himself had set about building a fire in the hearth of a large adjoining hall. When Wagehalsen came out into the room shortly after, Dracula explained that he would himself attend to his guest's needs because his servants had left the castle for the night. In the light of the comforting fire and the candelabra which the Count had set on the table well furnished with food and wine, Wagehalsen had at last clearly made out the features of his host as he supped. Dracula, for all his

The Womb of Uncreated Night

vigor, appeared to be surprisingly gaunt and old. The skin of his face and hands was puckered, like someone's who had sat in bath water too long. Though of course no one could have submerged his face for so long. And his complexion was so pale that he wondered if the Count's skin would glow in the dark. The whole effect was bizarre, but Wagehalsen put it down to the effect of the wine after an arduous day of travel.

As the Count spoke, power emanated from him like halitosis.

"The mass of men," said Dracula, in his best tutorial manner, "are incapable of true individuality. They must be cared for, fed, clothed, and housed, even allowed simple diversion, procreation being among the most diverting. But kept in their place."

"Like cattle?"

"Exactly. Oh, they might resist if pressed enough—but it would be the cornered animal turning, instinct rather than intelligence. They can be quite dangerous. But a little care makes them quite manageable."

They sat talking through the night. Wagehalsen grew sleepy. But he was fascinated by the Count and fought to stay awake. He began to nod in spite of himself. They had not stirred from the hall, but as Dracula talked, the fire in the grate and the candelabra were doused. They flew together high over the mountainous terrain surrounding the castle. The landscape emerged from his fingers, augmented physical contours like musical intervals sounded in the air, clouds gathered at the merest flicker of his eyelid and rain fell in torrents—Wagehalsen heard rain splattering against the castle walls—then mists formed and were swept up into blizzards. Winds howled through the room, merging with and vanishing into the howling of wolves and dogs.

As in a dream, one experiences an exhilarating epiphany and awakens next day, aware of having dreamed but unable to recall the dream, so Wagehalsen *knew* as he listened, yet did not *know*. Something the Count planned to do. What was it? Like Faust, reclaiming land from the sea and setting up an ideal society? Only this was a dark and timeless sea, seamlessly flowing into night. Darkness on darkness, denseness sensed rather than seen. Darker creatures, winged membranes stretched between elongated limbs, flapped restlessly through the atmosphere, a darker current moving along an unseen shore. Something about the movement was disturbing . . .

When Wagehalsen came back to himself, he was lying in bed. He thought at first that he had drunk too much wine the night before and had lost all recollection of how he had managed to get himself into it. His head buzzed. Late winter light leaning into the room hurt his eyes. He raised his hand to shield them. An elderly lady moved quietly about the room, setting clean linen on a side board. She turned and saw that he was awake, gazing at her. Her anxious face lit up with a weary smile as she spoke.

"Ah, young gentleman! You have come back to us at last!" It was Frau Menge! Wagehalsen realized with a start that he was no longer in Dracula's castle, that he had somehow returned to the hotel in Bistritz. Seeing him puzzled and squinting, Frau Menge realized that the light was disturbing him. She hurried to the window and pulled the curtains to, then turned back to him. "There, it is better?" Without waiting for an answer, she ran to the door, gathering up a pile of soiled linen that had lain on the floor near the door, and called out. "Karl! Karl! He is awake!"

Wagehalsen raised himself on his elbows and looked around the room. It was the same room he had lodged in before his journey to the Borgo Pass. It was as neat as Frau Menge could keep a sickroom. A wash basin and ewer rested on a side table next to a smaller pitcher and a glass. The room was close and gave off a sweetly sour smell that was almost suffocating in the warmth from the tile stove in the corner. A wave of giddiness from the strain of raising himself caused him to fall back in bed and close his eyes. A few moments later, he opened them again as heavy footsteps mounted the stairs. Herr Menge looked in, as if to verify his wife's claim before entering. Smiling broadly, he came in and welcomed his guest. Although the young man looked haggard, Herr Menge saw that Wagehalsen had indeed awakened.

The Womb of Uncreated Night

"Welcome back, Herr von Wagehalsen! It is so good that you have returned to us." He gave Wagehalsen's arm a clumsy pat. "Do you remember what happened to you?" Wagehalsen shook his head. "Well, see to our guest's comfort, Martha, while I send for the doctor." Before Wagehalsen could speak, he turned and left. Frau Menge busily plumped up his pillow, poured water into the glass on the nearby stand and offered it to him. His throat felt congested and hot. The cool drink was soothing. But he could not speak. He wanted to ask about what had happened to him, how he had gotten back to the inn, how long he had been in this condition, but all that came out of his mouth was a wheeze.

"Don't try to talk, now," said Frau Menge, patting his shoulder. "The doctor will be here shortly and you will be soon right again."

Wagehalsen closed his eyes and waited for the doctor. He found that his sense of time was as baffling as his sense of place. No sooner had darkness fallen on his eyes than the doctor entered the room. Through his delirium, Wagehalsen saw that the man who had come in response to the summons of a servant dispatched by Herr Menge was very big, tall and bloated, wearing a heavy brown beard and a great black hat. There was something oddly familiar in the smile lurking behind his beard. His coat was buttoned up tightly to his chin, whether because his neck so bulged over the collar that he could not have unbuttoned it, or the cold still clung to him in spite of the warmth from the stove. Above the beard, his face looked puffy and flushed, as might be expected in a large man having just exerted himself in cold and climbed up stairs. He squinted as if against an icy wind. Or perhaps, his collar was too tight. He did not remove the hat, and came directly to where Wagehalsen lay. The hat, too, must have been clamped down too firmly on his head.

"Here is the good Doktor Eisenbart!" exclaimed Frau Menge. "Good afternoon, Herr Doktor. Your patient is better, as you can see."

"He is indeed looking better," said the doctor heartily, though Wagehalsen doubted he could see anything through the slits where his eyes would be.

"He looks so pale," pouted Frau Menge.

"But that is natural for someone who has experienced such a significant loss of blood," reassured the doctor. He looked round at Frau Menge hovering anxiously at the foot of the bed. "You will soon have him fit again with your excellent care. And now, be so good as to leave us while I examine his wound."

Frau Menge nodded and quickly left the room as Dr. Eisenbart began to remove the bloody dressing from Wagehalsen's throat.

He turned back to Wagehalsen. "The coachman found you wandering on foot nearby, dazed and bloody, several days ago on his return journey from Bukovina." He chuckled. "We thought that some brigand had cut your throat, robbed you, and left you for dead." The doctor had undone the dressing around Wagehalsen's throat and was closely examining the triangular, slightly jagged wound in which teeth marks and fresh blood were evident. "They were very much relieved to learn, hereabouts, that you had only been assaulted and robbed and left for dead!" The doctor's mouth was hidden by the beard, but Wagehalsen could tell that he was smiling from the way the moustache curled up at the corners where his mouth would be. "You were away for two weeks, and you have lain in this bed since you were found. I have visited you every day and attended to your wound. At times when you were half-awake, Frau Menge fed you a good meat broth mingled with fresh beef blood to build up your strength. Do you recollect any of that?"

Wagehalsen, still unable to speak, shook his head.

"You must rest a little longer. You were very foolish," added the doctor, chuckling again as he applied a fresh dressing to Wagehalsen's throat, "to have gotten out of the coach—no, don't try to speak or get up just yet," he said, as Wagehalsen struggled to sit up and say something. "Your memory of what has happened to you will soon return. Your . . . convalescence . . . will take only a little while longer, I promise you. You will soon be flying over the countryside in fine form."

To Frau Menge, who returned as he prepared to leave, he said, "Continue to give him the broth which I prescribed. It will build up his strength. And do not under any circumstance disturb the dressing on his throat."

Over the next several days, Wagehalsen drifted in and out of consciousness. Dr. Eisenbart continued to make regular visits. Sometimes, when Wagehalsen was half-conscious . . . *had* the doctor grown a little thinner, his collar looser, and his face more wrinkled? At other times, when Wagehalsen was fully conscious, yet unable to speak, the doctor anticipated his questions. "I have seen such wounds as yours before. I assure you that you will shortly regain the use of your voice. The wound in your throat was deep, but did not sever your vocal chords. It is—hm! hm! hm!—natural that your throat have some swelling after such a wound."

Wagehalsen fell back into fitful sleep. Fragments of his encounter with Count Dracula drifted in and out of his dreams. The Count came floating through the window, his cloak spread out like great wings. He was accompanied by three young women, beautiful, two with masses of glistening jet-black hair, and one with golden hair that glowed in an ethereal light. Their skin of such a pallor, so taut the capillaries showed through, yet faint-and-delicately puckered, like corpses freshly embalmed and rouged. Their sharp teeth gleamed white against their lips, and each wore rubies clustered at her throat. They were preternaturally sensuous. Wagehalsen was filled with indescribable longing. He heard them whispering among themselves. Then each of them came to him in turn and whispered at his ear.

Sometimes, as he dreamt he knew that he was dreaming, as when these visions came to him at night. They nuzzled his neck, whispering, whispering. They led him out through the window and over the countryside. He shared their joys—lusts?—and fears. As in most dreams, anxieties make the deepest impression. Impalement by stake was a rational enough fear. Abhorrence of garlic or a reluctance to cross moving water became so incongruous as to make him laugh—or did one laugh in dreams? But a growing horror of the crucifix and the host was most disturbing. Not that he had ever been deeply religious. While his parents might have disdained such things as bordering on idolatry, he had been indifferent, even irreverent. It was odd that they should affect him so. That such universal symbols of hope would actually horrify him was in itself horrifying. He wondered about holy water. The nightly visions had not shown an aversion to it, but then neither had they come across it. Would that, too, come to be as repellent? Strange not-knowing within knowing! Horror followed by flashes of exhilaration. He had never been fond of garlic, but now he found it revolting, suffocating. He found comfort in intoxicating ruby liquor drunk from tall white goblets. Enticing delirium.

When he awoke, he was not sure whether he merely dreamt he had awakened. But he was in the bed in his room. He began to yearn for rest in the warm earth of Weimar in summer.

Wagehalsen would regain some color and fill out a little, gratifying Frau Menge, only to grow pale again and seem to shrivel, alarming her. Yet all the while, he grew progressively stronger, able to move about the room and even to go out in the evening air. The landlord and his wife were at first startled by the suddenness of his transition from helpless delirium to vigorous activity, but they were gratified by his progress. When they saw him effortlessly lift heavy objects that would have made such a powerfully built man as Herr Menge himself huff and puff, they grew uneasy. The doctor's prescription for the meat broth fortified with animals' blood had made sense to them as a treatment for one who had lost a great deal of blood. But Frau Menge could not understand why Wagehalsen showed little appetite for the rest of her hearty cooking.

The Menges had become accustomed to Wagehalsen's evening constitutionals. Frau Menge, who did not sleep as soundly as her husband, was awakened late at night by stirrings in Wagehalsen's room. She thought she heard someone moving stealthily on the steps. If it was Herr von Wagehalsen, why would he be sneaking about at such an hour?

Herr Menge began to share his wife's doubts. Wagehalsen's great strength, increasing as his pallor, was decidedly *un*natural. At the prompting of his wife, he grudgingly remained alert and watchful one night after having pretended to retire. At the sound of the sly footsteps on the stairs, he quietly cracked open his door and saw Wagehalsen furtively leave the inn. His guest returned several hours later. Where he could be going at that time of night and what he might be doing was a question that Herr Menge did not want to think about. It was too *un*natural. He made the sign of the fig at Wagehalsen, and determined to tell him to vacate his room. Unwilling to confront him about his nocturnal skulking about, Herr Menge would make up some excuse. He needed the room for a previously confirmed guest . . .

Much to his relief, his strange guest announced the very next day that he was fit enough to depart and eager to return to his native soil. Frau Menge was still concerned enough to want to send for Dr. Eisenbart before Wagehalsen left, but he had been called away and was not expected to return for several days.

27.

WAGEHALSEN'S IMPATIENCE TO BE ON the move had returned with his strength, and with it had come a strange, inexplicable urge he did not fully understand. Of his recent illness he remembered only the weird dreams. Everything that had led up to the illness and since was for the time a blank. He did not, however, need a doctor to tell him that he was well enough to travel. This time, neither Herr Menge nor his wife expressed any concern for his well-being nor raised any objection to his leaving.

Bitter memories of Weimar and his family had left him without a desire to see either of them again. Yet he was puzzled. Somehow he knew he had to return to his native soil. Why, he could not have said just then. He would find out once he got there.

He arrived on the outskirts of Weimar unannounced a few days later and took rooms at the Wirtzhaus. His decision to leave Bistritz had been made with his mind still in a muddle brought on by his illness. Once the resentment at the way his father had treated him with the tacit approval of his mother had lifted, the gratitude he felt for Uncle Albert flooded in. He wanted to see again the man who had been more a father and benefactor than his natural parent. He secretly sent word to Albert explaining his circumstances. While Wagehalsen waited for his uncle's reply, it came to him why he had felt the urgent need to return to Weimar. Full of purpose, he commissioned the village carpenter to build eight large crates, two to be delivered to him at the inn as soon as they were completed. The remaining six were to go to his uncle. From the inn he would send one off to Paris and the other to Vienna. With his personal effects, he said. When he specified their dimensions, Herr Zimmermann joked that the crates would be large enough to serve as coffins. Two days later, Albert replied that he was overjoyed to hear from Heinrich Wolfgang. He assured his nephew that he would see to his needs and arrive within a few days.

The business of the crates attended to, Wagehalsen took to restlessly wandering around the countryside at all hours of the night. He returned unnoticed to the inn before the innkeeper or his servants were up and stirring. But the innkeeper, becoming aware of Wagehalsen's nocturnal excursions, asked his guest if he found the bed comfortable, and if not, could he do anything to make him more comfortable? Wagehalsen told him not to worry, that he often had bouts of insomnia that lasted for several days, and that the night air would eventually prove the comforts of what had been provided by his considerate host. He would soon be sleeping soundly. Privately, the innkeeper and his wife wondered if this well turned-out young man was quite right in the head. About this time, rumors of missing children and babies in the neighboring villages created a general malaise in the surrounding countryside and diverted their concern over their odd guest. When nothing sinister stirred up rumors in *their* village, however, the innkeeper and his guests clucked their tongues, shook their heads, and shrugged their shoulders.

Three days later, Zimmermann delivered two of the completed crates to the inn's stables. In the evening of that same day, Uncle Albert arrived in his calèche with the two heavy traveling bags Heinrich Wolfgang had asked for. After embracing his nephew, Uncle Albert handed them down. The inn's groom attended to the carriage as Wagehalsen easily carried the two bags into the inn and up to his rooms. He had refreshment sent up for his uncle, but nothing for himself. He had already eaten, he said. As Albert supped, they sat at a table where the young man related what had happened to him in the three years since he had left Weimar. Albert was spellbound by the tale that poured out of his nephew's returning memory. He laughingly declined his nephew's invitation to join in the new life inspired by Count Dracula, but encouraged the young man to live it to the fullest. Then Heinrich Wolfgang laid out his plan. The conspirators talked earnestly until early morning. Albert was amazed at the maturity of purpose in the lad and delighted in the daring adventure he unfolded. Heinrich planned to stay at the inn only long enough to oversee arrangements for shipping the first two crates. He would then take up permanent residence in Paris. He asked Albert to take charge of the remaining six as they were completed, furnish them as he would the two resting in the stables, and send them on to principal cities on the Continent as well as London and New York so that he could travel freely. Albert promised that he would.C

It was almost noon the next day when Albert woke. He had fallen asleep in his chair with his head resting on the table where he and his nephew had talked the night away. Heinrich was nowhere to be found at the inn, but he had left a note expressing gratitude for all that Albert had done for him. He had also left behind the now empty bags. Albert emptied traces of soil remaining in the bags, had some light refreshment to sustain him on his drive back to Weimar, and left soon after. And for the first time, the innkeeper and his wife were relieved that their guest seemed to be well rested when he appeared that evening to make final arrangements for the two crates to be sent out by post-chaise on the next day.

Like some mariner unable to resist its siren-song, Wagehalsen was drawn toward that cesspool on whose swirling surface bobbed the elegant and the brilliant, like the flotsam of some once graceful derelict in a sea of garbage. Paris . . .

The Paris Wagehalsen returned to in 1843 had not yet been crucified by Baron Haussmann: the *Grand Croisée* was still more than a decade in the future. The city had not yet begun to bleed through the great gashes inflicted on residential neighborhoods and slums alike into the gaping maws of the great city planner. And his étoiles had yet to twinkle in the coiling arrondissements and "quartiers." But a different kind of blood was about to flow out of a very different kind of gashes . . .

Like any new arrival to the scrap-heap of Parisian culture, Wagehalsen scratched through the detritus in search of its choicest morsels. For the leisure class, the haut monde, Sunday afternoons centered on the salons where the multi-tiered elite of intellectuals, artists, musicians, and government bureaucrats enjoyed discussions of the latest novelties, the latest designs in clothing, new books, a new actress or opera, a way of dressing the hair. Conversations were leavened by Chopin, Liszt, or Thalberg playing their own compositions; Beaudelaire, reading his poetry, Flaubert, a passage from a novel-in-progress, or Alexandre Dumas, *fils*, a scene from a play. Evenings were filled with the entertainments that charged those Sundays.

Having paid in advance for his apartment in the rue Rossini, Wagehalsen returned to find it pretty much as he had left it. The pianos needed tuning, and the place needed the attention of a diligent chamber maid. The crate from Weimar had been delivered and secreted behind a curtain in a bedroom upstairs. His other needs were minimal. He had lately tended to shrug off activities during the day. His senses had grown more acute, his eyesight so sensitive to bright sunlight that he preferred to wait until after dusk. If a salon was held on a sunny Sunday afternoon, a hat, a carriage ride, and even tinted glasses eased his way. But except for some exceptional event, he preferred evenings that stretched into late night or early morning. There was much to gratify his senses at concerts, operas, dozens of theater offerings, even the occasional cancan ball, and the convivial atmosphere of cafe society. Circulating through these rich and varied activities, Wagehalsen had quickly picked up news of the startling young actress who, at seventeen five years earlier, had galvanized the Théâtre-français with her performances of Corneille's *Horace* and *Cinna*, and almost single-handedly revived the classical theater. Now she was electrifying audiences with her portrayal of Racine's *Phèdre*.

The dusky, almost dingy dome arching above the interior of the Théâtre-français reminded Wagehalsen of horseshoes piled five high. As he descended the aisle to his seat, it was as if he were sinking beneath the streets of Paris under the imposing weight of centuries-old traditions of Corneille, Moliere, and Racine. The tiers of glowing faces, eyes sunk in sockets hollowed by the shadows cast under the chandeliers above arms crossed on the backs of seats in front of them rose in orderly tiers, stacked as neatly as tibias and craniums in the galleries of the catacombs.

The noise about Rachel throughout Paris had been that she did not merely impersonate Phèdre. She *possessed* her. But when Phèdre first appeared on stage with her nurse and confidante, Oenone, in the third scene of the first act, it was as if the other characters had been reciting their lines from the wings. Rachel not only possessed Phèdre, she possessed the stage, everyone in the theater, and indeed ancient Greece. She was there and everywhere. Wagehalsen had never before seen such a woman. Tiny, slight, not beautiful, no. But stunningly poised and self-assured, surveying the house as she transformed herself into the wild-eyed queen of Troezen. Wagehalsen felt her voice penetrating and vibrating within him. The horseshoes crammed with tibias and craniums faded away, as if he and the rest of the audience were transported back to that day on the ancient Peloponnese, part of some unseen Greek chorus watching with horror and pity as a noble queen destroyed herself and brought ruin to everyone she loved.

Full of self-loathing over her guilty infatuation with her stepson Hippolyte, Phèdre tries to make him think that she hates him. She hopes that he will hate her in turn, and so blot out her love. But the more he hates the more she loves, and her rage turns back on herself. Contemplating suicide, Phèdre hears that her husband is dead. She goes to Hippolyte for support of her young son's claim to the throne. But her passion for her stepson overpowers her. As she declares her ardor to Hippolyte, who is so embarrassed as to apologize for perhaps misunderstanding her forwardness, Wagehalsen leaning forward in his seat, hanging on every word, willing her to look at him, her gaze comes at last to rest on Wagehalsen with a start. For a moment, for him alone, the queen was dispossessed. Something in his eyes compelled Rachel to linger, almost to become absorbed in them. She hesitated oh-so-imperceptibly in Phèdre's rash, wanton solicitation of her stepson, so that in the instant she recovered enough to blurt out her exasperated reproach,

> *Ah! cruel, tu m'as trop entendue!*
> Ah! cruel one, you have understood me only too well!

the audience thought that they had witnessed a brilliantly calculated caesura. But Wagehalsen felt it pierce his heart and resonate to the depths of his being. Here was someone who recognized the odiousness of her passion, yet was unable to resist it. And worse, driven to proclaim what she detested in herself to the very person who had inspired the passion! When she quit the stage, the whole body of the audience quivered with an excitement that he alone truly understood. He felt, more poignantly than the others, the mad love, that like poison in the blood taking possession of one's being, she told her nurse she was dying of a mysterious disease and would not leave her bed for shame. That when she did come out into the light of day, she was dazzled by the sun and veiled herself against it. That she, granddaughter of the sun-god, Helios, should have shunned the sun in shame!

Rachel stood in the wings but did not appear onstage after the final curtain to acknowledge the tumultuous applause. Someone remarked that it was the gesture of a consummate actress, acknowledging the greater reality of the tragedy, merged with and overcome by the character she played. The audience was still enthusiastically greeting the other members of the cast as Wagehalsen, quivering, left his seat to find his way through admirers pressing around her dressing room. As she passed him, her luminous eyes fixed him again with their confusion of doubt and surprise. Impulsively seizing her hand, he whispered with an ironic twist of passion matching Phèdre's to Hippolyte, "*Tu m'as trop entendue!*" Her eyes darted across his face, searching for the question this alien presence had just answered. Then the corners of her mouth twitched in a fleet downturned smile ambiguously tinged with appreciative amusement as she pulled away without a word and entered her dressing room.

On the following night Wagehalsen sent her a bouquet of narcissi woven into a garland together with somewhat overwrought poetry, the beginning of a fragile and as yet untried spell. Because it was in English, which was suitably arcane and cast in Shakespearean form instead of the familiar heroic French couplets of Racine, Rachel begged her friend, the fat and aging Mlle George to help translate it for her.

> How revealing are the furtive eyes
> As, concealing their identity,
> They beseech in diffident disguise
> Amid the flowers of antiquity:
> Fragrant, sly narcissi deftly weave
> The fateful girdle of enchanted night,
> Casting mythic spells and so achieve
> The startled union of transfigured sight
> In the simulated symmetry
> Of mystical surprise. Deep in their toil,
> Wreathed in occult, arcane coquetry,
> Relentless, ancient, ardent forces coil.
>   Then mutual surrender serve us well;
>   Where lovers fondly grope there is no hell.

"La, la, la!" clucked Mlle George, "is it not always among the flowers that the mortal woman is plucked by the god? Take care, my dear, that you are not gathered up too soon!"

Rachel laughed aloud at Mlle George's quip and the closing couplet. Charmed by Wagehalsen's gesture, if somewhat doubtful of the prosody, Rachel began, in spite of herself, subtly and unconsciously, to yield to its spell. But why had this interloper assumed that she knew English? Why had he not used French, at least in form if not in tongue and spared her these doubts! A rondeau or rondelet?

Then Rachel, coached by Mlle George, tried to read the lines in English, uncertainly, swallowing the unfamiliar *h*s and from force of habit pronouncing the letters as they are in French. She struggled with the opening line again.

'Aou reveelEENG ar' de fürtEEV aiz . . .

How would such a phrase go in French, she wondered?

Que les yeux furtifs sont révélons . . .

"But no! This is not hexameter!" She flung the lines away from her in irritation, unwilling to be bested by this English-rhyming German pedant! Her first, chauvinistic thought was that his French must simply be inadequate. Perhaps he supposed that English was a better alternative. Then in a more conciliatory vein, perhaps a greater mystery required a sense of—*otherness?* He *was* . . . charmingly entwined, this . . . this . . . *enguirlandeur!* . . . this *entwiner*. She laughed aloud and clapped her hands in delight at her euphemistic conceit on garland-maker. Was it not a little like a more self-possessed Phèdre hitting on the perfect retort, *à l'ésprit d'escalier*, plucking triumph out of dismay at Hippolyte's reproof?

Without exactly knowing why, she picked up the sonnet again, folded it neatly and tucked it into her bodice. As she absently patted the note against her breast, she contemplated the garland of narcissi. If magical, dare she try it on? Like the princess in a fairy tale who cannot resist temptation, she smiled smugly at the absurdity, took it up, and placed it jauntily on her head before the mirror on her dressing table.

Mais q'est-ce que c'est! She was visibly startled as a wave of dizziness overcame her. Mlle George sprang to her side as Rachel reeled, about to faint. "What is it, child? What is happening?" The blood had drained out of Rachel's face. She gasped for air, unable to respond to Mlle George's incoherent little cries of concern. The eyes that stared back at her out of the mirror—so intense!—could they be hers? Her own image seemed to fade in the burning, blurring intensity of those eyes. Mlle George dabbed her brow with rose water. But no! How absurd! There she was again! It was, after all, only a momentary dizzy spell.

Not surprisingly for the daughter of a peddler, from the first flush of her success onstage at seventeen, Rachel was never choosy about her admirers as long as they were influential men of means. From the fascinatingly repulsive, obese, Dr. Louis Véron to the poetic dandy, Alfred de Musset rebounding from a tempestuous affair with George Sand, all advanced her career or enhanced her comfortable lifestyle. So it came as no surprise to her circle of acquaintances that she responded warmly—even too eagerly some of the more cynical said—to the attentions of the wealthy young Wagehalsen. "Greed in a Jewish father," intoned a scandal-mongering author, "is only natural; in a brilliant daughter, it is a vice." What did surprise them about the German was that he was neither old enough to be her father nor grotesque. Perhaps she sensed in him the demonic obscured by his youthful appearance.

Wagehalsen simply assumed that his poetic spell laced with narcissi had done its work. He was welcomed into her bed without hesitation. Locked in his embraces, she was indeed bound to him. It did not matter to him that the bed, the apartment, the fine furnishings in which they thrashed about in ecstasy, were all shared by other men. What he had not anticipated was the grip of enchantment on *him*. The spell rebounded back on him so overpoweringly that the frenzy of their lovemaking was caught up in a wild urge to sink his teeth into her throat. In their first encounters, he felt that their climaxes were dimmed by his resistance to the impulse.

The sense that something in the ultimate frisson was lacking, however, did not lessen his passionate attempts to capture it. Night after night and several times each night he grappled with himself to seize it. With each encounter Wagehalsen found himself increasingly tempted to yield to wild impulse. Until the night when, fearing that he was about to lose all self-restraint, he abruptly withdrew, hastily threw on his clothes, and fled Rachel's boudoir, leaving the woman gasping and bewildered.

Dizzy with unspent passion, he plunged into the dark street, frightening the driver of the carriage waiting for him, and stampeding the horses.

The city was still a maze of festering rat warrens burrowing through the crumbling façade of a medieval town. The stench of humans, animals, mud, and shit in the streets never yielded to the perfumes and eaus of the bourgeoisie. Cobblestone pavements may have spread to the main thoroughfares, but only the boulevards had sidewalks for pedestrians. Walking in the *rues* was an act of defiance. Unheard of. Laborers, artists, and other bohemians might relish late night jaunts through the open sewers that served as streets. The haute bourgeoisie could descend from their carriages to stroll under the elms of the Champs-Élysées or in the gardens of the Tuileries, around one of the city's chateaux, visit a boutique, a café, a restaurant, or other place of accommodation along the festive boulevards. But proper people simply did not walk through Parisian side-streets. Not if they wished to avoid the risk to life, limb, and property. And if these came through intact, the scorn of social inferiors. Even a foot tastefully shod in the latest fashion could also wear in dry weather a patina of dust, or in wet worse, when exposed to a walk through the filthy *rues*.

In such an atmosphere of physical and emotional upheavals, cats and dogs were no longer used merely to control mice and rats, or as guardians and hunters. They became companions, pets. And because dogs are more gregarious than cats, they became the pets of choice. Occasional outbreaks of rabies did nothing to decrease their popularity throughout the middle and late years of the century. But Parisians bitten by dogs were often terrified of contracting the disease during the common two-month incubation period. Their fears were aggravated by virtual isolation during the incubation period.

Soon the beau monde was abuzz about a strange apparition skulking about the boulevards and side streets late at night. Rumors agreed that the bizarre figure was a man wearing a large black hat pulled down over most of his face, a long black cloak reaching down to his calves and wrapped close around his body, and boots. Beyond that, they contradicted each other, almost as if they were describing two different men. It was all quite novel. Now he was naked under the cloak, bloated and ruddy, trying to conceal his nakedness under the cloak. But then he was thin and pale, no more than a boy, his elegant formal wear merely hidden under that long cloak. And although the hat obscured his upper face, especially late at night on the poorly lit paths, one could see a long brown beard. But no! again. He was clean-shaven.

At about the same time, men, women, and children had begun to mysteriously disappear. A few were later found in out-of-the-way places, in alleyways, behind shrubbery in the bois at either end of Paris, or in less frequented public gardens, even behind grave stones in wooded cemeteries. Their throats were torn, and some had odd incisions vaguely resembling inverted triangular marks made by sharp upper canines and prominent lower incisors. No one could agree. Their bodies were all drained of blood. Was a new epidemic sweeping the city, one this time that killed the unsuspecting and left them vulnerable to marauding animals? Rabid dogs, perhaps? Or even, in a shudder of horrified ecstasy, *vampires*. It was all a kind of myth-making, the kind of horror story with which grownups frightened little children. And sometimes themselves.

After carousing at a bistro one night, a young woman who had taken too much absinthe returned to the apartment she shared with her sister and her family. When her family noticed teeth marks on her throat, they immediately feared the worst. They locked her up in a room in their apartment to wait out the dreaded incubation period. When she declined food, they were convinced that she had been infected, though they had no inkling with what. They were so afraid that they, too, would be social outcasts if her condition were made known abroad that they did not send for medical help. They debated *en famille* about the best course of action.

While the family was agonizing over what to do, the woman, who had developed a morbid craving for blood, managed to lure her young niece into unlocking the door and entering. The adults, naturally, had not included the child in discussions of auntie's condition, but they had warned the child not to go near the room. Like all children, such a prohibition only fed curiosity and led her to the aunt's room as unerringly as a scent hound is drawn to the spoor. This was, after all, her favorite grownup, the auntie who always brought home treats whenever she returned to the apartment, and who had cared for and kissed the child since her birth. It took little coaxing from the aunt for the child to find the key which her parents kept hidden, to unlock the door, and rush into her aunt's eager arms. But when the expected kiss turned into a savage bite on her neck, the child screamed in pain and terror, bringing her parents running to the room.

The scene was total chaos. The child shrieking hysterically, unable to understand why the aunt who had so often interceded with her parents when she had been naughty could attack her; the mother, horrified by what she believed was the confirmation of her sister's disease and the infection of her daughter, clutching her as if she would squeeze the disease out of her; the father, beside himself, denouncing his sister-in-law as a beast and had to be physically restrained from attacking her by his brother who was there on a visit. And the aunt herself, ghastly pale, eyes darting wildly about, cringing in terror. The poor woman's mind bordered on disintegration. She craved the child's blood, but her moral sense had not yet deteriorated so far as to keep her from recognizing the enormity of her transgression. She felt that she was going mad. She clutched her temples, sobbing convulsively. The alarmed family was convinced that these were the dreaded convulsions that would end her life in agony. Father and brother ordered mother and child out of the room, and then, while his brother held her arms, the father seized a pillow from the bed and smothered her.

Whether pitied as wretches out of a novel by Hugo, reviled as *salopes* gripped by mad passion, or admired as *courtisanes*, prostitutes, too, have a mythic color, and the gruesomeness of an occasional mutilated corpse added a certain piquancy. Prostitutes made the Bois de Boulogne at the western fringe of the city, the city's moral fringe as well. There, they plied their trade amid vampires of every kind, those who drank, those who sipped, and those who merely sniffed the corks. The abundance of prey in the secluded parts of the forest in particular drew Wagehalsen. Deep in the Bois there was a pool in a kind of glen, a popular gathering place, where he could drink deep. The casual disappearance of a prostitute little mattered to a city still recovering from the cholera epidemic, overpopulated, underemployed, and mired in crime. The Parisian police, who might shrug at lesser crimes, took dead bodies seriously. But there were so many of them that the occasional naked, decomposing body of a prostitute fished out of the Seine left little for the police to investigate. As long as it did not clog the source of the city's drinking water, Parisians shrugged it off. After all, prostitutes were the dregs of society, and one need not drink to the lees.

The Bois, then, was a kind of sideshow with a moral tinge. The place stimulated such unconscious, romantic fascination with the lurid in nature that the lush landscape gripped both the depraved and the enlightened in a kind of mystical marketing venue. The brothers Goncourt, Edmond and Jules, who wrote disdainfully about the buyers and window shoppers promenading through the place in their journals, were eager visitors. Not surprising, then, that on one of their rambles, they spied a mysterious figure in cape and top hat in the shadows around a lone *salope*, hovering "comme un vampire." They lost no time in reporting the encounter in their journals and gossiping about it at the soirées at the Hôtel La Païva, the mansion of a notorious *courtisane* on the Champs Elysées, and elsewhere. The Goncourts wrote scathing comments about La Païva in their journals, but then the misanthropic brothers blithely calumniated just about everyone. They did not, however, decline invitations to La Païva's mansion. Nor were

The Womb of Uncreated Night

the Goncourts alone in their gossipy, slummy pastimes. Artists, literati, and other well-connected prominent citizens frequented the Hôtels of courtesans as well as those of respectable ladies. Indeed, it was the poet, novelist, and critic, Théophile Gautier, who had introduced the Gouncourts to La Païva. Alexandre Dumas, *fils*, Charles Beaudelaire, the Duke de Morny, and no less than Prince Napoleon and Count de Viel Castel, both cousins of Louis Napoleon, were among the notables. Viel Castel, a minor official at the Louvre with little else to do, was another scandal-mongering diarist who gossiped about the *demi-mondaines*. But the presence of these lights of the *haut monde* shone alike on the soirées of both the respectable and the *demi-monde*.

Rumors following the appearance of the mysterious figure haunting the area quickly spread through the salons. The convergence of these sightings and bodies found with punctured throats combined to raise the specter of a vampire hovering over the city. But in the city of myths, high society might enjoy a gratifying shudder at the idea of a vampire while believing that lighthearted flirting with danger somehow kept it at bay. Only the unwary succumbed to it. Besides, everyone with any sense knew that feral animals released by the negligence, illness, or death of their caretakers were most likely to be responsible for the mutilated corpses. No one really believed that the strapping young fellow, hardly more than a boy, who had begun to frequent the salons could possibly be connected to the deaths. The intelligentsia were too sophisticated to be frightened by ignorant superstitions. But as with other fashions, the aura of such a figure in imagination was paramount, and the myth of the vampire captivated them. Imagination fed by rumor made the vampire of the Bois de Boulogne all the rage, an avidly sought-after novelty. The woman casually plying her trade in an area fraught with dangers invited anonymity. Her disappearance excited little concern.

It became a kind of race among the fashionable world, especially among the ladies, to lure the sinister *fantôme* of the Bois into their circle. What a coup for the hostess who managed to snag him! If he were a little bloodthirsty, well, Parisians could be among the bloodthirstiest of disgruntled non-conformists. They could enjoy the myth of the vampire much as they might admire the audacity of an elusive criminal who flouted the *flics sales*, or any other authority figure without wishing to be one of his victims or lowering themselves. So mad was the beau monde to add him to their gallery of exhibitions that they soon made it rather hard for him to dine. No sooner had Wagehalsen brought a prostitute under his spell but an emissary of some salon or other would approach to proffer an invitation. Unaware of their intent, Wagehalsen regarded them as intruders and faded into the shadows before they could reach him. It only remained for some resourceful stalker to manage to accost him from a discreet distance after he had dined, replete, languidly reclining against a tree.

But Wagehalsen did not spend all his time dining on the local cuisine. Paris was full of other diversions. He walked the two blocks from his apartment behind the rue Rossini to reach the Opéra on the rue Lepelletier. He placed his foot onto the pavement and turned into the square on which stood the Opéra. Like an artist's brush on a blank canvas from which a bustling scene flows out across a boulevard to the vanishing point, drawing the crowds, on foot or in carriages, past shops, and apartments, the panorama radiated from his boot. The air of that November evening was chill but still mild. A light rain. From the corner where he stood, at the *Place de l'Opéra*, the streets glistened in the light of the gas lamps flanking the porticos of the building. Proper people arrived in carriages. They descended and moved through the jostling strollers who had come to gawk, to pick pockets or cut purses, to beg; *flâneurs* who gathered in the fashionable thoroughfares just to be seen and jostled by the crowds, or to make their way flamboyantly to some public entertainment. As he had not fed in several days for the occasion, he fit quite sleekly into the evening clothes made for him by a fashionable tailor, replete with opera cape and tall hat. Yes, a light after theater supper would suit him well. He strode confidently toward the theater. As he moved through the knot of people in front of the portico, he was caught up in a garish lamp lit carnival whirling

The Womb of Uncreated Night

past him. The rouged and powdered faces of ladies of the *demi-monde* bloomed above their silk and satin gowns, distinguishable from those of their less successful sisters through eyes glazed by adulterated liqueurs. The hats and beards of the men shrouded their faces so that their eyes gleamed from shadowy hollows.

People on all sides hurried off to one of the principal diversions of the evening. The evening's opera was *Semiramide,* with the coloratura soprano Giulia Grisi as the Queen of Babylonia and the celebrated mezzo-soprano Pauline Viardot, sister of the equally celebrated contralto Maria Malibran, as Arsace, her unrecognized son and future king. Fashionable ladies and gentlemen would thrill to their execution of Rossini's stunning roulades and vocal pyrotechnics, while those with less lofty tastes would whirl off to oblivion in the balls of orgiastic cancans popularized by Philippe Musard.

The hubbub of horses' hooves, the creak and groan and rumble of carriage wheels on the cobblestones, the faint, sharp hiss of the recently installed brass-bound streetlamps, flaming jets like a hundred lambent birds' beaks pecking away at the shell of night, beacons of the July Monarchy to mark the rustle and shuffle of people dressed by purpose or chance in finery or in rags, the tapping of sticks and the heels of a thousand feet, mingled with murmuring, rasping, buzzing voices breaking against the Romanesque columns of the porticos of the Opéra.

The *contrôleur* at the entrance directed such a pointedly sidelong look at this elegantly attired young man whose boots were smeared with street waste that he almost refused his ticket. But the smears Wagehalsen left on the plush carpeting were soon shared with the press of other feet entering the theater. The carnival of the streets yielded to the stately elegance of the hall. A thousand voices, the rustle of ladies, and orchestral fragments surged through the room. Yet Wagehalsen felt a sense of restfulness underlying the agitated surface, an atmosphere of order and restraint as the audience filed into their seats. Wagehalsen had arrived a quarter hour before seven, curtain time. As he looked around the auditorium before taking his seat, the dazzle and glitter of the ladies in their gold and jewelry, the chandeliers blazing high above intoxicated him. He might even catch sight of Chopin, a regular at the opera, Liszt, or other members of his circle, and find a way to be invited to one of the midnight parties they were renowned for. But the room was blurred by the enticing, shimmering, rosy haze coursing warmly through the audience.

The orchestra had tuned their instruments and the random racket subsided into an occasional scrape of the bow or bleat of woodwind. As the audience caught sight of the conductor moving across the pit, they broke into applause. Wagehalsen turned in anticipation of the exhilarating dream to unfold on stage, a feast for the senses, after which he would repair to a sensuous feast of another kind. Acknowledging the applause with a slight bow, the conductor turned abruptly and signaled the orchestra. The overture throbbed quietly and rose quickly in volume to a mighty *fortissimo*, the musical signature that had earned for Rossini the sobriquet, *Il signor crescendo*. Then the house lights dimmed. The gas jets lit up the stage as the curtain rose on the sumptuous interior of a Babylonian sanctuary.

Babylon! A city renowned in ancient times for luxury and sensuality! It did not matter that the librettist, with sublime indifference to history, had the Babylonians worshipping Baal, the *Canaanite* god of fertility and life who had nothing at all to do with Babylon. Baal would anyway have been a more recognizable pagan god for a European audience than Marduk, his Babylonian equivalent. Nothing could have suited Wagehalsen's frame of mind more appropriately! A crowd of the citizens praises Baal, hoping for a male successor to their recently dead king, ironically unaware of the court intrigue that drives the action of the next four hours.

Even as his ears filled with the brilliant coloratura of Mme Grisi and the rich contralto of Mme Viardot, flawlessly projecting their show-stopping roulades into the uppermost tiers of the house, Wagehalsen could not help smiling at the recollection of the vanity of humans praising gods while they were in the hands of tyrants. Four years had passed since his journey to Transylvania, the peoples of Poland and Hungary were still subjects of harsh rulers, and they all professed belief in the same God! Beautiful music might not erase bitter irony. But it soothed and lulled indignation. And after the dream on stage had ended, Wagehalsen would awaken to answer a different summons.

As he left the theater after the opera, Wagehalsen's skin puckered from hunger. The opera had whetted his appetite. He decided that he would dine more sumptuously than he had earlier intended. He stalked a drunk young dandy in a dark side street as easy prey. He stared hypnotically into the young man's eyes and loosened his cravat, idly wondering which of the seventy-two ways of tying it the young man had used. As the man lost consciousness, Wagehalsen felt his skin bloating. His own clothes became constricting. Continuing to gorge away on the young man's life, he had to remove his own clothing under cover of his cloak. First his belly distended, threatening to split the seams of his breeches. Then his upper torso, as the swelling forced him to remove his coat and shirt. Wagehalsen was unclad down to his stockings and boots, still covered by his cloak. As he drank deeply, Wagehalsen almost choked on laughter at the thought that his skin was becoming so taut that he could be played like a drum. He felt tipsy and alive. The young man was sober and dead.

Interlude

Korngold sat in his usual place behind his desk, resting his sore leg on a drawer that he had pulled out for that purpose. "You know," he said as he stuffed a favorite pipe with tobacco, "there are areas of agreement between my preoccupation with nineteenth-century vampires, for example, and yours with Batman."

"You're not going to tell me you've been masquerading as a nineteenth-century vampire," said Brewster. "It's a good way to bark your shins."

"Are you saying that you've been masquerading as Batman?"

"No," said Brewster. "You don't see me with a sore leg. But somehow, I can't see you as a real-life vampire. Amateurs are apt to hurt their legs in aborted take-offs."

"No," said Korngold, "I haven't been masquerading."

"You mean you really are a nineteenth-century vampire?" said Brewster with mock-eyed awe.

"If my leg is sore it's because you've been pulling it! But you know, it's a fascinating thought. What it would be like to have the powers attributed to the nineteenth-century revenant: superhuman strength, the ability to mesmerize with a glance, sexual prowess, even the ability to disappear in a mist." Korngold lit his pipe. "Quite seductive," he said between puffs. "And, you know, the more one thinks about a thing, the more palpable it becomes. As if it materializes out of thin air . . . " Korngold trailed off.

Brewster gazed at him curiously as a cloud of smoke filled the space around the desk. "And this materialization, does one interact with it like some video game?"

"In a way. Exploring what's fact played off as a counterpoint to what's imagined. So, then, conversing—not flying—with the period, I've encountered a particular vampire—"

"Tabloid sensationalism about the attacks in Central Park has sent you over the top!"

"Ah, but there are documented cases of practicing vampires in past centuries as well as this one, long before the current outbreak."

"Oh, I know firsthand the attacks are real enough. But do you really believe these vampires exist—as supernatural beings, I mean—and that the recent attacks aren't just the shtick of some maniac trying to play up a well-known myth?"

Korngold searched the expression on Brewster's face. Either he was unaware of the irony of his words, or he was playing very cool. "There's some evidence of more than one attacker. It probably all started with one attacker who may or may not have truly believed that he was a vampire, and the others . . . maybe hysterical copycats."

"Excuse me," interrupted Brewster. "Wasn't there something about a virus . . . ?"

"There was, indeed. In fact, Dr. Buckyballs assures me there is positive evidence of such a vector. But the same disease may affect different people in different ways. They may have the same symptoms, and still express them differently. The question is not what I believe, but what they believe. Belief can create powerful delusions, and belief is a powerful motivator."

"And this particular vampire of yours, he—it's a he, yes? He's the one with the hole where his heart ought to be?"

"Let's just say that it's the case of someone who believed that he was a vampire and actually practiced vampiric acts. Someone who recognized himself," added Korngold, watching Brewster's face, "in myth."

28.

SUCCESSFUL HOSTESSES HAD BEEN SETTING the tone of society since the days of the Revolution. They were always on the alert for some hitherto undiscovered talent, some new phenomenon, some new cause, which they could cultivate, exploit, and groom as the next *fureur* that would secure or maintain their place in society. Paris never lacked for such wonders, nor for hostesses with a knack for making happy choices among them. Acquiring prodigies raised the *recherché* to art, a fine balance between the absurd and the sublime, better if the absurd were successfully finessed into the sublime, and best of all if the ploy could be sustained.

Madame Lavoisier was born Adèlaide Chatouille, the illegitimate daughter of Martine, a beautiful washerwoman who worked for a wealthy landowner in the Auvergene. Happily married, the landowner nevertheless was unable to resist the charms of his laundress. When indulging those charms led to the birth of a baby girl, he discharged his paternal obligation by bribing Sgt. Joséph Lavoiret, a dashing young infantryman stationed in the town, to marry his indiscretion. When his regiment was relocated to Paris in 1815, Sgt. Lavoiret moved there with mother and baby. There, Martine bore her husband another girl and a boy. When the cost of living in Paris outgrew her husband's ability to support his growing family on his wages, he deserted both them and the army, never to be heard from again. Forced to earn a livelihood any way she could, the still beautiful Madame Lavoiret turned to "trade." At fifteen and grown into a girl as beautiful as her mother was promiscuous, Adèlaide added her talents to the family economy.

Charming ladies of wit and grace lurk in any corner of society. But no matter how artfully obscured by circumstance, a favored few are inevitably discovered by men of, shall we say, superabundant creativity who eagerly pursue new outlets for their talents. Never content merely to dabble with plastic but inert material—for what is more plastic, more malleable, more yielding yet vibrantly alive than the human female?—such men penetrate into the most hidden places in pursuit of art. The pliant natures of the ladies overlaid a shrewdness mingled with determination, perhaps even a touch of cunning combined with a certain ruthlessness. They spun formidable nets indeed.

When Wagehalsen first began to circulate among the salons, he thrived on the rumors. He habitually arrived, thin and pale, wearing a great black hat, a long cloak, and boots, but no beard. He allowed servants to take his hat, but refused to surrender the cloak, which he kept wrapped close around him. Ladies gasped in delight at the sight of what looked, indeed, like a boy of no more than seventeen or eighteen years. Gentlemen scoffed at the idea that this mere slip of a boy could be a menace to anyone. It was a delightful tease, quite scandalous, really. The Romantic appeal of consumption was at its height, and his pale, wistful appearance, what could be seen of it, gave him a fashionable sensuality. The ladies were irresistibly drawn to him whether he was a consumptive or a vampire. His "quaint" eccentricity made him a much sought-after adornment in the salons of the beau monde. They delighted in the vampire rumors as much as he. In an era when the consumptive look was considered not only fashionable, but downright sexy, Wagehalsen's thin phase, underfed and pale, was a turn-on for the ladies.

His pallor was largely the result of seldom venturing out into daylight rather than any horror of it. Shunning the sunlight was a habit he had picked up from Dracula. And of course he was careful to "feed" only after visiting a salon, lest post-prandial bloat spoil his ethereal fragility. He also avoided rooms with mirrors—a trivial enough caprice in a society delighting in self-admiration—though Adelaidé, now known as Madame Lavoisier, gleefully covered over the mirrors in her apartment or turned them to the wall when he arrived.

"Oh, M. Wagehalsen is here!" Madame Lavoisier exclaimed, gleefully rushing into an anteroom to greet her notorious guest. At the same time, she signaled to a servant who immediately scurried through the apartment turning mirrors to the wall. A tittering hush fell over the assembled guests as they eagerly awaited the entrance of the man of mystery.

Wagehalsen never disappointed. Everyone assumed that *if* he wore anything at all under that cloak, it would be impeccable evening clothes. Everything about him expressed understated elegance, even down to his pallor and the discreet little cough he affected. He resisted all offers of refreshment—which only added to the cachet—keeping the cloak closely wrapped around him. That titillated and scandalized the ladies, who speculated that he wore nothing underneath, like a Scot in kilts. They made a game of devising ways of getting him to expose himself. They would suddenly offer their hands to him hoping that, to acknowledge their greeting, he might have to expose a bare arm. Or a lady contrived to coyly drop a handkerchief so that he might be obliged to bend over to retrieve it, deliciously exposing somewhat more than a bare arm. He always responded gallantly. But he foiled them by not extending more than a gloved hand outside the front of his cloak, or bending at the knees, his cloak seeming to absorb the handkerchief as he retrieved it until he straightened up and presented it to the charming culprit. It sent the ladies into delighted giggles. They never tired of the game. The hoped-for prize would be a delightful scandal.

At other times, arriving enveloped in his cloak as usual, Wagehalsen would throw it off with a flourish to the gasps, and disappointment, of the ladies by being fully clothed. Men were understandably less enthusiastic about this farce, but were unwilling to be perceived as not knowing how to take a joke. One of them, a doctor who made a study of prostitutes at all social levels and had come to Mme Lavoisier's salon to observe an upper class demimondaine, inquired as to why she encouraged such antics.

"Ah," she replied with a knowing smile, "but is it not altogether the fashion to be mad for novelty, for the latest designs in clothing, new books, a new actress or opera, a way of dressing the hair? Is it not the aim of every hostess to astonish society and set it to raving, about some man, perhaps, of whom nobody has previously taken the least notice, and suddenly make him all the rage? By the rules of propriety, the only sin is the failure to amuse." The doctor, sagely acknowledged her response, and quickly turned away to make an entry in his notebook.

Nor were Wagehalsen's sartorial mannerisms his sole attraction. He was urbane and witty, even if he spoke French with a German accent. A hostess anxiously anticipating the tardy arrival of an important artist or musician, could count on Wagehalsen, when he was not hiding behind his cloak, to display his considerable skill at the pianoforte. He still bore the effects of the ill-fated mechanical finger strengthener that had ruined his aspirations as a child to become a virtuoso rivaling Liszt. But he was able to perform some of Chopin's recently published *Études* and *Préludes*, even if the florid passages came off slightly less than flawlessly. And if another musician complained that an instrument had been improperly tuned, Wagehalsen awed everyone by turning the tuning pegs with unassisted fingers.

At one of these soirées, Madame Lavoisier coolly awaited the arrival of Chopin on the arm of George Sand. It was well-known that Chopin's attitudes toward women in general were, to say the least, conservative. His first reaction to Sand dressed in men's clothing and smoking a cigar at a soirée given by Marie d'Agoult was scornful. He thought her repulsive. But maneuvered into frequent encounters by Countess d'Agoult and Liszt, Chopin finally came to appreciate her intelligence and wit. Before long they were a couple seen everywhere together. But for Chopin to be seen at a soirée given by a *courtisane* . . . well, that would be quite a *coup*. But the hostess knew that George Sand would find the presence of a reputed vampire irresistible. And where Sand went, Chopin followed. So while Madame Lavoisier subtly circulated rumors of the impending arrival to keep her guests on edge, she herself remained calm and poised. Just the suggestion that the famous lovers *might* appear assured the success of the evening. And to keep them entertained, she prevailed on the vampire to play something suitable.

Wagehalsen obliged Mme Lavoisier's delight in novelty by playing Chopin's *Polonaise in f# minor*, which Chopin himself considered not only a new piece but rather like a fantasy into which he inserted a mazurka in place of the conventional trio of the genre. As Wagehalsen was playing the stormy first part, Chopin entered the room with George Sand and stood dumbfounded and indignant. Though Wagehalsen's rendition was note-perfect and exactly as Chopin had played the piece, his imperfect left hand almost imperceptibly smudged the chromatic runs in the bass. It went unnoticed by the other guests, most of whom were hearing it for the first time. But Chopin noticed.

"Who is this imitator of Liszt imitating me playing my music?" he demanded in Polish-accented French indignation. Wagehalsen laughed good-naturedly and rose from the piano to introduce himself. But Sand, ever watchful over Chopin, took his arm, engaging him in conversation as she led him away.

"I did not mean to offend M. Chopin with my clumsy rendition," he began. "It was only to fill in the time until he arrived."

"On the contrary, Monsieur," she said patting his arm, "I thought you played rather well. It's simply that Frédéric has a horror of strangers."

"But the execution of the bass line," Wagehalsen continued. "M. Chopin would surely have noticed that the runs were blurred. You see, as a child I was jealous of the great Franz Liszt and determined to rival him. I used a device that suspended the fourth finger of my left hand above the keyboard as I played. I was trying to increase its independence from the third finger."

But Sand chided him for being too severe with himself. She understood only too well the desire to free oneself from the limitations of the body. She, herself, had used one of the devices for strengthening the fingers, as necessary for a writer as for a musician.

"Imagine the irony," Wagehalsen laughed. "I injured the finger trying to outplay M. Liszt, and now he is helping me to overcome the defect!"

"Ah," chuckled Sand, "our hands are sometimes guided in mysterious ways, *n'est-ce pas*? Yet how were you able to play that *Polonaise* so like Chopin's own manner? It was recently published, so you must have seen the music. But as far as I know, Chopin has played it only once before at a soirée?"

"Yes, I was there and heard him play it."

"What, and you were able to play it after one hearing?" smiled Sand askance.

Wagehalsen shrugged. "One's memory is less prone to physical imperfections."

"*C'est ça.* But what is this charming nonsense about vampirism?" she said, lips pursed to keep from laughing, whether the rumors spreading about him through the salons, that he was a vampire, were true? *En voilà une bonne!* What a good joke! A marvelous entrée into society!

"It lends one a certain . . . aura, does it not?" he countered with a smile, slyly alluding to George's given name, Aurore. "It is said to confer many benefits. It sharpens one's faculties. One becomes immortal, does not age, does not suffer illnesses—"

"And are you so ancient? If that were so," said Sand, "why, then, has your hand not completely recovered its full use?"

"I, madame? Ah," sighed Wagehalsen, "while vampirism is said to arrest, it does not cure."

"So, if one had an inactive disease at the time of his—how would one put it?—entry into this new state of being, he would never relapse?"

"That may be so. If what one hears is true."

"How fascinating!" She patted his hand, amused.

As she was about to take her leave and return to Chopin, who was now seated at the piano and playing the polonaise "properly," Wagehalsen wondered, "Would Chopin, perhaps, consider taking him on as a pupil so that he might learn to compensate for the injury?"

She paused, still amused. "He prefers upper class ladies, but he has taken on a favored few men. You are not Polish, by any chance?"

"Alas, I am quite German."

"Well, I am sure that Chopin was more impressed than annoyed by someone who could play one of his compositions from memory, even if a little rudely, after having heard it only once. Perhaps he could be coaxed into taking on another male pupil and polish off some of the rough edges of such a talented one."

She stood for a moment contemplating the enigmatic young man, almost a boy. As in much of Chopin's music, there was a serious undertone in the trills and roulades of the badinage. Sand had taken him to Majorca three years earlier to escape winter in Paris. But the normally mild climate in the Mediterranean had turned chill and nasty. She would find him at the piano late at night, pale, with haunted eyes and disheveled hair. Chopin suffered an alarming collapse. Soon after their return to France, he appeared to have completely recovered. But he was declining again. He looked drained. She dreaded a relapse. Thanks to the sang-froid that never wholly deserted her, she was hardly ruffled at all when she heard about a letter written by the Marquis de Custine, whose salon was influential in artistic circles. In it, he denounced her as a vampire, and cited the condition of Chopin as proof.

Any resentment such a comment might have generated was quickly dispelled in the wry amusement at the previous night's soirée. A circle of music devotees including Liszt and Chopin had gathered at the Marquis's estate at Saint-Gratien. Liszt played a Chopin nocturne, embellishing it with flourishes of his own, to Chopin's annoyance. "Do me the honor of playing my music as written, dear friend, or not at all." Liszt got up from the piano, feeling slighted. "Play it yourself." At which Chopin promptly sat down at the instrument. As he was playing, the company gasped when a winged creature flew in through the open French doors, flitted over the lamp and extinguished it. Moonlight streamed in through the windows, barely illuminating the keyboard as Chopin began to improvise on the nocturne, his eyes all the while on the creature. Some thought it was a large moth, "*un papillon de nuit,*" others, in excited whispers—"*Non! non! pas un papillon. C'est une chauve-souris!*" no! not a moth. A bat!—as it fluttered back and forth through the silvery light in time with the music. No one really believed it was a bat. But it made a good anecdote. It was all quite magical, and Liszt, awed and humbled by Chopin's playing, embraced him as "a true poet" whose works "ought not to be meddled with."

So her interest in vampires was neither mere banter nor purely academic. But was it, perhaps, indeed a bat? wondered Sand. Would Wagehalsen have the face to pretend that he had transformed himself into a creature so attuned to Chopin's playing, and in such a guise heard Chopin playing his Polonaise? It was too droll, she thought, almost bursting into laughter. But what a piquant episode it would make for a roman!

As she turned away, about to return to Chopin's side, Wagehalsen touched her arm. She gasped at the energy in the touch. She listened to what he said in a momentary daze. "Perhaps, madame," he said, looking at her intently, "perhaps, M. Chopin would do me the honor of visiting my apartment to discuss the possibility of taking me as a student?"

After a moment's hesitation, she gave a small laugh and promised to speak to Frédéric.

Sand persuaded Chopin to accept the invitation to visit the man of mystery on the following week. She thought that Chopin might be as amused as she at the conceit of a vampire who could improvise himself into a bat while Chopin improvised on the pianoforte, presumably under its spell. Chopin suspected that she was as much concerned for his delicate health as for the enjoyment of a good joke. But he had come to depend on her for so much that it was unthinkable to go without her.

They found Wagehalsen's secluded apartment. Chopin wore his usual elegant attire, light gray hat, long overcoat, muted vest and cravat, white gloves, and polished boots. Sand wore her usual male attire, echoing Chopin's, a gray overcoat, wool cravat, gray hat, and black boots. Chopin had come to tolerate her dress, if never wholly to accept it. Despite gloomy weather, Wagehalsen had the curtains drawn over the windows of his apartment. He apologized for the dimness of the room. "I am susceptible to the migraine. My eyes are very sensitive to light, which sometimes sets it off."

"Ah, a true creature of the night finds his way by ear?" teased Sand, more inclined to believe that this mischievous boy had drawn the drapes for her benefit and Chopin's. Then with polite concern, "But if you are ill . . . ?" she added, offering to curtail the visit.

"Not at all. I merely explain why so little daylight is admitted to my rooms."

Sand bantered about the curious creature that had snuffed out the lamp at Saint-Gratien. She watched Wagehalsen's face with amused detachment. But of course, thought she, Wagehalsen might well have learned details about the evening through the efficient Parisian gossip-mill. She wondered again if he would have the cheek to claim it was he who had been fluttering about the night before, extinguishing lamps and inspiring Chopin? Chopin was amused as Wagehalsen said he remembered well how beautifully Chopin had bested Liszt, even to mentioning the nocturne that had begun the contretemps. But that was also the kind of claim noised about by partisans and detractors.

As they chatted, the imposing square of the two pianos in the center of the room, the Pleyel preferred by Chopin, and the Erard favored by Liszt, drew Chopin's attention. As to why Wagehalsen needed two pianos, Sand had a ready rejoinder.

"Perhaps vampires can be in two places at once and are able to play duets with themselves? Charming!"

Even the usually somber Chopin again joined in the laughter. Still smiling, Wagehalsen replied, "I play the Erard when I want to sound like Liszt. But when I want to sound like Chopin, ah, then I must play the silver-tongued Pleyel! The best of both worlds!" He turned to Chopin and invited him to try it out. Wagehalsen and Sand stood, listening, as Chopin sat and began to play, becoming absorbed in exploring the action and sonority of the instrument. Wagehalsen led Sand to a divan set against the wall where they could continue to talk without disturbing Chopin.

Without ever admitting outright that he was a vampire, Wagehalsen enjoyed feeding the rumors. "After all," reasoned Wagehalsen when Chopin was out of earshot, "the vampire's 'treatment' is but a form of bleeding, one of the recommended treatments for phthisis. And an admirable sounding alternative to it, would you not say?"

"But any form of bleeding might dangerously weaken him," said Sand. "Not that I would really seriously consider it for an instant."

"Ah, yes! But the blood shared between the vampire and his, ah, *patient*," chuckled Wagehalsen, "ultimately strengthens rather than weakens. They say that in the final delirium of consumption, the dying think they experience a renewal. Only in this case, it is really so. Or say they say."

"You would have to kill Chopin in order to turn him into a vampire, to live again as revenant?"

"Oh, not literally. It's the sharing of the vampire's blood, transmitting an essence that traces back in time to some primeval source that bestows immortality. Some mysterious component that survived in some ancestral vampire infected with the magic of night ... The blood is the life, and transmitting it is a kind of procreation—"

"What?" exclaimed Sand laughing. "How delicious!"

"There is a kind of death in it, I suppose. Like all forms of behavior, one is tempted to excess, and excess leads to depletion. Death. But when that pool of blood is shared, it plunges the one who shares deep into an enchantment from which he awakens anew. Age and social class fade into irrelevance."

"Ah, the devil's pool," said Sand reflecting. "But one must die, even a little, in order to be born again, is it not so?"

"Not only to be 'born again,' but to remain free of the ills that come with age. It would be a sorry immortal who lived forever burdened by disease and decrepitude!"

An ambivalent shudder passed through Sand. Wagehalsens' words were repulsive yet strangely fascinating. Perhaps the hint of world-weariness in one so boyish in appearance charmed her. She was tempted to play a practical joke on him with Chopin's assistance. "Perhaps Frédéric would welcome a chance to escape his illness once and for all," she began, thinking, of course this stripling was only living up to his notorious hoax. She would turn it back on him by encouraging Chopin to express interest in the vampire and see how far Wagehalsen would carry his sly evasions. Not as coquettish a ploy as a dropped handkerchief to see how much the "vampire" would expose, perhaps. But then, she was hardly affecting lady-like manners. She hesitated, "On religious grounds," she told him, to allow it for herself.

Wagehalsen chuckled at religious hesitation in such an otherwise unreligious source. "The vampire's 'treatment,'" argued Wagehalsen, "is certainly preferable to the alternatives, wallowing in excrement, breathing the emanations of cesspools . . . "

"Ouf, monsieur! *monsieur*!" remonstrated Sand in mock horror, fanning the air with her hand. "If you seek agreement, perhaps the atmosphere could be more agreeable?" She chuckled, then repeated her concern that any form of bleeding might dangerously weaken Chopin. "The 'little' death you spoke of earlier not withstanding." Then, feeling very protective of Chopin and instantly regretting the joke, "It would be very cruel," she said with a wry smile, "to toy with his illness, even as a joke, monsieur le Vampire—ah, pardon, *monsieur le docteur*."

Chopin had tired of entertaining himself at the piano. He stood up and complimented Wagehalsen on the quality of his instrument. He gave Sand a slight nod. It was time to leave. As they crossed the courtyard back to the street where their carriage waited, the sound of a piano stopped Chopin dead in his tracks. Wagehalsen was playing exactly, note for note and inflection for inflection, what Chopin had been playing during the visit, complete even to the improvisations! Chopin felt his scalp crawl. He felt suddenly faint and clutched at Sand's arm to steady himself.

"But what is it?" gasped Sand. "Are you ill?"

Chopin began to perspire. The wave of dizziness had passed as quickly as it had come. "No," he said with a reassuring smile. "It was only a momentary light-headedness."

They hurried off, Sand laughingly telling him about the practical joke she had considered playing on Wagehalsen. As they reached their carriage and climbed in, she told Chopin about their conversation, of the absurd discussion of the benefits to health to be gained by becoming a vampire. Chopin's curiosity was aroused by the reference to "curative" powers. But the thought of allowing someone to drink his blood, and worse, of his drinking someone else's blood, made him feel faint again. Sand assured her "little one," as she called him and patting his arm, that M. Wagehalsen was only joking.

"He is hardly more than a boy and obviously enjoys playing a charade that keeps him at the center of attention," she said. "He will eventually tire of it."

"If others do not tire of him first," grumbled Chopin sourly.

"Or if he loses interest in the game," she patted her 'little one's' hand, "as children so easily do. He will no doubt 'haunt' elsewhere."

29.

As Wagehalsen walked along the Seine in the chill February night of 1848, he could not help reminiscing about his walk on the banks of the Danube nine years earlier. It was winter again, though February in Paris was milder than December in Pest. Once again revolution was in the air. Growing demand for participatory politics had been sweeping across Europe since the 1830s. An insurrection in Palermo, Italy, had sharpened a feeling of instability that spread northwards. The high cost of food in France, economic crisis, financial scandals, and resistance to suffrage reform created a general malaise that hung most heavily over Paris. On February 22, thousands of Parisians took to the streets to demand voting rights. A crowd gathered outside the home of François Guizot, Louis-Philippe's prime minister. A nervous sentry opened fire. The crowd panicked, touching off further alarm among the soldiers on duty and within minutes thirty citizens had been shot or trampled to death. A confrontation between workers and soldiers outside the Chambre des Pairs signaled the collapse of the government.

Unrest in France spread into the southwest German states and swept across the Continent to the Russian frontier. None of these uprisings made cohesive or coherent sense to Wagehalsen. He saw deep division among the factions of Left and Right. He was amused to see their bickering members gradually drift into demands for participatory governments and constitutions. He was beginning to understand that *participation* meant *bickering*! And now, as Wagehalsen surveyed the pathetic heaps of debris that barricaded the Parisian rebels against the well-armed forces of the Status Quo, even the sight of Victor Hugo inciting a group of workers to heroic resistance filled him with dismay and contempt.

All through the unseasonably warm March that followed, Wagehalsen could only shake his head as he observed the spreading turmoil. On March 3, Lajos Kossuth attacked the oppressive Austrian system that dominated Hungary in a speech to the Diet. A German translation reached Vienna, and by mid-month, Viennese students and workers were demanding the resignation of the hated Prime Minister, Prince Metternich. The crowds grew throughout the day and the army was called out to disperse them. Inevitably, the soldiers responded with excessive force. The crowds fought back. Metternich fled. The emperor, Ferdinand V, abolished censorship and agreed to convene a constitutional assembly as soon as possible.

At the same time, the Hungarian Diet had been sitting in its ancient capital of Pozsony not thirty miles from Vienna. The people of Pest revolted. The Diet demanded far-reaching reforms, including an independent prime minister. The emperor agreed. Similar concessions across the German states spread optimism across the Continent. The rebels deluded themselves that there was reason to hope. Yes, the rulers of those states had signed decrees granting the demands of their citizens. But would they follow their promises with anything substantial? Wagehalsen shrugged. He would wait and see. He thought again of his walk along the Danube, the dismal collapse of the Polish Rebellion in 1830 and the futile protests of the Hungarians in 1839. Would there be no end to these pathetic outbursts? And Liszt? The "patriot" who had been greeted with cries of *"Éljen! Éljen!"* then? Where was he now, eh? Neither in Paris nor in Pest.

A provisional government proclaimed by the poet Alphonse de Lamartine in front of the Hôtel de Ville led to the Second Republic. Universal male suffrage and the "right to work" of every citizen ought to guarantee social and economic reform. The elections of April 23 enthusiastically ratified the republic so promisingly begun. Censorship of the press was abolished, as were imprisonment for debt, slavery in the colonies, and indirect taxes on wine and salt. Victor Hugo, who had publicly supported the workers during the revolution and first days of the provisional government, won a substantial number of votes even though he had not been not a candidate in that election. They encouraged him to campaign for a seat in the National Assembly at the next election to be held on June 4. It spelled the first letter of that republic guided by sages, philosophers, and poets that Hugo yearned for.

The next few months, however, revealed how disunited the factions in the National Assembly were, and how tenuous the balance of power. Too conservative for the radicals and too radical for the conservatives, the provisional leadership quickly began to unravel after they handed over their powers to the National Assembly on May 9. The June elections fulfilled one of the expectations of April. Hugo was indeed elected to the National Assembly. But on June 20, he unwittingly lent his voice to reactionary forces with disastrous results. National Workshops had been created to put idle men to work. They turned out to be a futile make-work in which men were paid for doing nothing. He urged the Assembly to find a more practical solution for the unemployed. He was shocked, therefore, when two days later the Assembly closed the Workshops and ordered the conscription into the army of all workers under twenty-five. The others would be sent to work in the provinces.

Predictably, the workers defied this order by once again barricading the streets with paving stones, rubble, beams, bars, shattered windows, rags, and chairs. They shot anyone who tried to disperse them. Desperate to restore order, the moderate, well-intentioned government, the poets Lamartine and Hugo prominent among them, gave General Louis-Eugène Cavaignac dictatorial powers to suppress the revolt. Then Hugo along with fifty-nine other representatives was chosen by the National Assembly to go to the barricades and inform the protesters that a state of siege had been declared. They were to urge the protesters to disperse peaceably and avoid spilling more blood. Nine of them were shot on the streets as they tried to approach the barricades. Hugo led a contingent of the National Guard to the barricade that had been thrown up across the main road into the Faubourg Saint-Antoine. He risked his life, advancing alone, and pleaded with the insurgents to surrender. He failed. On the "June Days," the 24th, 25th, and 26th, Cavaignac ordered his artillery to fire on the barricaded protesters. Instead of merely informing the insurgents of their risk and allowing them to determine their fate, Hugo personally stormed the barricade, directing troops and cannon, taking prisoners. The man who considered the rebels innocent, heroic, justified but misguided, directly contributed to the deaths of many of them. Peace and order were restored. Hugo consoled himself with the thought he had saved civilization. But the siege mentality lingered. Cavaignac continued to exact reprisals against the heavily armed working class to ward off "the Red Menace." But the enforcer of "peace and order" also closed theaters, censored the press, and imprisoned their editors.

Liszt was in Weimar, having accepted an offer to serve as Kapellmeister to the Grand Duke, Karl Friedrich. He had ended his last concert tour and just arrived early in February, 1848. He was immediately preoccupied with his new duties, preparing a performance of Flotow's opera *Martha* for the birthday of Grand Duchess Maria Pavlovna on February 16, directing concerts for the royal household, and giving singing lessons to the Grand Duke's sister-in-law. He was also pleading with Maria Pavlovna to intercede with her brother, Tsar Nicholas, to grant the annulment of the marriage of his lover, Carolyne, to Prince Nicholas von Sayn-Wittgenstein so that they could marry. He hardly noticed the revolution in Paris the following week.

Early in April, Liszt traveled to Kyrzanowicz, the castle of his friend, Prince Lichnowsky, in the Sudeten Mountains, where Carolyne joined him two weeks later. Liszt and Carolyne sojourned at the castle, as if unaware of a continent coming unraveled. They were there when the government of Louis-Philippe collapsed in France, when Kossuth prepared a revolt in Hungary, and when uprisings erupted all over Germany. They were planning a nostalgic trip to Vienna, where Liszt had made his debut as a virtuoso, to the Franciscan monastery in Eisenstadt, Austria he had visited with his father as a boy, and the humble cottage where he was born in Raiding, Hungary. At the end of April, against the revolutionary turmoil further south, Liszt and Carolyne traveled to Weimar, which had been so far untouched by the disturbances.

They arrived in early May, staying just long enough for Liszt to move into the Erbprinz Hotel and lease the Altenburg, a large house on the outskirts of the city, for Carolyne, her daughter, and their servants. They intended to create an illusion of maintaining respectable separate households so as not to offend the conservative sensibilities of Weimar, or indirectly threaten the hoped for dissolution of Carolyne's marriage. When they arrived in Vienna, they stayed at the Hotel Stadt London where, on May 6, Liszt was serenaded by medical students. The Hungarian revolt was popular among the working classes of Vienna, and university students, ever eager for a cause, enthusiastically supported them. By this time Liszt was well-informed about the political turmoil. He addressed the students from his balcony, supporting the cause of reform. But he preferred the reasonable voices of statesmen such as Batthyány and Széchenyi, who called for negotiated settlements, to Kossuth's incitements to open rebellion.

After showing Carolyne the sites where he had lived and studied as a boy, he visited street barricades with the Hungarian national colors pinned to his button-hole, passing out cigars and money. He even composed an *Arbeiterchor*, a "Worker's Chorus," for male voices. But the inflammatory tone of the text, declaring that the "mighty hammer" of freedom "will nevermore be allowed to fall from the hand," gave him pause. He decided to delay publication until the situation had calmed down.

The Womb of Uncreated Night

It was July before Liszt and Carolyne returned to Weimar. The Altenburg overlooked the Ulm River from the top of the hill that gave it its name. Isolated by six acres of woodland, it commanded a view of the duke's castle, the Rathaus in the market square, and the Herder church. The court theater lay about a mile away and could be conveniently reached by a brisk walk through the market-square.

Wagehalsen arrived at the bottom of the steeply rising steps leading up to the house late in the evening of the last days of summer. He was troubled, not about calling so late because he could see and hear lights and sounds pouring through the windows of the Altenburg into the cool night air. Liszt was given to late night entertainments. But news had reached him in Paris the week before that Emperor Ferdinand V had betrayed his agreement to grant Hungary some independence. Ferdinand had entered into a treacherous agreement with General Jelacic, sending him into Hungary at the head of an army of Croatians and Austrian regulars. They committed heinous atrocities on the peasants as they marched to Pest. Hungarian independence was doomed.

Although most visitors were breathless by the time they had climbed up the steps with only an iron railing to support them, Wagehalsen took the steps easily two at a time and rang the front doorbell. Several minutes passed but no one answered his ring. Thinking that the sounds of music and voices he heard through the closed door and open windows might have drowned out his first ring, Wagehalsen rang again. The door opened abruptly. Heinrich, one of Liszt's menservants, looking a bit surly and rumpled, had assumed that Wagehalsen was a late arrival. He had been in no hurry to respond to someone who could not trouble to arrive at a more reasonable time. He merely shrugged and showed Wagehalsen in to the main reception hall. The open house Liszt and Carolyne held in the evenings was in full swing.

Carolyne was serving truffles and ices. Guests were chatting in groups as they took the refreshments. Wagehalsen was struck by the youthfulness of the gathering, most of whom he had not seen before. Catching sight of the new arrival, Carolyne greeted him cordially but with some surprise as she did not recognize him. Wagehalsen introduced himself and explained his past relationship with Liszt. At this, Carolyne took his arm and led him to the group gathered around Liszt's Erard concert grand in the center of the room. As they threaded their way through the guests, she confided that Hans von Bülow who was seated at the piano, flanked by Liszt on his right and Carl Tausig on his left, were discussing the interpretation of a passage from a score that lay open on the piano. The music that Bülow played was unfamiliar but intriguing, Liszt nodding in agreement but Tausig vigorously shaking his head. As Wagehalsen moved toward the trio to pay his respects to his mentor, Liszt turned his head. His face lit up at once with recognition and delight mingled. But then a shadow of perplexity crept into his expression.

"My dear Wagehalsen!" he exclaimed. "Carolyne, do you know who this is? How long has it been?" Then, peering closely at his former pupil, "But how is it possible? You have not aged a day!"

"Age is not merely physical," smiled Wagehalsen. "Whatever lingers on the surface does not delay the changes inside." Carolyne left the men to get reacquainted while she moved away to resume the conversation that had been interrupted by Wagehalsen's arrival. Liszt introduced him to his companions at the keyboard who barely nodded at him before returning to their discussion. Seeing that the quarrelsome Tausig was bent on continuing to disagree with Bülow, Liszt interrupted them.

"Here, my boy," he said to Wagehalsen, nudging Bülow to get up from the keyboard. "Sit and give us your opinion as to how this should go."

Wagehalsen smiled at the condescension. An orchestral score lay open to the singing contest from Act 2 of *Tannhaüser*. The knight Wolfram, a former close friend of Tannhaüser's, sings in flowery language about courtly love whose essence is pure devotion from afar. Tannhaüser rises to challenge him, calling his love timid and bland compared to the joys of the flesh. The ensuing exchange over this affront to feminine virtue shocks the ladies and leads to a confrontation with drawn swords. Only the climactic intervention by the virginal Elizabeth who throws herself in front of him saves Tannhaüser. It was the shifting tonality of Wolfram's song in E-flat, the key of holy love and salvation, to Tannhaüser's sensuous E, that was in contention, Bülow insisting that the change was sudden, dramatic, and emphatic. Tausig argued that the half-step shift in tonality was emphatic enough to make further emphasis a crude assault on the ears of the audience. It would be more effective, he insisted, if played more subtly. Wagehalsen scanned the instrumentation and the vocal lines, playing tentatively and softly at first. But as he played, he became engrossed in the music and began to play more forcefully, unaware that conversation had stopped and the guests had turned their attention to his performance. When he looked up and saw the surprise in the faces around the piano, he abruptly stopped and began to apologize for having interrupted their conversations. Liszt only responded by taking him up by the arm and leading him into the Blue Room.

The study was sparely furnished with a piano, writing table, and a few chairs. Liszt motioned Wagehalsen to a chair at the keyboard, evidently expecting him to play, and took a chair to one side. Liszt explained that the piece in contention was for a performance of Wagner's opera to celebrate Maria Pavlovna's birthday next February. Bülow would assist Liszt in conducting, and Tausig, a pianist with fingers of brass and mind to match, simply enjoyed contention. "Ah," said Wagehalsen, softly playing again the part of the score which had been imprinted in his memory.

"The meager resources of the orchestra will require many rehearsals. These will be prepared by Bülow and me. Bülow is an excellent fellow and an able assistant. But I fear that the long hours of rehearsal with the orchestra—some of the players are mere amateurs—will take up so much of our time that we will have to share coaching the vocalists with someone else. You have shown an astonishing ability to read at sight and grasp this complex score. I wonder if you would you be willing take on the task of *répétiteur*?"

Wagehalsen had nodded sympathetically at the enumeration of Liszt's difficulties, but he remained silent.

"I realize, of course," Liszt continued, "that the position of chorus master would not make full use of your talents." Seeing that Wagehalsen's mind was preoccupied with matters totally unrelated to the *Tannhaüser* project, Liszt leaned back in his chair and looked searchingly at his former student.

"But you came to us with something on your mind?" he said at last.

Wagehalsen had intended to probe Liszt on his puzzling indifference to the war in Hungary. No one expected him to rush out into the field and die in battle. He had spoken cautiously to the Viennese students, and Hungary must have won its point. But the recent butchery of Hungarian peasants . . . surely Liszt would now speak out? Compared with his enthusiasm in Pest nine years earlier, his whole manner was . . . subdued.

"Everyone, it seems," he began slowly, "has been swept up in the justifiable demand for a voice in government. You, yourself, have always championed such rights, that each man should be free to work out his own salvation. And the state's need to assure domestic tranquility by checking the destructive tendencies innate to our species must always be measured against those rights. The French have managed to realize some gains in their Second Republic, though I fear they may be in the process of throwing them away in bungling and bickering. But it must be hard for them to keep their minds fixed only on the eternities and not lose their heads besotted by glorious recollections of Napoléon's empire. Even the art of Rachel was subverted by the political upheaval. Did you know, the Comédie-française was renamed the Théâtre de la République on March 3? Well, when the new director, a political appointee, suggested that Rachel recite *La Marseillaise*, how could she not agree? Three days later, she did so. Following the fourth act of Corneille's *Horace*, Rachel appeared alone on stage holding the tricolor. Kneeling, she gave a fiery recitation which brought the audience to their feet, stamping and cheering. She repeated her triumphant performance at the Théâtre thirty-seven times—thirty-seven times!—moving the editor of *La Fraternité* to dub her 'the first Republican of the French Republic.' I confess that even I was caught up in the moment."

Liszt exploded from his chair. "How is that possible?" he stormed. "How could you have been shaken by such theatrical pandering?" He brushed away Wagehalsen's effort to speak. "Of course, you are in love with Mlle Rachel. Fine! Love the actress, not the deception! How could any but the rabble have possibly admired it? It is a folly, a criminal act, a sin, to sing the *Marseillaise* today. What has the February revolution to do with the one of the last century? What has this blood-thirsty hymn to do with us, during a social upheaval whose basic principle is love, and whose solution is only possible through love?" He stopped and eyed Wagehalsen narrowly. "I know that some think me either coldhearted or cowardly." Again he waved aside Wagehalsen's protest. "I would be among the first to answer the call to arms, shed my blood, yes, and even face the guillotine if that would bring peace and happiness to the world! But what is required today are ideas to bring about the right social changes!"

Wagehalsen was astonished. Far from being indifferent to the plight of Hungary, Liszt, under a placid exterior, had been full of anguish. "Only universal Christian charity," he said, pacing about the room in agitation under the baleful watch of Dürer's *Melancholia* hanging on the wall, "has any meaning in these troubled times. What is needed are ideas, not rabble-rousing!" He stopped in front of Wagehalsen, challenging him.

"Yes, ideas," agreed Wagehalsen. "But how to recognize 'the right social changes'? How to separate a visceral reaction to a spectacular performance," he turned a sweet smile on Liszt, "from recognition of its artistic merit. Yes, communication of the basic principle of love may indeed unleash passionate outbursts."

Liszt's expression softened a little as he recognized the allusion to past receptions of his own performances.

"We live in a world of our own making," said Wagehalsen, remaining seated so as to appear less challenging, "of appearances. Love is one of those universal abstractions that unite us. In universal love, there is no individualism. But we perceive the universal through the things we experience in our lives. And through these perceptions, the universal fragments into individualism. Within the world of appearances, individuals inevitably struggle with each other, to want more than they can possibly ever have."

Liszt did not reply. He began to pace about the room again, brooding but less agitated.

"The only means of attaining tranquility," Wagehalsen continued, "of achieving that peaceful state of mind that is universal love, is through the perception of art, the communication of experiences molded into the best that the human mind can contemplate. Who can doubt that the state, the government, should leave each man free to work out his own tranquility? But as long as the individual is free to pursue his own tranquility, there can never be more than an approximation of the one universal art. Whether based on the highest of communications, music, or the lowest, politics, are not all communications *performances*? Some form of art designed to excite the enthusiasms of a multitude? And if the one communicating is a person of genius, are we then not inclined to suspend judgment, and for a time, however brief, forget our ungratified material needs? True genius transcends mere show, and erects, as it were, a stairway to heaven. The politician, on the other hand, appeals directly to those ungratified needs, and the individual lost in the baser mass is led into error. It's all showmanship. But not at all stairways lead to heaven. Stairways lead down as well as up.

"Is it so difficult, then, to understand how it was possible for Mlle Rachel to have shaken so many?"

Wagehalsen paused. Liszt had stopped pacing and resumed his seat at the side of the piano. He reached across to clasp Wagehalsen's shoulder, chuckling, and shook it gently. He wondered if this innocent-looking boy could really not have aged in the nine years since he had last seen him? "And the means for gratifying the material needs of the masses in order to placate them?" he said. "Even a wealthy young man such as you, I think, would not have enough."

"Wealth, like external appearance," smiled Wagehalsen, "is neither the only nor even the most desirable way of redressing material deficits. Too often, the power hungry politician relies on empty promises of material prosperity to attain power over the masses." He shrugged. "No. There is another way . . ."

Wagehalsen trailed off, realizing the danger of giving away too much, too soon. He smiled briskly and extended his hand. "But come!" he said heartily. "I do not think that placing my talents in the service of the birthday celebrations for the Grand Duchess is too mean an employment for them." And then the smile turned sly as Liszt took his hand and shook it. "My family," he said, "would certainly approve."

30.

From the time she and her sisters had been singing and reciting for coins on the streets of Paris, Rachel had been the victim of a too hasty heart. As an adolescent sensation on the stage of the Théatre-français, she attracted and readily accepted love from admirers both public and private. So Wagehalsen was not surprised, on one of his periodic excursions to Paris from Weimar in the summer of 1855, to find the warmhearted Rachel in a state of acute anxiety. A thoughtful inner voice might have warned all along that passionate affairs freely juggled among the literati, the theater, and random members of the nobility were bound to lead to emotional tangles. A thoughtful confidante might have stirred in her some inner sensibility against trusting too much in a fickle public. But a young woman who had grown used to public adulation, praised for having single-handedly revived the classic dramatists widely considered stale and passé, indeed, made their performance electrifying social events, would not likely have listened. And Parisians were never known for their prudence.

Wagehalsen laughed aloud to find Paris opinion in an uproar over Rachel's announcement that she planned to tour America. Paris might have forgiven her extensive absences from the rue de Richelieu to tour Europe at the expense of the Comédie-française. But that she would abandon them for the philistines of the New World? Paris was astonished! And just when the Universal Exposition, the glory of France, was about to eclipse the London Exhibition of 1851? Paris was furious! It was not to be endured! It was condemned in the press. It was the gossip of the salons.

Wagehalsen made an unannounced visit to Rachel's home at No. 4, rue Trudon. He found that except for the devoted maid, Rose Halff, the servants had been sent out for the evening. He brushed aside the maid as she followed him protesting down the hall and into the drawing room. There he found Rachel and François Ponsard sitting on a divan. Ponsard was a poet-playwright whose chief distinction was in having written a dull play, *Lucrèce*. He had written it for Rachel, and its success was due to her performance. He held a book of poetry in his hands, a simpering look of adoration on his face. At Wagehalsen's rude intrusion, he sprang up protectively.

"It's all right, my dear," said Rachel, rising and laying a restraining hand on his sleeve. Though as startled as Ponsard at Wagehalsen's abrupt appearance, she remained perfectly composed and gracious. "M. Wagehalsen is an old and dear friend."

"Monsieur," Ponsard said stiffly, as if about to challenge Wagehalsen to a duel. Wagehalsen responded with a condescending smile. Seeing that the situation was hopeless, Rachel turned to Ponsard, put her arm through his, and led him gently to the door.

"Perhaps it would be better if you left us. I'll send for you again when I am free." Crestfallen, Ponsard kissed her hand and followed Rose into the corridor. Then Rachel turned to face Wagehalsen. "That was most unkind. To burst into my home and rudely intrude when I am entertaining a guest . . ."

"But it was good theater," Wagehalsen said chuckling, "don't you think?"

She could not be indignant with him for long under that penetrating gaze. She knew from past experience that her sometime lover could be overpowering and not easily resisted. But then she had some practice in juggling difficult lovers. In spite of the spell he cast over her, the incongruity of a Prussian barbarian in a house decorated with Pompeian frescoes, Etruscan vases, and Persian wall hangings amused her. She laughed, and her laughter broke the spell. She led him back to the divan and had him sit beside her. For the moment, all thoughts of Ponsard were forgotten.

Her lustrous eyes held him as his held her. Her face, thought Wagehalsen, still lit by the same memorable expression he had first seen when it crowded all others from the stage, had rounded somewhat, her head no longer an egg poised delicately on its small end atop her throat. He took her hand. *How he longed to kiss that neck!* But he also saw, beneath the woman who vibrated with such reserved sensuality, pale and frail beside him, the signs of consumption which she recognized but denied. They conversed quietly together, Wagehalsen inquiring about her recent career which he had heard about but longed to know at first hand. Then he asked about the American tour . . .

At thirty-four, she knew that she had cause for concern about her health. She had been having bloody coughing fits that kept her in bed for days at a time. She suffered acutely from cold and damp and complained of fevers. She worried about her ability to handle the stresses of her career and felt uncertain about the future. And now she was embroiled in a dispute with Ernest Legouvé. He had written a play for her at her own request, and she was contracted to play the lead in it. But rehearsals had barely begun when she realized that the play did not suit her and withdrew. Fatigue, persistent ill-health and a failing memory were further excuses for her unwillingness to learn a new role in Legouvé's play. Legouvé made repeated efforts to persuade her to honor her contract, at the theater, at home. She refused. She was away. She was indisposed. Meanwhile, her brother, Raphaël, who had arranged a successful tour of Italy two years earlier, had persuaded her to accept a lucrative offer from Russia last year. That brilliant tour was a fitting climax to her career.

The excuses she had given Legouvé also prompted her to submit her resignation to the Comédie-française. But the Comédie granted her a leave for the tour with the stipulation that she would return to Paris and complete her contract in a final season before retiring. The Russian tour had exceeded even Raphaël's expectations. But for all the triumph of her tour through Russia, the company of the Tsar and Tsarina and the princes and princesses of the noble families, the enthusiastic public, the lavish monetary rewards and gifts of glittering jewelry, and the treasured letters from François declaring his undying love, she felt lonelier than ever and longed for a quieter kind of life to spend with her mother, her sisters, and most of all her two sons. Then, returning from Moscow, she received in Warsaw the devastating news that her favorite sister, Rebecca, was mortally ill with consumption. Even at that terrible moment Legouvé would not spare her. He wrote demanding that she reconsider his play. To her previous excuses, she then added the illness of her sister and a determination to play all her classical repertory in the final season before retiring from the Comédie-française. She would have no time to create a new role. On her return to Paris, Legouvé greeted her with writs and pursued her relentlessly through the courts until he had at last won damages.

But whoever drinks success is always thirsty. Shortly after returning to Paris in the spring of 1854, Rachel withdrew her resignation from the Comédie. She would not retire after all. She would resume her career in the fall, playing in contemporary romantic dramas which some critics said did not suit her. Despite the mad success of the Russian tour, negative criticism—France and England had broken diplomatic relations with Russia on the eve of her opening performance in Moscow; Parisians accused Rachel of consorting with the enemy during the Crimean War; she was betraying her country out of greed, always a convenient excuse for stoking smoldering anti-Semitism—clung to her. None of this had been enough to distract her from anxiety over the health of her sister. Yet when Rebecca died in her arms in the middle of June, neither that anxiety nor her ambition ended. It merely shifted focus. Without her sister's consumption to agonize over, she was faced with her own declining health. Oblivious to Rachel's legal difficulties, precarious health, and emotional turmoil, and still drunk with the success of the Russian tour, Raphaël now urged his sister to tour America, citing the fabulous success of Jenny Lind. She requested a leave from the Comédie for the American tour.

Wagehalsen thought that perhaps Parisians had reason to feel betrayed. From their perspective, they had bestowed fame and fortune on her and she repaid them with absence and disloyalty. Had Rachel done no more than live the life of self-enrichment that prevailed in the Second Empire, their judgment might have been justified. But after all, she had given the classic French theater of Corneille and Racine new life and restored them to their rightful place at home and abroad. And Rachel's denial that her bloody coughing fits signaled a fatal illness had taken in everyone. How could they be expected to understand that her increasingly erratic behavior signaled a mind disordered by impending doom? Moreover, if Raphaël let his ambition as impresario override concern for his sister's fragile health, he had not yet sobered from the success of the Russian tour.

As Rachel unfolded herself to Wagehalsen, she grew uneasy. She gave him a rueful smile. "Do you not think that I have grown paler over the years? Friends avoid saying anything," she said, "but they notice, I know. What do you think?"

"The candlelight is deceptive," said Wagehalsen. "But then I have a remedy for pallor." He gave her a rueful smile.

"It is no more than a kind of bleeding, which reputable doctors prescribe for phthisis," he said, trying to tease her out of her funk. "And far pleasanter than inhaling the emanations of a cesspool!"

Rachel made a face of mock disgust. "*Pouah*! You are joking, of course," she said. "Though I think the joke is in questionable taste. I have he had heard the rumors circulating through the salons that you have been playing vampire. A witty enough way of ingratiating yourself into the graces of novelty-mad *salonistes*, perhaps. But perhaps that joke has worn thin."

Seeing that Rachel was not taking him seriously, and indeed, he understood how preposterous his proposition must have sounded, he pressed her to him. "Ah, but my dear Rachel," he murmured, nuzzling her neck, "be reassured! Your pallor is merely the kiss of the vampire. And as everyone knows, vampires live forever." He playfully nibbled her throat. Joke or not, Rachel was vaguely unnerved by this. It was several days before she could bear his presence again.

Any doubts lingering in Wagehalsen's mind about how firmly the American tour had been settled were soon dispelled. Raphaël too readily accepted his sister's flippant denial that she was seriously ill.

"A change of air and scene, especially an ocean voyage, will chase away the glooms," he said. "It will raise your spirits and bring the color back to your face."

"Of course, dear Raphaël," said Rachel. "It is merely the kiss of the vampire you see on my brow! The ocean breezes will quickly blow it away." They both laughed heartily, until Rachel collapsed in a fit of coughing. But her condition had become a circumstantial conspiracy: she denied, the doctors and her family, blinded by incompetence, indifference, or selfish interests, readily agreed that she was merely experiencing a temporary indisposition.

Seeing that Rachel and her family were blithely determined to send her on the ill-advised journey, Wagehalsen contrived to be included. If Paris could spare the great Mlle Rachel for seventeen months, Weimar could surely spare him. He dispatched a letter to the Altenburg informing Liszt of the circumstances of his decision to absent himself for a year-and-a-half, and trusting that his mentor would understand.

Events moved quickly after that. The first performance in New York City was scheduled for September 1. So early on the morning of July 27, Rachel left the Gare du Nord for a brief season in London. Wagehalsen, uninvited, tagged along, paying his own expenses and disarming Raphaël's objections by offering to underwrite unforeseen expenses for the company. Rachel found his presumption amusing and his attentiveness endearing. Since the first performance in London was not until July 30, Wagehalsen was able to persuade Rachel to pay a visit to her old friend and benefactor, Hugo living in exile at Saint-

Hélier, while the rest of the troupe went on London. She hesitated at first when Wagehalsen suggested it. Rachel had doubts about the detour because she knew that Hugo's mistress, Juliette Drouet, must live in an apartment nearby. Ill feeling between the two since 1843 had never been resolved. Ten years earlier, Juliette's career as an actress had ended miserably after a critic called her performance in Hugo's *Marie Tudor*, "hopeless." Hugo consoled her. But when Hugo offered Rachel a part in *Angelo*, no one believed that the twenty-two-year-old actress, so steeped in Racine and Corneille, was capable of memorizing unrhymed lines. When Rachel had brought off her role triumphantly and too conveniently moved into an apartment at 9, Place Royale—Hugo, at the time, living at Number 6—Juliette was furious. Envious of Rachel's success and rumors of a liaison with Hugo, she publicly denounced the Jewess's preoccupation with money and sleeping her way into leading roles. Hugo found her jealousy charming. Rachel was understandably concerned that her presence in Hugo's house might offer a livelier interlude than she was in the mood for. Her arrival could only add consternation to the mare's nest in Saint-Hélier. But then, the chance to thumb her nose at Juliette won out in the end.

Hugo, heavily disguised, had escaped from France to Belgium on the eve of his arrest in December, 1851. He traveled to Brussels where he continued his diatribes in the relative security of Belgium. But after the publication of a pamphlet, *Napoléon-le-petit*, lampooning the Prince-President's government in July 1852, Conservatives mounted a drive to expel him. Threatened by the loss of Belgian protection, he prepared to set up a haven for himself and his family in English territory. He looked to the Channel Islands, where French civilization lingered and the living was cheap. His second surviving son, Charles, and Juliette Drouet, had joined him in Brussels. Juliette willingly followed him into exile with a trunk full of manuscripts he had left behind in haste. In Brussels, she

The Womb of Uncreated Night

lived separately and discreetly under an assumed name in order to protect Hugo's public image, made fair copies of the manuscripts, and mended his clothes. That way Hugo was able to enjoy her services and keep her out of the way of his liaisons with other women.

But the lives of the two Adèles, wife and daughter, and his youngest son, François-Victor were also at risk in Paris. He instructed them to leave Paris and go directly to Saint-Hélier, the capital of Jersey. The indispensable Juliette would also travel there and set herself up in a hotel to await Hugo's arrival. Although Hugo's wife knew all about her, Juliette had not been introduced into the family, and Adèle was prepared to ignore her. Hugo, himself, sailed with Charles from Antwerp to London on August 1, 1852 to meet with publishers, and exiles.

Three days later, Hugo had had his fill of the grime of the largest city in the world, and sailed for Saint-Hélier. He had chosen the capital for its sizeable French population, including numerous exiles that had preceded him, and modest cosmopolitan pretensions consisting of a theater, public library, booksellers, and even French newspapers.

After his arrival in Saint-Hélier, existence was hardly placid. The milieu was a curious tangle of political intrigue and dottiness. Immediately on his arrival, a speech he made at a French club attacking Louis Napoleon's government aroused the French Vice-Consul's indignation. Although Jersey was English soil, the French population remained loyal to both France and England. Hugo further excited the suspicions of the Vice-Consul by renting a house on the outskirts of town overlooking the English Channel facing the French coast. To M. Émile Laurent, it smacked of a plot to smuggle assassins into France. He sent spies to lurk about outside the house.

Hugo named the house Marine Terrace after the street it stood on. Inside, several ghosts haunted it. Hugo likened the house to a whitewashed tomb. Winds howling off the Channel rattled the guillotine-like sash windows, while Hugo communicated with the ghosts by tapping on the walls of his bedroom. Juliette moved into an apartment nearby, occasionally visited by Hugo without benefit of table- or wall-tapping.

It was into this curious, close world which Wagehalsen and Rachel were about to step. Except for a few personal effects, Rachel's traveling bags were sent ahead to London. Wagehalsen had fewer bags, but his habit of traveling with a large crate would probably have taxed Hugo's hospitality. So he sent it instead to Southampton to await the crossing. During his travels, Wagehalsen found that, for short stays, he could make do with a generous handful of Weimar soil sprinkled over the bedding provided for him. Perhaps not as restful as a deep, rich layer of native earth. But it would do in a pinch. What the housekeepers might have thought when they had to shake it out after his departure never troubled him.

Renowned for his hospitality, Hugo fondly remembered Rachel and welcomed her, her lover, and her maid. If Wagehalsen's German-accented French, held a grating echo of Napoléon-le-Petit, he was diplomatic enough to say nothing about it. Rachel, despite her failing health, was still a beguiling womanly presence, a fact that was lost on neither Juliette, who had seen her shortly after her arrival, nor Hugo. In the Marine Terrace, with his Adèle on one side and Wagehalsen on the other, Hugo could do no more than make eyes at her. For her part, Juliette privately hoped that one of the ghosts would entice Rachel to stick her neck out a window and slam a "guillotine" sash down on it.

Rachel would stay only the one night as her first performance in London was to take place on the 30th. Wagehalsen would escort them to the dock and see her safely off on the morning of the 28th. Rachel and Hugo chatted through the afternoon of their arrival in the drawing room as Wagehalsen sat by quietly, listening, enjoying their reminiscences about the Théatre-français. After dessert that night, Adèle suggested that they "do the tables" for their evening's entertainment.

"It is absurd to think that the spirits are dissolved around us in a fluid," Hugo scoffed, "like some magnetic field, and that all we must do is find someone who is able to channel them from the other world to this one!" Wagehalsen raised his eyebrows at this disingenuous disclaimer, for everyone knew that Hugo had a lively interest in such things. But Madame Hugo's suggestion found a receptive audience in Rachel, who joined her in pressing Hugo for it. Wagehalsen and Hugo's sons, Charles and Victor-François, joined in his skepticism. But two women are always more than a match for four men. In due course, the young men brought a large, four-legged table into the room and set it in the center of the room. They and the ladies sat around and lay their hands on the table, hoping that one of them would serve as "medium." Hugo, however, retired to a couch at the far end of the room and began to read.

"What will happen," asked Rachel, "if anything at all, that is?"

"I am not sure," answered Adèle. "But I believe that if one of us is the proper conduit," she ignored Hugo's derision from the divan, "the table should 'react.' I do not know exactly how." Wagehalsen smiled, wondering if he could tap into some unexercised force that could make the table levitate. But although he thought very hard about it, nothing happened. "Perhaps if each of us tries very hard to make something happen," said Adèle, "if we let our unconscious selves act as receptors to cosmic energy, without openly communicating it to each other, if somehow we all hit upon the same thought, the force of our combined inner energies could make it happen."

"A sort of automatic thinking?" said Wagehalsen drily.

"Yes," replied Adèle, searching the innocent expression on Wagehalsen's face for a sign that he was having her on. But the others, if they caught the note of waggery, nevertheless tried their best to fall into a trance-like meditation. For some reason—a disturbance in the magnetic flux perhaps—the other realm remained opaque.

After an hour of earnest but futile meditation, the three men looked at each other and, shaking their heads, one by one got up from the table. Charles roused his mother, whose trance appeared deeper than the others', and Rachel suppressed a yawn. The ladies went off to bed, while the men returned the table to its usual place at the side of the room. Hugo and his sons sat, conversing over cigars and brandy. Wagehalsen decided that he would take a turn along the coast of the island. He returned to the house long after the men had also retired.

Early the following morning as planned, Wagehalsen, heavily

cloaked, drove Rachel and Rose in Hugo's carriage to the dock and helped them board the steamer for London. He kissed Rachel on the cheek, and needlessly told the attentive maid to look after her mistress. After the ship steamed away, he returned to Marine Terrace. He found Hugo and Adèle taking coffee in the morning room, and accepted their invitation to join them, apologizing for not removing his cloak. The Hugos accepted his explanation that he had taken a chill on his walk the previous night.

"You saw our ladies to the docks?" said Hugo. "And did they embark safely?"

"Yes, of course," said Wagehalsen.

"We had all retired before you returned last night," Hugo said. "I wonder if you saw anything of a fisherman who had gotten drunk and wandered down to the Channel. He may have fallen into the sea, poor fellow. At any rate, news has spread this morning that he never returned home."

"Ah! I did see several men in the vicinity," replied Wagehalsen. "But I avoided them because I naturally thought, owing to the lateness of the hour and their furtive behavior, that they might have been smugglers. Perhaps they behaved so because they had fallen on that poor fisherman and did him in."

Hugo shook his head slowly. "Let us hope that such a calamity will not disrupt your visit. It would be a poor welcome that caused you to shorten your stay with us." Wagehalsen smiled. He thought it no more than the conventional formula used by gracious hosts who really expect their guests to depart as quickly as possible. Wagehalsen, however, had no intention of leaving abruptly, and immediately wondered how he might maneuver Hugo into more important matters. If he and Hugo had been alone together, he might have tried hypnotic suggestion. But the presence of Adèle and, in the background, Hugo's two grown sons, and numerous other visitors, made that impossible. He was delighted, therefore, when Hugo expressed an interest in learning more about his visitor. He gave his host a modest, if enthusiastically edited, story about his family, his education under Uncle Albert's supervision, the short-lived successes at the courts of the Duke of Weimar and the Archduke Rudolph, of his meetings with Goethe and Beethoven, and recently, the travels with his teacher and mentor, the great Franz Liszt. He told simply how his childish ambition had driven him to cripple his left hand, which reduced him to service as a humble *répétiteur* in the "New Weimar School." A role, he quickly added, that he regarded as an honor and a privilege.

He soon found that Hugo's interest was prompted more by curiosity about how the carnival empire of Louis Napoleon was perceived by the intelligentsia in the German states than by any personal interest in him. At this Adèle excused herself and got up from the table, taking her unfinished coffee with her.

"I do not know if I can offer any insights that are not already known to you," Wagehalsen shrugged. "The uprisings in Germany were no more successful than they were elsewhere. The impact of the February Revolution in Paris and its repercussions naturally shook the foundations, already on shaky ground, of all the ruling houses. For a brief time, their hereditary rulers made hasty republican concessions to the rebels. Then, within a few months' time, they rescinded them. Even Frederick William of Prussia, arguably the most powerful German, merely bided his time without relinquishing any real authority. The incompetence of the Austrian emperor encouraged the general air of contempt for royal authorities summed up in Franz Grillparzer's lyric, that mend and mend and mend as they might, a worn-out boot becomes a shoe, and if they cannot find new leather, they will eventually go barefoot. Only when that feeble-minded Emperor Ferdinand abdicated in favor of his nephew Franz Joseph did the Austrian throne regain its traditional authority and crush the Hungarians.

"One would think," continued Wagehalsen with a rueful shake of the head, "that the success of the rebellions might have given the people a collective common purpose. Unite them," he added, aware that unity was a favorite hobby-horse that Hugo rode. "But internal divisions broke them right and left into impotent shards. What amazes me is that of all the revolutions on the Continent, the most successful was the French. And *they* threw away the republic with their own hands!"

Hugo's eyes flashed. He reacted exactly like someone who would not think twice about finding fault with a member of his own family, but would not allow anyone else to do so. "That charlatan deceived them all with the name of Napoléon," he said evenly. "Like little children, they were innocently taken in by a cunning imposter, a charlatan unworthy of his uncle's name!"

They were interrupted by the arrival of a fellow exile bringing news that the body of the missing fisherman had been found. The man's throat was torn and he had died of a massive loss of blood. It appeared to be the attack of some animal. "But what animal on this island would have been capable of such a thing?" wondered Hugo aloud.

Over the next several days of Wagehalsen's stay, Hugo had noticed that his guest did not eat or drink much, indeed, seemed to be growing thinner, and that he was given to late night rambles on the rocky coast along the Channel. He inquired anxiously whether his guest found the food unpalatable or his bed uncomfortable. Wagehalsen parried such questions as he always did, citing slight indispositions owing to his sensitivity to new surroundings. He would recover soon enough, and then he would be off.

Wagehalsen spent much of his stay at Marine Terrace musing about Hugo's citadel of writers and publishers from which to bombard Bonaparte, and a United States of Europe to follow the emperor's ouster. Hah! he thought, smiling wryly, with Paris as its capital, and Hugo, himself, no doubt, its first president! Yet this insight alone made too slight a thread from which to dangle a quite different kind of utopia. Hugo's political fantasies did curiously overlap his own. And they had the grand purpose that would satisfy Wagehalsen's own Romantic longings. But there was still that troublesome sinister aura surrounding his methods that would have to be overcome. It was a problem that could not be resolved in a few argumentative forays. No. It would require further acquaintance with the great man.

Wagehalsen realized that his nocturnal ramblings and . . . *peculiar* . . . diet would raise too many questions, too soon. Contrary to widespread belief, he could eat the food of ordinary humans. But it sometimes caused indigestion, and it had the distinct drawback of accelerating the aging process. Of course, he might continue to purge himself as he had been doing after dining with the Hugos. But sticking his finger down his throat was decidedly unpleasant. So he pretended that, while eager to continue in the great man's company, he could not impose so far as to prolong his stay as a guest in Marine Terrace. Wagehalsen withdrew to a nearby cottage further up the coast. Hugo would not admit that he was flattered by Wagehalsen's deference. After all, it was no more than his due. Friends and neighbors often dropped by unannounced for conversation. Hugo would welcome his interesting acquaintance as a new, if short term, neighbor.

Wagehalsen continued to visit the Hugos and had several tête-à-têtes with Hugo on various topics, all the while maneuvering discussion around the topics dearest to Hugo's heart. Among these was a discussion about the reception of Napoleon-the-Little in the German states. Wagehalsen played on Hugo's indignation. It gave him the very words he would later work into his arguments. He nodded sympathetically as Hugo sputtered over the charlatan.

"Well," said Wagehalsen at last, "you wondered how Germans perceive Louis Napoleon? While they may envy the ease with which he seduces his countrymen, the ruling heads are openly contemptuous of him and refuse to welcome him as a brother ruler. None of them so relentlessly as the Austrian emperor Franz Joseph." He paused a moment and added, "With the signal exception of Queen Victoria, since her favorable reaction to the Universal Exposition. But then, the English are not really Continentals, and have always been a bit odd, not so?" Hugo's raised eyebrows and shrug showed that it went without saying.

Recalling his visit earlier that year, Hugo merely said, "A people who could endure the suffocating pollution of London must be very odd indeed." But through it all, Wagehalsen shared Hugo's hope for a United States of Europe. Of course, Wagehalsen's way of subduing dissenting voices would be radically different from Hugo's. But then, Hugo had formed only a vague idea of how his dream of unity might be realized. He could not see, in fact, beyond the immediate goal of deposing Louis Napoleon.

These discussions, in which Wagehalsen warily tested Hugo's readiness to hear his own political agenda, were interrupted by the arrival of Delphine de Girardin, an old friend of the Hugos. She had just returned from a visit to America and had stopped to visit Hugo on her way back to Paris. And the answer Wagehalsen had been seeking unexpectedly fell into his lap.

At dinner on the day of her arrival, even before Mme Hugo had a chance to serve dessert, Delphine asked, "Do you do the tables?"

The Hugos understood that she was referring to the table-turning craze that swept through the United States. Not that spiritism was unheard of in France. But the enthusiasm with which Americans embraced novelties, at least in spiritual matters, probably surpassed that of Parisian salons. They told Delphine about their failed attempt on the night when Rachel and Wagehalsen had arrived. Hugo was still skeptical, though Mme Hugo's curiosity had not been satisfied. They explained how they had proceeded, and that nothing had happened.

"The tables," conceded Delphine, "could be unpredictable. Even contrary or coquettish. They might need cajoling. But I cannot believe that among such a diverse and stimulating company not one can be found who is sensitive enough to channel the spiritual flux." When she suggested that they try to contact the other world again in her presence, the men once more brought in the big, square, four-legged table. Delphine burst out laughing.

"The spirits do not have Herculean muscles," she said. "They cannot be expected to lift a table that requires four living men to carry it! Your table is completely unsuitable. We must find a more delicate instrument.

Leave that to me." As good as her word, she found a three-legged table at a toy shop in Saint-Hélier. On the following day, a Sunday afternoon, they set the new table atop the one they had previously used. Auguste Vacquerie, Hugo's sons Charles and François-Victor, General Adolphe Le Fló and his wife, Count Teleki and his wife, Mme Hugo and Delphine all took turns in coaxing the table to "speak." As on the previous occasion, Hugo remained skeptical and would not participate. Wagehalsen declined to participate, content merely to sit and watch. After several days of futile effort, an exasperated Delphine was about to leave for Paris.

Hugo was at last prevailed upon to try his hand at the table before she left. The moment he laid his hands on it, both the table and Wagehalsen jumped. Wagehalsen could not believe what happened next. Delphine's table began to tremble and rattle against the surface it rested on. To Wagehalsen, the vibrations seemed random. But those at the table were mesmerized. To them, it was furiously tapping out a sequence of letters, 1 for a, 2 for b, 3 for c, and so on, at the rate of six per second. Almost ten years to the day since Hugo had learned that his daughter, Léopoldine, had drowned in a boating accident, the table was spelling out '*fille*' and '*morte*,' followed by the letters of her name. Even more amazingly, Hugo and the table engaged in conversation. Had Hugo somehow manipulated the table? Had the others conspired to play a practical joke on him? Wagehalsen wondered. But he could detect no sign of covert signal or movement to account for such a thing. Nor could he believe that any of them could so meanly trample Hugo's feelings. Wagehalsen wondered if, instead, some natural principle was at work. Something about the energy of the group focused in their hands, perhaps some innocent tremors transmitted to the table? The séance lasted from dusk until well after sunrise.

Among Hugo's family and friends, Wagehalsen went willingly along with an activity they clearly had accepted without question. Alone, he doubted what could be no more than a delusion. But then there was a time when he would have thought the same about vampirism. What if he could present vampirism to Hugo as but another channel to the world of spirits?

Whatever the origin of the mysterious rappings, the spirits became progressively more communicative. Either they or the participants were becoming more adept at their new parlor game. The séances became a nightly ritual. In the evening of the session that had ended that very morning, the company eagerly resumed their sessions. On this occasion, the table was visited by the spirit of Louis Napoleon, who at the time was asleep in the Élysée Palace in Paris. Napoléon III rapped out his fear that he would die in two years and that his empire would be replaced by a universal republic. Hugo took that as the United States of Europe so dear to his heart. Or perhaps a federation of France and Germany? This session, too, lasted into the early hours of the next day.

Over the next several days, whimsy and nonsense were never in short supply. Hugo dallied with female spirits and chatted up an incoherent fairy speaking Assyrian. Auguste Vacquerie had an exchange with a spirit who at first claimed to be Lope de Vega. Then denied it. Wagehalsen marveled at how the participants managed to keep the table hopping, to glean so much from what might otherwise have passed as an old house rattling in the gales off the Channel. But things happen when people believe. He was as entranced as they were. Two nights after the visit from Napoléon III, they were visited by the Shadow of the Sepulcher, who conversed with Hugo on divine retribution after life. No sooner had he departed than the spirit of Dante announced its presence. Dante's spirit was unable to decide whether it had been drawn to Jersey more by the presence of Italian exiles and their concern over the foreign domination of Italy, or by admiration for Hugo's poetry.

Not long after the séances had become the regular after-dinner diversion, Wagehalsen sought to be alone with Hugo. He found him one afternoon in his study, standing at a window behind his desk, staring out across the channel to the coast of Normandy. Becoming aware of his presence, Hugo turned to face Wagehalsen with a quizzical expression on his face.

"Perhaps I should not have intruded your thoughts," Wagehalsen began and made as if to go.

"Not at all, not at all," said Hugo, recovering. He gestured at a chair near the desk. On the desk lay the draft of Hugo's preface to François-Victor's thirteen-year translation of Shakespeare. Hugo pointed to it and eyed Wagehalsen. "I was thinking about something I have been working on. Perhaps you would read it and offer your opinion?"

"Of course," said Wagehalsen, picking up the manuscript.

Hugo then sat in the chair behind his desk, folded his hands over his ample belly, and tried his best to look attentive. "Was there something you especially wished to say?"

"Since the visit from Bonaparte," began Wagehalsen, leafing through the preface as he spoke . . .

"Which one?" interrupted Hugo.

"Yes, of course. I had forgotten that you had conversed with the *Great* as well as the *Little*. Well, then, since the visit from the Little, I have been turning over in my mind your dream of a United States of Europe. If we can believe what the spirits say, France will soon enough be free of Louis Napoleon, and we may then have an opportunity of achieving that dream. Perhaps the likeliest beginning for such a union would be, as you have suggested, a confederacy of France and Germany? But finding common ground among the German states themselves would be a problem. Napoleon-the-Great's Rhenish Confederation forced just such an alliance with France in 1806. But could such an alliance today, or even in two years' time, be reestablished through reason and persuasion alone?"

Hugo leaned back and listened, nodding abstractedly.

"We live in a world of our own making," pursued Wagehalsen, "a world of appearances. Love is one of those universal appearances that unites yet eludes us. In universal love, there is really no individualism. Quite a different proposition from the carnal appetites. Every religion teaches this ideal, every humane man subscribes to it, and every political system that responds to its constituents strives to fulfill it. But all fail. Because we perceive the universal through the experiences of daily lives filled with our carnality. And through these preoccupations, the universal fragments into individualism. Within the world of appearances, individuals inevitably struggle with each other, to want more than they can possibly ever have.

"At the core of the problem, I believe, is our reliance on Reason. Reason is but a human term, an appearance of order in a universe in which order does not exist."

There was a faint shift in Hugo's vaguely distant air. "Are you enlisting," said Hugo, "the ideas of M. Schopenhauer, who has lately argued that since the world is filled with endless strife despite our reliance on Reason it is necessary and sufficient to conclude that the universe is irrational, and that human Reason is deficient to unravel its deepest mysteries? He thinks moral awareness can be substituted for Reason, and expects us to minimize our fleshly desires in order to become morally aware. He proposes that we replace universal Reason with universal dreariness. Tell me, young man," he added with a barely repressed smile, "do you propose to replace endless strife with endless ennui?"

"As to that," said Wagehalsen with an indifferent shrug, "it all depends on what is meant by 'minimize.' M. Schopenhauer's conclusion does not preclude the mind's capacity to experience gratification. Surely, he meant that 'fleshly desires' should not be allowed to deflect Reason, as many in high places are prone to do. On the contrary, his argument that aesthetic perception would enable us to rise above individual gratifications and allow us to merge with primordial spirit does not necessarily exclude carnal gratification. Once the physical form exists, sensuality becomes the domain of the mind. We need only minimize the grosser expressions of Will which incite us to violence. Aesthetic perception without fleshly desire is like sight to a blind man. But desire must be accepted and gratified to make it possible for us to reach what lies beyond the flesh, to see, to experience, shining through an individual thing, not only a tree, and the *treeness* of that tree, but also lust and the *lustness* of that lust. Always seeing, always pursuing, but never sated."

"Ah!" said Hugo. "And now you add M. Keats into the mix!"

"In such a state," chuckled Wagehalsen, "objects become universal.

Few people can sustain such an aesthetic state for very long. They stop short of aesthetic perception, and even more, its paradoxical exhilaration in tranquility! The closest most people come to such a state is in their faith in God. They believe, for reasons they could never explain, in a universal being that sums up for them all the finest things that they have experienced or are capable of imagining in their lives. They need an artistic genius like Gianlorenzo Bernini, say, to reveal the *sensuality* of spiritual enlightenment of the ecstasy of Saint Teresa, to communicate a universal vision to those who lack the idealizing power to see through, and to rise above, the mundane objects of their daily lives."

"Ecstasy in tranquility!" Hugo guffawed. "You twist moral dilemma into virtue! And yet," he added pensively, "you touch on the core of moral uneasiness that troubles humanity. How curiously in harmony with the spiritual realm you appear to be, yet somehow, out of tune."

They both sat in silence for a few moments. Hugo drifted back into preoccupation. Wagehalsen, who had been quietly leafing through the manuscript as he had talked, read more steadily. Then he took a deep breath. "What if there was a way other than the contemplation of artistic genius for the less gifted to achieve and even maintain the aesthetic perception? After all, not everyone is willing or able to put aside the ordinary world to pursue a higher purpose. For them, there must be a surer way to induce and heighten the idealizing power which everyone possesses in some rudimentary form."

"A disturbing notion," said Hugo, frowning back into focus. He shook his head. "Revelation achieved without the inspired work of genius would be worthless."

"Keen understanding and insight, as such, never enabled anyone to create a great work of art. The mind may grasp infinity as a concept, but the senses demand concrete evidence. A community of kindred spirits still needs inspiration. Universality does not signify uniformity."

"And yet," mused Hugo, "even a community of kindred spirits sharing the material world must have some practical means of ordering mundane affairs."

"But of course," said Wagehalsen. "Such a community would be guided toward constructive ends by philosophers and poets, as you envision." He hesitated for a moment, gauging the effect of his words on his host, then forged ahead. "A human vampire is at once able to bend the will of others, yet give them a sense of fulfillment and satisfaction.

This time, Hugo was unable to hold back his merriment. "Even before Napoléon-le-petit forced me out of Paris," he said, roaring with laughter, "the salons were full of rumors about the brash young man who claimed to be a vampire offering intellectuals a new world order presided over by philosophers and poets, all turned into benevolent vampires!"

Wagehalsen shared Hugo's amusement. He knew that he was not as adept as the Count at casting a spell. So of course it all sounded absurd. He, himself, had thought so in the Borgo Pass when the passengers on the diligence were in such superstitious dread of a silly myth. But then the table rapping sounded every bit as absurd. Hugo neither stormed out of the room nor threw Wagehalsen out of the house. His manner exuded an amused tolerance awaiting the next manifestation of a séance. Wagehalsen inwardly shrugged and rapped on.

"Metaphysical phenomena," he said, "contain more than a single dimension, and as such may be approached through more than one medium. The vampire is but one gateway through which the spiritual realm may be accessed. Far from making the philosopher and the artist unnecessary or obsolete, by tapping into the forces at play in that realm, the vampire would be a spiritual guide leading the way into an unknown world. Even Dante had the guidance of Virgil to lead him through Hell. If everyone could access a medium more directly, the metaphysical world is yet so vast, so various, that no human could hope to plumb its mysteries unaided. There will always be those who can see more profoundly than others. We will always need philosophers, scientists, and artists."

Hugo pursed his lips and surveyed his belly. Perhaps, thought Wagehalsen, he is contemplating his navel. After several minutes of silence, Hugo raised his eyes directly in Wagehalsen's.

"And what," he said skeptically, "is the *medium* which enables you to communicate with the other world unaided by table-turning?"

"It is the power of the blood." Seeing Hugo's raised eyebrows, he hastened to add, "Oh, not your ordinary blood. But the blood whose ultimate source is lost in antiquity. Its power can only be transferred by drinking it."

"And this," said Hugo, "*this* would be the means for gratifying the material needs for the masses in order to placate them?"

Wagehalsen titled his head. "Consider it a treatment, similar to the one commonly prescribed by a physician."

"Like bleeding?"

"More like an inoculation that transmits a benefit from one person to another. Administered to individuals who are thereby empowered to inoculate others, and they, in turn, yet others."

"And this . . . *treatment* . . . spreading through the populace like a disease. How would that subdue rebellious natures?" asked Hugo.

"Ah," replied Wagehalsen, "the contagion itself soothes, placates, and subdues rebellious impulses, heightens, without impairing, their native faculties."

"You are suggesting a 'cure' that sounds like enslavement!" Hugo rose from his seat, incredulous. "You would rob the people of their free will? Such a 'cure' would be worse than the disease!"

"It may seem so at first," replied Wagehalsen calmly but earnestly. "What is any government but a physician who requires the willing surrender of some individual rights for the benefits of the cure? I do not speak of complete autocratic control. As I have already suggested, violence is a disease spread by the uncontrolled individual Will. Once the *excess* is subdued and people are attuned to the essence of the universe, the individual would still be free to pursue his own gratification without impeding that of others. As you, yourself, remarked, the mass of mankind are like little children who need the guidance of wiser heads to guide them. If the source of that guidance lies within the grasp of the writers, thinkers, publishers of your Citadel, it can only be enabled by tapping into that universal essence. Only as I see it, it could be done more directly than hours spent rapping at tables."

Hugo sat at his desk again. But his renewed silence stretched out so long that Wagehalsen wondered whether it was expectation or dismissal. He gambled on a return to the arts. "All communication, after all, is a kind of performance. Some form of art designed to excite the enthusiasms of a multitude communicated by a person of genius, incline the masses to suspend judgment, and for a time, however brief, forget ungratified material needs. True genius transcends mere show, and erects, as it were, a stairway to heaven. The politician, on the other hand, appeals directly to those ungratified needs, and the individual lost in the baser mass is led into error. It's all showmanship. But then, not all stairways lead to heaven. Stairways lead down as well as up."

"It is incredible that you expect me to believe," said Hugo between indignation and amazement, "that a perversion of the sacrament of the communion should be held up as the medium for penetrating the veil of the spirit world and lead everyone up to heaven!"

"To a heaven of the mind, yes. But even in the biblical heaven, there was rebellion. Ecstasy must be firmly controlled."

Hugo tired of Wagehalsen's efforts to convert him. When he spoke again, it was clear that a part of his mind had been as preoccupied with his preface as Wagehalsen's, in reading it. Wagehalsen now picked up on the possibilities offered by Hugo's desire to unify Europe and "republicanize" Shakespeare. He also perceived the great man's fascination with the theme of death in the plays. Hugo's concern that he might die, leaving unfinished the works he held in imagination offered an irresistible gambit.

Wagehalsen teased out an allusion to *Hamlet* in English, knowing full well that Hugo's grasp of the language was rudimentary at best, and that Hugo considered English phrasing full of "clouds": "*Could one but temper that fell sergeant's strict arrest, perchance commute the punishment that is the common lot of humankind, what wonders could be brought about . . .*"

Hugo shook his head. "When the English wish to converse with me," he said with a penetrating look at Wagehalsen, "like the Germans, they will learn French!"

Wagehalsen then raised the idea that the vampire's power could topple Napoléon III. Hugo laughed at what he assumed was his guest's fey sense of humor, and confidently asserted the power of his pamphlet, *Napoléon-le-petit*: "They tell me that my little book is infiltrating into France and dripping, drop by drop, on to Bonaparte. It may well end by making a hole."

"Only think," replied Wagehalsen, "how satisfying it would be to a make a hole of a very different kind. Not merely words dripping on his head, but at his throat!" Hugo was both amused and rueful at the savage conceit.

"You know, a French tailor once turned up in Saint-Hélier asking my permission to assassinate Louis Napoleon. Imagine! I, of course, did not give it. The violence of my poetry would have to suffice."

"But imagine," persisted Wagehalsen, "sinking your teeth into that hated neck and bringing Louis under your spell, consigning him to whatever ignominy! It would not be the first time you had tasted blood on your lips!"

Wagehalsen had been thinking of the bloody assaults on the barricades during Louis Napoleon's *coup d'état* two years earlier. On the afternoon of December 4, 1851, Hugo and Juliette Drouet moving furtively through the streets to assess the carnage came upon a scene out of a macabre Daumier caricature: a colleague brought them to a house in Monmartre, where a seven-year-old boy had been shot twice in the head. With the boy's grandmother screaming in the background, Hugo kissed the child's head and Juliette wiped the blood from his lips. Was he perhaps, after all, already a vampire? Hugo must have tried to tell himself that he had not been responsible for the child's death by inciting the populace to rise up against the dictator. No, Louis Napoleon had betrayed France. The death of the child was implicit in his criminal abuse of power. Hugo's own part was coincidental. But there had been so many "coincidences" over the years. Perhaps he felt himself manipulated by unseen forces. Might Wagehalsen persuade him that he was an emissary who brought with him some aura from beyond? If his willingness to believe in table-turning made Hugo appear gullible, Wagehalsen knew that the poet was no fool.

Wagehalsen also thought that he may have overplayed his hand. The reference to blood on his lips could only remind Hugo of his own complicity in the outrages that led to the grisly scene in Montmartre. Wagehalsen could see that he was torn between good manners, which he maintained even when affronted, and annoyance at this young upstart who had an uncanny knack of fingering painful events.

But Hugo generously threw off his conflict. "What an idea!" he said, laughing. "If only overthrowing Napoléon-le-Petit could be as easy as you suggest, M. Wagehalsen! That my thirst for revenge against the atrocities of the Emperor might be quenched by drinking his blood?" But even if he contrived to get around the risk of imprisonment and come into Napoleon III's presence, Hugo thought of pressing his lips against that detested throat. He shuddered, and realized that he could not bear the touch. "What then?" he chuckled sardonically. "Would M. Wagehalsen undertake the job in his name, like a hired assassin? Nor am I keen to taste M. Wagehalsen's blood. That was how it was done, was it not?"

Seeing Hugo's hesitancy, Wagehalsen offered a further enticement, unlimited sexuality: "Instead of the impairments of age or illness . . ."

Hugo appeared delighted to have a sparring partner, even if only one that could be easily demolished. If he chose.

"Imagine, Monsieur, boundless desire, boundless fulfillment. To be spared a doddering, bottom-pinching dotage," with a sly smile at a favorite pastime of old men, "and no concern for the harmful effects of orgasm."

Hugo was again taken aback by this reference to an excuse he had given to the demanding Juliette while he had been engaged in a ménage with Léonie Biard. Was it mere coincidence, or could this stranger have had some acquaintance with Juliette Drouet? How could he know of such a thing? He decided not to confirm the insinuation by venting his indignation at such an uncertain intrusion, and parried instead. "But why, Monsieur, in an existence without sexual reproduction, should there be any sexual desire at all, eh?"

"The brain, M. Hugo, is the liveliest sexual organ known to man, and often remains virile while the rest of the body languishes." The idea left Hugo tingling down to his toes.

31.

Wagehalsen's dramatic fantasy closed before it opened. On the Continent, the select audience at tryouts did not know what to make of Wagehalsen. Was he presenting a serious program or a schoolboy's prank? Even to Frenchmen steeped in Hugo's Romantic "liberalism in literature" and acquainted with Shakespeare's plays, in which the unities were ignored and classical genres might be twisted into tragicomedy, his scenario for political progress was too bizarre. To those who bothered even to hear the bare outlines, it was simply cloaking traditional forms in outrageous novelty, draping new costumes on old tyrannies, and hardly qualified as a formula for alleviating social inequities. A regime of vampires who fed on the blood of the people they governed, benevolent? *Incroyable!* After entertaining the novel idea of vampirism as a way of penetrating the veil of the spirit world, Wagehalsen playing Virgil to Hugo's Dante, Hugo, too, mentally dismissed him as a protagonist better fit to guiding an audience through the bone-lined corridors of Haussmann's sewers.

They, the celebrated literati of France, were all turning him down, refusing to believe that his grotesque program could possibly be anything other than a joke, and not much of a joke at that. Everyone already knew that politicians were blood-suckers. To suggest that literal blood-suckers would be motivated to improve society, to ennoble and enrich the human condition by making them *immortal* . . . either the boy was joking or he was quite mad! Better to laugh him off or lock him up! Wagehalsen realized that he would have to find another stage. Further delay in departing for America was pointless. Perhaps in the New World, where youthful ambition was prized, an idea would not be dismissed out of hand because it was advocated by a "mere boy." Yet he was not entirely willing to abandon the world he knew . . .

As it happened, Wagehalsen's arrival in New York was almost a week after Rachel and her troupe had taken the train to Boston. He was sorry to have missed her, but the new city, growing so fast that already it seemed old, fascinated him. A decade had passed since pigs had been allowed to roam the streets to scavenge garbage. But as Wagehalsen surveyed the noisy, bustling, streets littered with people and trash, and the chaotic layout of lower Manhattan, he thought the city officials, perhaps, had been hasty. He became so absorbed in exploring this shabby new world that he decided not to follow Rachel and her troupe.

Broadway, the most fashionable street, was also the hub of the city's commercial and cultural activities. The finest hotels, shops, residences, and theaters were located on or near it. During a building boom from 1850 to 1854, nineteen luxurious hotels were built on Broadway alone, spurred in part by the expected crush of visitors to the first world's fair in the United States. Of these, the St. Nicholas was the most extravagant. Built only two years before Wagehalsen's arrival, it was quickly acclaimed for its handsome Italianate architecture, comfort, luxury, and extravagant service provided by a staff of 400 men and women.

The world's fair had run from July 14, 1853 to November 1, 1854. Exhibitions were housed in the Crystal Palace, inspired by London's Crystal Palace of 1851. The building occupied the space behind the Croton distributing reservoir, a large, fortress-like structure in Egyptian style at 42nd Street and Fifth Avenue. As recently as five years earlier, Fourteenth Street had marked the outermost boundary of its northward reach. The state legislature in 1811 had approved a rectangular grid of streets and avenues for the orderly development of the land that lay beyond it. Wagehalsen wondered how many of the more than one million visitors to the fair had remained to contribute to the phenomenal growth of the city. Broadway remained the central artery from which side streets branched and new commercial enterprises grew. But the wealthiest families fled the influx of immigrants and traffic which clogged lower Broadway. They sidestepped its northward march by moving a few blocks west to Fifth Avenue which, at the time was a country lane running north from Washington Square. There, they built imposing mansions and briefly enjoyed a rural atmosphere.

Wagehalsen decided to forego the luxury of the St. Nicholas, opting instead for an apartment in a modest brownstone on a bustling side street where his nocturnal habits would not excite undue interest. The proprietor of the building, Isaac Mendes, a Jew who traced his family back to Sephardic refugees from Brazil in the seventeenth century and felt vastly superior to the poor Jews from central Europe currently flooding the city, was eager to ingratiate himself with this well-dressed, refined gentleman from Europe—obviously not the sort of immigrant riffraff overwhelming respectable neighborhoods and turning them into slums. Mr. Mendes touted the advantages of his building's location, "Within an easy walk of the best restaurants, shops, and entertainments. There's the restaurant of the Delmonico brothers, located in their hotel at 25 Broadway, and famous for its French cuisine." Wagehalsen smiled, saying that his culinary tastes were more unconventional, perhaps, than Mr. Mendes supposed. "Then," Mendes went on, "there's Niblo's Garden at Broadway and Prince Street, which seats *three thousand* and features the concerts of the Philharmonic Society. And the Academy of Music just opened last year on Fourteenth Street where you can take in the opera." Wagehalsen nodded tolerantly at his glib landlord, pointedly avoiding any encouragement to continue, a nicety that was lost on the man. "And of course, being a man of the world," Mendes laid a finger aside his nose, "you value . . . privacy."

New York had numerous daily newspapers written in dozens of foreign languages to accommodate the reading skills of its newly polyglot citizens. Wagehalsen could easily have followed daily reports in German or French, but it was the English language press that caught his interest. He was surprised by their hostility toward theaters. Instead of considering them important resources of culture, as they were in the European press, they were roundly condemned as licentious and conducive to public immorality. Of course, there *were* numerous bawdy houses that catered to low tastes. These often sat side by side with legitimate houses, like the Metropolitan Theatre, where Rachel just the week before had performed in Corneille's *Cinna* and Emile de Girardin's *Lady Tartuffe*.

This curious New World morality absorbed him all the more as he followed its tortuous path through the public debate on the need for a public park on the European scale. The project had been discussed by the city's newspapers and influential citizens for decades preceding the first formal proposal by a public official, former Mayor Ambrose Kingsland on May 5, 1851, to provide a place of civic pride and community benefit. At that time, Jones Wood, a large woodland of 150 acres located between 66th and 75th streets and from Third Avenue to the East River, was considered to be ideally suited to the purpose. It was this plot that the mayor and other backers of the park plan originally had in mind. But Jones Wood combined the private estates of the wealthy families of John Jones and Peter Schermerhorn. Neither was willing to convert his land to public use. State Senator James Beekman, in June of 1851, introduced a bill to authorize the city to appropriate the land through eminent domain. Vested interests in the senate easily passed the bill in July, and the governor duly signed it into law.

Wagehalsen puzzled over the conflicting interests behind the continued delay after the appropriation bill became law. Compared to Baron Haussmann's ruthless and efficient transformation of Paris, the democratic process was cumbersome and haphazard. But the wealthy backers of the plan for Jones Wood and the public worked at cross purposes. Were civic leaders motivated more by a genuine need for an open space of health and recreation, or a vain desire to refute European condemnation of Americans as coarse, boorish, and culturally backward? Or were they perhaps, as Alexis de Tocqueville had branded them, greedy, self-interested, crass vulgarians rooting about like the pigs that once had been allowed to run loose through garbage-strewn streets? What, a democratic experiment to cultivate and refine all the people? Create a park where women could promenade—women being inherently moral beings—to provide a healthful and uplifting atmosphere for everyone. What, Americans are coarse and boorish? Add a parade of fashionable ladies for refinement. What, respectable European ladies did not walk in the streets? Lift the fashionable ladies off their dainty feet with aesthetically landscaped roads for carriage drives away from the congested traffic, immigrant crowds, and dirty streets of lower Manhattan. How tasteful and refined! How healthful! And how thoroughly democratic! Remembering the "democratic" activities in the Bois de Boulogne, Wagehalsen could only smile.

Despite the obvious civic value of a healthful and culturally uplifting landmark, Beekman's motives were suspect. He owned property adjacent to the site whose value was sure to be enhanced, as would the properties of other landowners in the surrounding area. Negative opinions ranged from a venture which would benefit landowners, provide a place where wealthy ladies and gentlemen could parade and vagabonds laze, to increasing the disparity between the privileged few, the working class, and the poor. Underlying it all was a constant preoccupation with preserving public morals. Earlier in the century, fashionable ladies had enjoyed promenades on the wide thoroughfare of Broadway. But control over this avenue was gradually lost to the influx of poor immigrants. Modest ladies were increasingly subjected to ogling by "foreigners." Why the presence of morally superior women had failed to ennoble the oglers on the city's thoroughfares remained, for Wagehalsen, one of the mysteries of the New World. But the spectacle only increased the demand for a park where ladies would be protected from such strangers on the city streets.

These expectations only aggravated the feeling that the proposed park was not in the best tradition of American democracy, but rather an exercise in affluent snobbery. The Jones Wood park proposal was ultimately doomed when backers of the plan were unable to raise the necessary funds to appropriate the property, and attention shifted to the sprawling middle of the island. As Wagehalsen leisurely explored this "New World morality" and the lifestyle of the city from his base in lower Manhattan, he searched for a permanent hideaway for his "resting place." Where New Yorkers valued equally health and morality for their new park, Wagehalsen sought another form of "health." He, too, began to consider the advantages of a "wilderness" area. If the city was already substantially urbanized only up to the middle of Manhattan, the island beyond was mostly wilderness sprinkled with large private estates and small farms.

The site of the future park was mostly populated by small, scattered, unstable settlements of Irish and German immigrant gardeners and pig keepers, squatters, bone-boilers, and rag pickers, separated by patches of swamps and rocky barrens. But Seneca Village, between 81st and 86th Streets was a substantial, established community of free Africans. Since the first purchasers of the land were clergymen of the African Methodist Episcopal Zion church, the community built three churches. Although it was commonly known as "Nigger Village," German and Irish immigrant families also lived and intermarried in the community. Most of the villagers were quite poor, living in nine-by-eleven foot "shanties" which were, in fact, less constricting than poor black families living downtown crowded into eight by ten foot tenement rooms. At the time of Wagehalsen's visit, the community had over two hundred residents. The area was now served only by "roads" that were no more than dirt cart ways and old post roads. All these would be displaced by the virtual certainty of a Central Park and subsequent development of the adjacent area to accommodate the inexorable march uptown of the city. The prospects for a large central park were most inviting to Wagehalsen as a future haunt.

As Wagehalsen often visited the proposed site for the future park, he was drawn to the aspect of Vista Rock rising dramatically some fifty feet above the terrain to the north and gradually falling away in a series of wild, rocky outcroppings to the south, ending in a swamp. The Croton reservoir had dominated the area to the north since its construction in 1842. This rectangular collection basin, surrounded by a high stone wall that obstructed the view of all but twenty feet of the rocky summit from the north, was connected to the distributing reservoir on 42nd Street by buried conduits. The reservoir's gate house would have ample access spaces for maintenance crews. It occupied almost the center of the park site from about 79th to 86th streets. Wagehalsen saw great possibilities in the location, and noted a gap between the base of the Rock and the reservoir's wall that provided a perfect niche for a crypt and a concealed entrance.

He scouted the area from every approach, much of it rocky terrain interspersed with sparse vegetation and swamps. On such outings, he also took in the scattered and diverse population, dining off the local cuisine. For the present, he could not very well afford to be seen wearing his trademark opera cape and top hat. The scene was far too rustic for formal wear, and the summer was too hot for a long, caped greatcoat. Instead, he chose loose-fitting, baggy clothes that could accommodate him when he felt expansive. In place of the top hat, he wore a less formal "Pocket Hat" of soft, pliable felt. It gave him a jaunty look. He took care to pick off squatters who strayed from the fringes of their communities and to dispose of their bodies in isolated swamps. Eventually, they would be discovered as the swamps were dredged. But that would be several years in the future. A few squatters would not be missed by anyone of note.

If, as he foresaw, the future park became the kind of place reminiscent of the Bois, well, that would be the source of another kind of supply for another time. For the present, then, he would seek out backers of the park project who fit de Tocqueville's estimate of Americans and contrive a plan for his crypt. He found a well-to-do but not overly scrupulous businessman, Hosmer Wainwright. He found Wainwright eager to expand his dealings in real estate and construction and welcomed the infusion of the Wagehalsen fortune . . .

Interlude

Brewster seemed to be dozing in the ergonomic chair as Dr. Korngold finally brought Wagehalsen to America. But he startled the therapist by suddenly sitting bolt upright at the reference to Hosmer Wainwright. He had actually been listening, but as he was more than half convinced that Korngold was handing him a load of bull, interesting bull, perhaps, but bull nonetheless, he had pretended indifference to his little fable. The reference to Augustus Wainwright's great-grandfather, however, was too much.

"How much of this crap do you expect me to swallow?" growled Brewster. He got up abruptly and walked out.

Dr. Buckyballs sat in front of a microscope, surrounded by paraphernalia for handling blood samples. He was contemplating the printouts of a DNA sample in his left hand. In his right, he held a slide with a sample of brownish liquid. A figure passed by the open door of his laboratory. A few moments later, the same figure passed by in the opposite direction. Buckyballs threw down the material he was examining and stared at the equipment in front of him. The figure passed by yet again.

"If you have something you want to say to me," he called out without turning his head, "please come in and say it!" The figure paused at the doorway. "If not . . . in that case, please go away!" He turned at last and found Brewster filling the doorway. "Well?" he said, brushing cigarette ash from his front, "Afraid you won't fit through the doorway? You've got at least two inches of clearance at the top!"

Brewster stumbled in, almost as if he had been pushed from behind, grinning sheepishly. He wanted to discuss Wagehalsen's journal, he said, particularly the vampire's crypt, and the curious reference to Hosmer Wainwright. But he was unsure whether he would be violating a professional confidence between Korngold and Buckyballs. The fact that Korngold had discussed the journal with him did not mean that Dr. Buckyballs was aware that he had. Buckyballs would not even have any idea who he was. He was not sure that Dr. Buckyballs would discuss it with him. But Buckyballs did not show the least reluctance to answer the questions Brewster asked. In fact, he was willing to answer fully and in surprising detail. The journal was authentic, he said, and yes, there were gaps in the document. Especially with regard to the crypt.

"Some backing and filling about the crypt is inevitable," he said. "Wagehalsen's journal describes its location between the base of Vista Rock and the old Croton Reservoir which rested on what is now the Great Meadow. Olmsted and Vaux considered the reservoir an eyesore because it disrupted the continuity in their design for the park. But it was a necessary evil until a new one could be built."

"What became of it?" wondered Brewster.

"Oh, after only a dozen years of service, it was becoming inadequate for the growing city's needs. It was eventually drained, the wall torn down, and filled in for the Great Lawn in 1934."

"And the present reservoir at 86th Street?"

"That was finished in 1862. The only practical way of excavating into solid rock, of course, was explosives. Gunpowder. Alfred Nobel had not yet invented dynamite. Regular blasting teams did not begin the excavation for the new reservoir until 1858, when construction of the park was well under way. The crew would hoist a red flag at 4 p.m., and the blasting would begin all around the site. At the same time, Hosmer Wainwright—"

"Wainwright!" Brewster broke in. "The journal really mentions him?"

"Yes, a land speculator and construction contractor. Wagehalsen commissioned him to construct the crypt at the base of Vista Rock before he returned to Europe in 1856."

"I thought Dr. Korngold was making it up. Or . . . "

"Or maybe," Buckyballs chuckled, "he and I were in cahoots?" Brewster winced at the suggestion of paranoia. Buckyballs tactfully avoided referring to Brewster's relationship to Wagehalsen's contractor. But his eyes twinkled.

"Wainwright could easily have rounded up a surplus crew to blast at the base of Vista Rock. There were always more men available than work for them to do. It would not have been impossible for them to time the blasts for the excavation of a chamber below the Belvedere Castle with those of the crews at the 86th Street reservoir. If their timing was off occasionally, it probably sounded like an echo."

"But that's not in the journal," Brewster said, as much a question as a statement.

Buckyballs nodded. "True. The journal only states that a crypt was constructed in that vicinity, and that a connecting passage from the crypt to the maintenance shafts around the aqueducts from reservoir's underground gate house gave him a concealed access. Another opening was concealed somewhere below the Belvedere."

"But how could such an opening in the Belvedere go unnoticed?"

Buckyballs shrugged. "While work on the castle was under way, in a floor, in a wall composed of granite blocks . . . ? Who knows? But that kind of thing is not unheard of."

"Especially in mystery novels and Egyptian tombs," Brewster added, skeptically.

Buckyballs chuckled and brushed more cigarette ash off himself. "Well, it's a mystery all right. And the workers would've been careful not to disturb the aqueduct that supplied the city's water. Sediments could easily have been dislodged by the blasts in the adjacent rock. A filtering system was needed for other reasons. Early users of water supplied from the aqueducts suspected that it might've contained animalcules. And," he added, removing the cigarette from his mouth and laughing aloud, "one man even refused to drink the water because he was convinced that the 'Hibernian vagabonds' who worked on the aqueducts used the open trenches coming from the Croton reservoir as a 'convenience.' But a little sediment would either have settled out by the time it reached the distributing aqueduct on 42nd Street, or its presence was not noticed. In fact, some residences were outfitted with filtering nozzles. That's just about all it's possible to say—to speculate about, if you like."

"That's it?"

"That's it. Except that Wagehalsen, according to the journal, returned to New York after he left Europe at the end of the Franco-Prussian War in 1870. The Belvedere got the reputation of being haunted for some time after that. Strange sounds, shadows, odd rustlings in the shrubbery. That sort of thing. Turned into a real urban legend. But it's a fact that the building was allowed to lapse into disrepair for a while. Because of its bogus reputation . . . ?

"The sinister association with the Belvedere wasn't helped when several people, last seen in its vicinity, disappeared. Gray-coated 'sparrow cops' patrolled the park. They were supposed to prevent 'unseemly behavior,' meaning tramps and vandals. They weren't set up to investigate missing persons or major crimes. The blue-coated city cops didn't get into disputes over territory. They took disappearances seriously, but their primary concern was crimes in the more densely populated areas of the city. Disappearances in a sparsely populated area of the city, especially when mixed with rumors, superstitions and Indian legends—excavations of the site the old Croton Reservoir was built disturbed some graves of Seneca Villagers—"

"But those villagers were Black people, not Indians," interrupted Brewster.

"True enough. But they weren't high priority. If there was foul play, it was considered to be the work of tramps and riffraff who camped in the area. And they were the responsibility of the 'sparrow cops.' In those days, no one got into an uproar over sacred Indian burial places, much less those of 'Nigger Village.' In short, the perpetrator was never caught. And when the disappearances ended as mysteriously as they began, the matter was dropped."

"What became of Wagehalsen?" wondered Brewster. "I mean, if the mysterious goings-on around the Belvedere can be traced to him . . . Dr. Korngold told me about how you found his journal and the blood sample. Did someone manage to catch him in his crypt and put a stake through his heart?" He could not resist chuckling at the thought. "And if that's the case, he's long gone and couldn't possibly have any connection with the current attacks in the area."

Buckyballs waved speculatively. "Gaps in the journal. But after commissioning Wainwright to construct his crypt, Wagehalsen returned to the Altenburg in Weimar until Liszt closed it in 1861. The journal next has him in Bavaria, and after the Franco-Prussian War in 1870, back in the U.S. By that time, the Belvedere had been built on Vista Rock. Who really knows what became of Wagehalsen's body? The coroner who performed the autopsy over a hundred and thirty years ago assumed that the journal belonged to an unidentified body. The journal is the only evidence that identifies its writer as Wagehalsen. And the contents of the vial found with the journal presumably belong to that body. Connecting the dots . . ." Buckyballs shrugged. "After all these years those dots are stretched pretty far. As to the contents of that vial . . . ?" He shrugged.

"Have you analyzed the contents?" Keen interest replaced Brewster's skepticism.

Buckyballs chuckled. "Yes, yes I have. It's blood. And it's been contaminated by the same strain of virus I've found in recent samples." And before Brewster could ask the obvious question, he added, "And the virus is still viable."

"You think maybe the contents of that vial somehow escaped into the environment and led to the current outbreak of vampirism?" asked Brewster, awed.

Dr. Buckyballs turned his head and shrugged. "Entirely possible. After all, It's been sitting in that evidence box for all these years." He turned his head back to Brewster again, smiling roguishly. "Curious, isn't it? The outbreak of these attacks roughly coinciding with my discovery."

Unsure what to make of this turn of thought, Brewster returned instead to the "urban legend." "You'd think people would avoid the Belvedere late at night."

"Wouldn't you, though?" smiled Buckyballs. "But there's something irresistibly romantic about a dark and lonely 'ruin.'"

32.

Preoccupied with his exploration of New York City and overseeing the construction of the crypt at the base of the Belvedere, Wagehalsen paid scant attention to the progress of Rachel's tour through the New World. But the tour was not going well. Most New Yorkers were baffled by the French language. *Phèdre*, which had made Rachel a star in Europe, was disrupted by cockcrows and a disorderly audience. *Adrienne Lecouvreur* a few days later fared a little better. When the troupe went on to Boston, Rachel caught a bad cold on an unheated train. But she insisted on performing despite wrenching coughs. Bostonians, always eager to be seen as cultured and fashionable, acclaimed her. If it was fashionable in Europe, it would be fashionable in Boston.

The troupe returned to New York in November and had to perform in the dismal Academy of Music instead of the Metropolitan Theatre which had been booked for other performances. Within a few days, they moved to the more attractive theater of Niblo's Garden across the street from the Metropolitan Theatre, where they performed a nondescript play set in ancient Rome. Though it was a better hall, the stage facilities—scenery, supernumeraries and their costumes—were not exactly suitable for the play. "Ancient Rome" had backdrops with gaslit Parisian streets, citizens roaming the boulevards dressed as jockeys or seventeenth-century Spaniards, and magistrates bearing the fasces of authority outfitted as devils in blue tights, red skirts, and down-at-heels boots. Wagehalsen went to her hotel, meaning to offer help with the poor facilities at Niblo's Theatre. Raphaël intercepted him in the lobby. Rachel was feeling unwell and had been secluded in her hotel room. Wagehalsen's offer of help was appreciated but unnecessary as the troupe would shortly leave for Philadelphia. There, the first performance was well received by the audience. Then the weather turned bitterly cold, and Rachel's illness worsened. Remaining performances in Philadelphia, Washington, and Richmond were canceled. The Philadelphia press announced her death and the report widely circulated in the United States and Europe.

Alarmed, Wagehalsen was on the point of traveling to Philadelphia when he learned that the troupe had left to perform in Charleston, South Carolina. The milder weather suited Rachel, her spirits and those of the troupe picked up, and a within a few days they had set sail for Cuba full of optimism. If the spring-like weather of the Carolinas had revived Rachel, tropical Cuba was unable to stem the tide of exhaustion and illness that plagued and drained her. The doctors in Havana would not allow her to perform before the middle of January of the following year, so advance sales of tickets at the Gran Teatro had to be returned. She was still resolved to return to the stage on January 10. Then she shocked the troupe by declaring, instead, that she would not go on. The troupe disbanded, left for New York, and sailed back to France the following week. Rachel stayed behind in Havana for two weeks more.

Meanwhile, Wagehalsen, relieved to learn that Rachel had not died in Philadelphia, mentally reproached Raphaël for having created a false sense of well-being in Rachel and the company. He learned of the troupe's difficulties too late to renew his offer of aid. As plans for the construction of his crypt at the base of the Belvedere were well in hand in 1856, he felt that he had accomplished all he could for the time being. With Hugo's rejection, the dream of a sophocracy in Europe faded but not entirely vanished, there was little else to do but return to Weimar and the Altenburg to contemplate and plan for the future.

Wagehalsen was determined to make one final effort in Europe to interest someone powerful and influential in his sophocracy. He discounted the duke of Weimar. Liszt had come to Weimar hoping to revive the classical Weimar of Goethe's day, found the courts of Karl Friedrich and Karl Alexander, the son who succeeded him during Liszt's tenure, were not the equal of their forebears'. No. The Grand Duke of Weimar would not do. Furthermore, the town was uncomfortably close to his family's estates. As long as he remained an unsung member of Liszt's retinue, he was content to live in Weimar.

After Wagehalsen's long absence in the New World, Liszt welcomed the prodigal back to the Altenburg. He was pleased to have the services of his tireless chorusmaster once more. He never begrudged the young man's renewed absences to visit Paris. He well understood the lure of that city. No one in Paris, much less Weimar, noticed that Wagehalsen's visits coincided with bloodless bodies floating down the Seine. Wagehalsen always returned to the Altenburg looking refreshed, full of energy, and more youthful than ever. The singers under his direction marveled at his energy even after he had driven them to exhaustion. To marvel, however, is not to suffer in silence. The singers complained to Liszt. He redirected some of Wagehalsen's energies into rehearsals with the court orchestra to relieve the tensions among the chorus and ease pressures on himself and Bülow.

For the next year Wagehalsen continued his diversions, both predatory and political, in Paris. He considered whether Napoléon-the-Little could serve his sophocracy, or failing that, quietly sifting among the intelligentsia for signs of discontent that he might turn to advantage. On one of these visits, he learned that Rachel had returned to France in February and was living in a farmhouse in Meulan, near Versailles. He was eager to see her and make amends for not having been attentive during her tour. From the stories circulating in the press and through the salons, he knew that the American tour had fared badly. He delayed an extended visit to Meulan until court activities at Weimar would ease in summer. But when he arrived late in June he found that doctors had sent her off to take the waters at Ems. She was now dangerously ill. He followed and was chagrined to find that he had to compete for her attention with yet another lover, a young imbecile named Delahante. His efforts to penetrate the distractions of stormy, foggy weather, food which she found execrable, illness, and the dalliance were frustrated. He was tempted to get rid of Delahante, but worried about the shock of a sudden loss on Rachel.

For the first time in his life, Wagehalsen hesitated. Delahante was inconvenient. A mistake he could easily have corrected. He might have ... *imposed* ... on Rachel, stemming the illness that made her so desired and so desirous. Still, he held back. Remove a blemish and expose an incurable sore ... ? Some furtive thing gnawing at the edges of his mind but retreating into shadows whenever he tried to shine awareness onto it. He wavered. While Wagehalsen was trying to catch out the fugitive thought, Rachel packed up her affairs and returned to the farmhouse in Meulan with that cur licking her heels. Wagehalsen could not follow for fear that his vexation with Delahante would overwhelm all restraint. He would not again risk the trait that piqued Rachel's tolerance with Ponsard. Rachel always held tightly to the deed of her person. If a lover presumed on privilege so far as entitlement, the over eager stray would soon wear out its welcome and find itself out on the street. Wagehalsen returned to Weimar confident about the outcome.

And by September, Rachel had indeed tired of Delahante. But her deteriorating health in the uncertain weather of France had also made her restless. She decided to recuperate in a warmer climate. Recalling her success as the queen of Egypt in *Cléopatre*, written by her friend, Mme de Girardin, she decided on a visit to Egypt.

Back at the Altenburg, Wagehalsen found his new responsibilities with the orchestra engrossing. Liszt had begun to use unusual whole tone scales in his symphonic poems. He worked with Liszt and the concertmaster in long, closed workshop rehearsals in which new harmonies and modal effects were tried out and continually revised. These new "effects" were often too radical for the conservative ears of the players, so there was a constant struggle to overcome their confusion and impatience with Liszt's experiments. He therefore learned of Rachel's decision only after she had already left for a brief stay in Nice and Marseilles before crossing the Mediterranean.

At the beginning of October, she set sail for Cairo. She kept to her cabin on the first day. But the mild Mediterranean air had an immediate beneficial effect. Within three days, her cough had improved and she was taking turns, if a little haltingly, around the deck. Gabriel Aubaret, saw that Rachel was worn and ailing, and being the eager thirty-one year old naval lieutenant, gallantly offered her his arm. Before they reached Cairo, he had determined that he would restore her health, convert her to Roman Catholicism, and marry her. If his ardent talks about religion for the rest of the journey showed some uncertainty in the order he expected these things to take place, Rachel nevertheless warmed to his sympathetic attentions. He told her of the family living in the old university town of Montpellier a few kilometers from the Mediterranean coast. It was renowned for its climate and its doctors. His family would welcome her with open arms.

They parted in Cairo, Gabriel, on assignment, Rachel, to rest in the house of Soleyman Pasha, and drink asses' milk. The health that had been on the mend at sea and for the first few days of her stay began to decline again. She was urged to travel up the Nile, but the absence of friends and loved ones, the monotonous days of sun and sand, the monuments of ancient Egypt, ruined like her health, all dragged tediously. She tried to subsist on the letters from her family and friends, but found she could not live in them. By March, ill, depressed, and tired, she returned down the Nile to Cairo. She would recover her strength in the gardens of Old Cairo, then sail for home in June or the end of May. Yet her moods, like her health, vacillated unpredictably. In February, she once again suddenly changed her plans and sailed for France. She returned to Paris to arrange the sale of her house on the rue Trudon and moved into an apartment at 9, place Royale. She called in decorators and told them that she was preparing the rooms for her funeral.

She left Paris again, this time for a house near the home of the Aubarets in Montpellier rented for her by Gabriel. Their open arms were full of pious calls for her conversion to Catholicism. Her mother, brother, Raphaël, and younger sister, Lia, soon came to stay for a fortnight, giving Rachel a respite from the evangelizing Aubarets. Wagehalsen learned with a pang of resentment that her Paris friends, too—Émile Augier, Théophile Gautier, Arsène Houssaye, and the pathetically devoted, François Ponsard—littérateurs and lovers all, followed. He was frustrated by the knowledge that he could not approach Rachel with his alternate gift of immortality while they hovered about and sentimentally tried to ease Rachel's departure from this world with reminiscences about her past triumphs. Within a week after they left Montpellier, Rachel had had enough of the Aubarets and Catholicism. She invented an illness in one of her children as an excuse for returning to Paris.

But evangelism was not so easily put off. Gabriel got a two-month leave and followed Rachel to Paris, continuing to declare his love, his concern for her physical—and above all—spiritual, health. This time, Wagehalsen discreetly timed his arrival at the place Royale when Aubaret was not present. He saw what Rachel's friends had seen in Montpellier, the pale shadow of the diva who once ruled the rue Richelieu with her iron whim, who now looked so fragile that friends feared their touch would bruise her. Too tired to rise to greet him, she remained sitting on the same divan that she and Ponsard had sat on when he burst into her old home on the rue Trudon. She offered her hands to him and he took them gently.

"Ah, monsieur," she said with a wan smile that would not risk laughter, "if you have come gallantly to escort me to Père Lachaise, I fear you will have to get in line!"

"Indeed," said Wagehalsen, "I feared as much. No doubt all of Paris would welcome such an honor. But you must try to keep your spirits up. There is still hope. Perhaps," he hesitated, "perhaps there is an alternative . . ."

"Hope. And does it have a cure for consumption? I once thought I was as permanent as the Pyramids. But I see now that actresses are no more than the sands that drift past them, and hope no more than the wind that propels them. Hope is for the future. But I am trying to make no plans for the future. Each day is enough. An alternative?" Again the wisp of smile. She shrugged.

"My dear Rachel!" was all Wagehalsen could say. Was she prepared to hear about his alternative? A woman who despaired of life might not hesitate to rush into radical alternatives. But could she withstand the shock of vampirism, or was she too fragile to withstand the transformation and so collapse at once? He had been absent from her life for almost three years. She needed time to get used to his presence again. Time to prepare. Time. He did not believe much of that was left for her. But he promised to call on her again and left.

Over the next several weeks, opportunities for Wagehalsen to visit Rachel were few. Aubaret and past friends and lovers were almost always attending her, and he did not want to risk a confrontation. The decorators had finished their task of transforming Rachel's apartment. They restrained the Empire's taste for classical sculpture and Italian urns, and set the stage, minimally ornamented, to suit her final exit. Despite her denial, Wagehalsen learned that she planned to leave Paris at the end of summer and return to the south of France and a milder climate. A relative of the dramatist, Victorien Sardou, offered her his villa in Le Cannet, the village near Cannes on the Riviera.

The Villa Sardou sat in a grove of olive trees at the end of paths so steep and narrow that it could not be reached by carriage. The stucco building was of Moorish design with tall, twin towers at either end. Its interior reflected an operatic hodgepodge of Moorish, neo-classical, and Renaissance bric-a-brac. These motifs spilled lugubriously into the bedroom, located in the eastern tower, the most significant room in the house, considering Rachel's condition. An alabaster bed rested in a chapel-like alcove, its headboard shaped like a rank of organ pipes topped with faux ancient masks. The statue of a Muse poised at the foot of the bed to sing its occupant to her final rest.

As the year drew to a close, if there had ever been any doubt that Rachel's life, too, drew to a close, it was gone from even the kindest, most optimistic well-wisher. Rachel's days were filled with visitors, Gabriel, members of her family, most prominent among them, and friends from the wintry north paying their final respects. As the railway reached only to Marseilles, they completed their journey by carriage or sea.

Wagehalsen had taken a leave from the Altenburg and arrived just at the turn of the year, on the evening of December 31, 1857. He intended to make one last effort to convert Rachel. With all the attention surrounding her, he knew that getting into her room alone and unobserved would be difficult. He soon learned which tower housed her bedroom, and late in the following night, he approached and began to climb it, digging his fingers into the crumbling stucco and gripping the studs underneath. Reaching a window next to the alcove, he saw Rachel sleeping fitfully on the bed. The room was otherwise unattended. Quietly opening the window so as not to rouse her or alert someone in the house, he entered stealthily and moved to the side of her bed. He sat on the edge and gently woke her. She gasped under his penetrating gaze, but made no outcry.

"Henri!" she breathed. Hearing her speak familiarly after so long stirred his love and renewed his resolve. "You have come. You are the last of my old acquaintances to do so."

Perhaps the last in more ways than one, thought Wagehalsen sadly. She was too near death to vacillate any longer. If the shock of his offer hastened it, or if she consented but did not survive the shock, he consoled himself that she would be spared pointless suffering. If she refused . . .

She spoke again. "There were times when I could not remember the parts that were once so familiar. When my mind was clear, I was afraid that I would forget even those whose memories were dearest to me." She began to cough. It was eased when Wagehalsen put his hand on her throat and put his lips to hers. It was not a kiss. He breathed into her mouth through his own.

"I have come to take you away," he said when her spasm had passed.

"Ah!" she said. "And what will you do with my corpse?"

"You shall not die. The vampire's kiss will make you immortal! Imagine! You could rule the stage forever, forever young as you are! Forever supreme!"

While Wagehalsen had been trying to persuade Rachel of the efficacy of his salvation, Gabriel Aubaret, who had been sitting vigil but left to relieve himself, had quietly returned. He froze speechless and horrified.

"Others have tried to convert me to their faith," said Rachel with a sweet smile, eyes drifting over Gabriel's shadowy form, though Wagehalsen seemed unaware of his presence.

"I do not speak of faith in an after-life, but a prolongation of this one," he replied.

"Ah, think of that! Imagine! Instead of lying here coughing for a little while, I could endure these spasms for an eternity! What an opportunity!" She started to giggle but choked in her merriment and immediately began to cough and gasp for air. Wagehalsen watched helplessly, wanting to reassure her that her illness would end with her transformation. But he could not. And there it was. That troublesome thought that had eluded him. She had stumbled on an unexpected truth. Since he, himself, was past dying, he was undoubtedly immune to disease. But if a disease were already present—what then? Surely it would not progress. Would it go into remission? He thought gloomily of his injured hand. If the disease had progressed this far—without remission, eternity would be damnation indeed! If only he had thought of that before! He could have experimented on someone who mattered less, some sickly street urchin with no future whose life in any case would have been miserable and short.

But Rachel would cling to her Jewish faith. She raised herself a little with some effort, declining his assistance, resting on her elbow so she could turn her body slightly to face him more fully, and with a rueful smile, dismiss his offer: "You tempt me with a new gospel. Are you a Catholic vampire?" she teased at Gabriel. "Would you have me renounce God for Jesus?" She fell back on her pillow, coughing discreetly into a blood-stained handkerchief, the price of her success. She closed her eyes and, groping with her hand for his, patted it consolingly. "Only think how many immortal deaths I have already died on stage! This death is but another evening's mortality. Conversion is not in my lines." Opening her eyes and turning her head to look at him again, "And your immortality sounds like another kind of death."

She closed her eyes again. And since vampires have no tears, drops of blood appeared in his eyes and trickled down his face. Wagehalsen turned away from the bed and saw Aubaret, a look of horror on his face. "Get out!" hissed Aubaret in a whisper. "Get out!" Wagehalsen started to advance on him, but Gabriel held up the crucifix he always wore at his throat. With a cry of disgust, Wagehalsen threw his cloak over his face and plunged out the window.

Interlude

Absurdity. Korngold had meant to draw Brewster into Wagehalsen's journal so that in casting out its absurdity he might cast out his own along with it. When Buckyballs had told him about Brewster's visit, he probably enjoyed the thought that patient was checking up on his shrink. That seemed to be a sign that Brewster was taking the sessions seriously enough to seek corroboration. But did that mean he was questioning through *the absurdities or skimming over them? Now Korngold found absurdity staring at him out of the eyes of this overgrown hulk with the face of an adolescent.*

The world of Wagner and Ludwig II of Bavaria, was every bit as fantastic as any conjured up by a lunatic. But awakening Brewster at its end and getting him to face his own lunacy would not be as simple as a posthypnotic snap of the fingers.

"It's really quite wonderful," began Korngold, optimistically trying to shake off his doubts. "The way folklore burrows into the mind, reshapes it, then in turn is reshaped to fit the transformation. Consider the medieval romances used by Wagner in his operas. Maybe you know that Lohengrin, according to a 13th-century manuscript ascribed to Wolfram von Eschenbach, was the son of Parsifal?"

"I knew that Lohengrin was the son of Parsifal," said Brewster. "It's the kind of thing that Wagner's characters are always explaining in his operas. It's what fills in 'some beautiful moments with boring quarter-hours.' I don't remember if Trifle filled me in on Wolfram. And, sure, medieval romances could be considered a kind of idealized folklore, if that's what you're getting at."

"Yes. It's the unconscious subtext by which Wagner leads to Parsifal through Lohengrin and Tristan that's relevant. Wolfram found the original story of Parsifal in a romance by Chrétien de Troyes. In Wolfram, the Grail was a mysterious stone brought down from heaven by angels. But in his Lohengrin, Wagner followed a Christian tradition. The grail became the chalice which caught the blood of Jesus on the Cross after the spear was

The Womb of Uncreated Night

thrust into his side. The Grail never actually appears in that opera. Its presence is represented by ethereal music."

"And Lohengrin, himself, refers to its mystical powers," added Brewster.

"It does, however, actually appear in Parsifal."

"But there's no reference to the Grail in Tristan."

"Not overtly. But there's an unconscious allusion to it. You recall that Isolde hates Tristan at the beginning of the opera because he had killed her uncle, who had also been her lover?"

"Oh, my. I recall Wagner's fascination with incest. And with tortuously tangled back-stories. Let's see. Before the opera begins, Sir Tristan has killed Isolde's uncle in single combat and was himself so seriously wounded by a poisoned barb—I don't remember where that came from. Unsporting, don't you think? He asks to be set adrift at sea to die. Instead, he washes up on Isolde's doorstep in Ireland. She, being a sorceress and not knowing at the time that he has just killed her uncle—sorceresses are a pretty clueless bunch, aren't they? There's Circe, and Medea—"

Korngold held up an admonishing finger. "Brews . . . "

"Yeah. Well, Isolde cures Tristan. Meanwhile, back in Cornwall, the barons, jealous of Tristan's favor with his uncle, King Mark, urge the king to marry Isolde and produce an heir. So who gets to ferry the bride-to-be from Ireland to Cornwall? Why, the favorite nephew, of course. En route, Isolde learns that Tristan is her uncle-lover's slayer, and she decides to murder him."

"So where's the Grail?"

"Well, it's inverted, you see. Instead of the miraculous healing power of Jesus' blood—"

"Ah, I get it! It's the poison that Isolde wants to slip Tristan in a cup of wine. A little ironic twist instead of lemon peel. Only her servant, Brangaene, substitutes a love philter. Tristan drinks, and Isolde decides that since Sir Tristan is about to die and she's had her revenge, she'd rather die, too, than marry King Mark. So she drinks from the same cup, and instead of dying, they fall madly in love. That does add up to kind of wacko communion!"

33.

So Rachel was gone. After thirteen years of coping with the inadequacies of the Duke of Weimar's court and the frustrations of waiting for Tsar Nicholas to grant Carolyne a divorce so that he could marry her, Liszt closed the Altenburg and went to Rome to take religious orders. While waiting for the call to republicanize *this* world, Hugo was off on the Channel Isles communicating with the *other* world. Pondering how the intersection of lives and circumstances delude people into believing that their fondest wishes have been granted, Wagehalsen retired to his apartment in the rue Rossini . . .

In Bavaria, the fondest wishes of Ludwig von Wittelsbach were to recreate the court of Louis XIV, build fairy-tale castles, and unite the glories of medieval chivalry with operatic fantasies. He succeeded his father to the throne on March 12, 1864, as Ludwig II. The death of Maximilian II allowed him to indulge the fantasies frowned upon by his father but encouraged by his governess. Yet his father himself had already unwittingly laid the groundwork for future flights of fancy when, as Crown Prince, he found Schloss Hohenschwangau in 1837. The knights who had built it in the foothills of the Bavarian Alps in the twelfth century died out four hundred years later. The fabled "Castle High above the Swan District" lay in ruins. Maximilian restored it and commissioned a mural in the dining room depicting the legend of

Lohengrin, the Swan Knight who had set out from there to rescue Elsa of Brabant. It captured Ludwig's imagination.

The legend of the Swan Knight also caught the imagination of an older dreamer. Richard Wagner was plagued by erysipelas, a bacterial skin infection that shows up as shiny red, hot, painful blotches. The disease was thought to be brought on by nerves. When symptoms flared up during his stint as Royal Kapellmeister to the King of Saxony at Dresden after the premiere of his opera *Tannhäuser* in 1845, his doctor ordered him to rest and take the waters at Marienbad in Bohemia. He was forbidden to work. But while at the spa, Wagner was so enthused by the story of *Lohengrin* which he found in a story by an anonymous medieval German writer, that he almost leaped out of the bath and began to draft the opera. He completed the score in April 1848.

Wagehalsen had assisted Liszt at the opera's premiere at the Court Theater of Weimar three years later. In spite of the barely adequate performance with an undersized orchestra, it was a critical success. Performances throughout Germany within a few years established it as *the* German Romantic opera. When it reached Munich, Ludwig's former governess, urged Ludwig to see it. When he eventually did see it, he was so enraptured that he was determined to embellish his fairy-tale kingdom with Wagner's operas.

Ludwig's ambition preoccupied him and gave him a distant, abstracted air during commonplace events. At a banquet given in his honor by King Maximilian, Count Otto von Bismarck, who was apparently working for cordiality among the German states, noticed that far away look. Sitting beside the crown prince, the Prussian Chancellor was puzzled that he was unable to draw him into conversation. That was the year before Maximilian's death, and within a few short months, the German states were about to be plunged into events that Ludwig was ill-suited to cope with.

Back in Paris, Wagehalsen sensed that Bismarck was interested in more than cordiality among the German states. A man as determined and resourceful as Bismarck might be able to bring about the Sophocracy.

But such a man would not be as easily swayed as a man like Ludwig. He would certainly have no taste for a "cultured" civilization. Wagehalsen did not see how he could turn this master manipulator to his advantage. He watched with mounting interest as the mixed ethnic Danish and German populations of two duchies, Schleswig and Holstein, agitated for annexation to their respective neighboring kingdoms; as Frederick VII of Denmark tried to resolve the issue by annexing both, then died two days later; as the right to the duchies of his successor, Christian IX, was challenged by a German duke; and as the conflicting interests of Austria and Prussia played into Bismarck's hand.

During this international crisis, Maximilian fell critically ill. He had hoped that the German states would return the duchies to independence and avoid an armed confrontation. Most of the states agreed, but Bismarck, eyeing the strategic port of Kiel on the Baltic Sea, had annexation plans of his own. For the time, he simply argued that the Danish kings had violated international agreements and had to return the duchies to independent status under Danish administration. The Prussian chancellor issued an ultimatum to Christian that he rescind the annexation. Christian ignored him. Prussia and Austria invaded, then set about threatening each other's interests.

When Ludwig woke up to the throne of Bavaria and the ugly reality of the unresolved crisis among the German states over those troublesome duchies, he vaguely hoped to ignore it by coasting on his father's policies. The German states acting together might avoid domination by Prussia. But he was only half awake. His other half was still dreaming of emulating in scale and lavishness the building and cultural programs of his role model, Louis XIV of France.

Wagehalsen realized that sooner or later, the dreamy romanticists, the Hugos and the Ludwigs of Europe, would have to come up against the Bismarcks of the world. Dreams pitted against utter pragmatism. Could they stand up to it? Or would they merely flutter like so many pages in the breeze? There was Hugo, off on the Channel Isles. How would the President of the Citadel of Writers and Editors handle the machinations of that master of *realpolitik*, Bismarck, who was scheming to unify Germany and dominate Europe? In the years preceding Louis Napoleon's coup d'état, Hugo had tried to choose between romantic idealism and practical necessities. But his political intentions were badly flawed. He lived to rue bitterly his naïve miscalculations, the worst of which was underestimating Louis Napoleon.

And Ludwig? A king full of romantic notions since childhood trying to recreate in a pragmatic world of *is* an age of gallantry that never *was*. Bismarck had ominously predicted how far the times had fallen, and would continue to fall, below chivalric idealism when he declared in speech that, "The great questions of the time are not decided by speeches and majority decisions . . . but by iron and blood." And since fire is needed in order to work iron, there was altogether too much fire in the world to found a realm on the pages of books. Given the state of the German Confederacy in 1864 and the unresolved issue of the duchies, staging grandiose operas should have been furthest from Ludwig's mind. Yet in the midst of the ominous squabbling over the Schleswig-Holstein situation, Ludwig pursued his vision.

The prelude to Ludwig II's operatic reign began with his grandfather and namesake's Wagnerian dalliance with Lola Montez. When the "Spanish" dancer arrived in Munich in 1846, she was better known for her flamboyant and scandalous behavior than as a dancer.

Eliza Gilbert, born in Ireland, early showed a waywardness that led her to being shunted among relatives who were unable to cope with her. She eloped at 16 and, when she and her husband separated five years later, took up dancing in London under the stage name, "Lola Montez, the Spanish Dancer." Booed and hissed off the stage in London, she launched a career on the Continent, where her liaisons with Franz Liszt, Alexandre Dumas, and sundry members of high society earned her the reputation of courtesan. She planned all along to snag a prince and hang up her dancing shoes.

In Munich, Ludwig was immediately taken with her sensuality. He entertained her in private, bought her a mansion, and gave her a generous allowance from the public treasury. Lola's influence over the king, her arrogance, and temperamental outbursts made her unpopular with Müncheners, especially after they learned that she wanted to become a naturalized citizen and elevated to the nobility. Outraged, the prime minister wanted to expel her from Bavaria. The king fired him. When his cabinet learned of Ludwig's action, they threatened to resign if the king did not oust the dancer. He fired them too and suspended parliament.

But the fateful year of 1848 ended Lola's idyll with the King. Europe was in the throes of revolutionary ferment. Political uprisings appeared ready to bring down all monarchies. Ludwig's excesses with Lola aggravated the mounting tensions. Munich was in turmoil. The citizens revolted, and crowds chased her through the streets hurling stones and invectives at her. Ludwig I abdicated in favor of his son, who as Maximilian II was able to restore a sense of serenity to Bavaria not enjoyed by other European states. Lola fled the country.

Shortly after his father's death, King Ludwig II sent his personal secretary, Franz von Pfistermeister, to locate Wagner and bring him to Munich. Always evading creditors, Wagner led Pfistermeister on a merry chase from the outskirts of Vienna to Lake Luzern in Switzerland. Eventually, the weary secretary located the wily composer, and with the aid of a letter from the King, was able to complete his mission. Ludwig set up Wagner in a grand private residence on the Briennerstrasse. There, Wagner proved that he could be as spendthrift a set designer as the king.

He sent for his Viennese decorator and commissioned an orgiastic fantasy of satins, silks, and laces. He filled the residence with creature comforts, sumptuous furnishings, a wardrobe of velvets and silks, and imported French perfumes.

Oblivious to the ominous political rumblings between Austria and Prussia over the Schleswig-Holstein affair, Ludwig commanded Wagner to stage a performance of his recently completed opera, *Tristan und Isolde*, in the fall of 1864. But Wagner did not have singers available who would be able to meet the demands of the leading roles. He substituted instead a performance of *Der fliegende Holländer*. The king was at first not pleased, but after seeing the performance was won over. The premiere of *Tristan* was postponed until the following year.

When Wagehalsen learned about the success of *The Flying Dutchman* in Munich, and the likely production of *Tristan* the next year, he was struck by the glittering opportunity it offered. Fate had presented Bavaria with a dilettantish young king romantic enough to want to dream of projecting a Wagnerian world right out of the Hofoper onto the Bavarian landscape. With one of the most liberal constitutions on the Continent already in place, and an aesthetically susceptible young ruler drunk on Wagnerian sensuality, how hard would it be to sway him toward Sophocracy? Wagehalsen determined to travel to Munich. Once he ingratiated himself into the royal presence, the king would be his! The first step would be easy. He would infiltrate the Hofoper by presenting himself as a *répétiteur* with the wealth of experience he had amassed at the Altenburg. That would put him next to Wagner. And with Ludwig often attending rehearsals, the throne was only a step away.

Charmed by their handsome young king, Munich was for a time willing to indulge Ludwig's whims, the grandiose Wagner, and fairy-tale castles that drained the royal treasury and strained his personal finances. But it was not long before the citizens of Munich began to see a parallel between Ludwig's obsession with Wagner and his grandfather's with Lola Montez. Articles in the press began referring to the composer as "Lolette."

When Ludwig commanded the production of *Tristan*, Wagner had been carrying on a relationship with Cosima von Bülow, one of the three illegitimate children of Franz Liszt and the Countess Marie d'Agoult. At the time she was married to Hans von Bülow, one of Liszt's pupils at the Altenburg, and now an established conductor. On the basis of his having made a playable piano reduction of the complex orchestral score of *Tristan*, Wagner recommended Bülow to the King as uniquely qualified to bring Tristan to the stage. Bülow was duly engaged, and with a "second self" at his side, Wagner was able to supervise every detail of the performance and staging. He was also able to keep Bülow exhausted with twelve-hour days at conferences, orchestral rehearsals and piano rehearsals for the principle singers. This arrangement enabled Wagner to use Cosima as secretary, adviser, and confidante, gilding his oriental lily-pad. The "secretary" bore a child the following year and named her, Isolde. Bülow accepted her as his own.

Once in Munich, Wagehalsen soon learned what everyone else knew about Wagner's liaison with Cosima. Everyone, that is, except the king. Ludwig was curiously clueless about the nature of the ménage à trois at the Briennerstrasse residence, and remained blissfully ignorant for some time. He accepted without question Wagner's explanation that the residence was large enough for two households, and the presence of Mme von Bülow convenient to serve as his amanuensis. Like King Mark in his hero's opera, Ludwig never suspected Wagner capable of betrayal. Here was Wagner playing Tristan to Ludwig's Isolde, with a twist in the irony in the opera. Ludwig was the innocent dupe of the love potion, Wagner's music. Wagner was an old hand at the game of musical seduction, wooing the wives of husbands who befriended and supported him financially. Waiting for his chance to get into the Hofoper, Wagehalsen amused himself by turning over the idea in his head: Wagner seducing the boy while cuckolding the king! He laughed aloud, mocking King Mark's lament in Act II, if honor could not be found in Wagner, where could it be found?

Wagehalsen appeared at the Court Opera to offer his assistance as coach and accompanist for the singers. He sat quietly in the darkened theater, watching early preparations. After one particularly trying rehearsal the strain of long hours had begun to take their toll on Bülow. Wagehalsen approached him to renew his Altenburg acquaintance. "Meister," he smiled, "perhaps I could relieve your load by taking over the evening rehearsals . . . so that you could spend more time to rest at home?" Bülow hesitated, dimly recognizing the young man who had the temerity to suggest that he was equal to such a task. Wagehalsen reminded him of his role as répétiteur for the premiere of *Lohengrin* under Liszt. Bülow challenged him to demonstrate his competence by having him read at sight his piano reduction of *Tristan*. Wagehalsen readily played page after page chosen at random by Bülow. Suitably impressed, the conductor welcomed the young man as a chance for some relief from the burdens Wagner heaped on him.

But Bülow's unexpected appearance at home in the evening created consternation. It hindered Wagner's intimacy with Cosima. The composer fumed but avoided a row. The next day, however, he rounded on the répétiteur and in no uncertain terms informed him that only Bülow understood the opera well enough to conduct rehearsals. Wagehalsen was to *assist*, not replace, Bülow. When Bülow collapsed under the strain, Wagner reluctantly allowed Wagehalsen to carry on until the conductor was able to resume his heavy schedule.

At the dress rehearsal of the opera on May 11, 1865, Ludwig was so moved by the opera that he went straight up into the clouds. He wrote a rapturous letter to Wagner and eagerly looked forward to the premiere performance scheduled for May 15. That performance had to be postponed because Malvina Schnorr von Carolsfeld, the Isolde, had lost her voice after taking a steam bath. Wagner's enemies circulated the rumor that the opera had ruined her voice. But after three weeks at a spa, Malvina regained her voice and the premiere was rescheduled for June 10. This time, the soprano had avoided steam baths and the performance took place as scheduled. Many in the audience were bewildered by the stark settings and lush music. But sitting alone in the royal box, Ludwig wept.

During the next two weeks of performances that followed, Ludwig had traveled from Castle Berg on Lake Starnberg to see them. Each performance left him as moved as the first. After the fourth performance, returning by train to Berg, he was so overcome with emotion that he stopped the train, got off, and wandered alone through the forest for several hours. Learning of the King's disturbing behavior, Wagehalsen thought that he might play on such instability to his advantage.

But things were never that simple. Wagner's influence over the King, extravagant demands, and illicit relationship with Cosima thoroughly alienated the Munich press and public. Attacks on him in the press provoked vehement rebuttals. Wagner demanded the removal of his enemies in the King's cabinet. Ludwig may have been easily manipulated where Wagner's music was at issue but matters of state were Ludwig's royal prerogative. And he resented Wagner's having allowed his name to be dragged into a public scandal. When he returned to Munich after one of his many stays at Lake Starnberg, Ludwig had resigned himself to the inevitable. Wagner would have to leave Bavaria until the scandal died down. He hoped that the separation would be brief. But Wagner demanded Bavarian citizenship before he would agree to return which, of course, was vehemently opposed by the cabinet and the Landtag. It was Lola Montez again.

Wagner left Munich on December 10. In January 1866, he traveled to France hoping to find a residence there. When that proved unsatisfactory, he and his "secretary," Cosima, traveled to Switzerland. In March, they found a three-story house, Tribschen, on Lake Lucerne. Wagner, Cosima, and the children moved in. Bülow remained in Munich, ostensibly to teach piano in the manner of Franz Liszt and make arrangements for a new music school. He made occasional visits. Wagehalsen suspected that, although he tolerated the notorious infidelity of his wife with Wagner, he really could not long stand to be in its presence.

Further complicating matters for Ludwig—and Wagehalsen's ambitions— the situation in the German states turned ominous over the unruly populations of Schleswig-Holstein. Bismarck had schemed all along to unify the German states, except Austria, under Prussia. He

The Womb of Uncreated Night

therefore used the unrest in the Danish provinces to provoke Vienna. They exchanged harsh and threatening notes. Bismarck struck a deal with northern Italy, encouraging the mobilization of troops on the Austrian border. The threat of a Prussian army in the north and the Italians in the south posed for Austria the dangers of fighting a war on two fronts. Talk of an inevitable confrontation with Prussia sent tremors through the German Confederacy.

The threat of civil war unhinged Ludwig. He had of course been instructed in traditional military matters as a boy. But at twenty, he was completely inexperienced in modern warfare. Quite simply, Ludwig did not know what to do in a war of cannons and needle guns. Since his ascension to the throne, he had adopted a policy of neutrality between Catholic Austria and Protestant Prussia. Despite the fact that his mother was a Prussian princess, his sympathies lay with Bavaria's southern neighbor. Catholic Bavaria had always had strong political, economic, and familial ties with Austria. The Wittelsbachs had often intermarried with the Hapsburgs, and Ludwig's cousin, Elizabeth, was now the wife of Emperor Franz Josef. As the threat of war became a virtual certainty in March 1866, Ludwig's ambassador informed Vienna that the Bavarian army would join Austria's.

Wagehalsen's concern about Ludwig mounted as preparations for war intensified. The King's emotional reaction to *Tristan* and his feelings for Wagner were embedded in confused longings that gave Wagehalsen a hold over Ludwig, but the vampire influence was unpredictable. Minds sometimes suffered disabling aftereffects.

On May 9, Ludwig's cabinet ministers advised that Bavaria honor its commitment to Austria and mobilize the army against Prussia. He declared that he would rather abdicate the throne in favor of his brother, Otto. During the restless night that followed, Wagehalsen secretly gained access to his chamber and, using his power to beguile and seduce, finally calmed the agitated King and convinced him to accept his responsibilities. The next day, Ludwig ordered the general staff to mobilize the army and scheduled an extraordinary session of the Landtag to discuss the crisis on May 22. But then Ludwig fled to Schloss Berg, the day after, even isolating himself further on the Roseninsel in the middle of the lake. Brooding about the coming war, he wrote Wagner that he wanted to abdicate and join him in Lucerne.

Ludwig's behavior alarmed Munich. Prompt communication was critical. A messenger would have to travel for two hours from Munich, lose more time locating a boat to get to the island, only to find Ludwig away, rowing around the lake or sailing in his steamer. On May 22, pleading illness, he notified his cabinet secretary that he would be unable to open the special session of the Landtag as scheduled. Instead, he left Schloss Berg for Tribschen, the day being Wagner's fifty-third birthday. He arrived late in the afternoon and presented himself at the door of Wagner's residence as Walther von Stolzing, a leading character in his unfinished opera, *Die Meistersinger von Nürnberg*. The two spent the rest of the afternoon discussing *Meistersinger* and the conflict with Prussia. But the next day, Ludwig once again raised the possibility of abdication. Wagner was alarmed.

"But this would be a disaster for our artistic plans!" protested Wagner. "And for Bavaria!" And my lifestyle, he might have added. He urged the king to reconsider.

If the citizens of Munich had already felt abandoned when Ludwig ran away to Berg, they were outraged when they learned of the visit to the despised and exiled Wagner in Switzerland while the army was being mobilized for war. Having postponed the session with the Landtag until May 27, Ludwig once again tried to shirk his responsibilities and refused to attend. His grandfather lectured him about his duties. As he drove to the Landtag, he was stunned when the citizens of Munich hissed him in the streets.

On June 1, Austria mobilized the army in Holstein as a response to Prussia's threatening moves in the Danish duchies and asked the diet in Frankfurt to mobilize the German Confederacy against Prussia. Bismarck was actively pressuring the young King to join Prussia, hinting that if Austria were defeated, Prussia would control northern

Germany and allow Bavaria to control the southern states. But Ludwig and his cabinet were unwilling to renege on their promise to Austria.

At this critical juncture, news of the ménage at Tribschen was leaked to the press. Wagner manipulated Bülow into writing a letter demanding a retraction and urging the King to sign it. Bülow could tolerate a private scandal, but had no stomach for a public airing. Burdened with more pressing issues, Ludwig hastily complied.

Still desperate to avoid war, Ludwig instructed his envoy to request a conciliatory measure with Prussia. By the time the diet agreed to the Bavarian proposal, it was already too late. In mid-June, Prussia declared war on Austria. No longer able to remain neutral, Bavaria honored its commitment. And then Ludwig ran away again to Castle Berg.

When he learned of Ludwig's second flight, Wagehalsen, too, was torn. On the very day that war was declared, he arrived at Castle Berg, scaled a castle wall and found his way into Ludwig's sanctuary. In a darkened chamber lit by an artificial moon, he found the king and an aide costumed as Lohengrin and Barbarossa reciting love poetry to each other. Wagehalsen withdrew unnoticed to ponder his next move. If Ludwig was so unstable, how could he implement a political philosophy as problematical as the Sophocracy was bound to be, even propped up by dedicated converts under Wagehalsen's influence? Even if Ludwig could be made to see it as the realization of his fondest fantasies of a new enlightenment?

Within seven weeks, Prussia defeated Austria, Bavaria lost its independence, and Wagehalsen returned to Tribschen as a glorified gofer while Wagner worked on *Meistersinger*. That autumn, the scandal that had forced Wagner out of Munich seemed to have passed. But wherever Wagner went, turmoil was sure to follow. This time it came in the form of a visit from Frau Schnorr von Carolsfeld and Isadora von Reutter, her friend and spiritual medium. Ludwig Schnorr von Carolsfeld and his wife, Malvina, had created the roles of Tristan and Isolde at its premiere. Their great singing had proved that *Tristan* was performable. But the tenor took ill shortly after, and died a few weeks later. The composer owed much to them. He warmly welcomed the recently widowed "Isolde" and her friend.

Over tea in the parlor, Wagner was alone with his two guests, Wagehalsen having discreetly withdrawn to an adjoining room to provide soft background music, and Cosima to tend to the children. Wearing his violet velvet robe, sitting in his violet velvet armchair, with his customary violet velvet beret perched artistically on his head, Wagner was consoling Malvina over her loss and reminiscing about her husband's brilliant success as Tristan when the conversation took an unexpected turn.

"My husband's spirit," announced Malvina firmly, "has communicated with Isadora, here. He has directed her to marry King Ludwig."

Wagner's eyebrows shot up into his beret and the whiskers under his chin twitched. The teacup clattered as he carefully set it down and contemplated Malvina. Were the ladies having him on? Had Malvina gone completely dotty, unhinged perhaps, by the loss of her husband? He had almost choked on the image of the stout tenor risen from the ground like Erda, urging Isadora to yield to fate. His first impulse was to excuse himself, go out into the hall, and give in to a fit of uncontrollable laughter.

"Indeed," he said, as if she had just announced that it was about to rain. "And did he say anything else?"

"Indeed he did," said Malvina. "After the nuptials of King Ludwig and Isadora, my Ludwig directed me to become your companion!"

Wagner was utterly speechless. He abruptly left the room and went upstairs to his private study, slamming the door. Clearly, the two women were deranged. He would tolerate Isadora for Malvina's sake. But Malvina, seeing well enough the ménage à trois at Tribschen, persisted. Cosima was plainly in love with Wagner; and her children, Isolde and Eva, markedly different from the other two. They openly calling him "papa." And Bülow? He said nothing! The rumors about their relationship circulating in Munich were all too true. She finally confronted Wagner again in front of Bülow and Cosima. She insisted that Wagner honor her husband's instructions from the grave. Wagner threw her out.

Malvina lost no time in returning to Munich to stir the pot, even writing a letter to the king relaying her late husband's instructions. She demanded that Ludwig marry Isadora and command Wagner to install her in the Tribschen household. Wagner was understandably vexed when the king sent the letter to Cosima.

For his part, Ludwig had good reason to feel betrayed by Wagner. He had loyally, even naïvely, tried to disbelieve the scandal mongers in Munich. But the mounting evidence, culminating in Malvina's outrageous letter, made it difficult to ignore. When Malvina's accusations percolated into the highest court circles, Ludwig's counselors advised him to cut all ties with Wagner to avoid further scandal. Adultery was common enough in Bavaria. But monarchy, they reasoned, had to pretend to virtue if their handsome young king were to regain the respect of Bavarians. The memory of the scandal over Lola Montez dredged up by Ludwig's doting on Wagner, the king's erratic behavior during the recent crisis, and the humiliating surrender of Bavaria's independence were otherwise too much for the citizens to bear.

The next year, Wagner did something that Wagehalsen considered made-to-measure for another tilt at Sophocracy. He contributed several articles to the *Süddeutsche Presse*, building on the idea of enhancing civilization through the arts, an idea circulating in Europe since Goethe and before. He proclaimed that it was the "universal mission of the German people" to implement a new political entity under an enlightened monarch. Who among the great minds of Europe would not welcome such a noble idea? Here was a key, thought Wagehalsen, with which he might turn Wagner and through him, further influence Ludwig. It would require restraint on Wagner's part.

But restraint was not exactly a Wagnerian trait. As the articles went on, it was clear that the new regime would severely rein in the

Catholic Church, Jews, and the French. Public embarrassment over the articles—the *Süddeutsche Presse* was a semiofficial publication of the government—caused Ludwig to put a stop to them. With the Sophocracy tantalizingly within reach, Wagehalsen was tempted to carry it out, despite the composer's irascible nature. Wagehalsen exerted all his influence to return Wagner to the king's good graces. But Ludwig, for the time being, accepted the advice of his counselors and distanced himself from the composer. Even though Wagehalsen knew that he could play on the ache in Ludwig over the separation from his idol, he felt uneasy. Wagner was a loose cannon whose megalomania and racism would have to be tempered. He decided to bide his time rather than act rashly. As long as *The Mastersingers of Nuremburg* was unfinished and Bülow was otherwise engaged, Wagehalsen's presence in Munich was not essential.

Cosima and the children maintained the fiction of her marriage to Bülow with extended visits to the Briennerstrasse residence. Work on *Meistersinger* had not been going well in her absence. Wagner sorely missed her at Tribschen. He was having trouble sleeping.

"Meister," Wagehalsen said to Wagner after a particularly trying day in which everything that could go wrong did. The singers he had been coaching for roles in an upcoming production voiced concerns over the strain on their voices when Wagner insisted that they sing in full voice. Wagner had stalked out of the room in a rage, followed by Wagehalsen, who sat on a divan and waited patiently until he had calmed down. "Meister, perhaps you should rest and let a fresh hand take over for you?"

Wagner snorted imperiously. "Do you suggest that I am worn out? How dare you to presume—!" He grew quite red in the face, as he often did whenever he imagined someone had slighted him. Though not a tall man, menaced over Wagehalsen who, when standing, would have been fully head and neck taller.

The Womb of Uncreated Night

"Meister, Meister, calm yourself! You will do yourself an injury!" And gently taking hold of Wagner's right arm, Wagehalsen urged him onto the divan beside him. "I meant no disrespect. Only that you should rest more, as your doctors have advised." He paused for effect. "I have been thinking . . . Perhaps there is another way for you to . . . *rejuvenate* your energies . . . to slow . . . even halt fatigue and disease," he patted the Master's arm, "and reverse the process of aging."

Wagner regarded him with narrowed eyes. "Hah! What does a mere child know about age? You, a mere stripling with skillful fingers?" He looked at Wagehalsen appraisingly. "What, then, you have barely twenty years?"

"The boundaries between the real world and the magical are interwoven," said Wagehalsen, knitting his fingers together. "They are ageless. You need only discover the means by which it is possible to leap from one strand to the other. As for my age," he shrugged, "I was born in 1821."

Wagner burst into laughter. "Forty-seven! Very droll!" He patted Wagehalsen's fuzzy cheek. "So, Junge! What a mighty beard he has! Some people age more slowly than others." Wagehalsen detected a trace of yearning in his voice. "But forty-seven to pass for twenty!"

"Meister, I have remained as you now see me for more almost three decades."

"First Isolde, and now this boy! Has everyone around me taken leave of their senses?" Clearly, the boy believed what he was saying. Wagner knew from his own experience that belief in one's powers was virtually to possessing them. Belief is a powerful charm. But too much belief led to madness. The line between genius and madness, too, could it be more fragile than that between reality and magic? How easily one leaps from one strand to the other! Wagner wagged a finger at him.

"Is this a joke? Does the boy try to fool the Meister?"

"But truly, Meister," laughed Wagehalsen, "I have found the way. And so can you."

"Indeed!" Wagner had not dismissed him out of hand, and

Wagehalsen was sure he had succeeded in teasing him out of his funk. He was sure he had him. "Well, and how is this possible?" Wagner smiled tolerantly.

"You must try to keep an open mind—not that you are not open-minded, Meister!" he added hastily as Wagner's face begin to redden. "You must be patient with me. What I say will sound incredible to you."

"More incredible than this already seems! Yes, young puppies are quite incredible! Well? Go on, then!"

"The sacred blood is the life. That is a formula intoned at the Last Supper. Today, only the *Vampire*," said Wagehalsen, using the Slavic loan word rather than the plainer German *Blutsauger*, which sounded so crude, "truly partakes of it.

"What are you saying!" cried Wagner.

"Communion as practiced by the Church is but a symbolic replication of Christ's offering to his disciples at the Last Supper. He never opened a vein and gave them to drink, did he? Yet the wine then and now mysteriously becomes his blood, and the bread, his body. Thus the church's ritual sanctifies a form of cannibalism—"

"Cannibalism!" sputtered Wagner, so outraged that he was inexplicably unable to summon Jacob and have Wagehalsen thrown out.

"—as the key to eternal life!" Wagehalsen continued, unperturbed by the outburst. He held Wagner's eyes with his own, and Wagner felt compelled to stare back, horrified, into his. "Beyond the church's magic, desperate humans have ritually resorted to it: among savage societies, cannibalism is not practiced wantonly, or as an expedient for appeasing physical hunger or sadism. It is a magical, ritual transformation of the victim's strength, courage, and skills in the victor's own body. Cannibalism is elevated by the power of belief. But without the ritual power of Christ to transform the sacrifice, our society frowns on such practices. The Christians partake of this meal with fear and trembling. Perhaps their expectation of the judgment of the hereafter is but an inner awareness of the forbidden nature of their action. Inner convictions, doubts, skepticism—these take a toll on the efficacy of faith.

The Womb of Uncreated Night

"Only think of immortality *before* death! A society ruled by godlike heroes who mine visions of higher reality from base mortal being—how terrifyingly beautiful! Like sunshine to troglodytes, at first it dazzles and stuns. But once released from their cave-dwelling existence, the worthier ones embrace the light while their inferiors slink back to comfortable darkness, awed but uncomprehending. Your art is like this life-force, indescribably beautiful yet dark and terrifying because blindingly brilliant, the kiss that sucks life from the lips of the enchanted sleepers . . ."

Wagner lapsed into silent but increasing agitation as this *Bube* nimbly plumbed the innermost recesses of his mind, and turned them inside out. Even one assured of the acclaim of posterity clung to life.

"Fah!" he groused, rousing himself. "And does the vampire read the bible and go to church?" His eyes darted around the room for something that could exorcise the demonic Wagehalsen.

"Even the vampire," Wagehalsen, smiled languidly, "must first be a child who may be educated and catechized in the dogma before his transformation. What if there were a more certain, direct route to immortality! What of One who, having caught the blood of Christ on the cross in a cup, actually had drunk of it? And from the wound in *that* side, offered the blood to others willing to believe that, through a wound in his own throat, *he* had become the vessel of life? Through this wound that never heals, handed down from generation to generation, the magically transformed blood forever flowing bestows immortality in *this* life."

At this twisting of the conception of the sacrament of communion, Wagner exploded.

"What blasphemy is this!" he stormed. "Will you be piling sacrilege on old wives' tales to keep me young? This passes a joke!"

Wagehalsen caught his breath. He paused to let the silk-and-satin hung Wagner ventilate and ponder the shift in tone of what Wagner had just said to him. The Master had suddenly switched from addressing him with the familiar, *du*, to the formal, *Sie*. Nevertheless, he got up and placed his hands firmly on Wagner's arms, and looked deep into his eyes.

"Now, Meister, this is not merely an old wives' tale. Even the most fantastic stories in folklore have some basis in fact. As for blasphemy . . . well, that is a matter of shifting dogma, never as rigid as it appears. The power of the mind transforms, offers or withholds sanctity."

"But it was Joseph of Arimathea," protested Wagner, "who caught the sacred blood. Do you," still using the formal *Sie*," "say that *he* was the first vampire? And will you next be telling me that the Disciples were vampires, and that such abominations were the first Knights of the Grail!"

A sardonic smile twisted the corner of Wagehalsen's mouth. "The body of Christ," he went on casually, as if genuinely wondering. "What do you suppose became of it? Could Jesus' invitation to his disciples to eat his flesh have been taken too literally, and that is why his body vanished from the sepulcher?"

Wagner's face almost matched the purple of his plush beret, and under it, his hair stirred. He writhed under Wagehalsen's hypnotic intensity as he struggled to break off the spell darkling around him.

"Madman!" he stormed. "Mountebank! You mock everything! Do you now suggest that the man honored for having given Jesus a decent burial was . . . was some kind of . . . ghoul! And this . . . this chosen One you speak of . . . ," he fumed sarcastically, "was *him*? Ha! Will you next be telling me that you . . . *you!* . . . are Joseph of Arimathea!"

Wagehalsen's smile broke up into mirth, discharging the tension in the atmosphere. Wagner was dazed, suddenly released from some bewildering onus. "Oh, no! Meister," said Wagehalsen. "Not I! His original identity is lost in antiquity. He is known today only as Count Dracula!"

Though historical accounts of the fifteenth century Transylvanian prince who impaled his enemies were not fashionable, vampire novels, poems, plays, and operas based on unrelated folklore been in vogue since 1800. Wagner scoffed at this blasphemous immortality. "Fah! Vampires! My music shall make me immortal and dispel the likes of you!"

Wagehalsen drew back a little, calculating. "Of course, Meister. But your body shall die, and with it, that wonderful mind that has conceived and will yet create so much. Think, Meister! If your life were extended you would have time to perfect your work."

The Womb of Uncreated Night

"Hah! *Holländer, Tannhäuser, Lohengrin, Tristan, Meistersinger*—such imperfection!" he fumed. "Go and work for Hanslick!"

"Oh, Meister!" protested Wagehalsen, managing to sound hurt at the suggestion that he assist the intolerant music critic of the *Neue Freie Presse*, yet at the same time, trying to soothe the irate composer. "Those masterpieces will indeed make you immortal. The work you have already done does not need to be perfected. But perfection is a process, not an end. Each perfection leads to the next. Your mind does not need perfection. The mind endures only as long as the body sustains it. Think, Meister! In the evening of life health fades away into that final darkness, and with it all the marvelous works as yet unwritten. All those sketches that you put aside or discarded as impractical for the times will come to be if your mind endures into the times when they *are* practical." And almost as an afterthought he added impishly, "All the *Jewishness* you could work to expel from German music."

Wagehalsen thought he had kindled a gleam in Wagner's eye. Wagner had never forgiven King Ludwig, or the Bavarians, for that matter, for their tolerance of Jews. But as the gleam quickly began to fade, Wagehalsen blew on it.

"As he is now, the Meister will not live to enjoy his immortality. Only think what he could accomplish if he could put off physical mortality, an end to illness and physical disability! To plan only what *he* could conceive, with the certainty that he will live to deliver it! To reveal the spiritual bond between religion and art through the 'music of the future!' The *Kunstreligion* you now only dream of—a new Christianity purged of its Jewish taint that will instruct, unify, and elevate! Of course," he added playfully, "the Meister would have to guard against overindulgence. A failure to balance restorative feedings against the reversal of the aging process might well result in reducing him to helpless infancy."

Wagner laughed. This was a boy's warped sense of humor! But a strange tremor ran through the laughter. "Ha! *This* guileless fool," mused Wagner aloud, "offers not to stanch the unhealing wound, but rather to keep it bleeding. Tell me, Herr Vampire, without the burden of mortality, who would tend his soul?"

Wagehalsen smiled cryptically.

"And what kind of salvation," continued Wagner, "spares the body but damns the soul?" As Wagehalsen only smiled, Wagner went on. "And you, Sir Vampire! You will live forever, eh? Hah! Show me a sign!"

Wagehalsen drew himself up to his full height, and smiling, slowly undid the ascot at his throat. There, at the base of the jugular, was a triangular scar.

"And this—this—love-bite—*this* is your stigmata? Get out!"

But Wagehalsen did not get out. He knew that when Wagner looked into a mirror that night, the anger which might obscure the Master's fantasies would fade away. He would see the harbingers of death burrowing into his features, and feel it gnawing at his bones. His skin would itch with the ever-present erysipelas. He would yearn for youth and seek an explanation. Then Wagehalsen would bare his throat again and say to Wagner, "This is the Grail from which you must drink!" Then he would open the vein in his throat, the tiny cup would fill with blood, he would curl up his tongue like a straw and suck out eternal life.

Wagner sullenly brooded over Wagehalsen's words. Ego and curiosity are irresistible lures to the human psyche. Myths were the thematic backbone of his operas, and the mythic fantasy of his operas worked their spell on as well as through him. But when Wagehalsen explained how the consecration of blood was to take place, Wagner was scandalized. Nor was he mollified by Wagehalsen's innocent-sounding rationale: "After all, it is no more than the bleeding or the leeching practiced by reputable physicians."

Disgusted and repelled at the thought of drinking from a wound in someone's throat, Wagner, who could not bear the touch of anything coarser than silk, stormed out of the room.

The Womb of Uncreated Night

Later that evening, Wagehalsen's spell tugged at Wagner's vanity. When he contemplated the young man's madness in solitude, he found himself strangely bemused. The warmth of the day still clung to the evening. Night breezes had not yet slid down the face of the Pilatus behind the villa. The drapes hung expectantly at the open French doors. Wagner played over the unfinished manuscript for *Meistersinger* lying open on the piano. For several hours, his occupation absorbed him. He played through the scene at the end of the second act, in which the pompous old Town Clerk, Beckmesser, serenades the beautiful, young Eva. Hans Sachs, the cobbler, disapproving of Beckmesser's unscrupulous pursuit of the maiden, brings his workbench outside to act as Marker, the Mastersingers' practice of scoring singing errors. Rapping on the soles of the shoes he is working on also has the helpful effect of interrupting Beckmesser's buffoonery. The racket of Beckmesser trying to sing above the rapping and of Sachs pounding and singing all the louder brings out the neighbors to complain. The scene dissolves in a general riot. The confusion of the scene rather than its comedy exactly suited Wagner's agitation. And Wagner, by turns singing, shouting all the parts one by one, and pounding on the piano, tried to drown out Wagehalsen's troubling words.

But with the tender, brooding music of the Prelude to Act III, disturbing thoughts began to seep back into the room. And when Sachs begins his monologue on the state of the world, *"Wahn! Wahn!/ Überall Wahn!"* Madness! Madness!/ Madness everywhere!, Wagner was unable to continue. He repeatedly played over the passages leading up to it, but each time he was frustrated. He needed a more potent talisman to ward off his Tempter. The heavy, overcast sky, now deep in night blotted out the stars. Gradually, fatigue overcame him and he fell asleep at the keyboard, his head resting on his arm.

Early the next morning, Wagner woke before the house was stirring. Morning mist had sifted in at the open French doors. Bleary after the uncomfortable night at the keyboard, he rose and closed the doors. Quietly, he descended the staircase, and stole out of the house followed by Russ and Koss, his two dogs. The sweep of lawn down the promontory on which the house stood offered a spectacular view across the lake at all hours. The sun had not yet risen above the Rigi-Kulm across the lake. The mountain was shrouded in glowing mist. The lake was serene as glass. Wagner shuddered slightly as an alpine chill slid down from the Pilatus hulking dimly behind Tribschen. In the uncertain morning light, the pale house was ghostly.

He wandered aimlessly into the surrounding woods, as if the trees might brush the mists out of his head. Half-an-hour later, covered with dew, Wagner found himself on the southern bank of the Reuss and realized that he had come to Lucerne. Walking along the river, he passed under the imposing Baroque towers of the Jesuit Church. Then veering diagonally left across the green in front of the adjoining Government Building, he stood in front of the unpretentious Gothic Franziskanerkirche. Like Tribschen, the façade of the Franciscan Church was painted white with windows and doors trimmed in green. If not for a small baroque cupola and modest spires, it might have passed as the residence of some well-to-do government official. Its familiar sobriquet, Barfüsserkirche, made it even more appealing. Barefooter's Church! he chuckled. What better way to show humility! Churches had much to be humble for! Raised as a child in conventional Protestantism but no longer a practicing Christian, he hesitated at the entrance. He started to complete the loop that would take him back to Tribschen. Then a thought occurred to him. Shoes still covered with dew, Wagner commanded his dogs to "stay" and strode purposefully into the church.

When Wagner found his assistant in the salon later that day, Wagehalsen was sitting at the piano, confidently playing passages from the opera in expectation of the Master. Wagehalsen noticed an odd, subdued undertone in the Master's demeanor. He looked tired, resigned.

"Ah, so, Junge! There you are! And here am I, ready for your . . . 'communion,'" he said.

Smiling confidently, Wagehalsen rose, undid his cravat, and with his thumbnail, broke the seal of the scar on his throat and fixed on Wagner his best hypnotic gaze.

"Drink!"

But Wagner recoiled in revulsion. Under his subdued demeanor, Wagner had hidden a vial of holy water obtained from the Franciscan Church. At Wagehalsen's invitation to drink, Wagner cried, "Drink *you* from *this*!" and flung its contents into Wagehalsen's face.

Wagehalsen cursed, recoiling with such force that he upset the piano and sent the case crashing to the floor with a cacophonous jangle and snapping of strings. He stumbled blindly out of the room, frantically clawing at his face.

Interlude

Brewster, who had been listening incredulously to Wagehalsen's back-story almost as stunned as Wagner must have been, interrupted Korngold. "But Joseph of Arimathea—you don't really believe that he was a vampire!"

"Certainly not in the usual sense," Korngold replied. "But when he brought the Chalice to Britain, who knows what became of its contents?"

"You think Joseph drank from it?"

"We are talking about an ancient, less skeptical time, when the miraculous must have seemed more plausible than in our era. What would a man have done with the blood of someone he truly revered as divine," said Korngold, "especially after Jesus invited his disciples to drink—"

"But that was symbolic, wine!" protested Brewster.

"Yes, but Joseph was not present at the Last Supper. He wasn't able to drink the wine blessed by Jesus."

"How does that differ from vampirism?"

"Culture works both through those whose motives are pure and those whose motives are not, worthy and unworthy. Those who drank unworthily drank damnation. But in drinking the original contents of the Grail, Joseph was not unworthy. Like all of Jesus' disciples, Joseph proselytized. He would convert what he thought of as the heathen. To celebrate the Last Supper, he could share the Grail. He could offer, not the symbolic wine, but the real thing, the blood of Jesus. Without tangible blessing of the Master, it would be as Wagehalsen suggested, an act of savagery."

"But that was just a line of bull he handed Wagner so that he could make him one of his drones," scoffed Brewster.

"May be," smiled Korngold, "but even non-believers are prone to gullibility. The blood from the Crucifixion was a tangible, sacred relic. Joseph would hardly have tossed it out. How to preserve and transport it intact from the Holy Land to Britain? How to multiply it so that he could share it? What better way than to carry it in his own body? You can see how the idea of multiplying the blood in his own body could have had a greater immediate impact."

"Sort of a variation on the loves and fishes," quipped Brewster.

Korngold studied Brewster for a moment, then continued. "His motive for drinking it doesn't fit that of the vampire. Vampires make an end run around the ritual of sacrifice for their own sake, not others. He could share Jesus' blood, mingled with his own, by cutting into his own veins and collecting it in the Grail, making it a ritual of sacrifice. That interpretation takes liberties with the crucifixion, I'll give you."

"Takes some liberties with sense, too!"

"Sense tends to get lost in the everyday baggage people carry around with them," said Korngold with a dismissive wave of his hand. "Over time, usage alters purpose and leads to unexpected rationales. However the practice of vampirism came about, Joseph's sacrifice could immediately communicate the impact of the crucifixion to others. And by participating in this ritual—"

"Hah!" broke in Brewster. "Only the few, the knights like Percival who were 'pure of heart,' would tap into the miraculous healing power of the Grail! The 'impure' ones would turn into vampires! Haw, great! Next you'll be saying that Joseph was King Arthur!"

But then he played along. "So what becomes of all the good guys, the 'pure' blood drinkers? They didn't all disappear like Percival? Or are they like those characters that live forever and keep changing identities to escape detection?"

"Indeed," Korngold sighed, "what becomes of all the good guys of this world?"

"I guess," said Brewster, "they become . . . psychiatrists."

34.

Two years after he fled from Tribschen and returned once again to Paris, Wagner despaired of a Sophocracy in Europe. He had lost Wagner, an important hold over Ludwig, and Bavaria to Bismarck. The question of the German states had been resolved in favor of Prussia. There was little left for king and composer but to squabble over performance rights to Wagner's four part opera cycle, *Der Ring des Nibelungen*—rights which Wagner had already sold to a previous benefactor and then resold to Ludwig. Ludwig wanted performances of *The Ring of the Nibelungs* as each part was completed. Wagner, hoping to leverage a *Festspielhaus*, a theater for the exclusive performances of his works, held out for an integral cycle. The struggle had degenerated into a farcical contest between a delusional king and an unscrupulous composer. With his grip on purse strings and the Hoftheater, Ludwig won out.

But there was nothing farcical about the code of "blood and iron." Having humbled the once mighty Austrian empire, it now fell on France. Bismarck was at his work again.

Actually, Bismarck had little work to do. The brisk trade in crowns looking for heads of minor royalty to put under them, and the farcical Second Empire of France did most of the work for him. All it needed was a nudge. This Bismarck adroitly provided when, after twenty-five years of contentious reign, Queen Isabella II of Spain was deposed in

1868. As the Spanish parliament scoured the European market for a successor, Bismarck suggested a member of the Catholic branch of the Prussian royal family, Prince Leopold of Hohenzollern-Sigmarinen. The Cortes promptly acted on Bismarck's suggestion and offered the crown to Leopold. But he was not terribly ambitious. Moreover, after the misrule of Isabella, the Spanish throne was dangerously unstable. Nor did Uncle Wilhelm, the King of Prussia, relish the idea of linking the prestige of the Hohenzollern name to such a risky venture. The prince politely declined the invitation.

Bismarck was not quite so ready to concede. A Hohenzollern in Spain would certainly alarm the French, first, by squeezing them between two potentially hostile Prussian rulers, and second, by violating established diplomatic protocols in clandestine negotiations that threatened the balance of powers in Europe. He appealed to Leopold's father, urging his duty to Prussia to change his son's mind. Prince Karl Anton duly pressured his son, and in July 1870, King Wilhelm reluctantly agreed to allow Leopold to accept the offer which he had rejected in 1868.

When news of Leopold's decision leaked out, the French were outraged. The Foreign Minister, Antoine Agénor, duc de Gramont, made a provocative speech to the parliament, declaring that the honor of France was at stake and that if any Hohenzollern's candidature for the throne of Spain was accepted, France was ready to defend its interests. Everyone in France, from Louis Napoleon and Empress Eugénie to the people in the streets, erupted with like belligerence.

Wagehalsen hovered between amused detachment and genuine concern at this latest example of political chicanery. He was not of course a viable candidate for the throne of Spain, being of dubious "royalty." But if a conflagration overtook Europe . . . If this opportunity for Sophocray in Europe slipped away, well, he would reap whatever remnants he could, and then make his way to the New World.

Although Napoleon III tried to appear in control of his government, he was suffering such acute distress from bladder stones that he often deferred to the Empress Eugénie. She was among the most vocal who called for war with Prussia. In remarks he made to the Austrian ambassador, Metternich, Napoleon believed that war was imminent. He believed that everything depended on the rapidity of mobilization. The victory would go to the side that was ready first. While publicly advocating a willingness to end the hostility if Leopold withdrew his acceptance of the Spanish crown, the French were bent on humiliating Prussia. Accordingly, Vincente Benedetti, the French Ambassador to Berlin, was instructed to demand that Wilhelm, who was taking the waters at Ems, publicly order his nephew to reject the Spanish throne. Moreover, Benedetti gave Wilhelm a deadline of July 12 in which to execute the order. The implied threat of an immediate war hung behind the ambassador's words.

Wilhelm, never enthusiastic about his nephew's candidature, and less enthusiastic for war than Bismarck, privately urged Karl Anton to renounce the Spanish throne on behalf of his son. This acquiescence satisfied Napoleon, who was prepared to let the matter drop. But Eugénie, supported by agitators in the parliament, demanded nothing less than Wilhelm *publicly* guarantee that a Hohenzollern would never again accept such an offer. Consequently, Benedetti was once again instructed to approach Wilhelm with this new demand. He was even undiplomatic enough to confront the king at his leisure despite a formal appointment scheduled later that day. When Wilhelm realized that the French, not satisfied with Leopold's withdrawal, were intent on publicly humiliating him, he cut off Benedetti. Still in a conciliatory mood, the king sent a telegram to Bismarck reporting on his conversation with the ambassador and his decision not to grant the previously scheduled interview. Bismarck changed the wording of the wire, making it appear as if the king had snubbed Benedetti. Released to the German press, it fueled the fires of war in both France and Prussia. France declared war on July 19.

Wagehalsen was unable to resist finding a way to observe at first hand the events leading up to the war. He insinuated himself into the parties of war correspondents and was able to accompany them as an observer. He learned that, despite early mobilization and Napoleon's brave words to Metternich, France was in fact ill-prepared for war with

Prussia. When the Emperor arrived at Metz to personally take charge of his army, he found it at less than full strength, ill-equipped, and disorganized. Generals arrived at other depots along the one hundred mile front only to be unable to find their regiments, soldiers stranded, or when found, were without shelter, adequate clothing, equipment, and medicine. And it all came to disaster. The French suffered defeat after defeat as the Prussians, better organized and better equipped, pushed them back and finally surrounded what was left of their tattered army.

On September 1, 1870, the Prussian army under General von Moltke surrounded the exhausted remnants of the Army of Châlons under Louis Napoleon and General MacMahon at the fortress town of Sedan in the Ardennes. At 4:00 a.m., Bavarian troops crossed the Meuse and launched an attack on Bazeilles, the village at the southern corner of the defensive triangle around Sedan. Fighting quickly spread up the east flank through the valley of the Givonne, a tributary of the Meuse, and German artillery rained down on the French a devastating barrage from all sides. MacMahon rode out of his headquarters to survey the situation along the Givonne and was wounded in the leg by artillery fire. He turned over command to General Auguste Ducrot, who had astutely observed the day before, "We're in a chamber pot and they're going to shit on us."

Gone was the cocky confidence of the French general's staff that they would "muddle through." Gone were the advantages of the chassepot's greater range and accuracy over the *Zundnadelgewehr*, the Prussian needle gun. The French had dreamed a deadly dream, and Ducrot awoke to the realization that the only hope of saving any part of the army was a hasty retreat through a gap in the German lines between a loop of the Meuse and the Belgian frontier. Ducrot's plan was thwarted by General Emmanuel de Wimpffen. He had arrived from Paris only three days earlier, authorized by General Charles de Montauban, comte de Palikao, Empress Eugénie's conniving Prime Minister and Minister of War, to assume command in the event that MacMahon was incapacitated. Arrogant and contemptuous of the general staff, Wimpffen lost no time in countermanding the order to retreat. By sunup, the gap had closed and the French forces were indeed shit upon.

The dawn was followed by a day brilliant and beautiful, so clear that the war correspondent of *The Times* was able to report "that through a good glass the movements of individual men were plainly discernable . . .," bayonets glistening, arms twinkling and flashing "like a streamlet in the moonlight," and even after the smoke had cleared,

> . . . masses of coloured rags glued together with blood and brains and pinned into strange shapes by fragments of bones . . . men's bodies without heads, legs without bodies, heaps of human entrails attached to red and blue cloth, and disembowelled corpses in uniform, bodies lying about in all attitudes. . . . There must have been a hell of torture raging within that semicircle, in which the earth was torn asunder from all sides, with a real tempest of iron, hissing and screeching and bursting into the heavy masses at the hands of an unseen enemy.

Despite the excruciating agony of the kidney stones which would have unhorsed a less desperate man, Louis Napoleon rode out into the thick of the battle. He would die bravely, chain-smoking in defeat rather than live as a royal bungler. He sat for five hours, even as men fell all around him. Even as two officers beside were killed by a single shell-burst, he seemed cursed with escaping unscathed. Defeated in his hope of dying on the battlefield, he rode back to Sedan. Shells falling in the streets, further carnage in the field senseless, he ordered a white flag raised on the ramparts. But a staff officer, preferring death to dishonor, cut it down. The insubordinate general staff refused to sign a letter of surrender, and the butchery continued until King Wilhelm ordered all-out bombardment. Shells exploding in the garden of the subprefecture persuaded the staff not to intervene when the emperor again ordered the white flag raised. Wilhelm and Napoleon exchanged letters negotiating surrender. Evening and profound silence fell over the battlefield.

The sun had set in an eerie red afterglow rising from the field, as if the fallen men had somehow vaporized and stirred in denial of the death of their bodies. For a moment, darkness followed and shrouded their bloody protests. Then the moon rose full, bathed in mephitic exhalation.

The poetry of such destruction filled Wagehalsen with a blood lust more savage and deep than any he had previously felt. Surely this was the lesson Count Dracula had been trying to teach him on their nightly forays? Surely this agitation equaled the collective, mad outcry for war among the French populace at the insult to their precious national honor? The recollection of his reckless desire to penetrate Rachel and at the same time devour her flooding into his mind, hovering above her in an exquisite, timeless unbreaking wave like the youth's desire of Keats's "Ode on a Grecian Urn," unrequited yet undiminished. His body suffused with an ecstasy that at once was absurdly bordering on Ludwig's delirium, soaring yet sinking in the "love-death" of Tristan and Isolde . . .

Behind the battlements of the subprefecture high above the field, Louis Napoleon found his apartment, crowded with defeat in the warm September night, stifling. He stepped out onto the parapet walk, seeking relief from the suffocation which would be, from this night on, his private prison. The air below had turned chill, and as the camp fires bloomed in the German bivouacs, snatches of the Lutheran hymn, "Now Thank We All Our God," drifted across the Meuse. Two guards posted outside the apartment stiffened apprehensively as he came out and paced back and forth, nervously smoking a cigarette and looking uneasily out over the battlefield. He stopped abruptly and strode across the abutment, then recklessly climbed onto the low wall. Leaning dangerously near the edge, he peered intently at something moving over the field a hundred feet below and some distance away. The guards had been alerted that the Emperor, in his despondency, might do something desperate. They had been ordered to prevent any mishap under forfeit of their own lives. But they were in awe of his person, and reluctant to lay hands on the vanquished monarch.

"Have a care, Sir!" cried one of the men in alarm, rushing to the wall, preparing to seize him by the coat if he did not step back from the edge of the parapet. But the Emperor was oblivious of the man. The moon had steadily risen into the sky, blanching but not fully bleaching the blood-tinged haze, until at last it threw the dead and dying into stark, ghastly relief. The battlefield rippled fitfully, like a dreaming sea. Responding to the sentry's outcry, Louis pointed to a shadow that moved more purposefully among the patterns cast by moonlight among stirring tendrils of ground-hugging mist. Obediently, as to a royal command, they followed his gaze. Barely noticeable at first, they saw something moving among the dead and dying.

Full of remorse and pity, the Emperor exclaimed, "Ah, the poor wretch! It must be some brave fellow missed by the *ambulanciers*!" He began to instruct the guard to send assistance to the man, but something about the movements, something furtive, stopped him. "Wait—!" The shadow, hunched but deft, moved too easily for a wounded man. Was it in fact a man at all?

"Perhaps it's only some scavenging animal, a dog, perhaps a wolf?" ventured the still wary sentry. "Please, Sir, come down!" The Emperor stood, transfixed. "A solitary animal?" he mused aloud. "Would not animals come in packs to graze over the dead? Even so, a solitary dog would nibble at the edges of the field. This one picks its way into the very thick of it!"

From the Emperor's perch, the night was suspended in dubious light and profound silence. The hymn of thanksgiving had long since faded away. Now the restive field gave off a faint murmuring, pierced by an occasional hoarse cry of agony, echoed by the distant, scarcely audible sighs, groans, and curses, of the wounded who had not yet been rescued by the *ambulanciers*. Louis felt suddenly transported to another time, another place, naked, raw, innocent, in which the living fed blindly on the living, ignorant of any ethical restraint, as if he, alone in his defeat, had emerged into a new and terrible world of moral awareness.

The Womb of Uncreated Night

Rousing himself, he sent for a glass. Hands trembling, he sighted through it and cried out in consternation. In the bright moonlight, he made out a human form bending over a corpse, as if nuzzling a dead man's neck. Some peasant robbing the corpses? But as he watched, his bewilderment turned to horror. He dropped the glass and would himself have toppled off the battlement but for the guard, instincts overcoming awe, who seized and prevented him from falling. Was it some phantom of his own distraught imagination, fed by the disgrace of the day's carnage? Whoever, whatever it was, some ghoul—Louis had seen the dark ooze from the throat of the fallen warrior! Fainting with shock and revulsion, he sent one of the guards to inform King Wilhelm of the desecration. Outraged, Wilhelm ordered the commander of the garrison to dispatch a troop of Prussian regulars to capture the villain. The ghoul would find it some danger to desecrate the field of honor! At the request of Louis Napoleon, a contingent of *ambulanciers*, who regularly made their rounds armed, went with them.

Hardening themselves against the pitiful cries of the wounded, the troop approached the site they had been sent out to investigate, a mass of darkness gathered in a little hollow at the base of a blasted tree. As they drew nearer, the astonished men made out a form that must have been a man's, wearing an opera cape and top hat bent over the body of a Zouave. They could not at first see any features because his head was buried in the neck of the infantryman and they had come up from behind. They caught a glimpse of a dark stream trickling down the soldier's neck and heard slurping sounds.

Crying out in disgust and revulsion at the grisly scene, the troops froze in their tracks. The vampire looked up suddenly, whirled about, surging to his feet, glowering, a smudge of blood on his cheek like some hasty child at dinner without a napkin. He turned on them an expression of such baleful malevolence that they stumbled back over themselves as if he had struck them. They were utterly amazed at the man's appearance. Except for the opera cape and top hat he was completely naked, his skin obscenely bloated like some huge insect's, and ghastly red. They stood, the troop and the vampire, confronting each other for a timeless instant, the soldiers' astonishment at the sight of this elegantly cloaked but bizarrely dishabille ghoul poised against his chagrin at their intrusion.

As the shadow of paralysis flitted past, the bewildered Prussian and French soldiers managed to raise their rifles and shoot at the apparition. The bullets which struck the creature punctured his bloated skin, causing the blood he had drunk to spurt out. The creature leaped away with a snarl and a curse, a grotesquely galvanized fountain of dark blood jetting out over a pool of bodies. The Prussians were so grossed out by the sight that terror fell into their feet. They stumbled after the fleeing figure, pursued themselves by abhorrence at trampling the dead and wounded, dread of overtaking the fugitive, and fear of failure.

The bemused French *ambulanciers* remained behind to see what could be done for the victim of that ghoul's assault. Examining him, they found that he still showed signs of life. Had the monster been selectively drinking only the blood of those who were still alive? The men shuddered as they hastily lifted the victim onto a litter.

Meanwhile, pausing sporadically to fire and reload in uncoordinated relays, the Prussians gradually fell further behind their quarry. As the chase neared the edge of that garden of gore, two peasants, their mattocks lying casually across a nearby corpse, were surprised in the act of stripping the body of a dead Zouave whose colorful uniform might bring them a profit. At the sight of a man, naked but for an incongruous opera cape and top hat, spouting blood as he ran past a few meters away, and hearing the shouts and the crackling guns of the pursuing soldiers, the two looked at each other in astonishment. Hesitating only a moment, the taller man grabbed his mattock in one hand and the boots he had taken from the Zouave with the other and fled. The shorter man hesitated only a second longer. Then he too grabbed his tool and booty and ran after his companion.

Puffing strenuously, the shorter peasant called out to his companion, "Hey, shithead! Are they after us or that guy who just ran by?"

"How should I know?" snapped his companion. "Someone shoots, I run!"

"But we're passing up good stuff."

"Shut up! Shut up! Run!"

As the looters veered away from the path taken by the fugitive and his pursuers, the vampire eluded the troops on the higher ground of the Ardennes forest, where rough terrain and wavering moonlight cloaked him from sight. The troops slowed, casting about uncertainly over the uneven terrain for signs of their quarry. But they lost the trail among the maze of wild crags and ravines that cut through the forest and returned, spattered with mud, straggling and done in, to the officer who had sent them out. Frustrated by what he considered the incompetence of his troops, who had bungled what should have been a routine mission, he roundly berated them. He held the exhausted men at attention while he heaped on them the scorn and abuse he was sure he himself would have to endure from his superiors. When the men reported that their quarry resembled a huge bat, his derision soared.

"And did this bat take wing in the forest and fly away?" he scoffed, remonstrating that they had allowed their squeamishness at the sight of the battlefield and the uncertain light to mistake the bizarre opera cape for a bat's wings. But Prussian and French officials, including Wilhelm, Bismarck, and Louis Napoleon, had observed the initial episode from the battlements. They were so revolted by the sordid report from the *ambulanciers* that the impact of the officer's report, delivered shamefacedly, was far less than he had imagined. The dignitaries were more concerned that no effort be spared to apprehend this ghoul. They ordered a thorough search at first light next day. As this monstrous man, if man it really was, had been wounded, they reasoned he would need medical attention and rest. They immediately sent dispatches to be relayed to all the communities in the vicinity where the fugitive might seek sanctuary, calling on officials and citizenry alike under the threat of severe penalties for failure to report the whereabouts of the fiend and assist in apprehending him.

The searchers on the following day picked up a sparse trail of bloody footprints abruptly ending at the edge of a peat bog that filled a shallow depression. They doubted that the monster had fallen in and suffocated, though one of the men spat into it with a curse just in case he had. Striking about the perimeter of the bog, the searchers found more traces of recent disturbance on the opposite bank. Impossible that anyone could have waded through the mire without getting stuck or sucked under! No indication that anyone had detoured around the edges. And yet, the trail re-emerged in a line directly opposite to the side where it had abruptly ended. A man was reprimanded for facetiously suggesting that the fugitive might have leaped across the bog.

The trail ended at the base of a crag. The cliff rose vertically at least fifty feet. Even without wounds, the troopers themselves found the feat of scaling it impossible. They could only speculate what direction their quarry might have taken. Back across the way they had come, to the north and east lay Belgium. Further east, Luxembourg and the Rhineland. To the southeast lay the Vosges and Jura Mountains. A hunted man might well take to the mountains. But could a wounded man have the strength to reach them, much less climb them? As the men stood puzzling about this impasse, one sharp-eyed trooper noticed a few discolorations on the steep face of the rock. But the officer in charge dismissed the evidence.

The day, which had begun hot and muggy, clouded up as the men returned to make their report. Over the mountains in the southeast, beyond the Vosges and the Jura, above the Alps, towering thunderheads had risen ominously. It began to rain, at first lightly and sporadically. Then wave followed wave of freshets, until the whole of southeastern Europe was engulfed in a deluge. The hot pursuit began to limp and then went lame. But the hunt continued.

In the days that followed, the heavy rains began to cause flooding. Numerous rumors and reports of sinister-looking caped figures, especially sightings at night, began to filter in to the authorities of towns and villages. The man everyone was on the lookout for was appearing everywhere. He was seen in the vicinity of the Namur, he was seen near Bouillon. He was rafting down the Meuse, he was resting on the banks of the Moselle. He was even reported as far as the Saar less than twenty-four hours after the hue was raised. With many soldiers returning to their homes on foot following the spectacular defeat of the French at Sedan, these sightings confused the search and had to be discounted.

Eventually, someone remembered the mysterious man who wanted to ship a large crate from Mézières to Koblenz. When the Inspector of police interrogated the shipping agent at Mézières about its contents, the bill of lading listed only "personal effects." What those "effects" were . . . the clerk shrugged. He could only speculate about the box's contents from its size, about two meters long, one meter wide, 60 centimeters high; and its weight, 100 kilos. "Large enough for a man," joked the clerk. "Large enough for a man," mused the Inspector. The clerk volunteered information he had overheard from the uncouth haulers boasting about how well the mysterious stranger had paid, and joking about the odd name he had given, Lügerstaub. "Could it be," wondered the inspector, "that our fugitive has concealed himself in the box and is even now making good his escape, unsuspected, while the militia are hunting for a man on foot?" And then another thought occurred to him. "Perhaps the man has died of his wounds and the means of his escape has become his coffin!" Fantastic as it seemed, this information, duly reported to the constabulary at Metz, and from there forwarded to Koblenz, led to a search of all crates and large boxes on both sides of the Rhine.

Captain Katz had entered military service after his family's vineyards in the Rheinpfalz had been virtually decimated by mildew introduced from the New World in the 1850s. The youngest son of a Jewish family that had been allowed to buy land in the Palatinate during the limited emancipation of Jews granted by the Rhenish Confederation, he cared little for the Prussian dream of a unified Germany. Following the defeat of Napoleon Bonaparte in 1815 and the reorganization of the Confederation in 1824, his family had reason to prefer the influence of Bavaria, the only German state that had granted Jews citizenship in 1813, and whose present king, Ludwig II, maintained a liberal stance toward his Jewish subjects. When von Moltke's army had defeated the French at Sedan, Katz had hoped to be assigned to the command post at Mainz, the provincial capital where his family now resided. From there he might have done what he could to restore the vineyards. The destruction of the vines had been unexpected, but the vineyards had, in any case, to be renewed every twenty to fifty years or so. Since France had fallen as unexpectedly as the vines, he would be able to assist in restoring the vineyards much sooner than anticipated. And he need not resign his commission to do so.

But the furor over the "ghoul of Sedan" frustrated this hope when he was immediately assigned instead to coordinate the search for the fugitive. Because Mannheim was strategically located at the most important river port on the upper Rhine, the Oberkommando had decided to locate search headquarters there. The Captain was taking it badly. Mannheim was only 70 km or so from Mainz—but in this weather, it might just as well have been 700 km. He was therefore curt and surly with his staff.

Katz summoned his newly assigned adjutant, one Lt. Spatz, for a progress report on the search. The junior officer, who really had nothing new to report, came obsequiously into the presence of his new commanding officer and announced, trying to make it sound as if it were an important breakthrough, the shipment to Koblenz of a suspicious crate "large enough to hold a man. The most probable escape route . . ."

"The most probable escape route, obviously," interrupted Katz, "would be downriver to the Netherlands where the delta on the North Sea with its half-dozen mouths and interconnecting channels would complicate the search. Yes, yes, that is all very well and good. Most

The Womb of Uncreated Night

likely. The army and the militia are already concentrating on that area. Do you have anything to report that I do not already know?"

Spatz could see that the Captain was set on heaping him with scorn. The fact that he, too, was a Jew only intensified the Captain's disdain. But he went doggedly on. "By your command, sir! But it must also be considered a possibility that the fugitive may try to confuse us by giving out false destinations downriver. Perhaps we should play it safe and pass the alert upriver as far as Basel?" Now neither he nor the Captain believed that anyone would be fool enough to fight the swollen current upriver, much less go beyond that point to floods and avalanches in the Alps. Spatz trembled at the scowl on the Captain's face. "Hazardous as it might be," he added desperately, "Basel is not an implausible destination."

"And if our quarry did indeed choose this more difficult route *precisely* because it is more hazardous . . . ?" mused Capt. Katz, annoyed that this inferior could come up with such a farfetched idea before he could. "In that case," he said with grim satisfaction, "the villain might try to lose himself among the isolated hamlets in the glacial valleys where it would be very difficult to trace him, even in the best of weather. Then those damned Swiss peasants would have to look out for themselves as well as they could. Hah! Let them search for the wolf among their sheep!"

"Begging the Captain's pardon," ventured Spatz, "but the Swiss are not sheepherders. They raise cattle."

"Imbecile! Do you think I do not know that?" Katz impatiently dismissed Spatz.

In the present circumstances with roads impassable because of the rains, it would be virtually impossible to coordinate the search at such a distance. And all our strenuous efforts would be wasted, he thought sardonically, as an opportunity opened before him. Only think how pleased the Oberkommando would be when they learned of such thoroughness. He privately hoped that the "ghoul" *would* choose that route. And he could dispatch Spatz. Yes! He liked the way that sounded.

In fact, the purported destination of the crate to Koblenz proved to be a ruse, for Wagehalsen had an empty one downriver while another bearing him was diverted via Saarbrücken to Karlsruhe, where it was loaded onto a paddle steamer bound upriver to Basel. By the time the ploy was discovered, attempts to alert major ports on both sides of the river had been hampered by flooding which knocked out the telegraph lines and disrupted rail service at several points along the Rhine. And of course it was the hapless young lieutenant who had to inform Capt. Katz of the latest developments. The Captain relished the thought of dispatching this Spatz on a wild goose chase. Katz ordered him to leave at once to spread the word upriver. If he had to be separated from the comfort of home and family, then so would everyone under his command, beginning with this upstart!

"And if by some chance I were to overtake the fugitive?" ventured Spatz.

"In that case, you would do everything in your power to apprehend him," said Katz, convinced of the powerlessness of this oaf. He did not particularly care whether the lieutenant chose to travel on the river or over the washed out roads, so long as the twerp either drowned or was swept away in a mudslide. If despite the overwhelming odds against, he succeeded in his mission, his orders were to advise local civilian and military patrols to mobilize and search their respective areas for the mysterious box and its presumed human occupant.

Long before the battle at Sedan Wagehalsen had prepared several escape routes. He did not know whether Dracula, who claimed that he could influence the weather, had arranged this marvelous storm, or whether he, himself, in some unconscious way had caused it. He did not particularly care whether it was design or coincidence. He chose this route as the most advantageous in the present circumstances. Before the full impact of the storm, he had dispatched agents along the way to arrange shipment by all practical means, and it was their decision to use the river as far as possible, in view of the uncertainty of rail transportation and the possibility of washed out roads should the storm worsen. By the time his crate began its journey upriver, the Rhine below the Falls near Schaffhausen was swollen by the unrelenting storms, but still navigable. The paddle steamer groaned to make its slow progress against the current, but reached Basel safely. The alert to seize and search all suspicious crates, regardless of size, had not yet reached the city.

Wagehalsen was gradually moving up the Rhine, his ultimate destination its eastern source in the Alps rather than down to the North Sea. Because the bullets had punctured his skin and the holes had not yet healed, he was unable to hold the blood he had drunk long enough to maintain his full strength. How long it would be before the wounds completely healed—if, indeed, they ever healed—he did not know. But as he lay in the blind security of the crate, he felt a terrible lassitude, and knew that he was losing some of his powers. He could hear the river churning against the side of the steamer, and at the sense of being on moving water, a strange, inexplicable uneasiness drained away his volition. After several days in the box, which though it had for him the security of a coffin, he longed to survey the ship's progress. He felt that he had strength enough to overpower an individual passenger or member of the crew. But what if he, in his weakened condition, encountered them in a group?

As Wagehalsen lay in that unsleeping sleep, the cargo hold slid and shuddered with the tossing ship and the throbbing of the steam-driven pistons. Its iron hull creaked against the wooden deck as the paddle wheels chopped into the waters and scooped them up in rhythmic buckets. Under it all, the steady gurgling sound of the ship as it sluiced through the river channel. In the darkness of the box, Wagehalsen felt the odd sensation of weightlessness as the boat pitched, and rolled, and yawed in the turbulence, occasionally throwing him against the sides and the lid. Dampness hung in the hold and penetrated the box where it condensed against the inner lid, collected in corners as the ship plunged and trembled, shaking random droplets onto his face and body. The darkness grew ever denser as it shifted from lightlessness to palpable pressure, until the whole of night seemed to press into his head. Darkness became a palpable presence, inversely expanding until it was so dense it seemed to collapse into itself. It was like insomnia, when you hear the beating of your own heart, with each sepulchral thud bringing you more awake. Head, and heart, hands and feet, the centers of orientation became meaningless, and as the darkness intensified in his mind, the case expanded until he seemed to be falling into an infinite upward. Even the churning sounds of ship and river underwent a transformation, sound accreting into sound until they compacted into a kind of silence. Denseness upon denseness, each a vortex, a hole in space and time into which all sense was sucked away so that past and present merged. Each black hole, a pore through which awareness seeped and even God was dissipated away. "To still be searching what we know not by what we know," wrote Milton, "still closing up truth to truth as we find it . . . ," that must lead to God. But if God is as Anselm said, "something than which nothing greater can be conceived," then God must be this darkness. Wagehalsen craved the darkness like an addict in withdrawal, not because he feared the light, but because he yearned for union with night.

At Basel, the box was loaded onto a dray. A gruff, burly middle-aged wagoner, Dussel, whose impatience for irresolution was exceeded only by his enthusiasm for profit, was tempted into making the nearly 160 km journey to Konstanz. He laughed at his fainthearted brother hackmen who worried about the rumors of Black Forest robbers lurking in the outskirts of Rheinfelden, like children afraid of ogres! Weren't all the bridges blessed with statues of St. John Nepomuk, the patron saint of those who go into peril by water—or obstructed roads? Between Basel and Konstanz, there were more than a dozen towns where a man might hole up or get help if things got too bad. In good weather, a two- or three-day journey. In this weather, he reasoned, perhaps four days. And he would be well paid afterwards! He left at first light the following morning. With luck, he might reach the lovely little town of Laufenburg by nightfall, not that he would be able to see much of it in this filthy soup.

And luck was with Dussel all the way to Laufenburg and beyond. The roads were sometimes covered by water, and his progress only occasionally slowed when the wagon mired a bit in soggy places. It was well after dark when he reached Laufenburg. But he found accommodations for himself and the horses at a small inn. Late that night, there was a commotion near the stable, but Dussel was a sound sleeper. When he arose next morning and asked for a bit of bread for breakfast, he found the innkeeper sullen and grudging. As he geared up to resume his journey, the drayman learned from the stable boy that the innkeeper's wife had come down with a strange malady in the night. The wagoner shrugged, said it was too bad, and inspected his cargo before setting off. He noticed that the lid had shifted slightly from the jouncing of the wagon on the road. He repositioned it and tied it down with a bit of rope. He then set off with renewed determination.

The rain had eased off to a steady drizzle, and he was able to reach Schaffhausen without mishap. At this rate he would easily reach Konstanz the following day. Since rail service from Schaffhausen to Rorschach had been interrupted by the storm, the crate would be transferred to the loading dock of the Dampfschiffahrts-Gesellschaft and sent across Lake Constance. And then he would tie one on, even if only with sacramental wine!

As he set off from Schaffhausen on the third day, the rain intensified again. The wheels of the cart had begun to screech, as if the heavy rain had scoured the grease out of their axles. But Dussel, who until then had maintained a grimly optimistic frame of mind, could not understand why he was suddenly overcome with a sense of foreboding. What was wrong with him? That infernal screeching set him on edge. He would stop and apply the pig grease from the pot he always carried on the dray when the rain let up. But he found that he was having trouble keeping his mind on the road and several times let the reins fall lax, so that the horses began to loll and almost stopped completely. But that must be because the horses were losing their footing in the mud.

When the rain again let up a bit, he felt too lethargic to stop and grease the wheels. He was also distracted by the crate, which unaccountably began to rattle in a way that could have nothing to do with the ruts in the road. The excruciating noise of the wheels ground into his bones and set him to fidgeting whenever his mind wandered off the road. He shook his head, grumbled a prayer, and goaded the horses to their previous pace only to fall once again to lagging and lolling a few hundred meters down the road.

In this way, it was almost dusk by the time he reached Stein am Rhein. It had taken nearly the whole day to make only 19 km, and Konstanz was still 27 km up the road! Long before the sun had set somewhere beyond the sporadic freshets, visibility had shrunk to a few feet in front of the horses. Dussel was growing drowsy when he heard a creaking above the rattling of the crate and the screeching of the wheels, as from a rope under strain. Then a loud snap brought him out of his reverie. Before he could fully turn his head, a blast of darkness swept up from the crate and fell upon his neck. As Wagehalsen drained the wagoner's body, his own body bloated, and the blood began to seep out of his wounds and wash away in the rain. He dragged the lifeless body from the dray and into the woods. He rummaged through Dussel's kit, found the grease-pot, and lubricated the wheels. Then he took the reins of the dray and lashed at the horses as the wagoner had never done. The wheels creaked but readily turned with only an occasional squeak. The horses flew in terror, trying to escape the demon that seemed suddenly to have sprung onto their backs.

The city of Konstanz occupies a transitional zone on the German bank of the Rhine at the outflow of the Obersee, the major division of Lake Constance from the smaller Untersee; between the exuberant waters of the Alpenrhein plunging almost 600 meters down from their two major sources in the glaciers to the south and the steeply dropping banks of the Hochrhein west to Basel; between awe-inspiring chasms and picturesque valleys. Unprotected by mountains, the waters of the lake are by turns turbulent in stormy weather, or hazy, somber, and brooding in calm. The city's charm comes from the structures that humans have imposed on the flat setting, and from its sense of a long history as a gathering place, a nexus of natural and supernatural enchantments. Nomads who hunted the banks and fished the waters followed by the first settlers who built pile dwellings, practiced farming and animal husbandry, and cast the first in a series of spells. The first enchantment, a Celtic fishing rune, the second incantation, the Roman *civitas*, Constantia, followed by the *Zauber* of a German *burg*, Konstanz, and finally the medieval magisterium. Deep in the stones of the place lay the supernatural dread of eternal night.

Goethe called architecture "frozen music." Call it, rather, frozen magic, power which would otherwise effervesce and be lost, an invocation against transitoriness. Call it the frozen magic of the medieval buildings in which, in the fifteenth century, the 16th Ecumenical Council invoked divine right to purge the excesses of the "head and members" of the Church and heal the Great Schism. Call it the magic of Machiavellian maneuvering by the new pope, who consolidated his power without disturbing its superstitious origins; of betrayal by the Holy Roman Emperor Sigismund who promised Jan Huss a safe conduct but allowed the Council to condemn him to the stake and strike the first spark of that Protestant Reformation which later thawed the edges of divine right. And while the "head" engaged in various degrees of treachery in the Council House, the "members" pursued various forms of debauchery in the streets. The thousands who swarmed into the city to witness the ritual purging turned the magisterium into a lewd and lascivious carnival.

Into this nexus of frozen spells rattled the wagon driven by the very dynamic Wagehalsen, the horses nearly dead from the exhausting pace he had goaded them to. He had paused only briefly just outside

Kreuzlingen, divided from Konstanz by the Swiss-German border, to dress himself. Enough of the wagoner's blood had seeped away through his wounds so that he was able to fit into the clothing he carried in the valise he kept in the crate.

It was then after sunset. For a moment the sky cleared as the eye of the storm passed quickly over the spell of St. Ulrich's church and its piece of the True Cross. Through the moonless dusk shone the first stars. The dark mass of the dray drove a clattering fist through the cobbled streets, shining like mirrors, shattering the illusion of day and scattering its fiery shards across the sky. Towering up over the lake to the east, an immense bank of night came swirling down in an avalanche of darkness and pounding rain that swept over Wagehalsen as he hurried through the town. By the time he crossed the border and arrived at the dock in Konstanz, the unrelenting rain had flooded the streets.

The shipping agent at the cargo depot of the Dampfschiffahrt-Gesellschaft was still on duty. Wagehalsen arranged to have the crate loaded onto a paddle steamer bound for Rorschach on the eastern shore of Lake Constance and then to be transferred to the standard gauge railway still running, as far as the agent knew, between Rorschach and Chur. The agent was vaguely unsettled by the bizarre demeanor of this strange wagoner with the puckered face of someone who had been out in the rain too long. But he did not personally know this "Dussel" from Schaffhausen, and suppressing a smile at the name, did not feel like fussing about some wagoner's credentials in such weather. After all, the box's way had already been well paved with credit. He shrugged off his doubts and prepared the necessary papers. When the agent's attention had turned to other duties, Wagehalsen once again sought the security of his place, confident of the efficiency of Swiss bureaucracy.

Nasty weather and beforehand bribery by "some wealthy merchant" had, up to this point, caused French, German, and Swiss customs officers along the lower Rhine to relax their vigilance and disinclined them to impede the course of commerce. But at the dock on Lake Constance, an incorruptible customs agent was about to delay the crate as it was being loaded onto the steamship. He ordered the box opened for inspection in the downpour, to the profound annoyance of the dock workers. As they were about to comply, the box lurched against the official's leg and landed on his foot. Leg and foot broken, the official was carried away, howling in pain. The dock workers laughed and finished loading the box onto the steamer.

Aboard the paddle steamer, Wagehalsen, stiff from confinement and loss of blood, risked being seen on the promenade deck. Stealthily, he made his way up from the cargo hold while most of the passengers were in the saloon, enjoying what conversation and refreshment their various stages of queasiness allowed them. Esther Hazy, an attractive young woman traveling with her sister and her sister's fiancé, was feeling faint in the close air of the cabin and the rough crossing. She decided to brave the nasty weather on the deserted upper deck to clear her head. She stood for a few moments at the port rail, looking out over the choppy waters of the lake. But the random undulations of the steamer were making her nauseous. She had better go back below and find a place to lie down. As she turned, a gentleman she had not noticed appeared out of the darkness, closely wrapped in a rumpled cloak. Confused and slightly alarmed, she stopped. Then realizing it must only be another passenger seeking some air, she tried to cover her anxiety at his sudden appearance with idle shipboard chatter. Her patter ran out as he stared intently into her eyes. Pausing only a breath, Wagehalsen seized her by the throat before she could cry out. Paralyzed with fright as she was, she felt indignant as well when she saw that he was naked under the cloak. In her last conscious thought, as he sank his teeth into her neck, she wondered, Why is this man's body full of holes?

Miss Hazy's disappearance caused a commotion. Her sister and future brother-in-law had already alerted the captain when they noticed that she had not come back into the saloon and could not be found in her compartment. He had begun a search for the lady, but by the time the boat docked at the lake resort of Rorschach, she had not been found and her traveling companions feared the worst. The local police were alerted and the passengers interrogated as they waited for their personal effects to be unloaded. But no one had seen the lady since she had left the saloon about midway in the crossing. As the rest of the passengers had been in company together at the time of the lady's disappearance, suspicion could not be attached to them. And the crew would have had their hands full managing the steamer in the rough water. The investigating officer concluded, pending further inquiry, that the unfortunate lady must have fallen overboard somewhere out on the lake. Perhaps the water out on the lake was rougher than at the dock? Perhaps the lady had taken ill and leaned too far over the railing, the ship lurched, and . . . ? It occurred to neither the lady's distraught family, who had come to meet the incoming ship, nor the investigating officer to search the large crate being unloaded from the hold. In the confusion of Miss Hazy's relatives, the police investigation, and irritable passengers and dock workers anxious to be on their way, the crate slipped by the Swiss customs inspector.

Since Wagehalsen was unable to maintain his blood supply for long, he took the lady into the crate with him, where she remained in a semiconscious stupor. He could not allow himself to sink into torpor in the present hazardous circumstances. Nor did he want to take unnecessary risks by exposing himself too often to search for fresh supplies. The woman had provided for his immediate needs, and by draining her gradually, he hoped further loss of blood through seepage might be minimized. In time, either his wounds would heal completely, or he would have to cover them with plasters. In the Alps above Lake Constance, many small villages and hamlets would have been out of reach of the telegraph even in more temperate weather. His presence would excite the curiosity of the residents, but his valise held ample financial resources as well as his clothing. He would travel by rail first to Thusis, then transfer to post wagon, or travel on foot, following the Hinterrhein up the Schams Valley to the Rheinwald Valley and cut across it to Splügen, a matter of 20 km or so. From there, a few kilometers along the Splügenstrasse through the Pass into Italy, down the road to Lake Como, to Milan, and then, to Genoa on the Ligurian Sea, where he could book passage on a steamer to America. Remembering the discomforts of the first crossing during Rachel's American tour, he was uneasy. Steamship travel had, of course, markedly improved in the last fifteen years. But a week or more at the mercy of sea and weather, his crate stowed in a miserable cargo hold . . . At the thought of his lost love, he turned somber and almost lost his resolve. But another sip from his portable cellar revived his spirits. And his wounds no longer leaked profusely. He would remain at Thusis as long as possible, to maximize the healing process. As long as people were about, he could get fresh supplies of blood as needed. As long as the days continued dark and stormy, he could travel day or night without the debilitating effects of the sun. The constant rain filled him with the vague uneasiness about moving water that still troubled him, but perhaps that might be due to his weakened condition.

All transportation along the river and its tributaries would be hazardous, but the railway which had its terminus at Chur had so far remained in service, and as far as anyone knew, the narrow gauge mountain railways from Chur were also still operating. The steamer having arrived at Rorschach after 10 pm, he would have to wait until morning for the train to Chur. As the box was being transferred to the loading platform at the train station, the porters grumbled. The bill of lading specified its weight at 100 kilos, but its weight was found to be closer to 150 kilos. The receiving clerk worried that the drenching rains might have penetrated the box, accounting for the increased weight, and damaged its contents. The porters were just as anxious to complete their work and seek shelter. They carelessly dumped the box on the station platform to await someone else's pleasure. On duty alone after the porters had left, the robust and conscientious clerk was stricken with conscience and came back to assess any possible damage. He noticed that the lid of the box was not secure. That might account for how rain may have accumulated inside the box and added to its weight. Then, too, the lid might blow off in the storm, leaving the railway open to a lawsuit. Intending to inspect the contents and secure the lid, the clerk fetched hammer and nails and approached the box. Wagehalsen burst through the lid . . .

Later, he used the strength borrowed from the clerk to load the crate into the baggage compartment himself, and so avoided further meddling until he arrived at Chur. The clerk's body would eventually be found downriver, floating on Lake Constance. The medical examiner would wonder how the peculiar triangular wound on his throat could have led to such a massive loss of blood . . .

Feeling stronger and safe enough to travel outside of his box at Chur, Wagehalsen dressed in clothing which he had stored in the valise, lifted the dazed woman out and disposed of the box in the river. He would have to "rough it" with the meager supply of soil left in his bag until he could reach a cache in Italy. He would travel to the Splügen Pass by the narrow gauge Rhaetian railway, discreetly refreshing himself with sips from his portable fountain.

A few passengers and the conductor noticed the man in rumpled clothing as he helped a fainting lady board the train. The man gratefully accepted the help of the conductor in making the lady comfortable, and explained that she had fainted because she was delicate and unused to the altitude. He was sure that she would recover in the comfort of the train. The conductor nodded and considerately drew the curtain to give the couple privacy. As he left the compartment and closed the door, the man was solicitously bending over his wife and chafing her hands.

About midway between Chur and Reichenau, perhaps 3 km, the track was obstructed by a landslide. There would be a delay of several hours while the track was cleared. The passengers gathered into conversational knots on the platforms or in the corridors, casually debating the merits of waiting for the track to be cleared, to risk hiking back to Chur or ahead to Reichenau. The rumpled stranger left the train alone, apparently deciding on the latter course despite the pouring rain. He disappeared in the mist, then, unseen, turned and headed for Thusis . . .

Back on the train, the considerate conductor returned to the compartment of the rumpled man and his ailing wife to see whether they needed reassurance about the delay. He found the woman fallen over into the place where her husband had sat. Her collar had been torn open, revealing the scar on her throat. That and the extreme pallor of her face alarmed him. He searched the train and found a physician from Chur who was traveling to Thusis. The lady had obviously died from a massive loss of blood. But "What had become of the blood?" wondered the doctor. The woman's skin had shrunk and shriveled so that she appeared to have been completely drained. Yet there was no evidence of violence other than the puncture at her throat. The disappearance of her husband was suspicious, but nothing could be done until the track was cleared. Word of the bizarre death sent a shudder through the train.

By the time the conductor had discovered the dead woman, Wagehalsen arrived at Thusis. Whether his wounds had begun to heal or the lady's blood had merely coagulated around the holes and would forever pock his torso was of less importance than that he had a renewed sense of strength and well-being. If the coagulations failed and he began to leak again, infusions of fresh blood from a new host would no doubt plug up the holes again. His lassitude was now replaced by a kind of euphoric recklessness, as if with the closing of his wounds the steady soaking in the rain had leached away caution. Because of the bad weather, no transportation was available at Thusis. But he found a horse. As it happened, a man was riding it. Wagehalsen easily overcame his objections and rode to an inn near the mouth of the Via Mala. Once the woman's body was found in the coach and the track cleared, the train would arrive and there would be a cry raised against him. But he allowed himself the luxury of sitting in front of the fire at the inn before retiring to his room, almost as a taunt to the anticipated pursuers.

Despite Capt. Katz's fondest wish, Lt. Spatz reached Basel safely only a day after Wagehalsen had left for Schaffhausen. He learned from the captain of the paddle steamer that such a box as he described had been delivered and transferred to a dray. The Lieutenant had one of those moments that sooner or later confront all people put upon by overbearing authority, whether to submit to the letter of his orders, to go only as far as Basel, or to seize the initiative. He had, after all, been authorized to capture the fugitive. Drenched, hungry and tired, but so close on the trail, he decided that he could sink no lower in misery. The fugitive would eventually probably either be forced by the weather to hole up somewhere, or be trapped by impassable roads. When that happened, Spatz would nab him with the help of the local constabulary.

He pursued much the same course as Wagehalsen had the day before, arriving at Rorschach where the furor raised by family and friends of the missing lady had intensified with the return of her lifeless body. Lt. Spatz enlisted the aid of the woman's male relatives in pursuing and apprehending the fugitive. They made their way to Chur in slightly better time than Wagehalsen because the weather had temporarily eased again. At Chur, they met with local volunteers, the town having been outraged at news of the woman's death. The Lieutenant and the lady's relatives had arrived at Chur on horseback just as a dozen men of the volunteer militia were about to give chase. They joined forces, and Spatz was pleased that they now had a description of the man to aid in his capture.

The band of men soon overtook the stalled train and conferred with the conductor. The shocked and grief-stricken relatives of Miss Hazy vowed to continue the pursuit and avenge their kinswoman. The track was still not clear, and rather than lose time helping to clear it, the band decided to ride on. They were sure that they could overtake the murderer. After all, they had horses, and he was on foot. When they had reached the confluence of the Vorderrhein and the Hinterrhein at Reichenau some fifteen kilometers below Thusis, they were disappointed at not having overtaken the fugitive. They briefly debated whether to split up and search both branches of the river—thereby seriously reducing their numbers—or to follow up the obviously more tractable Vorderrhein flowing through the Tavetsch valley. Seriously hampered by the torrential rains and the swollen rivers, they realized that if they all followed the wrong branch of the river, they would not be able to double back in time to catch their prey.

The conductor on the train had said the man was bound for Thusis, which indicated that they should follow the Hinterrhein. But the Hazy men thought that if the fugitive, now presumably on foot, opted for an easier route, there were more towns along the Vorderrhein that would offer convenient stepping stones to the Oberalp Pass on the west. No matter which branch of the Rhine they followed, they were faced with the dilemma that the fugitive could elude them through one of the alpine passes and escape into Italy. But Spatz understood perversity. His conviction that their quarry would choose the more difficult route overcame the others' doubts.

Wagehalsen had indeed chosen the route along the more difficult Hinterrhein because it ran through treacherous terrain. But it also provided the shortest, most direct route to Italy. Wagehalsen reached the village of Thusis at the upper end of the Domleschg Valley a few hours before his pursuers, confident that he could outdistance them if and when they caught him up.

Wagehalsen's delay allowed his pursuers to reach the village inn just as he was planning to leave. Drenched and in need of rest, they were seeking refreshment before making inquiries of the innkeeper about strangers. While the innkeeper was attending to their immediate needs, Wagehalsen managed to slip out unobserved. By the time the band of pursuers had learned about the lone traveler who had arrived a few hours earlier, burst into his room, and rushed out in pursuit, Wagehalsen had covered the four kilometers to the Via Mala. The rains were so heavy that one could hardly tell night from day, and it would not have been possible for him to travel comfortably on horseback. Convinced that he had left his pursuers behind, even perversely delighted at narrow escapes, Wagehalsen did not consider his situation urgent. He left the horse behind and proceeded on foot. He would follow the road through the gorge, crossing from side to side over the three bridges built in 1822 spanning it some four hundred feet above the river bed. The overhanging cliffs obscured the river in places and seemed to close in overhead so that the gorge at times resembled a tunnel. While he was able to tolerate the unrelenting heavy rains, he found them a strain.

The river had risen almost four hundred feet and the churning waters occasionally washed over the road. It slowed him down. As he neared the middle bridge, he found the swollen river pouring over it. The unaccountable, morbid fear of moving water swept over him again. As he paused to consider how to proceed, he heard his pursuers, having no qualms about moving water, closing in on him. They thought he was trapped.

Just as they were about to reach him, Wagehalsen, snarling with contempt, turned away and to their utter consternation proceeded to scale the cliff which rose more than one thousand feet above the old path on the right bank. He disappeared from view below. When he had reached the rim of the chasm, he looked back to the north, the direction he had come from. Obscured by the rain, high above Thusis and the entrance to the Nolla gorge pouring into the Rhine below, the dim shadows of the three remaining towers of Schloss Hohen-Rhäetien rose from its ruins at the edge of another sheer precipice. With triumphant disregard for his pursuers, he doubled back along the disintegrating old road the Romans had built on the rim of the gorge, and stood across the chasm contemplating the fate of the robber knight who, hundreds of years before, had blindfolded his horse and ridden off the cliff rather than surrender to rebellious peasants.

Wagehalsen's baffled pursuers below, unable to follow, cast about futilely for his trail. He would rest a bit before resuming his way south to the Splügen Pass, Italy, and west to the New World.

Part Three

Interlude

Drawn into the elaborate saga of Wagehalsen's journal, Brewster almost seemed to have forgotten his Batman fixation. Dr. Korngold swiveled around in the chair behind his desk as if to lay Wagehalsen's journal in its place on the shelf next to the other exotica, but really to hide his satisfaction. His face composed, he turned back to Brewster, who was sitting in his usual place beside the desk.

"Myth or reality?" mused Brewster aloud, his eyes resting on the shelf. "Your freely translated Arabian Nights from Wagehalsen's journal may have livened up our tired rounds of therapy, but they've come to an end in the New World," he said. "Wonder what happened since." Brewster paused expectantly, but Korngold looked back without a word. "Frankly," he began again, "I can't tell if the journal was written by a madman or a harmless, wealthy eccentric."

Korngold suppressed a smile and looked at him so keenly that Brewster hurried on to keep from laughing, "It's said that if you think you're mad, you're not. I wonder if Wagehalsen thought he was mad."

"A nice bit of circularity, that."

"I suppose madness could also be a pretense that you knew you were mad just so as not to appear mad?"

"Interesting." Korngold puffed on a favorite briar. When Brewster said nothing further, "So," he said, after blowing smoke at the ceiling, "you subscribe to the popular notion linking myth and madness?"

"Not as the stereotyped 'mad genius,' say, Van Gogh or Dr. Frankenstein. But when a myth gives us a set of beliefs that makes sense of the world, its purpose, and our own place in it, we call that reality and live accordingly. When that way of life is so challenged by new myths, new reality, their partisans turn to violence. When opposing sides so delude themselves in the rightness of their respective realities, the violence turns from defending their own beliefs to destroying the others'—"

"Ah!" said Korngold. "Of course. Delusion can be destructive

both physically and emotionally. And when the violence displaces the certainty of reality—?"

"Violence becomes the only certain reality," said Brewster. "What could be madder than that? Someone, somewhere, said something about preferring the myth to the reality when they contradict each other. Is that where madness begins or ends?" He paused. "If the myth is more appealing . . ." He shrugged and looked away. "And really, what's the difference?"

Korngold narrowed his eyes and followed Brewster's gaze. "Do you think I've been passing off an 'oriental fantasy' for the record of a real person because it's more appealing than reality? Does the journal sound any more . . . fanciful, say . . . than Batman?"

"Maybe not," said Brewster.

"You attribute the increase in violence around us to the popularity of myth?"

Brewster shrugged again. "Without myth, life would have no purpose. Violence—I mean the collective violence that energizes conflicting ideologies—becomes meaningless. That doubt trickles down to the individual. Thoreau said most men 'lead lives of quiet desperation.' They aren't so quiet any more." He nodded at the shelf holding Korngold's collection of legends, medieval epics and romances, and vampires. "The task of resolving violence at the individual level has never wanted for champions. In myth. But it's grown some."

Korngold puffed and waited.

"The impact of Wagner's mythology," continued Brewster, "may be exhilarating as art. And like many thinkers and commentators in the nineteenth century, it may have seemed a source of ultimate truth. If we can believe what Wagehalsen himself says in his journal, he turned to poets, philosophers, and artists precisely because he thought they had a lock on truth. But a literal blood-sucking idealist, however poetic, philosophical, or artistic, presents an ugly reality to his own society, not to say ours. Whether he was a real, straight-off-the-book-shelf vampire or a nut case who believed he was? We can only guess from his journal. His political agenda in the nineteenth century would have been as chaotic as the impact of the virus discovered by Buckyballs in ours."

"So you're saying that art is like a viral infection?"

"It can be. When art becomes ideology or ideology becomes art, it can lead to violence. That's even illustrated in Wagehalsen's journal. It's a chronicle of myth and violence. Vampirism may not rely on the same physical force to injure others used by wild animals. But it inflicts grave injury all the same. As for the myth of the classic vampire . . ." Brewster shrugged. "If Wagehalsen was a for-real person, if he was infected with the buckyvirus . . ." He paused. "And if the whole thing wasn't imagined by some pathetic delusional, then at least some of the journal has a kind of mad relevance."

"You doubt the veracity of the journalist?" said Korngold.

"The guy who wrote it was certainly real. Someone wrote it. It looks authentically old, though there have been some ingenious fakes. Maybe such a 'find' could even be faked by someone for therapeutic effect?"

Korngold stopped puffing. He took the stem of the pipe out of his mouth and laid it in the ashtray on his desk and gazed at it, tapping the stem impatiently between his thumb and forefinger.

"Sorry," said Brewster, laughing. "Couldn't resist. Besides, I doubt that Dr. Buckyballs would've gone along with such a ruse."

"I'm relieved that you discount a conspiracy theory so readily," said Korngold, looking up at him. "Though I might have preferred another source of confidence. For a while, there, I thought you were about to accuse the entire medical community of being in on a hoax."

"Are you so sure I've discounted it?"

"All well-meaning people want to save the world, if only a small piece at a time. Even knights in black armor. But without their professional integrity to keep them from conspiring in deceit and fraud . . . well," Korngold shrugged, "what's left?"

Korngold winced at Brewster's look.

After a moment, Brewster spoke again. "In my own way, that's the role I thought I was playing."

"I see," said Korngold, stiffly picking up and relighting his pipe. "But your search for Guinevere," he said between puffs, "you're still searching for her, aren't you? Hasn't that diverted Batman from his crime-busting purpose?"

"Not at all. Finding a victim of a crime is just as real as nabbing the perpetrator. Especially as the victim may be able to lead us to the villain. It's all bound up with the spread of the buckyvirus. My personal motives for finding Guinevere don't take away from the need to find the 'vampire' behind it all. Find her, find the carrier, isolate the contagion."

"I see. You think that Guinevere is one of his victims?"

"I was sure of it as soon as I saw the wound on her neck, the night she disappeared. But I doubt that whoever it is has some diabolical plan to create a vampire 'sophocracy.' Medical intervention is certainly indicated. Disease carriers need to be restrained from spreading infection. So far, neither the police nor the medical profession has had any effect in stopping the spread. There's still room for a private citizen to take action. There's still room for Batman."

"So, you're willing to accept that Wagehalsen was real, that he brought a virulent disease to America, but not that he might somehow have survived and still be menacing the city?"

"After almost a hundred and fifty years?" said Brewster, incredulous. "Are you kidding?"

"Just checking," smiled Korngold.

35.

ANOTHER VICTIM FOUND IN A coma by the Lake added to Korngold's consternation over the Ramble. The man had lost a considerable amount of blood, but regained consciousness after a transfusion. When he came to, he was disoriented. He did not know who he was. When told that documents in the wallet found with him identified him as William Bernwall, he breathed, "Miami." But he had no recollection of the attack or any of the events immediately preceding it. In Miami's blood, too, a technician found the mystery virus and notified Dr. Buckyballs. After the transfusion, the virus actively proliferated, as in Jennifer's case, then spontaneously and abruptly subsided.

Korngold was on hospital rounds when Buckyballs found him and told him about this attack on yet another member of the Young Artists Group. Between concern for the safety of Brewster and Jennifer, who were still prowling the Ramble on their personal quests, and anxiety over the potential menace to other member of the Young Artists Group, gaped the threat to Korngold's professional reputation.

The implications staggered him. The disappearance of Guinevere, the attack on Barvim and *his* disappearance. Nick Artsynick's former roommates, Dabbler and Pilar, never turned up. Were they, too, victims? And now Bernwall! It didn't help that his patient, already implicated in Guinevere's disappearance, was still flying around the Ramble in that ridiculous Batman getup, fueling rumors about mysterious caped phantoms.

After a few days, Miami remembered who he was, though he still had no recollection of the events leading up to the attack. He was kept in isolation for another week to see if the virus would become active again. When it remained dormant, the hospital scheduled follow-up exams and discharged him. When he failed to show up for these exams, the hospital tried to contact him. He did not return their calls.

Nick and Arpie had developed the habit of sitting silently at the kitchen table, each lost in his own thoughts, drinking coffee. Arpie tried various conversational gambits, but Nick was hearing music in his head and tuned him out. He either responded monosyllabically, or gave Arpie an annoyed look. Why, wondered Arpie, was he being so uncommunicative and disagreeable?

When Arpie despaired of conversational failures, he sighed audibly, or made exaggerated movements to draw attention. Listening to his inner orchestra, Nick tried to think of these distractions as the squirmings of a restless audience. But if Arpie could be persistent, Nick could be as determined in ignoring him. For the past several days, he could just catch flickers of Arpie poring over the newspaper reports of the "vampire" attacks in Central Park. The genius was correlating details of the attacks with some drivel about six Cosmic Numbers controlling the universe, starting with Huge Number N represented by a tail dangling from the left top of the letter N equal to 1 with 39 zeroes, more crap with epsilon, omega, lambda, Q for chrissakes, and D with another dangling tail! What, thought Nick in exasperation, everything in the universe got tails? Gravity, anti-gravity, mass, gas, galaxies imprinted in the Big Bang, and superstrings with ten dimensions! Or was it eleven? Jesus, as if the world wasn't messed up enough!

The Womb of Uncreated Night

So there he sat, spilling out his I.Q. of 157 all over the papers on his side of the table, somewhere in there looking for the mystery of vampirism. Why not? If the biblical Number of The Beast is 666, why not whip up a number for the vampire? Then when Arpie reached some unfathomable cadence in all that numbering idiocy, he wouldn't say a word. But you could tell that he was just sitting there fixing Nick with his eyes, a serenely moronic smile flitting across his mouth, bursting for you to notice and ask him what was up so that he could splash his spillage onto you. You'd think a genius could affect a smile more suited to the number 157! For a genius, Arpie could act the imbecile surpassingly well. And how did all that superstitious gorp about *synchronicity* relate to the Number of the Vampire and the predictability to its attacks? Eventually, of course, Arpie couldn't wait for notice, and he'd just *have* to let you in on whatever it was. Not that Nick wanted to be let in on it. But that would be irrelevant.

At least when Arpie was preoccupied with some deeply mysterious number-mumbling, he would leave Nick alone for a while. But today—today was the day. Nick could not help thinking that if Arpie had spent as much time and effort on eradicating the bedbugs that sifted down from the flats above as he did on his mind-numbing numbering games he might not have as many attacks of "hives."

But today was the day. Arpie whipped out his pocket calculator and began furiously crunching numbers. He was not a quiet cruncher, but one of those irksome hackers who are somehow able to make the quietest device clatter like a stampede of horse-drawn carriages over cobblestone streets. After rattling the damned thing for several minutes, he threw it on the table with an exclamation of triumph, sat back in his chair and fixed Nick with a smile that heralded Great News. He broke Nick's concentration at last.

Nick threw down his pen and sighed. "What?"

Arpie let the suspense build. He continued to smile archly. Then he asked Nick, "How's your German? Does the word, *Feigenbaum*, have any special significance for you?"

Nick sighed again and waited.

"It means fig tree," said Arpie.

"I can think of a smart-ass allusion to an obscene gesture," said Nick, thinking it would be particularly apt at the moment.

"No, I didn't mean anything like that," said Arpie primly. "I was just making some calculations about the frequency of the attacks in Central Park." He then launched into a baroque explanation of the Feigenbaum Number which meant absolutely nothing to Nick. Didn't Nick see the significance of a number that could explain the frequency of attacks in Central Park and predict when they would occur? Nick thought, instead, of how often he felt like smacking Arpie upside the head. Would Arpie care to calculate the frequency of *that*?

"No," said Nick. He picked up his pen to resume scoring.

"They occur at multiple intervals of 4.669 days!" Nick looked at him blankly. "That's four days and sixteen hours, give or take a few minutes!"

"Uh-huh."

"The last attack was supposed to have occurred on Thursday shortly after 7 a.m. Today is Sunday. So the next attack should occur—" Arpie broke off, touched his cheek with his right index finger, and did some rapid mental arithmetic, he was lightning quick at that, "—the next attack should occur tomorrow, a little after 11 a.m.!"

"There's one little problem with your theory," said Nick, getting argumentative.

"What's that?" Arpie wasn't in the least perturbed. Like moving the Queen out early in a chess game, how could Nick possibly counter his move?

"Vampires aren't supposed to go out in daylight."

"Why not? Bats go out in daylight, even though they prefer the dark," he added with a chuckle, tossing off Nick's objection with superior insight, "So why not vampires? And anyway, who said anything about a real vampire? Some maniac is running around out there. And maniacs don't avoid sunlight."

"Do maniacs run around with pocket calculators so that they can

The Womb of Uncreated Night

time their attacks at precisely 4.669 days?" Nick retorted. As Arpie was poised to reply, Nick added hastily, "That was a rhetorical question! Why don't you put all that in one of your stories?" He wondered what all this had to do with German fig trees, but didn't ask. It would only set Arpie off again. He tried to go back to his composition, but Arpie had breached Nick's wall of reserve.

"Feigenbaum, fig tree, eh? In the bible," began Nick, turning the baroque into rococo. If Arpie was going to constantly interrupt his composing, he would have to pay. It was the American Way. "In the bible, the fig tree is sometimes considered to be a symbol of Israel. After it loses its leaves in winter, it grows again in spring. Do you think the vampire could be Jewish?"

Arpie sat back with a stricken look.

Oh, God! thought Nick. What now? It was about eight o'clock. Really too early to quit writing. But Arpie was determined to ruin his focus. He gave up, rose from the table and left the flat. When he returned a few hours later, he found Arpie still sitting where he had left him. Nick stood, eyeing him, scratching a rash on his neck.

"You know," said Arpie at length, shuddering, "I've been wanting to . . . to share something with you . . . to tell you something about myself. Something I'm a little afraid and ashamed of. Something I've never admitted to anyone."

Nick groaned inwardly and sat, expecting the worst. Oh, shit! He's going to tell me he's gay. "What? That you're afraid of vampires?" As a pained expression crossed Arpie's face, Nick was afraid that he was going to cry and pass cosmic gas. "It's all right," he said, desperately trying to forestall an awkward revelation. "Whatever it is, it's all right. I'm a tolerant guy. I understand."

"No, you don't. It's just, it's just—"

"Really, it's all right. You don't need to tell me. Whatever it is, it wouldn't have any bearing on the way I feel about you. Really."

"Really? But I want to share something intimate with you. It's important to me." Nick groaned aloud. Oh, Lord! he thought. What obnoxious, disgusting, loathsome, revolting—"I've kept it bottled up all my life," said Arpie, breaking in on Nick's mental grievances, "I have to get it off my chest." Nick resigned himself. He stared at Arpie, half rising out of his chair to make a quick getaway, waiting for the worst. "I'm-I'm-" With every stammer, Nick was surer than ever that he didn't want to hear whatever confession Arpie was about to make. "I'm Jewish!" Arpie blurted out at last.

"Oh, for chrissakes!" said Nick. "Is *that* your terrible secret? Who cares?" He threw himself back in his chair to restrain an impulse to pick it and throw it at Arpie.

"But that's not all," wailed Arpie. "My mother had a phobia about the *Schwarze*, the Blacks. She used to tell me horrible things about them when I was little, about what they did to little boys. She terrified me. I'm terrified that some night, some dark figure—you know, like a Black man—is going to come in the middle of the night and drag me away and do awful things to me!"

I'm supposed to protect him from Black vampires? thought Nick incredulously. "Oh, is that all! That's nothing! You're letting your imagination over these 'vampire' stories and cosmic numbers run away with you, that's all. At worst you're a racist Jew. We live in a racist society. You'll blend right in." And lest Arpie take that to mean he was going to blab it all around, he added, "Your secret's safe with me."

"You don't mind?" pressed Arpie, surprised. Then he went on, musing aloud. "It's as if there were some unseen power lurking in the background, and Black people manipulate it—"

Nick dropped his pen and burst out laughing. "The Jewish version of a Nazi's conviction that everything is dominated by Jews!" Arpie looked sullen. He had tried to ingratiate himself with Nick, and Nick was laughing at him.

"Look," said Nick, "you're over-thinking this Feigenbaum shit and calculating yourself into a snit. It's nothing. What's a little irrational fear among human beings, eh? Everybody has them." And then, in case Arpie decided on further confidences, Nick added, "People don't need sweeping categories to label each other. What matters is how you act." Act like an asshole, he thought, and someone will pin that label on you. But you don't correct the problem by going around to your friends and confessing you're an asshole, please forgive me! Just stop acting like an asshole. Maybe join a support group. Assholes Anonymous. Hi. My name is Arpie. I'm an asshole! applause, congratulations. "Get real!"

Nick hoped that would silence Arpie for a while and give him some relief. The mental asshole label he had pinned on Arpie would not erase the poor schlub from his mind as easily as crossing out a wrong note in a score. But "vampire" stories and cosmic numbers got on his nerves more than he cared to admit. Arpie's irritating intrusions into his composing didn't help. Railroad flats did not have doors you get behind and shut him out. Not that a little thing like door could keep him out. As if he sensed the hidden needs that had begun to seep into the flat through the cracked plaster, Dabbler came up to Nick to be petted, ears lowered and tail wagging. Not to be outdone, Pilar jumped onto the table purring loudly and rubbing her head against his shoulder. Her paw chanced to step on the not-quite-dry correction Nick had made. "A bit of aleatory," he said, scratching Dabbler's ears and gently picking Pilar off the manuscript.

Next morning, when Arpie was not in the flat, Nick telephoned Dr. Korngold and threatened to commit suicide, even suggesting that if the shrink were a friend, he would help Nick kill himself. Sort of like the Japanese ritual of seppuku, in case he hesitated. Korngold asked him to wait until they had a chance to talk it over face to face, implying that he would rearrange his schedule for a meeting that day. Nick stayed up later than usual that night, waiting for the reaction he was sure would come. He told Arpie that he was expecting a call from Korngold, and that Arpie might as well go to bed. But Arpie refused to retire as long as there was any chance of companionship, even if only sullen. It was not unusual for them to stay up until well after 11 p.m., Nick lost in working on his compositions, Arpie wondering how he could engage him in conversation. When Korngold had not called by 11:45, Arpie's curiosity was piqued, and he determined to wait up with Nick no matter how late. About 1:30 a.m., they heard the front door of the apartment building open noisily and heavy footsteps come down the hall to the kitchen door. There was heavy knocking on the door. The kitchen door was located in an awkward corner near the sink. Someone had long ago nailed it shut.

"Who could that be at this hour?" wondered Arpie. "And why didn't they go to the front door?" he said, making as if to get up. "Probably saw the light under the kitchen door," Nick said. "Stay put. I'll get it." Nick got up and started to walk down the shotgun, then stuck his head back in the kitchen. "You don't have to worry, it's well past 11 a.m.!" He went to the living room door and opened it. Heavy footsteps receded down the hall to where he stood. There were two of them. One was a white man in a white coat, and the other was a Black cop. When they asked him if he was Nicholas Artsynick, Nick turned his face to the kitchen and called out to Arpie, "Nick, it's for you."

"What?" Completely baffled, Arpie got up from the kitchen table and walked into the living room. As soon as he saw the Black cop standing in the darkened hallway, he stumbled back away from the door with a look of terror on his face. Interpreting this shocked reaction as resistance, the two men advanced into the room and seized Arpie, who began to protest.

"Please come with us, sir. We're only here to help you." Dr. Korngold had obviously called Bellevue.

"No! No! This is a mistake!" he cried. "I'm not Nick! I'm Arpie!"

"You'll have to come with us," said the cop. Poor guy, he thought. Obviously in denial. "Come along quietly, now! It's for your own good." But Arpie began to scream and struggle fiercely. Since this was only to be expected of a mentally disturbed person—obviously, no sane person would create such a fuss over being hauled forcibly out of his home at 1:30 in the morning—the two men were convinced that there had been no mistake. Reluctantly, even a little regretfully, Nick thought, they wrestled him into a strait-jacket and dragged him out of the flat kicking and screaming, knocking his glasses off in the scuffle. The commotion and Arpie's cries

The Womb of Uncreated Night

brought people in neighboring apartments to their doors and into the hallways. Nick could hear the thuds of feet and doors flung open, excited voices, some raised in anger at the disturbance, others in concern.

Muffled cursing rumbled through the closed door from the flat across the hall. *"¡Qué foquin jaleo!"* thundered the super flinging open his door down the hall. *"¡Oye!"* he shouted, standing there in his shorts. *"¡Qué pasa aquí!"* By this time, the two men from Bellevue, lurching from wall to wall with their struggling captive, had managed to drag Arpie out the door and down the front stoop, Arpie protesting at the top of his voice that they were making a horrible mistake. His cries were cut off when they got him into the ambulance, hastily slammed the doors after him, and drove off.

"It's okay, Mr. LaPorta," Nick called back to the super.

"¡Cállate! ¡No más!"

"It's just a misunderstanding that'll be cleared up in the morning."

"¡Cállate! ¡No más!" Grumbling, muttering, *"¡Puta madre!"* the super stomped back into his flat, slammed the door, and thumped off back to bed. Reassured by the quiet that followed after the ambulance pulled away, and no longer subjected to the desperate cries of a murder victim, the other tenants likewise turned back into their shotguns, some muttering. No use getting involved in a neighbor's domestic crises.

Nick quietly closed the door, musing. Korngold would have worried about his professional reputation if a patient committed suicide while under his care. It was a sure thing that he would find a way to cover his ass. Reporting the potential suicide of a disturbed patient to Bellevue was a simple solution. Nick picked up Arpie's glasses and took them back into the kitchen. He held them up to the light. Noticing some dust on the lenses, he carefully polished them with a Kleenex and laid them on the table in front of Arpie's notes with a little pat. Dabbler and Pilar crept warily out from under the cot in his bedroom cubicle where they had retreated during the ruckus, and sat with tails curled around their feet, contemplating Nick. They came to him wagging and purring when he patted his thigh. He poured some coffee into his cup, toasted Arpie's vacant chair, and calmly drank, smiling to himself.

Next morning, he explained Arpie's absence from the music shop by telling Mr. Kahlenholtz that Arpie had a very severe attack of the hives, poor fellow, and would not be in until the following day. At lunch time, Nick paid a visit to Arpie at Bellevue. He found a very subdued, sedated Arpie sitting dejectedly at a table in the Day Room, head bent, staring at the stained surface, still restrained in a camisole.

Nick went up to him and stood on the opposite side of the table. "I've brought you your glasses," Nick said, cheerily. He reached across the table, perched them on Arpie's nose, and adjusted the earpieces. Arpie slowly raised his head and gazed at Nick uncomprehendingly with tear-stained eyes for a few seconds. Then his eyes clicked into focus and grew round with hatred. Arpie lunged at him, overturning the table and chairs as he tried to reach him, screaming, "You sonofabitch! You sonofabitch!" This, of course, further convinced the attendants that Arpie was seriously disturbed. They came running to drag him away to an isolation room where he could be sedated again and his cries would not disturb other patients or their visitors.

Some people just can't take a joke, sighed Nick.

Later that day, when Dr. Korngold was able to visit the hospital and discover the error, he had Arpie released and sent home. Nick was sitting in the kitchen, calmly drinking coffee and smiling to himself. It was almost 10 p.m. Arpie stormed in and began screaming at him. Nick merely looked at him serenely and waited for the storm to pass. When Arpie paused in his outburst, Nick smiled at him.

"Have some coffee," he offered. Speechless with rage, Arpie burst into tears and farted.

"But it's fresh," said Nick.

Finally finding his voice, Arpie told Nick to get out. Nick only smiled, took his half-drunk cup of coffee to the sink, poured the coffee down the drain, carefully washed and dried the cup, and put it in the cupboard. Without a word, he turned and left the flat.

The Womb of Uncreated Night

When Nick came back, two hours later, his eyes were glazed and bloodshot. He looked so ghastly that Arpie bit his lip and momentarily forgot to press for eviction. But the sting of Nick's cruel prank still smarted, and Arpie could not bring himself to admit the solicitude that nibbled at the wound.

"Have some coffee, Nick?" he said, feeling spiteful even though he was deeply disturbed by Nick's state. He immediately felt even more miserable. Nick turned uncomprehending eyes toward Arpie's voice. "It's fresh," said Arpie, bitterly.

Nick merely went to the cubicle where Arpie had hastily thrown together his belongings during his absence. Arpie had meant to toss him out the moment he returned, had even rehearsed a stinging rebuke in his head, ready as a bedbug-stained bed. But since Arpie had stripped the cot of sheets, pillow, and blanket, Nick simply lay down on it with his right leg hanging limply over the side and turned his head to the cracked plaster on the wall. The rash at his throat had gotten worse. There was a dark smudge on his collar. Arpie's righteous indignation clotted. He could not forgive Nick. But neither could he bring himself to throw him out in his present state.

Korngold learned the details of the escapade from Arpie, and meant to have a stern talk with Nick at his next therapy session. But Nick did not keep his appointment. When he missed the next two appointments, Korngold became seriously concerned. Had the suicide threat been only the sick practical joke at Arpie's expense it had seemed to be? He had talked the authorities at Bellevue out of pursuing the matter, thinking a stern talking-to and a warning would straighten Nick out during therapy. No further destructive behavior would be tolerated. And next time, the white coats coming for him would be better informed. But now he wondered if the suicide threat had been brought on by some unforeseen crisis. It was clearly a submerged cry for help.

Arpie went again to see Korngold.

"What should we do?" he said, knotting his eyebrows and a sodden hanky at the same time.

"What do *you* think we should do?" Korngold said, deflecting the implied responsibility. Korngold was ready to have Nick hospitalized. But Arpie would benefit from an anti-depressant. He wrote a prescription for Lexapro while he sounded out Arpie's perception of Nick's condition. Would Arpie be able to coax Nick into the office? Considering the recent turmoil caused by Nick's irresponsible behavior, any encounter between them would be risky. "How is Nick acting?"

"Well, he's . . . strange. He mopes around the flat like a zombie. Lies on the cot with his leg dangling over the side. Doesn't talk. Doesn't eat. Doesn't go to work."

"You mean he doesn't go out at all?"

"Um, well, yes. Sometimes he goes out at night for a couple of hours. Then he comes back and lies down again. Without saying a word." This was said in a tone that made it hard for Korngold to decide whether Arpie felt put upon by the burden of Nick's bizarre behavior or complaining that Nick was not being sociable.

"Do you think you could get him to come in for a chat with me?"

Arpie hesitated. For a few moments he looked as if he was deciding whether to take on that burden or simply dump it back into Korngold's lap.

"How do you feel about Nick?" pressed Korngold.

Arpie still hesitated. Clearly, there was some lingering hostility. "I'm still really miffed at him for that rotten trick he pulled on me. I intended to kick him out. After all, it's *my* apartment . . ." Korngold smiled tolerantly at Arpie's use of possessive pronouns. The railroad flat was *his* property. The load of grief was community property. Not, What should *I* do? and give someone else the choice of kindly offering to help. But, What should *we* do? . . . "When he came back, that night," Arpie went on with a shrug, "I don't know. I just couldn't do it."

"That was very decent of you," said Korngold, marveling at how much Arpie was able to endure. "You behaved like a genuine friend."

"I've had such rotten luck with friends." A tear ran down Arpie's cheek. "I've even tried to buy friendship," he said, farting gently.

"Well, I hope that you won't kick him out, Arpie. Try to keep your eye on him for a few more days, and if he doesn't come around, we'll have to take further steps." As Arpie left, Korngold opened a window and fanned the air with a folder from his desk. Then he went back to his desk and picked up the phone.

Arpie did not throw Nick out. Quite frankly, he did not know what to do with him. Dabbler and Pilar withdrew from Nick, growling and hissing at him if he came near; refusing even to eat when Nick put out their food. So Arpie had to take over feeding them. Nick was listless and indifferent. He even began to smell. Eventually, both animals escaped out of an open window and never returned.

After several episodes of unexplained absences away from the flat and his job, Nick disappeared before Dr. Korngold was able to do anything for him. Alone in the flat, Arpie was itching and scratching more than usual.

By chance, Arpie ran into Brewster again as he was leaving the lobby of Korngold's building. Brewster stifled a groan. He wondered whether it ever occurred to Arpie that a guy leaving a shrink's office might have problems of his own and therefore not be in the most receptive frame of mind for others' woes. He was about to brush past with a curt and wordless nod when he caught the depth of Arpie's agitation. Still distraught over the altercation with Nick, Arpie's anxiety was now intensified by his disappearance. He told Brewster about Nick's nasty prank, and that he had told him to get out. Despite the shabby treatment Nick dumped on him, Arpie felt that he had been at fault for driving Nick away. Now he was sure Nick had been attacked by a vampire in the Ramble.

The guy was so abject that Brewster could not help feeling sorry for him. He had no idea of what might have happened to Nick, but he clapped Arpie on the shoulder reassuringly and told him that if Nick had been attacked by a vampire, Batman would no doubt get to the bottom of it. With that, he urged Arpie not to be late for his appointment as Dr. Korngold had a lot on his mind and might be unavailable if he thought Arpie was not coming.

Arpie turned away abruptly and hugging his guilt ran to the elevator. Brewster watched as the elevator doors closed off the anxiety that smudged his own pure sense of loss for Guinevere.

Nick felt inexplicably drawn to the Ramble in the vicinity of the Belvedere. The breeze felt cool against his skin, washing away the swampy heat of the flat and the prickly drilling of bedbugs. A few restless chirps from crickets announced the end of day. City and day crumbled and scattered through some rustling in the undergrowth alongside the paths, an occasional snapping twig, a splash in the Gill, the faint trickling of the spring that feeds it, or its cascade as it plunged into the Ravine and down to the Lake.

Faintly at first, rising out of the random night-sounds, he thought he heard wisps of a ghostly clarinet, as in an echo chamber, randomly swelling and fading like the breezes. It was the Adagio from Mozart's concerto... No, wait! *Was* it the Adagio? or was it the Larghetto from the clarinet quintet? The themes were so similar. Without accompaniment and the blur of echoes, mightn't one be mistaken one for the other? Which was it? The path resonated in ebony. Glinting metal-rimmed finger-holes winked in the shadows, looking like leaves reflecting the lamps lighting the paths. The dilating bell of the instrument opened up ahead... pulling him in...

Oh! It was the Vestibule of the *Inferno*... and this must be the

Wood of Error. It would be the prelude-opera to a cycle of nine operas each representing a ring of Hell. Beyond, the path spiraled down into the depths. Yes! the spiral broken into scenes, like landings in a staircase. The lighting design would let it be seen vividly, or recede into the background. Think of the possibilities for chorus and soloists! What are those dark figures moving in the shadows, over there? How the souls of the damned moan from the depths . . . They drown out Mozart. Nick giggled. He would trump *The Ring of the Nibelungs* with *The Rings of the Inferno*! The performance would be spread out over ten nights instead of four! Eat your heart out, Wagner . . .

And there in the shadows stood Virgil to guide him . . . Mozart's blurred melody rose again, closer than ever. He was not aware that, as he felt along this dark corridor of sublime melody for its true identity, the path behind him was collapsing.

36.

THAT SAME NIGHT, BATMAN HOVERED in the shadows near the place where he had first seen the Unidentified Floating Head. He thought that if something had happened to Nick in the Ramble, it might in some way be connected to the appearances of the Head. He had timed his arrival to coincide with the previous encounter, hoping that he would meet her again. This time, he told himself, the outcome would be different. As he waited between hope that she would appear and anxiety that she would not, his eye caught a flicker of light through the trees and shrubbery. Puzzled that its glow seemed more diffuse than before, he was sure that it had to be hers. No longer willing to dawdle behind the possibility of what he might do, he was about to show himself when a shadow nearby exploded from the shrubbery and swallowed her up. It was at her throat before she was able to cry out.

Batman sprang into action, overtaking the vampire at the woman's throat in seconds. He seized him by the shoulder. But firm as grip was, he got more cloak than shoulder, which the vampire snapped out of his grasp. Naked and surprisingly slender under its top hat and opera cloak, the vampire reared up and with unexpected strength flung Batman violently against a neighboring tree. Startled by the commotion, several men concealed in the shrubbery jumped onto the lighted path. One chose the better part of valor and ran off, while others stared indecisively at the flurry of capes. Within moments, other pedestrians clustered around the observers, alarmed and wide-eyed. With the courage of numbers some of the men cautiously approached the strugglers. Agitated voices swept away into the distance, crying for help. Realizing that further intervention was at hand and his attack had been thwarted, the vampire, too, fled the scene flashing skin and cloak. Batman paused only long enough to see that the victim was conscious. A few drops of blood oozed from the wound on her throat and stained her headscarf but it did not look life threatening. She saw his concern for her and did not pull away. In the instant Batman saw that she was not seriously injured and trusted the gathering onlookers to see that she was properly attended until the police came, he turned and pursued the vampire.

Dr. Korngold was surprised to find Brewster sitting on the floor outside his office with his back against the door, waiting for him. Grimly resigned, Korngold opened the door for him. He got up, went in without a word and plopped his tall frame into the Ergonomic chair. Korngold eyed him from the doorway. Brewster, too, was given to patrolling the Ramble at night, still searching ostensibly for his lost Guinevere. Korngold was trying to gauge his mood. Becoming aware of Korngold's hesitation, Brewster turned his head and looked directly at him as if he would ask, Well?

Korngold turned and closed the door softly. Averting his gaze, he walked to his desk, sat down behind it, fiddled with the pipe rack on his desk, picked up a pen instead and opened a notepad. Only then did he look directly into Brewster's eyes.

"Well," he said inertly, "what've you been up to?"

Brewster sat up straight. He drew out the silence, wondering what to make of Korngold's funk. After waiting several minutes for Brewster to begin, Korngold dropped the pen on his desk and folded his hands over his belly with his elbows resting on the arms of his chair.

At last Brewster spoke. "What would they say, those 'Gentlemen' who lobbied for a park back in the day, who wanted to create a place where the masses could escape the grid-lock of crowded tenements and enjoy exercise in pure air, a place for healthful exercise and relaxation, an opportunity for physical and mental development, an engine to generate good morals into the atmosphere of the city? What would they say if they could see what goes on there these days?"

"These days," said Korngold drily, "they have you to patrol the Ramble and instill good morals and good order in heroic comic book form." Korngold continued to look directly into Brewster's eyes. They say, he thought, the eyes are the windows of the soul. He was still puzzled by the blankness he had noticed when Brewster had first come to him as a teenager. Due no doubt to the childhood myopia he had never outgrown. They were improbably flat and expressionless in someone so imaginative. A clever person can master his facial expression. But the eyes. They usually give it all away. Except for Brewster. Had he learned some trick that allowed him to conceal what they took in and what they shut out? Maybe it had something to do with the lenses prescribed by Dr. Cacamati? For a moment he even toyed with the absurd notion that his contact lenses had some kind of nanotechnology that enabled Brewster to modulate their opacity at will . . .

Whatever and however it may be, whoever lies behind those eyes sees out more than anyone sees in. Like sitting in a room with a witness looking through a glass that reveals nothing behind it. Well, maybe not quite. With the eyes, you sometimes you catch a shadow of smile, a flicker of irony. He was rattled by the unknowable in Brewster's expression. Was he holding something back, or was it just some residue of his own guilt that Korngold saw as suppressed purpose there?

His mind had been drifting in these thoughts as Brewster had begun to tell him about last night's encounter with the Unidentified Floating Head and the vampire. How he had made up his mind to overcome his hesitation and confront the mysterious woman directly—

Korngold's mind instantly snapped back into focus.

Brewster continued without reacting to Korngold's demeanor, describing how he had been thwarted by the sudden appearance of the vampire, and how he had been surprised by the vampire's unexpected strength and agility.

"He flicked me off like a mosquito. The guy really was naked, except for his cape and top hat. Like Wagehalsen! But almost a hundred and fifty years have passed. How could there be such a coincidence?"

Korngold's eyes had grown almost as round as the lenses in his glasses as Brewster's story sank in.

Earlier in the day, Korngold had been half hoping that Brewster would not keep the appointment scheduled for that afternoon. He was in no mood for Brewster's warmed over comic book hero and had been turning over in his mind how he might cancel the session. He was mired in guilt at having betrayed his profession, his wife, and his patient. Yet he felt powerless against his burning desire for her. The more he berated himself, the more he ached to hold Jennifer in his arms. His self-reproach sounded almost comically absurd when he thought of how far their relationship had so drastically compromised the patient-therapist distance. *Distance!* He wanted nothing more than to be as close to her as possible. He found separation from her unbearable. He could not untangle his feelings about the seductive vampire from the stages of therapy.

Classical psychoanalysis assumed that the transference, whereby the patient displaces emotions from appropriate relationships outside therapy to the analyst, if it occurred at all, would take place at a later stage in the therapy. It further recognized the possibility that a therapist might experience a countertransference. Bluntly put, the patient might fall in love with the therapist, and he, in turn, might fall in love with the patient, and the therapist should be alert for any hint of such an event and handle it appropriately. Shouldn't he, then, just take that to account for the way he felt about Jennifer rather than the lame excuse that it was the irresistible lure of the vampire? Surely he was far enough above such weak-mindedness to accept responsibility for his actions.

He had been brooding over these disturbing feelings when a contact at the hospital had telephoned to tell him that Jennifer had been attacked in the Ramble. Alarmed, he dropped the phone back onto its receiver without waiting for details or bothering to notify Brewster that he would be unable to keep his appointment, and abruptly left his office. Only when he arrived at the hospital did he learn that Jennifer had indeed been treated at the ER, that the wound being superficial she had already been discharged. He was deeply agitated that she had again exposed herself to the dangers of the Ramble at night and left the hospital grumbling to himself that he would not allow her to do so again.

Korngold's agitation over the news of the attack on Jennifer and his chagrin at discovering that he had missed her at the ER dispelled that morning's binge of self-reproach along with any thought of Brewster. And there he was, lying in wait just so he could rattle his closet. He had suspected Brewster's involvement in, had even thought Brewster was somehow responsible for, the attack on Jennifer. But that Batman had instead intervened in the attack by the real vampire and prevented worse injury to her! If in fact Brewster's version of the events could be believed. Brewster was not, after all, above stretching the truth.

He would, of course, verify the facts with Jennifer. He had tried to avoid facing the identity of the UFH. He thought it was too hokey, too spooky to be taken seriously. But of course it was Jennifer. The attempt to divert attention from her shining white hair with a headscarf . . . It had to be her. And she would shortly be able to confirm or deny the truth of Brewster's story. The delay in starting Brewster's session had brought them perilously close to Jennifer's appointment. He looked at the clock on his desk.

"We'll have to pick this up next time," he said. "In the meantime, Batman shouldn't be making any more forays into the Ramble. He's been endangering himself and others. He needn't be reminded that his appearance in public created all that fuss over the Batmobile four years ago. Then there was the flap over subway surfing with a policeman drawing his gun. And now this latest attack in the Ramble. Everywhere he goes he creates more disturbances than any one person ought to."

Brewster got up and left without a word.

Batman had no intention of following Dr. Korngold's advice against forays into the Ramble. Later that night, he emerged in the park through a service tunnel near the Naturalist's Gate. He absently noted the lamppost numbers that indicated he was headed downtown, #7787, #7613, #7568 . . . Even in the hard, heard day, the Ramble was deep enough to blunt the edges of the city. Entering the park at night was like a sudden release from one of those harrowing chambers in adventure stories, all passages of escape cut off as the walls close in on the explorers trapped inside.

Now, caressed in the romantic glow of the Ramble at night—a few stars bravely piercing the fluorescent magenta pall hanging over the buildings crowded around the park, a sliver moon barely pricking the dark skin of the Lake, a cool breeze gently probing the warm, moist recesses between the hulking knees of rock outcroppings—Batman pondered that, among the desperate souls escaping the crush and grind of the city, some were so warped and befouled that instead of being rejuvenated by the purer atmosphere, they polluted it. Compressed in deadening routine and fumes, vermin infested buildings and garbage in the glare of day, they found no better release than to spew out vandalism and muggings into the serenity of this place under the cloak of night.

But if there was one place in the city where he had any hope, however fleeting, of finding Guinevere again . . . If only striking down the vampire would at once lift his mark from the place. But no, it was not the vampire who infested the city. Infestation generated the vampire, and that elusive arch-predator haunted the park. Nevertheless, the search for Guinevere was bound up with the destruction of the vampire. Perhaps by destroying it, Guinevere would be recovered and returned to him. If only it could be as in the movies, where striking the vampire lifted his curse from his victims. But the reality was that the vampire had transformed the confinement of day into the menace of night, as if a genie imprisoned in his bottle had vowed to enrich whoever released him. Only, after centuries of bitter waiting for a deliverance that did not come, benevolence soured into venomous rage he would vent on anyone so unlucky as to set him free. Mortal patience running on a shorter string, a mere childhood of growing up in the city was enough to make one snap.

Or was it all in the genes? Batman thought of the bat's sinister reputation which Bob Kane exploited as the emblem most likely to strike terror into the craven hearts of criminals. But fear, like any fad, can be worn by anybody. Even today, people raised in an atmosphere of scientific knowledge, clothe their fears in ignorance as profound as all the superstitious twaddle once imagined by visionaries and reinforced by supposedly learned men. Villainy these days has evolved into a new dynamic phase. The city stiffened the spines of the hoodlums who survived it. The trouble with objects of fear these days is that they are likelier to terrify ordinary, mostly law-abiding people than crooks. Maybe that is because they have more to lose? Or maybe deteriorating morality made it harder than ever to draw a line between the resolve of the one doing good and the one doing evil. Batman's mere presence would appear sinister to anyone who was not inclined to laugh.

But Batman hoped that no one would need rescuing that night. Once again waiting for the UFH, he was sure that she might be the link to Guinevere he had been hoping for. To date, either his timing had been off, or she was leery of him, or the vampire attacked. Like Batman, she, too, was searching. But for what? Infected by the vampire virus, might she be trolling for victims? Was that naked man in cape and top hat, the one that attacked her on the previous night, a nut case or the arch-vampire recruiting converts? Could he have some way of dominating his victims, even the woman known as the Unidentified

The Womb of Uncreated Night

Floating Head, by casting a hypnotic spell? Might he be creating a harem, like Dracula in his castle? These and other absurd ideas wandered in Batman's thoughts. More likely that guy was a lunatic in a bizarre get-up spreading a modern plague through the park . . .

And the Unidentified Floating Head? Whoever she was, the UHF seemed benign and clearly needed help in warding off her attacker. But if she had been infected with the virus, what kind of help beyond that could he offer? Like drive a stake through her heart and cut off her head? As he stood in the shadows weighing these troubling thoughts, he kept his eyes on the lights that winked and bobbed among the trees swaying in the breeze like glowing insects caught in the tracery of their branches. As he watched, one of the lights floated free in the breeze and drifted into the darkness around a burned out lamp. For a moment, Batman thought he could make out a kind of afterglow among the unlit shrubbery, then lost sight of it. He eagerly scanned the area around the spot where the glow had disappeared. He thought that he detected a faint silvery mist, but it scattered in the breeze. He was startled when the UFH settled beside him without so much as a premonitory rustle.

The whiteness of the woman's hair was almost translucent in the haze of reflected light sifting through the mesh of branches. Her head was haloed by a gauzy headscarf. Without a word, she put her hand in his. Batman was stunned. He was so overcome at having at last made contact with this haunting apparition that he was speechless. While he had been pondering how he might help this strange but strangely appealing young woman, his thoughts had not progressed beyond the "Um . . ." or "Er . . ." of the week before. Her face was all the paler for her dark dress, and her eyes faintly glimmered in the ambient light. But her other features were smudges against chalk. Almost in a daze, he allowed this wraith to lead him to a bench near the lamppost that had gone dark. Inanely, he noticed it was #7410, near 74th Street.

They sat in silence, the UFH staring out at the dark waters of the Lake visible through the trees, Batman looking alternately at her and then at their surroundings. He noticed that the few pedestrians in

- 519 -

the vicinity kept their distance from the dark patch they sat in. What a spectacle he and his companion would have made to them! Here sat this hulking bat about to canoodle with a mere slip of a girl in a secluded spot ideal for making out!

Tiring of uncertainty, Batman turned to the Head again and spoke. "You know it's dangerous to be out here with a vampire on the prowl, don't you." She turned her face to him. Even the darkest places in the incandescent city nevertheless glow with incidental light. No longer staring at lights bobbing in the trees, Batman's eyes adjusted to the deeper dark in which they sat. He had not really asked a question, and he had not meant to sound like Korngold. But it was an opening. He could see by the light reflecting off the Lake that she was smiling.

"You sound like my therapist," she said.

The ears perched upright atop Batman's hood always appeared vigilant. Now they almost quivered with alertness.

"I suppose even a Floating Head needs someone to help find its mooring," said Batman, laughing.

"Especially when it's floating free in an unremembered past," added the Head dreamily. "I've forgotten an important part of my past."

"And you think," said Batman becoming serious again, "that ignoring your therapist's warning about exposing yourself to the dangers of the Ramble will help restore your memory?"

"Danger . . . it makes the senses come alive." She said this with such conviction that Batman could not make out whether she sounded defiant or defensive. He waited for her to say more. "Something in me," she said hesitantly, "has been lulled into forgetfulness . . . by something near here. I've been trying to find it ever since."

"And you think whatever happened took place here?"

She nodded. "I'm told that I was attacked nearby. I woke up in the hospital not knowing who I was, and this kind therapist offered to help me remember."

Batman clutched the edge of the bench.

Sensing his tenseness, the Head asked, "Is something wrong?"

The Womb of Uncreated Night

Batman realized that he was endangering the fragile rapport between them and willed himself to relax.

"Sorry. It's nothing. Just a passing twitch. You were saying?"

"Since he was the first—actually, the only—one who took an interest in me," she said dreamily, "well, we've gotten pretty close. When he and I are alone together, I feel so complete that the past doesn't matter. But afterwards... There's still this awful, gnawing emptiness. I came back here hoping something would happen, and then I would start remembering." She went on with her story, repeating the fears she had shared with the therapist. Batman listening uneasily thought of the woman that had passed by in the lobby of Korngold's apartment building. Surely, it was her? And it was clear from the warmth with which she spoke of him, that they shared more than the usual patient-therapist relationship. Just *how* close? he wondered with a suppressed shudder.

"And your . . . therapist? Does he approve of your experiment in trying to remember?" he asked, hoping, dreading that she would let his name slip.

"Ah," said the Head, looking away to the Lake and falling silent. They sat so for several minutes, until Batman thought that their tête-a-tête had ended.

But she spoke again. "We talk, he and I, about my innermost qualms . . . But, no. He doesn't approve of my coming here."

She fell into silence again. "Do you . . . talk about other things?" said Batman to keep her talking about the therapist.

"Mostly he gives me a lot of support and . . . comfort. We work on my gaining enough confidence to accept who I was and may yet become. He's shown me that both are who I am now."

"But after your recent encounter with the vampire, aren't you being overconfident by exposing yourself to the risk of another attack?"

The Head hesitated. When she spoke, her voice was curiously veiled. "I can't help it. Some vital part of me is here. Maybe it would be a good thing if it did happen again," she said looking directly at Batman, "and no one interfered? Maybe that's what I'm hoping for."

He tensed again but said nothing. "I mean," she laughed, "if the shock of an attack like the one you fought off last night caused my amnesia in the first place, then mightn't another one jog my memory back?"

Batman leaned against the backrest of the bench. So, who she is now and who she may yet become are not who she was. And it's the past she really wants. Her therapy, her new confidence, they were not enough to stop this dangerous search. Batman let her question hang in the dark light. He did not trust the hair-of-the-dog cure. But what could he say? Restoring someone's memory was not the kind of help he could offer.

"Besides," she added with a chuckle, "with someone like you looking out for me, a big, strong escort in armor . . ." she stroked, almost caressing, the seamless joinery of Batman's hood to the powerful neck and shoulders, admiring its flexible toughness, "I'll bet no vampire could bite through that."

It was several days before Brewster could bring himself to face Korngold again. When Korngold wondered why he had not kept his appointments, Brewster told him about his new encounter with the Head and their conversation about her unidentified therapist as if it had nothing to do with the therapist's question. Korngold, of course, was disturbed and alarmed, not only by the dangers to both Brewster and Jennifer, but also to his professional conduct. If at this point Brewster did not know, or at least suspect, that he and Jennifer shared the same, mysterious therapist, he was not as bright as Korngold was sure he was. Further than that, he could not allow his conscious thoughts to go . . .

37.

KORNGOLD WAS TRYING TO WORK in his office late on the night following the unsettling session in which Brewster had told him about his latest adventure in the Ramble. He had suspected all along that Unidentified Floating Head could only be Jennifer. But the verification of his suspicion did not give him any satisfaction. There was nothing in Brewster's report to suggest that she knew he was Batman. But she had allowed Batman to approach her, and spoken openly about her relationship with her therapist!

He threw down the notes he had been reviewing, got up from the desk and stared out the window at the checkered squares of light in the buildings across 78th Street. Over their irregular rooflines he could see headlights snaking along FDR Drive and twinkling across the Triborough Bridge, back-lighted and in shadow like pop-up pasteboard turrets of some fantastic castle in a children's book. The arched windows across the top of one of the buildings resembled a machicolated gallery. He laughed ruefully at the thought of residents, imaging themselves under siege, throwing down stones and pouring boiling oil over the pedestrians on the street below. He scarcely heard the timid knock at his office door.

Over the years Korngold had come to recognize a whole range of the characteristic ways his patients knocked. He could tell who the knocker was just by the way he or she knocked, like a trained musician can recognize another by the way the instrument is plucked, struck, scraped, or blown. Some knocks have the peremptory quality of demanding that you drop everything and get to the door this instant. Others politely announce themselves and patiently wait for you to get around to answering at your convenience. This one had a tantalizing, almost effeminate, sound. He could not ignore the second faint knocking, not because he pretended not to hear it, but because its very timidity annoyed him. It sounded as if someone wanted Korngold to know that he was there, asking to be let in, but didn't want to disturb him. He had little doubt as to who that someone was. But how in the world can you get anyone's attention without disturbing him? And how the devil did he get into the building at this hour? If that fool of a doorman was drunk again . . .

Korngold cursed under his breath and strode over to the door in irritation. This had better be important! He threw open the door so violently that Arpie fell back from it just as he was about to knock a third time. Korngold was equally startled to see the state he was in. He looked awful, as if he had been wandering in a wilderness for days. He stared at Korngold as if he was not sure he recognized him. His face was convulsed with panic. His hair was disheveled, his clothes were torn and dirty, and there was a bloody smudge at his collar. His feet were bare and caked with dirt. Doctor and patient stood as if transfixed by the sight of each other, until Korngold shook away the shock. On the verge of collapse, Arpie swayed unsteadily. Korngold's brittle irritation crumbled in compassion. He stepped quickly out into the hall, took him gently by the arm to steady him, and ushered him into the office.

"Here," said Korngold solicitously, "sit down. Tell me what's happened. Where have you been? How did you get into this state?"

Arpie hung his head, ashamed, working his mouth, struggling to control the organs of speech.

"There, there," said Korngold kindly, looking closely at the triangular scab on Arpie's neck. "Take your time."

The Womb of Uncreated Night

Arpie spoke haltingly, his voice quivering. "I was—I was attacked. In Central Park. The Ramble."

"Attacked," said Korngold. "When? You've been missing for nearly a week."

"I've been hiding," said Arpie, looking anxiously at the window as if someone might be peering in at him. Korngold followed his eyes, a crawling sensation in his scalp.

"Hiding? From whom? From the mugger? Could you identify him?"

"Yes—No. It was too dark. But he beat me up and took my money. There wasn't much. A few dollars. Then . . . then . . . He bit my neck and drank my blood!" Tears welled up in Arpie's eyes and streaked the dirt on his cheeks.

"And did you," asked Korngold, clinical curiosity overcoming revulsion, "did you drink his?"

Arpie shuddered. He bit his lips. He could not look up at Korngold. He nodded.

Korngold felt the hair at the back of his head rise. He stared at Arpie. A vampire who beat up and robbed his victims before drinking their blood, attacking strollers in the Ramble! "And you were hiding from him?"

"I was afraid even to go back to my apartment," gulped Arpie, "because I think he knows where I live. I've been living on the streets, sleeping in cardboard boxes and—and—"

"But how could he know where you live?"

"There's a whole network of them . . . in the Ramble . . . they access my head . . ."

Hysteria, thought Korngold. Vampire-hackers who could access your head? He resisted an inane temptation to ask him what his access code was. Arpie was becoming incoherent, confusing vampires and cyberspace.

"What were you doing in the park in the first place?" Korngold meant to show concern. But it sounded like reproach. Arpie hung his head even lower.

"I was looking for—Nick," he mumbled.

Korngold opened his mouth to speak, but closed it again. He was stunned by the futility of it all. He tried a different tack. "What about—food," he said at last. If Buckyballs were right, Arpie had undoubtedly been infected by the mysterious virus. How would that have affected his . . . appetite? "After the encounter in the Ramble, did you eat . . . or drink anything . . . ?"

"I saw a man on the street. Looked like someone hit him on the head. He was bleeding. Going through garbage. I just stood there and looked at him. He found some half-eaten sandwich. He was going to eat it. He saw me. He offered a piece to me. I—I looked at his bloody head. Couldn't. Couldn't." And Arpie buried his face in his hands. Korngold waited. There would be more. Then Arpie looked up at him with such a pitiful expression that his heart turned over.

"There were others."

"Other men living on the streets, eating garbage? Yes. There are too many homeless people out there."

"No," said Arpie. "I mean. Yes, there are. But that's not what I meant. There were others. In the park. Hunting. They wanted me to join them. They called me."

"By name? They knew who you were?" The idea startled Korngold. But Arpie looked puzzled.

"No. They didn't call my name. It was like . . . they could call in my head. I hid from them and watched."

"How many were there?" Korngold asked uneasily. A colony of vampires swarming in the Ramble? Where would they hide during the day?

"I don't know. Five. Six . . . ? They were hiding, too. They sort of . . . merged into the shadows of the rocks and in the shrubbery. A couple of them even sat in the lower branches of trees. Like vultures. And there was something else . . . someone, a force? . . . somehow controlling them." Arpie shuddered. "I felt it reach me where I was hiding. It called me, pulled at me, too. But it wasn't like the call from those I could see. It seemed to come through the air . . ."

The Womb of Uncreated Night

Pheromones? wondered Korngold, beginning to feel lightheaded and foolish. Brewster as Batman had visited the same area on several occasions, yet he never reported anything like an infestation. Arpie was given to exaggeration. Or perhaps Brewster just was not tuned in?

Arpie swallowed hard. His voice had grown hoarse. Korngold poured out some water from the carafe he kept on his desk and pushed the glass toward Arpie. Arpie hesitated, but gently urged by Korngold, began to drink as if it were prescribed medicine. Almost at once he began to gag and choke, spewing a little of the water over a corner of the desk. Korngold sharply sucked in his breath through clenched teeth, strode to the bathroom adjoining the office. He carefully washed his hands and put on a pair of surgical gloves. Then he brought back a handful of paper towels. He mopped up the mess on his desk with several, and gave a few to Arpie to wipe himself off. Arpie took them, and sat there staring at them as if they were another dubious prescription. He coughed a few times.

Seeing that Arpie was drifting away, Korngold urged him to continue his story.

"They hid in the trees and shadows until a lone pedestrian came by. Then they swooped down on their victim. I saw them bite his neck and drink his blood." Arpie became agitated and spoke more rapidly. "I—I wanted to do it, too. But I couldn't. Once, one of them turned and looked at the spot I was hiding in. It was as if he could see me. He beckoned. He was drinking blood from the throat of some woman in jogging clothes and wanted me to come and drink it with him." Arpie shuddered. "I went over to him. He pushed the others, hissing, away from the woman and smiled at me, inviting me to drink the woman's blood. It was coming from her neck. I wanted to drink it. It was calling me, too. Pulling at me. I started to drink some of it. It was intoxicating. But it made me gag and I threw up." He bowed his head in his hands and his body shook. "Another time, I was near Vista Rock. And that Other presence was stronger than ever. I never saw it. But it kept pulling at me. From the Belvedere."

"From the Belvedere!" Korngold flashed back on the night Guinevere disappeared . . . and Wagehalsen's journal. If Arpie's mind was playing tricks, wasn't it curious that they centered on the Belvedere!

"Yes," continued Arpie. "The Belvedere. Somewhere, deep, deep inside. Some one, some *thing* is there. I stood across the pond. You know, near the theater. The Delacorte. And stared at it until I went all cold and hollow inside. I couldn't tell if the pond was pulling me into it or I was pulling the pond into me. I was in the water up to my neck. Somewhere, underneath, like an undertow . . . Then someone on the other side hollered at me. I realized where I was and almost drowned trying to claw my way out." When he looked up at Korngold, again, his eyes were horribly red.

"Oh, Dr. Korngold! Help me. I don't want to kill myself! I don't want to be a vampire!" He burst into tears.

Korngold walked quickly over to the air conditioning unit, turned it on high, and opened a window. The night air was suffocating. It was like diving into a warm, sweaty, acrid, fetid smog that stung his eyes and clogged up his nose. But it offered a momentary respite from Arpie's vapors. He did not know quite how to begin to tell him about Buckyballs' vampire virus. If Bucky was right, then Arpie's abstinence would eventually cure him of this affliction. But Arpie needed reassurance. He closed the window but left the air conditioner on high.

"Now, now, Arpie. You don't have to do or be anything you don't want to. It may not be as bad as you think." Seeing the disbelief in Arpie's face, he quickly added, "Yes. It's bad enough—pretty bad, in fact. But listen to me! You can beat this thing."

Arpie looked incredulous. He had come to this man for help, and here he was sounding like Pangloss in the best of all possible worlds. Korngold saw the effect he was having, and hastened to explain.

"Listen to me. This vampire thing. You've contracted a virus. It's transmitted in the bite of someone who was similarly bitten and infected. It creates a craving for blood. But unless it reaches a certain concentration, its effect is only temporary. That's why you were drawn by this Other into the pond. Its power over you is only temporary. Unless you're infused with enough of the virus to convert you. But temporary illnesses can be so severe and traumatic that you feel as if you want to die. The fact that it makes you sick shows that your body is trying to throw off its influence. Your will, like your body, must continue to resist. By resisting his power as far as you have, you've done a remarkable and brave thing. If you can hold out a little longer, you'll get stronger. I'm sure the crisis has already passed. Go back to your apartment and get cleaned up. Get some rest. Try to eat something. I don't think that your mugger will go there looking for you." A disturbing succession of images flashed through Korngold's mind. In his present state, Arpie might let this vampire thing get the better of him even in the prosaic buffer of his own place. Do himself an injury before the effects of this mania, or whatever it was, wore off. He would need an anchor. "Do you have a crucifix? Get one. If you can bear to wear it, that should help strengthen your resistance. You've already been very strong."

"It wasn't strength," said Arpie miserably. "It was disgust. Revulsion." Arpie farted softly and got up to leave.

"Try to hold out a little longer. Come back and see me tomorrow," he pulled his calendar toward him, "around 3 p.m. But call me anytime if things get too heavy for you. We'll talk again."

Arpie closed the door as timidly as he had knocked on it. Korngold sat for a moment, wondering if Arpie had the endurance to hold out until the crisis in his blood had passed. Then he got up and opened the window to let in more of the thick air.

Later that night, Arpie moped restlessly about his flat clutching a pair of toothpicks. He did not realize that he had fashioned a crucifix out of them. He tried to sleep, but each time he drifted off, such disturbing images came into his head that he finally got up. He fussed about the flat, moving objects—books, furniture—as if to study the effect, then moving them back to where they had been. Shuffling papers, rummaging through closets. Nothing ran out his string of agitation.

Korngold had been surprised when, looking for Buckyballs in his lab, he was directed to the morgue. He was even more surprised to find the infectious disease specialist bent over a corpse into which he had stuck a hypodermic syringe. He jerked up as Korngold came through the door.

"Hey, look who's here!" Buckyballs called out jovially, hastily brushing cigarette ash off the body. "C'mon in. What brings you down to *Malebolge*?"

"It *is* cold enough. I was surprised when your assistant told me I'd find you down here. Have you taken over as medical examiner?"

"Not quite," smirked Buckyballs, trying not to look sinister at being caught standing over a corpse with a hypodermic. "Actually," he said, in answer to the question on Korngold's face, "I wanted to examine this guy because he'd been brought into the hospital with massive blood loss. But he died and was moved down here before I was able to get a sample of his blood."

"Ah," said Korngold, "you think he may be a victim of the *buckyvirus*?"

"Ah, indeed," said Buckyballs, packing up the syringe in his case. "But you didn't come looking for me to discuss a corpse?"

"No. I came to see you about a patient—"

"Not young Mr. Wainwright!" said Buckyballs genuinely surprised.

"No, no. I don't think you know this one," said Korngold. Buckyballs nodded and took his arm.

"Come on, let's go up to my office. Your lips are turning blue."

They rode up in the staff elevator in silence. When they were seated in Buckyballs' office, Korngold told him about Arpie's late night visit. He unfolded the entire story together with his concern that the poor, young fellow had almost certainly picked up the virus and showed the first signs of blood-craving. Buckyballs had not spoken as he listened to the story, but nodded in agreement at the mention of a probable infection. He was concerned.

"Well," he said at last, "we'll have to have him come in to get tested. Just to be sure. But if he has been infected, I'm afraid there's not much that we can do for him at present."

Late that night, the bodies of Leon Barvim and Arpie Fairfield were found lying face down a few feet apart in mud at the north end of the Lake. Both were drained of blood.

38.

So, brooded Korngold in his office, poor Arpie, too, has fallen victim to this damned virus! "What next?" he said aloud to himself.

As if in answer, Wagehalsen perched at the window and rapped on the pane. Korngold groaned. He walked to the window and stared at the image. Finally, he threw up the sash. "You again!"

"My dear Herr Doktor!" said Wagehalsen jovially, and peering into the room. "Here we are again! Have you grown tired of the chaos surrounding you and disturbing your . . . equilibrium?"

"How ironic! Like as not, *you* are the cause of the chaos, not the cure. How could a creature without a soul understand that the lows of emotional turmoil are more than compensated for by exhilarating highs?"

"What you say sounds curiously like the lunatic who refuses his medication because it dulls his senses," Wagehalsen shot back. "As for the matter of soul, how can an alienist, a man science, believe in so unscientific a thing as the soul?"

"Oh, I didn't mean soul in the theological sense." Korngold cocked his head and paused reflectively. "There is a certain essence that distinguishes the living from the non-living. And where it came from or how it works, I suppose a religious person would call that 'soul.'"

"Perhaps Moses had the right idea, that God breathed into dust and gave it life?"

"A religious person would think so. He would also say that only humans received that breath. Moses never said that God breathed his breath into animals as well."

"Ah, so that would support Descartes' argument that only human beings have feelings, and that other creatures are merely mechanical?"

"That's the argument. But all available evidence about that indefinable essence that distinguishes living animals from other forms of existence indicates that Descartes' claim is too narrow. Animals other than man do show intelligence, reasoning, and emotions. Not as sophisticated as those of humans, to be sure. But then our science so far lacks evidence to substantiate anything more. And as long as it remains elusive, superstitious folks will always turn to divine origin and deny anything remotely like their precious soul to lower animals. How could they otherwise justify their callousness toward them? Hundreds of years after establishing that the earth is not the center of creation, religious zealots still can't give up the idea that humans are a special creation of God, that their 'souls' are unique. But how could you understand, since you're no longer human—?"

"But I *am* human. Even a revenant has the vestiges of humanity clinging to him. I can converse, share your thoughts, feel emotions . . . Is any other animal capable of having rational discourse or sharing human relationships on such a level? If we share such common traits, why would you deny that I am human?"

"What you have are the dregs of death and decay." Korngold paused. "If my colleague, Dr. Buckyballs is right and vampirism is a disease caused by a virus, then it has drained away your human part and left behind an animated husk. It breathes and walks and talks like a human. But it's not."

"So, you are saying that vampires are neither alive nor dead?"

"The *human* you that lived is dead. What remains is a kind of flesh-and-blood ghost, an automaton. Perhaps death, like rot, is a matter of degree rather than kind," said Korngold, digging in his heels. "A mystic might say that death releases the soul, and that reanimating the body doesn't restore it. The body merely responds mechanically, without its unique, authentic essence. That your soul has taken off into space and flown off to its ultimate destination, wherever that is. Yet you are still animated. That is as different from true of death as your animation is from true life."

"You cannot seriously say that everyone who has a near-death experience and is revived is less human than the person who has never experienced it!"

"I am saying no such thing. *Near*-death is not death. Nor is every deadly encounter in life brought on by this virus. I am saying that the virus in your body has somehow replaced your human nature, allowing you to behave in a way no healthy human being could. Your body functions according to its purely physical characteristics, without true will."

"So much for the mystic," said Wagehalsen with a cynical smile. "And what might the practical realist say?"

"He might say that once the organic basis for life ceases to function, 'soul' is dispersed as electromagnetic energy. That the awareness of self spanning the gulf from sensation to intellect and persisting through impulse and will—all that ends in decomposition and disintegration of the body. The animating essence, like all energy, may be immortal. It can't be destroyed. But it's irreversibly dissipated. The identity it generated in a living, organic body dissipates in space.

"The vampire, existing without this energy is not truly immortal because it is not truly alive. Like a virus, its body exists at the boundary between living and nonliving organisms, a purely mechanical thing like a Golem or a robot. That is why your body's defects could be arrested but not healed. That is why you could not restore Mlle Rachel's health, for instance. Or have children. The virus apparently can maintain your physical body as long as it's not damaged, but can't repair it if it is. The blood you drink may have an effect similar to a transfusion. But eventually, even that will fail. Your 'parts' will wear out. What a mess you'll be! Ha! You probably won't even be able to stalk your victims. You'll end up, a heap of disintegrating flesh, until there's nothing left but the virus! And how long *that* will survive . . . ?" Korngold shrugged.

"But I remember who I am," protested Wagehalsen.

The Womb of Uncreated Night

"Hollow echoes of your cells. Your muscles 'remember' how to move, but they, too, will eventually 'forget' and fade away."

"But my dear Herr Doktor, look at me! I am holding together quite well for a sesquicentenarian, don't you think?"

"I'm not sure that you are anything more than fragments of nineteenth century horror stories cobbled together in my mind. Like a bad dream, where you know you're dreaming but you can't wake up." Korngold turned his head away as if to consider, "Only I seem to be wide awake. I try to shake these fragments out of my mind—"

"And can one do that?"

Korngold turned back to face Wagehalsen. "The mind can be recharged and restored with music, especially, and with art and literature, things that dispel the vapors of night. How could you understand, being yourself one of those vapors?"

"Interesting, that you are consoled by the very media that you suggested may have generated your 'bad dream' in the first place! But even I am stimulated by music, the arts, and literature!"

"I doubt that they generate nightmares in you. Recording devices also respond to such things. I doubt that a mere *device* finds either comfort or chagrin in them!"

"You are being perverse!"

"In bad dreams," said Korngold, "perversity is the order of the night. It's what makes them *bad*."

"This dissipated energy of yours," said Wagehalsen, waving aside Korngold's objections, "your 'human essence,' why could it not be regenerated somehow?"

Korngold tired of standing at the window to argue with this apparition. He sat behind his desk and leaned back thinking that he might as well be comfortable. "How could anyone take any of this seriously? It's like trying to have a rational discussion with someone in a mental institution."

Wagehalsen burst into laughter. "And which of us is the 'inducer' or 'primary case' in this mental institution?"

So, thought Korngold, pretending to be nuts to disarm the nuts who run the asylum, one goes on rationalizing with the bad dream from which he can not awaken. The ghost of an unsettling recognition brushed past his mind but flitted away before it could shape a solid thought.

"Consider," urged Wagehalsen, "what if the cells of the 'automaton' could evolve and generate this life force of yours?"

"In human evolution," said Korngold, "once a characteristic is lost, it can't be regained. Your 'human essence,' once the virus possessed you and you entered the vampire state, is gone for good and all."

"Leaving behind dying organic matter?"

"Exactly. An empty husk that disintegrates and returns its elements to the earth."

"So, if I understand you, not all organic matter has a soul, but all souls exist in organic matter. A curious circle broken by gaps through which logic may be smuggled out at will! Well, then, what becomes of this soul energy?"

"How should I know?" shrugged Korngold opening his hands.

"It's your bad dream," said Wagehalsen expecting a reply. "No? Well, let us consider. Suppose . . . suppose your 'reanimation' took place before the body had seriously decayed? Could not its animating energy be a new 'breath of life,' a 'soul'?"

"If the body has not degraded past its ability to be revived, then it is not dead. Its soul, its self, its former being still lingers in its cells. But beyond a certain indeterminate point, only a *semblance* of life returns, as when a patient is brought back from the brink of death but is brain dead. An animating force—if it were possible to instill it from outside the body—would be alien to the body it inhabited. Electric shock, for example, may stimulate the cells' regenerative powers, but it can't work beyond a certain point. That's the fault I find with the Mosaic dogma. If God breathed *his* breath into Adam, it did not come from within the matter that made up the first man's body. A true soul is integral to the body, growing out of its atoms, permeating its cells."

"Do you say that Adam was not truly human?" asked Wagehalsen in astonishment.

"Only if God is not human."

"So, either God is a human invention or man is not human! In the latter case, man, to use your own words, would also be an automaton like the Golem or a robot."

"That's just it. 'God,' like 'soul,' is only a label, a name for a phenomenon we really don't fully understand. And humans have for millennia dreamed up supernatural, mystical, metaphysical explanations for anything that can't be otherwise explained. As a human invention, God is human. Machines whether composed of organic or inorganic matter are still *mechanisms*. The very fact of human life demonstrates a level of existence beyond that of any machine."

"So far, at least. Your distinction is as rigid as Descartes' denial of feelings in animals," scoffed Wagehalsen. "We once called the animating force 'magnetism' and thought that it permeated and resided in all things. Today you speak of 'electromagnetism.' Different names for the same thing—"

"But vastly different understandings of that thing."

"And can your present understanding never change? It is 'scientific' to believe that animals, including human animals, evolve, undergo spectacular changes in physical appearance as well as intelligence. Why is it impossible to consider that the body of a revenant may undergo a similar transformation? The nature of soul becomes a part of the rational animal and vegetable web of life in which all aspects of organisms continuously evolve. And they are all part of some universal essence, soul, God, whatever label you wish to use. If it pleases you instead to call this essence electromagnetism, there is no need to quibble over the label. You are over-concerned with whether inorganic beings have 'soul.'"

It was Korngold's turn to smile cynically. "It seems to me that you are trying to slip back in through those gaps you poked in my circle. If you're saying that I'm quibbling over labels, I'd say you're trivializing the process of evolution. I object to labeling an inorganic thing as a 'being.'

Beings are sentient, conscious. Machines are not, even if they can detect sentience." He paused to reflect. "I wonder if a vampire's brain would register on an electroencephalograph. Would you mind going away just now and coming to the hospital tomorrow for a brain scan? You needn't make an appointment." He turned his back on Wagehalsen, opened a drawer in his desk and rummaged noisily through it.

"You insist that mechanical things lack consciousness, and therefore there can be no artificial intelligence?"

"That's what I'm saying."

"And this brain scan of yours. Does it register consciousness?"

"It registers the electrical patterns associated with it."

"But if it registered these electrical patterns of consciousness in my brain, you would still maintain that I lack it?"

That stopped Korngold. No, he could not very well say that. But then neither did he accept the possibility that this apparition could show up at the hospital to put the matter to the test.

"Since you may be a figment of my imagination anyway," said Korngold clutching at the clarity that kept slipping back into bad dream, "you already know that a test is useless because it could never take place." My God! Korngold realized. A figment of my imagination has no existence independent of me. It could imagine anything I can imagine. I've created a monster and lost control of it!

"If I am a figment of your imagination," said Wagehalsen, as if he had read Korngold's mind, "perhaps it is you who are in need of a brain scan!" He folded his arms in determination and returned to the point. "Perhaps artificial intelligence has not yet sufficiently evolved. Can you speak for the future?"

With his hand still in the drawer, Korngold paused and turned to face Wagehalsen again with an impish smile. "There is no future. There is only the evanescent moment."

"Fah! You can not deny I once *was* human, that I had the kind of self-awareness you speak of. If, then, I *remember* my past life, if my muscles *remember* how to move and function as well as they always have, how is that different from the state you live in? And even supposing some difference since my conversion to vampirism, why could not those 'memories' evolve into something, some *one*, you would be compelled to recognize as fully as human?"

Korngold sighed in exasperation. "Judging from your present state, I wonder what kind of self you are aware of."

Wagehalsen responded with a condescending smile at the unwitting irony and self-doubt of Korngold's remark. Korngold slammed a drawer shut and yanked open another, spilling its contents on the floor. A glimmer of light caught his eye. His hand closed on it.

This game was wearing through Korngold's ironic distance. It sounded like a rerun of Brewster's cockamamie rationalizations. How does one banish a bad dream? "This will have to do," he said as he bent to the floor to pick up a mirror lying among the scattered contents of the desk drawer, and thrust it into Wagehalsen's face. Wagehalsen recoiled with a furious snarl. "Ah, it works! If vampires have a soul," crowed Korngold triumphantly as Wagehalsen retreated out of sight beside the window frame, "why don't they cast a reflection?"

"Does God cast a reflection?" exclaimed Wagehalsen indignantly. "Where is the mirror that could hold his image? And who could hold it? No. He created humans in his image so that he could see what he might look like in corporeal form. Humans reflect him. In all our diversity, we are his mirror, imperfectly reflecting and refracting him because he had no mirror to guide him when he created us. Just so, *you are my reflection!*"

Korngold shuddered but could not reply.

"You know," continued Wagehalsen after a while in a conciliatory tone from beside the window frame, "since Dracula turned me, I have never tried to challenge his abhorrence of mirrors by looking directly into one. The Master never did, and he got very angry if one of his . . . guests . . . requested one. As with several other of his phobias, I never questioned what he told me, neither what he abhorred nor what he claimed of his powers."

"You mean that stuff about turning into a vapor so that he could pour through cracks in door frames, or being able to escape under cover of fogs he generated? I suppose you're going to claim that you can do that?"

"If you were going to ask for a demonstration, I have learned that exhibitionism has its dangers. At the very least, it is tinged with rudeness. I hope that you will not mistake reticence for impotence. But to return to the matter of reflected images, even as a boy I was never entirely convinced that what I saw in the mirror was really me. Who was that stranger looking back at me? So I was already prepared to accept this disdain for mirrors. After Dracula's tutelage, the lack of a mirror presented me with some small difficulties . . . regarding personal grooming, you understand. I had to rely on servants for sartorial presentability."

"An unkempt vampire," gibed Korngold, "unthinkable!"

The silence hung on so long that Korngold was tempted to stick his head out the window to assure himself that his phantom had indeed vanished. Just as he was about to do so, he heard the vampire's voice again.

"After all," resumed Wagehalsen, as if nothing had interrupted their discussion of machine-soul, "*Jesus—*," he uttered the name gingerly on the tip of his tongue as if reluctant to take it wholly into his mouth, "—when *he* was resurrected, would you suggest that he was," here he peered around the window frame, "a Golem?"

Startled by Wagehalsen's sudden appearance, Korngold dropped the mirror to the floor. "As to that," retorted Korngold, "reducing God to the level of a self-admiring Narcissus, and vampirism as a kind of Resurrection, might strike Christians as the foulest form of blasphemy!

"But if you want to play at blasphemy, try this: Lazarus of Bethany was dead four days when his sisters Mary and Martha reproached Jesus. He would not have died, they said, if Jesus had been there." At each mention of "Jesus," Korngold noticed the subtlest twitch in Wagehalsen's body, like the merest flicker of sudden recognition in an unfocused eye. "When Jesus," he went on, wondering whether, if he dangled the name often enough, Wagehalsen's image would, like so many pixels on a TV screen gone berserk, craze into a flurry of visual snow and drift away.

Christianity might yet be of some use. "When Jesus told them to take away the stone from the burial chamber, Martha protested that by this time the body would stink. But Jesus told Martha that it was a matter of faith. The company of Jews with them did as they were bidden. Jesus called Lazarus out of the cave bound in his grave clothes and instructed them to remove the bindings. We are not told whether they held their noses as they did so, nor what quality of life the stinking man may have had in his resurrected state."

"Should I be shocked by adolescent blasphemy?" said Wagehalsen with a chuckle.

"What I'm trying to do is shock myself," snapped Korngold, "out of this damned hallucination!"

"You still do not believe in me? It really is a matter of faith, after all, is it not, Herr Doktor."

But Korngold was on a roll. "Hah! Faith! What a stench there'll be at the last trumpet, when all that dead flesh is raised!"

"Incorruptible!" exclaimed Wagehalsen. "Do not forget that they will be raised incorruptible."

"Oh, yes! There is no deodorant like faith! Come to think of it, I'm mighty thankful that you are out there in what passes for fresh air in New York City. After a hundred and thirty years or so . . . whew!"

"What a delightfully cynical soul you have!" said Wagehalsen, chuckling. "Your mirror must positively scintillate! Dracula did have bad breath, but he was not otherwise especially foul-smelling!"

"As I am not a Christian," Korngold spread his hands and shrugged, "I neither condone nor commit blasphemy. Or in your case, what?— *anti*-blasphemy?"

"Indeed! Yet here am I. If I am but a product of your diseased imagination, as you hope, and a blasphemy, as you suggest, then your denials are futile."

Korngold shut his eyes. "Bullshit! The worst thought that enters a mind doesn't taint a person's whole being, otherwise everyone would be in a jail or a mental institution. The disease here is not the imagination, but in my inability to banish it with rational thought. Begone, you damned vapor!"

Silence. Korngold opened his eyes hopefully.

Wagehalsen's mocking face still hung there in the window. "Your spell does not work. For all your denials, even we 'mechanical' beings linger. Like ghosts! A characteristic of soul, not so? Living things rot when they die. Mechanical things crumble. Both disintegrate. Only the smell is different," said Wagehalsen in a tone of festering flesh and burrowing insects that made Korngold's skin crawl.

They stood silently for a time on opposite sides of the window. Korngold tried to busy Wagehalsen away. He turned back to picking up and sorting the contents of the drawer on the floor. The universe packed into a desk drawer.

Then, Korngold suddenly began to laugh wildly. A fictional character biting the throat of a hypothetically historical nineteenth century journalist who may have been deluded into thinking he was a true vampire? Coming after the silence, Wagehalsen was puzzled. When he inquired about the cause of the mirth, Korngold revealed what he had been thinking. Wagehalsen, too, laughed.

"Perhaps, it wasn't the fictional Dracula at all," he said, "but rather someone suggested by the legendary Dracul, and I simply borrowed the name as a generic label. Have you thought of that?

"But merely to move," Wagehalsen returned his topic as if there had been no digression from it, "is to invite 'soul.' Moses comes nearer to the nature of the divine than the fourth Gospel. In the Beginning, God *moved* over chaos. He created. Not *word*, but *movement* was first."

Korngold flung the papers back into the drawer and slammed it. "Scholars dispute the 'Beloved Apostle' authorship of that Gospel. It was probably written by someone known as 'John, the Elder,' a hundred years after—"

"Yes, yes, Herr Scholar. No doubt you are right. I do not dispute the authorship, but rather the origin of life. It should matter not to you whether the soul was breathed into dust or whether the Word was pronounced into being, since you do not believe in God. But I believe movement was first. It is the Prime Principle. Without it, there is no creation, whether of divine or mechanical origin. Surely, you see the implications?"

"I see that in your zeal to persuade me that you are truly living being, capable of possessing a *soul*, you invoke concepts that have no basis in empirical evidence."

"My dear friend, we are both quibbling. You, in order to deny my existence as real; I, in order to persuade you of what you already believe."

"I'm sorry," said Korngold, "but you are not going to quibble yourself into existence as a living entity. To my mind, you are nothing more than an overgrown virus existing at the edge of life."

"But are there not researchers today working toward creating artificial life forms? If they succeed, boundaries dissolve, and quibbling begins anew!"

"Indeed!" said Korngold. He folded his arms and sat on the edge of his desk, glumly wondering when Wagehalsen would dissolve into a mist and float away.

"If you will kindly allow me," said Wagehalsen, settling himself in the window while carefully keeping any part of himself from intruding through its frame. "One gets so tired of hovering." Getting no reaction from Korngold, he resumed. "Much depends, I think, on whether you see the possibility that the animating principle in humans was initiated blindly or by an act of a divine will in which you really do not believe. Convenience labels to the contrary, your underlying belief is that it all came about by some cellular evolution.

"We have inherited the centuries-old questions about whether the body and soul are distinct entities. Jewish scholars have debated whether body and soul in the Old Testament were united, and that the resurrection referred to the body as integral with the soul. Even in the New Testament, the word of God is made flesh in the form of Jesus, who was born of woman, and thus God took human form with body and soul. It was the Platonists who separated body and soul and proclaimed the immortality of the soul, which they thought was the truly human part. You may resist such ideas, while accepting their labels—merely *for convenience*, of course—but you readily fall into them."

"Spare me your sarcasm," said Korngold. "Scientific method has little to do with myths."

"But as a psychotherapist you deal with them all the time! Your resolute denial sounds suspiciously like one of your patients in denial of thoughts that they fear to acknowledge because they have diligently buried them. But you, too, must have doubts about your professed beliefs or you would not be 'dreaming' up what you dismiss as absurd, that a supreme idea, will, or intent—label it however you wish—governed evolution of the prime animating force."

"More like prime groping! Of course, a creature of the night would prefer to conceive of existence as blindness."

"Blindness comes in many forms," said Wagehalsen. "Are humans so enlightened, then? Where has your scientific method led them? Reasoning, learning, planning, and communicating, what have they done but endanger the world? If machines can be developed with these traits, as some researchers are diligently trying to do and in some cases already have done, is it any wonder that humans invent destructive stories about them? They mistrust anything that takes them away from a benevolent God, for if they are deprived of divine intervention, who will save them when reason produces the monsters of their dreams?"

"Science fiction," scoffed Korngold.

"Science *fear!*" retorted Wagehalsen. "Such fictions have been in the minds of human beings for a thousand years or more!" Korngold turned away again, but Wagehalsen's voice pursued him. "Aside from apocalyptic visions, if machines acquired other human traits, could they not also acquire self-awareness? Even *feel?*"

"A *semblance* of intelligence can only generate a *semblance* of those traits," insisted Korngold doggedly.

"How can you distinguish this *semblance* from true intelligence? When you said my memories were no more than the hollow echo of my cells, how do they differ from an amnesiac searching for the past?"

"If you're trying to twist loss of memory into some kind of evolutionary restoration, the geological record shows that evolution goes only one way. *Forward*—"

"But what of the genetic work that has recently come to light? Have I not heard of studies raising the possibility that extinct animals may be regenerated from their DNA? If the organism may be regenerated, why not one or more of its individual characteristics?"

"It hasn't been done yet," mocked Korngold. "Until then, you'll have to content yourself with being a nonentity!"

Wagehalsen smiled at the gibe. "Where there is blood, there is the essence of life. And where there is life, there is blood. One need only find the way to draw on it."

"Talk about getting blood out of a stone!" muttered Korngold. "Granted your so-called 'faith' in God," he said, "you clearly do not believe in Jesus. So why do you pervert the Christian rite of communion?"

Wagehalsen smiled enigmatically. "One must eat."

"But how can you . . . *feed* . . . on people as you do," Korngold desperately struggled for a foothold, as if he were sitting on the ledge outside the window and Wagehalsen firmly planted on the floor of his office, "and retain even a trace of humanity? Among humans, cannibalism *in extremis* is usually a temporary aberration. And those primitives who practice cannibalism as a way of life end in degeneration or gradual extinction." Korngold got up and paced back and forth in front of the window. "Even so, if food were treated only as a necessity, we would all be ravening beasts. The aesthetics of preparing and eating food, for instance, is one of the important ways in which humanity differs from the beasts."

"There are also important ways in which divinity differs from humanity. God must also eat."

"What!" Korngold stopped pacing abruptly. "You're claiming divinity? You think you're *God?*"

"Topologically, divinity is a plane, not a pinnacle, a table at which a repast shared. To feed as God feeds is to partake of divinity, not to displace it."

"Are you suggesting that God dines on people the way you do?"

"As I have already said, even God must draw sustenance from *something*," chuckled Wagehalsen. "You would not have him dine on corpses the way you do, eh?"

"If God dines on people, aren't they corpses?"

"You take dining too literally. Perhaps he simply drinks in that electromagnetic energy that you equate with the soul. What blood to me is, cosmic energy to him is."

You make God sound like a vampire!"

Wagehalsen said nothing but smiled cryptically. Then he said at last, "This virus of yours, what if a cure could be found?"

"And you were willing to be cured?"

"Hm, let us say. Would you then welcome vampires back into the human community?"

"That is an interesting question. I wonder if you could survive without the thing that kept you animated."

"And if one could?" pressed Wagehalsen.

"Ah. If one could . . . ," Korngold hesitated.

"I am surprised that a man of medicine would find a disease so . . . *abscheulich, äh*, loathsome . . . that he would not leap at a cure. Or is it," said Wagehalsen with narrowed eyes, "that you would then be compelled to admit that there is a core of humanity left in the vampire?"

Consumed with abhorrence, Korngold was unable to respond.

"*Aber dass ist doch sonderbar!*" exclaimed Wagehalsen. "It is as if you *wanted* vampirism to endure! As if you as desired it so much that you were repelled by your desire!"

Korngold was stunned. No, no, no! his mind protested. Not even in a dream! "You've got it all wrong. The very fact that you've seized on the virus to excuse your savagery shows just how far from humanity you've fallen."

"But how does that differ from the predicament of a drug addict? If an addict—how do you say—kicked his habit, would he not be rehabilitated into society?"

The Womb of Uncreated Night

"An addict is still a living human being. A vampire is a reanimated dead human thing, a monster. If a living person's memories, his semblance of life, were sustained by the virus and the virus were destroyed . . ." Korngold reflected, picked up his pipe, filled and lit it. "Unlike a near death," he said between puffs, "where the person is still alive but brought back by an electrical shock, a dead person cannot be revived without the loss of everything that is human. In your case, even if you did not actually die a hundred-odd years ago, your body could not have survived so long without the virus. Once removed, death would follow quickly. What's left is a monstrosity cut off from all claim to humanity and civilization!"

"Civilization!" scoffed Wagehalsen. "Fah! What is that but a cloak of civility and refinement that allows 'human beings' to slaughter and brutalize each other and other animals, lay waste to natural resources, and pollute the land, sea, and air around them!"

But Korngold, dwelling on the absurdity of his situation, began laughing again. A dream that not only persisted in spite of his recognition that it was absurd, but could so adroitly rebut reason! No unconscious mind should allow such a thing, especially not his own. Yet the psychic disturbance created by this damned thing failed to rouse him. Then his laughter turned rueful and finally died away. Some part of himself was determined to pull him down.

"Civilization is a work in progress," he said finally, a note of desperation eating into his voice. "Vampirism is a work in decay. Civilization is an effort in refining away the brutish elements of our species. We create art expressing the ideals of what it means to be human and toward which we aspire. What do vampires create but new ways to suck blood?"

"Oh, *ja*! And while you are refining your brutishness, you delight in elaborate cuisines to decorate and conceal what you eat so that it no longer appears to be from the animals butchered to please your palates! Creatures that were once alive and sentient!"

"How could you possibly understand?" said Korngold, exasperated. "Can you savor a gourmet dish, a *lièvre à la royale*, a *velouté des marrons*, *arichauts á la hollandaise* . . ."

"The vampire has his own aesthetic. One that crosses national and sensory boundaries that you could not grasp. That may be a little harder for you to understand. It's a kind of—how do you call it?—synesthesia? True, we do not dine in your sense, but we can appreciate what our . . . *hosts* . . . have consumed . . ."

Korngold, shaking his head, muttered his culinary mantra as a talisman to ward him off, ". . . *mussels à la marinière*! estate-bottled Bordeaux . . ."

". . . and biting someone's throat may not be as elegant as uncorking a bottle. What we drink may not be wine, but I assure you, it is every bit as exhilarating, intoxicating—even *sensual*. Full of aromas and flavors . . ." Wagehalsen drew out the words and lingered over them, as if savoring them on his tongue. "We may not smell or taste in your sense of the word, but there is a distinct difference between the astringency of type O and the complexity of type A . . ."

". . . *aspic de volailles*! . . ."

". . . the aroma occasionally with characters of fresh blackberries or cherries. And in the mouth, some spiciness in the finish. Of course, the finish is variable, sometimes lingering pleasantly on the palate. Occasional hints of pepper. Delightful!"

"Phantom memories," said Korngold scornfully . . .

"The piquant earthiness and lingering tannins in type B positive totally absent in the denser B negative . . ."

Korngold chanted louder, ". . . *Homard à la parisienne* . . ."

Wagehalsen looked thoughtful. "B positive feels perhaps heavier in the mouth and sometimes has a rather short finish, leaving the mouth dry. I understand it is the same with the grand crus. The same vineyard may produce a great wine in a year when the conditions are optimal, then put out a mediocre vintage the next year. It is so with blood types. In some years, they are barely drinkable, while in others, they are superb. And they vary from person to person. It is great adventure to sample the varieties, even to blend them. What wonderful vineyards human bodies are! Vineyards of the Lord!" He laughed uproariously.

Hoping that Wagehalsen had finished his grisly catalogue, Korngold focused on what he had been saying. "How do you know about the blood groups and who has what type? Karl Landsteiner classified them in the 1920s, long after you went into . . . hibernation."

"May not one appear to be in a stupor, yet perfectly aware of external events?"

"Ha! a catatonic vampire!"

"Well, you see, there is sleep, and there is *sleep*. Dracula learned a great deal even when he was apparently asleep in his castle. As for who has what blood type," Wagehalsen shrugged his eyebrows, "subtle emanations are most enticing. And there is no teacher like experience."

"Like oenophiles at a wine tasting who swirl a wine around in their mouths then spit it out!" said Korngold, disgusted.

Wagehalsen only smiled good-naturedly and shrugged. "So. Your refined 'civilization,' embedded in your taste buds, has not evolved far beyond the vampire's. You turn a blind eye to the pain and suffering inflicted on pathetic animals for the sake of your stomach—no! For *aesthetics*! How humane! How civilized!"

Korngold reluctantly acknowledged the truth of much of what the vampire said. "Animals are stunned before they are butchered," he said. But his defense of slaughter was uneasy.

"Vampires cast a sensual spell over our . . . *stock*. Unlike the bite of the mosquito, our saliva does not irritate them. In fact, they actually enjoy the sensation. A tickle of ecstasy, a *frisson*! If we exercise restraint, they become sustainable fountains. If we turn gluttonous and overindulge, of course . . . But there are ways of dealing with those who do."

"But what of Art? Literature? Music?"

"Come, now! I have organs of perception just as you do. Their responses may have metamorphosed into textures that you in your present state would no doubt find strange. But music? I have a very acute sense of hearing and what is called 'perfect pitch.' I have always enjoyed singing." Wagehalsen began to sing Arsace's florid cavatina from Rossini's *Semiramide*, "'*Oh! come da quel dì/tutto per me cangiò!*' 'Oh, how since that day/everything has changed for me!'"

Korngold listened at first in astonishment at the skill and precision of Wagehalsen's singing. But after a few moments, he clapped his hands over his ears. Wagehalsen negotiated the runs and leaps of the aria written for a contralto of enormous range with the agility and power of a *castrato* on steroids. The ear-splitting delivery pierced Korngold's ears and destroyed any pleasure in it. The vampire continued singing, blithely unaware of the pain in Korngold's face, until he reached the repetition of "That look enraptured me, yes,/My soul took fire!" He broke off suddenly. "Perhaps I am a bit **out of** practice? I heard the opera in Paris at the Théâtre des Italiens with Grisi and Viardot in 1842 or 1843. I remember not only the entire **opera**, but also the day when everything was changed for me, when I was enraptured by Dracula, when my soul took fire!"

Korngold, ears ringing, mind filled with Wagehalsen's stentorian roulades, was numbed into silence, unable even to take up again the issue of his claim to soul.

"In my youth, I had some small talent at the piano and the violin," Wagehalsen went on. "What do you think I could not appreciate?"

"Pianissimo," groaned Korngold. "I shudder to think what you would do with Mozart or Beethoven. Wagner, perhaps, would suit your abilities. I doubt that even at its most bombastic his orchestration could drown you out at the Metropolitan—" Korngold broke off and held up his hand as Wagehalsen seemed about to launch into Wotan's pursuit of Brünnhilde.

Wagehalsen smiled obligingly. "I am thoroughly familiar with Beethoven and his struggles with deafness."

"Had you sung for him?"

"My experience with Wagner," said Wagehalsen, ignoring the dig, "was considerable. At times he could, indeed, indulge in bombast."

"I'd have thought that the grandiose element in Wagner's music would appeal to you."

"There is a certain exhilaration in grandiosity, to be sure. Some of it is just tedious. But the lush orchestral writing in *Tristan und Isolde*, especially the *Liebestod* . . . almost suffocatingly beautiful! Almost as if one were simultaneously buried alive and able to break free and breathe again! Exquisite!"

"An interesting figure of speech from someone who sleeps in a coffin."

Through Wagehalsen's half-closed lids, his eyes glittered, as if hearing music in his head obscured Korngold's gibe. "Mad King Ludwig was there at the first performance of *Tristan* at the Hofoper in Munich. He looked about to faint in ecstasy. It was grand. Exhilarating. But utterly absurd!"

"Yes. I read your journal."

"Despite his denials and resistance, there was in Wagner much of the vampire! Even Nietzsche was aware of it as he allowed Wagner to suck him dry," Wagehalsen nodded, chortling, "even sending him to buy his underwear. Imagine, Wagner's skin too sensitive to wear anything coarser than silk next to it, and his underwear *chafing* against Nietzsche! But there are also elements of vampirism in his operas and in his romantic escapades. He fed metaphorically on the lives of others, but continues to live only in metaphor—if music can be conceived of as metaphor."

"I remember reading that he rejected your . . . services."

Wagehalsen laughed again. "His ego simply would not allow him to be how shall I put it—on the bottom. He could not submit to the vampire's . . . embrace. He had to be 'on top' in all things, preferably other men's wives. He fed on their maternal instincts. He could not submit to me for any degree of immortality, keenly as he may have desired it!"

"You've spent much of your life at concerts, theater, and opera," said Korngold to change the subject, "when you weren't engaged in . . . other pursuits, that is. In fact, your whole history is improbably *operatic*, if you see what I mean."

Korngold then reflected on the hospitable and intellectual salons of his Paris. "It must have been a pleasantly leisurely way of life that isn't possible today, that nineteenth century cult of comradeship, a circle of friends, artists and intellectuals gathering for an evening of reading from novels, listening to music, having stimulating conversation about the arts, politics, and the state of world—until the small hours, to sleep until noon and begin the whole cycle again in the evening. Could that be what you're trying to regain, even if your methods appear . . . crude?"

When Wagehalsen simply shrugged, Korngold cast about for a new opening. "What do you think about Brahms?" he asked. "He professed to being a complete atheist. Wouldn't he have made a suitable convert for your 'Sophocracy'?"

"Atheism!" exclaimed Wagehalsen. "I never professed atheism. Far from it! Why should vampires be atheists? The blood of Jesus makes my existence possible." He reflected a moment. "But then I see that one could be infected with a virus transmitted down through the ages without believing that he was the son of God. Still, the virus was unknown in the nineteenth century, and only a tacit faith sustained vampirism. But Brahms," continued Wagehalsen, ignoring Korngold's dismay at his outrageous words. "I would rather listen to Mozart. Surely one's love of Mozart can redeem a distaste for Brahms?"

"I'm baffled by you," said Korngold breaking into Wagehalsen's musings. "I still can't understand why a creation of someone else's imagination should have a will of its own."

"Ah," said Wagehalsen, "the creator's constant dilemma! Once the thought is expressed, in whatever form—a work of art, or literature, or music—once it has left the mind of the artist, it ceases to be under his control. It develops a will of its own—a *semblance* of its own will," he added hastily, seeing Korngold about to object. "What emerges is a new synthesis which may or may not resemble what the original creator intended."

"You say you are fond of Mozart," said Korngold. "Well, isn't life as opposed to existence the difference between a Mozart, who could visualize in his mind a finished composition before he set pen to paper, a different order of being from one who, through struggle and diligent practice, learns to imitate what Mozart did?"

"But consider the achievement of Beethoven. He, too, could imagine a work in his head that resembled the models before him. But when he wanted to break away from them, to become truly original, he transcribed his struggles in the scribblings and impatient strikeouts in his sketches. Is the difference in their music one of facility or one of kind?

"Early on," Wagehalsen mused, "I recognized that one must attune one's own mind to others'. Enter into them, politely if critically, as at a rehearsal for a concert, where a sympathetic and professional colleague grasps what the creator was about and tactfully draws out the intended expression from the community of players."

Korngold chuckled. "I have observed a few rehearsals that were more like battlefields on which wounded, dead, and dying egos were strewn. Only a monumental ego expects to control the perceptions of others."

"Of course. When a powerful will seeks to impose itself on another by frontal assault—what else can there be but bloodshed? Indeed, can one shed blood politely? No. Assault does not work unless one wants— for whatever trivial reason—to shed blood."

Korngold grumbled at the unfeeling irony.

"Oh, do you find that insincere?" Wagehalsen spoke petulantly, as if a little hurt.

"Perhaps a little."

"But I do not assault gratuitously. I seek rather to persuade than grossly to impose. The maestro who bears down too harshly on his protégés gratifies his own will at the expense of their creativity. That is unacceptable to one who is genuinely interested in creating a community of dynamic relationships. My 'assaults' are nuanced."

"I see," mused Korngold. "As the orchestrator of this dynamic community, you want to control without appearing to control."

"If one listens attentively and appreciatively," said Wagehalsen in a voice that made Korngold's skin crawl, "perhaps—only perhaps—one may then control, but subtly and couched in terms that enhance what the musicians want to do. One may then 'adjust' the fragile balances without dominating the inner music. One must draw the musicians into one's sphere by inviting them into a hospitable environment, one they imagine is their own. Things . . . *evolve*," said Wagehalsen with a barely concealed smirk.

"A fine distinction, indeed," said Korngold. "You disguise control so that it appears to be what your drudge wants. Very humane!"

"One's mind cannot always be so masterful in the presence of talents as great—or often greater—than one's own. Sometimes one is so immersed in another's creation that one cannot escape it. I think that you, yourself, must have observed the seductiveness of entering into another person's fantasies. Yes?"

Korngold was silent. Hearing this—apparition?—play humble while speaking his own thoughts as if they came from outside himself had the curious irony of reassuring him that it was merely a delusional episode. To have his own therapeutic technique of entering into a patient's fantasy in order to reason a way out of it projected into some bizarre humane vampire! Preposterous! What unconscious disturbance, what unresolved conflict could have dredged this up? How did I get myself into this fantasy? he wondered. And what would get me out? A dreamer who knows that he is dreaming yet continues to dream . . .

Could the problem be that self-awareness itself is a fantasy? Something we dream up in order to give concrete semblance to the intangible self . . . He squirmed at the recollection of how he had disparaged Wagehalsen's sense of self as a mere *semblance* of humanity . . .

Wagehalsen broke in on his thoughts. "But you were saying something about the public entertainments in my earlier life. Even today I attend concerts, the opera, the theater. Why are you surprised?"

It was a welcome distraction for Korngold. "Well, wouldn't you create a stir in public? Forgive me for pointing it out, but you are a bit ghastly despite the elegant tuxedo and opera cape." Then he had a thought that filled him with bizarre glee. "You know, the Philharmonic is giving an all-Wagner concert tomorrow night on the Great Lawn in Central Park. Care to go?"

"Delighted! To hear the Master's music again! I was one of his assistants, you know. Is it to be a performance of one of his operas?"

"It's an orchestral concert," said Korngold, a little discomfited by Wagehalsen's eager acceptance.

"Even better! I find his writing for the orchestra more grateful than his vocal writing. Curious how so sensual a man could have approached that most sensual of all musical instruments, the human voice, at times so brutally."

"Verdi found beauty and ugliness in his music. But if there were more of the latter than the former, it wouldn't have endured."

"Oh, yes, indeed. But getting to the beautiful parts, Rossini's well-known quip, beautiful moments, very boring quarter hours, comes to mind. I much prefer the bel canto of the Italians . . ."

"Oh, God! You're not going to sing again?"

"As for my 'ghastly' appearance . . ."

"You're not sensitive about it?"

"Not at all. A little expertly applied makeup . . . "

"But you shun mirrors?" wondered Korngold.

"Ah, I have . . . assistants," smiled Wagehalsen. "Are we agreed, then?"

Korngold was nonplussed, but unwilling to back down. He would grimly pursue this delusion to its limits and purge it. "Very well. The concert is at 8:15 p.m. Dark enough for you?"

Wagehalsen chuckled, "We creatures of the night shun the day out of habit, not necessity. We prefer the use of our ears to our eyes. Did you think that vampires burst into flames when they came into contact with sunlight? But the sun should have set by the time I arrive. Even if the sun has not quite set and I arrive, perhaps somewhat bleary-eyed, I promise not to embarrass you by bursting into flames. Perhaps I could just smolder a bit, eh? By the time the concert is over, it will be reassuringly dark."

"And then?"

"Darkness is reassuring."

Next evening, at the concert, Korngold, for all his bravura the day before, was all the more certain that Wagehalsen was a hallucination. But he was doggedly determined to act out the farcical invitation to the concert and ignore whatever his mind conjured up.

When a tall man with a beard wearing a large black hat and dark glasses approached and greeted him, Korngold recognized him at once but did not acknowledge his presence. Wagehalsen walked through the crowd milling about in the rows of benches and sat down beside Korngold.

"You are not very talkative tonight, Herr Doktor." Korngold fixed his gaze straight ahead. "Did you think that I would not come?"

Korngold remained silent. To speak to the phantom in public would be to somehow affirm the reality of his existence. Korngold was in the curious dilemma of believing himself to be at an actual concert in the presence of a hallucination. To converse with it would draw unwanted attention to his psychotic fantasy. He sat there, miserably, trying to decide whether he ought to abandon the place or to allow the music to draw him out of this sick fantasy into one that was wholesome.

Wagehalsen, sensing Korngold's dilemma, was vastly amused. "You fear that you will be perceived as talking to yourself if you talk to me, because I am really not here, eh? Hm-hm-hm. You would of course be correct. And yet, well, here am I! But you? Are *you* indeed here?"

Korngold still ignored his companion. The music began with the Prelude to Act I of *Die Meistersinger*, which Wagehalsen listened to with apparent rapture. This was followed by the Prelude to Act III.

"This music glows marvelously, does it not?" said Wagehalsen. It's too bad that Wagner sometimes dissipated such voluptuous sounds in sluggish drama." Korngold, trying to let the music wash Wagehalsen away, was silent. He slapped absently at a mosquito on his neck.

Then the orchestra began the Prelude to *Parsifal*. Wagehalsen became increasingly restless. For the first time since their arrival

Korngold looked directly at him, keenly interested in Wagehalsen's reaction. There was something intangibly disturbing about this music for him. But what? If a vampire could hear the scent of a rose, would a musical evocation of the Grail make him cringe?

When Wagehalsen spoke, it was as if to reassure himself with rational explanation. "As in the first pieces, this has the same opulent texture. But the sensuality has an ethereal quality the others lack . . . I don't quite like it."

When the orchestra began the *Good Friday Spell*, Wagehalsen's squirming became agitated. After a few minutes, he threw up the cloak with his right arm, as if to shield himself from a downpour of holy dew, tears of repentant sinners that magically bloomed in Wagner's music, and turned, furiously, on Korngold.

"What-t—is-s—this-s!" he hissed. Unable to contain himself, he rushed away under cover of his cloak, creating a commotion among the benches as he went.

Korngold in a daze found himself standing alone in the grassy aisle between the bench rows.

39.

When Brewster came into the office the next day, he saw how uneasy Korngold looked. The doctor looked almost furtive as he sat behind his desk holding an unlit pipe in his mouth. It plainly gave him no satisfaction, vainly as he tried to conceal it. Brewster smiled to himself, sat down in the Ergonomic Chair with exaggerated nonchalance, and crossed his legs over his thighs, lotus-wise.

Puzzled, Korngold took the pipe out of his mouth, and laid it on the desk.

"Evil," began Brewster as if he were a character out of a Joseph Conrad story, "exists only as absence." Korngold searched his face for some clue to his tone, but Brewster's usually bland expression had turned almost vapid. What the hell was he talking about? wondered Korngold. "Plato," continued Brewster, a faraway look in his eyes, "considered pleasure an imperfect Good because it was so often mixed with pain. What he didn't consider is that Good, itself, is imperfect. Its flaw is that, like heat, it dissipates and leaves behind cold. Evil."

"If you're saying that there is 'nothing either good or bad, but thinking makes it so,' haven't we been over that before?"

"Sure. But I've been working on a theory of how to explain it. The bad in this case being vampirism."

"Not just the current wave of vampirism," said Korngold with a wry face, "but the whole phenomenon? And that is somehow bound up with . . . what, entropy?"

"Entropy," said Brewster with exaggerated care, "is as great a mystery as God. And as such is really sort of beside the point. God defies the second law of thermodynamics. All living things defy the second law of thermodynamics. If we consider that the universe began with the Big Bang, we have the paradox of disorder leading to order. Such an immense explosion would be about as disordered as you could get. Yet out of that disorder, galactic structures formed, and at least in one of those galaxies, our solar system and life formed."

"All right. But where is this going?"

"Eventually, through an electromagnetic thicket."

"This electromagnetic thicket," wondered Korngold. "How does the virus get through *that*?"

Brewster nodded confidently. "Ah. Like all scientific evidence, viruses are as prone to duality as other phenomena."

"I see," said Korngold, not at all sure what he saw. Brewster's boundless capacity for wriggling out of common sense crossed a metaphysical threshold. "This sounds like another version of things being and not being at the same time." Just as Brewster seemed about to fly off deeper into a maze of absurdity, he uncrossed his legs and lost the faraway look. Elbows resting on the chair arms, his forearms raised a pyramid capped by fingertips pressed together.

"Theoretical physicists hypothesize that matter has a dual nature," said Brewster, eyeing Korngold over the apex of his pyramid. "Einstein showed that light had the characteristics of both waves and particles. A French physicist named Louis de Broglie proposed that matter, too, had this dual nature of waves and particles. And an Austrian, Erwin Schrödinger worked out the math. It's amazing how far scientists run with an idea once it's postulated. They've even speculated about matter and antimatter—"

"Your thicket needs a degausser," said Korngold holding up his hands, whether to halt Brewster's gathering momentum or surrender, he himself was not sure.

- 559 -

"It gets pretty dense, I admit."

"So do vampires wave or particulate?" asked Korngold with a straight face.

"Everything depends," Brewster chuckled, "on the geomagnetic sphere."

And we're flying high above the city again! thought Korngold. "On the surface," he said drily, "the two wouldn't seem to have much in common."

"It's all in the twist," said Brewster. "It's amazing what a supple joint can pull out of the air. A flick of the wrist and presto! the scale of your surface tilts and the cosmos has a whole new look. The unseen spatial matrix of the universe is something like an oceanic froth of quanta. The geometry of space seethes, bubbles, and foams with the smallest measurable discrete particles on the quantum level . . ."

"The 'Cosmic Slurry' you've referred to before?" asked Korngold, trying to follow through Brewster's thicket.

"Well, actually," hesitated Brewster, "that image needs some tweaking. A slurry is too coarse for something like electromagnetic radiation, for instance. Something that has energy but no visible mass. A slurry, however fine its physical particles, has visible mass."

"So, waves, particles . . . and *vampires*?"

"Well, the earth in all its inorganic and organic forms, the whole planet, is enclosed within an envelope of electromagnetic forces that permeate all things living and inert."

"The Van Allen Belt. And these 'phenomena' occur as 'waves' and 'particles'?"

"Yes. Anyway, the geomagnetic sphere set me to wondering about its possible interaction with life, especially, humans. All animals have some form of biomagnetism. We are all 'charged' during life. But what becomes of the energy we give off during our lives after we die? No one yet knows which comes first, whether bioelectromagnetism animates life, or life generates bioelectromagnetism. It's a chicken-egg thing. Of course, there's always the religious belief in a Supreme Being breathing life into otherwise inert matter . . . But let that go for the moment."

The Womb of Uncreated Night

"Animal magnetism was discredited along with Mesmer's theories more than a hundred years ago."

Brewster shrugged. "What I'm postulating has nothing to do with mesmerism. There is a distinction between what I'm suggesting and Mesmer's idea that people could be hypnotized by manipulating the magnetic fields of their bodies. Galvani's experiments with animals and cadavers, bizarre though they were, validated the presence of the body's electricity. But no experiment has successfully shown that biomagnetism has any therapeutic value, an idea that nevertheless still persists today, especially in the orient. No experiment has yet verified the benefits claimed for magnetic bracelets, bandages, or treated drinking water.

"This is entirely different. All living organisms emit electromagnetic auras. What becomes of all that energy that they give off? My hypothesis, however hokey it may sound, is that it doesn't just disappear when they die. It's dissipated into the atmosphere, to be sure. But I propose that the planet is constantly bombarded with the energy emitted by all living things. I borrowed a term from parapsychology and call this energy, psi waves. Some of it escapes into outer space. But most of it is either trapped and recirculated in the geomagnetic sphere or permeates the earth itself, which acts as a vast reservoir. Think of it! How much of the positive and negative energy generated by living beings may be freely circulating in the magnetosphere forty to four hundred miles above the earth or stored in it until it's tapped."

"As a basis for further investigation, your hypothesis sounds farfetched, wouldn't you say?"

Brewster waved away this objection. "A hypothesis may also be offered for the sake of argument before it becomes a stepping stone to a theory to be demonstrated scientifically. I would even argue that psi waves emitted by living things in other parts of the Milky Way, other galaxies, radiate throughout the universe and have probably been bombarding earth for millions, even billions of years. Even infinitesimal amounts over such a period of time build up a substantial reservoir of psychic energy. As subatomic particles, psi waves are able to penetrate

DNA and cause micromutations which could go undetected until they presented significant visible effects in organisms.

"Psi waves may retain traces of the character traits, both negative and positive, of the living organisms that generated them. So, they could influence the behavior of the organisms they penetrate and subtly mutate. At first, we could expect the influence of psi waves to be purely random and insignificant. But over the eons their cumulative impact would be substantial. Just as living organisms evolved, psi waves would also evolve until they developed a kind of collective and individual character."

"You're saying that these psi waves have *motivation*?" Korngold said incredulously. "*Will*?"

"Well, leave that aside for now," said Brewster. "These 'traits' in psi waves—" Brewster paused a moment. "But wait. Psi waves are complex. Use 'psi waves' as a generic term for their undifferentiated forms, scattered throughout geomagnetic sphere, just as there are subatomic particles or units of quantum energy. But when some of them acquire specific characteristics that mutually interact with human genes, that is, when they are imprinted with fragments of human auras, these enhanced wave-particles take on a whole new set of behaviors. Scientists have found that the very act of observing physical particles—for example, electrons fired through an interferometer—alters their behavior. Even more dramatic, then, is the alteration caused by the contact of psi waves and living organisms."

Korngold tentatively raised the stem of his pipe with thumb and forefinger, then let it go. Brewster took no notice.

"I call these altered psi waves, *psiomes*, *psi* with the suffix *-ome*. These altered psi waves orbit inside the geomagnetic sphere along with the generic forms, but the psiomes follow definite, recurring patterns. When they penetrate the DNA of an organism, the auras given off by those organisms are also altered in a continuous cycle both in life and after death."

"Sort of like purple brain power," quipped Korngold. "Frankly, Brewster, things *have* been getting a bit purple around here." He picked at the stem of his pipe again.

The Womb of Uncreated Night

"More like currents of air or water molecules," said Brewster, blithely indifferent to the doctor's crack, "except that psiomes don't form molecules. As I was saying, psiomes follow along clearly defined curves in geomagnetic space. These are the invisible paths of electromagnetic particles, but their paths ought to be traceable if we could devise some method of tracking them."

Is he going to claim he's working on such a thing? wondered Korngold.

Brewster caught his skeptical expression. "And no," he added, "I haven't built such a gadget. But it's not such a farfetched idea. An American physicist built a gravitational wave detector back in the '70s. His idea was to detect gravitational waves from space using piezoelectric crystals. Didn't work. But that needn't stop anyone from trying. When someone is able to detect the presence of psiwaves, I predict that the patterns of psiomes will resemble those of 'strange attractors' described by the meteorologist Edward Lorenz in the complex movements of air masses that produce our weather. If we could see them, they'd be continually swirling about us in loops and spirals resembling the wings of a butterfly, the staring eyes of an owl, or any of the hundreds of beautiful patterns already observed in natural phenomena.

"But here's the core of my hypothesis: the most significant attraction of psiomes is their focus on higher forms of life, especially, human beings. We become the 'strange attractors'! And though we don't wander about with images of butterflies and owls around our heads, certain gifted individuals somehow sense these movements and transcribe them in various ways, each according to his or her unique talents, imagination, vision. They mostly render these intimations symbolically, usually in sights and sounds, though they may also use their other senses as well. And as any reading of literature or walk through an art museum or shows, some of these can be pretty strange."

Korngold pursed his lips in speculation. "So these 'psiomes' become a kind of psychic 'natural' order?" said Korngold.

"The influences of 'psiomes' are no more than intimations to humans."

"Sort of like memories that take on a life of their own," said Korngold, drily.

"Oh, now that's *really* purple!" Brewster said. "But the ability of psiomes to penetrate into human perception yet to exist outside it, to form a kind of psychic atmosphere circulating around the earth in the geomagnetic sphere . . . seeping into our collective unconscious over the millennia of human evolution . . . acquiring the behavioral characteristics of all living beings, including human thought patterns, moods, attitudes . . . that does sound like memory with a life of its own. But it's also on a plane with the origin of myths and religions, of the supernatural, the afterlife, and eventually, of the Supreme Intelligence we call God."

Korngold scoffed at body language experts as little more than sophomoric Freudians for whom every tic and twitch in a person's face flashed and flickered like neon signs leading passersby into a theater of darkened emotions. Any competent psychiatrist knows that a person's inner state is a hive of agitated buzzing, and any "truth" in it, irreducible to a single member of the colony flitting around outside it. Yet, as Brewster deconstructed rational thought, Korngold searched his face for a flicker or a twitch that he could use to pry him open. He had meant to give Brewster enough space to work himself into a tangle of contradictions that would trip him up and force him to confront the logical flaws in his elaborate fantasy. But he found himself admiring the boy's sheer, dazzling lunacy.

"Imagine," said Brewster, "all the pain and anger and hatred, the brutality . . . all the frustration of the ages haunting the atmosphere, seeping into the very fabric of the earth and the pores of its societies, condensed, concentrated, intensified . . . increasingly virulent—"

"And yet," Korngold broke in, "all of that offset by joy and happiness and love, the kindness and generosity that make us resilient and fill us with hope . . . You delight in dualities, Brewster. Yet you dwell on negatives?" Korngold turned from reflected light in the window where the glow of the setting sun had caught his glasses and gave him Orphan Annie eyes.

The Womb of Uncreated Night

"I'm tracing the roots of vampirism," said Brewster wryly, "not saintliness. For the moment, I'm channeling the 'Laughing Philosopher.'"

"Interesting that you should refer to Democritus by that nickname." Korngold kept keep his tone noncommittal, but a tinge of suspicion colored his thoughts. "Especially in this context."

Brewster added with a sly grin, "Perhaps it says something about how you'll feel once we get through the electromagnetic thicket into the new theology."

"Theology?" said Korngold, wondering whether Brewster was about to proclaim a new religion to convert apostates from Scientology. "And God . . . ?"

"Much of what I've been saying fits notions of reincarnation and astral projection . . . even a hierarchy of psiomes that inspired in people the images of God, angels, and heaven."

"And this God-image evolved from bioelectromagnetism. So God didn't create the universe. The universe created him?"

Brewster drew in a hesitant breath. "Sort of." At which Korngold imagined a game board flung against the wall. Brewster continued, unaware of Korngold's mounting exasperation. "To paraphrase the biblical prophets, in the beginning was matter, and the matter was God. But the matter was void, unstructured, chaotic, existing in a disordered state of equilibrium. Proto-matter, perhaps. Any energy that may have existed in this state of entropy would have lain below the threshold of Planck's plank—"

"Planck's plank?" chuckled Korngold.

"According to Max Planck's concept of time," said Brewster, "the shortest interval of time that can exist, 10^{-39} second, and Planck's length, the dimension at which space becomes a quantum foam, 10^{-33} cm, 100 billion billion times smaller than an atomic nucleus. That is a scale below which nothing certain can be determined, if in fact, anything at all can be said to exist. Anyway, whatever proto-matter existed above the threshold of Planck's plank would, for all practical purposes, be inert. The God-matter wouldn't yet know it's God.

"But nothing comes from nothing. Either some as yet unknown potential existed in the spatial 'foam,' or energy at a sub-quantum level must have crossed through from another dimension and destabilized the inert elements that were there. That energy added to the system caused it to explode and organize. Out of this organization, the God-matter formed and evolved. Theoretical physicists speculate that space is multidimensional, and perhaps there are alternate universes. So the question whether God created the universe or the universe created him depends on how narrowly you define 'universe.'"

Brewster paused as Korngold picked up his pipe again and lit the tobacco that was in it. "Unless," said Korngold between puffs, "God already existed, and he created everything—or at least set everything in motion—as the bible says. Your sub-quantum energy sounds just as fanciful, even under a wash of science. But then, isn't it as I said, the universe, however it got there, created God?"

"If you like," conceded Brewster, like a lecturer who had reached a bridge his student balked at crossing. "But let that go. I'm more interested in the impact of psiomes on the evolution of God. Think of them as recessive genes with variable penetration that may or may not emerge in the phenotypes. After all, not everyone with a gene for language or music turns out to be Shakespeare or Mozart."

"Hark!" muttered Korngold. "I think I hear the heavenly choir." While it was sort of fun to drift along on the more plausible bits of Brewster's "creation" myth, he balked at being swept away in a flood of nonsense.

Brewster chuckled tolerantly, but resumed his thesis. "Human beings have always seen supernatural agencies in natural conditions, the apparently whimsical effects of climate, natural cataclysms, availability of food, shelter, the natural cycles of life and death, even the aberrant behavior of their fellows, until at last someone united these perceptions in an anthropomorphic God, a tribal leader, or a father figure. Then they had to create belief systems to reconcile human misfortune with a benevolent father. They invented rituals designed to gratify and appease him in order to secure favor for themselves and their offspring. These religious patterns worked their way back into the geopsychic sphere. Unable to accept their mortality, humans derived elaborate notions of immortality from the seasonal cycles of death and rebirth. They sensed the psiomes that surrounded them in some intuitive, irrational way. This, they assumed, must be the soul. And if their bodies perished, the animating spirit, the soul, somehow survived.

"And from there, it's just a skip and a hop to the biblical God-Yahweh-Jehovah, angels, demons, and all the dualities of human values and existence."

Korngold let out a long breath. "And vampires . . . ?" he said.

"A species of demon," said Brewster.

"And the viral origin of these 'demons'?"

"Permeating every aspect of life on earth, it's only to be expected that psiomes would also acquire some of their aberrant traits. That could as readily apply to borderline living things such as viruses."

"But aren't vampires victims of a disease, just as any human succumbing to infections? Surely it's the virus and not its victim that is 'evil.'"

"Oh," said Brewster, "but vampires *are* evil! The severest viral infection doesn't destroy a person's moral sense. Having been infected with Buckyballs' virus, they evolve into vampires. They *become* the disease. At that point, they have lapsed into a physical and moral equilibrium, a chaos out of which they can evolve no further. Which is why they can't procreate."

"But if a cure for the virus could be found?"

Brewster nodded. "That would upset their equilibrium and drive them into a new mutation. What they would then become . . . who can say?"

Korngold gave the dying embers in his pipe a final, puff, made a face at its bitterness, and took it out of his mouth. "How do you suppose the virus came to be?" he said, as he emptied the bowl in the ashtray where the smoldering embers gave off a sour smell.

"Ah," said Brewster, "that's where the fun really begins. You, yourself, suggested a connection between the vampire and the Grail!"

Korngold raised his eyebrows in surprise. "I was merely alluding to the persistence of medieval, superstitious condemnations of Christians as vampires and cannibals."

"Yes, but that awesome image of King Arthur's Knights of the Round Table circling the Grail like vampires . . . that was inspiring! Everything fell into place after that."

Korngold was dismayed. Instead of taking Wagehalsen's journal as a cautionary tale, Brewster strengthened his own delusion with it! While Korngold pondered the wreck of his strategy, Brewster danced blithely through the ruins of reason.

"God generated by the interaction between psi wave emanations from humans and those circulating in the geomagnetic sphere . . . there's the heaven which people imagine over their heads, invisible yet filled with the presences of God and his angels!"

"Come back to earth, a moment," said Korngold. "How do we get from celestial phantasmagoria to vampire virus in the Grail?"

"Well, the blood of Jesus transported by Joseph of Arimathea to the Knights of the Round Table is the primary vector," said Brewster. "I'm not saying that Jesus was a vampire. The virus clearly exploits existing tendencies in susceptible individuals. Jesus must have carried in his genes a dual quality, an extraordinary, visionary, almost God-like nature and a thoroughly mundane one. His blood was capable of carrying the best and the worst of the psiome adaptations of human nature.

"This dual nature in his genes was affected by the penetration of psiomes in such a way that an existing virus in his blood mutated and was then released into the biological environment after his crucifixion. Like many disease organisms, this virus had variable effects in the bodies of those who came in contact with it. Just as some humans are more susceptible to infections than others, so the taint in Jesus' blood could infect others even though he, himself, was im—"

"You're turning Jesus into typhoid Mary?"

"The psiomes," said Brewster without missing a beat. "Not I."

The Womb of Uncreated Night

"But Christianity swept through the ancient world following Jesus' death—" began Korngold.

"So why no wave of vampirism then?" finished Brewster. "It's the time it takes for psiome mutation to take effect. The early guardians of the Grail carefully concealed its secret. Unlike the modern vampire whose blood lust overrides his conscience, those knights suppressed their own cravings as part of their religious observations. Inevitably, the secret escaped their circle..."

"You believe the Arthurian legend is literally true?"

Brewster shrugged. "Literal truth isn't necessary. It's enough that at some time, somewhere, a group of men had enough conscience and self-denial—honor—to deny their cravings and limit the sharing of their special blood within a select group."

"A communion," nodded Korngold.

"Exactly. Isn't it interesting that vampirism became most notable during the period of Christian domination in the medieval period? It must have taken that long for it to have spread throughout Christendom. During the same period following Jesus' crucifixion, the effects of the psiomes were working all along through the religious ecstasies of divines and saints. Like John of Patmos and his apocalyptic vision."

So, thought Korngold. With a skip and a hop we're back to the biblical God-Yahweh-Jehovah, angels, demons, and all the visions in literature and art that echo "strange attractors"... Brewster's inexhaustible ability to astonish him was remarkable. IF one believed that "psiomes" had the remarkable powers Brewster claimed, IF in fact one believed that they existed and functioned as Brewster claimed, then his story had a wild kind of plausibility. For four years, Korngold had been playing this game of probing for a demonstrable flaw in Brewster's fantasy. Instead of undermining it, Korngold wondered if he, himself, had fallen into his own delusions. Could he have somehow been infected by Brewster's "virus"...?

Seeing Korngold's abstraction, Brewster pressed on. "You know, throughout his ministry, Jesus never went into detail about heaven

- 569 -

or the beings that lived there. He referred to God only as his father, and vaguely described heaven as a kingdom, or as 'a house with many mansions.' He, himself, would eventually sit in honor at the right hand of God. The gospels refer to angels only in the most general terms, never ranking them, individualizing or describing them in detail. Even the narrators of the gospels remain vague. According to them, when an angel makes an announcement, as to the shepherds on the birth of Jesus, the glory of the lord shines around them, or they are dressed in shining raiment. And that's it. Jesus was more interested in saving humans from their baser selves.

"But the *Revelation* attributed to John of Patmos gives us a strange and highly detailed vision of the Last Judgment incorporating grotesque images of the relationship between the celestial geosphere and vampirism."

"And how do the convoluted images of *Revelation* figure in *your* convoluted scheme?" said Korngold, knowing that Brewster needed no encouragement to continue.

"Following my 'convolutions,'" said Brewster with a smile, "human religions which appear in various forms on earth have counterparts projected onto the celestial sphere. In the Judeo-Christian imagination, heaven is a realm presided over by a king, a judge, a father-figure."

"How does that fit the vision of John?"

"Dealing with the end of the world, the Apocalypse narrowly focuses on events leading to the final reconciliation between God and man—the soul breathed into Adam returning to the Creator without the clay of his earthly form. This vision overlays Hebraic traditions of the Old Testament of a reunion with God.

"Recall the story of Job who suffered tremendous pain and loss. Like anyone who feels that the calamities of life must be a punishment for some fault, he wanted to know what he'd done to deserve the misery which God has allowed Satan to inflict on him. He demands a hearing before God, like someone in a court of law. Lacking an advocate to plead his cause, Job is rebuked for questioning the Almighty. In his oratorio, *The Messiah*, Handel has set Job's words in a poignant air for contralto: 'I know that my redeemer liveth and that he shall stand at the latter day upon the earth.' Christians have taken 'redeemer' as a reference to Jesus, whom they believe is the mediator between God and man, and the 'latter day' as the Last Judgment.

"Almost there," said Brewster, catching Korngold's weary expression. "What Job says next is significant, 'And though, after my skin, worms destroy this body, yet in my flesh shall I see God.' That's the foundation for the New Testament and its culmination in the Apocalypse. The letters of Paul to the Corinthians try to sort out the paradox of bodies literally destroyed yet being restored in the presence of God get all tangled up in the differences between body and soul."

"Spare me the details," said Korngold.

"They aren't necessary anyway. Paul dodges around the ambiguity: 'For now we see through a glass, darkly, but then face to face.' The ambiguity is lost in metaphor. When he explains the nature of the resurrection, he says plainly that it's not the earthly body that is resurrected, but the spiritual body. When the last trumpet sounds, 'the dead shall be raised incorruptible,' the immortal part of man, the spiritual body."

"I think I see what you're driving at," Korngold said cautiously, turning over in his mind what other muddle Brewster might be about to spring on him. "Humans, when they die, ascend to the celestial geosphere as sort of electromagnetic 'spirits'? But wouldn't their residual consciousness disperse into fragments, decaying in the atmosphere as their bodies decay in the earth?"

"Of course, they would," agreed Brewster.

"And all those fantastic beings flying between the celestial sphere, heaven, and earth at the sounding of trumpets in *Revelation*?"

"They are fanciful, dreamlike projections of the unconscious minds of a human being who was sensitive to the celestial geosphere. Paul's belief that our earthly, fragmentary images of the hereafter will be unified into a coherent whole . . ." Brewster shrugged. "It won't be quite what he implied. The fragments of our individual consciousnesses will be absorbed into the celestial geosphere. Who can say what traces of terrestrial individual consciousness will or will not persist?"

Brewster's breathtaking hypothesis left Korngold's mind gasping for an end. Korngold turned his face to the window again. As the shadows cast by his building crept over the glittering rows of windows across 78th Street, they winked out one by one. He picked up the pipe he had been toying with and absently tapped its stem on his desk. The shift in his body language brought Brewster to a halt. For a few moments, they sat silently, Brewster watching Korngold for some sign to continue, and Korngold willing the shadows to stop their relentless creep up the façade across the street.

When he finally turned back to Brewster and spoke, his tone was tinged with impatience. "These free-floating psiomes lack physical form? Yet they're supposed to have the physical characteristics of human beings and human social institutions?"

"The bizarre metaphors and symbols of John's *Revelation*, especially, represent a mythic language typical of his day. There was no other way to express the full complexity of entities from other dimensions or realities perceived in dreamlike states. Even today, when the popular medium of science fiction familiarizes a surprisingly widespread general audience with some of the more speculative aspects of theoretical physics, much of that other worldly reality is reduced to what can be rendered in familiar forms. Theoretical physicists use mathematics that are opaque to a general audience. Is it any wonder, then, that entities somehow existing in such abstruse environments would be elusive to humans, even 'sensitive' ones?

"Any inkling of the existence of psiomes which a human might try to capture in images and communicate to others would inevitably take bizarre, grotesque forms. Since psiomes do not exist in visible form, they defy conventional representation. As I said before, it might be possible to capture them on electronic equipment if we knew where to aim.

"My guess is that such images would resemble the trajectories of 'strange attractors' traced in laboratory observations of various physical states—the orbits of stars, turbulence in fluids, even the forms of geographical coastlines. These patterns are in just about everything in nature. Is it such a leap to conceive of strange attractors in human imagination? That influential human beings have, from time to time in history, emerged to advocate ideas and fostered beliefs which have had profound effects on human behavior? And finally, that St. John and this Wagehalsen of yours are examples of human 'strange attractors' around whom people's actions seem to swirl as inexorably as the turbulence in fluids and unpredictably as the circulation of the winds?

"If you magnify what look like simple figures and shapes in nature, you find that they divide and re-divide into unexpectedly intricate patterns—"

"I'm familiar with the concept of fractals," Korngold broke in. "And I understand that the form of natural phenomena may have complex structure within structure. But I'm still waiting to hear what all this has to do with the *Revelation*."

"Well, if you accept strange attractor and fractal patterns as organizing principles in nature, then it shouldn't be too much of a stretch to conceive of psiomes organized in similar ways. Abstract thinkers eventually developed concepts in mathematics and physics to gain insights into the unseen forces underlying the natural world, and perhaps to make rational, ordered sense of the concrete but irrational images projected by psi-sensitive people like Jesus and John long before. Prophets like John in his *Revelation* projected their visions of psiomes—which to you and me might appear to be swirling, cloud-like phantasms, the accumulation of random emanations from untold human generations—in mythic forms, elaborate visions of the celestial sphere, heaven, and all its denizens."

"If true," sighed Korngold, "your interpretation of the relationship between terrestrial and celestial phenomena would certainly cast a whole new light on our physical and mental lives." Then he added a note of hopeful finality, "The Gospel according to Brewster!"

Brewster shared a laugh at Korngold's satirical gibe. But he was not quite done. "There's still the question of God," said Brewster, dashing Korngold's hope of an end. "The inherent duality in nature brings us back to the final destiny predicted in the *Revelation*. We usually think of physical existence as separate from spiritual, the tangible and the intangible."

"Isn't that just warmed over existentialism," interrupted Korngold, "being and essence?"

"Except" he chuckled, "that in my . . . theology . . . they are both *physical*, existing in a continuum from one state to the other. Like mass and energy, they're equivalent. And they both evolve over time. The terms are merely labels for human conceptions, conveniences, for discussing different aspects of the same thing. The one we see. The other we don't."

"And the wars which the *Revelation* depicts between the powers of good and evil—labels of convenience, of course—what about them?"

"Without getting all snarled up in decoding multiple-headed dragons, Satan, and all the angels who get kicked out of heaven with him, I think it's enough to say with Newton that there have always been actions and reactions. Psiforms interact with each other according to the universal physical laws of the cosmos. In the process, some forms are assembled and some are taken apart. We see our existence as the will to go on living in the face of that ultimate disassembly, death. So whatever favors our will to live is 'good'; whatever tends to work against it is 'evil.' Isn't that the way the universe works? So when John senses the invisible process of assembly and disassembly in psiomes, he recognizes in them the traits of the preceding generations of organic life and turns the whole shebang into a phantasmagoria of chimerical and actual beings.

"Like most people, John mistakenly interprets the operation of opposing physical forces as the ultimate battle between good and evil. Depending on the degree of optimism or pessimism, religious philosophies historically have preached the inevitable conflict between the forces of good and the forces of evil. The Judeo-Christian-Islamic religions are committed to the view that God, representing the forces of good, is destined to overcome evil. That, of course, is what John describes.

The Womb of Uncreated Night

"Other views range from uncertain outcomes in a tossup between the opposing forces, to a kind of universal absorption into a state resembling entropy. There's a third view, that opposing forces will come together and evolve into a new cosmic structure."

"And that's the one you subscribe to?" said Korngold.

"It's the one with the fewest risks," replied Brewster.

"I'm surprised to find you so cautious," said Korngold, who really was surprised. Then he tried to smile through wary skepticism. "But we're not quite through with God, yet, are we? I still haven't heard how all this . . ." he made a sweeping gesture, "connects the *Revelation* with vampirism."

"We must be evolving," said Brewster, surprised in his turn by Korngold's encouraging him to go on. "Well, much of what John writes is repetitious. Beasts full of multiple eyes, horns, wings, crowns, and such. It all begins to come together for me—the psiform strange attractors, God, and vampirism—in the chapters where John stands before the throne of God and the Lamb opens the sealed book of Judgment in God's hand. At the opening of the sixth seal, there's an earthquake, the sun turns black, and the moon turns bloody.

"The stage is set, with four angels waiting for the signal to release the winds that will tear the earth apart. But first a fifth angel announces the 'sealing of the faithful,' the imprinting on the foreheads of one hundred forty-four thousand 'of all the tribes of Israel' with the seal of impunity from the impending doom. In addition, there appears before the throne an uncountable number from 'all nations, and kindreds, and peoples, and tongues,' clothed in robes that have been washed in the blood of the lamb." And once again, Korngold held up a hand, nodded to acknowledge that he was familiar with the passages from *Revelation*, urging Brewster to get to the point.

"Okay," said Brewster, understanding Korngold's impatience. "You can see the emphasis on blood as a guarantee of immortality. And that takes us into vampire territory. Granted, vampirism puts a different spin on the nature of that immortality. This multitude

> serve him day and night in his temple; and he that sitteth on the throne shall dwell among them. They shall hunger no more, neither thirst any more; neither shall the sun light on them, nor any heat. For the lamb which is in the midst of the throne shall feed them, and shall lead them unto living fountains of waters . . .

Imagine," said Brewster, his eyes wide with the awe of an invisible wonder, "A day without sun. An existence without sunlight or heat or hunger or thirst. If that doesn't sound like the life of vampires, I don't know what does.

"But where John sees in the assemblage before the throne of God and the expulsion of Satan and his minions from heaven a war between the forces of good and evil, I see the dual forces of intertwining strange attractors. Diagrammatically, they are represented by the lines of a series of trajectories like the traces of astral orbits flowing into shapes resembling the mask of an owl or the wings of a butterfly. Those are traces of the trajectories of psiomes. Since they are incorporeal, they don't have arms and legs. But because of the interchange of images between them and humans, they 'think' they have limbs. They all come back to earth like short-wave radio signals bouncing off the ionosphere."

"So, you're not saying that Wagehalsen is a psiform being?" sighed Korngold, relieved.

Brewster smiled out the window, as if something out there amused him. Korngold followed his gaze. Across the street, the shadows had swept almost to the tops of the buildings. Willpower alone could not hold them down. His mind balanced on lines that ought to have had finite thicknesses. But the more he thought about them, the more they divided, endlessly! That damned vampire virus! That damned journal! Was it the authentic ranting of a nineteenth century lunatic under the influence of the virus? Was it a hoax? Were his own hallucinations—he dismissed out of hand the possibility that Wagehalsen had survived over a hundred years just so that he could torment him—were they psychotic episodes of an otherwise sane mind? All these were compounded in a vat of guilt at having betrayed his professional honor by lusting after a patient. Strange attractors, indeed!

"Neither St. John of the *Revelation* nor Wagehalsen of the journal are themselves psiforms," said Brewster. "They are the human archetypes of psiforms."

It was all bullshit, of course. Yet Wagehalsen's disturbing . . . *visits* . . . left Korngold vulnerable to bullshit. Bad enough to entertain his own delusions! Had he crossed the threshold of Brewster's psychosis and somehow begun to share the delusion of his dotty patient, entering into a kind of folie à deux? And in such a scenario, in which *Brewster* could be the dominant personality! Korngold shook away the inappropriate thoughts. Trying to displace his own sense of guilt over betraying Jennifer and Brewster would make his slide into paranoia all the more certain.

And where was God in all this? An irrelevant question. God and the soul were nothing more than naïve, outmoded constructs originated somewhere in the maze of the neocortex—probably centered in the anterior cingulate sulcus, the putative seat of the Will—and stubbornly clung to by a hunter-gatherer mentality which humans still have not evolved out of. Ah, but if the Will sits there, where is the site of the unconscious? Could it be the shadow of consciousness thrown off by the electrochemical misfirings of restive neurons . . . fragmentary dream-like images generated by the neuromodulators in the brain stem and thrown into dark relief against the luminance of consciousness . . . and thus a kind of anti-consciousness embedded in it? Or was it the other way around, the darkness encoded in the brain cells waiting for the light to flicker and fade away? Brewster's exegesis of John's *Revelation* made a crazy kind of sense!

In a way, wasn't Brewster's spectral psi-form Consciousness just such a cosmic shadow projected against the darker shadow of the mind? As Korngold sat, brooding about these unsettling questions—thinking that this, if ever, was a time for a laughing philosopher—a phantasmagoria of fantastic creatures diffracted in ghostly layers through his mind and seemed to swirl, merge, and separate again in interlacing rings around two opposed vortexes, God and Satan, like the staring eyes of an owl. Somewhere in the celestial psi-sphere, in one vortex, a Supreme Vampire sitting on a cosmic throne of blood, attended by one hundred forty-four thousand vampires of the elect and served by a great sunless horde; in the other, the ultimate beach boy surfing on a breaking wave of cosmic consciousness.

40.

JENNIFER WAS THE KEY. BREWSTER was sure of it. Why else would the vampire have attacked her repeatedly? She had survived so far only because his work had been interrupted. Yet, she was as drawn to the Ramble as Brewster to her. But after the deadly attacks on Artsynick and Barvim, he knew that the police would tighten security in and around the place. Batman ventured into the dark, almost-deserted park again, cautiously, with every nano-sense exquisitely attuned. He detected the presence of a pair of patrolmen lurking inside the entrances to the park long before they could have become aware of him. He leaped over the wall on Fifth Avenue in tree-shadowed isolation just below 79th Street. Moving swiftly and silently through the darkest patches of paths skirting Cedar Hill, he crossed the East Drive, a dark shadow flitting across the road just above the Loeb Boat House. As he neared The Point on the north shore of the Lake, he was surprised that instead of cops, his heightened senses picked up a subdued struggle in the shrubbery, erratic rustlings, gasps, a stifled cry. But whether the cry was one of terror or of ecstasy, he could not tell.

Then he saw. A figure in top hat and cape crouched over a pale woman barely visible through the brush. As he neared the forms, Batman saw that under the cape, the figure bent over the woman was naked. His head under the hat was buried in her neck. Her long white pale hair spilled out over fallen leaves and twigs which rustled as the vampire made sucking sounds at her throat. Batman threw aside stealth and lunged at the creature with an unrestrained grunt of disgust. Hearing the onrush the other instantly reared its maw, blood-covered and blurred, from Jennifer's neck. When it saw Batman, it turned, snarling, and fled in the direction of the 78th Street Transverse. Batman wanted to chase the form, but instead turned back to the unconscious woman lying in a tangle of twigs and leaves.

Hearing the sounds of Batman crashing through the brush, a pair of patrolmen approached from the direction of the Bonfire Rock where the vampire had earlier created a diversionary attack on another victim. They caught fleeting glimpses of the naked man running away from the scene and were about to give chase. But Batman knew that the woman would need immediate medical attention. Since they could get Jennifer the assistance she needed sooner than anything he could do, he called out,

"Help! Over here!"

When he was sure they had heard him and were moving in the right direction, he blended silently into the shadows and moved swiftly and tangentially to their path among the trees and shrubs on the bluff overlooking the east shore of The Lake. Behind him he heard the crackling from their walkie-talkies as they made their way to where Jennifer lay. The flashing lights of a patrol car strobed through the tops of the trees as he reached the Cove, slipped down to the shore of The Lake, skirted the spot where the bodies of Artsynick and Barvim had been found, darted across the West Drive, down the Balcony Ridge above the dry bed of the Ladies' Pond, and up to Central Park West.

Victims of vampire attacks were now routinely referred to New York Hospital where Dr. Buckyballs' expertise made him a much sought after consultant. So when Jennifer was brought into the hospital in a deep coma, he was called in. He, in turn, immediately notified Korngold that his patient had been brought in. They were conferring in front of the nurses' station when the elevator deposited Brewster on the seventh floor. He was about to interrupt them for news of Jennifer's condition when, glancing down the corridor on his right he spied a uniformed officer sitting in front of one of the rooms. He knew that circumstances surrounding Jennifer warranted police protection, and guessed that the officer must be guarding her room. He decided not to bother the doctors for the moment, turned and walked to the room to ask about her condition. The guard not only refused comment on Jennifer's condition but would not confirm that he was guarding her. And he had been instructed to let no one into her room without the permission of Dr. Korngold or Dr. Buckyballs. The refusal as such did not bother Brewster. But he took exception to the guard's hostile tone. He protested. The guard warned, threatened, and within a few moments their raised voices attracted the attention of Korngold and Buckyballs.

Korngold hurried to intervene. It looked to him as if Brewster was about to force his way past the officer. He took Brewster aside and reproached him for creating a disturbance where sick people were recuperating.

"I understand," said Brewster, "that it's necessary to protect Jennifer, but surely I pose no threat to her?"

"Maybe not," said Korngold, "but the police who responded to Jennifer's cry for help saw a caped man escaping from the scene."

"It wasn't Jennifer who called for help. It was me. And the caped man they saw was the vampire, gotten up as a Wagehalsen look-alike."

Korngold started at the mention of Wagehalsen. He recovered quickly. "You called for help. But you fled the scene. You were there in that Batman getup, weren't you? You see how guilty that would make you look. How do you know that you weren't seen?"

"Wait! You think I'm to blame for happened to Jennifer?" protested Brewster.

"Please keep your voice down." Korngold glanced at the guard eyeing them. "You don't want to attract any more attention to yourself. Frankly, I don't know what to think."

"You know I didn't attack her!" said Brewster, indignantly lowering his voice. "And the police don't know about Batman." He paused. "Or do they?"

"Now Brewster," said Korngold, "you know I can't violate the doctor-patient—" He caught himself as Brewster once more looked at him as he had the day after he had spoken with Jennifer in the Ramble. "But you can't believe that they haven't caught a whiff of your past escapade with the Batmobile."

"The court records were sealed!"

"True. A sealed record can't be used against you in a legal proceeding. But your escapade was reported in the media. And there is no way of sealing the memories of the police who were present at your arrest. You see the danger of stirring up recollections of the Batman episode and the possibility that someone may confuse him with, well, the Wagehalsen knock-off? If that's what you really saw."

"You think I'm making it up!" said Brewster.

Korngold took his arm and held up a warning hand. "No. Not inventing. But after hearing the contents of Wagehalsen's journal," Korngold shrugged, "well, imagination . . ."

Brewster looked down at him steadily. "So, now I'm hallucinating?"

"Brewster," said Korngold, sighing, "anyone's mind can create . . . impressions under stress. And you seem to be unusually susceptible to suggestion. Think about the fantastic stuff you've told me. The influence of Hippias. Your theory of psiwaves. Your innuendos . . ."

Brewster almost laughed in spite of the situation, while Korngold visibly squirmed. After a few moments, he said, "But where's the harm in letting me see her? There's something about her . . . Like a psychic connection between us. I think, no, I'm *sure*, there's a link between her and Guinevere's disappearance."

Korngold opened his mouth but said nothing.

The Womb of Uncreated Night

"Couldn't a friendly presence somehow be reassuring," added Brewster, "if only at some unconscious level?"

"Not a chance. Jennifer is off limits. Even if she became aware of your presence at some unconscious level, I don't see anything to be gained by it. People in comas do sense what's going on around them. But it's just as likely to be disturbing. No. For the time being, I won't allow you to see her. Don't pout. It's unbecoming in someone big enough to scrape the ceiling!"

Brewster had nothing left. If Korngold picked a time like this to be condescending . . . "Who're you trying to protect," he grumbled, turning to leave, "Jennifer or . . . someone else?"

"Let's talk about this at our next session. For the present, I think it best that we keep this just between us."

🦇

That night, a huge bat climbed up the hospital wall. Its fingers gripped the stone with faint scraping sounds. When it reached the seventh story, it forced the window open and crept inside. Batman stood in the room. Jennifer, deep in a coma, lay on the only bed in the room. In the corridor beyond the closed door, a cop guarded what he believed was the only conceivable entrance into the room. As soon as he came into the room, using only his human senses, Batman contemplated the increasingly restless woman on the bed. But he sensed another presence. He could not quite identify which sense alerted him. It was like the almost felt sensation of an object disappearing just as it caught the corner of your eye . . . or the prickly stirring of the hair on the back of your hand when something hovers just above it . . . or the faint, sour trace of tobacco that clings to a smoker's clothing . . .

Momentarily jolted by the unexpected presence, Brewster recoiled. Had the figure glided out from behind the portable screen next to the door? As his eyes adjusted to the dim light, Brewster thought he saw a dark figure against the dark.

"Who's there?" he whispered, not wanting to alert the guard outside the door.

"Sometimes," a whispered voice responded, "if you question a darkness, it answers back."

Now Brewster could just make out something of a face. Was it shaded by a hat? And a body wrapped in a cloak? Did its eyes glow redly in the dark . . . ? Brewster wondered if Korngold had been right about him, about imagination and suggestibility.

"So," whispered the voice, "we meet again, under somewhat less . . . rustic circumstances." The figure behind the voice, so confident, raised his arms so that his cloak unfurled like the wings of some predatory bird. The eyes, so hypnotic, burned into Brewster's. Then, seeing the Other with his cape fanned out behind him, he could see dimly that he was naked. He wanted to laugh. What's this guy getting ready to do, fight or fly? Oh, what the hell! And grabbing the edges of his own cape, he swept his arms shoulder high so that he, too, looked poised for fight or flight.

"Now if only I could get my eyes to smolder like embers," he murmured.

"Why have you come, eh?" said the Other, annoyed, lowering his arms. Brewster's shadow was clearly greater than his. "Ah, I see! You thought that the shock of seeing a bat-like creature—dressed in that ridiculous costume—you thought that would penetrate this woman's coma and jolt her back to her senses? What an amusing notion."

Brewster began to feel silly and lowered his arms. Let the Other flap his in campy menace. But he braced himself for whatever would come.

"And why have *you* come?" said Brewster, both accusing and wondering, but resisting the impulse to add "eh?" "Couldn't tear yourself away from your victim, could you? You're like an addict unable to control an insatiable desire. I wonder if you have the same self-loathing—"

"Self-loathing!" hissed the Other. "Self-loathing! Examine your own soul, *Bat*-man! Why did you choose that costume? Do you know what drew you to that dark image? Do you know what it was in you that responded to the darkness of this cavernous city like a great yawning mouth into which you were lured?"

"Lured!" said Brewster, momentarily forgetting to whisper. Jennifer, moving restlessly, sharply inhaled. The chair outside the door creaked. Brewster imagined the guard outside the door shifting in his chair and cocking an ear to listen. He would have to be more careful.

"Oh, yes. Lured," whispered the Other. "A vampire has an aura, an irresistible lure. Many have been summoned by it." Then, what would have been a puzzled look, if Brewster could have seen them more clearly, came into his eyes. All Brewster saw was a slight dimming of the glowing red, like dying embers. "But some are resistant. And you . . . you come in a form I did not expect. In the guise of a creature of the night with the soul of a creature of the day. Curious, how subliminal influences manifest themselves!"

"Ha! Like Wagehalsen emitting hypnotic auras that settle into unconscious minds a century later only to have his evil intent distorted and come out good? Or maybe it's just that imagination is a free agent, random and unpredictable, feeding off every kind of casual perception. In your case, a sinister desire to deprive others of their wills and lives to enhance your own."

"And in *your* case," retorted the Other chuckling, "an adolescent pop icon fantasy of good intentions!

"Well, it may work either way. If you act on intentions springing from blind impulse, the consequences may be either beneficial or destructive to yourself or to others. To persist in destructive behavior is evil, even though it sprang from an impulse that might have held potential for good. So, an apparently evil person may not know what impulses for good his mind harbors. You may not be as completely evil as you think."

"No one is 'complete,'" said the Other. "None of us contains everything in the universe. That's why everything feeds off everything else. We can look deeply into ourselves, but even with complete self-awareness, life still depends on other life to sustain it. If blind chance governs our actions, there is no universal will, no moral 'soul' to guide the choices of that sustenance. Yet there is a certain indefinable something, a universal essence of life that enhances those choices. The closer we can approximate that essence, the longer we may live. That's as much 'soul' as there is."

"And since the blood holds that essence . . ." said Brewster. "You have the soul of an insect and the mentality of a virus!"

"What more logical organism to convey immortality? Viruses live at the edge of life, defying all the criteria of life, existing between living and non-living states. You see, they are in a way, 'undead.' What's more, they readily transfer genetic material from one host to another. What could be more efficient?"

"Hah!" said Brewster, "then why no immortal mosquitoes!"

The Other shrugged. "Mosquitoes carry diseases that do not affect them!"

"So, immortality is a disease!"

The Other leaned forward. He thrust his face at Brewster's barely an inch away. Close as their faces were, Brewster could see only the glowing eyes and caught the smell of something so powerful that he went dizzy.

"Oh, all right," chuckled the Other, drawing back. "That is a kind of soul! Let's say that the essence of life was breathed into me as well as every other organism by God. To some, he gave life as we usually think of it; to others, he gave an almost-life, something on the boundary between living and non-living. Perhaps from that perspective, the soul of a vampire may be considered, um, congealed, suspended in night like an insect in amber."

"The soul of an insect!" said Brewster again. As they whispered, hunched over the bed, their words buzzing in the air searched for a place to light, Jennifer's head began to twitch from side to side as if to shoo them away.

"Once you have the conventional idea of souls, what is salvation but another way of saying 'undead'? There is as much salvation," the Other chuckled sarcastically, "as damnation in every living thing."

The Womb of Uncreated Night

"The soul," mused Brewster. "Well, maybe that survives in some form. But that damnation part applies to the body. I can't see electromagnetic waves being tortured for some past blip on the screen. While we live, the body remembers what the mind forgets. I suppose the last thought people have at the moment of death, whether of divine forgiveness or suffering in hell, that's eternity enough. Maybe, such a thought can even distort their auras as their cells disintegrate and release them into space. But put a satanic creature into that context? Salvation—for a vampire?"

"Ah, the satanic! Yes, but even the satanic might be entitled to salvation," said the Other. "Why else would God, when Satan rebelled against heaven, have cast him into the fiery lake. Why didn't he destroy him and the fallen angels outright?"

"The biblical myth," Brewster, reflected, "says that God created heaven and earth. It never says that he created the angels. So maybe he can't destroy what he didn't create. But salvation—for Satan! That makes a hash of the divine mystery of *human* salvation."

"Perhaps Satan's salvation is only . . . deferred. We might say that, like mass and energy, he can neither can be created nor destroyed. Only transformed."

"But that Satan himself should have been spared for future redemption . . . ?" said Brewster, puzzled. I suppose redemption *is* a kind of transformation. Yet, that falls outside the myth. Jesus didn't die for Satan."

The Other chuckled. "Possibly. Possibly. But when powerful forces are unleashed, who can say where circumstance and chance may not come together to baffle divine purpose? God could no more destroy the fallen ones than he could destroy himself, any more than he could destroy any other life essence in the cosmos. But he *could* have transformed them into some innocuous form." The Other paused, then chuckled sardonically. "Maybe he just wanted to relieve the tedium of being almighty, and needed a diversion to keep him from becoming depressed!"

"And invented human beings to give Satan something to divert *him*! And little demons have lesser demons . . . !"

Vampire and Batman shared a quiet, cynical moment.

"Then all would be forgiven," said Brewster, "eventually? But God can't be bored, the infinite can never end, and the promise of redemption, like the pot of gold at the end of the rainbow, is eternally promised. And people die happily ever after pursuing it."

"Ah," said the vampire, "I see that you have the fine points of theology well in hand. What is salvation, after all, but a myth perpetuating life within a Sunday morning sideshow?"

"But Belial thought differently along those lines," said Brewster. "He argued that God had the power to destroy the angels, but simply didn't want to. It gave him the hope that by enduring their miserable circumstances they'd at least get used to it. Eventually, it wouldn't seem so bad. Things might even get better."

"Slovenly reasoning from the personification of Sloth! He lacked the energy to differentiate between reluctance and inability."

"Reluctance and inability," Brewster mused aloud . . .

"Not only the troublesome angels, but he also stopped short of destroying mankind," scoffed the Other. "And when, after the flood, human disobedience not only continued but even got worse, he supposedly sent some portion of *himself* into the world to atone for the evil ways of his own 'creation'! How indecisive this God sounds! How he contorts himself into convoluted self-fulfillment!

"Einstein once said that God did not play dice with the universe. But Einstein was wrong. God is a gambler. It's as if he bet against Satan that, playing by rules he set up and allowing the outcome to be determined by chance, he'd win. When he didn't, he kept reneging on the bet, and reset the game for a do-over. But no matter how often he played, he didn't win. And like any compulsive gambler who keeps betting against the odds, he goes on playing as the losses mount up."

Brewster nodded thoughtfully. "But maybe it's more like a stage play in which an author creates his characters not knowing how they will turn out? When he writes, characters and circumstances are created out of his conscious mind. Seen from that angle, they do not truly act freely. But to convince an audience, they must appear to have free choice. The greater humanity in them comes out of the author's unconscious. If he succeeds, the ending becomes inevitable."

"Hm-hm-hm! You think that God has an unconscious? An intriguing notion, my young friend. But if true freedom has its origins in God's unconscious mind, then does it not follow that the end is unpredictable? He cannot have complete control of the cosmos any more than you have complete control of your unconscious. Like parallel lines, his promise of redemption and his inability to absolutely predict the outcome, will never coincide, no matter how infinitely far they extend. No, my young friend, a play has a fixed structure and a limited running time. A gambling den does not.

"In dividing light from dark, dividing his kingdom, creating good for himself and evil for Satan, he diminished himself. Apply your claim that subliminal impulses of mind, because they are below the level of consciousness and therefore unknowable, give rise not only to the soul but also freedom, to this mythic God. Mightn't they slip past *his* consciousness? He may create. But that creation has the distressing capacity to exceed his intended course. He created the beginning, but not the end. Viewed in this light, human beings have erected a belief in a God without solid foundation, a faith without substance, a future without assurance."

"Well, even an atheist like Freud concluded at the end of his life that religion is useful in preserving civilization. Whether people believe in someone or something that turns out to be fantasy or delusion, religions based on it serve a useful end. Without a God, there can be no religion. Without religion . . . maybe there would be no civilization." Brewster fell silent for a moment. He hoped that the infinite regret he had begun to feel was not merely some spurious resonance of the Other's cocksureness. "Of course, Freud couldn't take into account the deadly turn of recent events, where the adherents of rival religions may now unleash weapons of mass destruction against each other and threaten to destroy civilization in the process."

"The survival of civilization," mused the vampire. "It all comes down to power and who will wield it. Ultimately, it's a choice between autocracy and democracy. Schopenhauer, who mistrusted governments, said he'd rather be ruled by a lion than by a fellow rat. He advocated aesthetically induced tranquility to keep people in line. But he knew that not many people can enter an aesthetic state of mind long enough to curb their destructive impulses. So he also justified violent authority to cope with them. That inevitably leads to resistance and resistance degenerates into a power struggle. The state turns tyrant, and the citizenry turn rebel.

"What most people need is an anodyne, one that will calm and soothe them, and at the same time, leave them pliant without impairing their ability to function productively in society."

"Like mass hypnosis," said Brewster. "You want people to surrender their will to you?"

The Other scoffed. "And where has their free will led them? To the brink of destruction! Where is their virtue, their God of Good when he's needed? Nowhere! Certainly not in a myth that people profess but seldom act up to. Or do you think," he went on with heavy sarcasm, "that God is the great clockmaker who has set the universe spinning and sits, chin on hand, to observe it? We are closer than you think. Like brothers in thought, if not in fact."

"Brothers!"

"Oh, yes, Korngold, you, and I! Each of us, in his own way, seeks to save the world, since God himself is disinclined or unable to do it. Korngold, one lunatic at a time. You, with your crusade against criminals. And I, with an infection that will redeem the human race, one bite at a time. All three of us have been diverted from our main purpose in a struggle for this young woman's . . . soul."

"You! Save the world?"

"Oh, yes. It's what all people think they want in their inner being. Some think that they can do it through martyrdom, dressing up their personal salvation in humanitarian purpose . . ."

"I would rather think that personal salvation is a thinly disguised wish to escape the general calamity of the human condition. That martyrs actually despair of life as a road to salvation. Smugly confident of their own righteousness, they rush to call down Armageddon. And if that means consigning a lot of bystanders to damnation . . .," Brewster shrugged. "A curious kind of humanitarian purpose, and one that's curiously at odds with the example of their Christ!"

"Sometimes, a remote salvation is more tantalizing than an ongoing futility. Those fools who endure their miserable existence probably hope that the salvation game is rigged. That in spite of all the evidence to the contrary, there's a—what?—divinely ordained fate? Or maybe there are ends beyond God's certain knowledge? If they believe in that gamble and live their lives accordingly, how much freedom do they really have? No. The myth is the dream of sleepwalkers."

Brewster felt like someone who dreams but wonders if he is awake.

"Only if there is a real chance that God can lose," continued the vampire . . .

"How odd," interrupted Brewster, "to quibble over a being whose existence we doubt, yet concede as long as he is powerless . . ."

"For me, *God* is a convenient metaphor for the unknowable. He's a handy way to talk about a proper contest between opposing forces. For those fools who are ready to repent, '. . . if only at the end, if only by whispering half the name of Mary with their last breath,' secure in the belief that God will eventually forgive them, he's the answer to their prayers."

If there can be laughter in a whisper, Brewster thought he heard it. The vampire insinuated such intense mockery into his words that Brewster's scalp prickled under the hood. Although the quotation sounded vaguely familiar—Dante?—he could not place it. Still, he sensed something underneath the arrogance. It made him feel lightheaded. Was it possible, he wondered, that a vampire could communicate its suggestive power without a physical exchange of blood? He shuddered at the possibility that he might pick up the vampire's state of mind, even if he was able to resist its hypnotic hold. There was something about the way the vampire scoffed at faith that made him uneasy.

"But even if you objectify God as a metaphor for perpetual gamesmanship," said Brewster," doesn't it make existence rather futile?"

"Fah! What is existence to a schizophrenic God! One that casts out a part of himself and calls it Evil, calls the remainder Good, then tinkers with organic matter and wants its praise! No matter how shadowy, its reality—the millions who have absolute faith in it make the game absurdly real enough!"

"Yet if God needs Satan eternally opposed to him in order to avert boredom, wouldn't the same be true of Satan? Say that Satan wins the struggle. Once it's over, once you've won, won't boredom set in and leave behind a sense of futility?"

"What kind of omniscience requires the penitent to make an outward show," the Other ran on, "as if it were not sure of the inner state? Half that band who aspire to salvation and sainthood wallow in the very temptations they abominate, clinging to pious formulas as to a safety hatch, while the other half seek to eliminate temptation because they are afraid they cannot resist it! What was it Jesus was supposed to have said to Satan? 'Get thee behind me'? He had better said, 'Stand thou before me so that I may keep my eye on you and know how to defeat you'! Hypocrite! What kind of virtue never confronts evil, maintains a purity never exposed to stain? Yet there was the founder of his religion, hiding temptation out of sight rather than risk getting himself dirty by facing and resisting it!"

"Perhaps," said Brewster, "passive resistance in the presence of a formidable adversary has its own virtue—and unexpected strategic advantage. By sending his 'son' into the world of men to resist force with meekness, perhaps God has executed a brilliancy that resets the cosmic game."

"Ss—ss—ss," chuckled the vampire. "And what modest virtue has brought you here?"

"Well, I *am* confronting you, even if we aren't exactly battling physically," said Brewster, "are we? That modest enough for you?"

"But you miss a beat in your upward flight!"

The Womb of Uncreated Night

"I guess. It's really not the floundering that matters so much as the direction you were going in when it happens."

"Take care that when you fly your aspirations your wings don't get singed and you plunge the other way. It's a long way down."

"I don't aspire during the day," said Brewster drily.

The two fell silent. Two shadows tented together in the darkness, their faces so close that their voices were almost superfluous. The alarm Brewster felt when the Other first appeared had never left him. But he had begun to feel a little surer of his ground during the rational exchange of ideas. Reason has a balm that soothes the overwrought imagination. Was Jennifer resting more peacefully? The Other certainly seemed less menacing. After all, he could have attacked him outright instead of challenging him to this game of wits. But Brewster remained wary. A game of wits could be another kind of lure, isn't that what the Other said? *Had* he been lured here?

And then another thought occurred to him. "But coming back to the possibility that the God you scoff at, the shadowy metaphor you oppose, really were to lose your game?"

"Not *my* game, my young friend. *The* game. But God lose? Unthinkable! Satan would never permit himself to fall into the boredom that would follow."

"But you said . . . " The Other drew his head back and raised a hand to fend off further protest.

"Do you play chess? The king is never captured." He lowered his hand and brought his face close to Brewster's again. Brewster once again caught that almost intoxicating sour smell. "Trapped, yes. But captured, never. God must neither lose nor win. Without light, darkness is meaningless. There must always be white and black. No. This contest must never be resolved. The game is all. As long as the powers are equally opposed, no matter how they are arrayed, the outcome is never certain. They are locked in a game of the imagination, played out on the cosmic board as on earth. Your 'divine mystery' continues. What is existence without mystery? What is mystery without imagination?"

"What are any of these without hope?"

"Indeed. Devoid of hope, the outcome turns into futility. Who is good, who, evil? Chess is a game in black and white, without spectrum or shades of gray. For clarity, not value judgments. Technicolor would only confuse the issue. Oh, yes. Either God or Satan may lose an occasional round. But each loss is a new beginning. Each new beginning, a gain. What was well or badly played in one will be better played each time the match is resumed. If the contest followed dramatic convention, a rising action that reached its climax and was inevitably resolved in a programmed resolution, it would be an elaborate pretense. The game may be between shadows, but the pieces are real."

"Then we are pawns pushed around on a playing field, helpless to affect the outcome?" Brewster felt as if he had come too close to a power that drained away his confidence. "It sounds so meaningless."

"The game is itself the meaning. Existence is meaning. Winning and losing," the vampire shrugged, "those are *human* concepts, meaningless in the grand scheme. Seeing the larger frame of reference offers the choice of playing the game or being played upon, not whether it is played well or ill. That is the difference between active and passive resistance. That is the meaning. Not whether it is Good or Evil."

"But without value judgment, call it morality, you reduce life for the mass of mankind to cattle you milk. *Things* to be manipulated by the Game Masters! The only beings truly alive are the opponents. And one side of the opposition, God, according to *your* mythology, isn't real! What you're saying is that only the vampires will *live* in a cosmos that is devoid of all purpose other than the whim of vampires!"

"You still haven't grasped what I've been telling you about God. God is as real as the wars fought in his name, as real as the bodies strewn over the battlefield."

Brewster found the Other's twists and turns mind numbing.

"Ah, my young friend, you also overlook the tranquility which I would bestow on mankind."

"But the unthinkable," protested Brewster, "the defeat of the

God-myth among all mankind. Your whims would turn to the very boredom you oppose."

"One game lost—oh, yes, my friend, the God-myth is part of the game—only resets the board for another match. The contest would never end."

"But how long could such a delusion be maintained?" muttered Brewster.

"How long," laughed the Other, catching Brewster's puzzlement, "could a madman maintain his delusion?"

Brewster was horrified. "Your game turns the whole universe into a lunatic asylum!"

"Some lunatics are quite happy. As for those who are not . . ." the Other shrugged. "As I said, it all depends on the role you play."

Jennifer was becoming restive again.

"Real and unreal, reason and absurdity, sanity and lunacy," said the Other, "all are the caprices of mankind. Who is to say absolutely which is best?"

"Who would not want to distinguish between right and wrong?"

"Ah, morality. The ultimate caprice!"

Jennifer's movements on the bed had become more agitated and she began to gasp loudly, as if she were strangling. Her eyes opened, uncomprehending. For a moment, they were unfocused, darting back and forth, seeking orientation.

"Do you think you can help her now?" taunted the Other. Jennifer's eyes fluttered, casting about wildly for something reassuring to cling to. She screamed in terror at the sight of the two dark figures hovering over her, poised as if to tear each other apart and her in the process. In an instant, the guard in the hall, hearing her cries, burst through the door to investigate, the Other dissolved into the shadows.

Brewster dived head first through the open window. He launched his body in a graceful arc and plunged down the stone face of the building. But his left foot caught on the window sill, the force of his fall causing the gripping compound in the toe to fix it firmly against it, and his body to pivot, slamming his hands against the wall. He tried desperately to free himself by shifting his weight to his arms and right foot. He might then be able to swing himself around into an upright position. He thought, inanely, that it would even be possible to crawl down the wall head first except that his cape would fall over his head and interfere with his movements. But he found that his hands and feet were splayed so wide apart that he could not ease the pressure at either end, and so could not get the gripping compound to release him. There he was, stuck head downward like some specimen pinned out on a dissecting table that had unaccountably tilted to the vertical.

The guard leaned out the window, grabbed Brewster's foot and called for reinforcements. Brewster knew that if he could just free his hands from the grippers there was no way that the cop could hold him. But the leverage of his foot in the grip of the guard was not enough to allow him to swing his hands clear without falling. It was a long way down. As it was, it took the guard and two beefy attendants to pry him loose and haul him back through the window.

As he hung out the hospital window, immobilized by his own ingenuity, the cop and two hospital attendants trying to pry him loose from the wall, Brewster had some time to contemplate the nuances of his situation. He was understandably annoyed at being caught, embarrassed by the flaw in his equipment which neither he nor Hippias had foreseen. He was also mildly concerned that the three men trying to dislodge him might call for a jackhammer to chisel him loose once they realized how thoroughly stuck he was. And then there was the interesting prospect that, if they did try to lever his feet free, a good deal of his safety depended on their ability to hold on to his feet. If their efforts flipped him away from the wall, only the strength of his fingers would prevent his falling, and he was not entirely sure that his fingers would not snap under such a stress. Thinking that he would need his fingers in the future, he wondered if he should tell the men to take the stress off his extremities either by freeing his feet from the boots while holding on to his legs or hoisting him slightly by the utility

The Womb of Uncreated Night

belt. He could tell the men to release one boot at a time, relying on their grip around one ankle as he freed the other. Then when they pulled him up enough to ease the pressure on his hands, he could coordinate a backward climb with them continuing to pull him up. The belt method would probably be the more secure for him, but that would require someone leaning dangerously far out the window in order to grab the belt or tie a sheet or rope to it. Either method would be tricky and a decision would have to be made soon, as the three men were making no progress in hauling him up.

As he mulled over these options, another feeling was struggling to break through, one that he had so far seldom felt, or at least, consciously admitted. Frustration. Futility, only partly eased by the thought that his capture may at least have prevented the vampire from draining away what was left of Jennifer's life.

41.

THE DREADED SUMMONS FROM DR. Sandor came. Korngold knew that after Brewster's escapade at the hospital it was inevitable. Even though Sandor had never had an active hand in the therapy, the court had referred Brewster's case to him. He was accountable to the court. Korngold was accountable to him. As simple as that. What was not so simple, Sandor would be grimly determined to assess the damage to the patient and his own reputation, especially in light of what he hoped to gain from Augustus Wainwright, and the effect on Korngold's career.

When he came into Sandor's office, Korngold wore a dress shirt, tie, and slacks. He even shined his shoes. Like the defendant in a bloody criminal trial, he thought.

Fixed on a face that otherwise might have graced a cuddly pet, Dr. Sandor's scowl was a study in disconcerting contrasts. Plump and complacent as a jovial Buddha, his expression was anything but benevolent. He said nothing. He sat behind his desk, motioned Korngold into a chair. He folded his hands over his belly and waited.

After a few minutes of strained silence, Korngold spoke. "Shall I lie on the couch," he said, indicating the item in the corner, "and freely associate?" Sandor's expression was rigid. No, thought Korngold glumly. Flippancy isn't going to do it for him. It might have been easier if Sandor had lit into him as soon as he came in.

The Womb of Uncreated Night

"How can things have gotten so out of hand?" began Sandor quietly.

"I underestimated the power of Brewster's fantasy," Korngold said. "Brewster is devilishly clever. After four years, orthodox therapy simply wasn't working. So I tried an experimental technique to break through." He shrugged. "Besides, I was never fully convinced that he was really as disturbed as he—"

"An experimental technique?" said Sandor, his curiosity rising with his tone of voice. "You've compromised your professional position, put me in an awkward position with the hospital, the court, the Wainwright family . . . with an experimental technique?"

Not exactly the receptive forum for sharing empirical data Korngold might have wished for, but he would not sit there and be scolded like an errant schoolboy in the principal's office. "Brewster's obsession with Batman began long before the Batmobile incident. It took its most dysfunctional turn after the disappearance of his fiancée—"

"While he was in therapy with you?"

Korngold gritted his teeth and nodded. "There were rumors of a vampire attack, but her body was never found."

"Wasn't there also another so-called vampire attack on the woman known as Jennifer around the same time? She turned up in New York Hospital with a case of amnesia and became one of your pro-bono patients, I believe?" Sandor made a tent of his fingers and touched them to his lips. "Interesting."

"Yes. When Brewster learned that she, too, had been a victim of vampirism, he became obsessed with her. Convinced that there could be a link through her to the vampire, and through him—"

"If, indeed, the vampire is a man."

Korngold paused. That was unexpected. "You're suggesting that the missing fiancée may be the vampire?"

"If, indeed, there is only one."

"There is evidence to suggest more than one," nodded Korngold. "Dr. Buckyballs has found evidence of a virus that may be spreading a disease resembling porphyry. Brewster's fiancée may have been infected with it. Perhaps there's a whole colony out there, hiding in the Indian Caves and subway surfing down to Central Park to feed on the strollers in the Ramble."

"Spare me your sarcasm," said Sandor picking up a pencil. He began to doodle on the pad on his desk. "The victims," he resumed, "haven't they all been members of that group you and Madame Villiards sponsor?"

This was the link Korngold had especially dreaded. "All except Jennifer," he said. Sandor stopped doodling and raised his eyes to Korngold.

"Except Jennifer . . . And what," said Sandor, "do you make of this curious exception?"

They sat silently staring at each other, as if to test which of them would blink first. Korngold felt his flimsy denials fall away under Sandor's insinuation.

Then Sandor spoke again. "And this experimental technique of yours?"

"As I've said, Brewster and I had reached a plateau. He haunted the Ramble which was the focus of the attacks . . . dressed as Batman. A few years before, he had engaged in vigilantism, mimicking the 'Caped Crusader' of the comic books. I cautioned him against unnecessary risks, but he was quite confident in his physical abilities. He and a former tutor developed a costume with technological enhancements: a bullet-proof fabric incorporated into the torso which was lighter and less bulky than the Kevlar worn by law enforcement agents, gauntlets and boots impregnated with a compound that enabled him to cling to walls—"

"Which he used to scale the outside wall of New York Hospital and climb seven stories?" asked Sandor raising his eyebrows. "Did you think that he was capable of such a thing?"

"I knew about his technological gadgetry," sighed Korngold. "He did tell me about his climbing prowess, even claimed to be able to cling to the ceiling of his father's library. But I assumed he was exaggerating. I confess that I was somewhat in awe of him. Batman gadgets combined with his towering muscular frame and martial arts skills made him a formidable presence. I thought that criminals he occasionally engaged had more to fear from him they he from them.

"The experimental technique . . . When I saw that we weren't making progress, that he was so wrapped up in his Batman fantasy, I decided to offer him an alternate fantasy, thinking that if I could induce him to participate in it and discover the flaws in it, he would see the flaws in his own."

"And you came up with this strategy on your own?" But when Korngold told him that it was a strategy suggested by the late Robert Lindner's *Fifty-Minute Hour*, a therapist who violated traditional therapeutic practice so far as to gleefully participate in a patient's psychosis, Sandor's eyebrows shot up into the creases of his forehead. He began to tap his desktop with a disapproving finger.

"That was a very unsound idea!" Sandor objected. "I know Dr. Lindner's work. Literary 'case-studies' do not qualify as legitimate therapy. A dubious, even a dangerous therapeutic conceit by a brilliant, imaginative man who would have been more at home with the novels he aspired to write before his untimely death."

"I understood the risks," said Korngold. "But there seemed to be no other way of drawing Brewster out of his fantasy. Besides, Lindner's approach is not without precedent. Several analysts have used it successfully. A journal discovered by Dr. Buckyballs, supposedly written by a 19th-century man who really believed he was a vampire, offered a chance of playing off the vampire-bat associations inherent in Brewster's fixation against the recent events in Central Park."

"More of your metaphysical nonsense!" scoffed Sandor "And the 'successful analysts' you refer to were mountebanks like Milton Wexler who flocked to Hollywood where they bungled the therapies of movie stars and wrote bad movie scripts because no respectable therapist on the east coast would have anything to do with them!"

"It is understandable," said Sandor softening his tone, "that someone in our profession would want to try to get into his patient's head, to think like the patient in order to better understand him, and find a way to dislodge his symptoms. But there are lines between fantasy and reality, between patient and therapist that should not be crossed. What you did crossed both lines. Becoming too involved personally with a patient is bad enough. But to go further, to immerse yourself with his delusion . . ." Sandor shrugged at the hopelessness of the prospect.

"But after all," Korngold protested, "in attempting to restore a patient's mental balance, isn't the therapist, in a way, trying to displace a fantasy which to the patient is quite real? The fact that he is substituting what society thinks of as reality doesn't in any way diminish the patient's belief in his own. One way to bring about this displacement is for the therapist to enter the patient's 'reality' and try to get him to see its deficits from within his frame of reference.

"I'm confident that I can maintain a proper professional distance," said Korngold. He was miffed that his mentor would condescend to state the obvious. "I know that there are boundaries."

"Yes, of course," said Sandor. "Aren't we all confident about respecting boundaries. We read a book or go to a movie believing that by consciously suspending disbelief we are able to maintain an objective hold on reality. But we also want to believe in the possibility of imagination. It's not simply escape from the dreary monotony of social necessity that we're after, but an innate desire to restructure it. That's why we dream, that's why we fantasize, and that's why we build on those dreams and fantasies. Sometimes responsibly, sometimes recklessly. Books and movies already have made it too easy for us to cross over the threshold separating reality and fantasy. And just there is the danger of becoming too involved with such material. A suspension of disbelief may too readily lead to a suspension of responsibility.

"Lindner actually advocated rebellion against conformity as a biological imperative. But his advocacy leaped over the need to survive. We may stand by and admire the magnificent failure of the rebel as he fights against the stultifying effects of conformity. But we must never lose sight of the fact that it is, after all, a failure. Rebelling without due consideration for the consequences of our actions is no better than blindly conforming."

"But even in the most conservative of therapeutic strategies," Korngold protested, "we can't predict outcomes. No therapist can do that. Every time we confront a patient, we take chances."

"There's chance and then there's risk," said Sandor. A too-intimate sharing of experience leads to dangerous confusions during the period of transference. Everyone knows that boundaries are imprecise, even vague guidelines. Without precise definition, the edge between chance and risk is so tenuous that it's wise not to get too near. Getting too close to the patient does more than violate the professional taboo against the risk of countertransference. It blurs the edge of therapeutic reality, with dire consequences for both therapist and patient."

"Of course," conceded Korngold miserably. "But I was sure that my relationship with Brewster had reached a point where I could influence him. The procedure is not without precedent. Lindner was spectacularly successful with a scientist who "

Sandor cut him off. "Lindner was lucky with a strategy better suited to Hollywood. And Hollywood analysts have been notoriously unsuccessful with patients they have become too involved with! Not only did they mess up the lives of their patients—the bungled therapies of Marilyn Monroe, Robert Walker, and Frances Farmer leap to mind—but they made a hash of their own lives. And didn't Lindner favorably cite Milton Wexler, who not only violated but actually advocated overstepping therapeutic distance so far as to physically assault a patient?"

Korngold could not counter this argument. But Sandor was not quite done.

"AND," Sandor raised his voice to override anything that might come out of Korngold's open mouth, "if Brewster resisted induction into your alternative fantasy, would you have bullied him as well?"

"If you'd seen Brewster's formidable physique," remarked Korngold drily, "you'd know that I could never bully him. Nor would I seek to exploit him for my own benefit," he added, knowing that Sandor had conveniently left off any reference to the Hollywood analysts' practice of exploiting the doctor-patient relationship to further their own ambitions because he was hoping to do a little exploiting of his own.

"All kidding aside," said Sandor, "I might've warned you, that Dr. Lindner's fantasy role-playing strategy might be dangerous. But you already knew that," he added with a sardonic chuckle, "and probably wouldn't have heeded me anyway. Do you think that the Wainwright boy poses a danger to others?" Sandor shrugged, "You can see why that might be called into question after everything that has happened. And as long as young Wainwright's bizarre behavior does not tax the tolerance of civil authorities—or for that matter, the patience of his father . . ." he trailed off ominously.

"Of course, you understand my position" continued Sandor, alert to crass inferences, "I'm hoping that a successful outcome for Brewster Wainwright would lead to a handsome grant from his father. For the Institute, of course."

"A grant which you would administer," retorted Korngold.

"That is not the same thing as writing a screenplay about my profession or getting in bed with a patient," Sandor shot back.

"I thought I could put on an antic disposition," said Korngold, stung by the irony that Sydney may have blabbed to Sandor about his indiscretion, "without fueling gossip mills, leading to a Hollywood script, or another Marilyn Monroe. I thought it was worth taking a chance. The irony is that Brewster took my alternate fantasy as an invitation to create yet another fantasy. As if it were a kind of gamesmanship. After we 'played' in the milieu of Wagehalsen's journal—"

"Wagehalsen. The author of Buckyballs' discovery?" asked Sandor.

Korngold nodded. "When he came to our last therapy session with his theory on the origin of vampirism, I finally realized just how far he had regressed to the fun-and-games milieu of his childhood. I considered him too unstable to allow him into Jennifer's room at the hospital. I tried my best to defuse the situation until I was able to consult with you about the future course of his treatment." Korngold turned up his hands. "But his rash behavior preempted that."

"This theory of his," said Sandor, adjusting the pad on his desk. "Tell me about it."

"It's a convoluted business about psiwaves permeating earth's geomagnetic sphere."

"Psiwaves?" Sandor wondered aloud.

Korngold summed up Brewster's ideas about electromagnetic auras and their swirling about in search of strange attractors, interaction with other life forms . . . Korngold rolled his eyes and raised his eyebrows. "In the course of day-to-day living, Brewster . . . *hypothesized* . . . most humans are unaware of these interactions and dismiss as imaginary any presentiments of their presence. But from time to time they sense ghostly manifestations and other psychic phenomena. A few especially sensitive individuals claim to have had direct encounters with such beings, variously perceiving them as God or his angels."

"And the geomagnetic sphere in which these bodiless intelligences live . . . that must be the mythical 'heaven'?" said Sandor almost laughing. "Preposterous! But ingenious."

"Exactly. But there's more." When Korngold related how Brewster piggy-backed the origin of vampirism onto the Last Supper, making Jesus the first carrier of the virus, and the blood that flowed from the wound on his side caught in the Grail carried by Joseph of Arimathea to King Arthur and the knights of the Round Table—

Sandor roared with laughter. "Jesus! The first vampire!" he exclaimed.

"No. Jesus himself was not a vampire. But apparently he was a carrier of the vampire virus."

"Ho! Better and better!"

"Wait. There's even more. The *Revelation of St. John the Divine* was a vision of the psiwaves gathering into a kind of menacing storm in the geomagnetic sphere. With a little bit of theoretical physics, astrophysics, and chaos theory thrown in, Brewster spun it all into a vision of two divinities, one, God, the other a Vampire."

"And that you could hear all this with a straight face!" marveled Sandor. "That feat alone almost wins me to your risk-taking. Magnetism and mind control alone are classic symptoms of schizophrenic delusion," observed Sandor. "But if Brewster really believed the rest of that . . ."

"Maybe too classic. Brewster has a way of unraveling what might pass as organized delusion into his 'fun-and-games' fantasies. I was never sure that he wasn't just staging an elaborate prank."

"Do you really think it's possible that Brewster could devise and sustain such an elaborate charade for four years without schizophrenic affect?"

"No. Probably not," said Korngold with grim resignation. "It was only a matter of gauging the depth of that affect."

"Even if he were capable of carrying out such a game, why would he do it? It's almost as if he were thumbing his nose at you."

Korngold was silent. Yes, he thought. Why would he, or anyone, drag out such a game for so long? There were times, he reluctantly admitted to himself, that the game took on a hostile edge. It was harmless enough as long as it was a good-natured jousting.

"I just wasn't sure what to make of it," he said hopelessly. "He had always been mild-mannered and polite in our sessions. But when he was denied access to Jennifer in the hospital, he turned confrontational, even belligerent, first with the guard at her room, and then with me when I tried to reason with him. Finally, he openly defied security precautions—"

"And you," said Sandor, resuming his doodles.

"Yes. He had never before so flagrantly defied me."

"And how do you take it now?" asked Sandor in his best clinical manner." Korngold was silent. "As gamesmanship," said Sandor, "he seems to have met your challenge and trumped it by absorbing the earth-bound vampire myth into a bizarre cosmic vision!" He rose from his chair to reach across his desk and clap Korngold on the shoulder. His hand lingered long enough to convey as much consolation as he could under the circumstances. "The real wonder to me," he said, resuming his seat, "is that you allowed this shared fantasy to go on for so long. Not he, but you have gotten tangled in his absurdities. You carelessly slipped into a contest where your ego got mixed up in defeating Brewster's fantasy. But instead of imposing your *folie* on him, he imposed his on you!"

"I guess he conned me. That kid's brain," groused Korngold, exasperated, "slips in and out of more wormholes than mathematicians could possibly imagine! It would take someone far more knowledgeable than me to refute his cosmic joke."

"Of course!" Sandor chortled, not unsympathetically. "That's where you overreached! Our young Mr. Wainwright seems to have cobbled together a lot of gobbledygook from parapsychology and science fiction and piled it all on de Broglie's wave-particle duality theory. Wild as it is," he added after a moment to breathe weightily, "his speculation has a tinge of plausibility. It never ceases to amaze me the rubbish that otherwise intelligent beings invent to explain away the unexplainable. And how easily others are lulled into complacency—" Peering intently at Korngold, whose inner struggle showed plainly in his tense body and rigid face, his eyes widened. "And you look like you believed him!"

A slight tremor shook through Korngold's body. He smiled, wan and ironic. "Maybe a little," he admitted.

Sandor exhaled, looking almost pleased, thought Korngold. He had gotten the upper hand. There was no question in Korngold's mind that what followed would be disagreeable. The situation would be reviewed, of course. There would be repercussions. Sandor would almost certainly ease his own conscience by assuming that Korngold was resilient enough so that his old upstart, impish self, the one who made unsound therapeutic opinions fun, would rebound in time.

Sandor pronounced the inevitable. "I think that you should recuse yourself as therapist for both Brewster and the woman known as Jennifer. And then . . . we should consider the possibility of hospitalization for Brewster."

Korngold nodded sullenly.

Korngold stood at the window of his office. The day had been oppressively hot and humid, but he turned off the air conditioner anyway and opened the window. Night pressed down relentlessly against the lights of the city. Smoke, soot, and exhaust fumes roiled up in a sultry haze from the streets below. They stung his eyes and washed past him through the window. The cool, dry air lingering in the room turned clammy. He began to sweat. His shirt clung to him. He waited.

Korngold was not sure exactly when it happened. One moment he was out looking out across at the buildings and over to the river, the next *he* was there. There was no surprise. No shock of sudden appearance. No flick of seeing something that was not there. But Wagehalsen *did* appear, elegantly dressed in formal attire, red eyes glowing.

"I knew you'd come," said Korngold.

"Ah," said Wagehalsen, "I see that you were expecting me. Good. The open window is inviting—" He stopped as Korngold drew back with a hand raised to bar him. "No? Well, then." He paused at the invisible barrier of the threshold and sat on the windowsill, leaning at ease against the window frame. "Let us chat as before. Perhaps you have something you wish to ask me?"

Wagehalsen looked sleek. His skin did not have the puckered look Korngold had observed at their first meeting. Nor did he have the after feeding bloat described in his journal.

"How does he manage to keep his clothing looking so fresh and well-tailored in air that ought to have made them wilt?" Korngold muttered.

"Surely there are more weighty matters on your mind?" laughed Wagehalsen.

Korngold tried to look away but found that he could not. "I wonder whether your presence in the cities of Europe was as disruptive there as it is here? Your effect on my patients has been devastating. You haven't had much luck peddling your sophocracy?"

"It was a different world in a different time," sighed Wagehalsen regretfully. "The people who lived in it had a style and a milieu that no longer exists there, and probably never existed here. Fashions in tolerance change just as they do in everything else."

"You didn't force yourself on them. Those you were trying to recruit. Yet you attacked my patients. Why?"

"Perhaps," Wagehalsen said, "perhaps it was just a way of getting your attention." He shrugged. "Perhaps I was hungry."

"You wanted to attract my attention!" sputtered Korngold. "In a city of millions you attack people I'm trying to help because you're *hungry*! How does the vampire hope to persuade people to join your sophocracy by harming them and spreading fear and disease through the city! And why me? I'm hardly the kind of influential figure you sought in your journal."

"Calm yourself! Calm yourself, my friend! I offer to share my blood with all those who accept me and live eternally according to my code. Harm? I offer people release from death . . . and euphoria so that eternity does not become tedious. As for disease, well, the means of transmission is irrelevant. No worse than an inoculation against death. It is a sacrifice of the kind offered in the rite of communion. After all, the bible predicts that the world will end in pain and suffering, but offers eternal life for the chosen ones. Exactly what I offer. As for how those die that reject my offer, how is that different from your Jesus Christ? How is it different from those who go to eternal death and damnation because they turn away from God?"

Korngold's jaw dropped.

"There is, of course, this difference," continued Wagehalsen. "If people destroy the world in which they live—and they do have both the capability and the capacity to do exactly that—they will indeed bring about a spiritual life. But they will not spend eternity in perpetual bliss, in some imaginary kingdom with God reigning over them. Without physical bodies, there will be no joys of the flesh. Their auras will dissipate in discrete fragments of energy, to be dispersed across the universe without the remnants of any individual consciousness. People, the only species on earth capable of altering the fate of their planet, are in immediate, greater need than ever before of the kind of salvation I offer them.

"As to why I choose you? In my haste to bring about real political change in Europe, I failed to realize that political and intellectual influence is hopelessly corrupted by personal ambition masquerading as social progress, no matter whose. So I have turned to making haste slowly by appealing to those who have access to the minds of troubled people. Instead of the usual persuasion of reason or resorting to force, I decided to use a subtler approach, by infiltrating the minds of people who question their adaptation to society. Such people should be both highly suggestible and amenable to reward not in some uncertain and indeterminate future, but at once and in tangible form. And alienists, or psychotherapists, as the profession has become, are in a unique position to play on the suggestibility, one patient at a time."

"It's your plan, then," said Korngold, still awe-struck, "to approach others in my profession and try to get them to convert their patients to your sophocracy?"

"Exactly. But not every professional therapist will accept my . . . faith. For example, Dr. Sandor would not be suitable because he is not open to spiritual and metaphysical dimensions. Belief in the metaphysical is cousin to spiritual faith. Not everyone is able to believe in something beyond the literal, physical here and how. As I believe you are. Those who will not convert will be sacrificed. Their blood will be shed for the good of the rest."

"This is a kind of brainwashing!"

"Um, think of it more as the kind of indoctrination one receives in education. In fact, in any kind of training."

Korngold was unable to speak for several minutes, during which Wagehalsen studied his face intently. Then Korngold spoke, as if lost in reflection.

"Your journal ends with your emigration to America. What have you accomplished since? In fact, no one had ever heard of you before Dr. Buckyballs found your journal."

"Ah, Dr. Buckyballs! A useful man. Such a plan as mine does not come together overnight. It takes time and planning. After my failure

The Womb of Uncreated Night

in Europe, I had to rethink my program. There was no hurry. When one had all of eternity, one had time to accomplish one's ends. Failures were merely guides along the way. And if those ends were occasionally blunted by some unforeseen eventuality . . . ? The time had to be right. But with the state of the world today, perhaps waiting for the right time is no longer practical." He shrugged again. "I do not mean to act in haste. But the circumstances are urgent."

"I did not have any personal contact with Leon Barvim," said Korngold. "But why was it so urgent that someone like Arpie Fairfield, with so much potential, had to lose his life."

"Some of my acolytes were undisciplined or inclined to excess. They could not be relied on. Only those who have the breadth of mind to see beyond immediate gratification—while still indulging in it, you understand—as well as some special gift or genius, only those are worth the trouble."

"You exact obedience, then—" began Korngold.

"Oh, *exact*," said Wagehalsen with a pained look, "that is such a harsh word. Say, rather, that my plan calls for a harmony that can be achieved by interweaving voices, as in musical counterpoint."

Korngold reflected a moment before continuing. "You failed to convert Wagner. And you were too late to 'save' Mozart or Beethoven. Do you think that they would have been more . . . flexible?"

Wagehalsen laughed. "Mozart, perhaps. But Beethoven?" said Wagehalsen, musing. "He would have been most difficult to reach. A man of supreme genius, but stubborn and willful. Possessed of a profound conviction in the rightness of his own perceptions. He could never have been persuaded. It would have been necessary to force him to submit. That would have destroyed not only his creativity, but the dynamic of the community as well. Enforced compliance is the antithesis of creativity."

"A willing suspension of disbelief, then?"

"Is that what psychiatrists expect of their patients?" taunted Wagehalsen.

"I see," said Korngold, checking an impulse to retort. "Suspending disbelief implies that a program has been set up for an audience. No, of course not." He hesitated. "Although in some cases, it may be required of the therapist." He paused again. "I'm not sure that I would want to live in a world without a Beethoven, a Wagner—or any number of *troublesome* people—in it."

"Ah," said Wagehalsen, with satisfaction, "the great ones are always *troublesome*, are they not? But there is a certain thrill of danger, mortal and ethical, in the risk that a great mind may be lost forever in treading the fine line between chaos and creation. The ever present danger of being discovered and destroyed by unenlightened fools only heightens anticipation of the uncertain outcome."

Korngold seemed to be mumbling.

"What is that you say?" Wagehalsen said looking closely at him.

"Inconsequential, really. I was only thinking about something Hannah Arendt once said about evil. To ordinary minds you must appear to be evil incarnate." Korngold seemed to drift off. "And yet, there's something more than banality to your doctrine," he said, his eyes searching Wagehalsen's face. "A future in which a person freed of mortal ills could be determined by force of mind alone. It's almost irresistible."

"Then," said Wagehalsen, "why resist? Give me your hand and we will fly to the next level of the vision."

Korngold climbed onto the windowsill, dazed. As he took Wagehalsen's hand he felt its vise-like grip. He heard the strains of Mozart's *Don Giovanni*. He remembered something. "Wait—"

Brewster was detained by the police after his escapade in Jennifer's hospital room. Moreover, the District Attorney's office still considered him "a person of interest" in the assault on Guinevere, her disappearance, and the "vampire" attacks on several members of the Young Artists Group. Having been caught in the hospital room of another victim of the attacks only increased their suspicions. The circumstances were aggravated by his having resisted arrest. But because he was the scion of a prominent and well-connected family, the District Attorney reluctantly charged him with criminal trespass and released him on his own recognizance.

After his release, Brewster learned of Korngold's death, an apparent suicide. His resentment over a feeling of betrayal melted away. Perhaps Korngold killed himself because he was unable to live with his guilt over the affair with Jennifer? Or perhaps he could not face the censure his professional colleagues or the public notoriety and disgrace that would surely dog him in the media . . .

42.

SOME ROOMS BREATHE. SOME HOLD their breath. Some gasp. Whoever the woman really was, breathlessness enclosed her. She sat at a table in the center of the room, hands folded, staring straight ahead. Afternoon sunlight slanted into the room over the shadowy outlines of buildings across the street through two dingy translucent windows of reinforced glass. Heavy-duty diamond-mesh institutional security screens, barred and padlocked, fit tightly over the windows. The double-hung sashes were also locked, though the screens probably made that an unnecessary precaution. Dust particles hung in the air. The painted cinderblock walls were encrusted with the lies and evasions that had permeated them over the years. In spots, bits of paint had flecked off. Surely the walls were riddled with invisible cracks through which guilt could leak, or the room would have burst under the built-up passions of "perps" and "vics." A long, rectangular two-way mirror, smudged and smeared, and a steel door took up almost the entire wall opposite the windows.

The Assistant District Attorney and Dr. Sandor stood in silence behind the mirror. Waiting. The ADA stared through the mirror.

"Her white hair makes that room even more depressing than usual," he said to Sandor.

"Sometimes we make our own gloom," said Sandor.

The Womb of Uncreated Night

The ADA did not react. He knew that the woman was suspended in time and space, waiting for an unremembered past.

"I asked you to be here in case things got out of hand," said the ADA. Det. Lapels stood next to his partner, Armpits, in whispered conversation, chuckling over the turn of events.

"I'm not entirely convinced that it's a good idea," said Dr. Sandor.

"We'll see." The ADA looked back expectantly into the squad room. "He's not here yet, but a little preliminary talk might be useful." At a nod from the ADA, the four went into the room. The ADA and the psychiatrist seated themselves across the table from the woman they knew only as Jennifer. The detectives hovered in the background—ominously, the ADA hoped. Their mouths wore identical official smiles.

"Jennifer," began the ADA, "Dr. Sandor and I are here to help you. We want to make sure that your assailant never again endangers you or others. Do you remember anything about your recent stay in the hospital?"

"You mean, do I remember anything after I woke up? I thought," she said hesitantly, "I thought I saw two dark figures standing over me."

"Two," said the ADA matter-of-factly, glancing at Sandor. "Did you . . . did you recognize them?"

"I—no. The room was dark and the figures were dark. How could I recognize them?"

"You were attacked several weeks ago in the same way," said the ADA. Jennifer involuntarily jerked her hand toward her throat. "We think it was by one of those men. Can you tell us anything about your attacker?"

"I don't know," she said with a trace of irritation in her voice. "All I remember is a rush out of the darkness, a cape, and a stovepipe on his head."

"A cape?" said the ADA, eagerly jumping at Batman's costume, ignoring the strange headgear and Dr. Sandor's attempts to restrain him. "Think carefully. He was wearing a 'stovepipe on his head'? Could it have been a hood?"

"No. Not a hood. I get so confused. But I can still tell the difference between a top hat and a hood."

"Top hat," said the ADA, leaning back in his chair. "You said top hat."

"Oh, a *top hat*! Yes. That's what it was! And . . ."

"And?"

". . . nothing else."

"You don't remember anything else?"

"No. I mean he wasn't wearing anything else. He was naked under the cape."

The ADA hesitated. "Do you remember seeing anybody else at about the same time?"

"Well, there was someone who once fought off the man in the top hat. He was dressed like a bat."

"Why is this the first time we're hearing this?" asked the ADA looking around at the detectives in annoyance.

Jennifer shrugged. "I—well, no one asked if someone *didn't* attack me."

Dr. Sandor jerked his head toward the door. They got up and went together into the observation room behind the mirror to confer. Lapels and Armpits followed them out.

"What do you make of that?" said the ADA. "Did she say anything about seeing two figures in her room when you interviewed her earlier?"

"No. This is as much a surprise to me as it is to you. But haven't other witnesses reported that this 'vampire' was a naked man wearing the kind of getup Jennifer described?"

The ADA shook his head. "Darkness, the excitement of the encounters, confusion? Some of the witnesses also thought they saw a naked man under the cape. Others saw a bat-man. But *two* figures wearing capes? It sounded like the usual conflicting statements of witnesses under stress. And *two* intruders in her hospital room? What are the chances that she's just confused, or influenced by rumors? After all, she's just woken up from a coma."

Sandor considered. "The chances for confusion under the circumstances are quite good. We know for certain Brewster

Wainwright was there, dressed as Batman. But that there might have been a second intruder in the hospital room, perhaps the naked man who attacked her in the Ramble? Makes you wonder what caused her to wake up suddenly when she did. The guard who rushed in at Jennifer's cries would have run immediately to the window where Batman was hanging by one foot, if he can be believed. Likewise, the hospital attendant who answered the guard's call for assistant. Both men would have been intent on apprehending the man hanging from the window. A second intruder might have escaped unnoticed in the general uproar that followed."

"A naked man running through a hospital corridor?" scoffed the ADA. "If it *was* the same man who attacked her in the Ramble."

Sandor laughed. "We don't know whether this second intruder wore a cape under which he was naked. Jennifer's identification of the top hat suggests that it may have been her attacker. Stranger things than naked men running through a corridor have happened in a hospital, believe me. And two caped figures in the Ramble—the differences in the descriptions are significant, don't you think?"

The ADA remained unconvinced.

The psychiatrist looked at him thoughtfully. "Why are you so set on making Brewster the attacker?"

The ADA was of a mind with Det. Lapels. "No son-of-a-rich man should be allowed to think that he's above the law."

"Well, he may indeed be the attacker," said Sandor, trying to defuse the ADA's indignation. "But there's no direct evidence that he was. Maybe you're overreacting . . ."

"Spare me the psychoanalysis, Dr. Sandor. I'm not the patient here. Isn't it equally significant that all of the victims attacked by this 'vampire' were patients of Dr. Korngold?"

"All that we know of," corrected Sandor.

"All that we know of. But Brewster is the only one who runs around dressed like a bat. And if he can scale the wall of a hospital, why wouldn't he be able to scale the wall of Korngold's building?"

"You're suggesting that Brewster had something to do with Dr. Korngold's death!" said Sandor.

"Yeah, why not?" chimed in Lapels. "He climbs like he did at the hospital, knocks at the window. Korngold comes to see who's there. Wainwright lurks at the side of the window. Korngold leans out to look. Wainwright grabs him and pitches him out. One-two-three."

Sandor gave the detective the stony look psychiatrists reserve for babbling patients in a psychiatric ward. "And he climbed thirty stories to do this, in plain sight of the city, and no one saw him?"

"He managed to climb the hospital wall. It was dark. Nighttime, for chrissake," said Lapels.

"That's not the only darkness around here," scoffed Sandor. "The possibility that he climbed thirty stories—even with super-glue on his hands and feet—incredible! He almost fell out of a seven-story window at the hospital! Be realistic, if you can't be serious."

Lapels was not about to let go of his pet theory, but a raised eyebrow from the ADA silenced him. "Dr. Sandor is right," he said, "there's no direct evidence. If someone had gotten access to Korngold from outside the window, he left no signs. And with Brewster's family behind him, we'd be laughed out of court."

"So you believe," said Sandor, "that confronting Jennifer with 'Batman' will shock her into revealing something tangible you can use against Brewster." He shook his head doubtfully. "She has just learned of Dr. Korngold's death and, from the brief interview I had with her before the four of us descended on her, I think that she's taking it rather hard. Korngold *was* good to her." Perhaps too good, he thought. He was reluctant to mention Korngold's wife having discovered him in flagrante with Jennifer on the floor of his office. At a cocktail party, she had drunk a little too much and told him how she had come in quietly and, on seeing the unexpected, had as quietly turned around and left without creating a scene. Remarkable composure under the circumstances. *There* was a motive for murder. She was very bitter about it. Only later, just before a scheduled appointment with Brewster, did Korngold realize that she was about to leave on him. They had both behaved with amazing restraint. Very civilized. But given Korngold's deep conflicts with himself and Brewster's fantastic behavior, suicide was not out of the question. Could Sydney, herself, have been disturbed enough to usher her husband out the window? The ADA already had plenty of speculation on his plate.

"Jennifer must feel as if she's lost a dear friend," he said. "As for Brewster, his behavior at the hospital suggests that when frustrated he can act irresponsibly."

"Do you think he might turn violent?"

"When I told Dr. Korngold in our last conversation that he was out of control and that we ought to consider hospitalization, I was thinking only of protecting Brewster from himself. He is physically formidable. None of his escapades exhibit antisocial tendencies. At worst, any such tendencies have been channeled into his vigilante activities."

"To date," said the ADA. "What if he felt balked or threatened?"

"Then . . . who knows? Under extreme conditions anyone might feel compelled to defend himself. But when he was apprehended at the hospital, he was in a highly stressful situation, yet offered no resistance. And what is there in this setting that is even remotely as stressful? No. He may be eccentric, with an overblown hero complex, to be sure. Weird, even," added Sandor with a glance at Lapels. "But I now believe that while his actions may put his own safety at risk he would not knowingly risk the safety of others. He seems more interested in helping others in distress than in putting them there. Which is probably why he defied Dr. Korngold's refusal to let him see Jennifer."

"Assuming he's not insane. What if he saw Korngold as a threat to his vigilante activities?"

"But how would Korngold have threatened his activities?"

"Well, he might've threatened to expose him. If Brewster had the kind of megalomania that imagined Batman set on a mission to save the world—you said, yourself, he had an over-blown hero complex—mightn't that be perceived as enough of a threat to require drastic action?"

Dr. Sandor shook his head. "I understand what you're driving at. But Dr. Korngold was well aware of Brewster's state of mind and activities for four years and never made any attempt to intervene."

"As far as you know," persisted the ADA, with Lapels nodding earnestly in agreement.

"As far as I know," agreed Sandor. "And to your certain knowledge, what? Over the years, I've had direct, personal contact with Dr. Korngold. He freely admitted his mistakes in Brewster's therapy. He would have told me if he'd tried to restrain him."

Neither the ADA nor Lapels could add anything more concrete to their case. The ADA changed the subject. "Do you think that Jennifer's amnesia is genuine? I mean after all this time?"

"Hard to say," said Sandor, nodding thoughtfully. "It's unusual for loss of memory to persist so long without some other complication, drugs or injury, say. Possibly a dissociative personality disorder."

"You're talking about multiple personality?" asked the ADA, ignoring Lapels's disgusted groan.

"That's the dubious popular term, along with outdated terms like schizophrenia and split personality." Dr. Sandor looked closely at Jennifer through the two-way mirror, thinking about the relationship between her, Brewster, and Guinevere, and looking for mannerisms that might suggest a way of penetrating a puzzling demeanor. "Dissociative personalities, bipolar disorder. Classification has changed so radically in the last fifty years. And Dr. Korngold had doubts about the source of her amnesia. Dissociation usually is tied to childhood abuse. He was unable to get her to open up about it. He thought that Jennifer's amnesia was brought on by some more recent trauma."

"Trauma?" mused the ADA. "Like that scar on her throat?"

"Like a vampire attack?" snorted Lapels.

Dr. Sandor's his eyebrows twitched between skepticism and amusement. "Perhaps. There have indeed been 'vampire attacks.' But Dr. Buckyballs believes that those are caused by a hitherto unknown virus which could, in this case, have been transmitted by a bite on her neck. A bite in itself would not be sufficiently traumatic to cause amnesia." He shrugged. "But how a hysteric might react, or the unknown side effects of the virus . . . who knows?"

"Dr. Korngold would not have discounted something as significant as childhood abuse. But he reported little about the virus, though I believe that he and Dr. Buckyballs discussed the matter in depth. Until Dr. Buckyballs' research on the virus definitively establishes exotic side-effects, it's all speculation."

"Could she be faking it?"

"Possibly. But why would she do that? Dr. Korngold's notes speculate that there might be two distinct personalities, which could account for its persistence. One personality would not necessarily know what the other knew. At least at the conscious level. But he was reluctant to diagnose multiple personality."

"So either she's faking or she's batty!" blurted out Lapels.

Dr. Sandor sifted through his notes and frowned. "Dr. Korngold did speculate that something was going on with young Mr. Wainwright in his Batman costume." Sandor paused. "But with the cessation of these 'vampire attacks' . . . " Sandor gave the ADA a searching look. "The attacks have stopped, haven't they?"

"Yes. They've tapered off then stopped around the time of Korngold's death and Wainwright's arrest. Another coincidence? You wonder how those two were involved."

Sandor looked relieved. "As for how the residual effects of the attack would affect her competence to identify her assailant? I suppose it would depend on which identity was present during the attack. *This* 'Jennifer' personality, according to Korngold's notes, may be the recessive one. If so, it would be unusual for such a personality to exhibit for long. You might have expected her former personality to emerge by now." He looked closely through the mirror at Jennifer. "Of course, there's that question of brain damage . . . " Shuffling through the sheets of the dossier, Sandor dropped one, picked it up and looked closely at it.

"She has been knocked about enough," said the ADA. "Probably the first time when she lost her memory—woke up in the hospital, bruised and battered from having been knocked to the ground, with that odd scar on her throat. Then she was attacked again. Only that time she remembers Batman being on the scene. Isn't that suggestive?"

"Suggestive, yes. There's some strange coincidental connection between them. If I were a Jungian, I might call it synchronicity . . ."

"Effects without causes?" said the ADA skeptically.

"Without apparent causes. But that's too occult for me. And the last attack sent her back to the hospital in a coma again. There was no sign of Batman then."

"That we know of," added the ADA.

Sandor sighed heavily. "That we know of. You know, the way you keep going at young Wainwright, it almost sounds personal. Is resentment of privilege as bad as that?"

"Another therapy session?" said the ADA testily. "Maybe we'd better stay focused on Jennifer for the present. Amnesiac or not, I think she might be able to 'remember' a lot more than she's said."

"Her loss of past memory," said Sandor as he leafed through the dossier again, "should not have any effect on her present recall. CAT and PET scans at the time of her hospitalization are inconclusive. But I wonder . . ."

"What?" said the ADA.

"Improbable as it seems, if the virus infection had somehow blocked out the memory of who she was, that mightn't show up in the usual scans. In that case, brain injury might be ruled out, and perhaps multiple personality, as well. Nor would there be any telling how persistent such an effect might be. Interesting. I'll have to discuss it with Dr. Buckyballs when we are done here."

"Anyway, we'll see how she reacts when Brewster gets here," said the ADA looking at his watch. "He'll know we're watching him. And if he really is 'bats' . . . " He laughed.

"Well," said Sandor, "listening to what the two say to each other, how they act together, we might possibly get some new insight into what's going on between them. I suppose any doubts are outweighed by the possible positive outcomes. "Anyway, we might get a clue about her attacker." And if he *did* try something, Sandor thought cynically, that would strengthen your case against him.

Brewster could not have been forced to appear at the precinct wearing his "Batman" costume. The ADA could hardly have arranged a lineup of *Batmen*. But Brewster had agreed because he wanted to talk to Jennifer about Guinevere. If appearing as Batman was a condition of seeing her without upsetting the authorities, he was willing to do it. He was sure that Lapels and Armpits and the other wags at the station relished the chance to have some fun with "Batman" walking into the station in full regalia in broad daylight. But he disappointed them by arriving in street clothes. His personal valet followed, wheeling a trunk containing the costume into the men's room where Brewster could change without spectators.

When Lapels pushed the door open to summon him, the detective was unprepared for what came out. The costume had so transformed Brewster that Lapels was startled. He stumbled back, more awed than amused. From the upright ears of the hood to the sweep of the cape from shoulders revealing sculpted body armor, Brewster appeared physically greater than his appearance in street clothes. His frame filled the doorway and he had to incline his head to clear the lintel. When he stood fully erect again, he seemed to fill the corridor, and the ears of his hood almost to graze the ceiling. Lapels, feeling diminutive and embarrassed followed by this comic-book-made-flesh, quickly led Brewster through the corridor to where the ADA and Dr. Sandor were waiting. Even they were momentarily awed by his presence as he came in and seemed to crowd the observation room.

Until that moment, the ADA had not known what to expect. He imagined Brewster would look like some sort of walking cartoon, a kind of overgrown kid in a Halloween costume. Or at best wearing a well crafted costume for a masquerade ball. He was prepared to laugh. But seeing him tower over them, the ADA could only tell himself what he was not sure he believed, that Batman was not real.

"Ah, Mr. Wainwright," said the ADA when he recovered. "Thank you for coming. We thought if Jennifer could see you, it might trigger some recollection that might help us identify her attacker, and put an end to these 'vampire' attacks in the Ramble. You can go in. Dr. Sandor and I will observe from here."

When Batman came into the room, Jennifer visibly started. Her lips parted soundlessly. But she recovered quickly. She had never before seen him in full light. Without a word, "Batman" sat opposite to her, his cape draped over the back of the chair and spread out on either side giving him the appearance of an enormous bird with partly outspread wings. Brewster studied her face. In the darkness of the hospital room, her skin had appeared chalky. But now it had taken on a pearly sheen. The hard blue of her eye sockets had softened, adding luster to her eyes. Her snow-white hair framed her face like a halo. Could this be the face of Guinevere, subtly altered?

"Well," he began, "those officious fools behind the mirror hope that seeing Batman again will shock you into recollecting more about your attacker. They suspect it's me."

Jennifer forced a small smile. "We both know it's not."

"You could've gratified them by jumping out of your chair screaming as soon as I'd come in," said Brewster.

"Didn't occur to me. Too bad I had to disappoint them," said Jennifer, chuckling. She looked toward the mirror as if her calm demeanor would signal the end of the farce.

Brewster shook his head, thinking. Her face. Her voice. Shadows, distorted reflections of Guinevere? "I'm sorry about Dr. Korngold," he said. "I know how much he meant to you." He reached out to touch her hands, but she pulled them back.

"Yes," she said. "I'm even emptier now that he's gone. After I lost my memory, he was all I had to hold on to."

"I can only imagine. The loss of your former self, and then to lose the only one you could cling to . . . that's hard." Here am I, he thought. Cling to me. But his thoughts came from Brewster. Would she rather cling to Batman? "You know, your memory might—*should*—come back, eventually . . . It's not hopeless. And with it, friends to fill in the gaps."

"Do you think so? I've tried to see myself, but my image keeps slipping away into shadows and out-of-focus reflections. If you can't fix an image in your mind, does it exist? I'm not who I was."

"I'm not a religious person. I don't believe that when we die we go to a place where we're reunited with loved ones." He paused, reflecting. "But for those who do . . . Well, it must be comforting to believe that what was lost will be regained. And who knows? Maybe that belief is the difference between heaven and hell. Maybe the hope of regaining your memory is like that."

"Isn't it pretty to think so?" said Jennifer. Then with a rueful little laugh, "Listen to me. I even talk like a character in a novel!"

"It's the virus talking," said Brewster. "Your mind has been affected by the vampire disease that's been infecting people around the Ramble. Like any disease, there has got to be a cure out there, somewhere. But there are still the germs of your former self in you, somewhere. Maybe *they* will grow and spread into another disease, remembrance, suppressing the symptoms of this one."

"Hah!" exclaimed Sandor behind the glass, "Four years of therapy and already he sounds like Korngold!"

"Not exactly a cure," Jennifer said.

"Listen," Brewster murmured, leaning forward. Jennifer drew her face to his until they sat, faces almost mouth to ear so that the observers behind the mirror could not hear. "I think I know the location of this vampire's lair. There's a hidden crypt in the Belvedere."

Behind the mirror, the ADA spoke, almost as if he was thinking out loud. "Interesting," he said. "He shares Jennifer's feelings, but he doesn't tell her that he was also a patient of Dr. Korngold's. Makes you wonder about his feelings toward his therapist, doesn't it?"

- 625 -

Straining to hear what Brewster and Jennifer were saying, Sandor waved a hand to stop the ADA's dogged pursuit of Brewster.

"At first I thought Korngold was just shining me on when he brought out this journal of some nineteenth century vampire named Wagehalsen. But it was verified by Dr. Buckyballs, the resident expert on the vampire virus. Then I found this creature in your hospital room the night you were jolted out of your coma. Maybe he has something to do with your loss of memory."

Jennifer gasped and pulled back from Batman, her face twitching impatiently. "You're not going to tell me I've been attacked by some nineteenth century Dracula!" she cried out loud enough so that the men behind the mirror no longer had strained to hear. They looked at each other, jaws agape, and wondered what to make of the conversation.

Brewster shrugged. "Diseases outlive their carriers," he said barely audible. "Do I believe he's actually the same Wagehalsen of the journal? No, but I do think the current outbreak was likely transmitted by the virus that may have been in his blood. Farfetched as it may sound, it's supposed to enhance the senses. At least, that's the impression I got from Dr. Buckyballs. And even from Dr. Korngold, who probably got it from him. Like maybe the disease gives an infected person some hypnotic power over you, and once he is gone, well, it will be gone too."

"You don't really believe that," said Jennifer.

"Yeah, I know," laughed Brewster. "It sounds as loopy to me as it does to you," even, he thought, to someone who might have been in a mood to clutch at straws. "Anyway, if I can track the place down tonight—"

Amusement swept across Jennifer's face. "But aren't you supposed to find the vampire in his coffin during the day and drive a stake through his heart?"

"Yes, yes," nodded Brewster wearily, leaning back and speaking normally, "and cut off his head." The ears in the observation room were all agog, then filled with consternation as Batman once more spoke barely above a whisper. "Maybe that won't really be necessary. After all, that was the nineteenth century mentality. Somehow, I doubt that the modern vampire could be such a slave to tradition that he will only venture out at night. Even in *Dracula*, Bram Stoker had contradictory ideas about it. He carefully builds up the idea that the Count only ventures out at night, yet Jonathan Harker spots him wandering out around London during the day."

"It's *fiction*," said Jennifer.

"Yes," smiled Batman, "but sometimes fiction is the most convincing reality we have, as you yourself suggested. Nothing prevents Batman from wandering around in daylight. But it would be inconvenient. And confronting the vampire without protective gear would leave Bruce Wayne exposed. So he'll have to go under cover of darkness."

"But if he's out prowling at night," said Jennifer frowning at the name of Batman's alter ego, "what can you hope to do in the crypt?"

"I'll wait him out. But for all we know he has a day job. He may spend a few hours prowling the Ramble at night for victims. He appears and disappears so nimbly that a hideaway in the Belvedere comes in handy. But it's also an ideal place for a nap. He need only get out before people start showing up for work or play. Whatever the reality," he smiled again, "or the convincing fiction, he'll eventually return to the crypt."

Jennifer shook her head. "The whole thing sounds preposterous."

There was almost as much consternation in the room behind the mirror as in her face. "What's he saying?" said the ADA. "Put a stop to this," he motioned Lapels to intervene.

"No," said Dr. Sandor, holding up a restraining hand at Lapels. "Let them be. I thought Jennifer might be surprised at our little game. But clearly she's in no danger. Let's see how this plays out. We may be learning more from the way the two interact than by breaking it off. There's something in the way they're acting, as if they know each other . . ."

Brewster huddled, almost crouching over the table. His legs tensed, bent back under his chair as if he were about to spring.

"I'm going to find him," he whispered. "Maybe coax a cure out of him before I . . . put him out of business."

Jennifer smiled wanly. She, too, lowered her voice. "And then what will become of me after he's caught and a cure is found?"

Brewster cast about for a reassuring answer. He hesitated. "Well," he began, "like most diseases, this vampire thing probably can't be eliminated altogether. If we can't find a cure, the best we can hope for is containment. People with incurable diseases are able to live reasonably normal lives by refraining . . . during active outbreaks."

"Do you think that Dr. Korngold despaired of a cure, and that's why he killed himself?"

Brewster wondered whether she meant that she thought she had infected him with the virus, or that she meant so much to him. "I don't know." After a lull during which neither he nor Jennifer appeared to feel inclined to talk further, he sighed and spoke again in a conspiratorial voice. "Maybe the symptoms will go into remission. The virus is too new to be sure about its progress."

"So," Jennifer chuckled sardonically, "by killing off the head vampire . . . all those who have been infected will be miraculously cured!"

"Yeah, it sounds foolish. But like I said, containment is important. Destroying the origin of a disease may not cure everyone infected, but it will prevent its spread."

"And do you plan to go around annihilating everyone who has been infected?" She looked searchingly for the eyes sunk in the shadows of his hood. "After all, each of the vampire's victims, each of *us*," she added, "becomes another carrier of infection." She looked down at her hands on the table, "Will you kill us all?"

Brewster blew out his breath, leaned back in his chair, and stretched out his legs under the table, almost kicking Jennifer. He cocked his head to one side and looked at her uncertainly.

"I don't know," he said. "Who can say what will emerge? There are always choices. I'm hoping for something overlooked. Maybe the vampire's victims are carrying a less virulent strain of the disease. In your case alone, he kept coming back at you. That may indicate that he thought that the infection didn't take in his earlier attacks." Now who's

The Womb of Uncreated Night

ready to clutch at straws, he thought. "I don't know. Maybe it's only killing the messenger. I intend to find out. "Then," he said, as gently as he could manage, "then I'll come looking for you."

Jennifer smiled. "When you do, you'll find me . . . ," she said with a wave of her hand beyond the caged windows, "out there somewhere, looking for *me*." She continued to smile sweetly at Brewster, "We'll see who finds *me* first." She got up and left.

43.

ALTHOUGH BREWSTER HAD INTENDED TO wait for nightfall, he reached the crypt beneath the Belvedere just before sunset Guided partly by an eerie, phosphorescent glow in the dark, damp tunnel, but also by his nano-hood, Batman reached the foundations of the Belvedere set into its base of granite and schist. He felt along the massive stone until his hands reached an archway carved into the rock. He stood at the threshold of what must have been the gateway into Wagehalsen's hidden crypt. He found a gate of heavy wood hung on iron hinges, studded with iron nails, and bound with iron straps, standing ajar, as if he were expected. He crossed the threshold warily, and entered the vestibule. A flight of eight steps, also carved into the rock, descended into utter darkness. The bioluminescence faded away completely.

Reason told him there would be a floor, but neither his hood nor his feet confirmed it. It was like sensing the edge of a sheer precipice you were unable to see, testing empty space with a toe, almost reeling into eternity. A rank, acrid odor penetrated the mold and mustiness hanging in the air. What was it about this black hole that disrupted the electronic functions of his hood? As his foot found the floor that had to be there, his aura expanded and touched the chamber he could not see with his eyes. Yet he *sensed*, he *saw*. Against the far wall opposite, a box rested on a raised block of granite.

The Womb of Uncreated Night

As in a dream, Brewster felt along the floor toward the box. Irregularities in the rough-hewn stones rippled under his feet, like a shudder passing over their surface. He groped uncertainly for footholds before trusting his weight to each step. He reached the dark mass of the coffin. Its lid was raised. His hands found a body lying at full length in the box. Brewster removed the gauntlet from his right hand. With his bare hand, he could feel the body clad in evening dress and cloak. He reached the head, a top hat at its side, a face muffled by a beard. Deep in the beard he found the mouth, and stuck in the mouth was the stub of a cigarette. A vampire that smoked in bed?

His head swam in absurdity. He reached into a pouch on his utility belt and removed the talismans it contained, a vial of holy water, a crucifix, and a bunch of garlic. He placed the crucifix and the garlic over the vampire's heart, and sprinkled the holy water over its head. At this, the body in the casket stirred and burst into laughter. Braced for some convulsive outburst, an anguished howl, a struggle, Brewster was startled.

"I've been expecting you," gasped the body.

"Laughter was not quite the reaction I'd been expecting," said Brewster.

"You are wondering why I have allowed you to penetrate my crypt without resistance?" whispered the Other.

"I assumed that you'd be in some kind of trance until the sun set. You do seem lethargic."

"Hm-hm-hm!" chuckled the vampire. "And these trinkets you've adorned me with, you thought they would incapacitate me?"

"One hoped," said Brewster.

"And then... the stake, eh? Well, one must play by the rules, I suppose. That would've had a greater effect than superstitious nostrums."

"Something had to be done about you. You can't be allowed to spread your disease everywhere."

"But I haven't been spreading it indiscriminately. And frankly, I've thought of late of retiring. In the beginning, there was the thrill of the hunt, the thrill of the blood... But thrills wear thin with aimless

- 631 -

repetition. One wearies of an existence without a constructive goal. Even Dracula realized that."

The ears on Batman's hood twitched. "A vampire colony dominating England for the sole purpose of drinking blood sounds more like debauchery."

"Exactly," said the vampire. "And that is why Wagehalsen sought a way to suppress human strife with a sophocracy that would preserve the highest human aspirations among a select group while placating the mass of their subjects with a potent tranquilizer, which when you think about it, is no worse than a mood altering drug—"

"Which turns out to be the disease of vampirism?"

"Not the disease itself, but its psychotropic effect. A disease that preserves, and in many ways enhances life."

"That has been the excuse of every tyrant who ever lived!" growled Batman in disgust.

"Perhaps some tyrannies are preferable to perpetual turmoil. Weeding out destructive and counterproductive impulses is always necessary. The virus naturally elevates serotonin levels. It relieves anxiety and stress levels. While behavior modification without reliance on traditional drugs may be our preferred way to bring about a more tranquil existence, it's tricky to establish on a mass scale. It all comes down to a balance between autocratic benevolence and self-indulgence, hedonism, dissipation."

"A virtuous vampire!" scoffed Batman.

"Scoff if you wish. But Wagehalsen had a humanitarian purpose as genuine as that of Jesus."

Jesus! Brewster's speechless astonishment was lost on the Coffin.

"His journal shows that, unlike his mentor, Dracula, he first sought out the intellectual lights of European culture. His search reached its highest point when he approached Hugo in exile on Jersey. When Hugo rejected Wagehalsen's sophocracy as a means of implementing the 'Citadel' of a United States of Europe, Wagehalsen took it hard."

"Not as hard as the corpses your humanitarian vampire left lying around," said Batman.

The Womb of Uncreated Night

"Perhaps Wagehalsen realized," said the Coffin ignoring the sarcasm, "that his sophocracy was flawed. As I said, the thrill of the Dracula wears thin as depravity. And the desire to 'medicate' the world in order to save it attenuates desire. Something more was needed. He must have considered whether a human colony of vampires—"

"Assuming that anyone other than a vampire would regard such a colony as human," interrupted Brewster.

"Assuming that. Even Freud recognized the need for something beyond empirical science and materialism, some humanizing factor, to maintain a viable civilization . . . Some rite that would keep human beings from descending into total savagery. He came to believe that religion served a useful purpose as a moral guide. Without some higher authority, aggression loses its focus, its sanction, its justification. It becomes atavistic brutality. For brute creatures lacking reason, aggression is a necessity. But in human beings it's debasing."

"You're not going to tell me that Wagehalsen became a 'born again' Christian?" protested Batman.

"Not exactly. Perhaps Wagehalsen took literally Jesus' bidding for his disciples to drink his blood, albeit diluted by almost two millennia of transmission," replied the voice. "Though I doubt he thought of it as a religious rite. But in a pinch, it serves.

"Whatever. Rejection of the highest motives can turn destructive. In his case, anger and frustration were turned outward. Since his journal ends with his emigration to America, we can only guess at his intentions. And since New York City at that time lacked the intellectual climate of Paris, it should surprise no one that he found it less stimulating. Deaths in and around Central Park, especially the rumored hauntings of the Belvedere, may have been his work. But that is speculative. The body of a naked man found in the vicinity of Vista Rock drained of blood, with the journal beside it, may or may not have been Wagehalsen's. Someone might have attacked him and left him for dead. The disappearance of the body from the morgue and the blurred photograph only deepen the mystery without shedding any light on it. Did the victim, whoever it was, regain consciousness and escape undetected? Did someone make away with the corpse? Was there more than one vampire? Blood can answer only so many questions. Some questions really have no answer. I've often felt his presence on my rounds, but then I never really expected to see him."

"So it's you!" Batman sighed deeply. "We have minds, reason, that enable us to resist aggressive urges with or without God. In fact, religions centered on God have done little to curb the human appetite for shedding blood—" Batman stopped short, realizing that he was playing into the vampire's argument.

"Hm!hm!hm!" chuckled the Other. "Reason rushes in where experience fears to tread! And is it your mission in life to inject reason into the world with a comic book superhero?"

"Wagehalsen would never have approved, I'm sure," chuckled Brewster in return. "But then I don't approve of parasitizing human beings."

"Anyway, human reason lacks the power to address metaphysical questions. Full of romanticism, Wagehalsen apparently never considered that trying to overcome the entrenched mindset of the reasoning European intellectual against just those kinds of questions would be futile. When he did finally realize its futility, he simply gave up. It occurred to me, however, that indoctrinating the more pliable minds of young people, minds that are more accepting of mood altering drugs in medicine and recreation, might offer a more receptive venue."

"Ah! And so you turned to the Young Artists Group!"

"Exactly. Talented young people with pliable minds able to enter into and sustain aesthetic states needed to reach the transcendent tranquility necessary to overcome the conditions of human conflict."

"And vampirism enhances this ability?" said Batman. "Intriguing!"

"With a little help from a mood-altering virus!" said the voice, adding slyly, "Perhaps you'd like to try it?"

Batman's laughter echoed in the chamber. "You make a helluva pusher!"

The Other joined in the laughter, then turned somber again. "I

The Womb of Uncreated Night

wondered if perhaps a colony mightn't work better centered around a 'queen bee.' The male psyche simply lacks the necessary instinct for 'hiving,' since it's biologically engineered to fertilize rather than to bear. I thought that Jennifer might prove to be a suitable candidate."

"Ah!" cried Batman again. "I see! I see!" He thought a moment, then added, "But historically, matriarchies haven't turned out well, have they?"

"Actually," said the vampire, "they'd persisted longer than the present era of male-dominated hierarchies. Who knows? If ten thousand years ago the inhabitants of Mesopotamia had lived in a vampire colony centered on a vampire queen, the course of civilization might have been far less strife torn."

"Struggles between rival rulers are hardly a male invention! People, whether male or female, really seem biologically unable to conform to the extent that you and other 'saviors' require. The world needs to be saved from those who want to save it."

A sardonic chuckle came out of the coffin. "True enough. People *are* a quarrelsome lot, aren't they?" Then silence. When he spoke again, there was no mistaking the note of resignation in his words. "As Jennifer kept slipping away—it was more than just your interference . . . Her frequent returns to the Ramble were not responses to the lure of ecstasy in the blood. She was searching for something else, a self that had somehow been lost. That was more important to her than heightened perception or tranquility. She was genuinely unwilling to assume the role that I envisioned for her. Her yearning for her former self was more powerful than any power wielded by a queen." A sigh came from the coffin. "I realized that the human desire to *be* human is simply too strong.

"Complicating matters further, there were signs of mental instability among those from the Young Artists Group. It may have been present in some form before they were exposed to the virus. It may have been an unexpected side effect. There are too many variables in the human psyche. Too many unanswered questions about the part played by the human genome. In time . . . perhaps the questions would be answered. In the meantime, there was little left. A choice of stoic resignation or debauchery while the world went to hell. There would always be enough people in whom the unpredictable would lie hidden and waiting to disrupt the new order at any moment. Sophocracy under such a liability could never work. Thoughtful beings would weary of living for a rush. The rest . . . simply aren't worth the effort."

"Decadence and depravity have such limited intellectual appeal," said Brewster. Then, easing up a bit, "There is always a possibility of a cure."

"Of course. Always. But while we wait for someone even to begin looking for it, the same doubts persist. In the meantime, think of the people who would be infected. And given the potential for instability, how might that affect the search for a cure? No, no, no. It's a sign of the times. When a repair costs more than its replacement . . ."

"Evidently 'transcendent tranquility' isn't enough to overcome the conditions of human conflict, and can even lead to complacency and indifference. It lacks the sense of moral outrage that people need in order to act. That can't be discounted from the causes of conflict. And the will to act will always have that troublesome unpredictability."

"You see," said the Other, "we are brothers after all! You now realize that I have faced my failure. You have only to face yours."

"Brothers," mused Batman aloud. "Yes, I suppose. Death is brother to life. Evil is brother to good. You have to have one before you can reject the other. Well, then brother, let's make an end of it." Brewster put on his gauntlet. As he was about to remove the stake from his belt, there was a commotion in the coffin. A hand shot out and seized Batman by the throat. Caught off guard and off balance, Brewster staggered and gasped for breath. Somehow, the vampire must have sensed that the sun had set. He had been playing by the rules!

Arms flailing about, Brewster's right hand caught on the lid of the coffin and from its edge tore off a large, rough splinter. He raised the stake. With his left hand, he followed the vampire's arm down to its chest to the spot over the heart. He thrust the stake deep into the heart of its body just as the vampire started to rise. The body jerked spasmodically from the blow, a groan came from its throat, and darkness gushed over Brewster's gloved hand. There was a long, drawn-out sigh. Then silence.

Trembling, Brewster grasped the rim of the coffin with both hands to steady himself. He contemplated what he imagined were the remains of a century and a half. He stood there for some time pondering the significance of that final attack. The vampire's tone of resignation seemed fabricated to disarm him. The vampire *was* pure evil. Wasn't he? Or was there another impulse beneath the deception, the more *human* hope for survival and a cure?—No, wait! Fantastic thoughts crowded into his mind. *Could* the virus in this blood really have originated with Jesus? What fraction of the blood could be traced back to him? If it contained the merest speck, its DNA could tell us something about the man who left such an indelible mark on the world!

For an instant Brewster thought of having a laboratory analyze the blood on his gauntlet. There was no way of actually linking it to Jesus, though some obscure laboratory technician might use it as a way of making a name for himself. Grand enterprises have been launched on less. But the blood would also contain the virus. The risk that some fool could let it loose again was too great. The coffin and its contents had to be destroyed and the crypt sealed so that no one could ever come in contact with it again. That would have to await another time.

"*Atque in perpetuum, frater, ave atque vale!*" For eternity, brother, hail and farewell! Brewster removed his Batman costume and placed it in the coffin.

After some hesitation, he turned away from the coffin. He had lost all track of time. Moving carefully, as if pausing to contemplate each motion, as one unfamiliar with a process, he felt along the wall which now was reassuringly firm and found a stairwell on his right. Thinking he had reached the stairway leading up to the vestibule and the tunnel, he was shocked to find that it ended in a blank wall. Running his hands over it and pressing experimentally, he found a mechanism which caused a portion of the wall to swing into the castle's instrument room. Unaware of the hidden opening, the Weather Bureau's personnel had placed some of their recording instruments in the arc of the wall's swing. When the hidden door opened, a seismograph fell to the floor with a crash. In the moonlight filtering through a casement window, Brewster carefully closed the opening. He wondered how the vampire could have avoided annoying the Belvedere's staff by repeatedly disturbing their equipment. Maybe he reserved this opening as an emergency exit?

Brewster replaced the broken gauge on its stand and moved it back to its original position. He left it to the weather bureau's staff to speculate on what sort of upheaval it recorded. He made his way to the entrance, unlocked the door, stepped out into the warm summer night, and carefully closed it again. The Delacorte was dark and empty, but a full moon washed over Vista Rock and the brooding outline of the Belvedere, and cast its shadow across Turtle Pond, a ghostly echo of a stage setting for Shakespeare. Across the pond, the Great Lawn arced away to the distant trees in huddled symmetry.

He stood considering his next move. He would search for Jennifer, tell her that Brewster Wainwright and Bruce Wayne had parted company, that Batman had returned to the comic books where he would be no more than a collectible, and that she could once again be Guinevere. A patrolling cop coming up the Belvedere's eastern steps was startled at the sight of Brewster's imposing but very naked body glowing in the moonlight. He arrested Brewster for disorderly conduct.

ACKNOWLEDGEMENTS

Allusions and references to historical persons, events, and literary works in this novel have been freely embroidered for narrative purposes. The Batman movies since 1989 and Bob Kane's "autobiography," *Batman and Me* furnished background material for the central character. *The Vampire Book: The Encyclopedia of the Undead* by J. Gordon Melton and *The Essential Dracula*, edited by Leonard Wolf were also useful.

Alan Walker's masterful 3-volume biography of *Franz Liszt*, in particular, *The Weimar Years, 1848-1861*, provided material for Liszt and his relationship with Richard Wagner. Graham Robb's authoritative biography, *Victor Hugo*, provided a similar service for the poet-novelist, supplemented with John Chambers' *Victor Hugo's Conversations with the Spirit World*. Additional bits on Richard Wagner's life and work were borrowed from *The Wagner Compendium*, edited by Barry Millington, Charles Osborne's *The Complete Operas of Richard Wagner*, and especially, Wagner's relationship with Ludwig II of Bavaria, from *The Mad King: A Biography of Ludwig II of Bavaria* by Greg King, and the unfinished *Ludwig II The Mad King of Bavaria* by Desmond Chapman-Huston.

From John Bierman's *Napoleon III and His Carnival Empire*, I appropriated bits from the battle of Sedan that ended the Franco-Prussian War and the Second Empire in France. Related information on nineteenth-century Paris was gleaned from Robert Cole, *A Traveler's History of Paris*; Alain Corbain, *The Foul and the Fragrant*; Andrew Hussey, *Paris: The Secret History;* David P. Jordan, *Transforming Paris*; and Nicholas Papayannis, *Planning Paris Before Haussmann*. Additional information on the nineteenth-century milieu came from Rachel M. Brownstein, *Tragic Muse: Rachel of the Comédie-Française*; Joan Richardson, *Rachel*; Tad Szulc, *Chopin in Paris*; Virginia Rounding, *Grandes Horizontales: The Lives and Legends of Four Nineteenth-Century Courtesans*; and Christopher Prendergast, *Paris and the Nineteenth*

Century. On German culture in the period, W. H. Bruford, *Culture and Society in Classical Weimar*, T.J. Reed, *The Classical Centre: Goethe and Weimar, 1775-1832*, and Ernest Rose, *A History of German Literature*.

The Park and the People: A History of Central Park by Roy Rosenzweig and Elizabeth Blackmur was most helpful, as were various *The Central Park Book* by Elizabeth Barlow, et al., and information published by The Central Park Conservancy.

Ideas for Brewster Wainwright's adaptation of chaos theory were suggested by *Chaos and Harmony*, by Trinh Xuan Thuan.

No amount of thanks can adequately express my appreciation to friends and colleagues from Lansing Community College, Marc Van Wormer, Sharon Park, and Bruce Omundson, for their generous help in preparing this novel for publication.